Erotica Omnibus Four

Also available from X Libris:

Erotica Omnibus One
Erotica Omnibus Two
Erotica Omnibus Three

Erotica Omnibus Four

Sin and Seduction
Emma Allan

Cirque Erotique
Mikki Leone

Who Dares Sins
Roxanne Morgan

X LIBRIS

www.xratedbooks.co.uk

An *X Libris* Book

This omnibus edition first published by X Libris in 1998
Reprinted 2001
This edition published in 2002

A CIP catalogue record for this book
is available from the British Library.

ISBN 0 7515 2581 2

Photoset in North Wales by
Derek Doyle & Associates, Mold, Flintshire
Printed and bound in Great Britain by
Clays Ltd, St Ives plc

X Libris
An imprint of
Time Warner Books UK
Brettenham House
Lancaster Place
London WC2E 7EN

Erotica Omnibus Four

Sin and Seduction

Emma Allan

Chapter One

'WELL?' NADIA ASKED impatiently as soon as they sat down.

Angela grinned broadly. 'Well,' she said on a rising inflection. 'Where shall I start . . .'

A young, slim, curly-haired waiter arrived at their table. Nadia saw Angela's eyes roaming his trousers inquisitively, the way she always did with any man who was even vaguely attractive – and even with some who were not.

'What may I get you?' he said in a clipped precise English, avoiding, Nadia noted approvingly, any unctuous reference to their gender.

'Champagne cocktails for two,' Angela said.

The waiter nodded and walked over to the bar at the far side of the room. They were in the River Bar of the River Hotel overlooking the Tower of London and the Thames. The room was decorated in dark blues, with pictures of London river scenes on the walls. Comfortable armchairs, upholstered in a lighter blue, were placed around small burr walnut tables like the leaves of a quatrefoil. Nadia had selected a corner table though the bar was not crowded.

1

'Go on . . .' she urged. 'I want to hear all the gory details.'

'Perhaps nothing happenèd,' Angela said teasingly, the tip of her tongue between her lips.

'Not with that smirk on your face.'

'Perhaps he swore me to secrecy.'

'That's never stopped you before.'

'Well, the dinner was great.'

'Where?'

'Gavroche. *Soufflé Suisse, Canard Pot au Feu, Tarte Tatin.* Fourchaume Chablis, Cos-d'Estournel and . . .'

'D'Yquem.'

'How did you guess?'

'Modest little meal.'

The waiter returned with their drinks. He set two paper coasters, emblazoned with the hotel logo, on the table and sat two elegant crystal glasses on top of them. He added a trisectioned silver dish, its handle shaped into a fish, which contained pistachio nuts, black olives and little pastries stuffed with anchovies.

'Take those away, please,' Angela said at once. 'If you leave them I'll eat them.'

The waiter turned to see if Nadia agreed. 'Madam?' he queried.

'Yes, take them . . .' she said, a little surprised to be asked. Angela's personality was usually so forceful her demands were met without question.

'Will there be anything else?' he asked, scooping the silver dish back on to his tray.

'No,' Angela said, smiling at him sweetly, 'thank you.'

'Cheers,' Nadia said, picking up her glass.

They clinked glasses. Angela Barrett took a long

sip then settled back into her chair, crossing her legs. She was an attractive woman. Her red hair was her most striking feature, a red like a sunset, an iridescent colour cut into soft waves that fell to her shoulders. Her face was striking too, with emerald green eyes, their whites as clear as fresh snow, a large but well-proportioned nose and a fleshy rich mouth. She was slender and radiated health and fitness, everything about her body taut and well exercised. Her legs, which she flaunted in short skirts or skin-tight leggings, were long and shapely. Tonight, though she'd come straight from work, Angela was wearing a black Mani suit, its skirt displaying a great deal of thigh which was sheathed in sheer black nylon.

'So, obviously he asks me if I'd like to see his flat. Well actually he said apartment. But he is American.'

'And?'

'Did I tell you we're in his chauffeur-driven limo?'

'Naturally.'

'Well, the chauffeur takes us back to this building off Davies Street. Modern place, all black glass and stainless steel. He's got the penthouse.'

'Naturally.'

'It's massive. I mean rooms the size of a croquet lawn. I swear he's got two Picassos and a tiny Chagall and that's only in the hall.'

'And in the bedroom?' Nadia sipped her champagne, watching the bubbles eating away at the cube of sugar in the bottom of the glass.

'In the *sitting* room . . .' Angela insisted, ignoring her friend's interruption, 'there was a beautiful Edmund Cropper. He said it reminded him of his home town.'

3

'Can we cut to the chase,' Nadia said impatiently.

'Vicarious living?' Angela joked.

'Angela, you know that. If it weren't for you I wouldn't have any sex life.'

'It's sad, isn't it?'

'Very. So?'

'So. So I ask him if he's going to take me to bed. You know I don't like beating around the bush.'

'Did you want to go to bed with him?'

'Of course I did. He was gorgeous. He looked like Rossano Brazzi in *South Pacific*.'

'That dates you, doesn't it?'

'I saw it on television at Christmas. Anyway I was wet for him all evening.'

'Angela!' The shock was only feigned. Angela did not mince words.

'Well it's true.'

'What did he say?'

'He looked at me all serious, like he was going to tell me the meaning of life. He asked if he could trust me.'

'Trust you?'

'I said, of course he could, trying to be serious too. Then he goes all quiet. Gives me a glass of this wonderful Armagnac. He still looks serious, as though he's trying to make up his mind about something. I just stare back at him all wide-eyed, wondering what on earth's going on. Then, suddenly, he tells me he thinks I'm a very provocative woman.'

'Provocative?'

'He says he's a very rich man and that very rich men get used to having their own way in life. He says that he has got certain needs, certain special things he wants, very private things. Of course, I'm totally intrigued by now. My imagination's running riot. Then it's like he's made up his mind. He tells me he's sure he can trust me and he's looking at me with this really intense stare.'

'I'd have run away.'

'Don't be silly. Curiosity killed the cat. He takes my hand and leads me down the hall. It's a special room, he says. I mean, I'm imagining faked-up dungeons and whipping stools and mediaeval racks. So at the end of the hall he opens this door. The room's completely black – walls, floor, ceiling, everything. No window. There's a single divan dead centre lit by two spotlights overhead. It's covered in a black sheet. And there's a table, like an altar table against one wall with two massive white candles on either end. If there'd been a pentagram I'd have thought he was into black magic.'

'Weren't you scared?'

'No. He was harmless, Nadia.'

'How could you tell?'

'I don't know, just something about him. Anyway, I was fascinated. I wanted to know what he was going to do. Well, he asks me to take my clothes off, just like that, no kisses, no hugs. He had a lovely voice, very soft, like chocolate mousse. It made me shiver. So I ask him to unzip my dress – you know that yellow one with the spaghetti straps. He just shakes his head. So I do it myself. His eyes never leave me for a second, not a second. I'm only wearing stockings underneath, no knickers, no bra. There I am standing in my high heels and hold-ups with his eyes boring into me. And I'm throbbing. I mean palpitating. So I kick off my shoes and peel off my stockings.'

'And he's still dressed?'

'Oh yes, he's just standing there in his Huntsman's suit and Dunhill tie. He asks me to lie on the bed, on my back on the bed he says, and I do as I'm told. It's only when I lie down I realise the sheet is silk, really incredibly soft silk. He comes and stands over me, looking down at my body and for some reason I'm in a terrible state. My nipples are so hard they feel like cold steel and I swear I must be soaking the bed. And he hasn't even touched me. Must have been the way he was looking at me. Then he goes to the table and I hear him undressing. I could have twisted around to watch but for some reason I knew he didn't want me to. When he comes back he's wearing a short black robe embroidered with some sort of oriental serpent in red and gold. I can see his legs and they look strong and muscled. But as far as I can see he hasn't got an erection. He's carrying a black sheet, like the one on the bed. He flaps it out over me. It covers me completely apart from my head. I can see my nipples sticking out through it. He says very quietly that I must try to be still, as if I were in a very deep sleep, then he slowly draws the sheet up over my face.'

'That's creepy.'

'Creepy but exciting. The silk feels delicious against my body. So I'm lying there with the sheet over my face and I can't see a thing. I feel his hand tracing the contours of my cheek and jaw and down over my collarbone. Well, by the time it gets to my nipples my whole body's trembling. He just strokes them one after the other through the sheet. And I'm going crazy, moaning and gasping and only just managing to keep still. My clitoris is throbbing like a vibrator. The silk feels like oil against my skin, like I'm covered in oil. It was such a peculiar feeling.

What he's doing to my nipples drags the silk up and down all over me.'

'God, Angela, you're turning me on.' Nadia felt her own nipples stiffen in sympathy.

'So his hand eventually moves down to my belly. To tell you the truth I think I'd already had one orgasm just on what he did to my breasts. By the time he's got his hand on my thighs I'm completely soaked. I can feel it. And I'm squirming around like a fish, can't help myself. He puts his finger down between my legs, just one finger, pushing the sheet down with it and finds my clit instantly. I feel the silk working against it. And he's so good. What he does is perfect. Well, I'm coming again in seconds, really coming, screaming and moaning, writhing under the sheet, which only makes it worse because the silk feels so wonderful against my skin. He starts to push down until the sheet's dragged between my legs and I can feel him pushing it right up inside me. I'm so wet it's effortless. He puts his finger right up into me, covered by the sheet and, at the same time, his other hand is on my belly, another finger on my clit. It's amazing. I'm coming over and over again. Suddenly I hear him moan – well, cry out really – like an animal, a really strange noise. I feel his hands slip away. So I raise my head and the silk falls away and he's standing there with the robe open and the sheet is spattered with his semen.'

'But he had both hands on you.'

'Exactly. Spontaneous combustion.'

'Weird.'

'You can say that.'

'So what did he do then?'

'Like nothing had happened. He just leaves me in there. I get dressed and wander back into the living room. He's sitting there in a tracksuit with a glass of Armagnac and starts to talk about his investment portfolio. Just like it hadn't happened.'

'You can certainly pick them, Angela.'

'I know, but I'd never have guessed he was the type. The strangest thing was it turned me on so much. I mean, I was buzzing. Unbelievable.'

'Perhaps you've always had a thing about silk sheets and didn't know it.'

Sometimes Nadia wondered if the stories of the sexual exploits Angela came up with were, in fact, figments of her vivid imagination. But Angela was never short of suitors and it was equally possible that the outlandish details were perfectly true.

'Anyway, the chauffeur takes me home in the limo,' she concluded.

'Are you going to see him again?'

'Who knows? He's got my number.'

'And if he rings? Will you go?'

'I'll think about it.' Angela could not suppress a shiver. 'I might, I might not,' she said, grinning.

Nadia attracted the waiter's attention. She made a sign that they wanted another round of drinks and he nodded that he understood.

'You seem to attract them like a magnet.'

'Who?'

'Men who aren't the full sixpence.' Nadia had been friends with Angela since they worked together as graduate trainees on an accelerated promotion scheme operated by a firm of stock-brokers. They had shared everything, talked through every affair, every liaison and Nadia's disastrous marriage.

'I don't.'

'You do, Angela. You've had more than your fair

8

share. What about that guy who asked you to beat him with a school cane?'

'That was fun. He never called me again, though. I think I gave him more than he bargained for.'

'And the guy with the fur.'

'That's only two. Most of the rest have been normal.' Angela liked men. She had a voracious, almost masculine, appetite for sex. As she had never found a man who could satisfy her rapacious demands over the long term she had never been tempted to settle down. She liked all the games. She liked the variety. She liked the thrill of conquest – the female, in Angela's case, definitely taking the predatory role.

They talked about other things over their second drink, then divided the bill and left the slender waiter a five-pound tip. Angela had to go to the first night of a new opera at Covent Garden where the financial services company for which she worked was using its permanent tickets to do some corporate entertaining. As Nadia lived in Islington she offered Angela a lift, her car, a Mazda convertible, having been consigned to the hotel doorman.

'Are you going to the exhibition tomorrow?' Nadia asked as the doorman retrieved her car from the forecourt and drove it to the front entrance.

'What, the Jack Hamilton?'

Nadia slipped the doorman a ten-pound note as he held the car door open for her, then he raced round to do the same for Angela. They climbed in. 'You got your invite, didn't you?'

'Oh yes, but I've got Yamatso coming in at six. He usually wants dinner at Harry's Bar and brandies at the Dorchester. I can't do it. And I really wanted to meet him.'

Nadia pulled the car into traffic. 'Who?'

'Hamilton. Didn't you see him in the *Sunday Times*? They had him stripped to the waist. He's a hunk. Pumps iron and runs. Believes in the Greek ideal – healthy body makes for a creative mind. Well, he can have my body any day. And he's got these come-to-bed eyes . . .'

'Angela, you think any man under sixty has come-to-bed eyes.'

'Come on, I'm very selective. But he's really something.'

'Well, that means I'll have to go alone. Someone from the company's got to go – we're sponsoring it. Gordon can't, he's in Hong Kong.'

'Is he still on the board?'

'Retiring next year. He's the only one interested in art.'

'Sorry I can't come.'

'Can't be helped.'

Nadia dropped Angela at the bottom of Bow Street and drove around the Aldwych. The traffic was heavy but fluid and in fifteen minutes she was home. She had put down the deposit on the flat-fronted Georgian house three years ago with the proceeds from her first big bonus. It had been expensive but one of the advantages of working for a merchant bank was fixed and low-rate mortgages.

Nadia opened the front door, deactivated the burglar alarm and climbed two floors straight to her large bedroom and en suite bathroom which occupied the whole second floor. She had spent a lot of money having the house rebuilt to her specifications and the bathroom, in marble, had cost her the most. It was worth every penny.

Turning on the powerful shower, housed in its

own cubicle, Nadia stripped off her clothes and let the strong jets of water wash away the alcohol-induced tiredness that had suddenly seized her. She climbed out of the glass stall and into a white towelling robe, staring at herself critically in the large mirror behind the double wash-hand basins. She was thinking of Angela and the procession of men she managed to troop through her life. In contrast she had recently had only desultory relationships with one or two males, whom she cared about neither socially nor sexually.

She was no less attractive, she thought. Her flaxen blonde hair was expertly cut in layers and neatly framed her face. She had a small, slightly retroussé nose, high, sculpted cheekbones and a perfectly symmetrical mouth. Her lips were naturally a deep ruby red and her eyes a blue that had reminded past admirers of cornflowers. Nor was her body any less spectacular than Angela's. She was slender with a narrow waist, full hips and abundantly curved buttocks. Her legs were long and finely contoured and her breasts full and firm and very round, riding high on her chest in defiance of gravity.

It was, of course, nothing to do with appearance. It was a question of personality. Angela was outgoing to the point of being outrageous. She had no problem with going up to a man in a bar and asking him to buy her a drink, nor for that matter asking him to take her home to bed. Nadia had never been able to operate in that way though she had began to wish, especially after her divorce, that she could. Not that men were slow to approach her. She had enough offers, but they were frequently offers from the wrong men – men who were too old, too boring or too married, the last category

11

predominating. Had she been prepared to settle for an affair, to become a man's mistress, she could have chosen from a dozen candidates. But she was not.

She had done so once, and once was enough. After her divorce she had been courted by one of the senior partners of another merchant bank. He was elegant, worldly and sophisticated, all the things that her ex-husband was not. He had taken her to the opera and bought her little gifts of jewellery and clothes, all from the finest shops in Bond Street. He had made love to her with passion and enthusiasm and élan. He had told her he was married but Nadia thought she didn't care, that she would be able to cope with being merely his mistress, called on to perform whenever he was available and his wife was not. And for a while she had coped well, until one evening she had seen him, quite by chance, out with his wife, sitting in a restaurant where Nadia had arranged to meet a client. Suddenly the cosy accommodation she had come to with herself, the lies she had told herself and all the little deceptions they had practised on the pretty brunette she now saw for the first time, seemed sordid and despicable. Moreover she realised she loved the man and that her most profound emotion, as she watched the way his wife smiled and laughed and so clearly cared for him, was jealousy. It hurt her more than anything else had ever hurt her and she swore that was one mistake she would never make again.

Her divorce was not on the same scale of tragedy. She had married the wrong man for the wrong reasons. She had married a man with no ambition or drive because she wanted to be married. No other reason. She wanted to be married because it was like an insurance policy against the failure of her own career. As soon as it had become apparent she was not likely to fail her needs had changed. She had hoped he might change with her, that they could jointly bring a new dimension to married life, but it soon became apparent he was not willing to oblige.

Fortunately he had been tempted by the delights of a nineteen-year-old telephonist at British Telecom. Nadia and Doug's sex life had never been more than perfunctory. She was more interested in her career than sex and was glad that Doug appeared to be satisfied with very little. When he'd announced he wanted a divorce, her first emotion was relief, followed quickly by astonishment as he took great pleasure in telling her of his sexual exploits with Sharon, whom he had fucked and sucked and nibbled comprehensively, in every conceivable position in every possible location. With Nadia the limits of his endeavour had been the missionary position every Friday night.

Since her divorce, and her married man, Nadia's attitude to sex had changed and she found herself yearning for the sort of sexual adventure Angela apparently enjoyed. It wasn't that she hadn't had lovers. She had chosen one or two and they had been competent. They had performed adequately, indulging in foreplay and holding themselves back until she'd had her pleasure, as befitted a New Man. But she had hardly been driven wild, thrashing around and panting with lust. It had all been carefully controlled, calculated and, in the end, distant. And now, at this point in her life, Nadia wanted, and needed, more.

Wrapping the robe more tightly around her, she went down to the kitchen to make herself some tea.

13

She wasn't hungry. She had had lunch with a client at the Pont de la Tour. She sat at the breakfast bar in the kitchen and sipped a mug of strong tea. Once again Angela's story had left her restless. She glanced at the paper to see if there was anything on television that would distract her but there was nothing. She kept seeing an image of Angela stretched out under a black silk sheet being caressed by Rossano Brazzi.

Almost reluctantly Nadia walked back to her bedroom. It was nearly dark and she closed the cream curtains on the two large windows that overlooked the street. She didn't turn on the light. The gloom suited her purposes. She took off the robe and hung it on the back of the bathroom door. There was a tall mirror in the bedroom and she stared at her naked body. Her nipples were erect. She looked down at them. Their flesh was dark, a cherry red, and jutted out from the thin band of areola that surrounded them. She took her breasts in her hands and squeezed them gently.

'Damn Angela,' she said aloud.

She wondered if she would have become so concerned with sex if her friend hadn't regaled her with her sexual exploits quite so regularly. Was she just trying to ape Angela in some way?

Nadia lay on the bed. She had masturbated rarely in her early days. Now she found it more and more necessary. The strange thing was the more she seemed to need it, the less satisfactory it became. Her body was like a rarely played musical instrument. It was not capable of the demands made on it and did not respond well. Not only was her body out of tune when it came to the desires of her mind, she felt she did not know how to play the

14

instrument to its best advantage. Perhaps in truth masturbation was not to be her forte.

She could see herself in the mirror. It was immediately opposite the foot of the bed and she scissored her legs apart so the whole long crease of her sex was visible. Her pubic hair was soft and quite thick on her mons but did not extend down between her legs and she could see every detail of the deckled scarlet opening of her vagina. It seemed to be smiling at her, a mocking vertical smile.

She began to stroke the soft fur of her pubis, still debating with herself whether she should be bothered. As her finger nudged against the top of her labia she felt her clitoris pulse weakly, as if it too could not decide whether it was worth the effort to join in.

On impulse Nadia rolled over. There were two small chests of drawers on either side of the bed, in one of which she kept all her lingerie. She opened the bottom drawer and extracted a black satin slip. Lying on her back again she draped the slip over her body and raised her head to look at the effect in the mirror. The satin smelt of her perfume. She always kept her empty perfume bottles in the lingerie drawers. She could see her hard nipples sticking up under the material.

Closing her eyes she rested her head back on the pillow, inhaling her own scent. It smelt musky, more like an orchid than a rose. She could feel the silky satin against her body and remembered how Angela had described her experience. Was this how she had felt? What would it have been like? Her clitoris pulsed more strongly, deciding it did want to join the ceremony. She imagined Rossano Brazzi standing over her, stooping to circle her nipples with the palms of his hands, a knowing smile flickering over his face.

Nadia opened her legs. The hem of the slip was covering her pubis. She pushed the silk into her labia and found the cache of her clitoris. Delicately she rubbed it from side to side with the silk, and felt it respond with a frisson of pleasure. Her body moved almost unconsciously against the satin. Just as Angela had described, it felt deliciously sensual against her skin. Her clitoris pulsed strongly. She pressed it against the underlying bone, trapping it with the silk, then dragged it up and down. A wave of sensation made her shudder.

Closing her legs tightly she rubbed the tip of her thighs together so that her labia were trapped too, the satin caught between her legs. She could feel her wetness, leaking from her body. In the darkness of her mind she saw a big, circumcised erection edging towards her, a tear of transparent fluid escaping from the little slit that seemed to resemble an eye. It did not belong to anyone. It was anonymous and disembodied. It throbbed visibly, blood coursing through it, the glans smooth and pink in contrast to the shaft that supported it, which was rough and veined.

She eased her legs apart slightly to give her finger room to work on her clitoris. The spectre of the cock loomed large. Nadia imagined holding it in her hand, squeezing it, feeding it into her mouth, taking it in her throat, sucking it so hard it swelled even more. She imagined it pushing into her labia, testing her wetness, delving into the silky, pliant cavern of her sex.

What caused the change she didn't know. Suddenly the cock was not anonymous any more. It belonged to Doug. On the screen behind her eyes she saw Doug's body on top of her, remembered how she had looked up over his shoulder and watched his big, fleshy buttocks rising and falling as he drove his penis into her. He had a permanent pimple on his left buttock and it had often fascinated her. She had the feeling that it changed colour as he pumped away, fluoresced from pink to red, flashing like a lighthouse, a code in Morse she did not understand.

The thrills and trills of pleasure from her clitoris were lost. She manipulated it harder but only caused a wave of discomfort verging on pain. She tried moving her finger against it with the most delicate of touches, using the now wet satin, but that produced no feeling at all. It had become dulled and insensitive. It had no power, no dominion over her body any more.

Like a deflated balloon Nadia felt the excitement seeping out of her. She opened her eyes and looked at herself in the mirror, tearing the black slip away angrily. With both hands she grabbed her breasts, squeezing them hard then pinching her nipples, trying to get her body to respond. But all she felt was pain. She released them, white finger marks momentarily impressed on the pink flesh.

'Damn you,' she said aloud.

Chapter Two.

IT WAS CROWDED, so crowded it was difficult to see any of the pictures. They had not been roped off and the small gallery was so full of people they were practically touching the canvases. Not that anyone appeared that interested anyway. Most were there to press the flesh, to network among the critics and the journalists and members of the Arts Council who attended the event, or simply to gossip and grin and hear the latest news in the chattering classes. The champagne flowed copiously, and waitresses in short black uniforms circulated with trays of canapés that had been warmed and rewarmed so many times they had started to congeal and melt into the paper doilies on which they had been arranged.

She spotted him through the scrum. He had found a little corner at the back of the room and, even among so many, gave the appearance of being on his own. He was not quite as dark and brooding as Nadia had imagined from Angela's description, but she was certainly right in every other respect. He was a deeply attractive man.

A big buxom woman in a bright orange dress invaded the private space he had created and buttonholed him, trapping him against the wall. Nadia watched as the woman talked at him, emphasising her monologue with sweeping gestures at the various paintings. He had black hair, thick wavy black hair which fell, like a comma, over his forehead, occasionally brushing his bushy eyebrows. He would flick it back with a toss of the head. His eyes were the colour of burnished mahogany, a liquid mahogany that seemed to express an understanding of the profundities of life, and were, also, it seemed to her at least, etched with a kind of sadness.

He was tall and had the relaxed ease of someone who is happy with their body. He possessed a natural poise and grace of movement that was underlined by his obvious physical strength.

Excusing herself from the little group of people she had become attached to, Nadia squeezed her way towards Jack Hamilton through the crush of people. He saw her coming and fixed her with those eyes as she manoeuvred through the minefield of wine glasses and paper plates. As she got nearer she could see the eyes were quizzical. She read the question as 'What do you want with me?' and wasn't sure she knew the answer.

The buxom woman was talking earnestly, undeterred by Jack's obvious lack of interest. 'So I always see these things as a matter of form, not content, don't you agree? Oh look, there's Patrick. Do you know Patrick Proctor? He's wonderful, don't you think?'

'Yes,' Jack replied noncommittally.

'Must say hello. Excuse me, won't you . . .' And she bustled away.

19

'Hi,' Nadia said, taking her place. 'I'm Nadia Irving.'

'Hi,' he said with no enthusiasm.

'Aren't you enjoying yourself?'

'Would you?'

'It's your show.'

'You saw my picture in the catalogue.'

'Yes.'

'Not in the *Sunday Times*?'

'No.'

'Good. That bloody article has plagued me.'

'I've heard about it.'

'I should never have done it.'

'Why did you?'

'Pure foolishness. So what can I do for you? Please don't ask me some silly question about how I see the artistic process or why I only paint in oils or who my models are. If I could explain what I do I wouldn't have to paint.'

'I wasn't . . .' Nadia floundered.

'What then?'

Nadia couldn't think of a single thing to say. She had come over to him because he was the most attractive man in the room. She could hardly tell him that.

'I just wanted to tell you I thought your work was striking.'

'Striking! Well, that's a new adjective at least. Have you actually seen it?'

'Yes.'

'Have you? How can you in here?'

'I work for the company that sponsors the gallery. I saw the pictures at the preview last week,' she said assertively.

'I'm sorry,' he said at once. His eyes softened and

he smiled gently. 'I really am. I hate these dos. You spend three years of your life trying to say something, trying to do something and nobody even bothers to look at the pictures.'

'I looked. I think you're good, very good.'

He was. Hamilton's work was mostly figurative and he painted with almost photographic realism. But he had an ability to convey a mood and an atmosphere that suggested not only the situation in which his subjects found themselves but much wider issues. There was a resonance that spoke of the human condition, that touched a chord, or should have done, in anyone who cared to look.

'And what do you know about art?' The words were full of resentment again. He wanted to use her to prove a point to himself – that nobody understood what he was trying to do.

'I know I need to get an emotional response from a picture. I know when I find a picture moving. I know when I don't.'

'And you find my pictures striking?'

'I find two very moving indeed.'

'Do you? Which two?'

'The woman in the turquoise dress and the little boy with his mother.'

Jack Hamilton suddenly looked straight into her eyes. A broad grin broke over his face and he started to laugh. It was as though she had passed a test, a rite of passage to his respect.

'Absolutely right. The rest don't really work. But those two – I can't paint better than that.' His eyes continued to stare into hers, looking at her now as if to see into her soul. 'Can I get you another drink?'

'No, thank you.'

'So, Nadia . . .'

21

The words hung in the air. Despite the way he had treated her initially, or maybe precisely because of it, Nadia felt as strong an attraction for this man as she had ever felt in her whole life. She could feel her heart pounding and her pulse racing. And then, quite suddenly, she knew what she had to do.

'I don't suppose you would like to take me to bed, would you?' She had never said that to any man before, and never dreamt she would be able to. In fact, it came quite easily.

He grinned again, but with no smugness. His teeth were very white and regular. 'I'd like that very much,' he said quietly.

Nadia's heart was beating so rapidly it felt like a bird fluttering in a cage. What was she doing, what on earth was happening to her? She was mimicking Angela. But she realised immediately she had no regrets. She felt suddenly free and in control in a way she had never experienced before, as if heavy chains of restraint had fallen away.

'Would you like to go now?' he said conspiratorially.

'Don't you have to stay?' Was she hoping he would say that he did? She hadn't expected him to act so quickly.

'I don't think so. I've done my duty.'

'All right.' And she found it was all right.

With a gentleness that belied his obvious strength he took her by the elbow. It was the first time they'd touched. They were going to bed together and they had had no physical contact. Strangely the idea thrilled her. He led her through a small exit at the back and, in two minutes, they were standing outside on the street. Ten minutes later, courtesy of a black cab, they were drawing up outside a small

22

mews off the Fulham Road. The staircase of the mews was on the outside and he led her up the stone steps.

'My studio,' he announced as he opened the door.

Nadia walked into a large open space with windows set into the roof. The room must be wonderfully light during the day, she thought. To one side was a fully fitted kitchen and at the back, an alcove containing a double bed.

'Drink? Booze? Coffee? Tea?' he asked.

'No thanks.' Nadia had kept her mind in neutral during the journey, trying not the think about the implications of what she had done.

'Do you do this often?' he said.

'Do what?'

'Pick up strange men.'

'I've never done it before.' Her sincerity was obvious.

'Why's that?'

'I've never wanted to.'

'I'm flattered then. Why me?'

There was a big chunky sofa against one wall and he sat on it, inviting her to do the same. The studio was not what she might have expected, had she had time to think about it. It was not wild and untidy and dirty, but neat and well ordered and clean, everything in its place, canvases and materials racked and stacked, and books carefully shelved. There were bright coloured rugs on the stripped wooden floor. The white walls were covered in pictures but, in terms of style at least, they appeared to be the work of others.

'Could I change my mind?' she said as she sat down next to him.

'About what?'

'I'd love a glass of wine.'

He got up immediately and went to the kitchen. 'White or red?'

'Red, please.'

He took a bottle from a wine rack set under one of the counters and opened it, taking two glasses from a wall cupboard.

'So why me?' he said, handing her a glass then pouring wine into it.

'You're a very attractive man. You know you are. Shouldn't women be able to act on the same impulses as men?' That sounded convincing. She almost convinced herself.

'Of course they should.'

'Well then . . .' She raised her glass and clinked it against his. Half of her wanted to run away so fast and so far he'd never be able to find her again, while the other half wished she had the courage to ask him to take her straight to bed.

He sipped his wine. 'Let's take it to bed,' he said.

'Fine,' she said, trying to sound calm.

She got to her feet and he led her over to the alcove at the back of the room, putting the bottle and his glass down on one of the bedside tables. He operated a switch on the wall and dark grey blinds rolled out over the skylights. He turned on one of the small bedside lamps and turned off the lights in the rest of the studio.

He was wearing a white shirt, and dark blue slacks, the summer heat making a jacket unnecessary. Without the slightest embarrassment, he unbuttoned his shirt. His broad chest was covered in a thick mat of black hair, his arms shaped by hard, well-defined muscles. His hands, she noticed, were lined with prominent blue veins, the skin sprouting long but sparsely distributed black hairs. They were scrupulously clean, like a doctor's hands, and the fingernails were very regular and looked manicured. His navel was flat with deep hollows on either side carved out by his abdominal muscles. She could see why Angela had been so impressed with the photograph of him stripped to the waist.

He kicked off his shoes and pulled off his black socks, then unzipped his slacks, paying no attention to her, and pulled them down together with his white boxer shorts. His long legs were as muscled as his torso, his thighs, less hairy than his chest, contoured with taut, hard, fibrous tissue. His cock was slightly aroused, protruding from his curly black pubic hair, its circumcised tip as smooth as a billiard ball. The sac of his scrotum was comparatively hairless and hung down heavily between his legs.

Nadia sat on the edge of the bed. Her heart was beating so fast she was sure he would be able to hear it.

Again she realised they hadn't even kissed. The same thought seemed to occur to him. He came to stand in front of her and stooped to kiss her lightly on the lips, holding her cheeks in both his hands.

'You're very lovely,' he said softly. She had never been good at taking compliments but from him the words sounded absolutely sincere.

'Thank you,' she said.

'Would you like me to look the other way?' he said, the contrast between his nudity and her clothes stark.

'No, no . . .' she said, getting to her feet. It was the moment of truth, the point of no return. If she was going to run she would have to run now.

Jack stripped off the counterpane and bedding to leave only the undersheet. He piled the pillows against the wall at the top of the bed and propped himself against them, his legs crossed, his cock and balls sitting on top of his thighs.

With a coolness that surprised her, she pulled the simple white blouse she was wearing out of her skirt and unbuttoned it. She felt perfectly calm and committed. She had got herself into this and now she was determined to go through with it. If she regretted it in the morning, did it really matter? She had had so little to feel anything about recently, even regret would make a pleasant change. And it was possible regret would not be the emotion she would experience.

She unzipped her skirt. It was too tight to fall to the floor of its own accord. She had to wriggle out of it. She tried not to think, keeping her mind in neutral again.

Stepping out of her skirt she picked it up from the floor, only too aware of Hamilton's eyes following her every movement. She folded the skirt over the top of a nearby chair, conscious of the fact that he would be able to see her bottom, the way the white teddy she was wearing had dug itself into the cleft between her buttocks. She thanked some god somewhere that she was wearing decent lingerie, as she stripped her blouse off her shoulders and laid that on the chair too.

She didn't mind him looking at her. She was proud of her body. She wanted him to look. It excited her.

Very deliberately she peeled the thin white shoulder straps of the teddy down over her arms. The lacy cups that held her breasts fell away and she looked at her nakedness. Her nipples were puckered, her tan brown areolae dotted with tiny extrusions like pimples, born of her excitement. There was no doubt what her body wanted.

She pulled the teddy down, over her slim, waspie waist, down over the marked flare of her hips and the tight curves of her buttocks, down until its crotch was inverted, clinging to the plane of her sex as though reluctant to break the intimate contact with her body. With a tug she freed it and the silky white garment fell to the floor.

Her tights were a translucent grey, shiny and sheer. They did not hide the furry triangle below her belly, her short blonde hairs – if he had cared to think about it he would know she was a natural blonde – so neat they looked as though they had been combed to a point, a point that led to the junction of her thighs, like an arrow on the map of her body. She hooked her fingers into the waistband of the nylon.

'No,' he said.

'No?'

'Let me do it for you.'

'If that's what you want.'

'It is.'

She sat on the edge of the bed again and ran her fingers through her short blonde hair, feeling it spring back into place. Her display had swollen his penis. It stood up straight, projecting from the top of his thighs at a right angle. It was big and broad and long, the bulb of his glans like a giant acorn atop a shaft that was veined and rough-cast. As she looked she saw it throb, engorging more. She felt her sex throb too. She was barely in control now. She had succeeded in keeping her mind blank, in pushing reason and good sense aside, to get herself this far but she could no longer control the other side of the equation – her excitement. Doing what she had done had given her a sense of freedom that excited her almost as much as Hamilton had. She felt brave and independent. She couldn't distinguish her intellectual pleasure at what she had done from the strong physical emotions that pounded through her. She wanted this man. She wanted him now. She wanted to feel his hard, muscled body embracing her, wanted those arms wrapped around her, crushing her, wanted that cock, that big throbbing cock, bursting its way into her body, filling her, swamping her, drowning her in the same way she had already drowned in the dark abyss of his eyes.

She turned and ran her hand over his thighs until it brushed his balls. She wanted to take the initiative. His cock pulsed at the touch. She slid her hand down his thigh, caressing it with the lightest of touches. It twitched.

'Do you want me to suck it?' The sound of her voice betrayed her passion.

'Yes,' he said simply.

She knelt up on the bed, the nylon of the tights rasping. Perhaps that was why he hadn't wanted her to take the tights off. Perhaps he had no intention of fucking her; he was just going to lie there and expect her to take him in her mouth.

Sticky fluid had escaped at the tip of his cock, oozing out until it was the shape of a perfect tear, viscous and sticky. Nadine broke it with the very tip of her tongue, pulling back so the string of liquid was spun out, like a spider's web, connecting her lips and his cock. The string finally broke. She dipped again and repeated the process. This time when the connection snapped she plunged her head down on to the hard erect shaft, right the way down until his cock was buried inside her mouth and she closed her lips around its base and felt the curls of his pubic hair against her chin.

Her body churned. His cock was big and hot and so hard, hard like a bone. She sucked on it, sucking it without moving her mouth, feeling her sex throbbing as she imagined – not consciously but reflexively – how it would feel inside her, pressed deep inside her. Reflexively also she flexed her thighs to squeeze her labia together. She could feel the sap of her body spreading out from her loins.

She pulled her mouth back and began a rhythmic motion. He moaned slightly. She did not allow his cock to come all the way out, just to the gate of her lips where her tongue flicked at the slit at its tip, before she plunged down again, all the way down, until his glans nudged right up to the back of her throat. Then she pushed harder, controlling her gagging reflex, as she had learned to do in the past, and feeling his cock jammed hard against the ribbed wall of her windpipe. At the same time she fingered his balls, jiggling them against her chin.

'No,' he said suddenly, his hands gripping her face and pulling her mouth away.

'I thought that's what you wanted,' she teased, feigning innocence.

'You're very good at it . . .'

She was. Another man in her life had wanted nothing else.

'But that's not what I want,' he continued. 'I want to fuck you.' The word 'fuck' sounded different on his lips. It sounded as if it was something she had never done before.

He was pulling her down on to her back while he got up on to his knees. As soon as she settled he leant forward and kissed her lightly on the lips, his mouth just brushing hers, moving from one side to the other, his tongue darting out in little forays to penetrate fleetingly into her moist, hot mouth. Meanwhile the palm of his hand circled her hard nipples, one after the other. He moved his mouth to her neck, sucking and licking and nibbling at her flesh, making her arch her head back against the sheet, stretching the long sinews of her throat so they stood out like cords of rope.

She could hardly believe what was happening to her. She had never felt her body react like this. It was as though she were being strung out, each caress like the ratchet on a mediaeval rack, stretching her further. His mouth followed the taut sinews down to the hollows of her throat, over her collarbone, to the rise of her breast. While his mouth descended, one arm supporting his weight on the far side of her body, the other hand – just the fingertips of the other hand – caressed her belly, drawing imaginary circles with the faintest of touches. She had been caressed like this before but it had never caused her to feel what she was feeling now.

Nadia was on fire, her whole body quivering as his mouth approached her nipple. She could hardly wait for his lips to encircle the swollen, erect cherry that topped her breast. It seemed to be alive, wanting of its own accord, independent of her. Suddenly she felt his hot breath blowing on the puckered flesh and then his mouth sucked it in, not lightly now but hard and fierce, as though trying to encompass the whole breast between his lips, sucking in as much flesh as he could. Releasing everything but the tender puckered nipple, he held it firmly between his teeth. Then he repeated the process with the other breast. The tingle of pain was laced through with the exquisite pleasure.

Nadia's excitement was extreme and she struggled to understand it. Perhaps no more than an hour ago this man had been a total stranger. Now she was lying naked with him, his erection brushing her thigh, his eyes roaming her body. And it was all down to her, her idea, her initiative. She had taken the first step. Was that the cause of her passion? Was it the way she'd abandoned herself? Or was it Hamilton? His body excited her. It was hard and handsome and strong. His touch was perfect too, but she knew it had to be more than that. Her attraction to him was deep. What he was touching was not her body but her mind, stimulating the one part of her sexuality she had never been able to reach before. And the reason he could do that was what she could not understand.

She spread her legs and arched her body off the bed, giving up the attempt to analyse the whys and wherefores. She hoped he would see her need for him, her need to feel his cock plunging into her sex.

'Be patient . . .' he said, reading her perfectly.

His hand ran over her belly. The skin on his hand was rough, like a workman's hand, calloused and hard, and she could hear it rasping against the nylon of her tights. It caressed her thighs, smoothing over the contours of her muscles, down to her knees, then up again on the soft inner surface, until the side of his hand was pressing the nylon against her labia.

He moved his hands to the waistband of the tights and pulled it down over her hips. She co-operated, raising her buttocks from the bed so he could slide the nylon away. He rolled it off her legs one by one then gently opened her legs. She saw him looking at her sex. He was looking at it as she imagined he would look at one of his pictures, admiring, critical, approving, the deckled, wet, scarlet nether lips exposed to his gaze. She felt herself throb powerfully, as if his eyes were touching a raw nerve.

His finger slid into the crease of her labia, her wetness lubricating the movement. He looked into her eyes and she felt herself drowning again. She supposed she had never felt such a physical attraction for a man, uncluttered by social niceties. She had translated the attraction to reality, and now she knew her instinct had been right. She had never responded sexually to any man as she was responding to Hamilton, never, never, never . . .

His finger found her clitoris. She moaned, shaking her head from side to side, as if not able to believe what she was experiencing. Her sex seemed to have come alive, plugged into some source of power that filled it with energy.

Hamilton rocked back on his haunches. He watched her with studied interest as his fingertip brushed her clitoris, the only physical contact between their bodies. It was enough. As he moved the tip against the tiny nut of nerves he saw her arch up off the bed again and knew she was coming. He readied himself, readied himself to spring. He could see her angling herself towards him, almost imperceptibly, her body language artfully expressing her need, her sex open and vulnerable.

Nadia could hardly bear it. Feelings so sharp they were almost painful coursed through her body. His touch was perfect, the perfect pressure, the perfect movement. Men had touched her like this before but never with such finesse or understanding of her needs. It was as though he knew exactly what she wanted because he had complete empathy with what she felt. She managed to open her eyes to look up at him. His mouth was smiling, enjoying her pleasure. She looked down at his single finger moving so tellingly between her legs. It rolled over and around, pushing her clitoris against her pubic bone. Perfect. She felt the tide of orgasm engulf her, her eyes squeezed shut, her body shuddering, her mouth groping to express some sound or other, her nerves and tendons and muscles stretched to the limit.

Before she knew what was happening he had fallen on her like a wolf on its prey, riding up on the flood of her orgasm until his cock was buried so deeply inside her it would have taken her breath away, had she had any breath left. But she did not. She could hardly breathe at all. She was existing on sensation, the purest sensation she had ever experienced, a feeling so tangible, so real it was like a thing apart from her. It was a feeling she knew she would never forget.

She came again instantly, the second his phallus hit the neck of her womb, her whole sex contracting around his big, rock-hard shaft, squeezing it, milking it, the feeling of its strength reinforcing her orgasm, giving it momentum, making it explode higher and longer than she'd ever thought possible. As he moved in her, pumped into her, now with no subtlety or finesse, only hardness and vigour, using

33

all his considerable power to push deeper than she could ever remember any man being in her, Nadia did not know whether she was having one continuous orgasm or several, so close together there was no gap between them. All she knew was she never wanted it to end, and it didn't, not for a long, long time.

Eventually, though she did not know when, he must have come too. She would have liked to have felt him jetting inside her but she was too high, too overwhelmed, too far gone, too everything, to feel any more or react any more. She could not move; she could barely register conscious thought. But she knew one thing: she had never felt anything like this before in her life.

When she opened her eyes, he had rolled on to his side and was looking at her face. There was something in his eyes she had not expected to see, a vulnerability, an openness. She saw a little boy's face, a little boy who had been hurt by life but didn't like to show it. The aftermath of orgasm had exposed it, allowed a glimpse behind the face he presented to the world. Nadia put her arm around him and cuddled his face to her breast.

The light woke her. Or was it the need to pee? She had been asleep so deeply that for a moment she could not remember where she was, let alone what day it was. As she wrestled herself to consciousness the facts came flooding back, emotions in Technicolor, feelings in waves. The light was seeping through the blinds that covered the skylights.

She looked over at Hamilton. He was lying on his stomach, his head to one side on the pillow facing her, his naked body covered by a single sheet that

34

had been pulled down to his waist. His back was contoured with muscles and his scapulae stuck out prominently. His buttocks, under the sheet, were small and round. His face appeared to be in perfect repose, relaxed and remarkably childlike. She noticed he had black eyelashes so long they looked as though they had been curled with a brush.

Trying not to disturb him, Nadia slipped out of bed and looked around for a bathroom. There was only one internal door and she found a small white tiled shower room behind it, with a shower cubicle, wash-hand basin and toilet. The room had no window and she pulled the cord of the light switch which caused a fluorescent light to flick on with a hum, bathing her in a very white, very shadowless light.

There was a mirror behind the basin and she stared into it. There was no outward sign of last night's activities. Her body revealed no clues as to what she felt. But she felt as though she had been through an emotional wringer, squeezed dry and reconstituted. It seemed to her she *should* look different to match what she felt.

Sitting on the loo she peed long and hard. It was difficult not to think of sex, to start remembering what she had experienced. Immediately her body shuddered. Sex had been a problem in her life for so long, the gnawing inadequacies of her sexual encounters so much part of her personality that it was almost as if she had lost an old friend. Now the idea that she had cultivated and cherished, that some physiological mechanism was missing from her sexual loop, a short circuit in the connection between the erogenous zones and the cybernetics of orgasm, would have to be abandoned. The fact that the orgasms she had experienced before were light years away from what had happened to her last night could only be ascribed to one thing: for the first time in her life she had been with the right man. Even her married man, for all his sophistication, had never made her feel the way Hamilton had done.

She remembered a friend telling her, when she was fifteen and still a virgin, that women only had orgasms when they were truly, madly and deeply in love. She had believed it for a long time. She wondered if it still coloured her life. It was lust, not love that had motivated her actions. Curiously, despite what he had done to her, she did not feel any affection for Jack Hamilton. Knowing herself, however, she knew it would not be long before the spectre of emotional commitment, like an unwelcome ghost, appeared from the shadows.

After washing her hands, Nadia used a piece of toilet paper to wipe away the smudge of make-up under her eyes. She looked at her watch. It was six o'clock. Plenty of time to get home and change before work.

She opened the shower room door and padded naked across the studio floor. One of Hamilton's paintings was on a large wooden easel right under the skylights. It was an odd scene, half a room on one side of the canvas and half a garden on the other, with no dividing line between the two. In the foreground there was an outline of where two figures were obviously to be painted in.

'Morning.'

His voice startled her.

'Hello,' she said, feeling slightly coy about her nakedness.

He was sitting up in bed, smiling sympathetically.

'You found the loo?'

'Yes.' She got back into bed, propped herself up against the pillows and was just about to pull the sheet up over her breasts when some inner voice chided her for being so silly.

Hamilton ran the back of his hand over her cheek.

'You all right?' he asked.

She smiled weakly. 'You know, morning after the night before. I've got to go.'

'Go?'

'Work.'

'Ah, yes. The company that sponsors the gallery. What exactly is it you do there?'

'Actually, I work for a merchant bank.'

'Not just a pretty face. What does it involve? Arranging mergers and takeovers, that sort of thing?'

'That sort of thing exactly. I work in the acquisitions department.' That was definitely a point to him. When she told most men that she worked for a merchant bank they asked her what her boss did, assuming she was an assistant or secretary. It was a long time since Nadia had been either of those. In fact, if her latest venture was successful she would be put on the board and become one of the very few women holding a directorship in a merchant bank.

'Do you want coffee?'

'No, no thanks.'

He was looking at her breasts. Those big, liquid, mahogany eyes were staring at them quite unabashed.

'Do you like them?' she asked, feeling her nipples stiffen under his gaze.

'They're a lovely shape. Your whole body is really

37

exceptional.' He sounded as if he was discussing a painting, an objective assessment that appeared self-evident. Very gently he touched them, one after the other, moulding his fingers to their curves. 'Lovely,' he repeated.

The touch made Nadia's body hum, like a radio turned on but not tuned in.

'I've got to go,' she said weakly, suddenly feeling it was the last thing she wanted to do. She made a quick calculation. A cab to her house would take her thirty minutes, no longer at this time in the morning. She could shower and change and be out of the house in fifteen, and the drive to work was another ten. No more than an hour. It was six now. She didn't need to leave until seven-thirty. She could afford to give in to the impulse that his touch had created.

'I'd like to kiss you,' Hamilton said.

'Why don't you then?'

'I don't want to start anything I can't finish.'

'Oh, I think I've got time for us both to finish,' she said smiling, her pulse beginning to race as her body remembered what he had done to it last night.

He turned towards her and looked straight into her eyes. She felt like a rabbit caught in the headlights of a car, unable to move one way or the other, totally hypnotised. He caressed her cheek again then moved forward until his lips were brushing hers, the heat of his mouth radiating against them.

'Yes,' she whispered, 'oh yes.' The words made her lips move on his. Suddenly he took her by the shoulders, pulled her up towards him and wrapped his arms around her as he plunged his tongue into her mouth and squirmed his lips on hers.

Nadia felt a shock of pleasure. Her body lit up like a Christmas tree, every nerve tingling as if eager to establish that last night had not been a freak and they were capable of operating at the same level of intensity again, of giving and receiving pleasure at this new high frequency. She gasped, the sound gagged on his tongue. She felt her breasts being crushed against his chest, her nipples so hard they felt like pebbles trapped between their bodies.

He was pulling her down on the bed. In seconds he was lying on top of her and she felt his erection throbbing against her belly. He broke the kiss and began to move his mouth down her body, down over the tendons of her neck, stretched taut as her pleasure forced her head back. His lips were hot, planting tiny kisses at regular intervals. He reached her collarbone, then mounted the slope of her right breast. Her nipple throbbed as it felt his mouth approaching. He flicked it with his tongue then pinched it lightly between his teeth. His mouth moved over to her left breast, then gave that nipple the same treatment.

His hand was opening her legs, spreading her thighs apart. His finger nudged into her labia and found her clitoris. It felt swollen and hard. Slowly he began circling it, as his lips sucked on her nipple, coating it with saliva, letting the heat of his mouth engulf it.

'Jack, Jack . . .' she moaned. All the feelings she had experienced last night were back with a vengeance. Her body was energised, able to receive infinite sensation, an instrument that had been tuned up, for the first time, that could respond minutely to the most complex demands of its player. 'You don't know how good that feels.'

'What do you want?' he said.

'Everything, everything . . .'

She felt his finger working relentlessly against her clitoris and his mouth go back to her nipple. Another finger began to play at the gate of her vagina, stretching it and opening it. That was another revelation. She hadn't realised it was so sensitive, so adept at giving pleasure. It felt almost like a second clitoris, or was it just that she was so super-charged with feeling that anywhere he touched would react as though it were a new erogenous zone? She felt her body pulse and knew immediately she was going to come. She groped around with her hand until she found his erection, then grasped it tightly, letting its hardness and size and the memory of how it had been buried in her take her over the top, cresting a wave of pleasure as sharp as any she'd had last night.

He did not stop. His finger continued relentlessly. His mouth worked down over her navel and her body spasmed again as she felt his tongue, hot and wet, replace his finger at exactly the moment the fingers of his other hand, one, two or three fingers, she could not tell, plunged into her sex. She squeezed his cock hard as a response and felt another orgasm breaking through her as effortlessly as the first.

What had he done to her? How had he freed her body, connected up the missing neurons, achieved the ease with which she now mounted the heights she had never got near before? If she'd thought for a moment that last night was some sort of fluke, induced by a mad impulse, her body waking from a coma, only to sink back into unconsciousness again, she knew now it was not. The effect was irreversible.

Energy flowed through her like electricity, powering her pleasure. He was driving his fingers into her

40

in imitation of a cock as his tongue pushed her clitoris up and down. But Nadia wanted more.

'Come here,' she said, pulling his cock in the direction of her mouth so he would know what she meant. Without losing contact with her sex, he swung his thigh over her body and worked back on his knees until his cock was poised above her face.

'Is that what you want?' he said.

'Oh yes.' She pulled his big erection down and took it greedily into her mouth. It was so hard, she could never remember a man feeling so hard, hard like a bone. She snaked her hands around his buttocks as his cock slid into her throat. She felt it pulse. She wondered if she could make him come. She wanted to feel him spattering into her mouth, but she wanted him to come in her sex too. She simply wanted everything.

Nadia tried to concentrate on him, using her mouth as a substitute for her sex, making it cling to him as she sawed it in and out, taking him deep then pulling back until she could see the ridge of the glans at her lips. But it was difficult not to be distracted from her efforts by what he was doing to her. His artful tongue was moving sinuously against her clitoris, making it throb and setting the rest of her nerves on edge. The juices from her sex were so copious his fingers penetrated her effortlessly. As the two feelings coalesced and she felt, again, the first inklings of orgasm, he nudged a finger into the ring of her anus. It was wet from the juices that had run down from her sex. Before she realised what he was doing his finger was pushing forward. There was momentary resistance, then her body opened – not from any conscious signal but reflexively – and he plunged the finger into her rear, up alongside the

41

fingers that already invaded her vagina.

'God . . .' The word was gagged on the spear of flesh she held in her mouth.

She could feel his fingers sliding up and down inside her, the one separated from the others only by the thinnest of membranes, the movement lubricated by a new flood of juices that this extra intrusion had occasioned. Instantly, as he strained the tendons of his finger to get deeper into her, she came. This time her orgasm was like an explosion. It roared through her body with such intensity it was almost painful, the penetration of her vagina as complete as the penetration of her mouth.

Before men had laboured assiduously, even, occasionally, with art and finesse, to pleasure her. She would come, it was true. But not only were the sensations insignificant in comparison with what she was experiencing now, but her orgasm would be singular, her muted climax never to be revived. Now she was multi-orgasmic. She thought she was never going to stop coming. He had found a spot on her clitoris that made her squirm as though it were a button that he only had to push to bring her off. How was it that she had never found it for herself, nor any other man?

She sucked hard on his cock and felt it throb in response. She tried to clear her head, tried to think. Everything was happening so quickly. Suddenly she knew exactly what she wanted. She pulled away from him.

'Let me,' she said.

He raised his head. 'Let you what?'

She squirmed out from under him and came up on her knees. 'It's your turn,' she said, looking into his eyes.

'I've been having my turn.'

'Lie down,' she said. She wanted to show him she wasn't a naive innocent, however much that was what he made her feel. In her struggle to try and get her body to respond she had done what she did with everything else in life – worked hard at it. In business this dedication had brought her success. In sex it had failed – until now. She knew she could make him come for her; she knew what to do.

Hamilton lay on his back. His cock stuck up from his belly, glistening with her saliva. She looked down at him, the muscles of his abdomen as well defined as his biceps and pectorals. The hairs from his chest ran down to form a new pattern on his belly, all pointing inward, thickest in a line right down the centre.

Nadia felt her sex pulse as she looked at his cock. she took it in her hand, curling her fist around it so the glans stuck up above the ring of her thumb and forefingers. With her other hand she traced a finger over the smooth glans. The whole shaft reacted by spasming in her hand.

'God, I want you,' she said almost to herself.

Without letting go of his erection she swung her thigh over his navel and sat up on her haunches, poised above him. He was looking at her like an indulgent father prepared to put up with the antics of his child.

'You're very hard,' she said.

'You make me hard. You're a very sexy woman.'

'Am I?' Oddly she couldn't remember any man ever using that adjective about her before. She was used to 'lovely', 'beautiful', even 'gorgeous'. But not 'sexy'. She guided his cock between her legs and used it to open her labia. Her juices anointed it.

'You know you are.'

She sunk down on him, her thighs spread open, his cock plunging into her vagina, his pubic bone grinding against her clitoris. He filled her. He was so deep she could feel his glans touching the neck of her womb just as, minutes before, it had been forced down her throat. With all her energy she concentrated on squeezing him with her sex.

'Very strong,' he said, laughing.

She liked that. She laughed too. His laughter intoxicated her. She had never laughed in bed before. It had all been too dour and serious. Now she was relaxed and confident.

'I'm going to make you come.' She emphasised the word 'make'.

'Are you?'

'You want to come, don't you, come inside me?' The words made her whole body shudder.

'Yes.'

'Do it then.'

She began to ride up and down on him, sliding his cock in and out, squeezing it with her internal muscles, grinding her clitoris down on him. She took her breasts in her hands as the movement was making them slap against her chest. She played with her nipples and hoped he could feel the tremor this produced in her nerves. Releasing one breast she reached behind her back and captured the sac of his balls.

'Love that,' he said as he felt her fingers reeling it in.

She grasped it tightly, squeezing his balls firmly but gently. 'Like this?'

'You'll make me come.'

'That's what I want.'

'What about you?'

'Come for me.' Didn't he realise she'd come already more than she could ever remember coming in her life?

She jiggled his balls in her hand and felt his cock react. He reached out and held her by the hips, forcing her down on him and preventing her moving up again. He squirmed underneath her, forcing his cock from side to side, then stopped. He had found his place. Sure now that she understood she did not need to move, he put his hands on her breasts, caressing them with such tenderness, feeling their weight and shape, moving his fingers against the nipples, that Nadia's body trembled.

'So good,' she muttered.

'Yes it is.' And with that his cock jerked inside her, once, then twice, then in a continuous spasm as his hot semen jetted into the wet, silky caches of her sex.

From being in control, from wanting pleasure only for him, Nadia felt her body leap. She had never felt ejaculation so graphically, every inch of his erection touching her, every nerve of her sex so sensitised she was sure she could feel the semen spattering inside her. In her mind's eye she could see it, the jets cascading out from the little eye at the end of his cock, white semen washing down the walls of her sex. The image provoked her as much as the fact. A pulse of feeling, like a shock wave, flowed over her, cancelling everything but the sensation of hardness and power buried in the depths of her, depths it had turned to sticky liquefaction.

45

Chapter Three

'*PHONE CALL FOR* you, says it's personal,' Nadia's secretary told her.

'Thanks.' Nadia heard the click as the call was put through. 'Hello?'

'Nadia. It's Margaret.'

'Margaret, how are you?' Nadia had expected it to be Hamilton. Then she realised why Margaret was calling. 'Is there any news?'

'She's dead, Nadia. Died a month ago.'

'Definitely Nora Babcock?'

'Definitely Nora Babcock. They had a quiet funeral at Marie Ste-Eglise.'

'I bet it was quiet. Margaret, I owe you a big one.'

'Don't be silly, Nadia.'

'No, I do. I'll come over and ski in the winter and make proper recompense.'

'You don't need to do a thing. We're old friends.'

They chatted a while about the weather in Switzerland, where Margaret was calling from, but Nadia's mind wasn't really on the conversation. She was too busy thinking about the implications of what she had learnt. Eventually they said their goodbyes. Nadia found herself grinning broadly.

'What are you doing here?' The office door had opened as she'd put the phone down.'

Angela Barrett grinned as she stood in the doorway. She was wearing a dark green suit, the skirt of which was not much longer than the jacket. Her long legs were sheathed in very sheer, almost transparent nylon.

'As I was passing I thought I'd buy you lunch.'

Nadia was just about to protest that she didn't have time for lunch when Angela produced two paper bags from behind her back. 'Smoked salmon and cream cheese,' she said. 'And a half bottle of Chablis.'

She set the packets down on Nadia's large rosewood desk and fetched two cups from the credenza behind the door where a coffee-making machine was perched. A bottle opener was produced from her handbag.

'I had to see Travers at two so I thought . . .'

'What's Travers up to?' Nadia asked.

'He's looking for another acquisition apparently.'

'He's only just finished the last.'

'This one's much bigger. And the banks think he's the best thing since high fibre bread.'

'He's got the money?' Nadia was astonished.

'Every penny.' Angela unwrapped a sandwich from its cling film and passed it over to Nadia together with a cup of Chablis. 'Cheers,' she said, raising her cup. 'So how did you get on last night.'

'Fine,' Nadia said, trying to sound noncommittal. For once she didn't want to rush into telling Angela everything that had happened.

'Good pictures?'

'I'd seen them already at the preview. I think he's

47

very talented.' Oh yes, very talented, she said to herself, trying not to let the smug grin she felt on the inside spread to her face. 'There were a couple that are really moving. You should go.'

'Sounds interesting.'

'If I pull this deal off with Anderson I may buy one.' She hadn't thought about that until this minute but it was true. She would like the one she'd seen in the studio. It would remind her of what had happened, as if she needed any reminder.

'And did you meet the great man?'

'He was there.' Nadia hoped her voice didn't betray her.

'Gorgeous, isn't he?'

'He was OK.'

'Oh come on. Don't tell me you didn't find him attractive.'

'Yes, he was attractive.' Nadia tried not to give anything away but felt herself squirming unconsciously against the chair. She had a vivid image of Hamilton lying on the bed, his cock gripped firmly in her fist.

'Did you actually meet him?'

Nadia bit into her sandwich. It tasted delicious, slightly salty with the added smoothness of cream cheese. She felt her sex pulse. It didn't taste dissimilar from Hamilton's cock. 'Yes,' she said when she'd finished chewing. She sipped the Chablis.

'And his wife?'

The word made Nadia go cold. She felt a rush of adrenaline as though she had been startled awake from a deep sleep. She tried to put the cup down on her desk without making Angela aware that her hand had started to shake.

'His wife?' she said in a voice that was far from level.

'She's supposed to be a real beauty. Long black hair. You must have seen her. She's the face of Pandora.'

Pandora was a range of cosmetics that advertised heavily in magazines and on billboards, using the same model's face in all their photographs. Nadia passed one on the way to work, and could see the woman's face immediately. She was beautiful with long hair parted down the middle, her cheekbones high and hollow, her rather thin lips always pictured without the trace of a smile, her big dark eyes perfectly served by the company's products.

'Her? She's married to Jack?'

'Didn't you know?'

'I didn't know anything about him except what you told me the other day. Why didn't you tell me he was married?' The question came out all wrong: too much emphasis and too emotionally charged.

'Why are you so interested suddenly?' Angela said, picking up on her tone. They had been friends for too long for it to pass unnoticed.

It was no time to lie. 'Because I was with him last night, damn him. Damn him to hell.' A thought occurred to her. 'That's why he took me to his bloody studio.'

'You went to bed with him? You sly dog. Why didn't you tell me? You went to bed with Jack Hamilton. What was it like? Was it wonderful? God, I bet it was. I'm green . . .'

'Stop it, Angela. He didn't tell me he was married.'

'Oh Nadia, what does it matter? You had a good time, didn't you?'

49

'You know how I feel about married men.' The spectre of what had happened to her before loomed large. She had sworn she was never going to allow herself to be hurt that way again. Now, unwittingly, she had already committed the crime. The tingling that Hamilton's name had created in her body turned to hard-edged ice.

'Oh come on, Nadia . . .'

'And he lied to me.'

'Did he tell you he wasn't married?'

'No, but . . .'

'He probably assumed you knew. It's common knowledge.'

'Well, I didn't. I'd never have gone to bed with him if . . .' Suddenly she wondered if that was true. She remembered the strength of the impulse she'd felt when she first saw him.

'So he took you to his studio, and . . .?'

'Yes, presumably he takes all his bimbos there. Fully equipped. Double bed. Shower room. Kitchen. I even got freshly brewed coffee.'

'Why are you so cross?'

'I'm not like you, Angela, you know that. I find it difficult to be casual about sex.' Particularly wonderful, mind-bending, earth-shattering sex, she thought but did not say. 'And you know what happened with Jeffrey Allen.'

'I know, I know you were hurt.' She leant forward over the desk. 'But what was he like?' She almost whispered.

'Oh Angela, that's the trouble. That's the *real* problem.'

'What?'

'It was fantastic. I mean, like nothing I've ever experienced before, damn him.'

50

He'd got up after they'd made love, pulled on a short cotton robe and gone to the kitchen. He'd made a pot of coffee in a cafetière and squeezed her a glass of fresh orange juice in an electric juicer. He'd brought it to bed on a white tray. She had ten minutes before her seven-thirty deadline. He touched her face and looked at her in that way he had, as though he were looking at some peerless work of art. She had not recovered from their sex. Her nipples were still so hard she was beginning to think they would never go down and her clitoris seemed to be alive, pulsating constantly against her labia. She felt a sense of well-being that seemed to radiate from her like light from a lighthouse.

He'd told her to get dressed. As he watched her climb into her skirt and blouse he said she had a beautiful body and when she'd looked round again he was erect, his cock poking out from the folds of the robe, as he stroked it gently.

'See what you do to me?' he said.

The desire to take him again, to pull him down on top of her, was almost irresistible. But he could see what was going on in her mind.

'No,' he'd said firmly. 'Go to work. You said you've got to go to work.'

'I have,' she'd agreed. 'But I could . . .' She had *never* considered missing work before.

'No. If you do something you'll regret later then you'll associate that with me. It'll be my fault. I don't want to be associated in your mind with anything but pleasure. Sheer unadulterated pleasure.'

It was exactly what she'd wanted to hear because it implied they had a future.

'Will I see you again?'

'Of course. Don't be ridiculous. Give me your

number. I'll call you. As you can see, I can hardly wait.' His erection was testimony to that.

She'd driven home on a high. She'd been on a high ever since. She'd see him again, have sex with him again. Over and over again. She knew she'd never be satiated, not on what he made her feel.

'Christ, Angela,' she said, feeling betrayed. The tears started to well in her eyes but she fought them back. She wasn't going to let that bastard make her cry. 'What am I supposed to do now?'

'How did you leave it with him?'

'Oh, he was terrific. Took my number. Swore he'd call me. Said he couldn't wait. All that crap.'

'I'm sure he'll call.'

'So am I. Positive. Why wouldn't he? You're right. He'll have assumed I knew he was married.' She opened the drawers of her desk one after the other until she found what she wanted. The brochure from the exhibition was in the bottom drawer. She flicked to the back page where Hamilton's photograph stared back at her. The biographical notes ended with the fact that he was married to model Jan Hamilton. 'It's even in here. So he thinks I'm a willing accomplice. A nice juicy bit on the side, one in a very long line.'

'So? Come on, Nadia. What difference does it make? You say you had a good time. You're both adults.'

'No. He's married, Angela.'

'It's not going to be like Jeff. Just have a fling. As you say, there's probably been a whole netball team before you. I'd do it at the drop of a paintbrush.'

'Do what?'

'Go to bed with Jack Hamilton.' Angela took a large bite from her sandwich.

Nadia had lost her appetite. She felt angry and used. The night with Hamilton had been so special, she'd found it impossible to put him out of her thoughts all morning. It was not that she had become emotionally involved with him – though she knew in time that would have been inevitable. But she was physically involved and that was much worse. She had developed an instant obsession, an addiction, and weaning herself away from it was going to be hard.

'Got to go,' Angela said. 'Aren't you going to eat that?' She was looking at the half-eaten sandwich.

'No.'

'Don't mind if I do?' she said, reaching across the desk. She finished the sandwich in two big bites. All Angela's appetites were voracious.

'Thanks for the wine.'

'You in tonight? I'll call you.'

'No, I've got dinner at the Dorchester. Dick Cabot, that Canadian on the board of Tresko. He wants to sell.'

'Really?'

'I've placed the whole lot at quite a premium. The shares will jump.'

'I didn't hear that,' Angela said.

'I didn't say it.'

Angela waved and was gone, leaving Nadia staring at the files on her desk, her enthusiasm for work, as for everything else, suddenly flown out of the window.

It was twelve o'clock when Dick Cabot finally refused an offer of Hine Antique. Up to that point he had accepted gladly and often, and the bill, which Angela paid, was commensurately large. He appeared little the worse for wear, however, and courteously allowed Nadia to take the first taxi the doorman whistled up.

'It's good work,' he told her as she climbed aboard.

'I'll put it all in a fax tomorrow.'

'Great. Send it to Toronto. I'm leaving in the morning.'

It had been a good evening's work. The fact that she had been able to place the shares at such a good premium to the market price had so impressed Cabot that he had told her he would undoubtedly use her for his next major UK deal, which, though he would give no details, was already being planned.

But as the taxi wound its way along a deserted Oxford Street, Nadia could find no consolation in her business acumen. The spectre of Jack Hamilton continued to haunt her. She could see his face, the way those mahogany eyes had looked at her with such intensity, and his strong, naked body. She could see the way his laughter had wrinkled his face and the way he had looked at her as she'd sunk her sex down on to his erection. She could see every detail of his cock, its veins and contours like an animate relief map of her pleasure. She shuddered and, with an effort, tore her mind away from the taunting images.

'Damn you,' she said aloud.

'Sorry, miss?' the taxi driver said, thinking she was talking to him.

'Nothing. Talking to myself.'

'That's a bad habit, miss.'

'I know.'

Outside her house she gave the driver a big tip.

He didn't drive away until she was opening the front door, a gesture of consideration she appreciated. After turning off her burglar alarm she went straight up to her bedroom, stripped off the red silk dress she had been wearing and ran herself a bath. She needed to try and relax. She felt like the mainspring of a watch that had been wound too tight.

She lay in the bath and tried to concentrate on what she had to do the next day. A major takeover bid was due to be announced by the middle of the following week. Her clients had tried to negotiate with the company they wanted to buy, Anderson Aggregates, but all reasonable offers had been refused. They had decided to launch a bid which naturally Anderson's would oppose. There was going to be a major battle with the big institutional shareholders on both sides holding all the cards. But Nadia had developed another strategy. It depended on her getting to see Andrew Anderson in person and, as she was firmly in the enemy camp, there would certainly be no way he would agree to that on a formal basis. But the next day she was meeting a man who knew Anderson well and who had offered to introduce her casually, as if by chance. Then she would be able to see if the information her friend Margaret had given her that morning would be as valuable as she thought it was.

Drying herself quickly she walked back into the bedroom and got into bed. It had been a pleasantly warm night and Nadia had no need for more than a single sheet to cover her. She picked up her book from the bedside table and read a page or two. She caught a glimpse of herself in the mirror opposite the bed, the outline of her naked body – she always slept in the nude – under the peach-coloured sheet. It reminded her of Angela's story. She felt her nipples stiffen. She could see them clearly cresting the firm hills of her breasts. She opened her legs, creating a V-shaped valley, the sheet clinging to the roundness of her thighs.

And then it was too late. Too late to control herself, too late to do anything but plunge her hand down over the delta of her pubis, her fingers curving round the bone into the softness of her labia. She threw the book aside, her hand rigid against her sex. In the mirror she saw her middle finger move, crooking inward to find her clitoris, rubbing against the sheet.

'Damn you,' she said aloud. It had become her litany.

She pulled the sheet off her body, bent her knees with her legs wide apart and lifted her buttocks, staring into the open mouth of her own sex. Why was she lying here alone? Why wasn't she with him? She wanted to feel that big, incredibly hard cock throbbing in her hand. She wanted to suck it. She wanted it inside her.

With one hand she held her right breast, squeezing it tightly, while the other went back to her sex. Her body seemed to be mocking her, throbbing with the same anticipation she had felt with Hamilton. But she knew it would be useless. She would achieve nothing from masturbation but disappointment and anti-climax. Half of her didn't even want to try, just wished she could roll over and sleep. The other half sent her hand down over her belly, her finger parting her labia to find the promontory of her clit. To her surprise she was wet. Not just moist but soaking wet. She had never felt herself like this under these circumstances. She moved her fingers down to the gate of her vagina. Her whole sex was liquid. It felt different too, like a squashy, over-ripe fruit. She felt it throb at her touch, a surge of feeling so strong it made her gasp.

Of course, she was seeing Hamilton now. She could see him in the mirror standing by the bed, quite naked, his erection sticking out at a right angle from his body. He was looking down at her, with an indulgent expression on his face.

'Watch me, then,' she said aloud, opening her legs wider, arching her body up at the imaginary image, showing herself to him. 'Watch me.'

She plunged two fingers into her sex, pushing them in until the tendons of her hand were strained to the limit. But it wasn't deep enough. Her mind wanted the feeling of Hamilton's cock driving up to the neck of her womb. The odd thing was that she had never penetrated herself like this before. Occasionally she would put a finger into her sex but it had never excited her very much. Not like this. Now she wanted penetration. She needed something inside her, and needed it desperately.

Nadia looked around the room for some phallic object to serve as a substitute for Hamilton's presence. She had a small set of exercise weights stacked in a corner. The central spindle of the dumbbells could be disconnected to add extra weight. It was made from some sort of plastic and, apart from the ridges where the circular weights could be fitted, was perfectly smooth. She leapt off the bed, pulled the weighted ends off the spindle and carried it back to bed, resuming her position with her knees bent and her legs open. Her sex was throbbing. Her imagination made the spindle throb in her hand too.

She looked into the mirror. She touched the end of the spindle to her nipple, imagining it was Hamilton's cock. She pressed it down into the spongy flesh. The plastic was cold to the touch and made her nipples pucker even tighter.

Hamilton was looking at her again. He'd taken his cock in his hand as if to say, 'Wouldn't you rather have this?'

'No,' she said in answer to the unasked question. 'I don't need you.'

She trailed the phallus down over her belly. She wasn't seriously going to stick this thing inside her, was she? She'd never put any foreign object inside her vagina. But she needed it. She desperately needed to feel something hard and strong filling her, mimicking, however inadequately, the feeling Hamilton's cock had given her.

The end of the phallus nudged into her labia. She felt it butt against her clitoris, and used it to circle the little nut of nerves. She imagined she had Hamilton's cock in her hand and was manipulating his glans against her.

'Feels so good, doesn't it?'

Her masturbation had always been silent before. Now the words excited her. She moved the phallus down between her legs, her own juices lubricating its journey. She couldn't believe what she was feeling, the excitement that was coursing through her body.

'Come on then, put into me,' she said for her own benefit. 'Fuck me.'

She could see every detail of his cock. She could feel everything he had done to her, how his fingers had plunged into both passages of her body, how his tongue had licked at her sex, how his erection had overwhelmed her. With no hesitation she drove the spindle into her body. She was so wet it slid up effortlessly, until the end was deep inside her. The initial penetration produced a wave of feeling so strong it forced her eyes closed. She dropped her head back on the pillow. She imagined him looking down at her. Her sex contracted involuntarily, gripping the phallus as if to test its solidity.

'Yes, yes, like that,' she cried, forcing the phallus deeper.

And then the strangest thing happened, strange for her at least. She came. She came easily, with no exertion, no desperation, no prolonged, increasingly anguished striving. She came like she'd never come before by her own hand, a sharp, powerful orgasm that gathered in all her feelings and emotions and put them to work to pleasure her completely.

Her surprise was absolute. As soon as she could react consciously again she opened her eyes and looked into the mirror, seeing the astonishment written all over her face.

'Did you see that?' she asked her imaginary lover.

She was not finished. She knew that. She moved the phallus up and down. Her body was going to give her more. She could feel every contour of the object inside her. She could feel the silky wet walls of her vagina as it moved against them. As if to attract her attention her clitoris pulsed strongly. Holding the phallus in one hand she moved the other over her belly. Even the fur of her pubic hair seemed to be alive with feeling. She pushed her finger down into her labia. The breadth of the spindle had opened them and her clitoris was already exposed. It was swollen and incredibly tender. She stroked it gently and felt a surge of sensation course through her. It flashed down to her vagina and broke over the end of the phallus, causing another contraction.

'Fuck me then,' she said. 'Come on, fuck me.'

It was all so different. The words were provoking her. So was everything she could see in the mirror, the end of the phallus sticking out obscenely from the soft folds of her labia, the rest of it buried in her sex. She pushed the phallus in and out, imitating the action of a cock, of his cock, Hamilton's cock. The plastic had taken the warmth of her body. It had seemed to be alive. It was not difficult to imagine it was *him*.

She wished she could pinch her nipples. She wished she could push a finger into her rear passage. She wanted everything all at once. But this was enough. More than enough. She matched the rhythm of the penetration with the movements of her finger on her clitoris, suddenly adept and fluent, for the first time, at the rites of masturbation. She pushed her clitoris from side to side against the hardness of her pubic bone. Her whole body was alive, like it had been with Hamilton, so alive, so full of excitement, she found it hard to believe it had not responded like this before.

An orgasm flooded over her, sweeping everything aside but the intensity of pleasure. Almost immediately, as she continued to plunge the dildo to and fro, another began, this time swelling like a wave at the beach, gathering momentum, until it crashed over her, knocking her back into an undertow of sensation. She was writhing on the bed, tossing her head from side to side, her breasts slapping against each other. It was a storm, a cyclone of feeling.

Eventually the crisis passed. She could not take any more. She eased the spindle out of her body and looked at it curiously. It was glistening with her juices. Her labia and her clitoris felt a little sore, which was not surprising. She had been out of control and had hammered them mercilessly. But, as she looked into the mirror, she saw she was grinning.

She got off the bed a little unsteadily and went into the bathroom to pee. Her body was completely relaxed now, the mainspring wound down. She felt wonderful, little trills and remembrances of pleasure still occasionally jolting through her. Sex, she thought, must be like riding a bicycle. Once you learnt to do it you never forgot how. She laughed out loud. She had obviously never been taught properly before. She had assumed that whatever neural pathways Hamilton had opened would close again without his endeavours. She was delighted to find the effect he had had on them appeared to be permanent.

Getting back into bed she covered herself with the sheet. The touch of the cotton against her nipples gave her a tingling sensation. They felt incredibly sensitive. Her sex too reacted to the pressure of her thighs as she brought her legs together. She had gone from the sublime to the ridiculous, from the ice maiden to the fire queen. She was even tempted to touch herself again, exactly like a child with a new toy, who wanted to play with it, just one more time before bed.

The image of Hamilton hadn't faded. He was still there if she looked up into the mirror, his body turned sideways so she could see the projection of his cock jutting out from his belly, its curved shaft and the sac of his balls like some exotic fruit ripe to be picked. But, for all her passion, she was still furious with him for what he'd done.

The trouble was, it was probably too late to protect herself against him. Hamilton had already touched her in a way no other man had. He had reached into her libido and found the key to her sexuality. He had let the genie out of the lamp and now it roamed free, gaining strength and power and wanting to enjoy its new-found capabilities. It was difficult to stay cross with him. She saw his smile, and the warmth in his eyes . . .

'Damn you,' she said, chanting her litany. Why did he have to be married?

Chapter Four

ANGELA ANSWERED ON the second ring. 'Hello?'

'Hi, it's me. What are you doing?'

'Finishing up.'

'Do you feel like going out tonight?'

'Great. What time?'

'The Rencontre at seven-thirty.'

'The Rencontre? What's got into you?' Rencontre was in Berkeley Square. It was a bar and restaurant and was usually packed with women hunting in pairs among the prosperous male clientele. Women were allowed in free; men had to pay an exorbitant membership fee.

'You know exactly,' Nadia said pointedly.

'Oh right. Withdrawal symptoms.' Angela laughed.

'Get dressed up. I'm going to.'

'If that's what you want.'

'See you later.'

He had called her three times. Each time she had told her secretary to tell him she wasn't available. Each time the temptation to push the button on her phone that would put him through was almost irresistible. But she had resisted, just. She badly needed to take her mind, and her body, off him.

Two hours later Nadia sat on one of the barstools at the far end of the long bar of Rencontre, toying with a glass of champagne, and aware of the many pairs of eyes that roamed her body. She was wearing a black Ferragamo dress that clung to her figure. Its plunging neckline revealed the depth of her cleavage and a split in its skirt exposed a great deal of thigh. She wore a silver choker around her neck and had made herself up with less subtlety than usual: a heavy eye shadow to emphasise her eyes, a blusher to accentuate her cheekbones and a dark red lipstick to match the colour of her fingernails. She had sheathed her legs in sheer black tights that were woven with Lycra to give them a glossy finish and was wearing her highest high heels. She crossed her legs and let the split in the skirt reveal her thigh. It was an uncharacteristic gesture for her but oddly she found it exciting. She watched one man in a booth opposite staring fixedly. He was in his fifties with a bald pate and teeth yellowed by smoking. He was trying to catch her eye but she refused to play *that* game.

'Darling!' Angela exploded into the bar through the swing doors at the far end and pushed her way through the crowd. She kissed Nadia on both cheeks. 'Sorry I'm late, got a phone call just as I was leaving.'

'Don't worry.' Nadia signalled to the barman to bring two glasses of champagne without asking Angela what she wanted.

Angela squirmed on to the barstool Nadia had kept vacant for her. She was wearing a cobalt-blue dress that looked as though it had been sprayed on, no more than a tight tube of material clinging to her body from the top of her breasts to the middle of her thighs. On the front, over her navel, it was decorated with a figure of eight picked out in silver sequins. Her red hair had been pinned up to her head, rather severely emphasising her long neck and the bareness of her shoulders. Like Nadia she also wore Lycra tights but hers were patterned with a diamond motif. The blue of her high heels matched her dress. They had straps from the back of the heel around her narrow ankles.

'Have you sized up the talent?' Angela asked, blatantly looking at the ranks of men sitting opposite, only a very few as yet attached to female companions.

'Not really.'

The barman put the glasses of champagne on the bar in front of them. Nadia used the rest of her first glass to make the libation.

'So tell Auntie Angela all about it.' Angela had known her friend too long not to know what lay behind a visit to Rencontre, dressed up like a dog's dinner.

'It's Hamilton. I can't get him out of my mind.'

'He must have been good.'

'Can I ask you something really personal?' Nadia leant closer to her friend.

'Of course.'

'Do you use a dildo?' She didn't have to ask whether Angela masturbated. She knew she did. Angela had told her some time ago that she masturbated regularly, often as much as two or three times a week. She needed it, she had told Nadia, even if she had been having sex with a man. But the revelation had not included questions of technique.

'A dildo?' Angela repeated. The barman was hovering and smiled broadly but said nothing.

'You know . . .' Nadia tried to think of another word to describe it.

'You mean a vibrator . . . yes, of course I use a vibrator. They're wonderful. Don't you?'

'I . . .' Nadia faltered, suddenly wishing she hadn't brought up the subject. She took a sip of the champagne and lowered her voice, since the barman was clearly hoping he might hear further tit-bits of their conversation. 'No, I hadn't before.'

'What, you've just tried one?'

'I don't know what's happening to me, Angela. I'm just horny all the time. I never used to be like that.' Nadia had made a decision. She had to lay the ghost of Hamilton. She needed a man. She needed to find a man and sleep with him. That was why she'd invited Angela. She didn't have the courage to do it alone, but with Angela along it would be easy. Well, easier.

'And this is all down to Hamilton.'

'Yes.' She wanted to tell her everything.

'Angela, my dear girl . . .' A small, neat man in his late fifties had come up behind them. He had a prolific growth of totally white hair which years of combing in the same direction had laid into a set pattern and small green eyes that sparkled with devilment. His white moustache was slightly turned up at the ends. He wore a tweed suit, and despite the summer temperatures, a yellow camel-haired waistcoat. His Viyella shirt did not match his MCC tie.

'Georgie!' Without getting off the barstool Angela kissed him on both cheeks. His arm snaked around her back and stayed there. 'This is Nadia Irving,'

Angela said. 'Sir George Pontsonby.'

'Charmed,' he said, taking Nadia's hand and bringing it to his lips. 'And this is my nephew, Tony.'

A tall young man stood uneasily behind Sir George. He looked as though he found the décolleté dresses of both women embarrassing and wasn't sure whether he was supposed to look at them. Inevitably his eyes strayed downwards and came to rest on their bosoms.

'Hello, Tony,' Angela said, extending her hand. 'This is Nadia.'

'I'm very pleased to meet you,' he said earnestly, blushing a light shade of pink as he shook their hands in turn. He was no more than nineteen and wore a smart navy blue suit and a white silk shirt with a blue silk tie.

'Georgie and I met at the polo at Cowdray Park,' Angela told Nadia.

'Bloody awful game,' Sir George said immediately. 'Anything that involves horses involves shit and anything that involves shit is shitty.' His remark made him laugh. Angela laughed too. Tony and Nadia merely smiled politely.

'Why did you go then?' Nadia asked.

'Some damn Jap wanted to see it. Angie was the only compensation.'

'George is in property finance,' Angela explained.

'Trying to sell Buckinghamshire to the Nips. Not very sporting. But we all have to earn a crust.'

'And what do you do?' Nadia asked Tony, his attention having fallen to her nylon-covered thigh.

'Oh . . . oh . . .' He blushed again, caught in the act. 'I'm reading Greats at Cambridge.'

'Greats?' Angela queried.

'Classics.'

'Romans and Greeks,' Sir George explained. 'Best possible education for a man. I tell you, this country went to the dogs when civil servants weren't obliged to have Greats from Oxbridge. Essential. Teaches you everything. So are you on?'

'On?' Angela asked.

'On. For the evening. Car's outside. Got a table booked at Le Dernier Cri. Are you game?'

'Georgie, you can't take us there.'

'Can,' he said like a petulant schoolboy. 'Shall.'

'What is it?' Nadia asked.

'A private club with a very risqué cabaret,' Angela said.

'*Le plus risqué*,' Sir George added. 'Come on, dear ladies, no time to waste. The food is superb.'

'Well?' Angela asked Nadia.

'Why not?' Nadia said, putting aside her initial reluctance as she looked at Tony. He was undoubtedly attractive. His hair was blond and his eyes a deep, almost turquoise blue. He had a square set jaw, a fleshy mouth and a very clear complexion that looked as though he got a lot of fresh air, probably playing contact sports. He might be exactly what she was looking for.

'Right,' Sir George exclaimed, extracting a fifty pound note from his pocket and waving it at the barman to pay for the women's drinks. He helped them off the barstools and ushered them out before the barman could return with his change.

Good chauffeurs seem to have a second sense when it comes to knowing when they are required and, as the doorman at the club opened the outer doors for them, a Rolls Royce Silver Wraith glided up to the curb. A slender black chauffeur rushed round to open the nearside passenger door. He was wearing a grey uniform with a crossover front to its jacket and riding breeches for trousers. His black boots were spotless.

'I'll ride up front,' Sir George said as the two women sandwiched Tony between them on the rear seat.

As the car pulled away the glass partition that divided the passengers from the driver slid down and Sir George turned round, hooking his arm over the back of the seat.

'Did I tell you that you're looking particularly stunning, my dear? Stunning. Well, you both do. Don't they, Tony?'

'Lovely,' Tony agreed, only too aware of the two women sitting with elegantly crossed legs on either side of him.

'So what do you do, my dear?' Sir George asked Nadia.

'I work for Hill Brothers.'

'Oh jolly good. Like to see it myself. Women are a bloody underused resource in this benighted country.'

The Rolls halted in a small mews off Curzon Street. It was dimly lit with no functioning street lights and looked like a wholly residential mews with no sign of commercial activity, except for a discreet brass plate on the one building that was a good size bigger than the rest. The plate read: LE DERNIER CRI. PRIVATE MEMBERS ONLY.

As the black chauffeur let them out of the car the club door opened, no doubt alerted to their presence by the security camera mounted in the corner of the small forecourt in front of the house. A huge man filled the doorway. He was wearing a dinner suit and black bow tie, his shoulders so wide he would not have been able to get through the door without turning sideways. Incongruously he wore a small bowler hat.

'Good evening, Archibald,' Sir George said.

'Evening, sir.' The man's voice was falsetto. He stood aside to let them enter, closing and bolting the door behind them.

They found themselves in a small square foyer tastefully decorated with pale pink walls and red carpet. A large oil which Nadia thought was possibly a Pissarro dominated one wall. There was a single oak-panelled door behind a leather-topped Victorian partner's desk.

'Good evening, Sir George.' An attractive auburn-haired woman in a dinner jacket, white silk shirt and black bow tie sat behind the desk. She wasn't wearing trousers or a skirt and Nadia could see the 'shirt' was, in fact, a body worn over black fishnet tights. She typed Sir George's name into the computer that was perched on the desk. 'Three guests, sir.'

'Correct.'

'Very good, sir.'

The panelled door opened and a tall, long-legged, long-haired blonde held it open. She was wearing shiny, almost transparent tights and a leotard made from a fabric that glistened under the light and was coloured to look like silver. It was cut so high on the hip its crotch was no more than a thin thong of material barely covering the crease of her sex. The woman's breasts were large and they bulged out of the plunging neckline of the garment.

'Evening, Sir George,' she said, confirming the impression that he was a respected regular at the club.

70

They filed through the door and were led along a short corridor into a large room. To all intents and purposes it looked like a normal restaurant. There was a small bar area by the entrance which opened into a large space set with tables, glittering with crystal glasses and silver cutlery on pink table cloths. A huge display of flowers, mostly of arum lilies, stood on a table against one wall, individually lit by a spotlight overhead.

Beyond the tables was a dance floor and beyond that a small stage. A trio of musicians sat on the stage playing jazz versions of standard ballads. At the moment they were playing a version of 'Misty', the drummer and bass player providing a muted accompaniment to the skilful improvisation of the pianist.

'Have a nice evening,' the blonde said, making the twenty-pound note Sir George palmed into her hand disappear, as if by magic.

'Can I get you a drink before dinner?' A waitress had come over as they settled into the armchairs in the bar. She was wearing an identical outfit to the blonde's, except the colouring was gold. Sitting down Nadia found herself staring up into the girl's barely covered crotch. One thing was certain. The bikini line treatment for these outfits required complete depilation.

They drank champagne and ordered an extravagant dinner, urged on by Sir George. They were moved to a table in the restaurant where they feasted off oysters and fillet steak and vanilla soufflés, and drank Perrier-Jouet champagne and Romanée-Conti burgundy.

'My attitude,' Sir George declared during the meal, 'is that you should always have the best you can afford.'

71

The restaurant was busy. There were several Arab customers – men with swarthy complexions, silk suits in pale colours with lapels and facings edged with satin, and tieless shirts, their fingers beringed with gold, their wrists weighed down with elaborate watches, some encrusted with diamonds. The women that accompanied them were all European, all extremely attractive, and all wearing evening dresses in satin or silk or lace, tightly sheathing their bodies while giving tantalising glimpses of breast or thigh.

The maître d' was a woman, though she was dressed in a very masculine dinner suit, with her hair cut and parted exactly like a man. In fact, Nadia had noticed, the entire staff of the club, apart from the bouncer outside, were women. As they finished their meal and were served coffee the maître d' stepped across the dance floor, mounted the small stage and took a microphone from its stand.

'And now, ladies and gentlemen . . .' she said, turning to the audience. 'Le Dernier Cri is proud to present for your entertainment this evening the singular talents of Madame Morceau and Monsieur le Count.'

There was a smattering of applause. The lights in the restaurant dimmed. The band began playing a version of 'Unforgettable' and two of the waitresses placed a small round table and a gilt chair in the middle of the dance floor which was bathed in a bright, very white light.

Nadia settled back in her chair, glancing across at Angela who was watching the dance floor intently. So far the evening was exactly what she had hoped it would be: an escape from the realities that beset her – well, one reality in particular. She had no idea

72

what to expect next.

A woman appeared on stage. She was wearing a catsuit made from the sort of denier of nylon usually reserved for tights. It was shaded cream but hid little of her body. The woman's blonde hair was pinned tightly to her head and she was wearing heavy, dramatic make-up, especially around the eyes. In her hand she held a leather loop attached to a chain leash. As she walked on to the dance floor she tugged on the leash and a man appeared. He was dressed in black evening trousers, a white tuxedo and black bow tie, and moved on all fours like a dog, the leash attached to a studded collar strapped around his neck. The woman sat on the gilt chair, crossed her legs and tugged on the leash so the man would come to kneel in front of her.

Immediately he began kissing and licking the white high-heeled shoe on the floor while his hands caressed her ankle. Apparently satisfied with the work he had done on one, the woman put the other foot down. The man eagerly grasped it and licked the white leather. The woman opened her legs to allow him to kiss the inside of her calves and Nadia could see a lush growth of pubic hair trapped under the nylon gusset of the catsuit. Its dark colour was in contrast to the blonde hair on her head.

The man worked his hands up her legs, until they were caressing her thighs. She allowed his hands to reach up, over her hips, and then to circle her breasts. Nadia could see them clearly under the sheer nylon. They were not large and her nipples were minuscule.

She seized the leash again at the point where it was attached to the leather collar and pulled the man's face up to hers, kissing him full on the mouth.

Nadia glanced around the table. Sir George had turned his chair around to face the spectacle and was watching intently, his features wrinkled in a broad grin. Tony had not bothered to face the stage and was staring into his coffee cup. It looked as though he was blushing again. Angela sat back in her chair. She gave the impression of having seen it all before.

Nadia heard a moan of pleasure and looked back at the dance floor. The man's face was now buried between the blonde's legs and she had clamped it there firmly with her thighs, her fingers laced into his dark hair pulling him forward rhythmically as she thrust her pelvis to and fro with the same tempo. She moaned continuously, faking – or perhaps it wasn't faked – the sounds of orgasm, until she reached a crescendo and the man was pushed away, splaying back on the wooden floor.

The man got to his feet, an erection jutting from his trousers. Slowly he took off his jacket and stripped off his shirt with his back turned to the audience. In the same position he kicked off his black patent leather shoes and unzipped his trousers, letting them fall to the floor. As the trousers fell a roar of surprise came from the audience. The man was wearing black stockings and a black lace suspender belt. He turned and Nadia saw, strapped around his hips, an inflatable rubber tube that had been used to produce the erection. She also saw a pair of very female breasts. The 'man' was, in fact, a woman.

Pulling off the rubber prosthetic, the newly discovered woman lay across the table, face down, her buttocks towards the audience. The blonde got to her feet. The audience's attention had been on the

74

'man' but now there was yet another surprise. Sprouting from the blonde's loins, pressed up under the tight nylon, was the outline of a penis, fully erect. Freeing a hidden seam in the catsuit the blonde extracted the phallus and stroked it with her hand. How it had been hidden in the thick pubic hair Nadia did not know but there was no doubt the 'woman' was a man, or more accurately, a slim-hipped eighteen-year-old boy.

Standing behind the woman on the table the boy pushed himself between her buttocks, the erection sliding between her legs. At that moment there was a total blackout. When the lights came up again both performers had disappeared.

The audience had been so mesmerised by this turn of events they had forgotten to applaud. But that was soon remedied. Two or three of the Arabs got to their feet and began clapping wildly, the rest of the audience joining in with more circumspect appreciation.

'Jolly good, jolly good,' Sir George said, turning his chair back into the table. 'Would never have guessed. Did anyone guess? I mean, that boy made a damn fine woman. Must have been on hormones or something.'

'Definitely,' Angela agreed.

Normal service in the restaurant was resumed. A waitress arrived with a silver pot of coffee and refilled their cups. Nadia accepted Sir George's offer of a brandy and selected a Vieux Armagnac from a trolley laden with every conceivable liquor. She drank it rapidly, trying to calm herself down. The show had affected her more than she could believe. Her sex was throbbing and she knew it was moist. She felt hot and uncomfortable. Angela caught her eye and smiled knowingly, as if to confirm her reaction was the same.

'Well, shall we stay for the second act?' Sir George asked, puffing on a large Montecristo cigar.

'No, I'd like to go now,' Tony said decisively, asserting himself for the first time.

'Didn't you enjoy it, old boy?'

'No I did not. It was disgusting. Degrading. This whole place is disgusting, girls dressed like . . . like . . .'

'Just a bit of fun,' Sir George said quietly, looking a little shamefaced. 'What do you think, ladies?'

'I thought it was exciting actually,' Angela said.

'And Nadia?'

'I'd like to go,' Nadia replied, sidestepping the question.

'Righty-o. Back to my place for a nightcap then.'

No bill was presented or asked for. In a matter of minutes they had decamped to the Rolls, this time with Sir George sitting between the two women and Tony in front, his anger still simmering. Angela made it very clear to Sir George that she expected him to take full advantage of the feelings that the cabaret had aroused in her. By the time the car turned into the curved gravel driveway of a house in one of the larger avenues of Hampstead, the two were wrapped in each other's arms, the skirt of her dress rucked up around her thighs, their mouths glued together. They seemed oblivious to the fact that the car had stopped.

'We're here,' Nadia announced helpfully.

Tony had got out of the car and opened the front door, the chauffeur opening the passenger door on Nadia's side.

'Come on, old girl,' Sir George said. 'Making a bit

76

of an exhibition of ourselves . . .'

Tony took Nadia into the house, not waiting for his uncle. It was vast, a dining room capable of sitting at least thirty people on one side of the hall, a sitting room on the other. The decor was rather masculine with walnut-panelled walls and leather sofas. Pictures, lit individually by brass lamps, decorated all the walls. There was a Sickert and a Whistler in the hall and Nadia recognised another Whistler over the Adam fireplace as Tony led her into the sitting room.

'Another Armagnac?'

'Yes, please,' she said.

He went to an antique escritoire that had been converted into a drinks cabinet. He poured her brandy into a balloon glass and poured himself a Ty Nant mineral water. 'I didn't mean to be rude in the club,' he said, handing her the glass.

'You were only expressing an opinion.'

Nadia heard the front door close but neither Sir George nor Angela appeared. She thought she heard footsteps on the thick carpeting of the stairs.

'I suppose I'm just not very . . .' – he blushed again – '. . . worldly. That's why I love the classics. I'm more at home with ancient scripts.'

'I don't believe that.' Nadia heard a heavy thump from somewhere upstairs.

'It's true. I've never been very good with women.'

'Why is that?' Angela sat down on a well-used black leather Chesterfield. The split in her skirt revealed her thigh. She had had a lot to drink but whereas it usually made her woolly headed and confused, tonight it appeared to be having the reverse effect. She knew exactly what she wanted and the role she would have to perform to get it. It was not a role she'd played before and that excited her.

'I don't know,' Tony was saying. 'I always seem to say the wrong things. And I never know what to do.'

'Do?'

'Like whether to hold hands or kiss her. If I kiss a girl without asking first she'll be the type who wants to be asked. If I ask first the girl's sure to be the type who wants men to be aggressive. I never get it right.'

'What type do you think I am?' Nadia said, measuring the tone of her voice precisely. She saw Tony looking at her. For the first time that evening it registered with him that Nadia was not just a companion to make up the numbers at dinner but a woman and a beautiful woman at that. Perhaps he'd imagined the age difference between them pre-cluded anything else. As he realised it didn't he blushed a crimson red.

'I don't know,' he said, trying to hide his embar-rassment by taking a long drink of water.

'Well . . .' She ran her finger around the rim of the balloon glass. She had set out this evening with the express intention of getting a man into bed. The show at the club had excited her, but the image of the woman who had pretended to be a man bent over the table naked and exposed had only added to her needs, not created them. Her desire for Tony had mounted throughout the course of the evening and now she was surprised how easy it was to translate that desire into actions. She was behaving like a man. No, that wasn't true. She doubted a man could cast the sort of spell she intended to create. 'I'm the type who likes to be very open and honest about sex. I see no point in beating about the bush.'

'No . . .' he said uncertainly.

'You're a very attractive man, Tony. I'm sure you don't find me unattractive.'

'You're beautiful.'

'Thank you.' She uncrossed her legs. His eyes fell to the valley of her thighs. 'So you see what I want is very simple.' She paused, letting the words hang in the air.

'What's that?'

'I'm sure this great big house has a nice comfortable bedroom with a big double bed. I'd like you to take me upstairs and . . .' She was going to say 'fuck me' but changed it to '. . . make love to me. Is that clear enough?'

'Oh yes.' He didn't look particularly delighted at the prospect. In fact he looked nervous and apprehensive. 'You *are* very beautiful.'

'I'm glad you think so.' Nadia got to her feet. She stood looking into his big serious eyes. 'I'm the type who likes to be kissed straight away,' she prompted.

'Oh . . . sorry.'

He took her cheeks in his hands and kissed her on the mouth, plunging his tongue between her lips, then wrapping his arms around her, hugging her to him, squeezing her so tight he almost took her breath away. His body was hard and strong. Nadia's sex throbbed and, for the second time that evening, she felt it moisten. Her hands caressed his buttocks; they were firm and knotted with muscle.

'Mmm . . .' she said, breaking the kiss. 'You're very strong.'

'I work out,' he said with pride.

'I love it. Come on . . .' She took his hand, enjoying the fact that she had the initiative. 'Let's find a bedroom.' She was beginning to understand how much fun Angela must have had playing the vampish role for so many years.

She led him into the hall but at the bottom of the stairs he pulled her back, circled his arms around her and kissed her again, pushing her back against one of the two elaborately carved newel posts. His tongue was hot and large. She sucked on it and felt her body pulse again. She wanted sex badly. If she had doubted that her sexual renaissance would last, she knew now the doubts were unfounded. Whatever shields had masked her receptors of pleasure, like hardened lacquer shells, had been melted away by Hamilton. The feelings just this embrace were provoking proved that. She was open and receptive now to the slightest stimulation.

Tony's penis had unfurled against her belly. It made her impatient. She broke away and took his hand again. 'Come on . . .'

They got to the top of the stairs. 'Which way?' she asked.

He led her down a corridor to the right. They passed a large pair of double doors and Nadia thought she heard Angela's voice talking softly. Tony led them through a single door at the far end of the passageway.

The large room was decorated in greens. The walls and carpet were a dark forest green while the counterpane and the upholstery of a small sofa were a check in light green and black. There were two mahogany bedside tables and two large bedside lamps with shiny green shades. Tony switched on one and used its built-in dimmer to reduce the illumination to a pleasant glow, as Nadia turned off the overhead light.

'Very comfortable,' she said, sitting on the edge of the bed. 'Is this your room?'

'God, no. I've got a little boxroom at the back for when I come to stay. I prefer that. There's a bathroom over there.' He indicated a door on the far side of the room, his nervousness very apparent.

'Why don't you undress me,' she suggested. She raised her leg and rubbed her shoe against his trousers. He stooped to pluck it off her foot. She raised the other leg and he obliged again, this time taking her foot in his hand and caressing it. 'Now my zip. It's at the back,' she said, turning to one side.

He sat on the bed behind her and found the little plastic tongue of the zip. The zip sung as it parted. His hand slipped on to her back below the strap of her bra, smoothing against her flesh.

'Why don't you undo my bra too?' she said.

His fingers fumbled with the catch, then succeeded in opening it. His hand caressed her back where the strap had been.

'You are so soft,' he said.

Nadia thought she heard Angela's voice cry out in a paroxysm of pleasure. It made her shudder. She got to her feet a little unsteadily. The feelings she was experiencing were similar to being intoxicated. She had never behaved this wantonly with any man, not even Hamilton, and it was making her giddy with excitement. She pushed her dress off her shoulders and let it fall to the floor. It made a whispering sound as the silk lining rubbed against her body and the nylon tights. She stepped out of it and picked it up, draping it over the small sofa. She shucked herself out of her bra straps and let the cups fall away, seeing his eyes looking at her breasts.

'Do you like them?' she said.

'I've never . . . they're lovely.'

Nadia walked up to the bed and stood in front of

him, so close her legs were touching his knees. Feeling her heart pumping in her chest, she ran her hand into his blond hair and pulled his face into her cleavage, holding him tightly to her bosom. He moaned.

'I'm so excited,' she said.

His hands found the waistband of her tights and began pulling them down over her hips. She released his head so he could finish the job. She was wearing black panties under the nylon, no more than a triangle of lace covering her pubic hair, supported by thin satin straps. As soon as he had wrestled the tights off her feet he straightened up, her breasts in front of his face again. This time he kissed them, one after the other, his tongue hot and wet against the spongy flesh.

'Your turn,' she said. She sat on the bed and began unbuttoning his shirt. He got to his feet, took his jacket off and wriggled out of his tie. He completed unbuttoning the shirt and pulled it off. His chest was broad with muscle lining his ribs.

'I've got to go to the loo,' he said, disappearing through the bathroom door in a flash.

Nadia got up and pulled the counterpane and bedding to the foot of the bed. The bottom sheet was cream. She propped two pillows against the mahogany headboard and rested against them. She opened her legs slightly and stroked the soft fur under the black lace of her panties. Inevitably her sex throbbed but she avoided the temptation to touch it.

When Tony emerged from the bathroom he was wearing a small white towel around his waist. His body was much beefier than it had looked in clothes, the muscles of his legs thick and well defined.

'Come over here,' Nadia said, patting the sheet beside her.

He came over to the bed and stood looking down at her. 'I'm really nervous,' he said.

'I know,' she replied quietly.

'I haven't had much experience.'

'Everyone has to start somewhere. Don't worry. Now sit down here.'

He sat down on the edge of the bed next to her. She sat up and ran her hands over his back.

'Big strong boy,' she said. She pressed her breasts into his back and he shuddered. Her nipples were as hard as pebbles. They cried out for attention. 'You're allowed to touch,' she said, lying back again.

Half turning he put his hand on the upper slope of her left breast and slowly moved it down until his finger brushed the puckered nipple.

'Mmm . . .' she said with exaggerated enthusiasm, wanting to encourage him. 'So nice . . .'

'Is it?' He rolled her nipple between his fingers more confidently. 'They're very hard.'

'I'm excited. You excite me, Tony.'

'I do?' He sounded astonished.

'Why wouldn't you? You're young, attractive, strong.'

'I try to keep really fit,' he said earnestly.

'I can see that. Why don't you take my panties off now, Tony?' she said, a huskiness creeping into her voice that reflected her excitement. She could feel her pulse rate racing and her breathing getting shallow. She scissored her legs apart until her left knee touched Tony's back. He stood up, the towel around his waist tented by his erection. Kneeling on the bed beside her he reached for the thin satin waistband on either side of her hips. As he drew it down she closed her legs and arched her buttocks off the bed. He pulled the lace clear of her sex and down her thighs. She was in such a sensitised condition even this produced a surge of feeling. Stripping the panties from her ankles he stared at the soft blonde hair that covered her mons. He ran his hand over her belly and stroked the hair as though he were stroking a little animal.

'I'm very . . . I haven't . . . it's just that . . .' he mumbled, trying to find the right words, anxiety etched into his features.

'Sh . . .' she said.

For Nadia his obvious inexperience was exciting, or was it just his youth? The aura of freshness and health he radiated, the sheen that glowed from his flesh like a perfectly ripe peach, unblemished and unwrinkled, thrilled her at a physical, animalistic level. But psychologically too there was something about his gawkiness and innocence, about the way he was looking at her, his expression torn between a sort of disbelieving adoration and raw lust.

Lust won. In one, almost balletic movement, he pulled the towel away, swung on top of her and pushed himself between her legs. She felt the crown of his erection butting into the folds of her labia. Finding the passage he plunged inside. There was no resistance. Under these circumstances Nadia did not need foreplay. Her sex was already wet.

'God,' he cried, his hand fumbling for her breast between their bodies, his face buried in her neck. 'Oh God, oh God . . .'

He rode up into her, his whole body tense, his strong muscles driving his erection back and forth. He had only achieved three or four strokes when Nadia felt him shudder, a tremor so profound it affected every part of his body, and his cock spasmed inside her, jerking against the silky walls that sheathed it so tightly. He made a noise that was halfway between a sob of despair and a cry of anger and immediately rolled off her. He lay on his side with his back towards her, curling his legs into a foetal position.

His attack had been so sudden, and ended so quickly, Nadia had barely had time to react. His cock had felt wonderful for the few seconds it was inside her, hard and strong and big, but she needed more, much more. She considered getting up and going home. But what would that achieve? Her frustration, the needs that had sent her out hunting in the first place, would only be compounded.

'I'm sorry,' he muttered.

'For what?' she said gently. It was certainly no good being angry with him. He needed coaxing. Young boys were supposed to have phenomenal recovery rates, weren't they? Wasn't that one of the advantages of younger men, according to the various magazines aimed at the liberated woman? Well, it was time to put the theory to the test.

'I mean . . . I just couldn't . . .'

'Sh . . . you felt wonderful, Tony.' She turned on her side and pressed her body into his, spooning it against him. She didn't know whether she was acting cynically in her own interests or genuinely trying to spare the boy's feelings. It didn't matter. The result would, hopefully, be the same. 'You just got over-excited. It's a terrific compliment.'

'I just . . .'

'Sh . . .' she insisted. 'There's no hurry. Now it's my turn.'

'What do you mean?'

'Does this feel good?' She pressed her firm breasts into his naked back.

'Yes,' he said without conviction.

'Can you feel my nipples?' She squirmed her breasts against his shoulder blades.

'Mmm . . .' he said with rather more interest.

Nadia ran her hand around to his chest and found his nipple. She flicked it with her fingernail, then pinched it between the nails of her thumb and forefinger quite hard. She felt him react, his body trembling.

'Nice?' she asked, moving over to the other nipple and giving it the same treatment.

'Yes,' he acknowledged with surprise.

She kissed his neck and let him feel her hot wet tongue against his skin. Nadia had never played the seductress before and had never thought of herself as particularly experienced sexually. But compared with his total inexperience she knew enough to give him the impression he was in the hands of an expert. She brought her mouth up to his ear, bit his lobe then pushed her tongue deep into the inner whorls.

Emerging from his foetal cocoon, he straightened his legs. Nadia pushed her belly against his buttocks and felt them push back in return. She rubbed her thighs together, squeezing her clitoris between her labia. It felt as hard as her nipples. Her labia were wet and she could feel a trail of moisture leaking on to her thigh.

Gently she rolled Tony on to his back and came up on to her knees at his side. She saw his eyes looking at her breasts and held them both in her hands, pinching her own nipples as she had done his. His cock stirred very slightly.

'Open your legs,' she said.

'What for?' He sounded momentarily like a petulant schoolboy. She cast the image aside quickly, not wanting it to interfere with her scenario.

'Just do as I say.'

He spread his legs apart. Nadia shifted down the bed and knelt between them. It must have been obvious what she planned to do because he said immediately, 'I don't think I can . . .'

'Sh . . .'

'But really . . .'

'You have no choice,' she said sternly, surprised at her own decisiveness. 'I told you, it's my turn.'

His guilt made him unable to argue with that assertion and he lay still, his eyes torn between pleading with her to stop and studying her breasts.

Nadia leant forward, took his cock in her hand and fed it into her mouth. She tasted her own juices. She sucked it all in. Not satisfied with that, she captured his balls between her lips too.

Tony moaned. His hands went to her head as if to pull her away but then he felt a sudden quiver of excitement from his cock as Nadia's tongue licked the pronounced ridge at the base of his glans. The quiver became a spasm, the spasm a steady pulse. Slowly and inexorably, as Nadia worked her hot wet tongue over the same spot, his cock began to engorge.

'Mmm . . .' she muttered, wanting him to know she could feel it.

'Yes . . .' he said in wonder at his own achievement.

It was only a matter of seconds before his erection filled her mouth and she could no longer contain his balls. They spilled from her lips one by one, as she concentrated on the rest of his phallus. He was hard now, and throbbing. For a moment he pulsed so strongly she thought he was going to come again. But he didn't. The convulsions came under control.

'So good,' he said.

She pulled her mouth away, holding his shaft firmly in her hand, proud of her creation. 'You see,' she said. He had passed the test. It was true what they said about young men.

'You're wonderful,' he told her. His attitude changed with his erection, his confidence in his masculinity miraculously restored.

'It's still my turn,' Nadia reminded him.

'Yes.'

She moved forward, straddling his hips until her sex was poised above his cock. She guided it between her labia and used it to stroke her clitoris. She felt a jolt of pure pleasure so powerful it forced her eyes closed and almost made her lose balance. She stuck out her hand to steady herself against his belly.

'You're a very sexy man,' she said, whether for his benefit or hers she was not sure. She squeezed his cock in her hand to test its hardness. It was adamantine.

Tony bucked his hips, anxious to get inside her, but Nadia resisted. She wanted to tease herself first, feel the sensation flowing out of her clitoris as she stroked it against the smoothness and heat of his glans. She had been so concerned to resurrect Tony's erection she had not thought of herself. It was nice now to be able to revel in her body's sensitivity. It felt so alive and so sexy. That was the difference from what she had felt in the past. Not only did she want sex – she had always *wanted* it –

but now she seemed to have the ability to satisfy her own desires. Her body was all charged up, sensitised and sensitive to every provocation.

'Do you want me?' she said.

'You know I do.' He reached up and took her breasts in his hands, trying to use them to pull her down on him.

At that moment she heard a loud scream of ecstasy, hardly muffled by the intervening walls. It was the word 'yes' repeated three times in quick succession, the sound so distorted by passion it was hardly a word at all.

That was the last straw for Nadia: she could hold out no longer. For a second, in her mind's eye she saw Angela being taken by Sir George. She saw it quite graphically, her friend lying on her back with her legs sticking up in the air in a giant V, Sir George buried at the apex of the angle. She could see the expression on Angela's face, her eyes wild, her mouth open and slack with passion. Instantly she dropped herself on to Tony's hard phallus. It rammed into her, filling the depths of her vagina, taking her breath away, and provoking a surge of feeling that shook her to the core.

She squirmed down on the sword of flesh inside her, taking possession of it, making it her own. All the old feelings were revived. Not that they were really old at all. She had wondered if any man could make her feel what Hamilton had made her feel. Now she knew even this callow boy could. Hamilton had been the progenitor of her passion but was not its sole master.

Instantly Nadia felt the first stirrings of orgasm, not muted, distant feelings, a ghost that had to be searched out, but wild, rich currents of sensation, pounding in her blood so strongly that the gap between the realisation that her body had begun the circle of climax and the climax itself was only a matter of seconds.

Driving herself down on Tony's hard cock, spreading her legs apart so her clitoris could grind against his pubic bone, using every muscle to push him into her, Nadia's orgasm flooded over the crown of his cock. Her sex seemed to open, as though there were a secret barrier, another level into which he was permitted only as she came. It was more real than imagined perhaps but it added impetus to the core of feeling that raced through her.

Before she knew what was happening, before she'd even begun to regain her senses, Tony seized her by the shoulders, rolled her over on to her side and then on to her back and fell on top of her, plunging his temporarily disconnected cock back into her sex. He began pumping to and fro, arching his whole body to push deeper then pulling back until his glans was kissed by her nether lips. Not satisfied with this, he grabbed her legs under her knees and pushed her thighs back towards her torso, changing the angle of her sex and enabling him to penetrate deeper still.

Suddenly he stopped dead. Nadia felt his cock pulsing inside her. She thought he was going to come. He thought he was too. He lay perfectly still, trying to control himself, before gingerly beginning to move again. The pulsing eased. He moved slightly faster, testing himself. His confidence grew. He was in control again and every stroke proved it. He pumped as hard as he had before with no loosening of the bonds of restraint. It was a major victory. It made him feel powerful and masculine. Using his well-trained muscles he plunged deep, as deep as before, but though the clinging, hot, velvety walls of her sex gave him exquisite pleasure as he stroked against them, though the temptation to press his glans into the absolute depths of her and spill his seed was almost irresistible, it could be resisted. He was a man now, not a boy.

'Yes,' he said triumphantly.

'Tony, Tony,' Nadia muttered.

Almost before her first orgasm had faded a second broke over her. She wrapped her arms around his back and clung to him as though she were drowning, her body quivering with feeling. His muscles were like steel. It was not only his cock that was hard. His whole body was like a giant phallus.

'I could feel that,' he said proudly, his belief in his own prowess flooding through him as strongly as his pleasure.

Nadia wallowed in her feelings, squirming and writhing under Tony's body, tossing her head from side to side, loving it all. Suddenly she found herself seeing Hamilton, looking into his mahogany eyes. They were looking at her knowingly as if to say, 'I told you so'. She remembered that first night, how he'd used the tip of his finger to circle and tease her clitoris. She remembered the absolute shock of the pleasure that she'd felt.

She tried to put the image aside, tried to concentrate on Tony and forget about Hamilton. But there was no escape. His eyes hypnotised her. Like the spectre at the feast he lingered. She heard his voice questioning her. 'Isn't it me you really want?' it said.

'Yes, yes,' she cried aloud, hoping the words would rid her of the ghost.

But they didn't. He was inside her. As Tony's cock pressed ever deeper into her sex, opening her out, it was Jack Hamilton who really possessed her, whose throbbing erection was making her come again, whose hands held her legs so firmly, whose mouth sucked at the long sinews of her neck, who pitched her into orgasm and made her scream for release.

He was coming inside her. She felt his cock begin to throb again but this time he did not try to stop it. His pace slowed then stopped completely. Involuntarily Nadia's body convulsed around him, clinging to his hardness like a limpet. A spasm jerked his cock violently inside her, then another. Semen jetted out of him.

Nadia was defenceless against it. He had opened her up completely, exposed the raw nerves. Each jet hit her with the force of a tidal wave, throwing her back, pitching her into an abyss of pleasure. She screamed again, this time with sheer delight.

'Jack, Jack, Jack,' echoed in her mind, though whether she screamed the words out loud she could not tell.

Chapter Five

'THAT'S HIM.'

Kurt Froebel was indicating a man sitting on his own at a large window table. They were in Le Grand Chiffre just off Bishopsgate, a purpose-built restaurant on the top floor of one of the most lavish new office developments in the city. Its plate-glass windows overlooked a throng of city workers busily going about their short lunch breaks, rushing around the streets with little packets of sandwiches.

Andrew Anderson was a small, slender man with a beautifully tailored grey suit, a blue handmade shirt and a patterned Sulka silk tie. His black shoes were handmade too. He had neatly cut short fair hair that was greying over the ears and a rather feminine face with a small nose and chin and soft, dove grey eyes.

'Introduce me then,' Nadia prompted. She had dressed for the occasion, a St Laurent flannel suit in a Prince of Wales check.

Kurt Froebel attracted the attention of one of the waiters, who was dressed *à la française*: white shirt, black trousers and a white linen *tablier* tied around his waist.

'Take Mr Anderson a glass of champagne with my compliments, would you?'

'Certainly, sir.'

They were standing by the bar at the far side of the restaurant. The waiter ordered the champagne from the barman, placed the glass on his silver tray and marched over to Anderson's table. They saw him gesturing towards Froebel, obviously indicating whence the drink had come. Anderson immediately gestured for Kurt to come over.

'Kurt, how are you?' he said as soon as they were in earshot. He got up from the table and shook Froebel's hand.

'Andrew, nice to see you, old friend. May I introduce Ms Irving?'

'How formal,' Nadia mocked. 'Nadia Irving,' she corrected, holding out her hand. Anderson shook it lightly, his grip rather weak.

'Won't you join me? Kurt and I go back a long way, Ms Irving.' He emphasised the 'ms'.

'Nadia, please.'

'What a lovely name.'

'My parents were great romantics.'

'Please, you must sit down.'

'Actually, I have to rush,' Kurt said. The introduction made, they had agreed he would make himself scarce.

'Let's have lunch soon. Give me a ring,' Anderson said.

'Love to.' Kurt bowed slightly then winged his way across the restaurant.

'I must go too,' Nadia said.

'Please stay. I always seem to end up eating lunch

on my own. It would be nice to have company.'

'It's very kind of you but I really ought to go.'

'And if I insist?'

He summoned a passing waiter who pulled a chair out from the table, waiting for Nadia to sit down. With what she thought was an appropriate show of reluctance she gracefully acquiesced.

'A drink?' Anderson asked while the waiter still hovered.

'I don't drink at lunchtime.' She noticed the bottle of mineral water on the table.

'Neither do I, but as Kurt has bought me a glass of champagne I certainly don't intend to waste it. Join me in one glass and then we'll be good.'

'You've convinced me.'

Anderson nodded to the hovering waiter. Nodding his understanding, the waiter hurried away.

'So what can I do for you, Ms Irving?' he said, pointedly changing the mood.

'What do you mean?'

'Oh please, you wouldn't have gone to all the trouble of dragging Kurt in here to get yourself introduced if you didn't want something from me. Poor man's not even allowed to have any lunch.' He had seen through the subterfuge immediately but was intrigued. He also found Nadia an extremely attractive woman.

'Very astute.'

'That's what I get paid for. So?'

'I work for Hill Brothers . . .'

'Oh, I see.' His face clouded with anger. 'Well, in that case I think we'd better make small talk and have a very quick lunch.'

'Can I just ask you one question?'

'No, Ms Irving, you can't.'

'Did you know,' she continued regardless, 'that Manny Tomkins is going to drop his entire holding into our lap?'

'Manny told me personally he was absolutely committed to me.'

'Manny is a two-timing shit. The whole city knows that.'

'True,' he conceded.

'It is agreed. That gives Manson's control.'

'So if you've already got control, why come to me?'

'Because I see another alternative.'

'What's that?'

'That our clients don't take you over at all.'

The anger on Anderson's face dissipated as the waiter arrived with Nadia's champagne.

'Tell me more,' he said as soon as the waiter had gone.

'Our clients want an aggregates company, *any* aggregates company. It's a good fit for their business, lots of synergy, economies of scale, and distribution.'

'I've heard the pitch.'

'But you're not the right company. You're too big. If they mount a hostile takeover their gearing will go sky high. They have three institutional shareholders who I know would start getting very unhappy about their holdings.'

'Why tell me this?'

'Because I want to do the best for my clients. If they end up with your company but with a falling share price compounded by all the publicity of a hostile bid, they are not going to be very happy.'

'I should give a damn.'

'But you should. You own a holding in Babcock Minerals, don't you?'

'You've done your homework.'

'Babcock's is exactly the right fit for Manson's – not too big, and the right mines in the right places.'

'Go on.'

'Babcock's is controlled by a family trust. They hold sixty-six per cent. It's takeover-proof. That's why its share price hasn't moved in ten years.'

'I wish I was in the same position.'

'No you don't. Your share price has quadrupled in the last five years. Your share options alone made you one-point-six million last year.'

'You *have* done your homework.'

'So all you have to do is persuade Babcock's to sell to Manson's.'

'Look, Ms Irving, this is all very commendable work, but do you really think that if I could get Charlie Babcock to sell I wouldn't have done it already? It's a non-starter. He wouldn't sell at any price.'

'Charlie Babcock is an old man. His son is ambitious. Very ambitious.'

'But,' he said, as though trying to explain to a ten-year-old child, 'it's a trust. His son can't sell without the whole family's consent.'

Nadia paused for dramatic effect. 'He can,' she said after a long beat. 'Put it another way. Nora Babcock is dead.'

'What!' Anderson's voice was so loud it startled the diners at the next table. 'How do you know that?' he snapped.

'She was in a sanatorium in Switzerland. They buried her there.'

'Unbelievable. You sure about this?'

'I've a friend in Geneva. She's married to a doctor, Nora Babcock's doctor.'

'It changes everything. Charlie's lost control.

Jesus, I've been trying to get hold of that company for years.'

'So give it to Manson's and they're off your back. They only need to offer the son a good job, share options, all the usual perks. He'll take it like a shot.'

Anderson looked at her intently. 'Why didn't you just take this straight to Manson's?'

'Firstly they might not have taken kindly to being told they were biting off more than they could chew.'

'And secondly?'

'You own a good chunk of the shares. I'd like to do a deal for them. And thirdly . . .'

'Yes?'

'I thought you'd be grateful.'

'How grateful?'

'Grateful enough to transfer all your business to Hill Brothers.'

'Done,' he said immediately, picking up the glass of champagne and beaming like a man who had just had a death sentence lifted. She raised her glass too and clinked it against his. 'On one condition.'

'What's that?' she asked.

'That you have dinner with me next week.'

'No conditions,' she said firmly.

'All right, no conditions. So will you have dinner with me next week?'

'I'll think about it. Can we order? I appear to have developed a very healthy appetite.'

James Hill burst into her office without knocking. He was middle-aged, running to fat and had pernicious bad breath. He obviously didn't have a friend in the world to tell him about it.

'Where have you been?' he said.

'At lunch,' she said.

'It's four o'clock.'

'I was just coming to see you,' Nadia said calmly, ignoring his anger. 'I think it's time we discussed my contract.'

'If you're going to stay out at lunch till four . . .'

'Three-thirty,' she corrected. 'I was back at three-thirty.'

'Three-thirty then. If that's what you think we pay you for then I think it's definitely time we discussed your contract.'

'I was having lunch with Andrew Anderson.'

'What?'

'You heard.'

'Anderson. What was the point of that?'

'And then I rang George Manson. You're expected there at five.'

'What are you talking about?'

'Anderson is going to sell his Babcock shares to Manson. Manson's is going to buy Babcock's instead of Anderson's.'

'What?'

'You heard.'

'But it's not possible.'

'It's a done deal.'

'It's absolutely brilliant, that's what it is,' he said as the implications of what she had told him sank in.

Helpfully, she spelled them out for him. 'The institutions won't worry any more. Manson's share price will rocket and so will Anderson's. And Anderson's going to bring all his business to us.'

James Hill looked nonplussed. 'Come to my office in fifteen minutes,' he said brusquely. 'I need to talk to my brother.'

'Certainly, sir,' she said emphasising the 'sir' with a degree of irony.

If Angela had answered her phone it wouldn't have happened. Not that night anyway. Perhaps it was inevitable, like the invisible attraction of a magnet, something she could not resist. She would have been pulled back inexorably in the end. But more immediately, as Angela wasn't in, Nadia had no one to celebrate with.

She sat at her kitchen table feeling sorry for herself, when that was the last thing she should have been feeling. James and Cameron Hill had agreed she would join the board of Hill Brothers in November. From that time she would have a share option package and a percentage of the profits. Her plan had worked out perfectly. Manson's were delighted and, so, after she had talked again on the phone to him, was Andrew Anderson. The Hills had had no choice but to concede graciously that it was a considerable coup and to reward her endeavour accordingly. Nadia Irving was the toast of the city. But she had no one to propose the toast.

She could have called Tony, of course. But though physically their encounter had, eventually, been a success she had no intention of getting involved with someone so much younger than herself. She had told him there could be no future for them and he had accepted it reluctantly but without argument. If she called him now and started the whole thing up again it might not be so easy to disentangle herself. She had used Tony for her own purposes. He was a distraction, nothing more.

She picked up the phone and dialled the number, then crashed the receiver down before it started to ring. Her secretary had noted each of his three calls on pages torn from a little yellow message pad which she had left on her desk, as any call to her at Hill Brothers would have been. Without consciously wanting to, she had remembered the call back number, presumably the number of his studio, not his home. She dialled it again. She was just about to crash the receiver down for a second time and curse herself for her foolishness when she heard the line begin to ring.

'Hello,' he answered on the second ring. She had forgotten the sound of his voice. It was rich and melodic like the low register of a viola.

'It's Nadia,' she said weakly, not having prepared what she was going to say.

'Oh . . .' He didn't sound pleased to hear from her.

'I'm sorry I didn't . . . I've been . . .'

'What do you want?' he snapped.

'To see you.' She couldn't think of any other way to put it.

'Why didn't you call me back?'

'I had to sort myself out, Jack.'

'What does that mean?'

There was no way she could avoid the truth. 'I didn't know you were married. I wasn't sure what my attitude was. I had to work it out.' There was a silence at the other end of the line. 'Now I have,' she said, rushing to fill the vacuum.

'I understand.' His voice softened.

'Would you like to have dinner?'

'Yes. Why not? When had you got in mind?'

'Actually I just had some good news at work. I was thinking of celebrating.'

'Tonight?'

'Yes.'

'All right. Shall I come to you or do you want to come here?'

Nadia suddenly saw the ruffled bed in the studio. She shuddered and felt her sex pulse.

'Why don't you come here? There's a good restaurant . . .'

'Not a restaurant,' he said definitely, with no explanation.

'I could cook something then.'

'That would be good. I'll bring the champagne.'

'Done.' She remembered Andrew Anderson saying the same word over lunch. It was a word that had already changed her life. She jerked herself back to the present and told Jack her address.

'What time?'

'Eight.' It was just gone six.

'Fine.' She heard him hesitate. 'And Nadia . . .'

'Yes.'

'I'm glad you rang.'

'So am I,' she said but as she put the phone down realised she was not at all sure that it was true.

But she was committed now. There was no going back. She looked in the fridge and decided she needed to get some food. There was a supermarket around the corner and she ran out of the house, glad of the distraction of dreaming up a meal, saving her from thinking about the consequences of what she had done. She needed something simple and easy to prepare.

In an hour and a half she had done the shopping, set the table in the dining room at the back of the kitchen and prepared the food. She had twenty minutes to prepare herself. She had a quick shower and put on her make-up, while she thought what to wear. It needed to be simple, like the food, and easy

102

to discard. She opened her lingerie drawers. What she was going to wear underneath had to be considered too. After all, she thought, hardening herself to the idea, she was about to embark on an affair with a married man. Sex was its *raison d'être*. It was too late to agonise over whether she should or she shouldn't. That was a decision she had already made.

Her doorbell rang at five minutes past eight. She looked out of her bedroom window and saw a black cab pulling away from the curb. She checked her hair in the mirror. She had chosen a waisted red dress with a flared skirt. It was very plain but the colour suited her blonde hair and the style her narrow waist and the fullness of her bosom and hips. She walked downstairs, trying to keep calm and avoid the temptation to run. She could not stop her heart pounding against her ribs.

'Hi,' she said opening the door.

'Hi.' Hamilton stood on the front step. He was wearing very clean faded blue jeans, docksider shoes in light blue and a military-style beige shirt, with breast pockets on both sides. He held a plastic carrier bag in one hand.

'Come in.'

Rather self-consciously she kissed him on the cheek.

'This is nice,' he said looking around, examining the lithographs she had on the wall.

'Come through.' She led him through the kitchen and dining room and out into her small patio garden where she had laid a small cast-iron table with a flowery green cloth. She'd put out two champagne glasses, a wine cooler filled with ice and a bowl of black olives.

'Shall I open the champagne?' he said, extracting a bottle of Moët Chandon champagne from the off-licence carrier bag. He opened it expertly with no fuss, twisting the cork out without a pop and pouring the wine into the glasses. She picked them both up and handed him one as he slid the bottle into the ice of the cooler.

'Cheers,' she said.

'Cheers,' he repeated, meeting her gaze briefly. 'So tell me what we're celebrating.' He sat down on the little white cast-iron bench that matched the two chairs positioned around the table.

'Just a coup at work. It's not very interesting.'

'Tell me,' he insisted.

She did. To her surprise he seemed genuinely fascinated, asking her questions about how family trusts worked and why the institutions had been so against Manson's taking over Anderson's. She found herself explaining the technical details of gearing and prices to income ratios.

'No wonder they've given you a directorship,' he commented when she'd finished.

'It was just luck really, finding out about Nora Babcock.'

'Don't put yourself down,' he said.

He got up and wandered around the garden, looking at all the plants, naming most of them and even telling her where they originated in the world.

'You know a lot about plants,' she said.

'Good for the soul,' he replied.

She had the feeling there was a vast chasm between them, a lack of spontaneity, that had not been there on the night they had met. She knew it was a chasm she had created but suddenly felt resentful that *she* was being put in the position of having to bridge it. She had thought she could hold her anger at him in check and rely on her passion, but he appeared to feel it was she who should say sorry.

'Do you have a soul?' she snapped.

He looked at her long and hard, then sat down on the cast-iron bench. 'Sit here with me,' he said softly.

'I'm not sure I want to,' she said like a petulant child, her mood entirely changed.

'Please, Nadia. There's something I want to explain.'

Nadia sipped her champagne, then sat down next to him. He turned towards her, those big brown eyes dazzling her again.

'So what upset you?'

'You're married. Why didn't you tell me?'

'I assumed you knew. It was in the art gallery profile.'

'I know.'

'Nadia, I didn't lie to you.'

'How many affairs have you had?'

'That's a silly question. I hope I'm selective.'

'Oh, I'm sure you are.' Nadia practically spat the words out.

'Look, perhaps this is a bad idea.'

'Yes, I think it is.' She hadn't thought beyond her lust. She wanted him more than she'd ever wanted any man. Not an hour had gone by without her thinking about him and craving for him. She'd thought she could cope with the fact that he was married to someone else, that she was and would only ever be a casual affair, that, above all, he was the sort of man who could betray his wife, but she couldn't. She couldn't respect him. She had felt all these emotions before with Jeffrey Allen, trying to kid herself that she didn't care, trying not to face the unpalatable facts for the sake of being with him.

He put his glass down, got up and walked through the French windows into the house.

'Don't go,' she said. She had felt all these emotions before with Jeffrey but he had inspired no sexual passion. She caught up with him in the kitchen.

'I thought . . .'

'For Christ's sake, Jack, just fuck me. Fuck me, Jack, please.' She threw herself into his arms, a flood of emotion washing over her. As she kissed him full on the lips, as their tongues met, both wanting to penetrate the other's mouth, as his arms wrapped around her and crushed her into his body, Nadia experienced the whole gamut of emotions: hatred, self-loathing, fear, anger and resentment, but most of all passion, a passion that coursed through her body like a crimson tide, a tsunami of passion that swept everything else away.

'Jack, Jack . . .' she said while their mouths were still joined, her tongue and lips moving against him.

He hoisted her into his arms, as if her weight was of no account, cradling her like a baby. He started upstairs.

'It's two floors,' she protested, breaking the kiss, but he had already breasted the first flight. He took the second at the same speed.

In her bedroom he laid her on the bed, not at all out of breath. Then he was kissing her again, rolling on top of her, pushing his hard body down against her softness, crushing her breasts. His hand worked up her leg, caressing her thigh.

'Are you going to fuck me, Jack?' she asked

unnecessarily, but wanting to hear the words.

'Yes.'

He rolled on his side and began unbuttoning the front of her dress. She wrestled with his belt. The fly of his jeans was buttoned and she yanked it open easily. She reached inside and grabbed his cock, pulling it from the front of his crisp white boxer shorts. There was no time to be civilised, to get up and undress and fold their clothes away.

He freed the buttons of her dress and laid it open. Nadia was wearing a black satin teddy, with lace cups over her breasts. His hands kneaded the pliant flesh as Nadia found the clasps that held the crotch in place. She felt the heat and ripeness of her sex as she tore the fastenings apart. He rolled on top of her again, his cock nudging into her labia.

'Let me . . .' she gasped, pulling at his jeans and shorts. He raised himself from her body so she could wrestle them down over his buttocks but as soon as they were clear of his cock he fell back on to her. In one fluid stroke he was deep inside her sex.

'God,' she cried in surprise. It was surprise at herself. She had never been so wet. She felt as though her vagina was flooded.

'You see,' he whispered, knowing the effect he had on her.

'You bastard,' she said, hating him again. She tried to squirm away from him, but the movement only increased the rush of feeling his cock was creating. 'You bastard,' she said again, this time because the words excited her. Whatever he had done to her body, whatever key he had found in the depths of her libido, the door he had unlocked with it was wide open. Already the inescapable momentum of orgasm had started forward.

He didn't do much. He seemed able to sense what she needed. He just pressed forward, the muscles of his buttocks holding his cock deep inside her, up against the neck of her womb.

He was so hard. So hot and hard. He seemed to fill her completely as though he had been carefully moulded to fit every crevice of her sex. Her orgasm gathered impetus. He was supporting himself on his elbows, looking down into her face. She looked into his eyes.

'Kiss me,' she said, her resentment melted away by the heat of him inside her.

He dipped his head immediately, kissing her very gently on the lips. At the exact moment the wave of her orgasm broke over her, his tongue plunged between her lips, in imitation of his cock. She gasped, her hot breath expelled into his mouth, as she clung to him for support, her body trembling uncontrollably. Teasingly he withdrew his tongue and kissed her with his lips, with the lightest of touches, the sweet delicacy of it in such contrast to the pounding waves of pleasure from her sex. As she felt her body relax, the tension of her climax draining away, he broke the kiss.

'I wanted you too,' he said softly, beginning to pump his cock in and out of her. He dropped his mouth to her neck and began kissing and licking at her flesh. 'I wanted you very much.' He was moving gently but firmly, the hard phallus surrounded by the clinging glove of her vagina.

Nadia raised her legs, bending her knees, angling her pelvis up at him, wanting to give him pleasure now. She ran her hands down the back of his shirt and on to his naked buttocks, caressing them, then turning her fingers into talons to urge him on. But she was not immune. The feeling of his hardness sliding in and out of her was too provoking. In her fevered imagination it seemed she could feel every inch of him, every contour of his erection, every ridge and vein. She could certainly feel his balls slapping against her labia. They were heavy and full.

'You're making me come again,' she told him.

'I know, I can feel it,' he said.

'Do you want it?'

'Yes.' He crushed his body down against her in response, writhing his chest against her breasts, making her nipples prick with feeling. Her orgasm took hold of her, like the hand of a giant picking up a rag doll, and shook her violently, overwhelming her with raw sensation. But, at the centre of it all, at the moment she thought it could not be any more exquisite, she felt him find a place in her sex. Almost of its own accord her vagina seemed to open around him and close on him too, at the same time, trapping him as his cock began to spasm and semen spattered out into the cache it had created.

They were both gasping for breath. Sweating, their clothes making them hot. Coming up for air, they disentangled themselves, lying, exhausted, side by side, with not enough energy to discard the clothes that were uncomfortably rucked around their bodies.

Nadia only realised she must have dozed off when she woke up having trouble, for a second, remembering where she was. She saw Hamilton was asleep too, his face turned towards her. He looked like a little boy, the wrinkles and tensions of age dissolved by the effects of sleep, not a care invading his world.

Getting off the bed without disturbing him, she tiptoed into the bathroom and stripped off the damp and crumpled dress, then pulled the satin teddy over her head. The bathroom was cooler than the bedroom, where the sun streamed in through the west-facing windows at the end of the day. Naked she sat on the loo, the effects of passion giving way to a thinking woman's doubts. Sex had never ruled her life before; she had never allowed it to compromise her, or make her do things she found reprehensible. On the other hand she had never had sex like this before.

'What are you doing?' his voice said from the bedroom.

'Trying to cool down.'

He appeared in the bathroom doorway. 'Let's take a shower.'

'Good idea.'

She got up, opened the shower cubicle and adjusted the mixer tap until the water ran lukewarm, all the time aware of his eyes on her body. She stepped into the stream of water as he stripped off his clothes. The water cascaded over her, splashing on the ridge of her breasts, running down her body to be funnelled by the creases of her pelvis into her pubic hair.

He stepped in behind her and closed the cubicle door. Immediately she felt his hands cupping her wet breasts and his navel pressing against the sharp curves of her buttocks.

'You feel so good, so soft,' he whispered in her ear. 'I needed you so badly.'

Like you need your wife, she thought but did not say. How could she let herself do this? The answer unfurled between her buttocks. It appeared it was not only the young who could recover with alacrity. The feeling of his erection growing against her, such tangible proof of his desire, made her sex pulse.

He picked up a bar of soap from the little metal tray at the side of the tap and began running it over the front of her body, up around her neck, all over her breasts, down to her belly and over her thighs, the lather it created making her body slippery and soft. He moved it to her mons then down between her thighs, the edge of the soap parting her labia, catching against her clitoris.

'Oh . . .' she moaned.

He pulled back from her and brought the soap around to lather her shoulders and her spine and the pliant flesh of her buttocks, running it down the back of her thighs then up between her legs again. The lather was thick and white.

'You're so beautiful,' he said, pushing into her back again.

'Please . . .' she said, water splashing on her face. She didn't know whether it meant please stop or please take me again. Her body was less ambiguous. It was rocking against him, her buttocks moving rhythmically.

His cock slipped down between her legs. The water had washed away all her natural juices and, perversely, made her dry. He tried to force himself up into her sex but she was sealed against him.

'Have to force it,' he said.

'Yes, do that.'

She felt the tip of his glans prodding at the gate of her vagina. It managed to force past the initial resistance. Beyond, on the inside, was a lake of sticky wetness, as hot as molten lava. It lubricated his cock instantly and allowed him to push deeply

111

into the centre of her.

'Lovely,' he said.

He used the tapered edge of the soap to open her labia, then rubbed it against her clitoris. Water running down her body caught on the soap and was directed on to the nut of her clit, forming a lather as he moved it. The feeling of it slipping and sliding against her was delicious.

He was making her come again, so quickly, with so little effort. Standing like this the penetration of his phallus in her sex was not deep but all she needed was the feeling of the breadth of him, stretching her labia apart. She braced herself against the cubicle with her arms, needing support, as her body churned.

'Oh God . . .'

'Feels good,' he said.

'Oh Jack, what have you done to me?'

She wriggled her buttocks from side to side. He cupped her breast with his free hand and pinched her nipple. The soap worked relentlessly. It was so easy. Like the first time with him. In seconds she felt herself buzzing, her clitoris spewing out feeling into the rest of her nerves, her orgasm rising like a flood tide, forcing her eyes closed, its eddies and currents carrying her helplessly into a whirlpool of pleasure, the water hammering down on her body only increasing the illusion that she could drown in exquisite sensation.

As her senses returned he opened the cubicle door and pulled her out. Even if she had wanted to resist she had no energy. She had no energy even to stand and he carried her, dripping wet, into the bedroom. He lowered her on to the bed then rolled her over on to her stomach, pulling her up on to her

112

knees and kneeling behind. His hard cock prodded into the cleft of her buttocks again. Instantly he slipped inside her, deeper inside this time, deeper than he'd been all evening.

She felt his cock pulse. He stroked it in and out slowly, feeling the way her wet flesh parted to admit him, folding around him, then closing on itself again as he withdrew.

'So lovely,' he said, 'like silk.'

'Oh, Jack.' It was like when he kissed her earlier, so infinitely gentle, so sweet. Her wild swings of emotion were out of control. She'd gone from hatred to anger to lust and now to what felt like tenderness. She would have done anything for him.

'Let me do it,' she said decisively.

'Do what?' he said.

'Do anything, Jack, anything you want.'

'I want this. You feel wonderful.'

He didn't stop. His pulsing erection stroked forward. She reached down between his legs and caught the sac of his balls in her hand. She squeezed it gently and his cock reacted, jerking strongly in her sex.

'Like this?' she asked, delighted to have found a way to please him.

'Oh yes . . .'

'Come then.' She knew at once she had the power to make him come for her. She squeezed harder and pulled the sac down away from his body.

'Oh yes.'

She felt his cock spasm. She squeezed once more and, as though she were milking the spunk out of him, his cock erupted, jerking wildly inside her for the second time, his spending seemingly as urgent and as copious as the first.

They sat in the garden drinking the champagne. They had picked at the food Nadia had prepared but ended up eating no more than salad and cheese. It was a balmy night and Nadia felt perfectly comfortable in the short white cotton robe she'd wrapped herself in to cook the meal. Oddly she seemed to have come to terms with the problem she had wrestled with all night. It didn't seem to matter any more. Her body was sexually replete, the aftermath of the shocks of sensation that Hamilton had provoked leaving her with a sense of contentment that nothing could disturb. Or so she thought.

'Tell me about your wife?' she said, as if to test herself, to see whether her new-found indifference would last.

'She's very beautiful,' Hamilton said. He had put on his jeans and shirt but left the latter unbuttoned.

'Yes.' Nadia had seen the latest set of pictures, a fashion layout in *Vogue* – dresses and suits in black and white, the colours of the new autumn season. Jan Hamilton had long legs and a small but shapely bosom. Her face was angular and sharp and inimitably photogenic. 'And?' she asked.

'She's not like you. She's quite cold, actually. And unforgiving.'

'She knows you have affairs? I'd like the truth.'

'Oh yes. She has them too. Sometimes we share,' he said, almost as an aside.

Nadia thought he was joking. 'Very convenient.'

'My wife is bisexual.'

It took a minute for Nadia to connect the remark with the idea of sharing. When she did her reply exploded, 'You share lovers!'

'Yes. You said you wanted the truth.'

She had failed the test. She found that her hand was trembling and her heart beating at an accelerated pace. She gulped at her champagne.

'In the same bed?' She tried but did not succeed in keeping her voice at a normal pitch.

'Sometimes.' He looked unfazed.

Nadia felt she had stepped into quicksand and was sinking rapidly.

He could read the expression on her face. 'There are no rules, Nadia. Life can be very complicated, *is* very complicated. Women are liberated now. Look at you. Even ten years ago a woman wouldn't have done your job; it just wouldn't have been allowed.'

'What's that got to do with it?'

'Everything. Women have taken responsibility for themselves. They're allowed to express their own desires, not have them subordinated to the desires of men. That's what you did with me, after all. It seems churlish for men to object after so long in the driving seat.'

Nadia suspected that was just intellectual sophistry, but she was too emotionally involved to argue logically. 'How many lovers do you have?'

'Jointly? Not many.'

'And singularly?'

'It's not a competition.'

'Are you happy?'

He laughed. 'Happy. That's a bit bourgeois, isn't it?'

'Will you stay together?' Nadia persisted.

He had been looking at a big rhododendron bush that grew in a terracotta pot opposite the bench, its shiny leaves lit by a floodlight from the wall above.

115

He turned to look directly at Nadia, his eyes burning with fierce intensity.

'Now that *is* a good question. You said you wanted the truth. The truth is I married her for her money. I was literally starving. Well, not quite literally, but I couldn't sell a painting to save my life. Jan came along. Wanted a very unconventional lifestyle. Wanted an artist. I often think it wouldn't have mattered who; it was just good for her image, I think. I was available and quiescent. It was nice to be able to eat and I have to say the idea of having some of her friends join us in bed was not . . . unexciting. Now I don't need her money.'

'Or her?'

'That's the big question, isn't it? And I don't know the answer.'

'Don't you have to go home?' She hoped he would say yes. She needed to be alone.

'I do,' he said simply.

She couldn't sleep. Sweat ran off her body and she tossed and turned, unable to turn off her mind. It had only happened once. She'd forgotten about it. No, that was absurd. She hadn't forgotten about it at all. What she had done had been to build a wall around it, a thick, high, impregnable wall, waterproof, soundproof, memory-proof. It worked most of the time.

But as she had sat out in the garden with Hamilton, his words had brought it back so strongly, so graphically, it seemed it had happened just yesterday. The wall that kept it separate had preserved it, too.

It had been the summer, like now, hot and humid, making sleeping difficult. She could hear her voice.

116

'Are you awake?'

It was a huge Tudor house with countless bedrooms. She was eighteen. Her best friend at school had invited her to stay for the weekend. Her parents were rich. It was the summer before they would be parted to go to different universities.

'Yes.'

The huge, stripped oak floorboards creaked as Barbara slipped into the bed beside her. There was a full moon outside, the ghostly grey light streaming through gaps in the curtains. Barbara was upset.

'Did you see what Greg did to me?'

'He's a pig.' Greg had spent dinner ogling a friend of Barbara's mother and had taken her home in his MG instead of staying the night. Greg was supposed to be devoted to Barbara.

'Oh Nad, I can't stand it.' She started to cry, wrenching, convulsive sobs.

Nadia put her arm around her for comfort.

'All men are pigs,' she said.

'Pigs,' Barbara agreed.

As the weeping subsided gradually Barbara nestled her face to Nadia's neck. She began kissing her. It seemed a natural thing to do. She kissed her cheeks and then her mouth, but only little, pecking, affectionate kisses. Her hand slipped on to Nadia's breasts, pushing against them gently. She untied the ribbon that held the neck of her broderie anglaise cotton nightdress together.

'What are you doing?' Nadia said, only then feeling any alarm.

'I need it, Nad,' Barbara whispered into her ear. Her hand became more insistent, kneading Nadia's flesh, pinching at her nipples. She stripped back the top sheet, and before Nadia really had any idea

117

what she was going to do, prised her thighs apart, and planted her hand over her sex.

'Oh Babs . . .' Nadia said, caught between wanting to push her away and wanting more of the delicious feelings Barbara's fingers were producing.

'I need it, Nad,' Barbara repeated. She trailed her mouth down Nadia's body and in seconds it was on her sex, her tongue circling Nadia's clitoris. It was the first time she had ever felt a mouth, any mouth, down there. The combination of heat and wetness created a wave of feeling she didn't understand but wallowed in. 'Do me,' Barbara said. 'Please Nad, do me.'

Barbara swung her thigh over Nadia's face and pulled up her nightgown until it was around her waist. Slowly she lowered her sex on to Nadia's mouth. Nadia remembered exactly how it had felt, hot and incredibly soft, and molten inside. She knew they shouldn't be doing this, that it was wrong, but the guilt seemed to make the pleasure sweeter. What Barbara did to her she mimicked on Barbara. *Soixante-neuf* – they had giggled about it in French class. It felt so good, so real, so comforting. They shuddered and trembled and rocked together on the bed, and came together too, with an intensity Nadia had never experienced before.

She had never wanted to see Barbara again. They had not mentioned what had happened the following day and Nadia refused all Barbara's subsequent invitations, until, eventually, Barbara had taken the hint and stopped asking.

But she had never experienced pleasure like it. Until now. Until Hamilton.

Nadia tossed and turned, unable to get comfortable, too hot with a single sheet covering her, too cold without it.

Every time she closed her eyes she saw an image of Jan Hamilton. She was lying propped up against the pillows of the bed in the studio, her long legs crossed, her dark eyes containing a question. It was not a question Nadia wanted to answer.

Chapter Six

STRIKE WHILE THE iron is hot. Was that what he was doing? He'd called her at work. They'd only picked at the food last night. Why didn't she bring what was left over to the studio? They could finish it off. Waste not want not, he'd said. And he wanted a lot of her. They could spend the night together. His wife was off on a shoot for a magazine.

She'd agreed.

He told her he had to go to a gallery first. There was a key hidden under the third step on the exterior stairs where a piece of concrete had worked loose. She could let herself in.

She had.

It felt strange to be in his studio alone. She prowled around looking for evidence, though of what crime she did not know. She was glad he'd called. She wanted to see him again, there was no question of that. The fact that his revelations had stirred such memories was nothing to do with him, or what she felt for him. She had made her decision and she was going to stick by it. A time would come, inevitably, when the advantages of passion were outweighed by the disadvantages of the lies and deceits it involved. But that time was not yet.

Nadia was firmly in control of herself. She knew what she was doing and why. As for the wall around her memory of Barbara, that could be rebuilt brick by brick. Or perhaps it didn't need to be. It was years ago. It had definitely been a trauma in her life and she had hidden it away for fear it meant more than she cared to admit. But now she knew herself better and the fear seemed faintly ridiculous.

He'd told her he'd be there at eight. She'd put the food in the kitchen and a bottle of red wine on the work surface. At ten to eight she stripped off all her clothes and lay naked on the bed. The studio was hot and she did not cover herself. It was exciting. Her nipples were hard and corrugated. She opened her legs wide and bent her knees as if to practise what she would do when he arrived. She could not resist the temptation to touch herself and found her clitoris was as hard as her nipples. She heard his footsteps on the stairs outside.

It was all like a dream from then on.

He opened the front door. Seeing her on the bed he came over and stood looking at her. She did not close her legs. She wanted him to look at her. She knew she was wet. She hoped he could see that. He looked at her intently, examining every detail of her sex, the deckled outer labia, the scarlet oval that was the gate to her vagina.

He pulled off shoes, trousers, shirt, dropping them on the floor, his cock emerging from his clothes already erect. He leapt on her, covering her, his strength pushing down against her, the hard muscle of his body a perfect match for the hardness of his cock. In seconds they were joined and his cock stabbed into the depths of her, filling her completely, a rod of hot steel her body clung to compulsively. Her first orgasm came so quickly it was almost painful, forced out of her before she had time to catch her breath.

They rolled and writhed on the bed, each desperate to give the other pleasure, each finding reasons to take their own. Hamilton was relentless. He hammered into her body, prising it open like an oyster to get at its soft, defenceless heart. She lost count of how many times she was racked with pleasure, her nerves stretched out like the strings of a harp, thrumming in harmony. Unashamedly she ground her clitoris against the base of his phallus, rocking her hips from side to side, revelling in the feeling of being penetrated so comprehensively.

It was entirely possible that they came together. Since she could hardly remember a second when she was not coming or beginning to come again, his orgasm must have overlapped with hers. She felt him slow, make space for himself in the cavern of her sex, and spasm, his cock kicking against the tight confines of the sheath that surrounded it. But by that time Nadia was too high, too intoxicated by passion, to separate these feelings from the general melange of pleasure she was already experiencing.

Eventually, exhausted, they rested. Nadia brought chicken and salad to the bed and they ate and drank the red wine, picnicking on the tousled sheet, their eyes never leaving each other's naked bodies, their arousal still not flagging, the food hardly tasted at all, just necessary as fuel.

'I've never wanted a woman more than I want you,' he said.

'I've never wanted a man more either,' she

replied. At least she thought that was what they had said. Later she could hardly remember any words being exchanged. She knew she *had* never wanted a man more. No man had ever made her feel what Hamilton made her feel. No man had ever reached down into the secret mechanisms of her libido and found the switches and levers that controlled it. No man had turned every gesture, of hand and mouth and eye, into a eulogy of sex, a secret, private oratory to some sensual god.

She did remember what they had done after that. She'd taken the food back to the kitchen. She'd glanced at the painting on the easel which for some reason she had not registered when she'd been alone. One of the shadowy figures in the foreground had been filled in, a striking, rather masculine woman, her hair and dark complexion suggesting Pre-Raphaelite influences. The other figure, though now clearly a woman, remained obscure. Her head had been painted but not her face.

Hamilton lay on the bed watching her as she stood by the easel. 'Come back,' he said.

And then it was as though they had never been parted. He pulled her down on to the bed, lay her on her back and began kissing her body, running his lips over her breasts, sucking her nipples into his mouth, moving down between her legs, finding her swollen, eager clitoris and renewing all the feelings that had swept over her before.

She spread her legs wide apart, allowing him to tongue the whole plane of her sex. He pushed his fingers inside her, creating a jolt of pleasure that made her gasp. Licking her labia from top to bottom first, he narrowed his attentions to her clitoris,

123

circling it with the tip of his tongue, prodding it, provoking it, causing her eyes to close as she wallowed in sensation. In the darkness she felt the beginning of an orgasm throbbing in her body like an engine. That was why she hadn't seen her, of course, but she would never be able to understand why she hadn't heard her opening the front door or walking across the studio floor.

'He's good at that, isn't he?' she said.

It was so perfectly timed. Nadia opened her eyes but even the shock of seeing Jan Hamilton standing looking down at her could not stop the flood of orgasm as Jack's tongue swept, like a tiny brush, over her clitoris. In fact, she knew later, the way the woman's dark eyes had flicked approvingly over her naked body had sent her orgasm into overdrive. She writhed on the bed, the dark eyes following her, unable to do anything else.

'Well, quite a performance,' she said as soon as Nadia was still.

Jan Hamilton was, if anything, more beautiful than the hundreds of photographs of her suggested. She was tall and slim, with long black hair that shone with health. Her Mediterranean complexion made her very regular teeth in the large but thin mouth seem translucently white. Her face was striking, the angular contours of her brow, cheeks and chin giving her an air of severity that was counterbalanced by the warmth and brightness of her dark brown eyes.

She was wearing tight Lycra leggings in pure white, and black thigh boots folded over above the knee like a pirate. The leggings were so tight they had dimpled into the crease of her sex. Her black blouse, a blouson design, was made from chiffon with very full sleeves. Nadia could see her white lacy bra underneath.

'I got your note,' she said to Jack.

Hamilton raised his head as his wife sat on the bed. She took his cheek in one hand and kissed him, deliberately letting Nadia see her tongue lap up the wetness that clung to his lips.

'Mmm . . . Tastes good,' she said, looking at Nadia.

It was at that moment that Nadia had to make a decision because it was then that Jan stretched out her hand, the hand that had held her husband's cheek, to touch Nadia's breast. As if in slow motion Nadia saw it moving towards her, feet, then inches, then a hair's breadth. Her mind was in turmoil. She did not know what to think or do. But she did know that if those long, beautifully manicured fingers, their nails varnished a deep dark red, touched her she would have no control.

She had seen a movie once where a woman had died. Her spirit, in the shape of a white image of her body, had peeled away from her supine form, sat up, got up and walked away. That was exactly what she felt like now. She wanted to sit up, to push Jan Hamilton's hand away, to get to her feet and dress calmly but with dignity, and walk out of Hamilton's life forever. That was what her spirit wanted but it had no corporeality. Her body, on the other hand, was firmly rooted in more mundane realities, in the throes and thrills of passion and self-gratification. She was not dead, nor could she split herself in two.

Jan's hand cupped her firm round breast.

'No,' she said as a reflex.

'No?' Jan queried, smiling a knowing smile, as though she already knew Nadia's secrets. She did not take her hand away.

125

It felt as though the fingers that gently squeezed Nadia's pliant flesh were plugged into some source of electricity. Tingling shocks of sensation spread through her, over to her other breast, out through already over-wrought nerves. Her nipples, though rock hard, puckered further, the corrugations in the pink flesh cutting deeper, pimples on her areola forming in profusion. The electricity coursed down to her sex, her clitoris experiencing the same engorgement, swelling against the hood of her labia. Inside her vagina she felt the pulse that usually accompanied a flood of juices.

She should get up and walk away.

'You're quite lovely,' Jan said, trailing her hand from one breast to the other. In the world Nadia was inhabiting, a world turned on its head, where implications and consequences were suspended, up to now, she had made no commitment to what was happening. She had merely acquiesced. But now that changed. As Jan moved her mouth towards her lips, Nadia raised her head to meet it. She plunged her tongue into Jan's mouth and felt its softness, and heat. The kiss went on for a very long time. It sealed the silent contract she had made with herself. There was no turning back now, and no desire to do so.

Jan got to her feet. She stripped off her blouse and unzipped the boots. She peeled the tight leggings down to her ankles and sat on the bed to pull them off her feet. She was wearing white silk panties cut high on the hip.

Nadia looked across at Jack. For a second she thought she saw a flash of regret and resentment as if he didn't want his wife to be there. But it melted away. They both looked at Jan. Her body was flawless, every limb perfectly shaped, perfectly proportioned, smooth, seamless curves, rotundity and softness balanced by angularity and firmness, her whole body supple and lithe. She had a grace and economy of movement that matched her elegance.

Jan unclipped her bra and let her breasts fall free. They were small but very round with neat, dark red nipples. It was as Nadia watched them quiver slightly at their freedom that she felt the first pang of desire. She wanted to feel that long slender body pressed against her own, to feel her breasts and navel and sex, to do things she had only done once before, and had never thought to repeat.

They kissed again. Jan knelt at her side, Jack watching her intently. She trailed her mouth down the sinews of Nadia's neck, over her collarbone, down between her breasts. Nadia knew where the trail would end. She opened her legs as a way of telling the woman she did not mind, as if her whole body wasn't telling her that anyway, communicating with the language of need, her flesh trembling, her mouth mewing little gasps of pleasure.

Jan's tongue toyed with her soft, furry pubic hair. Slowly, as if deliberately teasing her, it descended lower, kissing the flesh on either side of her labia first. Then, after what seemed like forever, she centred her lips on the labia themselves. Nadia moaned loudly as Jan's tongue eased the yielding flesh apart and searched for the little bud hidden underneath. Jack's mouth had done exactly the same thing moments before but it was nothing like this. Jan's mouth was supple and smooth and incredibly soft. It seemed to mould itself to Nadia's sex, clinging to it limpet like, while her tongue worked away inside, stroking at the clitoris. Strings of febrile memory stretched back to another place and another time, reinforcing the sensation.

As her mouth worked ceaselessly, Jan's hand slipped under Nadia's thighs. The fingers of one hand found the portal of her sex but instead of penetrating into her vagina they stretched it open, scissoring her fingers apart. At the same time Nadia felt a finger testing the ring of her anus. It had no difficulty penetrating the little puckered circle, the juices from Nadia's sex having collected there. As this finger pushed home the others thrust upwards, coming together to form a phallus in her vagina, mimicking the action of a cock – just as her husband's had once done.

As the fingers drove into both her passages, the tongue stroked harder at her clitoris. Nadia was torn between the exigencies of the shock of feeling Jan was creating and the vivid memory of what it been like before, of Barbara's tongue and mouth, the first time a mouth – let alone a woman's mouth – had touched her sex. She remembered the hot, sweet, almost sickly passion, mixed so strongly with guilt. Was knowing that it was wrong what made it feel so exquisitely right? Was that why she had exactly the same feeling now, her sexual passion mixed with the guilt of knowing she should not be allowing herself to take part in a *ménage à trois*?

Her eyes had been closed by the shocks of sensation. But she forced them open. She looked at Jan's slender body, her legs bent up under her, the silk panties stretched tightly over her buttocks. She looked up at Jack who was kneeling too, on the other side of her, his erection projecting from his loins. She tried to read the expression on his face. It seemed, for a moment, to be anger.

Nadia was coming. A wave of sensation forced her eyes closed again and in the crimson darkness of her mind she saw images of Barbara, the forbidden memories fusing with the current feelings, until she could not tell one from the other. It didn't matter. All she cared about was the sweet, rich, dark pleasure that erupted inside her and spread out rapidly to every last nerve, wiping out the need to think, or do anything but feel.

A weight moved on the bed. She sensed the warmth of Jan's body. When her crisis had passed and she could open her eyes again she saw Jan was straddling her face, her legs open, her sex covered by the crotch of the silk panties. In the miasma of feeling her brain refused to work. She couldn't understand how Jan's fingers were still inside her yet at the same time peeling the crotch of the white panties aside, until she realised it was Jack's fingers moving the silk and that he had come to kneel behind her head. As he revealed Jan's sex he moved his erection towards it. Jan's labia were thin and neat, rather like her mouth, and, whether naturally or not, completely hairless. Nadia stared as they parted to welcome Jack's glans, just like a mouth pursing in a kiss.

Hamilton plunged forward, his cock disappearing into the maw of his wife's sex. Nadia's body pulsed over Jan's fingers. She had never seen anything like this and never realised how exciting she would find it, how her sex would react as if the cock were penetrating *her*.

Instantly she felt another orgasm spring up from the fathomless well of passion she appeared to have become. She had stopped struggling with her conflicting emotions. There was nothing she could do about it now anyway. This was not the time for moral judgments. This was not the place to sort past from present, nor tell herself what she should or should not be doing. At this moment it didn't matter. All that mattered was the glorious feeling of sex, the feeling she had missed for so long. There would be time for regret later, no doubt.

Clutching at the sheet, clawing at it with her hands in a desperate need to hold on to something, she came again, over Jan's artful tongue and adept fingers. She fought to keep her eyes open, knowing the view of Jack's cock sliding effortlessly into Jan's sex would only deepen what she felt.

Recovering slightly, Nadia raised her head off the bed, pushing her mouth up against Jack's cock. She saw him shudder as her lips sucked at the underside of his phallus.

'Oh God,' he groaned.

Nadia tasted the sap of Jan's body. Though it was years ago she could still remember the taste of Barbara's sex, just like this, sweet yet salty at the same time. The breadth of Jack's cock had spread Jan's labia wide apart and Nadia could see the little nut of her clitoris, pink and swollen and glistening wet. Inching forward she brought her tongue on to it, her chin butting against the sac of Jack's balls.

As a reaction she felt Jan's tongue go rigid. Aggressively, using the same motion Jan had employed on her, she prodded and stroked her clitoris, making her moan.

It was too much for Jack. Nadia's hot breath and the movement of her lips was making him come and he didn't want that, not yet at least. He pulled out and shifted around to the side so he could watch.

With her husband gone Jan could sink herself more fully on to Nadia's mouth, and Nadia, in turn, had access to her lower labia. Nadia moved her hands round Jan's buttocks using one to pull the crotch of her panties aside, as Jack had done, so she could get her tongue into her vagina. She circled the entrance first, then plunged inside. She lapped there for a moment before pulling back to Jan's clitoris and pushing the fingers of her other hand where her tongue had been, one into the small ring of Jan's anus, two into the heat and wetness of her sex.

It was a perfect circle. As Nadia's tongue stroked the swollen gland of Jan's clitoris, her own was similarly assailed. As she felt Jan's body tense and knew an orgasm was about to strike, so her own pleasure gathered with renewed force. Together the two women quivered and shook, their feelings mirror images, their bodies pressed together, every sensation magnified and multiplied by the fact that what one felt was instantly transmitted to the other like an echo trapped in a mountainous canyon, bouncing from one wall to the other, seemingly without end.

Finally the echo died; the shackles of passion that held them so tightly loosened their grip. Jan rolled off Nadia. They lay side by side, wet with sweat and their own juices, finally replete.

But there was still Jack. He was kneeling up on the bed, his erection glistening and hard, its veins standing out like cords of string, distended by his need. He moved up the bed until his cock was lying across his wife's lips.

'Feeling left out, are you?' she mocked, letting the words move her lips against his flesh. She sucked

131

on the underside of his cock then squirmed back until her head was forced between his thighs and her flawless, lithe body lay out in front of him. She locked her lips around the sac of his balls and sucked it into her mouth. At the same time she circled the shaft of his cock with her right hand and began pumping the ring of her thumb and forefinger up and down, concentrating on the ridge of his glands.

Nadia watched. She saw Jack's eyes close as Jan's ministrations caused a jolt of pleasure. Not wanting to be left out of the final denouement, Nadia got up on to her knees. Crawling behind him she pushed her breasts against his back and sunk her mouth into his neck. At the same time she found his nipples and pinched them quite hard. He shuddered, driven that much closer to his climax.

Jan released his balls from their toothsome prison and juggled them instead with her tongue, the rhythm of her head incessant. Over his shoulder Nadia saw the head of his glans swell to even greater proportions, glistening and smooth, and the slit of his urethra open, like a tiny pleading mouth. Almost immediately a string of semen shot out of him, describing an arch in the air, and splashing down on Jan's trembling breasts and her belly and even, one or two drops at least, on the white silk of her panties that still veiled her sex.

She unlocked her car and sat in it without starting the engine. The interior of the car was familiar and comfortable. Eventually she drove home, concentrating on her driving, doing it with clipped precision, priding herself on the way she handled the sporty car, the way she cornered and positioned it on the road. It was a means of distracting herself from thinking about anything else. There was little traffic and she watched intently for signs of the police as she drove well above the legal limit. She played a tape of Itzhak Perlman performing a Bach solo violin partita, playing it so loud the sound almost hurt.

At home she went straight to the bathroom, stripped off her clothes and stepped into the shower. She avoided looking in the mirror. She soaped herself vigorously then let the water wash the lather away.

She was exhausted physically and emotionally. She towelled herself dry and went to bed, covering herself with a single sheet. She knew she would not be able to sleep, that now, with nothing to distract her from her thoughts, nor the images that played in her mind, like pictures on a cinema screen, she would toss and turn, plagued by implications and consequence. Strangely she fell asleep almost before her head had touched the pillow.

On another day she might have thought twice. But not today.

'Hello?' She hoped it wasn't Hamilton. She couldn't remember whether she'd given him her home number.

'Can I speak to Nadia Irving?'

'You are.'

'Oh, hello, it's Andrew Anderson.'

'Mr Anderson, how are you? How did you get my number?'

'I know it's an imposition. I'm afraid I badgered James Hill.'

'That's all right,' Nadia said.

'I'd have waited to catch you at work but it was rather urgent.'

'Oh . . .'

She hoped nothing had gone wrong with her grand scheme.

'Not business,' he added, obviously picking up her anxiety. 'Purely pleasure.' He realised that sounded wrong and corrected himself. 'I mean I wanted to ask you out.'

'That urgent?' she said rather sharply.

Angela was sitting on the large cream Chesterfield in Nadia's first-floor sitting room, a glass of gin and tonic in her hand. She swirled the ice in the glass and mouthed, "Who is it?" to her friend.

Nadia mouthed back, "Anderson".

Angela made a ring of her thumb and forefinger and pumped her fist up and down. Nadia ignored her and turned her back.

'Well, it's just I've got tickets for the first night of the new Stoppard at the National. I remember you said at lunch you were mad about Antony Sher.'

'I am.'

'So I thought you might like to come. They say the rest of the run's sold out. But it's tomorrow night, you see, I thought you might be . . .'

'Tomorrow's fine and I'd love to come.' She wasn't sure she'd love to at all – Andrew Anderson was distinctly not her type and held little fascination for her – but she certainly wanted to see the play and she certainly did not want to stay at home on her own.

'Six then,' he said.

'That's early.'

'Starts at seven. Press nights are always early.'

'Six then.' It wasn't a problem. Working in the city

she started early but finished by five.

'Wonderful. I'll come and pick you up.'

'That would be nice.' She gave him her address.

'And dinner afterwards?' he asked tentatively.

'Can we take it one step at a time?' she said, not wanting Andrew to get the idea that he was to be anything other than a convenient companion.

'Of course,' he said.

They exchanged goodbyes and rang off.

'Andrew Anderson's got the hots for you, eh?' Angela guessed as Nadia sat down opposite her on a matching Chesterfield.

'So it appears. Wants to take me to the National.'

'Well, you could do worse.'

'It's the theatre, not a proposal of marriage.'

'He's single and rich.'

'And I'm not the slightest bit interested in him, Angela. Other than as a client.'

'What's the matter with him?'

'Absolutely nothing, except I don't find him attractive.'

'Not like Jack Hamilton?'

Nadia got to her feet, took Angela's glass and her own and refilled them with gin and tonic. She dropped in ice from an ice bucket and set them on the large coffee table between the two sofas.

'No, not like Hamilton.'

'So, where were we?' Angela sipped her drink. 'You're in the studio . . .'

Nadia had called Angela first thing that morning, the morning after the night before, and told her she needed to talk. Angela, perhaps hearing a note of distress in her friend's voice, had volunteered to come round that evening. For the last hour Nadia had poured out the whole story, everything that had happened with Jack since she'd first met him. She'd got to the part where she had arrived at the studio on her own when Anderson's call had interrupted the flow.

'Can I ask you something really personal, Angela? I mean, we've been friends for a long time but we've never discussed it.'

'Discussed what?'

'Have you ever . . .' Nadia wasn't sure how to phrase it. She was going to say "made love to a woman" but that didn't sound right. "Have you ever had sex with a woman?" sounded wrong too. She settled for the familiar euphemism. 'Have you ever been to bed with a woman?'

'God, no,' Angela said rather too quickly. Nadia knew her too well. She knew immediately she was lying.

'Then you're going to be shocked.'

'Shock me.'

And she did. Angela's mouth fell open as Nadia related the rest of the story, telling her how Jan had let herself into the studio, and what had happened on Hamilton's bed.

'I only remembered what she'd said this morning. She thanked him for the note. She was supposed to be off on a photographic shoot, but he must have left her a note telling her about me. It was all planned. Like the others.'

'Others?'

'He told me they'd shared women before.'

'His wife's a dike?'

'Bisexual. That's the trouble.'

'What is?'

'I think I am too.'

'What, bisexual or a dike?' Angela tried to make a

136

joke of it.

'It's not funny. I enjoyed it, Angela, I mean really.'

'What's wrong with that?'

'Nothing, I suppose. It's just confusing.'

'You said Hamilton's had a terrific effect on you, got you all pumped up. It was probably just that you got so turned on she was like an extension of him.'

'Maybe.' She hadn't told her about Barbara, and the sticky sweet feeling that memory had provoked.

'Actually . . .' Angela said, her tongue between her teeth, 'I lied.'

'About what?' Nadia said as if she hadn't guessed.

'I have been to bed with a woman.'

'Recently?'

'You're right, we've never talked about it, have we?'

'We don't have to now if you'd rather . . .'

'Actually, I've been to bed with several women if you want the truth. Jan Hamilton was your first?'

'First *woman*.'

'Explain?'

'At school. Well, between school and university.' Nadia told her about Barbara. It was turning into a night of true confessions.

'Oh, my first experience was much more menial,' Angela said when Nadia had finished. 'It was when I was at Drew's. You remember my boss, the head of the bond department? Well, his wife propositioned me at the Christmas party. She knew I was up for promotion. She told me she was going to tell her husband she thought I was unsuitable.'

'And what? You didn't complain?'

'What could I do? Her word against mine. Nobody would have believed me. But that wasn't the point. I suppose that's why I've never talked about it with you. You know the way I am with men? I love having sex with a man, with lots of men. I didn't have any idea I wanted to do it with a woman too, not until this woman came along. But I wanted her. She was beautiful. Oh, ten, maybe even fifteen years older than me, but she was gorgeous. Really long blonde hair, very slim with fabulous clothes. She always wore Joy 1000. It's supposed to be the most expensive perfume in the world.'

'And?' Their third, or was it their fourth, gin and tonic had disappeared. Nadia refreshed their glasses.

'She was very experienced. Very . . . adept. She knew all the right buttons to push. Oh, I was ripe for the picking but she was just so damn good at it.'

'And after her?'

'After her I have been very discriminating. The point of my telling you all this is that it hasn't made one iota of difference to my relationship with men. Never has and never will. That's what's worrying you, isn't it?'

'Yes, I suppose that's exactly what's worrying me.'

'I felt the same. I wanted it, I was desperately curious, but I was shit scared. I didn't want to turn into some bra-burning dike with a moustache, greased back hair and a man's suit. But it doesn't work that way. You know I love sex with men. I love it. Having sex with a woman is different, but in a way it's exactly the same. The pleasure comes from the same thing. I doesn't make you a bad person. In fact, as far as I'm concerned it makes sex better – the contrast, I mean.'

'Variety's the spice of life?'

'Right.'

'Why did you lie just now?'

Angela laughed. 'Well, firstly because I wasn't sure

what you were going to say and secondly because . . .' She reached into her handbag and took out a long, narrow parcel wrapped in red wrapping paper. 'After our last conversation I bought you a present and I didn't want you to take it the wrong way.'

Angela handed Nadia the package. 'The wrong way?' Nadia said.

'Open it.'

Nadia peeled off the red paper. On the inside she discovered a long yellow rectangular box with a transparent plastic window along part of one side and lettering that declared it contained a DREAM LOVER, THE ULTIMATE VIBRATOR (BATTERIES NOT INCLUDED). Fascinated, she extracted a cream plastic phallus from the box.

'I put batteries in,' Angela said.

'Where did you get it?'

'They have them all over the place. Twist the end.'

Nadia saw a gnarled knob at the end of the dildo. She turned it and the whole stem started to vibrate. She turned it off quickly because the action transmitted a jolt of sensation through her hand to her sex.

'You use one of these?'

'It's better than some of the men I've had.'

'What do you do?'

'Put it inside you. Put the end on your clit. Anything. You don't need instructions. Whatever's good.'

'And it makes you come?' Whether it was the drink or the subject of the conversation Nadia wasn't sure, but she was becoming very hot. She also thought she was blushing. She couldn't remember the last time she'd blushed.

'So, you see, I didn't want you to think I had an ulterior motive.'

'Ulterior motive?' The gin had affected her brain. She knew Angela had said the present might be misinterpreted, but, for the life of her she couldn't remember why.

'If I suddenly told you I'd been having sex with other women, then produced a vibrator, you might think . . .'

'Oh right.' The penny dropped. 'But you don't?' That remark slipped out before she realised what she'd said.

'Don't what?'

'Want to have sex with me?'

There was a silence. The words seemed to sober both women up.

'I think that would probably spoil a very good friendship,' Angela said earnestly.

'Probably?' Nadia queried.

'Yes.' Angela stared at her intensely.

'Meaning if it wouldn't spoil our friendship . . .' The words hung in the air. Both women realised they had taken a step on to territory they had never explored before.

'Let's talk about it another time. What are you going to do about Hamilton?'

'Nothing. I can't see him again.'

'Why not?'

'Oh Angela, I'm not like you. I scared myself. I scared myself badly. I should have got up and walked out.'

'Has he called you?'

'Twice. I got my secretary to say I was out.'

'But I thought you had a good time with him. In bed, I mean.'

'I do. I did. But I'm not going to become part of their *ménage*. I was used. He set me up for his wife. I know he did.'

'And if it were just him on his own?'

'Damn him. Why did he have to do it? I've never wanted a man more in my life. Christ, you don't know what it was like.'

'What do you mean?'

'Well,' the gin was making her loquacious, 'I was never very good at it. Sex, I mean. I never seemed to be able to get the hang of it. I thought it was me – that I wasn't very proficient. Then with him I went wild, really wild. Now I'm a different person. It's like I was asleep and he's woken me up.'

'I'd love to go to bed with him. I think he's so sexy.'

'He is.'

'So why don't you *use* him? As long as you know you're doing it. Men use women for sex all the time.'

'I just can't. I wish I could.'

'I've got to go,' Angela said, looking at her watch. 'I'll leave you to practise.'

'Practise?'

Angela indicated the dildo. For the second time that evening Nadia blushed.

'I'll call you a taxi.'

They chatted amiably while they waited for the taxi to arrive. At the front door they kissed each other on the cheeks.

'Thanks, Angela, you always seem to have the habit of saying just what I want to hear.'

'If you begin growing a moustache then you can start to worry.'

'Thanks for understanding.'

'I understand only too well.'

141

And that, Nadia had been surprised to discover, was undoubtedly true.

When she woke it was just getting light, fingers of light creeping around the gaps in the curtains, the room suffused with an odd cream tint. She was still wearing her bra and panties. The alcohol she had consumed with Angela had left her too tired to be bothered to strip them off.

She glanced at the clock on her bedside table. It was six-thirty. Next to it was a long rectangular box which she didn't recognise, until, all at once, it came flooding back to her, the gin-soaked confessions and Angela's gift.

She reached out and extracted the plastic cylinder from its wrapping. It felt cold and hard. There was enough light filtering through the curtains to see it quite clearly. The top was tapered and smooth, but two thirds of the length was moulded with little ribs circling its circumference. She was about to put it back when she felt her sex pulse, as though to remind her that, after a period of getting considerable attention, so far in the last twenty-four hours it had got none.

She stroked her pubic hair through the silky nylon of her panties, thinking she would go back to sleep. But her clitoris responded immediately. She could feel it swelling. And suddenly sleep was no longer on the agenda. Quickly, a little annoyed with herself for having started the process, she slipped out of her knickers, throwing the sheet that covered her aside. Remembering what Angela had said she trailed the dildo down her body until the tip was resting on the top of her thigh. Again she was aware of its coldness, in such contrast to the heat and life of a cock.

Without raising her head to look she groped around for the gnarled knob at the end of the phallus and turned it. A high-pitched humming noise filled the air and she felt her thigh vibrate. The vibration spread out like waves on a pond, and reached her labia. She experienced a delicious tingling sensation.

Nosing the dildo closer to her sex, she opened her legs. With one hand she pulled her breast uncomfortably from the silky nylon cup of her bra, squashing it down against her ribs, while, with the other, she directed the dildo into her labia. The vibrations extended all the way along the crease of her sex, affecting her clitoris too, but she didn't want to concentrate on that just yet. She wanted to feel it inside her. Slowly she moved the smooth cream plastic down to the entrance to her vagina. She remembered how Jan's fingers had stretched the opening apart, and used the tip of the dildo to do the same, circling it and pulling the pliant flesh this way and that. She felt a strong pulse of pleasure.

'Come on then,' she said aloud. Words seemed to have become an aphrodisiac.

She plunged the dildo home, right up into her body, objective experiment giving way to raw need. Her sex reacted to the intruder by going into spasm, contracting around it, gripping it tightly to feel its hardness.

'God,' Nadia gasped.

What Hamilton had done to her body, whatever process of atrophy he had arrested, seemed to override the guilts and confusions of being with his wife. The sexuality Nadia had so recently seen blossom remained in flower. Her senses reeled under the assault of the vibrator humming deep inside her. Almost unconsciously she began moving the phallus up and down in imitation of a cock. She felt her sex flooding with her juices. The spindle of the dumbbell had satisfied a need but this was so much better. She could feel blood pumping into her clitoris as it sent out urgent messages, pleading with her to bring the vibrations closer, wanting to be at the epicentre of the shock wave, not on the outskirts.

Nadia knew moving the dildo to her clitoris would make her come. For a while it was possible to tease herself, to hold the demands of her clitoris at bay and enjoy the pleasures emanating from her vagina, as the phallus stroked in and out.

But the storm of orgasm gathered more rapidly then she would have thought possible. The vibrations made her tremble, made her flesh quake, her breasts and thighs and buttocks alive. The dildo, almost of its own accord, slipped from her body and moved up, parting her almost hairless labia until the tip of the cream phallus butted hard against the pink wet promontory of her clit. She gasped with the jolt of pleasure it produced. The vibrations engulfed it. The feelings were so intense it felt as though she had been punched, a raw shock of energy that took her into an orgasm quite unlike anything she had experienced before. At its centre were the endless vibrations, tendrils of sensation that reached into every nerve, her body arched off the bed like a bow, her legs wide open, her muscles as rigid as steel.

It was the first time she'd come since she'd come with Jan. But fortunately for Nadia the rush of pleasure was so intense that it blanketed her mind. She'd feared she would see Jan's face or the image of her body, her thin, hairless labia and the open maw of her sex. She'd feared she would not escape the vivid emotional impact the experience had left. But, as the trills of vibration carried her down into a trough of pleasure, there were no mental pictures to reinforce the sensation. Her orgasm, like its creator, was completely disembodied.

Chapter Seven

AT EXACTLY SIX the doorbell rang. Nadia was
waiting in the kitchen. She was dressed in a slinky,
tight, dark blue dress that clung to her bosom, waist
and hips. Its skirt was short enough to reveal a great
deal of her slim, contoured thighs, and its scoop
neckline, similarly, showed off the ballooning
curves of her breasts. She loved this dress. It was
comfortable to wear and immensely flattering and
she was in the right mood to flaunt herself. Ultra
sheer, glossy black tights and dark blue high heels
completed her outfit.

'You're very punctual,' she said as she opened the
door.

'It was bred into me from an early age,' Andrew
Anderson replied. He was wearing a beautifully
tailored double-breasted evening suit and a black
bow tie. His cummerbund was cherry red.

'Do you want a drink?'

'I'd love one but I think we'd better go. The
traffic's terrible at this time of the day.'

'Fine.'

She quickly set the burglar alarm, picked up her

small evening bag, preceded him out of the house, locking the front door after them. Parked a little way down the street was a silver Mercedes 500SL.

'Gave the chauffeur the night off,' he said as he opened the passenger door for her.

They drove through the traffic, crossed Waterloo Bridge and parked in the underground car park of the National, talking all the way: a little about the fact that Anderson had helped Manson's to negotiate a contract for Babcock's son to take a seat on the Manson board and a lot about the theatre and plays they had seen. Anderson was knowledgeable and astute and Nadia was impressed with his cultural expertise.

The foyer was crowded with glitterati and Anderson seemed to know a lot of the people who milled around, introducing her to one or two as they sipped a glass of champagne. The critics, with their dowdy suits and weary expressions, kept to themselves and took their aisle seats only at the very last minute.

The play was entertaining, for which Nadia was grateful. She had had a busy day at work, with only a sandwich at her desk for lunch, but that was exactly what she'd wanted. She'd had no time to dwell on the whys and wherefores of Jack Hamilton and his beautiful wife. She had reached one very simple conclusion, despite what Angela had said, with very little internal debate. With or without his wife, she never wanted to see Jack Hamilton again. She had lived dangerously, well beyond the pale of anything she would have thought herself capable of. Well, like a child who had strayed too far from home, all she wanted to do now was run back to safety.

By the end of the play Nadia was completely absorbed in its complexities. She had managed not to think about Jack Hamilton for at least two hours.

On the way out in the crush of people she took Anderson's arm.

'Thank you,' she said, smiling at him.

'My pleasure.' He returned the smile. For a moment their eyes met. 'How would you like me to take you home?'

'No,' she said definitely. 'I would like you to take me to dinner.'

'I took the precaution of booking a table at the Connaught Grill Room, just in case.'

They drove through Whitehall and Pall Mall. Outside the hotel a doorman sprung to open each door of the car, then, as soon as they were out, valet parked it. Nadia discovered she was ravenous. They ordered quickly, barely glancing at the menu, opting for *coquilles au gratin*, and chateaubriand with *soufflé, aux pommes*, a speciality that few restaurants could afford the manpower to prepare. Anderson ordered Tattinger champagne and a Margaux.

As the evening progressed Nadia found she liked Andrew Anderson more than she had thought she would. He was attentive and interesting, and though she had been put off in the first place by his rather weak appearance, she found it grew on her. He was not an unattractive man.

'Have you ever been married?' he asked after the coquilles had arrived.

'Yes. You?'

'Yes. A bad divorce. All my fault.'

'Children?'

'No, thank God.'

'Me neither.'

'Shall we compare divorces?'

'Too depressing.'

'Would you mind if I told you I find you very attractive?'

'Thank you.' She had the impression he wanted to say something else. 'And?' she prompted.

'Oh, nothing . . . It's all so difficult – well, I find it difficult.'

'Difficult?'

'What used to be called the mating game. Men and women. I'm too old to call it dating. When you were young you were allowed to be gauche and green. Youth was the perfect excuse. At my age you're supposed to know everything, exactly what moves to make, what to say, what to do.'

'And?'

'And I know nothing. I feel completely lost.'

'What did you want to say?'

'I want to say I'm extremely attracted to you.'

'You said that already.' That came out more churlishly than she'd intended.

'You see, I'm getting it all wrong . . .'

'Andrew . . .' It was the first time she had used his name. 'Perhaps I can make it easier for you. I've just been through a very bruising affair. I feel completely betrayed. I'm not ready; I'm not capable of going to bed with another man at the moment. When I am, if I am, I'll let you know.'

'That's very clear.'

'Sorry . . . I didn't mean . . . That area of my life's been very screwed up recently.'

'I understand. I appreciate your honesty.'

'Good. I'd like to do this again.' She wasn't sure whether that was true.

'So would I, very much.'

They ate the rest of the meal with gusto and ordered vanilla soufflé for dessert. The air had been cleared as far as Nadia was concerned and she could relax. Anderson, too, seemed to be more at ease having got the subject of sex off his chest.

It was well past midnight when they got back into the Mercedes and Anderson drove her home. He found a parking space almost outside her house and came round to the passenger door to open it for her.

'Well, good night, Nadia. I've really enjoyed your company.'

But Nadia found she didn't want the evening to end there. 'Come in for some coffee,' she said. It was Friday, after all, and she didn't have to be up at the crack of dawn.

'Are you sure?'

'Just coffee,' she said, smiling.

'That would be nice.'

Inside he stood in the kitchen while she filled the coffee maker and switched it on. She took out small white cups and saucers and set them on an oak butler's tray.

'Do you want a drink?'

'Better not,' he said. 'I don't think I should be driving as it is.'

She poured herself an Armagnac and put it on the tray. Upstairs Anderson settled on one Chesterfield and Nadia sat opposite on the other, the tray on the table between them.

'Do you want to talk about it?' he said, 'Or have you talked about it so much you're sick of the subject?'

'Talk about what?'

'Your bruising affair.'

150

She found she did want to talk about it. She leant forward, poured the coffee and pushed a cup across the table towards him.

'For the first time in my life I let myself go,' she told him. 'I took a risk, and lost.'

'What sort of risk?'

She looked across at Anderson. His neat, small face was serious and concerned. She couldn't help thinking of a small boy who had found his mother in tears and was trying to comfort her.

'I just wanted a man . . . I thought I was . . . what's the expression . . . past caring.'

'And he let you down?'

'Yes.'

'Did you love him?'

'No, curiously I can't say I did. I can't say I even cared for him very much.'

'Then why were you so upset?'

It was a good question. She wasn't sure she knew the answer. She hadn't felt love for Hamilton at any stage, though she knew love would be a natural development from what had happened between them. She supposed the reason she was upset by what had happened was that she felt used, that instead of responding to what she had thought was something special he had merely treated her as another affair, another prize to be shared with his wife.

'Because he used me,' she said after a pause.

'Used you how?'

'Do you want to know the truth?' She hadn't imagined telling Anderson such intimacies but she realised she didn't care enough about him to hide anything. If he was shocked and put off by it, she really didn't mind.

'If you want to tell me.'

'He shared me with his wife.'

She expected shocked horror. She expected him to ask when and how and why. Instead he said quietly, 'He must be a very arrogant man.'

Nadia laughed. 'Yes, you're absolutely right, he is.'

'And is that the sort of man you like?'

'What, arrogant? No, I don't think so.' She drank her brandy. Confession was good for the soul. The way Anderson had handled the news pleased her; it made her feel as though what she had done was not so beyond the bounds of acceptability after all. 'You're a very unusual man,' she told him.

'I take that as a compliment.'

'It is.' Nadia was looking at Andrew through different eyes. For the first time she wondered what it would be like to go to bed with him. The talk of Hamilton had inevitably put sex back on the agenda. 'Come and sit over here with me.'

Giving her an old-fashioned look, Hamilton got to his feet and came round the coffee table to sit beside her.

'Is that better?'

'Are you a gambling man?' she asked.

'No.'

'Oh, what a pity. I was going to offer you a gamble.' It was extraordinary. It was as though her body had changed gear. One minute she was calm, rational and objective. The next she felt a knot of anticipation cinch itself tightly in the pit of her stomach, and a wave of desire wash over her. She wasn't sure whether it was desire to have sex, or desire to have sex with Anderson. She knew it was desire to have sex with a *man*.

'What sort of gamble?' he asked.

'I was going to say that if you kissed me I might like it and if I liked it I might change my mind.'

'About what?'

'About what I said in the restaurant.' She was playing the vamp again. It appeared to be a role she enjoyed. 'On the other hand ...' She smiled coquettishly. 'I might find the whole thing totally uninteresting and make you go home.'

'Quite a gamble.'

'But you're not a gambling man.'

He turned towards her, pushed her back against the Chesterfield and kissed her on the mouth. His tongue probed between her lips, but she pushed it aside with her own and penetrated his mouth. His hands caressed her shoulders very lightly. She felt her nipples pucker.

He sucked on her tongue gently then broke the kiss with an audible pop. 'Well?' he said.

Nadia got to her feet. The excitement she felt made her a little light-headed. She wasn't sure whether it was the kiss that had engendered it or the way she was acting. 'It pays to gamble, you see,' she said, extending her hand.

'You're very beautiful,' he said, taking her hand in both of his and rubbing her fingers very gently in a circular motion.

'Take me to bed, Anderson.'

'I thought you weren't ready?'

'I've changed my mind.'

Without another word she led him upstairs. In the doorway of her bedroom she turned and kissed him again, wrapping her arms around him under his jacket and pressing her body against his. She wasn't sure why she had suddenly been overcome by an urgent sexual need, apparently with no cause, but it had seized hold of her so strongly that her body was already tingling.

'The zip's at the back,' she said, turning her back to him.

'I noticed. It's a beautiful dress.' He caressed the material lovingly, smoothing his hands down on either side of her waist where the dress clung to her hour glass figure. 'Lovely material,' he said indistinctly, before pulling the tongue of the zip down. He folded the shoulder straps over her arms so the dress could fall to the floor. As Nadia stepped out of it he stooped to pick it up, and laid it carefully over the bedroom chair. Apparently not satisfied it was crease free, he shook it out and lay it across the chair a second time.

Nadia was wearing a black bra and matching panties under her tights. She stripped back the bedding, turned on the bedside lamp and drew the curtains. Taking a red scarf from a big mahogany chest of drawers, she draped it over the light. The bedroom was plunged into a rosy glow.

'You know, I was quite prepared to . . . I mean, you didn't have to . . .' Andrew said, taking off his jacket.

'I want to, Andrew. Women are allowed to want.'

She kissed him again. His hand found the catch of the lacy three-quarter cup bra and undid it. He pulled back from her mouth and eased the bra away from her breasts.

'Lovely,' he said. As he appeared to be paying more attention to the bra than to the breasts, Nadia wasn't sure whether he meant her or the garment. He put it on the chair, alongside her dress. 'Sit on the bed,' he said.

She did as she was told and he came to kneel in

154

front of her. Taking her left foot in his hand, he eased her shoe off. 'Such beautiful ankles,' he said, running his fingers around them. He bent his head forward until he could kiss the top of her foot. Then he took off her right shoe and kissed that foot in the same way. His hand smoothed against the glossy nylon.

Anderson got to his feet. He unbuttoned the gold studs that held his evening shirt and stripped it off. His chest was slender and hairless. He kicked his shoes off, peeled away his socks, reached behind him to unhook the cummerband, then unzipped his trousers. He was wearing shiny red silk boxer shorts. He was not as meticulous with his own clothes as he had been with Nadia's, merely leaving them where they fell on the floor.

Nadia lay back on the bed. She extended her foot and touched his thigh with her toes, working them up under the leg of the shorts. His legs, like his chest, were not defined by muscle, and were, oddly, completely devoid of hair. His body looked weaker and slimmer than it had looked in clothes, almost like the body of a young boy. She found herself comparing him with Hamilton. Damn Hamilton, she thought, consciously excising him from her mind.

'Help me with my tights,' she said.

Anderson knelt on the bed beside her and hooked his fingers into the waistband of the sheer nylon. Slowly he pulled them off her hips while she raised her buttocks. Instead of throwing them aside, he folded them as neatly as he could and laid them on the bedside chest.

The triangle of her lace panties barely covered her pubis. Strands of blonde pubic hair had meshed with the nylon. She was about to take them off herself.

'No, let me,' he said. His fingers caressed the lace, smoothing it against Nadia's mons. She saw him close his eyes momentarily as if to concentrate on the feel of it. 'Is it silk?' he asked.

'No, I don't think so,' she said, thinking it a strange question.

His hand slid down between her thighs, pushing the material into the crease of her sex. The gusset of the panties was made from a silky satin. As Nadia opened her legs he ran a finger along it.

'Take them off, Andrew,' she said.

With a certain reluctance his hands skimmed the panties down her hips. When they were clear of the ankles he brought them up to his face, rubbing them against his cheek. 'I'm sure they're silk,' he said, folding them carefully and putting them on top of her tights.

His hands cupped her firm, round breasts, squeezing them gently. He kissed her again on the mouth as his hand descended to her belly. A finger inveigled its way between her labia. Conscientiously he stroked the nub of her clitoris, while his mouth kissed her neck and worked down to her nipple. She felt his lips close on the hard puckered flesh and suck on it, covering it with saliva.

Nadia had the feeling he was making love to her by rote, as if he had read somewhere this was what a woman wanted, not because *he* wanted to do it. While she had been clothed his caresses had contained a certain electricity; now she was naked that spark had gone. She felt her excitement draining away. She wanted to be fucked; she wanted to be taken and possessed. Like Hamilton had possessed her. Damn Hamilton. It was no good expecting every man to be like Hamilton. Tony had been like him, at least in strength and power, but he was more likely to be the exception than the rule. 'What do you want?' she said. She had the feeling Andrew wanted something he was not prepared to ask for.

'I want you,' he said.

She sat up, wrapped her arms around his neck and kissed him full on the mouth, moving her other hand down into the fly of the silk boxer shorts. Her hand closed on his cock. It was erect but only partially so. He was not circumcised and his foreskin still covered his glans. She pulled it back and he moaned against her mouth. Her finger rubbed the tender flesh of his glans and she felt it swell.

'Take your shorts off,' she said.

'Would you mind if I kept them on? I love the feel of silk.'

She answered by pushing him back on the bed. It was an odd request but it hardly mattered. His erection poked through the folds of red silk. She circled it with her fist and moved her head up and down. It was harder now and she could feel it pulsing.

'If you like silk . . .' She reached over to the bedside chest and caught hold of her panties. She dropped them on his chest and used them to caress his nipples. Instantly she felt his cock throb strongly in her hand. She brought the panties down to his erection and wrapped it in them. His cock jerked visibly, harder and bigger now.

'Oh Nadia, that's so lovely.'

'Good.'

There was a time when she would have settled for less, when she would have accepted a sexual encounter full of fudges and compromises. But not now. Her body demanded more. She wanted to excite Anderson because she wanted to excite herself. She swung her thigh over his hips and poised her sex above his prettily packaged phallus.

'You're really turning me on,' he said.

'Do they feel good?'

'Oh wonderful, so soft.'

'Smooth and silky?'

'Yes, yes . . .'

She pulled the panties away and nudged his glans into her labia, using it, at first, to prod at her clitoris. A wave of feeling swamped her, together with a sense of relief. This was not going to be like Hamilton but it appeared she had managed to resurrect her excitement. With Hamilton she had been out of control. Tonight, her pleasure was going to come from her own machinations.

She sunk her sex down on to Andrew's cock, wriggling her clitoris against his pubic bone. She could feel the shiny silk against her inner thighs.

'Feels good,' she said, squirming against it.

'I love it,' he said. His erection throbbed inside her. He extended his hands and ran them over the sides of his boxer shorts, caressing the silk as he bucked his hips to ram his cock into her more deeply.

'Yes,' she said to encourage him.

She leant forward, supporting herself on her left hand. With the panties in her right she brought them up to his cheek and rubbed them against it.

'You'll make me come,' he whispered.

'I want you to come.'

'Do you think I'm terrible?' His face looked anguished.

'No. Why should I think that?'

'For wanting this.'

'I like it.' It was partly true. The oddness of the experience was exciting.

'Do you like to be licked?' he asked, looking into her eyes.

'I love it.'

'Let me do that first.' It was a little cold, these premeditated negotiations in what was supposed to be the heat of passion, but better that, Nadia thought, than a quick fumble and an even quicker ejaculation. He appeared to care what she felt.

She swung off him, expecting him to sit up.

'No, come up here,' he said, wanting her to sit astride his shoulders. 'So I can see you.'

'Like this?' she said, kneeling above him, her legs wide open, her sex inches above his face, open and exposed.

'It's so beautiful, Nadia, like an orchid, a rare orchid.' His hands came up to her thighs and held her firmly. He looked at her for a long time, then pulled her down·on to his mouth. The first touch made her shudder, his tongue prising open her labia and finding the portal of her sex. He circled it, provoking all the sensitive nerves concentrated around it, then pushed inside, straining his tongue against its tendons, to get as deep as he could.

He was very good. His tongue was strong and articulate. It caressed and dallied with every part of her sex, exploring every nook and cranny. He pushed it into her vagina, he stroked it against the long slit of her labia, he butted it against her swollen clitoris. His cock pulsed. Nadia had the strange

159

impression it was like a ritual, an act of worship, an adoration at the altar of her femininity.

Whatever it was, he was making her come. After covering every inch of her pudendum he concentrated on the clitoris. He seemed to know exactly where the most sensitive nerves were sited. His tongue swept over them, dwelling just long enough to provoke, then moving on, round in a circle, to return again. With absolute regularity he completed his tiny circuit, each sweep making Nadia's body grate with pleasure, creating the incessant rhythms of orgasm. The tempo was relentless and monotonous and perfect. Each circuit produced a moan of pleasure from Nadia, each moan louder and louder. Her body was trembling, her breasts quivering so much they were slapping against each other, producing yet more sensation.

She found herself grinding down on him, wriggling her buttocks from side to side, wanting to feel her labia against the bones of his face, and her wetness all over it. But she did not disturb his rhythm. Inexorably his tongue circled the button of her clit, a little faster perhaps as he sensed she was approaching her climax. She moaned again, a continuous wailing now. A part of her mind thanked Hamilton for what he had done to her, another part cursing him as it fought to exclude his image from a causal relationship with her orgasm. She looked down at Anderson's slight body, his cock projecting from the folds of red silk, stained and damped by the sap from her body, trying to concentrate on that as the totem of her pleasure.

As her orgasm escaped, driving through her body with the power and energy it had so recently discovered, she tried to think of Anderson. But she could not. Her mind was too full, too crammed with images of Hamilton and, worse, of Hamilton's wife. As she heard the wailing sound of her own voice reach a crescendo, she quite unexpectedly saw the cream-coloured phallus being pushed between her legs. The hand that held it was not hers. In her mind's eye she saw the long, carefully manicured fingers of Angela Barrett.

'No, no, no,' she cried, shaking herself violently, trying to rid herself of the spectre that had so unexpectedly appeared at the feast, at the same time wringing every last ounce of feeling from the final throes of her climax.

She felt release from the rack of pleasure that had stretched every tendon in her body, but did not relax. She pulled herself off Anderson's mouth, swivelled round and slammed her body down on to his cock, with no subtlety or finesse.

'Your turn,' she said rather aggressively, riding up and down on him, making his cock slide to and fro inside her, feeling the wetness of her sex running, like a river, over the whole length of him.

'Lovely,' he said. But he didn't sound convinced. His cock was hard but it was not throbbing. He moved one hand around to his belly and stroked the silk of his boxer shorts. His head twisted to one side, looking for her panties. They were lying on the sheet. He stretched out his hand but could not quite reach them.

Nadia saw what he was trying to do. She pulled herself off him, grabbed the panties, then sunk back down on him again.

'This is what you want, isn't it?' she said, not moving now, just holding him deep inside her.

'Yes.' The anguished look had returned to his

face, as thought he were admitting to a mortal sin.

She rubbed the panties against her breasts. His eyes watched avariciously. The satin gusset felt cool against her super-heated body. She dropped the panties on to his chest then rubbed them against his nipples one after the other. His cock immediately jerked inside her.

'You want that, don't you?' She moved the panties up to his face.

'Yes.' His expression was a turmoil of emotion, caught between anguished shame and extreme pleasure.

Nadia stroked the panties against his cheek.

'They smell so lovely,' he said.

'I always keep my empty perfume bottles in my lingerie drawer,' she told him. His eyes seemed to note this information as though it were something he needed to remember.

'You're wonderful, Nadia.'

His cock was throbbing strongly. She ground her sex down on it and used her internal muscles to squeeze it. She moved the panties down to his lips. He kissed them, pursing his lips against the lace. Nadia pushed the material into his mouth and he sucked on it. She saw the whites of his eyes roll up in an expression of ecstasy and felt his cock spasm, spattering out his semen into the cavern of her sex.

Chapter Eight

'PLEASE.'

She did not reply. There was nothing she wanted to say to him.

'Pretty please . . .' he said, trying to charm her. It did not work.

'Look, Hamilton, I've told you. I'm not interested. Not under any circumstances.'

She was looking at the largest bouquet of long-stemmed red roses she had ever seen. They had been delivered a minute after she'd got home from the office, the van driver waiting outside. The note read: ''You're wonderful. Andrew.''

'Nadia, I need to talk to you,' Hamilton was saying. He'd called her three times over the weekend. The first time she'd put the phone down then set her answerphone to monitor her calls. He'd called her at the office four times during the day but her secretary had been there to intercept. She answered the phone as she got home, thinking it would be Andrew.

'There's nothing to talk about,' she said.

'But there is. You think I planned it, don't you?'

'You did.' That was a mistake. She should have just put the phone down.

'No, Nadia. I told you Jan was supposed to be away on a shoot.'

'It doesn't matter. You're married. I don't go out with married men. I was stupid to agree to it. I've only got myself to blame.'

'I can't talk over the phone.'

'Good, because I told you I have nothing to say.'

'Just a drink somewhere, anywhere, just for half an hour.'

'No. How many times have I got to say it? No. And please don't call me again.' She slammed the phone down, its bell tinkling at the impact.

It rang again instantly.

'Look, I told you . . .' she shouted, grabbing the receiver off the hook.

'Nadia?' It was Andrew Anderson.

'Oh hi . . . sorry, someone's been pestering me about double glazing.'

'Did you get the flowers?'

'There was no need.'

'There was every need.'

'They *are* beautiful.'

'I meant what I said, Nadia. I haven't been able to stop thinking about you.'

For different reasons, she was sure, Nadia had not been able to stop thinking about him either.

'I have to go to Rome on Saturday. I wondered if you'd like to come with me. We could make a weekend of it.'

'Rome?'

'Leave Friday night, back Sunday night.'

'Sounds lovely,' she said. The idea of a weekend in Rome, far from Jack Hamilton, was enticing. She wasn't at all sure what she felt about Anderson, but did that matter? He was pleasant company and, though he had been rather odd in bed, he had also been conscientious. And he had, as the Americans said, given very good head. She smiled at the thought.

'Does that mean you'll come?'

She hesitated a full half second. 'I'd love to.'

'Pick you up at six. There's an eight o'clock plane.'

Three days later she was parking her car outside her house. It was the first time all week she had come straight home from the office. There had been a reception at the American Embassy on Tuesday and a leaving party for one of the employees at Hill Brothers on Wednesday. She was relieved to have the whole of Thursday evening to pack for Rome.

She locked the car and extracted her house keys from her handbag.

'Nadia.' Jack Hamilton came up behind her as she walked towards her house. He must have been waiting for her out of sight round the corner, since she hadn't seen him as she drove up.

'What are you doing here?' She tried to sound angry but the wave of purely physical pleasure she experienced at seeing him again took her completely by surprise.

'I told you, I had to see you.'

'I've been busy.'

'I know. I've waited here every night.'

'Jack.' She tried to put aside the way her skin had turned to goose pimples and her heart raced. She tried to discount the fact that she was having to remember to breathe. 'Jack, I've got nothing to say to you.'

'Nadia, something happened between us, didn't it? Tell me honestly that you didn't feel something special and I'll go.'

'What do you mean?'

'For God's sake, Nadia,' he said angrily, attracting the attention of a woman walking a Yorkshire terrier on the other side of the road. 'You know what I mean.'

'You're married.'

'And if I wasn't?'

'You are. End of story.'

'If I got a divorce?'

Her heart was pounding so hard against her ribs she was surprised she couldn't see it bulging from her blouse. She wheeled round and stared at Hamilton. He was wearing his usual washed-out denim jeans, with a blue shirt and a white T-shirt underneath. His black hair hung down over his forehead, almost falling into his left eye. He brushed it aside with a characteristic shake of the head.

'You're not getting divorced. You're happily married, remember? I saw it for myself, Jack. You do everything together, you *share* everything.'

'I didn't plan that.'

She could feel sweat breaking out on her upper lip. The late afternoon sun was shining straight into her face. There seemed to be a buzzing in her ears as though some sort of flying insect was trapped there.

'I was there. You left her a note.'

A tubby little bald-headed man marched up the street with a determined stride. 'Excuse me,' he said as he walked between them.

Jack looked blank. 'A note?' he queried.

'A note, Jack. She said she'd got your note. Don't you remember? What did it say? I'm at the studio with a new girl, come right over?' Nadia stormed through her gate and up the path to her front door, her anger at last winning out against her other emotions.

'Nadia.' He charged after her and caught her by the arm. 'I left a note to say I'd gone to Manchester, just in case she got back early and thought of coming to the studio. She was being ironic.'

'Can't you do better than that? Leave me alone.'

Another passer-by, a young man in a black leather jacket, stared at Hamilton aggressively, then stopped at Nadia's gate.

'You all right, love?' he asked.

'Fine,' she replied, not wanting any interference. 'Just go,' she whispered to Jack. She put her keys in the door. The young man sauntered off.

'Nadia, this is ridiculous.'

It all happened at once. She opened the door and before she could stop him he had pushed inside and slammed the door behind her, pulling her into his arms and kissing her on the mouth. He crushed her against the hall wall, her breasts pressed against his chest, his erection engorging against her belly.

'Get out,' she spat, trying to free herself from his grip and tearing at his shirt.

'Nadia,' he gasped as she began raining blows down on his back. 'Can't you understand, I need you. I know you feel the same.'

He brought one hand up to her face, caught her by the cheek and forced his mouth against hers. She tried to squirm away but it was too late. Her body was already beginning to respond to Hamilton, the effect he had at a physical level overriding her rational response.

'No,' she said, tearing her mouth away.

'Yes,' he insisted, his hand twisting her back to face him, his mouth closing on hers. He had felt her body's reaction.

As his tongue plunged between her lips she felt her body channel the passion of anger into lust, hard, hot, throbbing lust. It took her by surprise with its intensity. Her hands, instead of clawing at his back like talons, held him tighter. Her sex pulsed. She kissed him back, pushing her tongue past his, vying for position in his mouth. Hungrily she tore his shirt out from the back of his jeans, wanting to feel his flesh. She had never wanted a man more in her life.

He was kissing her neck and her ears, his tongue hot and wet. His hand found the catch of her bra under the white cotton blouse she was wearing and snapped it free with dexterous, practised ease. He started to open the buttons at the front of the blouse, then, with frustration at the slowness of the process, grasped the two sides of the garment and ripped it apart, pulling her bra up to reveal her quivering breasts, their nipples already stone hard. His hands engulfed them, squeezing and squashing the firm orbs.

Nadia was fighting with his belt. She dropped to her knees, ripped his flies open and pulled his jeans and white boxer shorts down together. His cock sprung free and without any hesitation she took it greedily into her mouth, glorying in the feeling of its hardness and size. She took it right down her throat, sucking on it hard, and felt a response from her sex as though it were buried there too. He moaned as she sucked him again, not caring if she hurt him.

Seizing her by the shoulders, he forced her down on to the hall carpet, his cock plopping out of her mouth. She was wearing a cream linen skirt and white panties. He pulled the skirt up to her hips and caught the front of the panties in his hand, rucking up the material until the crotch was no more than a thin string. Pulling this to one side he forced himself between her legs and drove his cock into her labia. She was wet. On the tide of her juices his cock slid back easily, found the entrance to her vagina and, in one effortless moment, rammed into her.

For a second he did nothing, the haste and urgency that had gone before overtaken by blind pleasure, both of them wrapped in the same exquisite folds of feeling, animation suspended by ecstasy.

The second seemed to last forever, gathering in layers of emotion, febrilely connected to everything that had happened between them, every touch, kiss, caress, every deed and sensual perception.

It was ended by need. The rhythms of their bodies asserted themselves, pulling them back from the lofty spiritual plane to the grinding tempo of urgent desire. Nadia felt him begin to pound into her. She was uncomfortable, the floor hard and unyielding, her bra up around her neck, its wired cups digging into her throat, the thin string he had made of her panties cutting into her buttocks. But none of that mattered. All that mattered was the sword of flesh that invaded her, filled her, focused her every sense on her sex.

It was not a question of technique or size. What Hamilton did to her could not be explained rationally. His cock inside her simply *was*. It fused with her, as though he was not only inside her body but inside her mind. She knew she had started to come the moment he'd forced her back against the wall. Her sex had throbbed so strongly she knew he had felt it. By the time he was inside her the nerves of her body were knitted together in tight spasms, each one a stepping stone to the next, taking her higher and higher, as the hardness of his erection arched up into her. She could feel the velvety wet walls of her sex clinging to it. At the zenith of his stroke the neck of her womb seemed to open for him, like another tiny mouth pursed to welcome him.

'Jack, Jack . . .' Her hands clawed at his flesh under his shirt, her voice strangulated by passion. The back of her head was forced against the floor, at a right angle to her spine, the sinews of her neck stretched and prominent like cords of rope.

It was only seconds, only four or five strokes of his erection, and her orgasm was born, breaking over the crown of his cock, spreading out through her body so fast every nerve experienced the explosion at the same moment. Instinctively he did not pull out of her, but pushed his cock deeper instead, using all his considerable strength to thrust it further up, knowing this would reinforce her pleasure.

But there was more to come. Her orgasm was so long and detailed, each graduation in it separate and distinct, that it felt like a thing apart, able to grow and function independently. As Jack arched his cock into her, her orgasm rippled and bucked, seizing her body with a new wave of pleasure and taking her on to another plane.

'No, no, no . . .' she screamed. She was stretched out so tightly she thought she might snap. She wasn't sure she could take any more.

But she could. Her entire world had narrowed to

the tiny compass of her sex. Not even her whole sex, just the clinging niche at the top of her vagina, that gloved his glans. She could feel it minutely, every contour and line. It was throbbing. She knew he was going to come. He had crossed the invisible line between control and reflex. She knew he was going to jet his semen into her. She had never needed anything more desperately.

She could see, in her imagination, his glans, the smooth pink flesh glistening wet, the little mouth at its tip open and waiting. As she felt him spasm, jerking against the silky cell that imprisoned him, she was sure she could feel each jet of spunk splashing into her, each globule like a spark of life creating a new erogenous zone wherever it landed.

Did she come again or was her orgasm just propelled to new heights by those incredible feelings? Did it matter? All she knew was that her whole body was trembling uncontrollably, that she was moaning and tossing her head from side to side, that here, on her hall carpet, Hamilton, once again, had wrung feelings and sensations from her body she had never known it was capable of delivering.

At that moment an ear-splitting noise erupted in the hallway. Nadia's body reacted instinctively to the deafening cacophony of high-pitched sound, tensing as the adrenaline rushed through her. Her mind was so isolated from reality it took her seconds to realise its cause. She had forgotten to turn off the burglar alarm.

There was undoubtedly a tension in the air, an atmosphere that could be cut with a knife. Neither woman was relaxed, their body language tense and

171

defensive, though both were equally determined, consciously at least, not to show it.

'Smells good,' Angela said. The weather had broken. After two weeks of heat and balmy evenings, a cold drizzle lashed at the French windows. Angela sat at the dining-room table watching Nadia putting the final touches to their dinner, in the kitchen. A big blue china bowl on the cherrywood dining table contained a green salad. Alongside it was a wooden cheese platter covered with a thick glass cloche, four French cheeses laid out underneath. There was a good bottle of burgundy already opened, a bottle of mineral water and two glasses at each plate setting.

Nadia brought in a white bowl of pasta with prosciutto, peas, shallots and cream. She divided it between two deep oval white plates and offered Angela freshly grated Parmesan cheese from a specially designed glass and stainless steel dispenser.

'So tell me about Rome?' Angela said.

'I didn't go.' Nadia poured the burgundy and tasted it.

'What . . . I thought . . .'

'I cancelled.' Nadia hadn't seen her friend since the night they had had too many gin and tonics. Angela had been away on a weekend residential course on the international futures market and had only spoken to Nadia briefly to tell her she would be away. At that point Rome with Andrew Anderson had been very much on the agenda.

'Why?'

'You have one guess.'

'Hamilton.'

'Got it in one.'

'Hamilton what?'

'Are you ready for this? He told me he wants to get a divorce.'

'A divorce!'

'Not entirely on my account. But he says I'm the catalyst that's made him realise his marriage is over.'

'When was this?'

'Thursday night. He was waiting for me when I got home. We spent the weekend together.'

'Jesus, Nadia, I had no idea. So, what, he's really serious about you?'

'He says so.'

'And what about you? How do you feel about him?'

Nadia didn't respond immediately. She wound her fork into the tagliatelle and took a large bite, then chewed thoughtfully while Angela watched her with mounting impatience. Finally, after a sip of wine, she put her friend out of her misery.

'I'm not sure yet. I've heard it all before, Angela. He was only with me this weekend because his wife was away in Poland working. I'm not kidding myself. When it comes to the crunch I have no idea what will happen. If he actually leaves her then it'll be a different matter. Until then . . . I'm keeping all my options open.'

'Including Anderson?'

'He's a nice man.'

'Nice? Nice is practically pejorative.'

'If I hadn't met Hamilton I think I could be really quite involved with him.'

'But?'

'There's something missing.'

'What?'

'I don't know.' Nadia knew precisely but wasn't

173

sure she wanted to broach the subject of sex. Sex was, she knew, the reason for the tension that laced the air.

Angela was less circumspect. 'He's not good in bed?'

'Yes. No. I don't know, I just get the feeling he wants something more . . . something else.'

'Mmm . . . Interesting. So what have you told him?'

'I lied. I told him I was going on a course about the international futures market.'

Angela laughed. 'Sounds familiar. But you can't put him off forever.'

'I suppose I'll have to tell him the truth.'

Angela chewed on the pasta. 'This is delicious. So what truth are you going to tell him?'

'That I've met someone else.'

'You think Hamilton's serious?'

'I haven't the slightest idea. But if he behaves himself, if he actually does what he says he's going to do . . . then who knows what might happen.' Nadia grinned broadly.

They changed the subject and talked about work as they ate salad and the cheese, then a pear and almond tart Nadia had made. She served it with chilled Beaumes de Venise.

'That was really great,' Angela said, finishing her second slice while Nadia put the coffee on. 'Can I have another glass of wine?'

'Help yourself. And pour me one.' The dessert wine was in a cooler on the table.

They took the wine and the coffee upstairs to the first-floor living room. Nadia realised, after she'd done it, that sitting on the same Chesterfield as her friend was a deliberate gesture.

174

'So what happens now?' Nadia said, emboldened by the wine – at least, that was her excuse. Hamilton had not only changed her sexual perceptions. It seemed he had also given her a hardiness she had never had before.

'Is something supposed to happen?' Angela replied, feigning innocence of the subject that was on both their minds.

'You tell me?' Angela's cautious response during their last conversation in this room hadn't killed Nadia's interest in the idea. Almost unconsciously, she had found herself thinking about what it would be like to have sex with her friend. The idea had slipped into her mind while she was with Anderson and had remained firmly lodged in her libido, resisting all her attempts to shake it free.

She looked at Angela with admiration, noting the way the one-piece tailored pants suit in a subtle beige suited her figure, how beautifully her red hair caught the light, and how her green eyes sparkled with life. She was not slow to realise it was not admiration she was feeling but desire.

'I thought we'd said it would be a bad idea.' There was no need to define what "it" was.

'You did.' Nadia picked up the glass of wine and sipped it. 'But now I'm not so sure.' She looked straight into Angela's eyes, wanting to see her reaction. There was no sign that she was shocked.

'You don't think it would spoil our friendship?'

'I'd like to try an experiment.'

'What sort of experiment?' Nadia thought she saw the expression in Angela's eyes change. They dropped to her bosom and seemed to be examining the cleavage that peeked out from the V-neck of her peach-coloured dress. She had tucked her legs up on the sofa and saw Angela's eyes sweep over them, too.

'I told you I had an experience with a woman before Hamilton's wife. I tried to forget about it. It frightened me. I thought it was like a virus, that I'd become infected . . .'

'I know what you mean.'

'Then with Jan Hamilton, well . . .' She took another sip of the sweet golden wine.

'Well what?'

'With Jan Hamilton I could pretend I was doing it for Jack. I still don't know.'

'Know what?'

'If what you said is right – that it wouldn't take over my life.'

'It doesn't.'

'Because if it didn't I think it could be very pleasant. Very.'

'I don't want to lose you as a friend,' Angela said earnestly.

'You won't. That's too important.'

'Promise?'

'Cross my heart and hope to die.'

Angela got to her feet. She picked up her cup of coffee, finished it and looked down at her friend. 'Last chance to ask me to go,' she said.

'Stay,' Nadia said firmly, her pulse rate instantly racing.

'Give me five minutes then.'

Angela turned and walked to the door. Her footsteps mounted the stairs, then crossed the floor to the bedroom above, and went into the bathroom. Nadia felt remarkably calm. She had rehearsed what she was going to say and when she was going to say it and Angela had reacted exactly as she'd expected.

She had decided that it was time to get to know herself, to put an end to the uncertainties she had felt since she had been to bed with Jan Hamilton. The skeleton of Barbara had been hidden in her cupboard for too long. It was time it was out in the open, especially if she ended up making a commitment to Hamilton. That would involve forswearing *all* others.

Was that likely? Did she even want it? She did not know the answer to the first question but the answer to the second was very definitely, yes. No man had ever made her feel what Hamilton made her feel. She was in danger of admitting to herself, after their weekend together, that she could easily fall in love with him.

The five minutes had passed and there were no more footsteps echoing from the bedroom. Nadia finished her coffee, took a deep breath, and walked upstairs.

Her bedroom door was ajar. She walked inside and closed the door firmly behind her.

Angela was lying on the bed, her head propped up against the pillows, her ankles crossed, the triangle of pubes that nestled at the top of her thighs a mass of thick, unruly red hair. Her fingers were pressed together, as in an attitude of prayer, their tips resting against her bottom lip.

'Take your clothes off,' she said firmly. 'I don't want any fumbling.'

Nadia's breathing was shallow and her pulse continued to race. She had seen her friend naked before but the context had been different. Now she was looking at her as an object of sexual desire. Her body was beautiful, full and rich, plumper than her own, but not fat. Angela's body was a symphony of curves and cambers, the convexity of her breasts and hips and belly counterpointed by her long lithe legs and the narrowness of her waist.

'Where's the vibrator I gave you?' she asked. Nadia unzipped her dress. She slipped it off her shoulders and let it fall to the floor. She was wearing white panties and a matching bra.

'In the drawer.' She indicated the top drawer of one of the bedside chests.

As she unclipped her bra and shucked it from her shoulders she felt her nipples stiffen. Angela extracted the cream plastic phallus. She uncrossed her legs and opened them slightly, pushing the tip of the dildo into the crease of her labia, then closed her legs, trapping it so tightly it stuck up vertically from her thighs.

'Did you use this?' Angela asked.

'Yes.' Nadia pulled her panties down and stepped out of them. She picked up her dress and hung it on the back of the door. She left the panties on the floor, suddenly remembering the way Anderson had handled them.

'And?' Angela prompted.

Nadia sat on the edge of the bed. 'I never imagined it could affect me so much. Do you want to know the truth?'

'Yes.'

'I imagined you holding it in me.'

'Mmm . . . come here.' Angela took Nadia's arm and pulled her on to her side on the bed. Rolling on to her side too, the dildo still projecting from her thighs, she arranged herself in front of Nadia, their breasts touching, the base of the dildo brushing Nadia's pubic hair. They stared into each other's eyes, knowing it was the point of no return.

Angela leant forward and brushed her lips against her friend's without kissing her, as her hand cupped Nadia's breast. She squeezed it gently and moved it so the tips of their nipples were touching. Nadia felt a rush of pleasure out of all proportion to the caress. Her body shuddered. She pressed against the butt of the dildo.

'Open your legs,' Angela said. As Nadia did as she was told she felt the cold plastic slide against her labia, and Angela's thick pubic hair grazing her own. 'Turn it on, then close your legs tight.'

Nadia reached behind her back. The gnarled knob at the end of the vibrator was sticking out from the cleft of her buttocks. She turned it and the phallus began to vibrate strongly, its motor humming.

'Harder,' Angela said.

Nadia turned the knob to maximum and the vibration increased, the humming noise getting louder. She closed her legs and gasped as the vibrator was suddenly trapped against her sex. Her clitoris pulsed. Angela pushed her belly closer. It was fleshy and round in contrast to the flatness of Nadia's and felt wonderfully soft. Her pubic bone was hard, however, and Nadia could feel it grinding against her.

'Oh, it's good . . .' Nadia gasped.

'Yes . . .'

Angela wrapped her arms around her friend's waist and pulled her even closer. She brushed her lips against her face, kissing her cheeks and her chin and her throat, avoiding her mouth for fear that a full-blown kiss would turn her off. But Nadia had no such inhibitions. With both hands she held Angela's cheeks, staring at her intently for a moment, before she pulled their lips together and plunged her

179

tongue into Angela's mouth.

The kiss made her shudder, the pleasure from her sex arcing to join the heat and passion from her mouth. At once, as simply as if someone had thrown a switch, she felt her body falling towards orgasm, the ceaseless vibrations impossible to resist. As Angela sucked on her tongue, Nadia trembled like a feather in the wind, the feel of Angela's belly and breasts against her deepening the pleasure that exploded in her body.

'God,' she said, panting for air.

'How delicious, I felt you come.'

'Again . . .' Nadia said, feeling Angela pushing the vibrator forward as if it were a cock, so it was pressed even harder into Nadia's clitoris. A second orgasm, distinct and quite separate from the first, sprung through her. But this time she felt Angela's body tense too. Just as passion flooded over Nadia, she felt Angela's reaching fruition too. They clung together, both needing support, the feeling of their bodies pressed together adding to the pleasure. They quivered and shook and slid against each other until they could stand it no longer. Almost simultaneously they opened their legs and let the dildo roll on to the bed.

'Well,' Angela said. 'How's the experiment progressing?'

'I think I need more data before I can evaluate it properly,' Nadia replied, running her tongue against her friend's lips, before rolling on to her back.

Angela trailed her finger down Nadia's body until it reached her pubic hair. Nadia eased her legs apart and the finger continued downward until it was coated with the sticky juices from Nadia's sex.

Angela brought her finger to her mouth and sucked on it with an exaggerated gesture.

'So sweet,' she said, getting to her knees. She bent forward and kissed Nadia's breasts one after the other, then trailed her tongue along the same route her finger had taken.

Nadia felt the surge of excitement. 'Oh Angela,' she gasped as she felt hot breath against her sex.

'You want it, don't you.' It was a statement, not a question. Nadia's sex had angled itself towards Angela's mouth, her buttocks raised from the bed, her legs wide open. She could feel her clitoris throbbing and her wetness leaking from her vagina.

Angela stared at the rough-hewn folds of her friend's sex. Slowly, with the tips of the fingers of both hands she drew Nadia's labia apart so she could see the scarlet interior, glistening wet. The mouth of her vagina was open, the entrance an irregular oval, the cavern beyond an inky black. It seemed to be breathing, the deckled edges of the vertical mouth contracting regularly.

Dropping her lips full on to Nadia's sex, Angela kissed it as though it were a mouth, plunging her tongue into Nadia's vagina, lapping up her juices, and feeling Nadia's body clench with sheer pleasure. She licked from front to back, long licks using the whole width of her tongue, like a child licking an ice cream cone.

Nadia gasped, the shock of sensation mingling with a wave of affection for her friend. 'Together, ' she insisted, sitting up. For a moment the sight of Angela's head bobbing between her legs produced such a strong pulse of feeling it interrupted her purpose. 'Together,' she repeated when it had passed, pulling at Angela's leg.

181

Angela swung her leg over Nadia's shoulders, her sex open and poised above her friend's head. Her tongue began to concentrate on Nadia's clitoris, licking it with the very tip of her tongue, pushing it this way and that. Slowly she lowered herself on to Nadia's waiting mouth.

As Nadia watched the descent her body shuddered. Her excitement was intense. She didn't need to think about the implications and consequences of what she was doing. She had worried about destroying their friendship but the ability to give each other such intense pleasure was not going to be detrimental. It was like an affirmation of what they had always felt for each other.

Angela's sex was plump and hairy. As its softness pressed against her mouth, as she felt how wet she was, the sensual circle was complete. Nadia kissed the intimate flesh, her tongue separating the labia to find the nut of Angela's clitoris, ready to mimic what her friend was doing to her. Pushing it against the pubic bone, Nadia felt Angela do the same to her. The shock of sensation produced in one immediately translated to the other, amplifying the frequency of pleasure as it reverberated between them.

They wallowed in it. Nadia's orgasm blossomed in her body like a flower photographed by time lapse cameras, from bud to full-blown petals in seconds. But as it opened, as it spread through her it was communicated instantly to Angela by the flesh that was pressed against her, by Nadia's mouth, and tongue, and quivering breasts. The provocation tipped Angela over the edge too, orgasm seizing her just as surely and sending new shocks of feeling back to Nadia, exchanging everything they felt.

They shuddered and shook, coming together then separately, as one asserted an ascendancy, licking and sucking and nuzzling the soft, sweet flesh that melted over their mouths, contracting helplessly as it was moved by the tides of orgasm. Sweat created by the heat of their bodies meant they could slip and slide against each other, feeling their breasts ballooned out against each other's belly, their nipples as hard as pebbles.

Quite suddenly a new element entered the equation. Angela's fingers had lighted on the dildo. She slipped it into her hand and brought it down between Nadia's legs, pressing it into the portal of her vagina, watching as the cream plastic shell disappeared inside.

'God,' Nadia groaned. She hadn't realised it until that moment but she was missing the feeling of a hard phallus buried inside her. The vibrator was not perfect – what Nadia really wanted was a hard, hot, living cock, Hamilton's cock – but it was good enough to kick her up to another level, a higher plateau. Her sex clung to the intruder, contracting around it, and, only seconds after Angela turned it on, the vibrations reaching in to what seemed like the very centre of the sex, she came again, her body stretched taut to extract every last ounce of pleasure.

As soon as she could, as soon as the pleasure released her from its tyrannical grip, she groped between her thighs. She pushed Angela's hand away and pulled the vibrator out of her body, bringing it up to Angela's sex, the hum of its motor changing pitch as it was freed. The plastic was wet. Renewing her assault on Angela's clitoris, Nadia poked the slanting tip of the phallus into the gate of her vagina, the labia pursing around it as it sunk deep. The pitch of the humming was lowered. Nadia felt Angela's body tense, her muscles go rigid, just as hers had done, and, in seconds, she was caught in the inescapable tendrils of vibration.

'Oh God,' she gasped, the words pronounced against Nadia's sex, her breath panted out and hot. With the last of her energy she butted her tongue against Nadia's clitoris and allowed herself to be overcome in a wealth of feeling, her body convulsing, her mind blanked of everything but exquisite pleasure.

They rolled off each other and lay side by side. Slowly their heartbeats returned to normal, their breathing deepened and the sweat on their bodies dried.

Nadia was the first to speak. Getting up on one elbow she looked at the naked body of her friend and was relieved to find that she felt no regret, or shame, or anger. She felt only affection.

'I think,' she said steadily, 'the experiment was a success.'

Chapter Nine

IT HAD BEEN two weeks. He had stayed with her for four nights. She had stayed at the studio twice. They'd spent another weekend together. The rest of the time Nadia had been catching up with her sleep because sleep was difficult to come by when she was in bed with Jack Hamilton.

Her experience, the experiment with Angela, had produced no discernible effects except an overwhelming need to be fucked. That was how she thought of it. Not a need to make love but a need to be fucked. In her mind they were two different things.

Jack had obliged. Like overdosing on anything – booze, cigarettes, coffee – the most intensive period of sexual activity in her life had left her strung out, shaky and more than a little dissociated, her mind not quite able to grasp what her body was doing. But despite their over-indulgence Nadia's need had hardly slackened.

It was not all to do with Angela, of course. What had happened with Jack over the last two weeks was, she knew, just as much to blame. The depth and intensity of her sexual pleasure continued to improve and she knew it was because she was becoming emotionally, as well as physically, involved with him. That was a mistake, but he insisted as soon as his wife returned he was going to tell her he wanted a divorce. Jan Hamilton had flown from Poland to San Francisco, where she was to be photographed to promote a new range of Pandora cosmetics.

But Nadia's sexual need was primarily a physical thing. Like a toothache, it throbbed. It was so strong and robust she felt she should be able to take it out and handle it, easing the pain with her hands. Unfortunately she could do no such thing. It was buried deep inside her and could only be mitigated by a single remedy.

She parked the car and looked at the clock set in the dashboard. It was seven o'clock. She couldn't remember ever doing anything as blatant as this before but she was a different person now, different sexually, at least. The genie Hamilton had released from the bottle had grown up, become adult, established its own demands.

Getting out of the car, she was acutely aware of the silk of her dress as it rubbed against her nipples. Her imagination – the graphic images of what she was going to do – had made them hard. She wasn't wearing a bra. She wasn't wearing anything under the simple shift dress. Blatant. She had planned what she would do. The violet-coloured dress was loose. She had only to slip the shoulder straps off and it would cascade to the floor and pool at her feet. She had practised in the bedroom mirror like a child practising a curtsey for some visiting dignitary.

186

Her heart was pounding as she mounted the concrete steps of the mews, her bag bouncing against her hip. She rang the doorbell and unconsciously ran her tongue over her lips, making them glossy and wet. She heard footsteps on the wooden floor. Hamilton opened the door.

'Nadia,' he said with surprise, his eyes taking in every detail of her appearance. 'I thought you wanted to be alone tonight.'

'Aren't you going to ask me in?'

'Come in, of course . . .' He stepped back and she walked into the studio. 'I thought you needed to rest.'

'I changed my mind. Women's privilege.'

'Do you want a drink? That dress is wonderful. The colour's perfect with your hair.'

'Thank you, red wine would be nice.'

Nadia walked over to the easel to look at the painting. The two women in the foreground were almost complete now, one distinctly more worn-looking, a trace of world weariness in her eyes, while the other was more innocent, her face open and very much alive. It was a ravishing picture.

He got the wine from the kitchen and brought it over to her.

'Cheers,' he said, clinking his glass against the side of hers. 'So what made you change your mind?'

'It was an emergency. Needs must where the devil drives . . .' Just as she had planned she slipped the thin straps of the dress off her shoulder and it floated to the floor, the silk whispering against her body. She stepped out of the violet pool at her feet. 'I'm getting very demanding, aren't I?'

'Oh,' he said. 'I . . .' He was clearly at a loss for words.

187

'What's the matter, Jack? Don't tell me you're shocked?'

'No, it's just that . . . I . . . I'm all dirty. I'd like to clean up. Have a shower. Why don't I come round to your place . . .'

'Here is just fine.' He had obviously been working. His jeans and shirt were old and spattered with paint, and there was a streak of orange oil paint on his cheek. 'Well, are you going to kiss me?'

He was not usually so reluctant. All the signs were there – the way he looked at his watch, his hesitation and uneasiness. It was just that Nadia chose to ignore them.

'I'd really rather . . .'

She gagged his mouth with hers, hugging him to her, plunging her tongue between his lips, squirming her naked body against him and feeling his erection unfurl against her belly. Breaking the kiss, she dropped to her knees in front of him. She opened his flies and fished inside for his cock. It sprung free of his boxer shorts and she took it into her mouth greedily, pushing it down into her throat.

Jack took her by the shoulders and pushed her away.

'No,' he said.

'What, then?'

She ran over to the bed, threw herself down on it and opened her legs as wide as they would go. He stared at her naked body. 'You want to watch me?' she said, opening her legs and moving her hand to her sex. The heels of her shoes dug into the sheets, rucking the material around them. She had never done this for him. She let him see her finger find her clitoris, while the other hand dallied with the opening of her vagina. 'Does that excite you?'

'Yes,' he said. He was lost then. He began ripping off his clothes, his eyes riveted to Nadia's sex. 'Does it feel good?'

'It's very good.'

'You're wet. I can see it.' He knelt, naked, beside her.

She pushed first one, then two fingers into her vagina, letting him see the way her labia parted to admit them. She saw his cock pulse with excitement as the penetration made her moan.

'You like that. I can see I'm going to have to do this for you again.'

'Yes,' he replied.

She was watching his face, the look of lust she had created, a hunger as great as her own. Her body clenched with pleasure. Once she had striven and struggled to find a masturbation ritual that would bring her even a modicum of satisfaction. Now whatever she did to herself brought her to a pitch with careless ease. The instrument of her body was at last highly tuned.

Plunging her fingers in and out she strummed her clitoris with no subtlety but with considerable speed, her hand a blue of motion. She saw him glance up at her face before his eyes returned to the drama of her sex.

'Oh, oh God, what have you done to me, Jack?' she managed to say as her orgasm overtook her. She knew it would be quick. Since she had parked the car her excitement hadn't stopped building. 'Oh God.' It was the way he was looking at her that produced the final kick of pleasure. Her hands stopped moving, clutching at her sex instead as though in a desperate attempt to prevent her orgasm seeping away.

'Beautiful,' he said. He had forgotten the time, forgotten the other imperatives. He was engrossed in her. Without thinking he stooped and took her left ankle in his hand, easing off her shoes, kissing the top of her foot, then the slender ankle, then her calf. He kissed her thigh, up along the femur and down into the soft inner flesh. But he avoided her sex. He moved his mouth to the other leg and began a downward journey this time, kissing and nibbling and sucking every inch of her flesh. He took off her right shoe.

'Turn over,' he said as he reached her right ankle.

She rolled on to her stomach, bringing her hands up to her head, lacing her fingers together and resting her cheek against the back of them. She kept her legs wide open.

His mouth sucked on her Achilles tendon, worked up along the back of her calves and dwelt on the hollow at the back of her knee. He kissed and nibbled her thigh, tracing the crease where the top of the leg tucked into her buttock, then delved deep into the cleft of her bottom. Just as the tension of her orgasm ebbed away she was strung out again by his ministrations. His tongue explored the valley of her buttocks, but did not dip into her sex. Instead it traced along the other thigh and back down the leg to suck on the Achilles tendon of the other ankle, a journey of exploration completed, both limbs treated precisely equally.

She felt him shift on the bed, then his mouth planted itself in the small of her back, licking up along her spine. He followed the knobbly vertebrae up to her neck then worked his way out along one arm as far as the elbow, which was bent. He worked back the way he had come then over and out to the other arm. She felt his erection nudging against her shoulders. It was gorgeous. She felt her whole body coming alive.

His mouth descended to the base of her spine again, gliding over her skin with little sucking kisses. His hands caressed the two globes of her buttocks, smoothing and kneading the soft, spongy flesh as he moved to kneel between her legs.

'You're so beautiful,' he said.

'Mmm . . .'

He leant forward, lying on top of her, his cock immediately brushing against her labia. Her masturbation had made her wet but he had made her wetter, a trail of juices running on the top of her thigh.

As the crown of his cock, hot and as hard as steel, parted her labia, she felt her clitoris pulse wildly. This was what she'd come for, after all. If she were truthful with herself not an hour had gone by since she'd met Hamilton when she had not thought of him doing this to her. It was what she dreamt of and what she craved.

He held her by the hips and drove his bone-hard cock into her vagina. The feeling took her breath away, the inward plunge so long and so deep it filled her completely. He did not withdraw. He held himself there, letting her sex close around him, squeeze on him, feeling the breadth and power.

Nadia trembled. Her clitoris spasmed. The trail his mouth had left across her body was burning, as though scorched into her flesh. Every inch of it provoked her, adding to the almost unbelievable heat and passion. He was a wonderful lover. He was everything she'd ever wanted.

'Fuck me, you bastard,' she gasped, wanting

191

precisely that, wanting to come over his pounding cock, wanting him to take her without giving any quarter.

He pulled out. He had another surprise. Before she knew that he was doing, or could protest, his hands spread her buttocks apart. He centred his glans on the ring of her anus and, with the lubrication her own juices had provided, pushed into it. He did not penetrate far. He held himself there just long enough for her to feel an enormous jolt of sensation, then pulled out and plunged straight back into her sex, as deep as he had been before. Nadia's body spasmed in surprise. The initial shock of pain turned so quickly to pleasure, a raw, indefinable pleasure, that she cried out loud. She was melting, turning to liquid, no muscles capable of working, a delicious weakness spreading through her, speared at its centre by the hardness of his cock. As he started thrusting into her she could still feel the shadow of his erection in her rear, the nerves there tingling with an odd mixture of pain and pleasure. On the flood of these feelings her orgams washed over her, not sharp and forceful this time, but soft and mellow and incredibly deep, like a heat that penetrated through to the bone, turning her into a lake of molten lava, simmering with pleasure, seemingly without end.

'Again,' she said, once she was capable of speech.

He laughed. 'Again?'

'What have you done to me, Jack?'

She grasped his cock with the muscles of her sex and squeezed it as hard as she could. Damn Hamilton – that mantra again – damn him for reducing her to this.

Just like the last time she didn't hear the front

door open and couldn't see it from the bed. She didn't hear the footsteps across the wooden floor, though the high heels must have made quite a din. It was only when she heard the voice that she looked around in alarm.

'Well, Jack, you are being greedy.' Jan Hamilton was wearing Lycra leggings and body in a leopard skin print, her feet zipped into red patent leather ankle boots with a spiky high heel. Standing next to her was a young, petite blonde, in tight blue jeans and a dirty black T-shirt, her small breasts and large nipples clearly outlined underneath it. Jan had one arm around the blonde's shoulders. 'And I told you I was bringing you a present.'

'You're early,' Jack said with an air of resignation.

'Looks great,' the blonde giggled. 'I love it.' She peeled off the T-shirt, kicked off her scuffed, black leather high heels and began unzipping her jeans. Her eyes were roaming Nadia's body.

Nadia struggled to roll out from under Jack. Before she could stop her the blonde had sat on the edge of the bed and cupped Nadia's left breast in her hand. Nadia slapped it away instantly, the heat of her breast turned suddenly to ice.

'That's not very friendly,' the blonde said in a voice with a Cockney accent. She moved her hand to Jack's erection. He did not react. The blonde crawled forward. 'Lovely big cock, just like you said,' she told Jan before sucking it into her mouth.

Despite herself Nadia felt a pulse of desire. She scrambled to her feet.

'Don't go, honey,' Jan said, catching her arm. 'If I'd known you were going to be here I wouldn't have brought Eve. But there's plenty to go round. You know Jack.'

Nadia knew Jack. She shook Jan's arm off, picked up her dress and pulled it over her head. She collected her shoes and bag, and marched to the front door, slamming it closed after her. She didn't put her shoes on until she was standing beside her car.

The anger was transitory. As she got behind the wheel she felt remarkably calm. There was no decision to make, no agonising over what she should do, what would be right or wrong. Jack had made that decision for her.

The Guildhall sparkled like the inside of a jewel. Silver candlesticks stood on every table, the polished Georgian silver catching the light from the crystal chandeliers. The dresses of most of the women, too, and their diamonds, glittered and twinkled in contrast to the plain black and white of the men's formal suits.

After the long, indigestible and – by virtue of the fact that the kitchens were so far from the long lines of tables – partially cold meal, the speeches too appeared interminable. Nadia had looked at her watch several times and on each occasion it gave her the sad news that the event was nowhere near its completion. James Hill, on the other hand, who had insisted on her coming to the banquet, appeared content to listen to the pontifications from the top table, though he had sequestered his own bottle of Remy Martin to refill his frequently empty glass.

Eventually it was over. The last speaker sat down to a chorus of polite applause, frock-coated waiters served the last of the coffee and people began drifting away, a fleet of chauffeur-driven cars lining the street outside.

When he got to his feet James Hill discovered he was a little the worse for wear and headed off to the toilet, leaving Nadia in the anteroom outside the dining room.

'Hello.' He had come up behind her without her being aware of it. She spun round to face Andrew Anderson.

'Andrew.' She was surprised. She hadn't seen him in the dining room. 'I didn't know you were here.'

'That's a beautiful dress.' It was. The strapless boned bodice in a crimson satin clung to Nadia's bosom. It was shaped into her waist and finished in a little peplum on her hips, under which the ankle-length skirt stretched tightly over the rich curves of her buttocks and thighs.

'Thank you,' she said, not quite sure how Andrew was going to react. She had aborted the trip to Rome with the flimsiest of excuses and since then had not returned any of his calls. He had very quickly got the message that he was surplus to requirements.

'And you look stunning, Nadia,' he said earnestly. 'I mean it.'

'That's very nice of you.'

There was a silence, neither quite sure what they wanted to say next.

'I . . .'

'It was . . .' They both spoke at once.

'Go ahead,' he said.

'I was going to call you,' she said weakly. 'I didn't behave very well, did I?'

'No,' he said, smiling, 'but it doesn't matter. It's just nice to see you again. You're here with James, aren't you?'

'Yes.' She suddenly wondered if this whole thing

had been engineered, if Anderson had persuaded Hill to bring her. 'But he's suffering from an overdose of Remy Martin.'

'Can I take you home then?'

It had been four weeks since she had seen Anderson. Her experience with Hamilton had wiped the memory of him away. She remembered telling Angela that, if she had not met Jack, she would have felt differently about Andrew. She wondered if that was true.

'That would be very nice,' she said and discovered she meant it.

They found James Hill, who was delighted the Hill Brothers' Jaguar was not going to have to take a detour to Islington. He appeared totally uninterested as to why Nadia should want to go off with Anderson and accepted his explanation that her house was on his way home, though if he had cared to think about it, it was not.

'Would you do me a favour?' Nadia said as they settled into the back of a chauffeur-driven Rolls Royce.

'Of course.'

'Would you take me for a drink first? I don't feel like going home yet.'

'It's gone midnight. Most bars are closed. What about my place?'

'Fine. If you don't mind.'

'It's not far.'

Anderson had the penthouse flat in a mansion block just off Cadogan Square. It was vast, with tall ceilings and large, imposing rooms, all decorated with meticulous attention to detail. The furniture was an eclectic mixture of antique and modern, and the paintings that littered the walls were equally varied, from Russian icons and Victorian landscapes to abstracts by Hartung and Rothko. The living room, which had a spectacular view of London, was lined with oak shelves crammed with books. In the kitchen, fitted by Gaggenau in black and stainless steel, Anderson put on the coffee and poured Nadia an Armagnac.

'Can I ask you why you didn't return my calls?' he asked tentatively.

'I was taking the coward's way out. I'm sorry. It was rude.'

'It's all right. It was my fault.' He was looking at the stream of liquid filtering into the coffee jug.

'How was it your fault?'

'I know my limitations.'

'Limitations? What limitations?'

'Sexual limitations.'

'Is that what you think? Do you think the reason I didn't call you was because of what happened in bed?'

'You know it is.'

'Andrew. Please. I enjoyed our sex.' It was true but not the whole truth.

'Really?'

The coffee machine finished. Anderson took the pot and two cups and saucers and put them on a tray together with the bottle of Armagnac, then led her through into the living room. They sat side by side on a large, comfortable sofa.

'The reason I didn't call was that I got involved with someone else.' She decided she should tell him the truth. 'I told you I'd had an affair?'

'Yes.'

'Well, it broke out again.'

'The same man?'

197

'Yes, and I made the same mistake. It was a disaster.'

'I wish you'd called me.'

'I just thought it was a bit much . . .'

'I'd have understood. I do understand.'

In the short time they had been together Nadia's feelings for Anderson had rekindled. There was a certain lack of masculinity about him that was positively refreshing after Hamilton. On impulse she leant forward and kissed him on the cheek. Before she could pull away again he caught her face in his hand and kissed her on the mouth. His tongue darted hesitantly between her ' lips and before she knew what she was doing she found herself sucking it in hungrily.

Pulling herself up, Nadia got to her feet. She walked over and examined a Paul Nash landscape that hung on the opposite wall, wanting to give herself time to sort out her feelings. She felt Anderson's eyes watching her but he said nothing.

She tried to analyse what she felt about Andrew. Of course she had been tempted to call him soon after the debacle with Hamilton, to let his company and his wealth distract her, to allow good food, fine wines and visits to the opera and theatre wash away her sense of disappointment. But the reason she had hesitated was not only because she had thought he might take a jaundiced view of her sudden change of heart. It was something more fundamental. What he had said in the kitchen was true. Their sexual encounter had been limited.

Perhaps before she had met Hamilton she would not have minded – it was possible she would not even have noticed. But there was no turning back the clock. Hamilton had charged her sexuality and she had no intention of returning to the good old, bad days. Sex, for her, had become like an unexplored desert island. She had already started to chart its territory, map out its hills and climb some of its mountains. She had no intention of going back to the beach, getting on the boat and rowing away.

If she was going to have a relationship with Anderson then the "limitations" as he had called them had to be dealt with. She turned and walked back to the sofa, sitting down next to him and taking a sip of her Vieux Armagnac.

'A lot has happened to me recently, Andrew,' she said. She crossed her legs, making the satin rustle. She saw him looking at her black suede high heels. The strap over the arch of her foot was decorated with diamanté. 'I've realised that for a lot of my life I have accepted compromises in my relationships. I've been prepared to settle for things I should not have done. Can you understand that?'

'I think so.'

'Well, I've decided I need to change that. I'm not going to compromise any more.'

'I understand that.'

'What you said in the kitchen . . . about sex, I mean. Do you want the truth?'

He looked a little frightened but he nodded.

'I had the feeling you were holding back. If we're going to have any sort of relationship you have to be honest with me about what you want.'

'You might not care for it.'

'That's true, but then at least we'd know, and we wouldn't be fumbling about in the dark pretending.' It was odd, she thought, how her new sexuality seemed to have made her assertive, too. It was a trait she'd admired in Angela but been unable to exercise herself – until now. 'Do you agree?'

He didn't reply. There was a long silence as he stared down into his lap.

'Perhaps this is a mistake,' Nadia said finally.

'No. No, you are absolutely right. I know you are. What is the point in fudging around things?' He looked up and into her eyes and she could see him taking a deep breath. 'There *are* certain things I like, I need, in bed, things I find difficult to ask for.'

'I'm very open-minded, Andrew.' She wondered if that was true.

'Are you?' An expression of anguish was etched on his face. He searched her eyes as if looking for some clue as to how she might react.

'Tell me what you want.'

'I've always had this problem, Nadia. I've had to live with it.'

'You were married . . .'

'Oh, my wife made it quite clear she wasn't going to help, and she didn't know the half of it.' Anderson sat up, took a sip of coffee and looked at her intensely. The expression in his eyes had changed. Nadia could see he had made a decision. 'You really want this, don't you?'

'I told you, Andrew, there is no point in a compromise.'

'It has to be now. I couldn't spend two or three days thinking about it, worrying about it.'

When Nadia had asked him to take her for a drink she hadn't had the slightest intention of going to bed with him. But then she hadn't had the slightest intention of having this conversation either.

'I can understand that,' she said. 'I'm not going anywhere.'

'You'll have to give me twenty minutes.'

'What do you mean?'

'If you want to know about me, Nadia, it's better I show you.'

'All right,' she said, trying to sound positive.

'Twenty minutes.'

He got to his feet and strode out of the room without looking back, afraid the slightest hesitation might change his mind.

Nadia finished her Armagnac, poured another coffee and wandered around the room. Glancing at the small brass carriage clock on one of the book shelves, she saw it was eleven-ten. She listened intently for any clue to what was going on but could hear nothing.

The trouble was, of course, she hadn't expected this reaction. She had expected him to respond either by telling her that he realised there was a problem and that there was nothing he could do about it, or by saying that they would work on it together to make it right. But clearly, she thought, as she roamed the room looking at the paintings, fingering the objects d'art, without seeing or feeling either, Anderson had some sort of perverse fetish. He wanted to be whipped or tied to the bed. Nadia hardly knew what to expect.

The twenty minutes passed slowly. At eleven-thirty Nadia drank the last of the coffee, then ventured down the hall. He hadn't told her where the bedroom was and all the doors in the long corridor were closed. She tried the first one to the left and discovered an elaborate bathroom. The next door down on the right was a small guest room decorated in a flowery wallpaper.

There were two doors at the far end of the hall. She tried the first, which opened on to a large

201

bedroom. The decor was a symphony of blues: heavy drapes over the big windows, the bed stripped back to a pale blue undersheet, and the light from the dark blue shades of the bedside lamps dimmed to a pleasant glow.

But Nadia thought she must be in the wrong room. Sitting on the edge of the bed in a long-sleeved, polo-necked cream silk cocktail dress was a pretty, fair-haired woman. Her legs were sheathed in tan-coloured nylon and she was wearing cream suede shoes with an ankle strap. She had three rings on her left hand and a gold bracelet sparking with diamonds on her right wrist. Her make-up was heavy, a thick pancake, with eyelashes that were clearly artificial, dark eye shadow and very red lipstick. Her hair was permed in an old-fashioned style, curls framing her face right down to her shoulders.

It took Nadia minutes before the penny dropped. Suddenly she realised the hair was a wig and the ''woman'' was Andrew Anderson.

'My God,' she said under her breath.

'I'm not homosexual,' he said firmly.

Nadia wasn't at all sure what her reaction was. Her initial surprise became horror, then turned to fascination. She studied Andrew's face, trying to see his masculinity behind the mask of what was a totally feminine appearance. He made a very convincing woman, his small-featured face and slight body fitting the role perfectly. His legs were slender and shapely and his ankles and feet dainty in the high heels.

'You're beautiful,' Nadia said, meaning it.

'Thank you.' She had obviously said the right thing. The remark gave him confidence. 'Are you shocked?'

'Of course,' she said. She was remembering how he had handled her clothes so carefully. Had he been imagining how they would feel on him?

'I've never let anyone see me like this,' he said.

Nadia sat on the bed beside him. 'What do you want me to do?' she said. She put her hand on his knee, rubbing her fingers against the silk and the nylon. She'd thought it odd that he had such hairless legs; now she wondered if he shaved them.

'I'm not homosexual,' he repeated. 'I only want to have sex with a woman.'

'Dressed like this.'

'Yes. I just love the feel, the softness. I always have. My wife caught me one day putting on some tights. That was the end. She'd never have sex with me again.'

Well, Nadia thought, she had asked for it. She'd asked him to tell her the truth and now she had the truth in spades. He'd exposed himself to her completely, holding nothing back. Now she had to make a choice. She could get up and walk out. She could say, politely, thank you but no thank you and walk away. Or she could stay. Whatever she did she knew she must be careful. Andrew's secrets were laid open and he was as vulnerable, emotionally, as he would ever be.

'You'll have to help me, Andrew,' she said finally. 'I've never . . .'

He put his arm around her. Experimentally he kissed her on the mouth, very lightly, without using his tongue. The silk of his dress rustled against the satin of her own. She felt his obviously padded bosom crushing her breast on her left side. Putting her hand around his neck under the wig she pulled his lips on to hers more fiercely, putting her tongue

203

into his mouth.

'What do I call you?' she said. It appeared she had decided to go through with it.

'Andrea.'

Nadia got to her feet, the range of emotions she felt still not focused on any one. She felt sympathy and compasion, a strong streak of absurdity and more than a little excitement. She felt no disgust.

'Are you going to take your dress off, Andrea?' Nadia reached behind her back and undid the long zip of her dress.

'Yes,' he said, his eyes looking at her with a mixture of gratitude and apprehension. He got up and stripped the dress off, draping it, as carefully as he had once dealt with Nadia's clothes, over a small button-backed armchair. He was wearing a tight, white all-in-one corset with satin shoulder straps and a diamond-shaped satin panel over his navel. Suspenders from the base of the corset held up tan stockings, pulling the tops into chevrons on his thighs. The bra of the corset contained two flesh-coloured flexible plastic bags which looked to be filled with some sort of liquid. A small pair of white French knickers covered his crotch but Nadia could see his erection outlined underneath them.

'Pretty,' she said. She felt a strong pulse of desire as she looked at the bulge in the knickers.

'Thank you.'

'You want to do it like this?' she asked.

'It's ridiculous, isn't it?' The shame-faced expression she had seen on their first night together returned.

'No,' she said forcibly. She stood in front of him. 'I want you. I want you to fuck me. Let's not think about anything else.' It was true. The shock and surprise of all this had apparently not affected her basic instincts. She kicked off her shoes and pulled her dress from her shoulders, stepping out of it. She draped it over the chair Andrew had used for his dress. Brusquely she unclipped her bra, stripped her tights down to her knees then sat on the bed to roll them off her legs completely. She wore no panties.

'I haven't worn stockings for ages,' she said.

'I love them. They feel so sexy,' he said in an uncharacteristically light voice.

'Do you shave your legs?'

'Only a bit. I've never had much hair.'

'I always have to shave mine.'

'You don't have to shave your face,' he replied with what sounded a little like envy.

'Are you going to lie back now, Andrea? Let me get at you.'

'Yes,' he said breathily.

'Come on then. Come on, Andrea.'

She could see the name gave him a frisson of excitement. He squirmed back into the centre of the bed. Nadia ran her hand up his leg to the French knickers. The sac of his balls was confined tightly under their gusset. She ran her hand over it and he moaned.

'Shall I take your panties off, Andrea?'

'Please . . .'

She pulled the waistband over the corset as he raised his hips, and skimmed the knickers down his legs. They caught on the ankle strap of his shoes but she disentangled them carefully then threw them aside. His erection had embedded itself under the front of the corset and she had to pull it out. Unsurprisingly it was harder and bigger than it had been before.

'Oh, darling . . .' he moaned at her touch.

'You have to fuck me hard, Andrea,' she said, meaning it.

'I will.'

Nadia knew she was already moist. There was undoubtedly something erotic about this bizarre situation. She gave up trying to work out how it could be sexually exciting for a man to want to have sex with a woman, dressed in woman's clothes, but exciting it clearly was. Anderson's cock was throbbing visibly.

She swung her thigh over Anderson's hip. Her breasts quivered. She settled the tip of his glans between her labia and felt her own wetness leaking from her body. She looked down at Anderson, for all intents and purposes a woman, a woman with a cock but a woman nonetheless.

Was that it? Nadia thought. Was that why she was not revolted or turned off by all this, because she had learned to express desire for a woman without fear? She felt her sex throb as she remembered the almost impossible softness of Angela's body against her own.

She realised she couldn't see Andrew Anderson any more, could not make the intellectual leap of looking through the woman she saw in front of her eyes to the man who had sat with her thirty minutes before. There was no need. She was quite content with the woman. She leant forward and traced the contours of a woman's face with her finger. She ran the tip of one finger over a woman's lips.

'Lovely,' she said.

The word made Anderson's cock pulse.

A woman with a cock. She allowed her body to drop, falling on to the hard shaft. Anderson moved

206

his hands to his sides, smoothing them against the corset.

'Hard,' she said. Pressing herself down on him she was completely confused now. Was the swelling, increasing urgent desire she was feeling for a man or for a woman? Did it really matter? It was the same thing, the same result, her body already seized by the rhythms of orgasm. Wasn't that what Angela had said – it was all the same thing?

He began pumping into her, bucking his hips, forcing his cock up into her, moving his hands on to her thighs to hold her down on him, grinding his pubic bone against her clitoris. His cock was like a rod of steel.

'Yes . . . yes . . .' she cried.

His body strained against the tight corset, the suspenders pulling at the stockings as he squirmed deeper.

It was a contradiction, a contradiction of opposites. Andrew's hardness at the centre of her sex, and his femininity surrounding it, the one caused by the other. Giving up any attempt to sort them out, Nadia simply surrendered to her feelings, getting her excitement from the woman who lay underneath her *and* from the man who pumped away inside her. She felt her sex spasming, contracting around the shaft of the flesh that invaded it and sending a wave of sensation up through her body, enveloping her like a rising tide, forcing her eyes to roll back, blacking out the vision of a woman and making her concentrate on the essence of a man. As she wriggled and writhed to the dictates of her orgasm Andrew pounded on, faster and harder, sensing her pleasure, feeling the top of her sex melting because of it, opening for him, giving him space to shoot his seed. The walls of her vagina were as silky and smooth as the clothes he loved to wear.

He stopped, held her thighs tightly with fingers of steel and came, his body trembling, the female clothing clinging and coaxing his flesh, the sound of his name (his real name, what he wanted to be) on her lips.

'Andrea,' Nadia cried as she felt him climax inside her.

'It's quite common, apparently. I read up about it.'

'Really? I thought it was just gays.'

'They're not gay at all. They want to have completely normal heterosexual relationships.'

'Wearing women's clothes?'

'Exactly.'

'Weird. I think I can understand a man wanting to be a woman, wanting to have his dick cut off and all that. But logically, in the end, he'd be having sex with a man.'

'That's transsexualism,' Nadia said. 'Transvestites are different. They just like the touch and feel of women's clothes. That's their turn-on.'

'And you used to say I was the one who always got the weirdos,' Angela said. It was true. For once it was Nadia with a long story of a sexual adventure, spiced with sexual foibles.

'B H I would have run a mile.'

'B H?'

'Before Hamilton . . .'

'But you didn't.'

'I told you. It was quite sexy in a peculiar sort of way; I suppose mostly because he was so turned on.'

'But it wasn't like having sex with Hamilton?'

'Nothing's like that, Angela.'

'You lucky bitch. He's just my type, too. Why didn't I go to that bloody exhibition? Anyway, what are you going to do?'

'About Anderson?'

'Of course about Anderson.'

They were sitting out in Nadia's patio garden. It was Sunday evening and, according to the weather forecast, had been the hottest day in London since records began. The television news had shown pictures of thousands of people lying head to toe in Hyde Park, girls diving topless into the Serpentine and eggs being fried on the pavements in Oxford Street. Even now, with the sun low in the sky, heat radiated from the stone flags of the patio and the walls of the house and it was impossible to get cool.

Nadia got up and refilled their glasses. They were drinking from a carafe of white wine and lemon juice Nadia had mixed and left to marinade in the fridge overnight.

'You know what I'm going to do.'

'How extensive is his wardrobe? Perhaps he's got some nice dresses you could borrow.'

'It's not funny. I just couldn't face it.'

'You said it was exciting.'

'I said it was peculiar. It was the sort of excitement you get when you've stolen a sweet from a sweet shop. It tastes better because it's stolen, but you know it's wrong. I feel sorry for him but that's not the basis for a relationship.'

'He's very rich, Nadia.'

'What difference does that make?'

Angela was laughing. 'You could go on a shopping spree together. Get him to take you to Fifth Avenue, or the Via Condotti.'

'Be serious.'

'Have you told him?'

'I told him on Friday. He was expecting it. To tell you the truth I wish I could have been more understanding. I like him.'

'And Hamilton? What are you going to do about Hamilton?'

The answer was not as simple as it would have been had Angela asked the question immediately after Nadia's last visit to his studio. Then she would have said that she had no intention of ever seeing him again. But since her night with Andrew/Andrea she had been thinking a lot about Hamilton.

Previously, she had assumed that in order to have a sexually meaningful relationship with a man she also had to have an emotional commitment to him. Since the emotional commitment had never materialised – except in the case of her married man, when she had fought tooth and nail not to become involved with him – she had drawn the conclusion that this was the base cause for her sexual inadequacies. She had reasoned from this that unless there was a chance of an emotional commitment developing in a relationship there would be no chance of sexual fulfilment. Having sex with a man who meant nothing to her would therefore be fruitless. Casual sex, for her, unlike Angela, had always been ruled out.

The force of Hamilton's personality, or the sheer physical attraction she had felt for him, or both, had broken the mould. But she had assumed that because they had great sex, they also had to have an emotional commitment. She had kidded herself that she was falling in love with Hamilton, but the fact was that all she actually felt for him was unmitigated lust. She was immensely relieved to find she was not in love with him.

If she were honest with herself, what she had felt when Jan Hamilton had arrived at the studio with the blonde had been, quite simply, nothing. But she had reacted as if she had been rejected. She'd acted as though she were jealous. Hamilton, of course, had compounded this travesty by pretending he wanted to leave his wife. Even if he had been genuine in that desire, Nadia should have realised that he would find it impossible to give up the sort of sexual menu his wife was offering him.

What her experience with Tony and the bizarre experience with Andrew had taught her – to say nothing of what had happened with Angela – was that there was no connection between sex and emotion. She had been able to indulge Andrew's outré tastes and enjoy herself and yet feel no emotional ties. Conversely the opposite would not have been true. If she had cared for Andrew, if she had fallen in love with him, her ability to cope with his revelations would have been severely limited. It was not caring that had freed her.

So it was with Hamilton. In the beginning, in the gallery where she had propositioned him so brazenly, she didn't know him or care about him. It hadn't spoiled her enjoyment; in fact, she realised, by the same token it had enabled her to be totally uninhibited.

The truth was that, as much as she had tried subsequently to persuade herself that she cared for Hamilton, based on a perverse misunderstanding of her own psychology, she could never do so. She had run away from him because she feared a repeat of what had happened with her other married man. But she knew now she would never become involved with Hamilton in that way. There was therefore, she had concluded with a certain amount of glee, nothing to stop her using Hamilton for her own purposes, using being the operative word.

'I wanted to talk to you about that,' Nadia said in answer to Angela's question. 'There was something I had in mind.'

'Tell me more.'

'Let's eat, I'm starving,' Nadia said. She had two large cold lobsters in the fridge and had prepared a salad of lettuce, mache and rocket.

'Me too,' Angela agreed.

They walked into the house together.

Nadia's feelings for her friend, she was glad to say, had not been changed by their intimacy. Both had enjoyed the experience. For Nadia it had played an important part in sorting out her sexuality. It had even occurred to her that the fear she had hidden for so long over what had happened with Barbara was partly responsible for her sexual hiatus. Whether that was true or not, she had confronted her fear and used Angela as a way of sorting herself out. How big a part women would play in her future sexuality she had no idea. At least she had no idea in the long term. In the short term she knew more or less precisely.

Angela sat at the table as Nadia laid out the food. She opened a bottle of Chablis and poured it into the glass she had set on the table.

'So,' Angela said. 'Are you going to tell me what you've got in mind?'

The front doorbell rang at exactly the prescribed hour. It was getting dark, the summer evening beginning to pull in. Nadia had watched Jack Hamilton get out of a taxi from her bedroom window. She

212

still felt the same pulse of excitement she had always felt every time she had seen him. But this was different. This was on her terms.

He'd sounded puzzled on the phone. He tried to apologise and invent some explanation for what had happened and was obviously nonplussed when Nadia appeared totally uninterested. She'd asked him if he wanted to come round to her house that night. He'd said he did. He'd said he couldn't think of anything he'd rather do.

Nadia walked downstairs slowly. She was wearing a black lace teddy cut so high on the hips it revealed most of the crease of her pelvis. It also gave tantalising glimpses of her breasts under its lacy cups. Her nipples were so hard they felt like round glass beads.

'Come in,' she said, opening the front door.

Hamilton walked inside, not smiling, his eyes riveted to her body. He was wearing a pair of beige cotton slacks, and a white shirt. The front of his black hair fell on to his forehead and he flicked it back with a characteristic gesture. 'You look wonderful,' he said.

'Thank you, I thought you'd appreciate it.'

'Look, I know I owe you an explanation . . .'

'Jack, you owe me nothing.'

'It's just . . .'

'Sh . . .' She put her finger to his lips. They felt hot. She ran her finger across his mouth then pushed it between his lips. 'Aren't you going to kiss me?'

He wrapped his arms around her, his hands caressing the silky nylon of the teddy as his mouth closed over hers. He kissed her hard, hugging her to his strong body, his cock immediately unfurling against her belly.

Nadia felt her body throb. She pushed her mons

213

against his erection, letting a wave of sexual energy wash over her.

'Come with me,' she said, finally breaking away. 'I've got a present for you.'

She took his hand and led him upstairs, making him follow her so his eyes could feast on her long legs and her buttocks, neatly bisected by the black material. Her excitement was compounded by the fact that she was in control, that this was her scenario they were playing out.

Outside the bedroom door, which was firmly closed, she turned around, resting her back against it.

'What is it?' he said.

'I told you, I've got a present for you.'

'A present from you is the last thing I expected, Nadia.'

'I owe you a lot, Jack. More than you will ever know.' She meant it because it was the truth. She reached out her hand and touched the bulge in his flies but when he tried to kiss her again she twisted away. 'Open the door,' she said.

He turned the handle of the door and went in. The curtains were drawn and the bedside lamp, draped with a red scarf, cast a dim but rosy glow. There was enough light to see Angela clearly. She was lying on the bed naked apart from a pair of tiny black silk panties that barely covered her thick growth of red pubic hair. She was holding the cream plastic vibrator to her lips, licking it like an ice cream cone.

'I almost started without you,' she said.

Cirque Erotique

Mikki Leone

Chapter One

AS DUSK QUICKLY gave way to night Danni Appleyard perched herself on the windowsill of her bedroom and gazed with secret pleasure at the view from the picture window. Although she lived in a nondescript part of West London, the vista was so magnificent she could have been watching the sunset anywhere in the world. It was a real shepherd's delight of a sky. Marshmallow clouds, tinted orange, streaked an endless backdrop of red-gold, the horizon marked by a dark crenellated skyline of factories and tower blocks. Further into the distance the glowing crescent of the setting sun hovered for a while before sliding lower and lower to disappear from view.

Night had finally descended.

Danni loved this time of the evening but for her it was still far too early to think of going to bed. Though Tam, her boyfriend, had other ideas. His job was a bloody nuisance, she thought, as she wandered over to the dressing-table and sat down. Working as a sound technician on one of the breakfast television programmes meant he had to be up at four-thirty every morning to get to the studio. For Tam his job was exciting and challenging, but as far as Danni was concerned it was a pain in the neck.

In fact, she mused, as she leaned forward and peered at her round, wide-awake face in the mirror, their whole relationship was starting to get her down. There were all sorts of little things that bugged her about him, particularly those stemming from a chauvinistic attitude that left her feeling as though her place was in the wrong. And, if it wasn't bad enough having to go to bed ridiculously early, she was forced, by the minuscule dimensions of her flat, to listen to his ritual 'bathroom sonata' beforehand . . . every night.

As she gazed into the depths of her jade green eyes and flicked a long tendril of tawny-coloured hair away from her face, she cocked an unwilling ear to Tam's latest 'performance'. First came the loud, off-key singing in the shower, either operatic arias or a selection of Queen's greatest hits – *Mama mia, Mama mia . . . Mama mia let me go . . .!* Then there were the five minutes – and not a moment less – of dutiful teeth-brushing, followed by a stomach-churning series of gargling noises . . . And so it went on until he finally appeared in her shades-of-blue bedroom looking well and truly scrubbed clean, his fair skin all pink and shiny, his perfect teeth positively blinding in their whiteness.

She only hoped to God that tonight he wouldn't come in and start flossing his teeth in front of her or she would throw up.

Tam was fanatical about a lot of things but dental hygiene was the worst of them. He was so fastidious that he flatly refused to give *her* the sort of oral attention she craved. He claimed it simply wasn't healthy. Although, she mused wryly as she wiped off her makeup, his distaste for such a practice didn't stop him encouraging her to do it for him.

She smiled at her own reflection, noting how her wide, generous mouth curved at the edges, dimpling the hollows beneath her rounded cheeks. Her eyes held a definite sparkle, she noticed, although goodness only knew why. What is it about me? she asked herself. I've got a boyfriend who is totally devoted to himself, practically no social life, and I'm always flat broke even though I work myself to death.

'What a life,' she said aloud as she stood up and slipped off her bathrobe. 'Twenty-six? I feel more like ninety-six.'

'Talking to yourself again, darling?'

She glanced up as Tam came into the room looking lean, healthy and disgustingly pleased with himself.

'Why not? You never do,' she countered, immediately regretting her words.

Having treated her to a condescending, thin-lipped smile that infuriated her, he dropped to the bedroom floor to do his customary thirty push-ups before retiring for the night.

Sitting down on the edge of the bed she contemplated the movement of his muscles as they bunched and relaxed under his pale, hairless skin.

'I could slip under you and make your exercise routine a bit more interesting,' she offered. She deliberately tried to make her tone of voice light and hoped she didn't look as exasperated as she felt.

'Uh? Oh, yeah, in a minute,' he puffed. 'Must just – oof, ah, that's it, all done.' He jumped to his feet and rubbed his hands together in a familiar, self-satisfied gesture that made Danni feel like screaming.

She couldn't help noticing that his dedication to his appearance was paying off despite the irritation it caused her. He was looking a lot more toned these days. His daily exercise routine and regular swimming sessions lent his physique an enviable inverted triangle shape. At about five feet ten with thick, dark blond hair, he came pretty close to her physical ideal. Although at only five three herself she often felt dwarfed by him.

'You should think about doing some exercise, you know, Danni,' he remarked as he wandered over to the bed and pulled back the blue and cream striped duvet. Without looking at her he picked up the clock, wound it and set the alarm. 'Your bum's looking a bit lumpy.'

Danni bit back an instant retort but as she climbed into bed beside him, he reached out and pinched the top of her thigh. 'Is that cellulite?' he continued mercilessly.

Wincing, Danni glanced down and pushed his hand away angrily. 'No it bloody well isn't! Leave me alone.'

'You don't mean that.'

She noticed his voice dropped an octave as the same hand slid over her hip, into the indentation of her waist and up over her flat torso to cup one of her full, rounded breasts.

'No,' she admitted, sighing as she reclined against the pillows, despairing of her own weakness, 'you know I want you.'

She watched the way his hazel eyes darkened and his petulant lips formed a self-satisfied smile as he lay back, clasping his hands behind his head. Leaning over him she kissed him, her tongue forcing its way into the dark wet cavern of his mouth. Her tongue recoiled slightly as it tasted tangy peppermint. Hot and sharp, the flavour of his mouth made her delicate tastebuds zing.

'Bloody hell!' she exclaimed, breaking away from him. 'How much toothpaste have you used tonight? Half a tube? Why can't you taste of beer or cigarettes just for once?'

He looked affronted. 'If you'd rather have a lager lout for a boyfriend—'

'Oh, Tam, come on,' she interrupted, despairing of the notion that he was about to launch into one of his lectures instead of sex.

Realising that actions always spoke louder than words, she didn't bother to continue but instead walked her fingers teasingly across his chest. Hearing his soft sigh of pleasure she began to toy with his left nipple, pinching and tugging at it until it hardened, then rolling the little bullet around and around under the pads of her fingertips.

She eased herself further over him, her other hand travelling down, skating the hard flat plane of his stomach, stroking over his hip and down the outside of his thigh. Feeling her own desire mount she ran her palm over the taut mound of his thigh muscle to slide into the warm nest of his groin. Cupping his balls and then sliding her hand higher up to stroke his stirring penis, she simultaneously lowered her head to suck his nipples and lathe his chest with the flat of her tongue. She licked, she nipped at his skin with her teeth, she breathed her warm breath on his damp flesh. Presently she was rewarded by the sound of an anguished groan.

He surprised her by pushing her abruptly away from him and rolling her onto her back in one swift movement. Covering her with his body he ground her breasts beneath his hands, his palms moulding the pliant flesh while his fingertips plucked fervently at her nipples.

Tongues of fire licked at her nipples from the inside, fanning out from the hard, elongated nubs to inflame her whole body. Between her legs she felt wet and hot. She imagined her labia swelling with arousal, opening out to reveal the true extent of her desire. Her clitoris pulsed, an urgent tingling started in her vagina and she felt her juices trickle from her. She gasped, feeling overwhelmed by the surge of passion that gripped her.

It was always the same story with her, moving from feeling nothing, or almost nothing, to full, throbbing, panting lust in a matter of seconds. Tam often called her insatiable. She preferred to think of herself as normal.

'Please,' she moaned, pushing down on the top of his head.

He looked deep into her eyes, the definite shake of his head frustrating her. 'No, you know I don't like that.'

'All right then, touch me,' she gasped, unwilling to let his intransigence mar her desire, 'stroke me down there instead.'

Knowing he knew what she meant and how desperately her body craved such intimacy, she found it all the more frustrating that he didn't comply straight away. Instead he kissed her, his tongue, still sharply minty, darting around inside her mouth.

Feeling desperate, she wrapped her legs tightly around his waist and urged her pelvis up, rubbing her swollen clit shamelessly against his cock which was now rock-hard. Whimpering with desire she allowed her hands to slide over the thin film of perspiration coating his shoulders. His breath was warm and arousing as it stroked her ear while his tongue laid a damp trail down the length of her neck and along her collarbone. Using the index fingers of each hand she followed the bumpy ridge of his spine, smoothing the flesh either side of it until she reached his coccyx. Then she flattened her hands and grasped his buttocks hard, her short rounded fingernails digging into them.

'I want you,' she urged breathlessly, rubbing

herself more ardently against his cock. 'Finger me, fuck me, fill me up.'

Though heavy-lidded, her eyes couldn't fail to notice the flicker of distaste that passed over his face.

'That's not very ladylike,' he mumbled, burying his head in the crook of her neck.

She almost hit him then. 'Sod being ladylike! We're in bed now, remember? We're supposed to be able to express ourselves any way we want to.'

'Well, I don't like you telling me what to do and when to do it.'

Slowly, Danni unwound her legs. All at once she felt her passion for him abate. She pulled his head back up and looked at him with tears of frustration and disappointment glistening in her eyes.

'This just isn't working, is it?' she said in a cracked voice. 'I mean all this, you and me, living together and everything. It just isn't working out the way I'd imagined.'

'Nor for me either,' Tam replied evenly. 'You're always moaning.'

'I am not!' Feeling furious now, Danni struggled out from beneath him and sat up, cross-legged, on the bed. She felt a bubbling anger replace the churning heat of desire that had filled her a moment ago. In some ways, she realised, the two sensations were quite similar.

Glancing down she noticed that her labia were still puffy. The hard bud of her clitoris, all red and swollen, peeped through the darkness of her pubic hair. Ignoring Tam, she reached down tentatively and touched herself there, her fingertips skimming over her desperate flesh. Sliding her fingers down the moist slit between her labia she slipped one finger inside herself. Capturing a small amount of her juices with her fingertip she slicked it over her clitoris, her fingers working to a familiar rhythm. Gradually she felt her desire mount again until her need for satisfaction became urgent, her responses sending a raging heat through her lower body. Her clitoris began to throb and she felt her breath becoming shorter. With her heart hammering behind her ribs she stimulated herself, sliding the delicate little hood of skin back and forth over the tip of her swollen bud.

She didn't look up at Tam but watched with glazed eyes as his fingers covered hers, pressing them harder against her clit, rotating slowly, then faster and faster. When he pushed her back again she didn't bother to protest but uncrossed her legs and spread them wide, bending them at the knees, all the time maintaining the stimulation of her own body under Tam's guidance. She whimpered when she felt a couple of his fingers plunge inside her vagina. It grasped desperately at them, her inner walls delighting to the sensation of his stroking fingertips.

Shamelessly she churned her hips, grinding her lower body against his fingers and her own. She felt wide open and sopping wet, her vagina swallowing his probing fingers, craving more. Dark thoughts invaded her mind, snippets of fantasies ... being tied up ... faceless people obscured by shadow watching her and Tam perform for them . . .

She heard herself gasping as her free hand roamed her own breasts, her fingertips pinching and tweaking at the nipples until they became hard and swollen. Her breasts ached with longing as passion clutched at her. For long delicious moments it held her in its grip, squeezing every ounce of lascivious pleasure from her writhing body.

Her climax, when it came moments later, rose and peaked quickly, her internal muscles spasming, gripping Tam's fingers.

'Fuck me now,' she cried, forgetting all about his earlier complaint until the words had already been torn from her throat.

This time, to her relief, he complied straight away and without comment. Kneeling between her widespread thighs he lowered himself until the smooth knob of his glans touched the entrance to her body. His fingers slipped out of her with a soft sucking sound to be replaced by the more satisfying girth of his cock.

As he placed his hands either side of her to take his weight, she wound her legs around his waist again, slamming her body up against his, matching him stroke for stroke. She felt the wiry bush of his pubic hair brush over the sensitive tip of her clitoris, filling her with renewed lust. Gripping Tam's upper arms she arched her back, rubbing herself against him, feeling the warmth of his harsh, rapid breaths on her torso until she felt the first burning waves of a second orgasm.

He continued to move inside her at a more leisurely rate then upped his tempo again. This time she watched as Tam's expression exploded in a look of pure ecstasy. She felt him pump hard, his cock swelling momentarily before erupting inside her. For a few moments he rocked his pelvis back and forth, the continuous movement allowing her to coast on the level wave of a third, far less intense orgasm. Then she felt him come to a gradual halt, resting inside her for a minute or so longer before sliding out of her.

'That was great, darling,' he murmured breathlessly, pulling her into the crook of his arm and nestling her head against his shoulder.

For a little while Danni allowed herself the luxury of basking in satiated bliss, simply listening to the harmonious rhythm of their breathing as it slowed and became even. Then she glanced up at Tam from under her eyelashes, intending to suggest that they start all over again.

With a wry smile she noticed it was too late. Although the clock on the chest of drawers beside him showed it was only a little after ten o'clock, he was already fast asleep.

The next couple of days followed their usual uneventful pattern. Work for Danni meant a half hour Tube ride into central London, followed by eight hours filing, typing and answering customer enquiries at one of the big insurance companies. Then came another Tube ride, only this time at the height of the rush hour, squashed amid a crowd of perspiring bodies while her feet were trampled on.

Tam, who finished work at twelve-thirty, would usually be waiting for her when she got home, although invariably he hadn't got around to tidying the flat or preparing dinner.

Wednesday, though, was different. First of all Danni received a memo from her company's personnel department informing her that she must take two weeks of her holiday entitlement before the end of the following month. Then, when she got home, she found it was deserted. Instead of being confronted by the sight of Tam lolling about on the sofa listening to CDs, she discovered a note propped up against the kettle.

To Danni, it said simply on the plain white envelope. Opening it while she shrugged off her leather jacket, she glanced at the hastily scrawled contents. It was from Tam, of course.

Dear Danni, it read, *hope you are well* . . . She smiled, realising it was the first letter he had ever written to her. *I'm sorry I'm not there but Jake offered me a freelance trip to Hong Kong to do some documentary or other about Chinese rule. Anyway, couldn't turn down a chance like that, could I, so I've taken a bit of leave that was owing to me. I'll be back in about three weeks or so. Don't know when or if I'll be able to call. Take care. Oh, and by the way, the gas and electricity bills just arrived. Be a love and sort them out, would you? Bye for now. Love as always, Tam.*

She reread the letter once more then put it down on the counter. Totally enraged by Tam's thoughtless behaviour – he could at least have called her at work – she picked it up again and carefully tore it into tiny pieces which she flushed down the loo.

Later, when she had calmed down, she sat and thought about what she should do. Tam's unexpected departure had left her in a bit of a quandary. She had hoped he would use some of his holiday entitlement to go somewhere with her.

Picking up a framed black and white photo of her old childhood dog, Rufus, which sat on the little round table beside her, she gazed at it, feeling wistful and more than a little sorry for herself. 'Well this is just great,' she said aloud to the photograph, 'I've got all this time off, no money, nowhere to go and no one to go with. Bloody marvellous – whoopee!'

She sat clutching the photo to her breast until she noticed that the shadows cast across the pale peach sitting-room carpet were lengthening. As she glanced over her shoulder in the direction of the window she realised that it must be getting quite late. With no Tam around she had no one to remind her of the time. All at once she found herself missing his company, which she had taken for granted. Perversely, she even missed the prospect of his night-time ritual.

Sighing, she set the photograph back on the table. 'Suppose I'd better make myself something to eat,' she muttered. Floppy-eared and wearing a dopey expression, Rufus's image gazed mutely back at her. She glared at him, then smiled. 'Fat lot of help you are.'

In the end she settled for a cheese and chutney sandwich, which she took to bed with her along with a couple of magazines she had pinched from the reception area at work. As she munched, she flicked idly through one of the magazines. It seemed full of nothing but advertisements featuring beautiful, smiling people who made her groan with envy. Then, right near the back, she came across a feature about a circus school.

The article stirred a latent interest in her. It took her right back to her childhood, to her eleventh summer when she had played circuses almost every day. Sometimes, she recalled, she had been the ringmaster, striding around in a red tailcoat, wearing a top hat and cracking a long whip – all imaginary of course – or sometimes she had cast herself in the role of a trapeze artist, a lion tamer, or a clown. Most of all, she remembered now with a smile, there were three things she had longed to be able to do: eat fire, juggle and do backflips. How wonderful it would have been to amaze all her friends with her skill and daring. Now, she realised as she felt a familiar excitement stir inside her, the desire to show off was still there. And what better way to boost her self-confidence than to learn these tricks, she mused. If nothing else they would certainly help to get herself noticed at parties.

The image of herself at a lavish society bash – not that she had ever been invited to any – suddenly backflipping across the ballroom, or juggling with the contents of the fruit bowl, made her laugh aloud. I really want to learn how to do something like that, she told herself. However pointless it might seem, even if I never get a chance to show off my skills in public, at least *I'll* know I can do those things.

Despite Tam's absence, or perhaps because of it, she slept really well that night, the magazine left open on the bed as a reminder to do something truly positive with her life for once.

The next morning Danni awoke with a tingle of anticipation without knowing the reason why. Then as she threw back the duvet, knocking the magazine to the floor, she remembered what she planned to do today. Jumping up, she wandered around the bed to where the magazine lay. Pausing for a moment to rub the sleep from her eyes she read the bold type at the bottom of the article. No address was given but there was a name, Fauve Legère, and a telephone number.

'I'll fake a forgotten dental appointment and go into work late,' she told her reflection as she sat down at the dressing-table and began to cleanse her face. 'If I don't get this over and done with, I'll probably let it slip like everything else.'

Procrastination, Tam often told her, should have been her middle name. And she could remember her mother saying time and time again to her, 'I don't mean next week, Danielle, do it now!' Even her boss complained that hers was the only in-tray which had more in it by the end of the week than at the beginning. In return, Danni tried to justify herself through a whole gamut of excuses which sounded lame, even to her own ears.

Her real problem was that she was a daydreamer. There were far more important things to life than reality. Running away with the circus appealed to her sense of adventure like nothing ever had before.

For once she didn't wait until she had showered and dressed before picking up the telephone. 'Do it now,' she urged herself, reaching for the receiver with a trembling hand. 'Ring these people before you lose your bottle.'

She dialled but the phone just rang and rang, increasing Danni's frustration and leading her to wonder if fate really intended for her to do this. Then, just as she was about to give up, it was answered by a woman with a delicately husky voice.

''Allo, Fauve Legère, 'ow can I 'elp you?'

Danni swallowed deeply as she gripped the receiver. 'I'm just ringing up about your circus school. I saw an article in—' She didn't get a chance to finish.

'Ah, I know it. You are interested to learn *l'art du cirque, non?*'

'*Non*, I mean, *oui*, I mean—' Danni broke off. She had exhausted the limits of her schoolgirl French and wasn't at all sure what she was agreeing to anyway.

Fauve's voice was calm and reassuring. 'Do not worry, *ma chérie*, it is my fault for not speaking in English. Tell me,' she continued, ''ave you tried anything like this before?'

'No, but I really want to,' Danni said excitedly. 'I've loved the circus since I was a child.'

'Ah, a love of the circus, that is good. That is the first step, no? I tell you, my dear, I 'ave loved the circus since before I talk, or walk. It is – 'ow you say? – in my blood, I think.'

Danni laughed. She liked the sound of this woman and was becoming more determined to join the circus school by the minute.

'How much is it?' she asked hesitantly. 'I mean, er – I might not be able to afford all of the courses. And I only have two weeks.'

'Two weeks from when?' Fauve replied, ignoring her question about the cost.

'Well, I, er, from this Saturday I suppose.'

'That is excellent.' Danni could hear an excitement in Fauve's voice that seemed to match her own. 'It would be perfect. By the end of your stay you would be ready for one of our grand performances.'

'Really?' Danni sat down on the arm of the sofa. She hadn't imagined the course would involve a real live performance . . . in front of other people.

'Yes, really. It is a special thing we like to do.'

'But how much will it cost?' Danni persisted.

To her dismay, Fauve mentioned a sum that was way beyond her means.

'I'm sorry, I've been wasting your time,' Danni said. 'I couldn't possibly afford that much, even a tenth of that would be stretching it.'

She heard Fauve laugh. 'Stretching it – that is a funny English saying, no? Please, my dear girl, do not worry about the money. I never worry about such things.'

Danni thought privately that the only people who never worried about money were the ones who had plenty of it.

'I want you to come,' Fauve continued, 'I like the sound of you. You are young, yes – and pretty?'

Pursing her lips, Danni thought about herself for a moment. 'I'm twenty-six, which I suppose is youngish,' she said, 'and other people tell me I'm pretty, so I suppose—'

'Describe yourself,' Fauve interrupted.

'Oh!' Danni felt taken aback. 'Right, OK. I'm quite short, only five feet three, I've got quite a nice figure—'

'Stop there,' Fauve interrupted again, only more firmly. 'I don't want to 'ear this *quite nice*, I want to know exactly. Tell me, my dear, 'ow does your figure go – out-in-out, or out-out-out?'

Despite her nervousness, Dannie laughed. 'Out-in-out. I haven't measured myself lately but I usually wear a size ten, or occasionally a twelve if the bust is a bit tight.'

'So you have quite large breasts then, yes?'

For some reason she couldn't fathom, Danni found herself blushing. It seemed very odd to be discussing her breasts on the telephone with a woman she hadn't even met.

'They're ... generous,' she said, hedging a bit. 'My boyfriend likes them, at any rate.'

'Your boyfriend?' Fauve sounded surprised. 'He will be coming with you to the school?'

'No,' Danni said. 'He's away for a few weeks. That's why I'm feeling a bit miserable at the moment. I was hoping to go on holiday with him.'

'So you are missing him then – you are very much in love?'

'To be honest, no,' Danni surprised herself by saying. 'I'm starting to think our relationship is a mistake. It's actually quite a relief to be on my own again.'

She heard Fauve mutter, 'Interesting,' and all at once she got the impression that someone else was listening to the conversation.

'So,' Fauve continued, 'you 'ave this delicious figure, yes – and what about the rest of you, your 'air, your eyes?'

Danni stood up and walked over to a tall glass-fronted cupboard which housed her meagre selection of wine glasses and tumblers. She could see her reflection in the glass and so proceeded to give Fauve as detailed a description of herself as she could manage. When she'd finished she heard the other woman mutter something and then her ears picked up a responding voice in the background. A voice that was dark, interesting – and definitely male. Unaccountably, Danni felt her pulse quicken.

'We think,' Fauve said after a few moments had passed, 'that you would be most welcome here. Pay what you can afford. The rest you can, 'ow you say – work off?'

Danni couldn't help noticing the *I* had suddenly changed to *we* but she was too stunned by Fauve's generosity to give it much thought.

Instead, she stammered, 'Are you sure? I mean—'

The answer was firm. 'We're sure.'

While she was still grappling mentally with her unexpected good fortune, she managed to take note of the address that Fauve gave her and promised to turn up by lunchtime on Saturday. Which, she realised as she put down the phone with a sigh of satisfaction, gave her just under two days to shop, pack and generally prepare herself for realising a long cherished dream.

Chapter Two

SUNLIGHT DAPPLED THE bonnet of the red minicab as it wove its way from the station along a series of leafy lanes. Sussex, Danni decided as she gazed out of the passenger window at the passing scenery, was a beautiful county. They had already passed through a couple of tiny, picturesque villages and now they were approaching a third. The thirty-mile-an-hour signs instructed the driver to slow down and told Danni that she had almost reached her destination.

Having felt relaxed during the train journey from London and the fifteen-minute taxi ride, Danni now felt her heartbeat quicken. She felt as though she were heading for the unknown and suddenly remembered that she hadn't let anyone know where she was going.

As she was expecting to return before Tam, she hadn't bothered to leave him a note similar to the one he had left her. But, she realised on reflection, she should have at least phoned her mother, or her best friend Linda. Supposing these circus people turned out to be maniacs, or if she injured herself in some way, who would know of her plight? And if she never returned home at all no one would know where to start looking for her. Unnerved by the possibilities that now occurred to her, she resolved that, at the earliest opportunity, she would walk down to the village and send a post-card to her mother. That way she wouldn't feel stranded. Or, better still, the school probably had a pay phone she could use . . .

'Nearly there, love,' the driver said to her, turning his head for a moment and giving her a friendly smile.

She nodded. She had opted to sit in the front seat and was grateful that the driver of the minicab was genial without being too talkative. Although she had already spent the previous couple of days and the whole of this morning mulling over her telephone conversation with Fauve, she was still glad of the opportunity to be left alone with her thoughts. She felt as though she were preparing herself mentally for something momentous and now, as her suppositions were about to become reality, she found herself filled with an equal mixture of excitement and trepidation.

There had been something about the way the Frenchwoman had spoken to her – the combination of her low, seductive voice and the intimate way she had questioned her – that made Danni's intuition quiver. And the presence of the mysterious third party in Fauve's office, the one who had been listening to her describe her appearance, including the size and shape of her breasts, filled her with uneasy anticipation.

She knew the listener had been a man. As though an invisible thread connected them she had felt his 'vibes' – kind and sensitive yet also darkly, deeply erotic – and her body had automatically thrilled to them. Intuitive and dreamy by nature, Danni felt as though she were about to enter a realm of discovery that involved far more than simply learning a few circus skills. Is this the point in my life where I finally leave my childhood behind? she asked herself, while answering her own question with a certainty, deep inside, that she was poised on the brink of a new self-awareness.

The village they had now entered was every bit as picture-postcard perfect as the others she had seen. Stone cottages, some of them thatched, lined the winding street that led through its centre. There were two pubs, she noticed, and only one grocery shop-cum-Post Office and newsagent. She saw a couple of men and a woman standing outside the shop talking and, further along the street, where it opened out on the left – to what she assumed was the village green – she observed a handful of children playing, while mums with pushchairs sat on wooden benches, toasting bare white arms and legs.

It was late May and extremely warm. The sky was an unbroken canopy of blue and the tarmac-covered road ahead shimmered in a haze of heat. Undecided at first as to what to wear, Danni had finally opted for a pair of loose black cotton trousers and a cream top, which she wore with a pair of black wedge-heeled sandals to make her look a little bit taller. She had brought very little with her in the way of clothing: a few pairs of leggings, half a dozen T-shirts, some underwear, a couple of cotton dresses and one pair of shorts, all of which she had packed into a single holdall. At the station she had bought a couple of paperback blockbusters, a few bars of chocolate and a couple of bottles of flavoured mineral water – just in case the school was a long walk from the shops. Now, she realised as they drove out of the village and turned right up a steep, narrow lane, she had been right to take such precautions; late-night chocolate binges were one of her many weaknesses.

'The place you want is just up here a-ways,' the driver said as though he could read her thoughts. He pointed. 'See, it's over there.'

Following the direction of his finger, Danni glanced up and to the right. On top of the hill she could make out a cluster of brick farm buildings, behind which she could just see the white canvas top of what looked to be a huge marquee.

'That must be where they put on their performances,' Danni said excitedly. 'Have you ever been to one?' She assumed the driver lived fairly locally. However, he shook his head as he turned off the lane, drove through an open gateway and continued up a rutted track.

'No, it's not for the likes of us. By invitation only apparently. That Madame Legère can get a bit sniffy if folks start poking their noses into her business.'

'Oh dear, really?' Danni didn't really know what to say. She had assumed that circus people were naturally friendly and would make an effort to get on with the locals. Still, she supposed, this was a circus school, rather than a real circus and Fauve *was* French. She laughed to herself then, wondering why she thought it was quite normal for foreigners to be a bit standoffish. 'Perhaps she's just shy,' she offered.

To her surprise the taxi driver gave a spluttering laugh. 'Her – shy? You must be joking. From what I've heard, them in there' – he cocked his head in the direction of the farm which they were just approaching – 'don't know the meaning of the word.' He lowered his voice to a conspiratorial level. 'There are lots of stories flying about these parts and most of them concern some very rum goings-on. Very rum indeed.'

Danni felt her heart start to pound. It was too late to feel afraid, she told herself, and far too late to turn back now. The car was already pulling into a central courtyard.

A couple of dogs, one a large black labrador, the other a white and tan terrier, ran up to the taxi and started barking. As they drew to a halt Danni glanced nervously at the driver.

'Do you think—?' she started to say, but the driver was already opening his door and shooing the dogs away in a loud, firm voice. As he went around to the back of the car to unlock the boot, Danni climbed out of the passenger side. She

241

closed the door and stood with her back pressed against it as the dogs danced excitedly around in front of her.

'Regis, Delilah, come here – at once!' The stern command came from a small dark woman who appeared from around the side of the main farm-house.

Danni watched as the dogs immediately stopped barking and walked obediently over to their owner, their tongues lolling and eyes rolling in a slavish expression. Despite her nervousness, Danni laughed.

The woman bade the dogs to sit and stay, then walked towards Danni, her hands outstretched.

'Hi there. I am Fauve and you must be Danni,' she said, smiling brightly and gripping Danni's hands between her own.

Danni nodded, then turned to the mini-cab driver as he put her bag on the ground beside her. 'There you go, miss,' he muttered. 'That'll be eight pounds fifty.'

'Oh, right, thanks,' Danni said.

Fumbling a bit, she dug into her shoulder bag for her purse, pulled out a ten-pound note and told him to keep the change. She couldn't help noticing how he cast a wary glance at Fauve before getting back into the car. Flashing Danni a smile, which to her looked falsely bright, he turned the car around and drove out of the courtyard. Raising her hand, Danni watched the rear of the car as, in a cloud of dust and straw, it receded down the track towards the lane. Unaccountably, she felt a sinking feeling, as though she had just waved goodbye to her last contact with reality.

'So, *ma chérie*, you are 'ere at last.' Fauve's voice broke through Danni's thoughts and she turned to look at the petite Frenchwoman, who had a half smile on her face.

She had tried hard to imagine what Fauve must look like and as far as age and colouring went, she saw straight away, her assumptions had been spot-on. However, she had imagined Fauve as a much taller woman and also that she would have long hair. In fact, the older woman's dark brown, almost black, hair was cut in a gamine style that feathered around her exquisite, slightly pointed face and swan-like neck. She was, Danni estimated, somewhere around her mid-thirties, although she also had the appearance of someone who was ageless. Her figure was trim without being too thin and she was clad in a flatteringly cut pair of black jeans, worn with a short-sleeved ribbed jumper, also in black, which seemed to mould itself around her small, rounded breasts and fitted snugly against her flat torso and tiny waist. On her feet she wore a pair of flat-soled sandals with braided black leather thongs.

At first Danni found it strange as she experienced the unusual sensation of looking down on another woman from a greater height; she was so used to everyone being taller than herself. Then gradually, as Fauve picked up her bag, took her arm and began to lead her towards the farmhouse, chattering all the time about the wonderful weather and so forth, she found herself warming to her hostess.

Although the farmhouse was nothing special to look at from the outside – just a brick oblong with a red tiled roof and white window frames that looked as though they could do with a fresh coat of paint – the interior took her breath away.

The ground floor had obviously been extensively remodelled, Danni noticed. Most of the internal walls and the ceiling above had been demolished to make one vast, sparsely furnished room which seemed limitless in height. The floor was polished wood, the walls simply rough, cream-painted plaster which were dotted here and there with paintings and framed photographs of circus performers. And, as Danni gazed up to the exposed rafters which supported the high sloping ceiling, she found herself reeling with a sensation she could only liken to vertigo.

'Steady on, little one,' a deep voice said in her ear, surprising her almost as much as the strong hands gripping her shoulders.

Feeling dazed, she turned her head slowly and found herself staring into the deepest, most startling pair of blue eyes she had ever seen.

'Ivan, darling, this is Danni. Remember – she called us a couple of days ago?' Fauve smiled over Danni's shoulder at the man who gradually released his hold.

Danni noticed he didn't look at Fauve but watched *her* intently, keeping his hands raised as though poised to catch her again should she falter.

She swallowed deeply, finding his attentiveness reassuring yet also a little disturbing.

'I remember,' he said as he held out his hand and took Danni's holdall from Fauve. 'She of the modest nature and wonderful breasts.'

Danni couldn't help blushing as he spoke, particularly as he cast his eyes appreciatively over her at the same time.

Fauve laughed lightly. 'Ivan, stop it,' she admonished, 'you are embarrassing the poor little thing.'

Fauve's description of her as 'little' struck Danni as amusing. She laughed nervously, glancing from Ivan to Fauve and back to Ivan.

He was, she decided, the most beautiful man she had ever seen. Tall and broad-shouldered, he held himself proudly erect. His tanned face was both strong yet finely chiselled, as though created by a master sculptor, with a straight nose, full, sensual mouth and those eyes ... Oh, dear God, those eyes ...

Danni found herself sinking into them once again and only with the greatest effort managed to tear her gaze away. She had the impression that he was capable of mesmerising her. Not only were his irises as startlingly brilliant as sapphires but his gaze was direct and unblinking, making her feel as though he could see right inside her and thrilling her to the core. The other part of him which she found almost equally amazing was his hair. A shocking white blond, it was layered at the sides to sweep over and behind his perfectly shaped ears to fall just below his shoulders.

It was a habit of Danni's to liken people to animals and she found herself doing it now with Ivan and Fauve. He reminded her of a pure-bred stallion. Screaming virility from every pore, his body was firm and strong with skin the colour of toast, his carriage erect, his movements supple and fluid, the whole magnificent ensemble crowned by a silky white mane. By the same token, she decided, Fauve was strongly reminiscent of a gazelle. Her figure was delicately proportioned, her movements lithe and graceful and her face, with it's long-lashed, almond-shaped eyes and tiny pink mouth, was so feminine it made Danni almost weep with envy. As for herself, she felt as ungainly as a hippo in comparison.

Thankfully she had no time to ponder her own disadvantages. Fauve led her over to a large group of soft, white cambric-covered sofas where she instructed her to sit. On a low table in front of her Danni could see a collection of old circus programmes and magazines. Leaning forward she picked one up and began to flick idly through it as Fauve and Ivan stood a little way off, talking quietly.

Glancing surreptitiously over the top of the magazine, Danni found her gaze drawn once again to Ivan. He was dressed all in cream, his trousers and casual shirt cut from a fine silky fabric that seemed to flow over his hard, taut body yet disguised nothing. She fancied she could see every ripple, every curve and delineation of his

246

musculature beneath his clothes. All at once she found herself growing very warm and had to fan herself with the magazine to stop herself from feeling faint again.

Unable to bear the physical torment of looking at Ivan any longer, she closed her eyes, revelling instead in the peace and quiet that surrounded her and the scent of fresh flowers which the outstretched arms of a warm breeze carried in from the open windows. Finding herself lulled into blissful contemplation, Danni was surprised when she felt the seat beside her give a little. Opening her eyes she found Fauve was studying her, her expression inscrutable yet bearing the merest hint of a secretive smile. Automatically Danni smiled back at her then glanced up and immediately felt a sharp pang of disappointment – Ivan was nowhere to be seen.

'Oh, he's gone,' she said without meaning to.

Fauve patted her hand indulgently. 'I thought you would take to Ivan. 'E is nice isn't 'e? 'E 'as agreed to be your tutor and mentor during your stay 'ere.'

Danni didn't know whether to laugh or run away. Nice, the woman said, nice? He was gorgeous. And here was Fauve suggesting that she would be spending the next couple of weeks under his metaphorical wing. Quickly, Danni mentally altered Ivan's similarity to that of a golden eagle.

Her smile turned to a grin as she gazed back at the Frenchwoman, noticing for the first time the light floral perfume she wore. 'You'll have to forgive me if I seem a bit nervous,' she said by way of a convincing explanation for her behaviour. 'I haven't ever done anything this daring before.'

'Ah!' Fauve laughed and clapped her hands delightedly. 'You do not know the meaning of daring yet, my dear. Wait until Ivan 'as started putting you through your paces. You will amaze yourself. I guarantee it.'

'I hope so,' Danni said. 'You've been so kind to me already, what with letting me come here at a reduced rate and everything. I promise I'll do my very best and won't let you down.'

Glancing down, Danni watched as Fauve's hand left hers to squeeze her knee reassuringly instead. 'I'm sure. But please don't be too grateful yet, you're 'ere to work as well as 'ave fun, you know.'

'Oh, yes,' Danni agreed, nodding enthusiastically and trying hard not to feel discomfited by the Frenchwoman's overtly tactile gestures, 'I'll do the dishes, cook, make the beds, whatever—'

'You'll do nothing of the sort,' Fauve interrupted her. 'When I say work, I mean at your lessons. 'Ere you will learn skills you never thought possible. And I also 'ope,' she added, in a slightly lower tone, 'that you will discover many new things about yourself at the same time.'

Danni shivered at the way Fauve spoke. Again, her tone and the implication behind her words seemed strangely intimate. All at once, she found herself wondering what it was exactly Fauve and Ivan had in store for her.

'Where will I be sleeping?' she asked to break

the thread of apprehension that threatened to strangle her.

'Oh, my dear, I am so sorry. You must be anxious to – 'ow you say? – wash your hands.' Fauve laughed again and stood up. 'Come with me, Danni.' she said. 'I will show you to your room. Then a little later Ivan will come and get you and show you around properly. The sooner you feel relaxed and at 'ome 'ere the better, no?'

'Yes,' Danni said, thinking she sounded as relieved as she felt, 'thank you. I'm sure everything will be just perfect.'

In the predominantly white bedroom which Fauve had allocated to her – where wide French windows on one side of the room gave her such a feeling of light and space that she felt as though she and the surrounding countryside were one – Danni realised the true meaning of perfection. Everything around her bore the hallmarks of Fauve's style.

At that very moment she was reclining on a huge double bed covered in fine white broderie anglaise which matched the drapes that hung from a brass pole above her head. These were caught either side of the bed by huge bows of oyster ribbon fixed to brass rings, which in turn were cemented into the white plaster wall. The floor was covered by thick, cream carpet. And opposite her was a long pine dressing-table and drawer unit. A white painted door led to a large bathroom complete with a deep claw-footed bath with a shower, a shell-shaped porcelain basin, matching lavatory and a bidet.

So French, she had mused to herself the first time she noticed the bidet. Whereupon she had found herself wondering if she would actually use it for the purpose it was intended, or if she would end up soaking her smalls in it instead, like most English people who were unused to such continental luxuries.

There and then she had resolved to watch Fauve and try to imitate her. It wouldn't do her any harm to learn a little finesse, she decided. If just a tiny amount of the Frenchwoman's chic rubbed off on her it would be to the good. She could just imagine Tam's face if she returned home looking as though she had stepped elegantly from the pages of a French fashion magazine. For a start she would try to do something more interesting with her hair. Although she couldn't imagine herself with a style as short as Fauve's, she could practise pinning it up, or at least braiding it. Long flowing locks, she decided, would definitely be a hindrance to some of the things she planned to learn – like fire-eating for instance. She shuddered as she imagined accidentally setting her golden brown tresses alight at her first attempt.

'Are you cold, Danni – in this heat?'

The voice, all too familiar already, set her pulse racing. Turning her head almost unwillingly, she noticed that Ivan had stepped into her room through one of the pairs of French windows.

'I, er, no, I was just imagining setting my hair alight,' she replied instantly. She felt foolish as she answered him and wondered why she felt compelled to be quite so honest sometimes.

His seductive mouth curved into a smile as he sat down uninvited on the edge of her bed. 'Really, are you that bored?' he said.

Danni gazed back at him. The look he gave her was so lambent she fancied she could feel herself melting from the inside out. Somehow she managed to shake her head.

'No, I—' she began before quickly giving up trying to explain. Instead she said, 'Fauve mentioned something about a guided tour.'

'Ah, yes.' Ivan continued to smile at her, his eyes making an appraising sweep of her reclining body which now stiffened. 'I keep forgetting you are new to all of this. Somehow,' he paused and reached out to stroke a single finger along the sole of her bare foot, 'I feel you are already a part of this – us. You have a certain – oh, I don't know – I suppose Fauve would call it *je ne sais quoi.*'

Danni's eyes widened and she tried not to wriggle her foot. 'Do I?'

'Oh yes.' Ivan's finger moved to her other foot and this time, when he had finished stroking up and down the sole, he began to circle her ankle. 'I see great things for you and me. We will make a good team, I know it.'

As Danni concentrated on the mesmerising effect of his finger, she couldn't help noticing for the first time that he also had a slightly unusual accent.

'Are you French too?' she asked.

'No.' He laughed and to her disappointment took his finger away. 'I am stateless, timeless and therefore ageless.' He stood up and to Danni's surprise stretched his arms wide in a theatrical gesture, as though he were trying to embrace the world. 'This whole earth is my birthplace. I belong wherever I am. And I am whatever I want to be.'

Danni shook her head, wondering if she had actually fallen asleep and was now lost in the depths of a particularly vivid though confusing dream. His laugh brought her back to reality with a jolt.

'Come on,' he said, reaching out a hand to her, 'you must not let me distract you from your reasons for being here.'

'I'm not quite sure what they are, to be truthful,' she admitted, struggling to her feet and casting a searching gaze around the floor for her shoes. She spotted them tucked under a low, armless chair covered in oyster sateen. As she slipped her feet into them she glanced up at him. 'I want to learn as much as I can. I don't know if Fauve told you but I've loved the circus since I was a child.'

'You along with many other people,' Ivan said, leading her through the doorway and around the long, single-storey building. 'The only difference is, you have the courage to explore your dreams.'

Exploring my dreams, Danni mused as she followed him – is that what I'm doing? She realised she felt strangely detached from reality. She hadn't eaten since early that morning yet felt no hunger. Nor was she thirsty. Like Ivan, she simply *was* . . .

He took her across the closely mown field behind the farm buildings to the marquee. It looked much bigger close to, Danni realised, than it had from the road. Inside, it was everything she expected from a circus tent, albeit slightly scaled down. From the high canvas ceiling hung a trapeze and two ladders, between which was strung a high wire. Quite a distance below a large orange net was suspended from tall metal poles sunk into the ground. As they drew closer to it, Danni saw that the net was still a good metre or so above her head.

'I will take you up there tomorrow or the next day,' Ivan said, pointing to the top of the ladder where the platform looked about as large as a postage stamp.

'Oh no, I don't think—' Danni started to say but Ivan interrupted her.

'You will trust me, I hope, Danni,' he said. 'No harm will come to you if you place all your faith in me – only pleasure.'

She thrilled to his words and the darkly promising way in which they were said. Trust him? she thought. To trust another human being that much, particularly a man, was asking an awful lot of her.

Fleetingly she recalled a very old memory she had thought was lost to her for ever. It was of her father repeatedly throwing her into the air and catching her again. Then once, just once, he had turned at the last minute, distracted by something her mother called out to him and Danni had fallen to the ground. Fortunately, the grass had not been mown and was long and soft. Nor had she fallen very far. But it had been enough to make her wary.

Years later, when her father had left her and her mother to live with another woman, his betrayal had been enough to revive her mistrust of men and she had vowed from that day forth always to expect the worst and withhold a tiny part of herself from other people. That way they could never hurt her, never let her down.

'You look doubtful,' Ivan said, interrupting her morose thoughts. 'I will cure you of that.'

Oh yes, Danni wanted to retort, suddenly angry with him through no fault of his own – how? But she remained silent in what she hoped was an enigmatic but still interested way. Though she felt angry with men in general, the last thing she wanted to do was put Ivan off her. At least, she reasoned, not until she had given him a fair chance to prove himself.

Chapter Three

DANNI WAS IN the shower when she heard the insistent tapping sound. Turning off the powerful jet of warm water she cocked an ear and listened. There it was again, the sound of knuckles rapping on glass. Quickly she grabbed an oyster pink towel from the rail. Wrapping it around her, she went into the bedroom. Outside the French windows to her right, which she had prudently locked before taking her shower, she could see Ivan with his fist poised to rap on the glass again.

Feeling as embarrassed as a schoolgirl, she hugged the towel closer to her body. Securing it firmly around her bust, she rushed to the window. She fumbled awkwardly with the lock and eventually was forced to stop holding the towel with one arm so that she could turn the handle and open the door.

'Yes?' she said, hovering nervously on the threshold.

She trembled as she stood there, the wet ends of her hair straggling over her shoulders and dripping down her back. As she was barefoot Ivan seemed even taller and more intimidating than before. And though she felt the warmth of his gaze as it cast across her bare throat and shoulders where droplets of water still clung to her lightly browned skin, she couldn't help shivering.

Just as she opened her mouth to repeat her question, he spoke.

'Fauve asked me to tell you that dinner will be served in the main hall at eight,' he said.

Automatically Danni glanced at her bare wrist and realised her watch was lying on the dressing-table, where she had put it before taking her shower.

'It's only a quarter past six,' Ivan supplied for her. 'You've got plenty of time.'

'What do people, er, that is—' Danni cursed herself for stammering. 'What should I wear?'

Again, Ivan treated her to a warm appraisal. This time though his eyes swept the whole of her body in a long, lingering way. Danni felt instantly embarrassed. Although the towel covered her body from bust to knees she still felt incredibly under-dressed.

Apparently ignorant of her discomfort, Ivan leaned casually against the door-frame. 'I would suggest you wear a bit more than that towel,' he said in an amused tone.

This time Danni blushed. She could feel it starting at the tips of her toes and spreading like wild-fire to the roots of her hair.

'I, I wasn't – I'm not—' she stammered again.

She flinched as Ivan reached out and touched her shoulder.

'You are tense, aren't you, little one?' he said.

Danni felt her throat go dry. His voice was as much of a caress as the fingers stroking her bare shoulder. She tried to shrug and regretted it immediately as the top of her towel slipped a little. She felt the flush across her throat increase as Ivan glanced down. Above the edge of the towel the upper swell of her breasts was clearly visible. Gulping, Danni hitched up the front of the towel again and tried hard to look unconcerned.

'I suppose I am a bit wound up,' she admitted when she finally found her voice. 'It's been a long day and this is all so strange.' She glanced around him to suggest that she was referring to their surroundings.

To her embarrassment, Ivan reached up with his other hand and began to stroke both her shoulders. His touch was warm and soothing and Danni could feel herself melting a little as his fingertips started to knead the taut muscles. He was right, she realised, she *was* feeling tense.

'I am an excellent masseur,' he continued immodestly but in a way that made Danni instantly believe him. 'If you like I could prove it. You would feel so much better, I promise you.'

For a moment Danni hesitated, weighing up the situation. Although part of her felt nervous about allowing him to touch her, another part acknowledged that she had always wanted to experience a proper massage and his touch was not unpleasant by any means. There was also the question of having almost two hours to kill before dinner.

'OK,' she agreed. As she nodded she took a step back. Now her body no longer blocked the doorway it was an open invitation to Ivan to enter.

She continued walking backwards and Ivan followed her, stooping as he entered through the French door. Glancing around hurriedly, Danni realised the only place she could lie down comfortably was the bed. The thought sent a shiver of apprehension through her, then she reminded herself that she was an adult and there were other people around. If Ivan did anything she didn't like she only had to yell and someone would probably come running. Not that he would anyway, she told herself firmly as she lay face down on the broderie anglaise bedspread and rested the side of her face on her folded arms, She was far too unsophisticated to interest a man like him.

From her prone position she watched as Ivan closed the door carefully behind him then reached for the tasselled cord hanging beside it. A pair of self-striped oyster silk curtains swished across the glass wall, casting rosy-hued shadows across the cream carpet. She noticed how he glanced around, his noble brow creasing in confusion.

'Is something the matter?' Danni asked from the bed.

He turned his head to look at her and she felt her breath catch as it did every time he fixed her with those piercing blue eyes.

'I was wondering if you had some body lotion,

or oil of some kind,' he said.

'There's a bottle of baby oil on the shelf in the bathroom,' Danni offered, 'or I think I've got some—'

He didn't give her chance to finish her sentence. 'Baby oil will be perfect,' he said. Turning away, he walked into the bathroom and returned a moment later with the clear plastic bottle in his hand.

She felt the mattress give as he perched on the side of the bed. Then he uncapped the bottle and poured a little of the oil into the palm of his hand. Putting down the bottle on the bedside table, he began to rub his hands together lightly.

'I'm just warming the oil,' he explained. 'If it's not at body temperature the shock of it can make you feel even more tense.'

Danni nodded gravely. She felt as though her gaze was transfixed by the sight of his long fingers glistening with oil, knowing that in a moment they would come into contact with her bare skin.

In the next moment, as his oily palms swept across her shoulders, the breath she didn't realise she was holding was expelled from her lungs on a long sigh. The pressure of his hands was light but firm, the fingertips moulding themselves around the contours of her muscles, kneading them until they felt as soft and pliable as Plasticine.

'Good?' he asked softly.

Danni felt as though she hardly had the strength to nod. His breath was warm upon her ear. It excited the delicate membranes there, making her shiver inside.

'Very,' she gasped. 'I didn't realise how good a massage could feel.'

'Most people don't until they experience it for the first time,' Ivan said, continuing to knead her shoulders. The pads of his thumbs began to follow the ridges of her spine, smoothing and circling. 'But that can be said of many things,' he added. 'Now, could you lift up your hair – I want to massage your neck.'

Reaching behind her, Danni gathered up her hair obediently and swept it upwards, piling it up on top of her head and holding it there. She kept the side of her face pressed against the pillow. As Ivan's thumbs travelled further up her spine to the very base of her hairline, she felt her eyelids growing heavy. In fact, she mused dreamily, her whole body felt heavy. Leaden with drowsiness, it seemed to be sinking deeper and deeper into the mattress.

His touch was magical, driving away all traces of the strain and pressure which had taken their toll over the past few months: work, lack of money, her problems with Tam . . . All at once, Danni felt a flare of warmth in her lower belly. Ivan's fingertips were still massaging her neck, gently easing the taut muscles at the base where it met her shoulders, but now it seemed as though small threads made a direct connection from her neck to her lower body. The nape of her neck was an erogenous zone, she knew that full well, but she hadn't realised how sensitive it was until this moment.

The desire she felt was unmistakable. Its

warmth flooded her, melting her from the inside out. She could feel gentle trickles of moisture seeping out of her as it gathered in her newly awakened vagina. Pressed against the soft towelling, her clitoris began to swell and pulse. Oh, God, no – not now, she prayed silently, wondering how her body could betray her so readily when only a short while before her mind had been concerned about Ivan taking advantage of her. He had continued to behave like a perfect gentleman, confining the promised massage to her neck and shoulders. Whereas she seemed to be behaving like a depraved beast. Despite her best intentions her body worked of its own accord – blossoming, moistening, becoming warmer and warmer and no doubt giving off the unmistakable scent of arousal.

'I think that will do,' she gasped hastily, struggling to sit up.

Ivan's palm flat against her upper back pinned her down. 'Nonsense,' he said. 'I haven't done your arms yet.'

'My arms are fine,' Danni insisted, still struggling. 'Please!' She felt the release of pressure as Ivan took his hand away and sat back. When she rolled over onto her side, she noticed that he was looking at her with a curious expression.

'What's the matter?' he asked simply.

'The time,' Danni said lamely. 'It must be getting late.'

She felt completely flustered as she watched him glance at his wristwatch again.

'It's only five to seven,' he said. Although he

looked perplexed he made no further comment. Instead he stood up and returned the bottle of baby oil to the bathroom. Then he hovered by the French windows, where the curtains were still drawn. 'I'll see you later, at dinner,' he murmured to her as he reached into the gap between the curtains for the handle.

Still lying on the bed Danni watched him push open the door. For some reason she felt guilty, but couldn't understand why.

'Yes, OK,' she said, clearing her throat, which felt extraordinarily tight. Then, almost as an afterthought – by which time he was halfway through the door, she called out, 'And thank you – for the massage, I mean.'

His white-blond head swivelled around and she noticed, with relief, that he was smiling as he looked at her over his shoulder.

'Don't mention it,' he said lightly. 'Any time.'

It was only when dinner-time finally arrived that Danni realised she had no idea where the 'great hall' was. She knocked tentatively on the front door of the main farmhouse and when there was no reply walked around to the back where she found that the stable-type kitchen door was standing wide open. As she popped her head around she saw two identical young women standing side by side chopping tomatoes and red peppers. The colour of the vegetables, she noticed, almost matched the shade of their straight, shoulder-length hair.

They glanced up and the one nearest to the door smiled at her and said, 'You must be new. Are you lost?'

Danni nodded. 'I'm looking for the great hall.'

The young woman put down her chopping knife and picked up a blue and white checked towel. Rubbing her hands on it she inclined her head towards a heavy wooden door on the far side of the huge kitchen.

'Straight through there,' she said amiably. 'I think Fauve and a couple of the others are already waiting.'

Murmuring her thanks Danni walked across the wide expanse of red flagstone covered floor, noticing on her way that the kitchen was typically rustic. Heavy oak beams supported the low ceiling and were festooned with strings of garlic and dried herbs. Along the wall to her right oak cuboards sat either side of a huge black kitchen range. And in the centre of the room stood a long, scrubbed oak table surrounded by matching wheelbacked chairs.

The twin girls were standing in front of another range of cupboards which were topped by a white marble work surface and a double sink. In one of the basins a stainless steel colander was heaped with lettuce leaves, on which water droplets still clung, glistening like fat diamonds. The other basin contained an assortment of dirty cooking utensils. The two young women looked very youthful indeed in their pink overalls, which somehow failed to clash with their hair, and very slim.

263

'Do you need any help?' Danni felt compelled to ask. It seemed to her that, depite Fauve's protestations, she should be doing more to pay for her keep than enjoying warm showers and long massages.

The two shook their red heads simultaneously. 'Oh, no, you're here to learn, not work,' they chorused.

Danni couldn't help noticing how they glanced at each other straight afterwards and seemed to share a knowing look. It made her feel distinctly uncomfortable without knowing why. Take no notice, it's just your overactive imagination at work again, she told herself firmly. Nevertheless, as she pushed open the door and stepped through it, she was sure it wasn't her imagination when she heard one of them say to the other, 'Like a lamb to the slaughter.' Nor did she imagine the light tinkle of girlish laughter that followed.

As she stepped into the room beyond, closing the door hastily behind her to block out the echoes of laughter that seemed to follow in her wake, she realised the term 'great hall' was an anomaly. Hardly larger than the bedroom she had been allocated, this room was perhaps the most sparsely furnished she had seen so far – with only a round polished table encircled by eight straight-backed chairs. The walls were natural brick, relieved only by a few strategically hung paintings, and the flooring was bare wooden boards. Only the fire burning merrily in a cast-iron grate gave the room any feeling of warmth and habitation.

Another door on the far side opened at that

moment and in walked Fauve, dressed in smart black trousers and a matching silky blouse. A smile lit up her face as she noticed Danni hovering uncertainly and she extended a fine-boned hand in greeting.

'Danni, 'ow lovely you look, come and sit,' Fauve said.

Danni glanced down at herself. Compared with the chic Frenchwoman she didn't feel all that lovely. Unsure what she should wear, she had opted for one of her two dresses. T-shirt style, it was made of white ribbed cotton and had shoe-string straps and a scooped neckline. As she had forgotton to pack any tights she was bare-legged. Her only concession to dressing up had been to put on a pair of gold high-heeled sandals.

'I didn't know what I should wear,' she managed to blurt out, 'especially as I hadn't thought to bring any smart clothes.' Crossing the room, she sat on one of the dining chairs and clasped her hands demurely in her lap.

Fauve took the chair next to hers. Pausing to smooth imaginary creases from her trousers, she crossed her legs elegantly and turned her body slightly so that she was facing Danni.

'What you 'ave chosen is *parfait*,' she said, reaching out to finger one of Danni's shoestring straps. 'That colour, it look so good with your tan and it 'ug your figure like a lover.' Danni blushed at the comparison and forced herself to remain calm as one of Fauve's pink-tipped fingernails scraped lightly across her throat. 'It just lack the jewels,'

Fauve added, 'do you not 'ave any – a gold chain perhaps and some earrings?' She flicked Danni's tawny hair over her shoulder as she spoke, exposing a bare earlobe which she regarded with a narrow-eyed look of dissatisfaction.

Danni used the shake of her head to dislodge the Frenchwoman's hand. 'I'm not really a jewellery person,' she said, 'but I normally do wear earrings. I just forgot to put them in after my shower, that's all.' She watched as Fauve sat back and appraised her thoughtfully.

'Are you pierced anywhere else?' Fauve asked out of the blue.

Taken aback by the question, Danni found herself blushing and stammering as she answered, 'No, I haven't – I couldn't—'

Fauve laughed huskily. 'It can be very becoming,' she assured Danni, 'the nipples, the labia, even the delicate little clitoris can all look very pretty when adorned.' She paused and raised her head, glancing toward the doorway as Ivan entered. '*N'est-ce pas*, Ivan?' she said, drawing him into the conversation as he took the empty chair next to Danni.

'What is that, *ma chérie*?' he asked.

Smiling at him, Fauve repeated what she had just told Danni.

'Oh, yes,' he said, nodding his affirmation to Danni, who blushed even deeper. She wished fervently that they weren't having this conversation 'Such beautiful parts look even more beautiful decorated with gold and precious gems,' he continued.

'I don't really think that's for me,' Danni said, clearing her throat hastily. She glanced around, wishing she had something to drink. Her throat felt awfully dry. It was the fault of her damned imagination again. Conjuring visions of all the naked women Ivan must have seen, all of them wearing gold hoops through their pretty pink nipples and their labia studded with diamonds. She forced her mind to dispel the image. 'But then each to his or her own,' she managed to add lightly. She allowed her brave words to die away, realising that Ivan and Fauve were both gazing at her intently.

Thankfully, at that moment, the door opened again and a thin young man appeared. Like Fauve he was dressed all in black and his collar-length hair was as sleek and dark as his clothing. As she watched him sit next to Fauve, Danni realised that the red-headed twins were the only two people she had seen so far at the circus school who looked and sounded English. She could tell by this young man's olive complexion and his chocolatey irises that he was foreign.

Fauve smiled at the young man then turned to Danni. 'You haven't met Guido yet, have you, *ma chérie*?' she said. 'He is Italian and absolutely superb on the high wire.'

Danni thought Fauve made it sound as though being Italian and a trapeze artist was a natural combination.

'Really?' she said, reaching across Fauve to offer Guido her hand. 'Nice to meet you, Guido.'

To her delight, the young Italian didn't shake her hand but raised it to his lips. As he cast his eyes down, Danni noticed how thick and silky his lashes were. Inside she felt an envious yearning that almost overrode the flicker of desire she felt as his sulky lips caressed the back of her hand.

Suddenly, it seemed the room was filling with people. The red-headed twins were the next to arrive. They had dispensed with their overalls and were now dressed identically in loose tie-die cotton dresses that reached their ankles. Then two other men entered. Both of them wore dark blue casual trousers and light coloured shirts and both were in their late twenties, Danni estimated. One looked distinctly Scandinavian, if his colouring was anything to go by, and the other had long chestnut hair, caught at the nape of his neck in a ponytail. They also had a similar physique: fairly tall and athletic with muscular arms and shoulders, and flat stomachs that tapered to narrow hips.

Danni couldn't fail to let her interest show. As far as she could remember, there had never been a time when she had been surrounded by such exclusively beautiful people. Usually at social gatherings her lot was the fat, balding accountant, or the hairy macho type. Even the women she normally encountered were flawed in comparison to the female company present tonight. If only I could be like them, she mused ruefully to herself as Guido reached across the table to pour her a glass of wine. She nodded her thanks and was gratified to receive a wolfish smile in return. Whatever her own failings, she told herself as she raised the glass to her lips, things were definitely looking up.

Her attention was diverted by Ivan as he leaned across the space behind her chair to speak to Fauve. One of his hands rested lightly on her shoulder and she couldn't fail to pick up the enticing scent of his citrus and musk aftershave. Trying to ignore the fingers that seemed to be branding her bare skin, Danni concentrated on sipping her wine – a rich, fruity red of some kind – and pretended to study a painting of a circus horse which hung on the far wall. Despite the babble of lively chatter that circulated the table, she couldn't fail to hear what Ivan and Fauve were saying to each other.

'Who is serving dinner tonight?' Ivan asked in an undertone.

'Meah,' Fauve replied. 'She arrive from Mauritius last night. All day she sleep, now she is awake and ready for some fun.'

Danni heard Ivan's low burst of laughter. It sounded indecent somehow, as though Fauve had made a suggestive remark.

'That's good,' Ivan said, 'it seems like a long time since we last had the pleasure of Meah. What a wonderful pupil she turned out to be.'

'Ah, *absolument*,' Fauve agreed, '*mais notre petite amie*, she will appreciate such fun?'

Her words ended on a questioning note and although Danni's French wasn't all that good, she recognised enough to know Fauve had some misgivings that concerned her. A sense of intrigue mingled with that of trepidation, caused Danni's stomach to churn. Fortunately, she didn't have long to ponder her fate. At that moment the door opened again and this time a young woman she hadn't seen before entered, pushing a trolley laden with food.

Dressed in a traditional French maid's costume, with a skirt that was barely decent, the young woman had a wonderfully exotic appearance. Skin the colour of tobacco shimmered like silk over slender limbs. Her face was a beguiling heart shape in which almond eyes were set like jewels either side of a small, neat nose. Her mouth, painted a deep plum colour, was generous and bore a slight pout that Danni would come to recognise as natural. But her hair was her crowning glory in every sense: long and dark, it flowed over her shoulders and down her back like a satin sheet, the wispy ends just reaching the base of her spine.

As she reached the table with the trolley, she stood up, showing how the mass of frothy white petticoats under the black silk of her skirt barely reached the tops of her thighs.

Glancing first at Fauve and then at Ivan, she licked her plummy lips provocatively. 'Dinner is served,' she said in a thickly accented voice. She waved a slender hand over the feast. 'Please, *mesdames et messieurs*, enjoy.'

All at once the dull little room was filled with the lively chatter of cutlery on porcelain. While

Guido and Ivan began to lift the heavy dishes from the trolley and place them on the table, the maid stalked over to the fireplace on impossibly high black heels. There she picked up a silver candelabrum and brought it back to the table, where she lit the five red candles.

Moving to the far wall, she flicked off the electric light and all at once the room was cloaked in intimacy. The light from the candles and the flickering fire now cast a rosy glow over the plain white tablecloth, glinting off the heavy silver cutlery and turning the cut-crystal glasses to rainbow-hued prisms.

Already feeling light-headed from the potency of the wine on an empty stomach, Danni almost reeled from the effect. Even though it was a good seven or eight feet away and was blocked by the bodies of the twins, the fire seemed to be giving out a lot of warmth. Without realising what she was doing, Danni pulled at the front of her dress where it seemed to be sticking to her breasts.

'Interesting,' Ivan said in her ear. 'No bra.'

Yet again, Danni felt herself blushing furiously. 'I can't wear one with this dress,' she said in a deliberately casual tone. 'It's the straps.'

'Then we should all thank the good Lord for your straps,' Ivan said to her, raising his glass as if in a toast.

Disconcerted by his interest and by the way her body was betraying her – her sex moistening and sending out urgent signals – Danni lowered her eyes to her plate and pretended to become absorbed with the food in front of her. At any other time she would have been delighted by the food: a harmonious concoction of thinly sliced chicken breasts in a cream and mushroom sauce, generously laced with white wine, heaped over ribbons of garlic and herb tagliatelle. As it was, she could hardly remember tasting a thing. Ignoring the crisp green salad that was served the French way, as a second course, she reached greedily for one of the bottles of wine that seemed to be circulating freely.

'I'd go easy on that, if I were you, it's potent stuff,' an unfamiliar voice said in her ear.

Turning her head, Danni noticed that the Scandinavian was hovering by her shoulder. Ivan was talking with one of the twins, who had moved to sit next to him while they were waiting for dessert to be served, so Danni flashed the newcomer an encouraging smile.

'Dutch courage,' she said, waving the bottle. 'Are you Dutch?' She noticed, when he grinned broadly, that he had very white teeth. Instantly, the sight of them reminded her of Tam and she found herself backing off a little mentally. With his floppy blond hair, he reminded her quite a lot of Tam, she realised.

'No, Norwegian,' he said. 'My name's Randi, what's yours?'

Despite her intention to stay cool, Danni laughed. 'Danielle,' she said, 'although everyone calls me Danni.'

His eyes were the colour of denim, she noticed

as they creased up at the corners. 'Why did you laugh, Danni?' he asked.

For a moment she couldn't remember and she gazed blankly at him. 'Oh,' she said as the memory came back, 'it was your name.'

He cocked his head to one side, looking endearingly puppyish. 'Randi is a funny name?'

'It is for someone English,' the twin who had been talking to Ivan cut in from across the table. 'Mind you,' she added, giving him a frank look of appraisal, 'it suits you.'

Feeling as though she were caught up in a game of verbal tennis, Danni glanced from one to the other.

'I'm Lettie, short for Letitia,' the twin continued, shifting her gaze to Danni, 'and that's my sister Rose sitting over there talking to Aldous. Our parents were only prepared name-wise for one red-haired baby and Rose came out first, so she got the name they had chosen.'

Danni smiled at Lettie, thinking how nice and normal she seemed compared with Fauve and Ivan, even Guido and Randi. 'Do you come from around here?' she asked.

'Just up the road,' Lettie said. 'When we saw that the circus school had started up in the village me and Rose ran away from home.'

Marvelling at the sisters' daring, Danni said, 'How old were you when you ran away?'

Lettie sat back and gazed blankly up at the ceiling, giving the impression that she was counting in her head. 'We'll be twenty this August,' she said finally, reverting her gaze to Danni, 'and this'll be our second summer, so we must have been seventeen, nearly eighteen.'

All at once Danni felt quite old. She could just about remember turning twenty.

'And you, my dear Danni, how old are you?' Ivan interrupted as though he could read her thoughts.

As if a light had just been switched on inside her, Danni felt herself warming instantly again. 'Twenty-six. An old woman,' she joked. To her delight, Ivan took her hand and cradled it in his own.

'Not old, Danni,' he admonished her gently, 'but certainly old enough.'

Thrilling to the dark promise that lurked in his tone, Danni found herself once again drawn to his gaze. It was true, she told herself, she was old enough. Certainly of an age where she could stop acting like a gauche teenager and start appreciating the attentions of a charming, not to mention extremely gorgeous man.

Chapter Four

DESSERT WAS A fresh fruit salad, served in cut-glass bowls, with a generous dollop of whipped cream on top. Danni eyed the temptation put in front of her by the exotic Meah and in an unconscious gesture patted her stomach.

'Worrying about your figure?' Ivan whispered in her ear.

Glancing sideways at him, Danni gave him an abashed smile. 'I've been watching my weight lately,' she admitted, 'my boyfriend—'

'Must be an idiot if he doesn't appreciate you just the way you are,' Ivan finished for her, adding, 'You're gorgeous, every inch of you.' His smile was slow and warm as he picked up her spoon, scooped up half a strawberry and a little of the cream and held it to her lips.

Danni hesitated. She wasn't used to such blatant flattery, nor to being spoonfed by a virtual stranger. Still, she opened her mouth obediently and experienced a delicious thrill of pleasure as the succulent fruit slipped onto her tongue. As she chewed and swallowed she kept her gaze locked with Ivan's. For just that moment it seemed as though they were the only two people in the room. Everything, everyone else receded into insignificance as she felt herself drowning in his deep blue eyes. Seemingly of its own accord her body inclined towards his. She realised she would have to relax and learn to trust him, as he had suggested. Otherwise the next two weeks would be a waste of everybody's time, not to mention Fauve's generosity.

'You're too kind,' she murmured, accepting another mouthful of fruit from the proffered spoon. Her teeth clashed on the silver spoon, sending a frisson through her.

Putting down the spoon, Ivan picked up a napkin instead and dabbed at the corners of her mouth.

'Not kind,' he said, 'merely honest.' He laid the napkin back down but continued to gaze intently at her. 'I don't ever say things I don't mean.'

As Danni nodded, she acknowledged how desperately she wanted to believe him. For most of her life she had felt at a disadvantage because of her figure. In the early days of puberty her child's body had seemed to suddenly transform itself into that of a woman in one gigantic leap. Not for her a slow series of changes: the budding protuberances of breasts, the delicate fuzz of hair that gradually thickened. Overnight, it seemed, she had become a fully fledged woman.

Along with the change wrought on her had

come a host of confused emotions. Grown men started taking an interest in her, making her feel at a terrible disadvantage because her body responded in ways that her mind could not cope with. Later, when she finally ceded her virginity at the ripe old age of sixteen and a half she had immediately embarked on a sexual spree, bedding nearly every man or boy who showed an interest in her. Then had come a couple of years' remorse and near celibacy, followed by her relationship with Tam.

Now, she realised, she had never really allowed herself the luxury of proper sexual adventure and by that she meant slow seduction and true sensuality. After her early forays, she had settled for the sort of half pleasure Tam had offered. All at once she saw that her feelings for Tam had been based on gratitude. Gratitude for saving her from the twin evils of promiscuity and celibacy. Her feminine instincts told her that another kind of erotic enjoyment existed. She just hadn't discovered it yet. Somehow she recognised that perhaps Fauve and Ivan and their oddly assorted troupe held the key.

She gave Ivan a lopsided smile as he softly spoke to her again.

'I'm sorry, I didn't catch that,' she said.

His fingers stroked the length of her bare arm, the tips of them stopping at her wrist to describe small circles on the sensitive flesh there.

'I asked you where you had gone,' he said gently. 'You looked as though you were away with the fairies.'

Danni chuckled. 'I was indulging myself in a bit of introspection,' she said. Several glasses of the heady wine meant her tongue had difficulty forming the word.

'And what was your conclusion?' Ivan asked.

He looked intently at her, she noticed, as though he was genuinely interested in the workings of her psyche.

Her natural diffidence made her hesitate. 'I just came to the conclusion that I haven't really learned how to live,' she confided after a moment. 'But that stops as from now.'

She watched as his eyes darkened slightly, the pupils expanding, the colour of the irises deepening to navy. That and the wolfish curve of his lips made her feel warm and desirous. Beneath her dress she felt her breasts swelling. Glancing down, she wasn't surprised to note that her nipples were jutting unashamedly through the thin white cotton.

It was with a certain amount of relief that she saw Fauve lean across to interrupt them.

'We are talking on the subject of *la sensualité*,' she said in the husky voice that Danni envied. 'Guido claims the Italians are masters of the art.'

Beside Danni, Ivan gave a throaty chuckle. 'You would say that, wouldn't you?' He directed his words at the young Italian, who gave a knowing smirk. 'Personally, I think people of all nationalities are capable of great sensuality – even the English.'

Danni noticed how he winked broadly at the

twins. as though he knew what sort of reaction his statement would provoke.

'Pig!' Lettie retorted, 'You foreigners don't have the monopoly on sensuality. Rose and I have learned how to appreciate the finer things in life – as well you know.' The two girls shared a knowing smile which they then flashed around the table.

Only Danni felt excluded.

'Then give me six examples of a truly sensual experience,' Ivan challenged. Resting his forearms on the table, he clasped his hands together and gave the twins a defiant look as he added, 'Non-sexual.'

A whisper of admiration ran around the table but the twins apparently refused to let Ivan's challenge faze them.

'Well, let's see.' As Rose and Lettie spoke they reclined in their chairs in perfect harmony. Then they turned their faces up to study the ceiling, as though the inspiration they sought was written across it.

'Wet leaves,' Rose said, looking forward again. Her green eyes sparkled. 'Remember what it's like to walk in the woods on a crisp autumn morning? The smell of damp leaves and bracken is delicious.'

'And the scent of the earth beneath them,' Lettie added enthusiastically, 'so peaty. Oh, and the texture of it – do you remember that time we stripped off and rubbed it into our bodies, Rose?'

Danni shifted uncomfortably on her chair as she watched the young women go into raptures over the shared reminiscence. It seemed their experience went far beyond the simple strolls through the woods she had enjoyed. All at once she envied them their imaginations and their spirit. Since when would she have thought of rubbing damp earth into her naked body? Glancing hastily sideways she noticed Ivan appeared rapt.

'Go on,' he said. 'That's one.'

'Two,' the twins chorused.

'OK,' Ivan conceded, 'two then. But I still want to hear four more examples.'

Lettie giggled. 'Only four – we've got heaps.'

'The sun,' Rose chipped in suddenly. 'Glowing heat caressing your naked body.'

'Or snow,' Lettie interrupted. 'Rolling around in it in the buff last winter was wonderful.'

Rose nodded, her expression showing how much pleasure that particular recollection gave her. Then she added, 'Chocolate fondue's another one. Letting it cool a little then dripping it slowly onto breasts and thighs—'

'Then licking it off. Mmm . . .' Lettie made a noise of appreciation and licked her lips lasciviously.

Danni glanced around wildly, wondering if everyone was starting to feel as hot and uncomfortable as her. Good God, she asked herself, does everything they do involve them being naked?

'One last one,' Ivan said, appearing unperturbed by the mantle of eroticism that seemed to have descended over the small gathering.

The twins pretended to think hard, although

Danni could tell they were not short of ideas.

'Sawdust,' they said in unison, reminding everyone that they were at a circus school. 'Falling into a huge pile of it from a great height,' Lettie added.

'Don't tell me,' Danni interrupted in an ironic tone. 'You have to be naked to appreciate it.'

The silence that followed was deafening. Then Ivan turned his head slowly to look at her. 'The expression that seems most apt at this moment,' he said smoothly, 'is don't knock it until you've tried it.'

There was no censure in his voice but Danni felt as ashamed and embarrassed as if he had lashed out at her physically. Speaking without thinking was another of the things she loathed about herself.

'Excuse me,' she said hoarsely, pushing back her chair, 'I think I've probably had too much to drink. I should go to bed.'

She missed the raised eyebrows as she stumbled to her feet and made for the door. Grappling with the knob she turned it and headed left down the passageway. It was several minutes later when she realised she didn't know where the hell she was going. I'm lost, she wailed silently, leaning against the wall. Huge tears of frustration ran down her cheeks and she dashed them away angrily with the back of her hand.

'What's all this, Danni?' a familiar voice said. It came to her out of the shadows. 'There was no need to run away. We are all friends. We can take a joke without any hard feelings.'

'It just slipped out,' Danni mumbled. 'I didn't mean to be rude.'

She was relieved when Ivan stepped out of the darkness and put out a hand to stroke her hair. 'Of course you didn't,' he said. 'We understood that. It is clear you do not have a malicious bone in your body.'

A harsh laugh tore from her throat but she still managed a wobbly smile. 'I wouldn't say that exactly,' she said. 'I can be a terrible bitch.'

She glanced down at the pale carpeting beneath her feet. 'But I didn't mean to be bitchy then.'

Ivan's hand continued to stroke her hair. 'I know,' he said soothingly, 'don't worry.' His hand left her hair to trace the soft line of her jaw. Three slender fingertips tilted up her chin. 'Do you want to come back with me, or shall I escort you to your room?'

She shook her head regretfully. 'I can't face them again tonight,' she admitted in a small voice. 'I feel like an idiot. Hopefully they'll have forgotten all about it by the morning.'

Gazing deep into her eyes, he smiled. 'You can be sure of that,' he said. 'They are nice people. They don't take offence. Now,' he paused to take her arm and glance around, 'we need to go this way.'

Feeling embarrassed, Danni tried to shake his hand off. 'You don't need to take me,' she insisted, 'just point me in the right direction. Then you can go back to enjoying yourself.'

He regarded her with a quizzical expression, then said something that made her stomach turn to water. 'If you think I don't enjoy being with you, Danni, you are very much mistaken. You are the loveliest young woman I have met in a long time – outside and in,' he added emphatically. 'You are too hard on yourself and I think you have been hurt, no?'

At that moment, Danni thought, he sounded more French than Fauve. 'Yes,' she said, nodding, 'but I'll get over it. I'm almost there already.'

They began to walk down the long passageway, turning right and left at intervals. As they walked, Danni found herself confiding in Ivan about her earlier reminiscences, particularly her confusion at being transformed from a child to a woman in one fell swoop and the pain she had felt. It seemed completely natural to be talking to him in that way. She supposed it was because he was so easy to be with. To her, he wasn't a man she hardly knew but a compassionate person who offered her friendship. Although perhaps, she dared to admit to herself as they left the farmhouse and walked across the courtyard, she wouldn't mind if he offered her something more.

When they reached her room Ivan seemed in no hurry to get back to Fauve and the others. He took the key from her trembling hand and unlocked the door. Stepping into the room ahead of her, he walked to the bedside table and flicked on the lamp. The red bulb, which Danni hadn't noticed before, immediately cast a rosy glow upon the white walls and ceiling. Then he walked around the bed and switched on the other lamp.

Now the room that was bright and airy by day seemed cosy and womb-like. As Danni glanced around she couldn't help noticing how soft and inviting the bed looked. Like the rest of the room, the broderie anglaise covering was cast with a blush pink hue that beguiled her. Heedless of Ivan's presence, Danni kicked off her shoes and sat on the bed. After a moment, while he stood in the centre of the room, she reclined back on her elbows and regarded him thoughtfully. His gaze as he stared back at her was so lambent she felt her body melting. She remained unaware that her desire glowed around her, reaching out to him with ethereal arms.

'You are so beautiful, Danni,' Ivan said in a voice filled with wonder. 'If only you could see yourself as others see you.'

'Now that's a gift everyone would like to have,' she replied in a tone so light she marvelled at her capacity for sounding cool when inside she felt volcanic. Emotion churned inside her in a way that it never had before. She wanted Ivan, she realised. She wanted him to stay and talk to her some more. She wanted him to hold her, caress her, make love to her. Suddenly she shivered, thinking he must be able to see the desire in her eyes and the way her body sent out voluptuous signals.

Glancing down she noticed how far up her thighs her dress had ridden. Another inch and she would be displaying the semi-transparent whiteness of her knickers. When she looked up she noticed she had unintentionally drawn Ivan's attention to her bare legs. She kicked her feet idly, enjoying his attention.

For once, she realised, she felt completely calm and in control. It was as though she had known all along that they would reach this point sooner or later. And she thanked her lucky stars that it seemed to be sooner. The monotony of working in a stuffy office and travelling on the Tube every day seemed such a stark contrast to the sophisticated yet relaxed atmosphere around her now. It was as if the very act of enrolling in the circus school had helped her cross an invisible chasm between the mundane and the new and exciting.

'Would you like a drink?' she asked, wondering why he was still standing a few feet away from her when it was obvious that she wanted him to be much closer. Daringly, she patted the space beside her on the bed. 'If you want to sit down I'll get us something.'

'Just a soft drink,' Ivan said, moving to the bed.

As he sat down Danni got up. She felt the warmth of his gaze on her back as she opened one of the cupboards under the long dressing-table and took out a couple of glasses and one of the bottles of mineral water she had brought with her.

'That's just as well because this is all I've got,' she said with a broad smile as she held up the bottle.

He returned her smile full measure as he nodded. 'Perfect,' he said, 'just like you.'

Danni felt her cheeks dimpling with pleasure and her hand shook slightly as she poured the water. Walking back to the bed, she sat down tentatively and handed Ivan his glass.

'Cheers,' he said softly, touching his glass to hers.

They sipped in silence for a while, allowing themselves to become immersed in the mood of the late evening. The air temperature was still balmy and through the slightly open French window came the rich loamy scent of the surrounding fields and the faint bleating of sheep.

'This is idyllic,' she said, allowing her head to drop back. 'It's so peaceful here, not like London.'

'I can't imagine living in the city,' Ivan said as he put down his glass. 'There is so much pressure and the noise—' He made a disparaging sound and shook his head as if to dispel the unpleasant image.

Danni smiled. Copying Ivan, she put down her glass. Then she turned to him, the expression on her face an open invitation.

'I think I'm going to really enjoy the next couple of weeks,' she said frankly, 'and I don't just mean because of the surroundings. The people too are—' She was forced to break off suddenly as Ivan reached for her and pulled her into his arms.

That first touch of his lips as they met hers was so piquant Danni heard herself groan with longing. Wrapping her arms around his neck she pulled him to her fiercely, her passion surging. She kissed him back forcefully, her tongue darting into his mouth, thrusting and parrying with his as their lips ground together. Locked tightly together, she could feel her breasts pressing against the hard wall of his chest. All at once the thin layers of fabric between them seemed like an unwelcome barrier between pleasure and pure bliss.

Now Danni felt a real empathy with Lettie and Rose's delight at being naked. Only the sensation of her bare skin touching Ivan's, she thought, could improve on the wonder of his kiss. Scrabbling hungrily with her fingertips, she managed to pull his shirt free of his waistband and she sighed softly as her hands encountered his bare flesh. Smooth and hairless, it felt like silk under her fingertips. As she slid her palms up his back as far as she could reach, she delighted in the sensation of his hard musculature and the ridges of his spine. Her hands roamed his back feverishly while his mouth continued to press hot and wet against hers. In the next moment his fingers began raking through her hair and caressing the sensitive area of bare skin between her shoulder-blades.

Heat flared inside her, the plaintive bleating from outside now echoing her own whimpers of arousal. Please, oh yes, her mind urged. Never had the need for physical contact been so strong, she thought. She fancied she could feel him restraining himself, as though he feared he might frighten her if he were to let loose the full force of his passion.

'Don't hold back,' she murmured, pulling her mouth away from his. 'I want you, all of you.'

With a groan he pushed her away from him,

throwing her back against the bed. Taken by surprise, she fell, gasping for breath, her legs sprawling. Excitement churned inside her as she felt his hands roaming her body over the top of her skimpy dress. Her chest heaved and she felt her breasts swelling as his hands covered them.

'My God, Danni, you're gorgeous,' he said huskily, 'so ripe, so delectable.' As he spoke his fingers moulded the pliant flesh of her breasts, his palms rubbing her nipples into ardent little bullets that seemed to be forcing their way through the thin cotton.

'Suck them,' Danni cried out, her own hands pulling down the neckline of her dress. Hungrily she thrust her bared breasts into his face. 'Please, suck them.'

Darts of pure eroticism flashed through her entire body as she saw the darkly passionate look in his eyes and felt the luscious warmth of his lips as they enclosed one nipple. He sucked greedily, drawing the sensitive little nub of flesh into his mouth and lathing it with his tongue. Danni writhed against him, drawing her fingers through his long hair as he mouthed each nipple in turn.

Her dress had ridden right up over her hips by this time and as Ivan finally pulled away she noticed how his expression darkened even further as his glance swept over her body. Following his gaze she saw how flushed and swollen her breasts looked, the nipples so hard and distended it seemed they might burst at any moment. Below the wide ribbed cotton belt that had been her dress, she could see her white knickers stretched tightly across her hips. The dark blonde thatch of her pubic hair showed clearly through the gauzy fabric that clung damply to her crotch.

'My God, Danni,' Ivan said again and she marvelled at the way a man as eloquent as he could suddenly become lost for words. It thrilled her to realise that she was the reason for his loss of speech. The knowledge making her feel even more aroused.

Squirming voluptuously on the bedspread, she spread her thighs a little wider, tilting her pelvis to make him an offering of her body. Look at me, she demanded silently, take this gift and enjoy the pleasure. Although she behaved with a wantonness she had almost forgotten existed, Danni felt strangely submissive in Ivan's presence. Willing and wanting she might be, but she craved the luxury of being erotically dominated. She wanted him to take her and bend her to his will. From that point on she realised that, for as long as he desired, she would be his willing pupil and a slave to his passion.

'Do you want me?' she asked thickly, thinking, please say yes, I want you to want me.

To her relief Ivan nodded, his expression wolfish as he looked deeply into her eyes. The understanding that was transmitted silently between them was unmistakable, a pact that was sealed and remained only to be delivered.

She felt herself trembling as he glanced down and ran his palm possessively over her lower belly.

Slipping his hand between her thighs he rubbed the damp cotton against her crotch.

'Naughty,' he said, darkly. 'So innocent and yet so wet.'

Danni whimpered, feeling herself melt under the heat of her desire for him. Digging her heels into the bed she raised her hips, rubbing herself urgently against his hand. She moaned when he slipped a finger between her outer labia, pressing the thin fabric into the groove between them and caressing the sensitive flesh. A rush of warmth flooded her pelvis as she felt his fingertip stimulating her clitoris. Then shame gripped her as she felt a surge of her own juices soak into the crotch of her knickers, knowing that he would quickly discover the way her body betrayed her.

As his finger slipped lower, urging the sodden fabric into the grasping entrance of her vagina she writhed against him, moaning incoherently. The curve of his lips and the flash in his deep blue eyes were as thrilling as they were wicked.

'You are a tempting little morsel, aren't you?' he said, his fingers working inside her. 'You don't know how difficult it's been for me to resist you. I wanted you the first moment I laid eyes on you.'

Hearing the proof of his desire for her, knowing now that she hadn't imagined the charge of eroticism that had flared between them the moment they met, sent a further rush of pleasure careering through her. She answered him with a groan and churned her pelvis more anxiously, grinding herself down on his probing fingers. The crotch of her knickers was sodden now, the material slippery with her own juices as he rubbed it against her inner walls.

At that moment he hooked his fingers and, probing still further, found the sensitive place high up behind her pubic bone. As he caressed it with knowing dexterity she felt herself soaring on a great wave of pleasure. A pleasure so poignant it was almost painful in its intensity.

'Aah!' she cried, writhing against him. Almost demented with arousal she clutched at her own breasts, massaging the naked orbs urgently between her hands. Plucking at her burning nipples she felt them harden and lengthen even more.

'There is just too much of you to cope with, isn't there, sweetheart?' Ivan said softly. Withdrawing his fingers, he began to tug at the waistband of her knickers. 'Come on, my love, lift your *derrière* – I want to take these off.'

Danni raised her hips obligingly then, and after he had pulled the damp scrap of material down her legs, kicked her panties off. She didn't bother to look and see where they landed but threw herself against him, her fingers fumbling with the clasp on his belt. After a few frustrating moments she managed to work it free and unfasten his trousers. With shameful eagerness she plunged her hands into his pants and was delighted to find that he was already hugely erect.

'What a compliment,' she murmured as she smiled at him.

Her glance took in the mirror over the dressing-table on the far wall and she couldn't help noticing how wanton she looked. Her hair, which was difficult to tame at the best of times, was totally tousled, her eyes sparkled above flushed cheeks and her lips looked so swollen they lent her mouth an insolent pout that was pure sex. Wow, she thought, transfixed for a moment by the sight, even *I* fancy me.

The thought made her giggle and she noticed the questioning look on Ivan's face as he reached out to caress her naked breasts. Rolling onto her side she pressed her breasts into his hands and stroked his hard cock. Her exploring fingers told her instantly that he had been circumcised. She could feel the smoothness of his shaft, with just the slightest ridge where her fingertips encountered a swollen vein and the taut bulb of his glans. As she stroked around the rim of his glans she heard him groan softly.

'That's a very light touch you have there,' he murmured hoarsely. His glance dropped to her mouth. 'I can't help wondering how your lips would feel on the same place.'

She smiled mischievously. 'Care to find out?'

Without waiting for his answer she scrambled down the bed. As she moved he quickly divested himself of his shoes, socks and trousers until he wore just a small pair of black Calvin Klein's, above which the top of his cock reared up.

'Very impressive,' she commented impishly, without making it clear whether she meant his designer label or his erection, 'but I think I'd prefer to see all of you.'

The black pants quickly joined the pile of clothing on the floor and in the meantime Danni pulled her dress off over her head and dumped it unceremoniously on top of the heap. Then, pressing her hand lightly but insistently against his chest, she pushed him back until he lay flat on the bed. Devoid of any restriction his cock reared up, a small, glistening tear of pre-emission emerging from the tip of its bulbous head.

Kneeling between his spread thighs, Danni leaned forward, her palms positioned either side of his hips to take her weight, and flicked out her tongue to lap up the drop of viscous fluid. She was gratified to hear Ivan groan with pleasure as she flicked her tongue experimentally around his glans and then slid her wet lips up and down his rigid shaft. If there was one thing she knew she was good at, it was giving oral pleasure. Her only hope was that he would not be like Tam and decline to give her the same in return.

Just thinking that he might actually treat her to the indulgence she truly craved sent her soaring to even greater heights of eroticism. Grasping the base of his cock with one hand she covered his glans with her lips, feeding more and more of his delicious length into her mouth until she engulfed him entirely. Then she sucked just a little harder as she slid her lips up and down his shaft.

She felt the slight tug on her hair as his hands delved into the silky mass, urging her mouth lower. A moment later, as she continued to lick and suck with increasing fervour, one hand left her hair and slid over her shoulder and down to cup her dangling breast. She gasped as Ivan's fingers pinched her nipple. Then he rolled the sensitive bud between finger and thumb, sending frissons of delicious pleasure coursing through her.

The blissful sensation of pure lust swamped her as she felt his cock expand within the wet cavern of her mouth. She could sense the excitement surging through him, feel the blood pumping beneath the fragile covering of his tautly stretched skin. A moment later a warm jet of salty fluid spurted into her mouth. Although she swallowed as quickly as she could a small amount escaped her lips and dribbled down her chin. Sitting back on her heels she wiped away the glutinous trail with the back of her hand, all the time smiling at him and feeling flushed with pleasure.

She couldn't help noticing how blissful his expression was. His eyes were heavy-lidded as he gazed back at her, his body relaxed, one lean, lightly tanned leg bent at the knee. At the apex of his thighs, his cock, still erect although not looking quite as rampant as before, jutted from a well-trimmed nest of silky hair. His scrotum looked loose and heavy, the skin dark and wrinkled in comparison to the smooth hairlessness of his upper thighs.

'You're beautiful,' Danni breathed as she gazed at him in wonder. It was the first time she had ever considered a man to be more than merely handsome but in Ivan's case she felt *beautiful* was the only way to describe him. Not only was his lean physique achingly desirable but his face was arresting in its perfection. His lashes cast long shadows over finely sculpted cheekbones and just beneath them she could make out the fiery glitter of his sapphire eyes.

'No, *you're* beautiful,' he insisted, stretching out a hand to her. 'Come here.'

Leaning forward again she moved up until she was lying full length on top of him. She could feel her breasts pressing into his chest and his cock nudging her belly. A sigh of pleasure escaped her lips as he cupped the back of her head and pulled her face close to his for a deep, searching kiss. At the same time his other hand stroked her shoulders for a moment before following the length of her spine and curving over the swell of her buttocks. While he continued to kiss her he stroked her bottom, occasionally sliding his fingers between her legs to tantalise the sensitive folds of her blossoming sex.

Feeling a renewed warmth, she squirmed against him, her breath hot against his ear as she told him how aroused she was feeling.

'As if I couldn't already tell,' he said lightly as he slid a couple of fingers inside her hungry sex and scissored them insolently. 'I think it's your turn for some pleasure now.'

Chapter Five

HARDLY DARING TO hope for too much, Danni allowed Ivan to roll her over on her back. He kept his fingers inside her as he moved and with his other hand patted her thigh.

'Bend your knees, darling,' he murmured. 'That's right, open your legs wide. I want to see all of you.'

Whimpering with barely contained longing, Danni complied with his request. She felt a flush of embarrassment mingled with lust suffuse her entire body as she watched him spread her labia wide open.

'Wonderful,' he said, 'so ripe and juicy.' Glancing at her face, he licked his lips suggestively. 'With such a succulent banquet on offer, I must sample it.'

Danni felt her stomach clench at the promise underlying his words and as he lowered his head between her open thighs, she found herself holding her breath. The first touch of his lips on her inner thigh was magnificent. So tormenting in its delicacy was it that she let the breath out of her lungs on a long gasp of pleasure. For what seemed like an eternity, he continued to kiss and nibble at the soft flesh of her thighs, while the silky ends of his hair whispering across her belly and the delicate flesh of her vulva tantalised her even more.

Panting with arousal, she had no option but to allow her body to cede to the demands of his mouth. Fire licked at her from the inside, while his tongue lapped delicately at her swollen folds and flicked insolently over her clitoris. As he drew back the tiny hood of flesh that concealed the sensitive tip of her clitoris and touched it with the end of his tongue she cried out, unable to bear the exquisite torment. The dark velvet cloak of eroticism descended over her, shrouding her naked body with ill-concealed passion.

'Oh, yes. Oh, God, yes!' she moaned hoarsely as the delicious thrill of orgasm overtook her.

It burned its way through her lower body, encouraging her to writhe her hips in the agony of ecstasy. With her arms stretched wide she clutched mindlessly at the bedspread, crumpling the pristine cotton into her palms. The waves of pleasure did not peak and abate instantly, but continued. Pressing the soles of her feet into the bed she opened her legs as wide as they would go and raised her hips, urging her desperate sex against the lush, warm wetness of Ivan's mouth.

He obliged her as she instinctively knew he would, cupping her buttocks in his hands and drawing every last ounce of pleasure from her body with his lips and tongue. When at last she felt the final tremors of her multiple climax ripple through her and dissolve, all the tension seemed to leave her body. With no strength left in them, her legs sprawled carelessly on the coverlet. Her arms felt limp and lifeless, the whole of her body as languid and amorphous as melted ice cream.

'Another time I will make love to you properly,' Ivan whispered to her, 'but not tonight.'

As she started to protest, although feebly, he added, 'It is already so late and we have to be up early in the morning. Or rather today.' He glanced at his wristwatch then turned his arm and held it to her face. 'See, it is already past two o'clock.'

That late! her mind registered with some shock, wondering how the time could have passed so quickly. She nodded weakly, ceding readily to the belief that he knew what was best for her.

'Eight o'clock at the latest for breakfast,' he told her as he rose from the bed and began pulling on his clothes. 'No slacking now, especially not on your first full day. Fauve will never forgive me otherwise.'

'OK,' she murmured tiredly, 'I'll be there.'

Just before he left he bent to kiss her one last time. As he did so Danni couldn't help noticing the sweet honeyed taste of her own juices on his lips. Around his mouth the skin, which was darkly shadowed with stubble, glistened with her moisture. Smiling, she reached up and rubbed her fingers over it.

'Can't have you leaving here looking like the cat

298

that's just got the cream,' she said, chuckling softly at the image.

He smiled back at her then, his eyes still dark and heavy-lidded with latent desire. 'Really?' he asked, 'Why not? Everyone will simply recognise that I have been a very lucky man tonight.'

Glowing inside at his compliment, Danni waved feebly to him as he left through the French window, drawing it closed behind him. For a few moments she simply lay where he left her, luxuriating in the unfamiliar sensation of feeling totally replete. Then, as she felt her heated body cooling in the night air, she crawled up to the top of the bed and slipped under the comforting warmth of the quilt.

She was asleep within moments of her head sinking into the pillow.

The next day dawned too quickly for Danni at first. Then, when she realised where she was and recollected the events of the previous evening, she suddenly felt a renewed vigour. Throwing off the quilt she sprang from the bed and enjoyed the powerful jets of warm water from the shower for a few minutes until she felt fully awake. Afterwards she wrapped her hair and body in towels and went back into the bedroom where she pondered her meagre selection of clothing.

Just as she was trying to decide whether she would be better off wearing shorts or leggings there was a knock at the door. Thinking it would be Ivan, Danni flung the door open and was surprised to see the diminutive figure of Fauve standing on the threshold.

'Oh,' Danni exclaimed, clutching the towel tighter around her.

'Do not bother to explain yourself, *chérie*,' Fauve interrupted as she walked boldly past Danni into the room. 'You thought I would be Ivan, no?'

Danni had the grace to blush.

'Well, no matter,' Fauve continued with a slight touch of imperiousness, 'I just come to give you this.' From behind her back she produced a leotard. Made of stretch fabric with a satiny sheen, it had short sleeves and consisted of horizontal stripes of pale blue and pink.

For a moment Danni felt lost for words as she took the garment from Fauve. 'It's, er, lovely,' she murmured as she found herself wondering how on earth she was going to fit all of her into it, 'but I'm not all that sure if it is my size.' She tried in vain to find a label.

'Then try it on, my pet,' Fauve said reasonably as she sat down on the end of the bed.

Danni hesitated, wondering if she should go into the bathroom to change. The last thing she really wanted to do was reveal her naked body with all its imperfections to Fauve's critical gaze. Nor give the chic Frenchwoman the benefit of watching her wrestle with the tiny garment. However, Fauve looked as though she had made herself comfortable and Danni felt rooted to the spot by indecision.

'Come on, *chérie*.' Fauve urged, 'we 'ave not the

whole day. Even as we speak, our *croissants* they go cold.'

With a mental shrug, followed by a physical one, Danni allowed the towel she was wearing to fall to the floor. She was startled when she heard the sharp clap of Fauve's hands.

'Ah, my dear, what a *fantastique* figure,' the Frenchwoman exclaimed. Temporarily struck dumb, Danni just stood there and watched as Fauve stood up and walked over to her. The older woman wandered around Danni, appraising her body thoroughly and dispassionately, as though she were a mannequin in a shop window. Then she smiled warmly. 'Such hips,' she enthused, 'such a lovely round bottom.' Danni flinched as Fauve's hand stroked across her buttocks. 'Oh, and those breasts, they are *magnifique*.'

Worried that Fauve was about to touch those as well, Danni stumbled back and mumbled something about having to hurry. Bending forward she stepped into the leotard and was surprised to find how easily it slipped up her body. Still, she felt quite red-faced when she straightened up and slipped her arms into the short sleeves. When she was standing upright she realised how high the leotard was cut on the legs. Glancing down she couldn't help noticing that a generous amount of curly hair was visible either side of the deep vee that just about covered her pubis.

'I'll need to get my bikini line done before I can wear this,' she mused aloud.

To her discomfort, Fauve squatted down in front

of her and stroked the curls absently. 'Do you have a razor?' she asked, glancing up at Danni's face, which now glowed an even brighter crimson.

'A – a Ladyshave,' Danni muttered, 'in the bathroom.' As she paused to glance over her shoulder Fauve sprang to her feet.

'*Un moment*,' she said, 'I will fetch it.'

While Fauve was in the bathroom, Danni – still feeling shaky by what had just transpired – turned to look at herself in the mirror. She was surprised and pleased to note how flattering the leotard was to her figure. Somehow it seemed to emphasise the good points about her shape, namely the high roundness of her breasts and the way her waist curved in then flared out sharply again at the hips. Even her legs looked longer and more shapely. Just as she was straining to look over her shoulder to see what her bottom looked like, Fauve came back into the room brandishing the little battery-operated razor.

'*Bon*,' she said, 'we soon make you as smooth as a baby's bottom, no?' Chuckling softly she squatted down in front of Danni again and flicked the switch on the shaver.

'Oh, no, I can do it,' Danni exclaimed quickly, trying to grab the shaver from Fauve's hand.

'Shush,' the Frenchwoman said, swatting Danni's hand away as though it were a fly, 'you cannot see properly to do it. Allow me.'

Opening her mouth to protest, Danni closed it again just as quickly. What was the point? she thought. Although she was small, Fauve was certainly a force to be reckoned with. There was little to be gained by arguing. All the same, she couldn't help feeling horribly embarrassed as Fauve began to stroke the head of the shaver over her curly thatch. When she thought Fauve was finished, Danni made to walk away but the Frenchwoman stopped her with a firm hand on her upper thigh.

'A second shaving is most important,' she said, ' 'ere, feel how the skin is still a little, er—' With a typically Gallic shrug she gave Danni a questioning look.

'Bristly?' Danni suggested, touching the places that Fauve's fingertips had skimmed over.

A smile lit up Fauve's delicate face. 'Yes, bristly,' she said. She gave Danni a look of apology. 'Five years I am in your country and still I do not speak perfect English.'

'Oh, but you do,' Danni insisted, forgetting her embarrassing predicament for a moment, 'and you put me to shame, honestly. I can hardly understand a word of any other language.'

'You are too kind,' Fauve said, continuing to smile. 'Perhaps I teach you a little French while you are 'ere, yes?'

'That's nice of you to offer,' Danni replied with a sheepish smile, 'but I'm far too slow to learn another language. I just can't seem to get the hang of it.'

Fauve made a tutting sound and looked disbelieving. Then she said, 'You must not describe yourself as slow, *ma chérie*, you are beautiful and no doubt talented in other areas.'

'Well, if that's the case I don't know what they are,' Danni laughed. 'All I seem to do is manage to make a mess of things. Even last night at dinner—' She allowed her words to trail away, remembering her rude outburst.

'Ah, last night,' Fauve said, applying the shaver to Danni's almost smooth skin once again. 'We were most disappointed you went to bed early. Meah especially.'

'Why Meah?' Danni asked, feeling confused. As far as she could remember, all the young Mauritian woman had done the night before was serve the food. They hadn't even spoken to each other.

A secretive smile touched Fauve's lips. 'That girl, she provide some very good entertainment. Last night was *formidable*. So good that tonight she will serve our meal again. But this time you will stay, no?'

'Oh, yes,' Danni said, nodding enthusiastically. She couldn't help wondering what sort of entertainment Meah provided. Perhaps she was a singer or played the guitar or something.

'That is good,' Fauve replied, interrupting her thoughts. 'We, that is to say, Ivan and I, want you to get the most enjoyment from your stay 'ere.'

'Well, that's very kind of you,' Danni began. She broke off as Fauve switched off the shaver and began stroking her fingertips across the areas of smooth skin either side of her groin. 'All done now?' she forced herself to ask lightly.

She wanted to take a step back, to get away from

the feather-light caresses that, to her discomfort, felt extremely tantalising. No other woman had ever touched that part of her body before. Chaste kisses on the cheek and the occasional hug by a good friend was all she had ever experienced. And all she had ever wanted to experience.

'Gosh, I'm starving,' Danni said, moving purposefully away, 'and I really ought to comb my hair through before it dries into tangles.'

'*Mais oui*,' Fauve agreed, appearing unconcerned as she straightened up and put the shaver on the dressing-table. 'Breakfast is always served in the kitchen – you know where that is, *n'est-ce pas*?'

'Yes.' Danni nodded and unwrapped the towel from her hair. 'I shouldn't be long.'

She watched Fauve cross the room to the door and in a moment, the petite Frenchwoman was gone. Only then did Danni feel her body sag with relief.

The kitchen was deserted when Danni wandered into it about ten minutes later. Her hair was still slightly damp but looked clean and healthy as it tumbled over her shoulders in thick tawny waves. To keep her warm in the cool farmhouse and to protect her modesty, she had pulled on a pair of black leggings and a baggy cream sweatshirt over the leotard. She hoped there would not be too many people present in the circus tent when she took them off for her first lesson. The garment, although flattering, was still far too skimpy and revealing for her liking.

The pine clock on the kitchen wall showed it was almost eight o'clock already and so she abandoned her idea of a leisurely breakfast. Instead, she quickly gobbled down a delicious *pain au chocolat*, spurning the idea of a second one and settling for a banana instead. Then she washed her breakfast down with half a mug of lukewarm filter coffee.

At just a few minutes past eight, Ivan appeared at the back door. As usual he looked gorgeous, Danni thought. Today he was dressed in a pair of black athletics shorts and matching vest. Although simple, the outfit set off his tanned skin and lean physique magnificently. She wondered if he would make any comment about the night before but her hopes were quickly dashed when he rubbed his hands together briskly and asked her if she was ready to get started.

'As ready as I'll ever be,' she said, standing up. She noticed he was regarding her quizzically. 'What's the matter?' she added when he didn't say anything.

'I thought Fauve was going to find a costume for you to wear,' he said. Then he shrugged, much in the same way as Fauve had done earlier, Danni noticed. 'Ah, well, it doesn't matter.'

'She did,' Danni said, following him to the door. 'I'm wearing it underneath.'

All at once Ivan smiled at her over his shoulder and she felt her breath catch at the warmth which enveloped her instantly. To her surprise and pleasure he stopped and put out his hand. Then he

306

stroked her hair softly and cupped her chin, forcing her to meet the full impact of his gaze. Her knees felt weak and she gripped his wrist to steady herself.

'I forgot to mention – you were superb last night,' Ivan said softly as the pad of his thumb brushed over her lips. 'You are beautiful and thoroughly enjoyable.'

The effect of his words was cataclysmic. Immediately, Danni felt like ripping off her clothes and throwing him down on the kitchen floor. Instead she opened her mouth and drew in his thumb, sucking on it suggestively as her gaze remained locked with his.

Much to Danni's dismay, the 'Big Top' was already a hive of activity when she and Ivan arrived. There were quite a number of people she didn't recognise: some juggling and performing gymnastics, a couple swinging backwards and forwards on the trapeze, and a tall young man with fiery red hair, swallowing a long sword, the broad flashing blade of which he then withdrew with a flourish.

'How on earth does he do that?' Danni asked, wide-eyed.

'Relaxation of the throat,' Ivan replied simply. 'You should be good at it. I've been told it's like going down on a man.'

Danni blushed deeply, recalling the previous night and how delicious Ivan's cock had felt in her mouth.

'Well, I might give it a go then,' she said when she could speak again.

Ivan's brisk handclap shattered her reverie. 'Let's go over there and find out what else you can do already,' he suggested. He led her to one side of the circus ring where several padded mats were laid out next to each other on the floor to form a brightly coloured patchwork. 'How are you at gymnastics?' he asked.

Danni shrugged. 'I used to be able to turn cartwheels and do handstands when I was about ten years old,' she said. 'Other than that . . .'

Ivan brushed aside her doubts. 'Well, take those heavy clothes off and let's see if you can still do them,' he suggested.

Self-conscious, Danni pulled off the sweatshirt and leggings. When she straightened up she noticed Ivan was looking at her in much the same way Fauve had earlier.

'Do I look OK?' she asked tentatively as she pulled at the tight elastic that gripped her bottom and clung to her hips and groin.

'No,' Ivan said to her surprise. Then a smile lit up his face, the outer edges of his sparkling blue eyes crinkling. 'You do not look OK, Danni, you look fabulous. What a lucky man I was last night. And will be again, I hope.'

'Oh, you will,' Danni assured him, feeling her passion for him soar all over again. In a fit of elation she skipped across the layer of mats and executed three perfect cartwheels in a row. She straightened up, arms held out straight to the sides, and bounced lightly on the balls of her feet. 'I can still do them!' she cried, feeling flushed with success.

As Ivan gazed at her, noticing her bright pink cheeks, her tumbling hair and the way her breasts bounced as she moved, he had difficulty reminding himself that she was a grown woman and not a particularly precocious child. She brought out the masterful streak in him and seemed to delight in it, he recalled, thinking of the night before. When he had gone back to his room, he regretted that he had not stayed and made love to her completely. But that was just one night, he reminded himself – there were plenty of others to look forward to.

'OK, Danni,' he commanded briskly, turning his attention back to the present, 'how about those handstands you mentioned.'

To Danni's chagrin, she wasn't able to balance on her hands as easily as she had as a child. However, Ivan was patient with her and held her legs lightly until it became easier to keep her balance for longer periods of time. Finally she fell to the mats, feeling red-faced and short of breath.

'I'm knackered already,' she said, smiling up at Ivan.

'Knackered?' he asked. He squatted down beside her, his leg muscles bulging as he did so. Feeling tempted, Danni put her hand on his thigh and stroked it. His skin felt satin-smooth, the colour and texture reminding her of Belgian chocolate.

'Old English expression – you must have heard of it,' Danni said with a chuckle. 'I also feel starving again.'

Ivan laughed. 'My, my, you are a greedy thing, aren't you? Food and sex, is that all you think about?'

'I do now,' Danni replied pertly.

By lunchtime she had managed to accomplish a perfect sequence of tumbles. Under Ivan's careful instruction she learned how to perform backflips and couldn't believe how truly circus-like she felt. Sitting cross-legged on the mats she asked Ivan what other things he might teach her during her stay.

'That depends on what interests you,' he replied, 'and what is practical. Some things you cannot master in a matter of weeks.' He leaned forward and patted Danni's knee, trying not to allow his gaze to stray too obviously to her groin. When he had happened to glance there, he couldn't help noticing how the lips of her sex bulged enticingly under the tightly stretched material of her leotard. 'Let me see,' he continued. 'Can you ride a horse?'

'Sort of,' Danni said. 'I haven't ridden for a couple of years.'

'How about lion-taming?' he asked while forcing himself to keep a straight face.

Danni's eyes widened. 'Really?' she gasped. 'Do you have lions here?'

Laughing gently, he shook his head. 'No, not really,' he admitted. 'I was just teasing.'

'Pig,' she said with a broad grin. 'I always fancied having a go at that as a matter of fact. Mind

310

you,' she added, leaning forward conspiratorially and deliberately treating Ivan to a good view of her cleavage, 'I've always wanted to be a ringmaster.'

'Ah, that you cannot do,' Ivan said firmly.

Danni felt intrigued by his swift reply. 'Why not?'

He smiled. 'Because that is my job,' he said, 'I enjoy cracking the whip.'

Danni sat back and regarded him thoughtfully. I'll bet you do, she mused, surprised to feel a small quiver of excitement inside her. All at once she found herself wondering if her food had been doctored in some way, or if there was some kind of stimulant in the drinking water here at the farm. Her appetite for sex now seemed to be matched by a sudden interest in *kinky* sex. Feeling herself blush, she got quickly to her feet.

'Shouldn't we go and get some lunch now?' she said briskly as she glanced around the empty marquee. 'I can't help noticing the others went ages ago.'

Lunch was light, just salad, granary bread and fruit, although Ivan pointed out how sluggish they would all feel if they ate anything heavier.

'You may indulge yourself properly tonight at dinner,' he promised.

'It doesn't matter,' Danni said, patting her stomach and thinking how empty it still felt. 'I could do with losing some weight.'

Ivan's response was gratifying in its immediacy.

'No, you are lovely just the way you are. You wouldn't be Danni without all those delicious curves.'

Danni felt herself blushing and wondered if her inability to take a compliment was something she would ever grow out of. 'You're too kind,' she murmured, echoing Fauve's words earlier that day.

'No,' he said, taking her hand to lead her back to the circus tent, 'not kind, just truthful.'

Before their afternoon session began, Ivan asked Danni about some of the things she hoped to accomplish during her stay.

Impulsively, she said, 'Lots of things, but I've got a real urge to be able to ride a unicycle.'

She didn't know where the idea had suddenly come from. No doubt it was something she'd had locked away in her psyche since childhood, she realised. Glancing up at Ivan, she followed his movements with her eyes as he stood up and brushed away the few strands of straw that clung to his nicely rounded behind.

'No problem,' he said. 'Just give me a moment to get the necessary equipment, then I will teach you.'

He returned within moments, carrying a silver-framed unicycle with a black leather-covered seat.

'Here,' he said as he handed it to her, 'a bicycle made for one.' He paused and craned his neck to look around her. Then his face broke into a broad, crinkling smile. 'I really envy that saddle, knowing it's going to have your delicious behind resting on it.'

312

Danni's only comment was to blush profusely. He flattered her dreadfully but somehow always managed to sound completely sincere. Resting the unicycle against the blocks that edged the ring, she slipped off the elastic band which she wore around her wrist.

Scraping her hair into a high ponytail, Danni turned back to look at Ivan. She couldn't help noticing that he was staring at her with an odd expression that was halfway between amusement and desire.

'What's the matter?' she asked, trying to ignore the tightness in her chest.

To her relief he laughed aloud as he shook his head. 'Nothing,' he declared, grasping her lightly by the shoulders and gazing down at her. 'Only that you look about sixteen years old with your hair like that.'

She fluttered her eyelashes and pouted her lips coquettishly. 'Am I right in thinking you fancy me as a schoolgirl?' Glancing down to his groin, she was certain she could detect a certain tumescence there she hadn't noticed before.

'Don't tempt me like that, it's not fair,' Ivan said with a groan. 'I fancy you, as you put it, regardless of how you wear your hair. But right now I could—'

'Yes?' Danni butted in hopefully.

Instead, Ivan seemed to pull himself together. 'I could teach you how to ride the unicycle,' he said. 'Now hop on. I'll hold it steady for you.'

Steadying herself with a hand on Ivan's arm,

Danni climbed awkwardly onto the saddle. Even though Ivan was holding the back of the saddle firmly with one hand, the unicycle wobbled the moment she took her feet off the ground.

'I don't know if I'm going to be able to do this,' she said doubtfully. 'Like everything else, it's obviously harder than it looks.'

'You can ride an ordinary bicycle, can't you?' Ivan said over her shoulder.

'Yes, but this is a lot different,' she countered. 'There's a wheel missing for a start.'

'Just start pedalling,' he suggested. 'Even if you do fall off you won't hurt yourself on all this sawdust. Use your arms for balancing.'

'Like this?' Danni spread her arms out gingerly, wobbling the whole time.

'Perfect,' Ivan said encouragingly. 'Now, just pedal.'

Working her legs slowly at first, Danni started to pedal around the edge of the ring with Ivan running behind her still holding the saddle. Gradually, as she became more confident, she found her legs pistoning up and down, her speed becoming faster and faster. She used the gap in the ring wall as her marker and when she had done a second fast circuit she suddenly became aware that Ivan was standing a little way off, just watching her, with his hands on his hips. Immediately, she stopped pedalling and came to a wobbly halt. Putting down one foot to balance herself, she slid off the unicycle.

'I did it,' she cried, her face glowing with

triumph. 'I really did it, first go.'

She noticed Ivan looked as pleased as she felt and right at that moment what she most wanted to do was fling her arms around him and hug him half to death.

'Yes, you did,' he said as he planted a benevolent kiss on the top of her head. 'But you have to keep practising in order to be perfect.'

Two hours later, Danni felt as though she never wanted to ride the unicycle ever again for the rest her life. Her neck was stiff and aching, similarly her behind and her leg muscles were screaming from unaccustomed use. Also, she felt very thirsty.

'I've had it,' she complained, rubbing her saddle-sore backside. 'Could we get something to drink?'

He glanced at his watch as Danni bent forward and began to massage her thighs. 'I think we can call it a day,' he said. 'You've worked hard. I'm very proud of you.'

Although he made her feel the age he claimed she looked, Danni still felt extraordinarily pleased – and relieved that lessons were over for the day. Right at that moment she ached all over. The handstands and cartwheels she had done earlier that day had taken their toll on her body as well.

'I'm so unfit!' she wailed as she shuffled beside him back to the farmhouse. Her legs were stiffening up and there was a burning ache in her lower back.

'You'll get used to it,' Ivan said, without a hint of compassion. Then he glanced at her and added, 'I really meant what I said back there. You're proving to be an excellent pupil.'

'Well, thanks,' Danni said, trying not to look too pleased. 'Now all this excellent pupil needs is a long cold drink, a warm bath and about ten hours sleep.'

Smiling at her, Ivan glanced at the kitchen clock. 'Four hours maximum,' he said. 'Fauve wants to eat early tonight. I understand she has plans.'

Although she thought this sounded mysterious, Danni hadn't the energy to pursue the conversation. After a long drink of fresh lemonade, she made her way back to her room, bathed away her aches and pains, then fell into a deep, dreamless sleep.

Chapter Six

REVIVED BY HER sleep, Danni got up and slipped on her only other dress – loose yellow cheesecloth with buttons down the front from the deeply scooped neckline to the ankle-skimming hem. She felt a tingle of anticipation as she dressed, wondering what might happen after dinner. Hoping the evening would end up in bed with Ivan again, she switched on the bedside lamps in readiness and added judicious squirts of perfume to every erogenous zone. Satisfied that she was ready at last, she made her way to the inappropriately named Great Hall.

The same people were gathered there again: Lettie and Rose were seated either side of Randi, with Ivan next to Lettie, then Fauve on the other side of him. The only free seat was between Aldous and Guido. As Danni sat down she flashed a smile across the table at Ivan, wishing he wasn't seated quite so far away from her. The power of the smile he gave her in return nearly knocked her backwards. He was dressed in a black shirt and trousers and his hair seemed even whiter, his eyes even bluer and his skin even more tanned in contrast.

By way of a change, Fauve had ditched her usual black clothing in favour of red – a short silk shift worn with matching high-heeled sandals. Matte lipstick of exactly the same colour made her small mouth look lush and pouting. Danni felt an irrational stab of jealousy as she eyed the other woman surreptitiously. If it wasn't bad enough that she looked so chic and sexy and vibrant, she was also seated where Danni would like to be – next to Ivan – and kept touching him every other minute, it seemed.

Right now, Fauve's hand rested lightly on Ivan's shoulder and her face was animated as she leaned across him to talk to Lettie.

A moment later, Danni's disturbing thoughts were interrupted by a deep voice with an American accent.

'You look lovely tonight. Like a daffodil in full bloom.'

Danni started in surprise at the unexpected compliment. She had been so enthralled by watching Fauve's movements that everyone else in the room, apart from Ivan of course, was temporarily forgotten.

'I, oh, thank you. Thank you very much,' she gasped as she turned her head.

It was Aldous who had spoken and the first thing that struck Danni as she looked at him was the brilliance of his smile. Full pink lips stretched wide over a perfect set of teeth, the whiteness of which seemed startling against the olive canvas of his complexion. Like Ivan, he had long hair that reached past his shoulders, but his was dark and curly. She seemed to recall Ivan mentioning that Aldous was a New York Italian, which would explain both the accent and the Latin looks.

'Don't mention it,' he said reaching for his glass of wine. He paused to sip it then asked, 'How did your first day go? I saw you tumbling on the mats this morning – very impressive.'

Danni blushed and, grabbing her own glass, gulped at the wine hastily. The way he spoke made her wonder if it was her acrobatic skills he found impressive, or the sight of her jumping about in her skimpy leotard.

'Ivan's a good teacher,' she murmured.

He grinned broadly then and squeezed her upper arm lightly. 'Ah, but it's the quality of the raw material that really counts.' He leaned back and appraised Danni blatantly, in a way that made her feel instantly defensive. She wanted to wrap her arms around her body but steeled herself to resist the temptation. After a moment, Aldous nodded appreciatively. 'I'd say the raw material looks pretty damn good from where I'm sitting.'

'Thanks,' she said again, not knowing what else to say.

She cursed herself inwardly for not being sophisticated enough to accept a compliment graciously and for being unable to indulge in witty repartee. Glancing across the table she noticed that Fauve obviously had the talent she so badly lacked. The Frenchwoman had nearly everyone else in her thrall and Ivan was laughing openly and smiling at her in a way that was so intimate it made Danni's chest ache to see it.

'Fauve and Ivan are old friends,' Aldous said, following Danni's gaze.

'So I understand,' Danni answered before taking another large gulp of her wine. This evening it was a dry, crisp white. 'Have they always run the circus school together, do you know?'

'Yes, I think so.' Aldous nodded. 'As far as I understand it, they have worked together all over the world. Ivan's knife-throwing act is internationally famed but now he prefers the role of ringmaster.'

'Yes, he told me,' Danni said. 'And what about you – what do you do?'

He shrugged. 'Juggle, tame lions, walk the tightrope . . . A bit of everything really.'

Danni smiled. 'There are no lions here, are there?' she asked, already knowing the answer.

'No way,' he said, 'but jeez, there are a bundle of other things for me to do around here. Plus I handle all the choreography.'

'Choreography – what for?' Danni asked.

'The shows,' Aldous replied, giving her a vaguely curious look. 'Every special show is choreographed. They are more like modern ballet than circus performances. Artistic – you know. Basically, the movements need to be smooth and sequential.

And erotic, of course.'

Danni felt her stomach do a backflip of its own. 'In what way do you mean erotic?' She was surprised when Aldous made a sort of growling noise. Then she saw he was laughing.

'I can't believe you just asked that,' he said. When he saw that Danni's blank look meant she truly didn't understand, he added, 'What do you think *Cirque Erotique* means?'

'I don't know,' Danni began, but immediately comprehension dawned and she added, 'Although I think I'm just beginning to get the picture.' Swallowing the rest of her wine she nodded as Aldous picked up the bottle and made to refill her glass. 'Thanks,' she muttered. She took another gulp just to calm her churning stomach, then said, 'Do I take it that everyone involved does – well – erotic things as part of the performance?'

'Got it in one, sweetpea,' Aldous said.

Despite her growing anxiety, Danni couldn't help asking, 'What sort of things?'

'Sensual things,' he replied. 'Caressing, stroking, generally giving each other pleasure. Then there's a grand finale where everyone gets involved with everyone else.'

'In front of an audience?' Danni asked, unable to believe what she was hearing. The quick shake of his head that she was hoping for didn't materialise. Instead, to her dismay, he nodded.

'Oh, don't worry,' he said airily. 'The audience don't walk in off the streets. They're all carefully vetted by Fauve and Ivan. Some of them travel thousands of miles just to see the spectacle.'

Danni felt as though her head was floating a long way above her shoulders. What Aldous was suggesting seemed like part of a bad dream. In a moment she would wake up and Ivan would be beside her, telling her that *Cirque Erotique* was simply an ordinary circus, just like any other.

With hope in her heart she glanced across the table at the man she so desperately needed to talk to. Unfortunately, he was deeply involved in a discussion with Randi. By the gestures he was making, it looked as though he were describing some sort of acrobatic sequence.

'OK, Aldous,' Danni said after fortifying herself with another gulp of wine, 'tell me what all the other people here do. And how come there were so many people in the circus tent today that aren't here tonight? I don't really understand the set-up.' She shifted uncomfortably in her seat as Aldous slipped his arm across the back of her chair.

He leaned towards her conspiratorially. 'First of all,' he said, 'call me Al. Second of all, everyone here is either instructing or being instructed by someone else.' He glanced across the table then back at Danni. 'Lettie is instructing Randi, Rose is instructing Guido and I am instructing Meah, who's just come back for the second time around. You know Ivan is your instructor, which just leaves Fauve to handle all the administration and stuff. She and Ivan take it in turns to instruct. It's always boy-girl you see.'

'And the others?' Danni prompted as she tried

to assimilate what Aldous, or rather Al, was telling her.

'Experienced performers, sweetpea,' he said. His arm moved from the back of the chair to drape lightly around her shoulders. 'They choose to live either on the farm, or outside in one of the surrounding villages.'

'And do they take part in the special performances?'

He smiled. 'Some, not all. It depends how many people are needed and if there is a broad enough range of skills. It is still a circus performance when all said and done, just with the erotic slant, that's all.'

That's all! Danni thought, wondering how quickly she could pack and get away from there. Her hopes for a wonderful couple of weeks had taken a nosedive. Wasn't it typical? Just when she'd finally got up the courage to do something entirely for herself. And found a man she really fancied . . .

When she glanced up she was surprised to see Ivan gazing at her across the table. He knows, she thought wildly, feeling stupid for believing he could read her mind, yet believing it all the same.

Feeling like a condemned woman, she ate a hearty meal. In all honesty, she thought as she speared a tiny Jersey potato with her fork, the food was too good to ignore. Tender spring lamb heavily flavoured with garlic was served with new potatoes cooked in their skins, a medley of wild mushrooms and a crisp green salad. She washed down the excellent meal with copious amounts of Chardonnay – having made a point of looking at the label on the bottle nearest to her, just so she knew exactly what she was getting drunk on.

All the way through the meal she was aware of Ivan's gaze upon her. He watched her cut her meat – the knife sliding through it like butter – raise her fork to her mouth, chew, swallow, sip some wine . . .

Don't keep looking at me, she willed him silently. Despite her best intentions her body seemed intent on betraying her. There was a warmth in her pelvis that was achingly familiar, as was the tiny pulse of her clitoris which beat insistently. There was no way of ignoring her body's responses to him. And no way of denying her intention to get him back into her bed that night.

There was something so sensuous about his gaze. Like a caress, it warmed and tantalised her body. She could feel it, like fingers, sliding under the flimsy lace of her bra and stroking her breasts. Down over her stomach it slithered, touching, teasing, energising her flesh. All her nerve endings were tingling. The moisture flowed freely from her body to soak the crotch of her cream satin and lace knickers. She closed her eyes trying to block out the image of his lambent gaze. Don't, she prayed silently again, don't just look at me, touch me . . .

The fingers stroking the nape of her neck came as a blessed relief. Was it Ivan? Turning her head she was surprised to see not the object of her desire but Fauve, looking secretive and excited all at once. Glancing back, Danni noticed that Ivan was still sitting across the table from her. Only he was no longer looking at her but in deep discussion with Guido. It shocked Danni to realise that she hadn't exchanged a single word with the nice young Italian, let alone noticed him move from her side.

Fauve took the seat that Guido had vacated. She smoothed her fingertips along the length of Danni's arm, the tips of her nails scraping lightly down the outside of Danni's breast.

'Ready for dessert?' the Frenchwoman asked.

Danni swallowed, feeling her throat go dry and her head swim. It wasn't just the wine having that effect on her, she realised with a jolt of surprise – she was actually enjoying Fauve's innocent caress. The Frenchwoman's light floral scent filled her nostrils and she was surprised to notice how easily she detected the faint undertone of feminine musk. Whether it was Fauve's or her own she couldn't be sure but the aroma tantalised her, flickering around the sensitive membranes of her nostrils and flooding her head.

Gradually, the smell of sex and the heat of it enveloped her.

'What is for dessert?' she managed to blurt out.

She couldn't help noticing how Fauve's liquid brown eyes darkened as she replied, 'The most succulent fruits imaginable.'

As if on cue, Meah reappeared. Danni glanced at her without surprise. It was as though she knew all along what was about to happen and was party to all the secrets contained within the sensual philosophy of *Cirque Erotique*.

Looking even more exotic than the evening before, Meah's eyes sparkled and her full mouth glistened under a coat of plum-coloured lipstick. Expertly smudged kohl rimmed her almond-shaped eyes, making them seem even darker and more shadowed, above which her sable brows were plucked into fine arches. Glancing over the young woman, Danni couldn't help noticing how curvaceous her figure seemed in the black and white maid's uniform. The mass of white petticoats frothed over the tops of endless black-stockinged legs and the frilled neckline showed a generous amount of dusky cleavage. In contrast to her voluptuous appearance, her glossy dark hair was tonight pinned up in an elegant chignon and she wore a pair of diamanté earrings to match the collar encircling her slender throat.

'Over here, Meah,' Fauve ordered softly, crooking a finger.

The young woman seemed to glide across the room, her grace unimpeded by the four-inch black patent stilettoes she wore. Fauve moved her chair back from the table and turned it slightly, motioning for Danni to do the same. In the gap between them Meah stood motionless. Her demeanour was submissive as she clasped her hands in front of her and lowered her gaze.

Danni glanced at the young woman, then turned her attention to the other occupants of the room. The atmosphere was electric. Everyone seemed to be watching, waiting for something to happen. Erotic tension gripped her as she caught the flash of Ivan's smile. There was something knowing in his eyes and just the merest suggestion of assurance. It was as though his sultry gaze conveyed the message, 'Enjoy this for now but don't forget what you have to come later.'

All at once, Danni realised that being given licence to enjoy herself, to let herself go, was exactly what she needed. She wanted to please Ivan and please herself. There was nothing to fear. Even the unknown held a beguiling promise.

Tearing her gaze away from Ivan's with difficulty, Danni noticed that Fauve was stroking Meah's thigh. The Frenchwoman's fingernails – tonight painted a glossy red to match her outfit – skimmed lightly over the dark welt of stocking top and scratched the olive skin above. Up and down her fingertips travelled. It mesmerised Danni, who felt her own body responding as if it were she who was being touched.

'Raise your skirts,' Fauve murmured to Meah.

Danni felt her breath catch as, unhesitatingly but with provocative slowness, the young woman gathered the froth of petticoats in her slender hands and lifted the front of her dress.

A triangle of glossy dark hair showed. Perfectly trimmed, it concealed the womanly pouch of flesh beneath. Meah stood perfectly still as Fauve reached out and stroked the curls covering the young woman's mound. The red fingernails raked through them, pulling and parting.

Gradually Danni became aware that Meah was breathing heavily. Her eyes were heavy-lidded, she noticed as she glanced up at the young woman's face. And her plummy lips were wet and slightly parted.

Moving her hand away from Meah's pubis, Fauve patted her on the top of the thigh. 'Go and show the others, Meah,' she commanded gently. 'You know they're waiting.'

Dry-mouthed with anticipation, Danni watched the young woman move away. Still keeping her dress raised at the front, she walked around the back of Danni's chair and stood in front of Al.

'Lovely, sweetpea,' he said in an appreciative tone.

He slid the palm of his hand over her glossy thatch. Then his middle finger burrowed into it, sliding into the crevice between Meah's outer labia.

With a sense of disbelief at what she was witnessing, Danni watched his finger stroking up and down. Crossing her legs she clenched her thighs together, anxious to quell the dull throbbing of her clitoris. There was no need to draw her eyes away from the hypnotic movement of Al's finger to glance at Meah's face. She could feel the young woman's excitement. Heat mingled with erotic yearning emanated from her in waves. And the scent of her arousal was unmistakable.

Danni felt a rush of her own moisture and ached to put her hand between her legs. Her breasts swelled beneath the tight confines of her bra and she had difficulty in controlling her breathing. Putting up a hand to her forehead, she wiped away a few trickles of perspiration.

The next thing she knew, Ivan was by her side. Squatting down between Danni and Meah, he hardly glanced at the exotic young woman but turned his full attention to Danni.

'Feeling warm, darling?' he asked as he slid his hand along her leg, from hip to knee.

She looked down at his hand as it rested there and, involuntarily it seemed, her crossed legs slid apart. Almost in a trance, she watched as his fingers worked the material of her long dress up her leg to expose her bare thigh. Then his hand caressed her, squeezing and massaging the warm silky flesh he had uncovered.

'I, I—' Danni gasped, feeling lost for words.

'Don't fight it, darling,' he murmured. 'We're all friends here. Everyone just wants you to have a good time, however much or as little as that may mean.'

'I don't want to make a fool of myself again,' Danni admitted in a hoarse whisper.

Ivan resisted the urge to laugh, knowing that it would be inappropriate when Danni looked so bewildered. Coming to terms with one's own erotic desires was not something to be taken lightly. He remembered his own early experiences only too well and empathised completely with the lovely woman by his side.

'There is no right and wrong when it comes to sensual discovery,' he said gently. 'At least not among consenting adults. Wickedness is the denial of pleasure, not the exploration of it.'

'I wish I could believe that,' Danni answered.

Her cheeks felt flushed with shame and confusion. She noticed how Ivan's fingers had started to describe small circles on the inside of her thigh, just above her knee. His caress was so chaste and felt so achingly delicious that Danni wondered why she felt she should be stopping him. What if his hand moved higher up her thigh? she asked herself, would that make a difference? In her heart of hearts she knew it wouldn't. She trusted Ivan and felt confident that he wouldn't push her, or do anything which he knew would embarrass her in front of the others.

Danni's inner conflict was apparent on her face, Ivan noticed. Yet he sensed how her resolve not to enjoy herself was weakening.

'Just go with the flow, Danni,' he said. 'Don't push it but don't fight it either. Simply take each moment as it comes.' It was then he turned his head and glanced at Meah. 'Look at her,' he continued. 'I mean really look. Does she seem as though she's hating the attention she's receiving?'

Against her better judgement, Danni looked. To her surprise she noticed that Lettie had taken Al's seat and it was her hand that now caressed the dark triangle of curls. Fauve was standing behind Meah, stroking her throat below the diamanté collar. Meah's head was thrown back, touching Fauve's shoulder and the expression on her face was one of pure bliss.

A tight knot of erotic tension gripped Danni as she watched, enthralled. Fauve's hands slid lower, palms flat, her fingertips inching under the frilled neckline. Meah arched her back more and Danni could see Fauve's hands working beneath the black satin, her fingers flexing as she massaged Meah's breasts.

'Oh, God!' Danni heard the gasp and wondered for a moment where it came from. But as Ivan's grip intensified on her thigh and she heard him whisper, 'It's OK, Danni, just let yourself go,' she realised the exclamation had come from her own mouth.

She gazed at him, though her glazed eyes hardly registered his features. The temperature surrounding her seemed so warm all of a sudden that the thin dress she was wearing stuck to her and seemed like an encumbrance. With trembling fingers she unfastened the top couple of buttons and blew down the front of her dress.

Beside her she could hear Meah panting and whimpering. The young woman had spread her legs wider apart and now she was teetering on the high heels, her legs trembling so hard Danni could see the muscles quivering. Her pelvis was thrust forward, Lettie's fingers working between her legs.

'Let's see that naughty little clitoris, shall we?' Lettie murmured, parting Meah's outer labia.

To Danni, the intimate flesh thus exposed looked red and swollen, the folds glistening with Meah's own juices. The young woman shuddered as Lettie plunged a finger into the hungry wetness of her vagina and slicked another trail of moisture over her inner folds. She took care to coat the swelling bud of Meah's clitoris, Danni noticed, rubbing her finger around and over it in tight little circles.

Knowing how good it must feel, Danni sensed her own clitoris responding. She could feel her sex swelling and becoming wetter. The crotch of her knickers was saturated and she could feel her clitoris throbbing mercilessly. The temptation to grab Ivan's hand and put it between her legs was overwhelming. She turned to him with an anguished expression, hoping he could read the unspoken message in her eyes.

'Feeling a little horny, are we, sweetpea?' The runny-honey tones of Al's voice touched her ear and she noticed that Ivan was standing up, to be replaced by Al.

Not you, she wanted to cry, I want Ivan! But the object of her desire was already moving away, leaving her with a lascivious wink and the mouthed words, 'Later, darling.' Her body cried out to him not to leave her. It seemed cruel but she couldn't help wondering, in the next instant, if he was trying to tell her something. Perhaps he thought she was growing too dependent on him already.

Stop it! she told herself sharply, you are a grown woman with no ties. No one is here to judge you, why not just make the most of what's on offer? Realising she may never get an opportunity like this again, or at least not for a long time, she resolved to try and loosen up. Just to help ease her inhibitions she reached for her wine-glass.

'I'm not sure if I'm cut out for this kind of thing,' she admitted to Al, who was now squatting by her side where Ivan had been moments before.

He smiled warmly, his hand mirroring Ivan's caress on her thigh. 'Sure you are, sweetpea,' he assured her. 'Everyone is if they bother to explore their needs properly.'

She shook her head, noticing how fuzzy it felt. 'But that's the trouble, I don't know what my needs are. Not really.'

'Do you need an orgasm?' he asked, shocking her.

Danni knew her cheeks had turned pink. Full of shame, she nodded. Her breath caught as she felt his hand sliding over her thigh, delving under her dress.

'You're wet,' he commented, as if she didn't know. He put a finger to her lips as she opened her mouth to reply.

Moaning quietly, Danni felt his fingertips brushing her inner thigh. They touched the cream lace covering her mound and slid over the wet satin clinging to her crotch. The fingertips eased under the satin to stroke the blossoming lips of her sex. Groaning, Danni clutched at the edge of the table with one hand and with the other raised the wine-glass to her lips and tipped the contents down her throat.

She put the glass down shakily, wishing she could have a refill. Alcohol was not ideal but at that moment she would have been grateful for anything which could dull the burning waves of eroticism that were sweeping through her body. Her nipples felt as though they were on fire. They chafed uncomfortably against the cream lace of her bra and without thinking she tried to adjust it, pulling at the strip of satin which linked the cups. As she tugged, the front fastening sprang undone. The relief was exquisite. Her breasts felt liberated, though the hard buttons of her nipples now rubbed against the cheesecloth dress, their outline clearly visible through the thin fabric.

'Go with it, sweetpea,' Al urged as his fingers stroked her sex.

He reached down with his other hand and began unbuttoning her dress from the hem upwards.

Stop it! Danni wanted to cry out. Her hand fluttered to his wrist and tried ineffectually to stop him. Instead, she found her fingers moving away from his wrist and sliding over her belly to her groin. She could feel the movement and breadth of his fingertips under the damp scrap of satin as they stroked her clitoris and the rim of her vagina.

Her flesh seemed hypersensitive. The warmth and wetness emanating from the pouch of flesh between her legs was unmistakable. The tropical sensation of her arousal transmitted itself to her fingertips, encouraging her to slide her hand up over her torso to cup one of her breasts. Under the thin cotton she could feel its roundness and its weight. The nipple was hard and swollen, the

334

sensitive bud becoming even more aroused as she rubbed her palm over it.

All at once, it seemed, her senses were alive and flooded with inspiration. Although Al's body partially blocked her view she could see that Meah was having a good time. With legs spread wide she was enjoying the oral attentions of Lettie, while Fauve had somehow released her breasts from the tight confines of her dress. Full and olive-skinned they filled the Frenchwoman's tiny hands, the nipples and surrounding areolae as sweetly enticing as chocolate buttons.

As she gazed at them Danni was surprised to feel a rush of desire. She wanted to take those nipples between her lips and lathe them with her tongue. Somehow she imagined that they would taste as delicious as they looked and she found herself longing to give another woman the sort of pleasure that she herself enjoyed.

To Danni's surprise, Rose came up behind her. The young woman's hands slid down the sides of Danni's neck to ease the loosened neckline of her dress over her shoulders. As the young woman caressed her bared shoulders Danni couldn't help marvelling at the delicacy of her touch. Light and feminine, Rose's fingers with their short rounded nails skimmed over the golden brown skin which lay like sculpted satin over the upper swell of Danni's breasts.

The whimper that escaped Danni's lips was unstoppable. She felt a tremendous surging excitement that at the same time seemed limitless. There was no rush to take her pleasure, she realised, relaxing further into the chair and spreading her legs wider. True sensuality had no respect for the passing of time.

Where do I get all these ideas? She wondered at that moment. Was it really the case that *Cirque Erotique* had already begun to work its magic on her? Could it happen that quickly, or was this merely an expression of her true desires? Desires that had, without her knowing it, been sublimated beneath the outer mantle of duty and the code of ethics that had been taught to her. Normal, wasn't that what she was? If so, what was normal?

A moment later Ivan came back to her. He stood by her right shoulder. Danni felt a sense of relief and watched as he bent over her. His breath was warm on her bare shoulder as he kissed it and lathed his tongue over her burning skin. Between her legs she could feel her vulva responding to Al's touch, her vagina welcoming the intrusion of his fingers eagerly, her clitoris swelling under the practised manipulation by his thumb.

'I'm proud of you, Danni,' Ivan murmured quietly to her, 'you seem to be really enjoying yourself.'

In answer, Danni moaned and arched her back. Touch me, her body screamed. Ivan, Al, Rose, anyone – just touch me!

Danni heard the harsh cry of Meah's orgasm and felt her own body respond. Her clitoris pulsed hard. Her vagina, wet and stretched wide open by Al's broad probing fingers, spasmed and grasped at the digits inside her. One breast was enfolded by the delicate softness of Rose's hand, the other by the familiar palm of Ivan. Unknown fingers plucked at the remaining buttons on her dress, the material drawn back to expose her scantily clad body. Her breasts were bared, her vulva only just concealed by the damp scrap of cream lace and satin.

Rose and Ivan took their hands away from her breasts simultaneously, each of them moving so that they could lean over her.

Glancing down through eyes heavy-lidded with arousal, Danni saw her own torso, curvaceous and golden brown. Her breasts looked full and ripe, the nipples swollen and hard like underripe cherries. The kneeling figure of Al was all but blocked out by Rose's slight frame but Danni could feel him. Oh God, could she feel him. He knew the workings of a woman's body, she realised as she felt the pad of his thumb caressing her clitoris in maddeningly tantalising circles.

The moment she felt her nipples being enclosed by the warm, sucking mouths of Rose and Ivan, Danni felt her body go into a spasm of lust. It oozed outwards from her solar plexus in continuous waves of warmth. Abandoning all shame, she cried out and ground her sex ardently against Al's fingers. A strong spear of heat shot up inside her and exploded. Behind her closed eyelids she saw white lights. Every part of her body seemed gripped in the poignancy of sensual abandon.

She came back down to earth shakily and with a

flutter of shame at having let herself go so easily.

'You are beautiful, *chérie*,' Fauve said, surprising Danni with a kiss on the cheek and a deft stroke of her elegant hand over Danni's left breast. She tweaked the stiff nipple and smiled warmly. 'Tomorrow night you will enjoy even more, yes?'

Tomorrow night? The prospect seemed tantalising. But there was still the rest of this night to consider and Danni hoped fervently that Ivan wouldn't assume that she was already satisfied.

She needn't have worried, she realised, as he bent to whisper salacious promises in her ear.

'Come,' he said, taking her hand and helping her to rise to her feet. 'I will take you back to your room.' Danni wobbled unsteadily as she stood up. With a docile air she waited as Ivan fastened her bra, wrapped her dress around her again and fastened most of the buttons. 'You'll do,' he said with a smile. He patted her bottom indulgently and took her hand again. Then he commanded softly, 'Bed, young lady.'

Chapter Seven

IN SHARP CONTRAST to the orgiastic nature of the evening, the couple of hours that Danni spent with Ivan afterwards were as intimate and seductive as they could possibly have been. And it came as no surprise to Danni that he turned out to be a incredible and tender lover.

He took his time to undress her, kissing every minute portion of her flesh as he exposed it. Then when he finally made love to her he did so gently, urging her to lie back on the bed before sliding smoothly into her.

She was so aroused that her body was a wet and willing vessel. As soon as she felt the delicious length of his cock enter her, she wrapped her legs around his waist and urged her pelvis to match him thrust for thrust.

As he moved inside her, he raised her arms over her head and pinned them there with one hand, his grip light but firm. It was this that disintegrated the last of Danni's inhibitions. Her last vestige of reserve turned to voluptuousness as she moved beneath him. To cede control to him was a delicious luxury. He would give her pleasure, *was* giving her pleasure, lots of it. If she learned nothing else during her stay at the circus school she would know from now on exactly how much of a sexual, sensual woman she was.

Sunlight streamed through the thin silk curtains at the bedroom window, casting a diffused golden light over its stark whiteness. Luxuriating in the warmth and the contentment she felt from her new experiences, Danni lay on her back and gazed up at the delicate canopy above her. This is not a dream, she told herself for the umpteenth time since she had woken up that morning. Incredible as it seems this is all real and this – she paused in her thoughts to stroke a hand voluptuously over her naked breasts – is the real me.

The coming day stretched out before her full of promise. She was going to ask Ivan if he would let her try the trapeze. The wonderful, confident feeling that enveloped her made her sure of her own capabilities. And if she proved to be a failure on the trapeze? Well, she would just try something else.

Instead of leaping from the bed with her usual exuberance, she slid gracefully from it. She intended to make a conscious effort to behave in a more sophisticated fashion. *Sensual woman* was her key phrase. The one that she hoped would eventually prove to be an apt description of her. Character traits such as *scatterbrained* and *impetuous* would now be anathema to her personality. She would be elegant. She would be serene. And above all, she would be supremely, sublimely erotic.

Skipping breakfast, she went straight to the marquee behind the farmhouse. There she found Rose, Lettie, Randi and Guido already hard at work. Lettie was teaching Randi how to juggle a set of brightly coloured hoops, while way above their heads Rose was shouting instructions to Guido who swung on the trapeze.

'Ready to work, little one?' Ivan said, coming to stand beside her.

Turning her head slowly – gracefully does it, she reminded herself – Danni smiled at him.

'As ready as I'll ever be.'

He stroked a finger along her arm. 'Sleep well?'

Her smile broadened. 'Like a top. And talking of big tops, I wouldn't mind having a go up there.'

Ivan followed her gaze to the small platform way up near the roof of the tent where Rose was waiting for Guido. As Danni and Ivan watched, the young Italian swung up to the platform and grasped the ladder rail. Rose caught the trapeze and secured it with a rope as Guido climbed off.

Danni noticed Ivan flash her a curious look. 'Are you sure you feel ready for that, Danni?' he asked, 'I don't want you to rush things and risk scaring yourself.'

'I'm not frightened,' she insisted. 'I'm dying to have a go.'

She was displaying more bravado than she felt.

Behind her ribs her heart was thumping and her stomach felt knotted up with anxiety just at the thought of climbing the ladder. Nevertheless, after Rose and Guido had descended, at Ivan's instruction she started to climb.

It was important to take it one step at a time and keep looking up, Danni told herself. She chuckled softly to herself. Somehow, it seemed an appropriate course of action for her to follow regardless of whether she was on the ladder or with both feet safely on the ground.

'Nearly there, Danni,' Ivan said encouragingly from below her.

Danni blushed when she realised what a wonderful view he must be getting. To her surprise, that morning she had discovered a small pile of freshly laundered clothes on her dressing-table. These included her leotard which, despite her missing breakfast, was still much too tight and revealing. Now she was aware of the way her bottom and hips bulged and was certain that the clinging fabric showed the outline of her vulva and the groove between her buttocks to perfection.

Unable to resist it, she called down, 'Enjoying the view?'

Ivan's deep, throaty chuckle was immediate. 'I'd be lying if I said I wasn't.'

When Danni finally reached the small platform she waited for Ivan to join her. Risking a glance down, she watched the top of his white-blond head rise up, closely followed by his shoulders and then the rest of him. Once again he was wearing black shorts and vest and looked superbly lean and athletic. Feeling the tightness in her stomach turn to melting warmth as she looked at him, she couldn't help putting a hand on his forearm. It was lightly furred with hair so fair it was almost invisible and the muscles were hard and well-defined beneath the toasted brown skin.

'Don't look down until you feel fully confident,' he told her.

Danni laughed nervously. 'I wasn't going to. I was just looking at you.'

Now she was up where she had wanted to be she wished she was back on the ground. The space separating their platform from the one on the other side of the ring seemed vast – unbridgeable.

Picking up a broad leather belt attached to an elasticated rope, Ivan told her to hold her arms out to the sides.

'You look worried,' he murmured gently. 'Here, let's put this on you. It should make you feel a lot more secure.'

She glanced at the band of brown leather and then up at his face. 'What is it?'

'A safety lunge,' he said, fastening the belt around her waist. 'Although the net would break your fall this is additional precaution. It's especially useful for complete beginners.'

Feeling grateful to him, Danni stood obediently with her arms held out. As he put his arms around her to circle her waist with the belt she breathed in his special scent and luxuriated in the warmth and masculinity emanating from him.

'Could you imagine having sex up here?' she joked as she considered the improbability of achieving such a feat.

Ivan glanced at her face as he straightened up. A wolfish smile touched his lips and his blue eyes glittered. 'It *is* possible,' he said, sounding mysterious and full of promise all at once.

He's done it already! Danni realised straight away. To her surprise she found that she didn't feel any twinge of possessive jealousy, only curiosity. Not to mention excitement at the possibility of trying it for herself.

'Later then,' she said boldly, 'once I've got my bearings a bit.'

Ivan laughed and he slapped her buttocks lightly as he turned her around to face the trapeze. 'My, my, you are becoming adventurous,' he said.

'Of course,' Danni replied, tossing her head with feigned aplomb, 'I intend to become the original daring young woman on the flying trapeze.'

Ivan smiled. 'That wasn't what I meant.'

She was delighted when Ivan put his arms around her. He squeezed her waist, then slid the palm of one hand up her torso to cover her breast. He held her against him tightly, her back pressing against the hard wall of his body. Danni sighed with pleasure. She could feel an unmistakable tumescence nudging her buttocks. Then his other hand slid down her body to press against her belly, his fingertips cupping her pubis.

His breath was warm on her neck as he bent his head to kiss her there. He nibbled her shoulder and

Danni sighed again, pressing herself back harder against him. Squirming her hips, she rubbed her bottom deliberately against his erection.

'Later, Danni,' he groaned, his fingers massaging her breasts and sex, 'I promise you, tonight it will be just us.'

Thrilled at the prospect, Danni turned her head and offered her mouth to his. Their kiss was deep and passionate, kindling a fire deep inside her.

With obvious reluctance, Ivan relaxed his hold around her. 'Come on,' he said gruffly, 'we should start your first lesson.' Untying the rope that tethered the trapeze to the ladder, he held the bar steady so that Danni could climb onto it. 'Just treat it like a children's swing,' he advised her. 'You saw what Guido was doing?'

Danni nodded dumbly. Her whole body was trembling as she sat gingerly on the narrow bar. Reaching out, she held on to the sides of the trapeze with both hands and watched as the blood drained quickly from her knuckles.

'Relax,' Ivan urged, 'this is no worse than a fairground ride.'

'I hate fairs,' Danni muttered. 'The rides scare me to death and so does this.'

Ivan pursed his lips, though his eyes were smiling. 'In that case,' he said, 'I'd better be cruel to be kind.' With that he pushed Danni away from him and before she knew what was happening, she was swinging in mid-air. 'Work your legs and body,' he called to her. 'That's right, backwards and forwards. Go on, keep it up, you're doing it.'

As she huffed and puffed, trying to work up some impetus, she suddenly felt as though she were flying. The relief and sense of freedom it gave her were indescribable. Up there, way above the circus ring, with the white canvas roof just a little way above her head, she felt as though she and the trapeze were one. Swooping back and forth, faster and faster, her body and limbs moved like pistons and she had the overwhelming sensation of being truly free and capable of anything.

She glanced over her shoulder at Ivan's smiling face and returned his smile broadly and confidently. A moment later she risked a glance down. Everything below her swam. She could see people moving about on the ground. The orange mesh of the safety net became a blur. For a moment her arms and legs stopped working and she felt frozen by panic. The trapeze, having lost its motivation, wobbled. Consequently Danni wobbled with it. Her palms, damp with perspiration lost their grip. Then she was falling . . . down and down . . .

Like a bungee, the safety lunge reached its limit then slackened. Her body jerked upwards and as she bounced up and down on the end of the lunge she felt as limp and helpless as a rag doll.

From somewhere above her head she heard Ivan shout, 'Hold on, I'm coming down.'

If she hadn't been so shocked by what was happening, she might have laughed. Hold on – to what? She was suspended in mid-air by a length of elastic. What did he think she was going to do apart from dangle?

Rose and Lettie joined Ivan as he climbed onto the net and reached up to unfasten the safety lunge around Danni's waist.

'Just drop into my arms,' Ivan instructed as Rose unfastened the last buckle.

Danni did as she was told, dropping like a dead weight into Ivan's outstretched arms and causing him to topple backwards into the net. They lay in a tangled heap of arms and legs, Danni crying with relief and also embarrassment at having fallen from the trapeze.

'I mucked it all up,' she wailed, gulping back her sobs.

Ivan's hand was soothing as it stroked her hair. 'Rubbish,' he said firmly. 'Everyone takes a tumble at one time or another.'

Through wet lashes, Danni gazed at him.

'Even you?'

His smile warmed her and he nodded gently. 'Yes,' he said, kissing her forehead. 'Even me.'

It didn't take Danni long to get her equilibrium back and by lunchtime she was quite ready to join the jolly group gathered around the kitchen table. To her surprise she found that she was starving. Temporarily forgetting about her desire to achieve a figure as sylph-like as Fauve's, she tucked into the simple meal of ham, granary bread and salad with gusto.

Lettie and Rose were quick to reassure Danni about her acrobatic abilities, insisting that they had both been terrible on the trapeze at first.

'I won't go up there now unless I have to,' Lettie

347

confided in her. 'I came to realise quite early on that I was much better suited to other ground-based things.'

'Lettie's a bit of a contortionist,' Ivan supplied as he winked at the young redhead. 'It must give her lovers a thrill.'

You mean you don't already have firsthand experience? Danni wanted to say but she kept her mouth shut and instead smiled at Lettie.

'Well,' Ivan went on, glancing at the clock on the wall, 'I think that's enough conversation, we've got work to do.' He rubbed his hands together and looked meaningfully at Danni, who popped the last piece of her bread into her mouth and stood up.

'Are we going back up on the trapeze this afternoon?' she asked as they walked back out into the sunshine.

Ivan raised his eyebrows as he looked at her. 'On a full stomach?' he said.

Part of Danni was relieved, yet she felt anxious to get back on to the trapeze before she lost her nerve.

'Tomorrow,' he promised her when she told him how she felt.

'This afternoon I plan to show off a bit.'

He told her to go over to the mats and just do some gentle stretching exercises while he sorted out his equipment.

Danni sniggered in a very unladylike way when he said this and wondered immediately afterwards if she would ever get the hang of being sophisticated. When he came back he was wheeling a large round board and over his shoulder was slung a green canvas bag. The board was painted red, with a large white star in the centre.

'What's that for?' Danni called out to him as he adjusted the castors on the board frame so that it stood firm on the ground.

'You will see, Danni,' he replied mysteriously. 'Just you concentrate on warming up your muscles. I want you to practise your backflips in a moment.'

Danni immediately regretted the amount she had eaten for lunch. Reaching forward to her toes, with her legs spread wide, she glanced sideways to see what Ivan was doing. She noticed that he had opened the bag and was now taking out a handful of long, broad-bladed knives. It was then she remembered Al telling her that Ivan was famous for his knife-throwing act. Wondering who he used as his assistant – or rather victim – she grasped her left ankle and bent her neck, easing herself down until her forehead touched her knee.

Just as she held the pose, two hands followed the curve of her waist and hips and slid along her thighs. 'Lovely and supple,' Ivan murmured approvingly in her ear.

Her face was hidden by her hair, allowing Danni to smile secretively to herself. She felt instantly warm again, as she always did when Ivan touched her. As she straightened up, she glanced at him over her shoulder.

'Fancy a quick tumble on the mats?' she asked provocatively.

They both glanced around. For once the circus tent was empty of people other than themselves.

Ivan smiled as he slid his hands back up over her sinuous torso and cupped her breasts. 'Don't mind if I do.'

Feeling only slightly concerned that someone might interrupt them, Danni quickly stripped off her leotard. Lying on her side on the mats, her head propped in her hand, she watched Ivan undress. He wore nothing underneath his shorts. And as he pulled them down, she was gratified to see how eagerly his cock sprang free and how hard it was already.

Telling her to stay on her side, Ivan gently pushed her knees up to her chest. Her sex pouted invitingly and it took only the briefest of caresses for Ivan to make her properly wet and eager for him to enter her. As he pushed hard inside her welcoming vagina, Ivan reached up with one hand and stroked her breasts. The nipples sprang to attention and he pinched and pulled at them gently as he ground more deeply into her.

Pulling her knees back towards her chest even more, Danni opened up to him completely, working her hips so that her body and Ivan's ground against each other in perfect harmony. As their tempo increased, Ivan was forced to use both hands flat on the mat to support his weight.

Gazing through her lashes at him, noticing the way his stomach muscles rippled as he moved, Danni felt consumed with lust. She twisted her body at the waist so that her shoulders lay flat against the mats. Sensuously, provocatively, she caressed her own breasts, noticing, when she glanced at Ivan's face, how his gaze darkened as she did so.

He moved then, freeing one hand which he stroked over the curve of her hip. He caressed her buttocks, avidly watching the way his cock slid in and out of her moist opening. The slick wet proof of her arousal rimmed the base of his cock and glistened on the stretched outer lips that surrounded her vagina.

'Beautiful,' he breathed, sliding his hand over her hip and buttocks again, 'exquisite.'

Danni felt the warmth of her arousal flood her and she urged her body against his. Knowing that he was watching his cock move in and out of her made her feel even more aroused. She wished then that they had a mirror, so that she could witness the phenomenon for herself. Just imagining it pushed her over the edge into orgasmic bliss.

Ivan came a few moments later, encouraging Danni to murmur, 'You're beautiful,' as she watched his face transform into a blissful expression. To her he looked like a god, or a figure from a great work of art. His features were so finely sculpted, his expression so otherworldly that he didn't seem real.

As they came slowly back down to earth and Ivan held her in his arms, her head nestling on his shoulder, she told herself what a lucky girl she was. If Tam hadn't gone off like that ... if she hadn't happened to read that magazine ...

'It must be fate,' she murmured quietly to herself. Then she turned her face up and smiled at Ivan. 'Thank you,' she said softly, shaking her head when Ivan asked her what she was thanking him for. 'Just – thank you,' she repeated.

And Ivan, knowing better than to try to fathom the workings of this extraordinary young woman's mind, merely smiled and accepted her words as the compliment they were intended to be.

Their interlude was brief. Being the hard taskmaster that he was, Ivan was soon urging Danni to get back to work. And, after an hour or so of tumbling about on the mats, Danni sprang to her feet and declared that she had had enough. Even though she felt exhausted, her face was flushed with vigour and her eyes sparkling as she smiled triumphantly at Ivan.

'Well done,' he said, smoothing back her hair which tumbled haphazardly around her shoulders. He bunched her hair into a ponytail and held it away from the back of her neck as he kissed it.

Danny felt a small thrill run through her and she stroked her palm across his chest. 'More?' she asked, knowing he would realise that she didn't mean backflips or somersaults.

Dropping her hair, he shook his head regretfully. But he smiled as he said, 'Not just now. I should really put in a little practice. I haven't thrown in over a week.'

He took her hand and led her over to the circular board. Then he positioned her in front of it.

Immediately, Danni stepped away from it. 'Oh, no,' she said. 'Don't think for one minute that I'm going to—'

'Please, Danni,' Ivan interrupted. He put his finger to her lips to quell her protests, then led her back to the place he had put her before.

Shaking her head, Danni protested, 'I can't. I'll move and get my arm chopped off or something. I don't want to die this young.'

Ivan couldn't help laughing. 'I can assure you, sweetheart,' he said, 'you will not die. Nor even lose as much as the tip of a finger.' He moved her arms and legs so that her body formed an X-shape. 'I am the best knife-thrower in the world. You must learn to trust me.'

'I do,' she protested, 'but not with sharp instruments. Not when it's my body at stake.' She glanced at the pile of knives lying on the floor and added pleadingly, 'Look, I know what's going to happen. As soon as you throw one of those things I'll try to move out of the way. It's instinct, isn't it?'

'Instinctive,' Ivan corrected her grammar.

Danni found this amusing considering that she was the one who was English and said so.

'Don't use me, please,' she added, laughing, 'I mean it. I'll only muck it up.'

He looked at her levelly. 'Do you really think you would move?'

'I'd run a bloody mile,' Danni answered with feeling.

'Then there's only one thing for it,' Ivan responded, advancing towards her.

Glancing around, Danni felt a surge of expectation. What was he planning to do? To her surprise he grabbed one of her wrists and secured it to the board with a leather cuff. Then he did the same with her other wrist.

'No!' Danni shouted, trying to squirm. 'This is a joke, isn't it, Ivan?'

'No joke,' he said, strapping her ankles in a similar fashion, ignoring the way she tried to ward him off by kicking out at him.

Strapped in a spread-eagle position on the round board, Danni glared furiously at him. It annoyed her the way Ivan treated the whole thing as a game and yet at the same time she couldn't help feeling deliciously helpless. He could do anything to her while she was like this, she realised with a thrill of nervous anticipation, and she wouldn't be able to do a damn thing to stop him.

'You are just planning to throw knives at me, aren't you?' she said, thinking, '*just* knives!' and almost laughing at the ridiculousness of her predicament.

'No,' he replied with a shake of his head. He reached into the green holdall and took out a set of wicked-looking implements that Danni recognised from watching old westerns on TV. 'I thought I'd practise with the tomahawks as well.'

Then she did laugh. She continued laughing until tears of disbelief at what she'd got herself into ran down her face and Ivan told her to stop because her shoulders were shaking.

'You must remain perfectly still,' he warned,

coming over to her and placing his hands on her shoulders and stroking them until she calmed down. 'Please, Danni. No harm is going to come to you and playing the hysterical female doesn't suit you one bit.'

Danni hung her head in shame. Hysteria had almost got the better of her and now Ivan was treating her like a frightened animal. His touch was soothing and soon she felt herself relax and simply give in to the pleasure of his caresses. When she stopped shaking, his hands slid across her collarbone and then down over the wall of her chest to her breasts.

She sighed as he moulded them gently and whispered soothing words in her ear.

'I'm not going to hurt you, Danni sweetheart,' he said. 'Please believe me, I have spent many years practising this art. I am the best.'

There was nothing modest about his claim and yet he made it without a hint of conceit.

'I'm sorry, Ivan,' Danni said finally as she raised her head to look him in the eye.

He smiled a crinkly, sparkling-eyed smile that melted her heart and the rest of her insides.

'Don't be,' he admonished her gently, 'I've said it before and I'll say it again – just trust me.'

'I do,' she said earnestly, knowing deep down that she meant it, 'it's me I don't trust.' She paused then added, 'It's a bit like – oh, I don't know – a bit like when you're standing on a station platform and you know the train's coming and all of a sudden you get this wild urge to jump onto the track.'

'You do?' He sounded amused.

'Well, I do,' Danni asserted, 'I suppose that makes me sound a bit mad.'

Ivan's hands left her breasts to stroke her hair and follow the contours of her face. He cupped her face in his hands and looked levelly at her.

'I suppose it does,' he said with a straight face, 'after all, anyone who is prepared to stand there and let me throw knives at them must be completely crazy.'

'Careful,' she said, laughing all over again, 'otherwise when I get free of this thing I'll throw a few knives at you.'

As it turned out, Ivan proved himself beyond a shadow of doubt in Danni's mind that he was extremely skilful. He threw the knives and tomahawks apparently casually but with accurate precision so that they dug into the wood just fractions of an inch from her body.

After he had got into his stride and when Danni assured him that she now trusted his skill completely, Ivan went on to the next stage of his act which involved rotating the wheel.

As Danni spun round and round she felt herself becoming dizzy. So much so that the sound of the blades whizzing towards her and digging into the wooden board hardly compared with the tide of blood rushing in her ears. It was as though someone had stuck a couple of seashells to the sides of her head. In the end she gave up trying to fight the sensation and instead closed her eyes. She kept them tightly shut until Ivan was satisfied that he had had enough practice for one day.

As he slowed the spinning board and brought it to a halt with his hand, he said, 'You can open them now, it's all over.'

'Thank God,' Danni responded with a huge sigh of relief. 'Now you can get me out of these things.' She pulled ineffectually against the wrist restraints.

Just as Ivan reached up to unbuckle the first one, they were interrupted by the arrival of Lettie and Rose. The two young women were both dressed in jeans and cropped white T-shirts that showed off their narrow midriffs.

'Phone call for you, Ivan,' Lettie said.

He glanced over his shoulder at her and stepped back. 'Oh, really? I had better go and see who it is.'

'What about me?' Danni said, trying not to sound plaintive.

Lettie grinned at her and then at Ivan. 'Don't worry,' she said to Ivan, 'Rose and I will sort Danni out for you. You'd better not hang about, I think the call is long distance.'

As soon as Ivan had gone Lettie turned to Danni again. 'You're brave,' she murmured approvingly. Then she nodded in Rose's direction. 'Isn't she brave, sis?'

Rose said she was and then to Danni's complete surprise, walked up to her and ran a hand assessingly over her torso. 'Do you know what, Lettie?' she said, reaching for something in the back pocket of her jeans, 'I think it's a bit too soon to undo those restraints. Danni deserves some fun and relaxation after allowing herself to be put through such a dreadful ordeal.'

'Oh, no, it wasn't that bad—' Danni started to protest but her words evaporated into thin air as she caught sight of the long, white, ribbed plastic vibrator Rose was now holding.

Lettie grinned at her sister, then at Danni. She took the vibrator from Rose and turned the base. As the vibrator whirred into life Danni sensed their purpose and felt her stomach turn inside out. This was no premonition. There was no mistaking exactly how the twins planned to help her to relax. And she was totally powerless to stop them.

Chapter Eight

THE SWEET WOODCHIP smell of sawdust mingled with patchouli oil would always remind Danni of that afternoon in the circus tent. Both twins favoured the scent of patchouli. They told Danni that they wore it as a sort of homage to their mother, who had been an original sixties flower child. Free love, they said as they caressed Danni's body over the top of her leotard, was an expression of everything beautiful.

If Danni hadn't felt so helpless, or so full of anxiety about being left at the tender mercy of the two young women, she might have laughed at this.

As it was she said, 'I really don't think this sort of thing is for me.'

Rose glanced up at her wide-eyed. She was kneeling in front of Danni, her pale fine-boned hands exploring the contours of her legs.

'How do you know until you've tried it?' she asked simply. 'You enjoyed last night, didn't you?'

Danni sighed and tried to organise her thoughts

and feelings so that she could express them as succinctly as possible without sounding hurtful.

'Yes, I did enjoy it,' she said finally, 'but that was different. I'd had a lot to drink and Al—'

'You liked it regardless, why deny it?' Lettie cut in, running the tip of the vibrator back and forth across Danni's throat and the upper swell of her breasts.

'I'm not denying it,' Danni insisted, trying to twist her body away from the vibrator and finding herself hopelessly pinned down, 'I'm just explaining why it was different then compared to now.'

'But now it's just us,' Rose said soothingly. 'No audience. No men.' She stood up and took the vibrator away from her sister. Over the top of Danni's leotard, she circled each of her breasts with the throbbing instrument. The circles became smaller and smaller until they were concentrated around Danni's nipples. 'There's no need to feel embarrassed,' she added, still in a gentle tone.

To Danni's shame, she felt her body respond to the tingling vibrations. It wasn't the first time she had experienced the inanimate pleasure that a vibrator could give her. But before, she had always been the one in charge of the device. Herself alone, locked in her own private world of self-induced gratification.

Now, it seemed, as far as her treacherous body was concerned, the inclusion of other people didn't make the slightest difference to its responses. She could feel her torso start to hum, echoing the erotic tune the vibrator plucked from her sensitive nerve endings. Her nipples stiffened and, further down, her sex began to tingle as her vagina moistened.

Don't do this to me, body, she moaned silently. A gasp of surprise escaped her as Lettie's fingers slid under the scrap of fabric covering her pubic mound. The fingers stroked her pubis and gently pulled the skin upwards, parting her outer labia. Then Lettie slid her hand all the way between Danni's legs, her knowing fingers spreading the labia wider apart and skimming tantalisingly around the sensitive flesh rimming Danni's vagina.

Danni tried hard to stifle a whimper. She could feel her body answering Lettie's caresses with a continuous pulse of excitement. And she could sense the way her outer labia swelled and opened out like petals to reveal the dewy, sensitive flesh beneath.

'What a shame she's wearing this thing,' Lettie said with a glance at her sister.

Rose nodded. 'I know, it's a nuisance, isn't it?' she agreed, 'mind you, if it were to tear—' She broke off to pull experimentally at the neckline of the leotard.

To Danni's relief, although she thought she felt it give slightly, the fabric stayed in one piece. Her relief was short-lived. In the next moment Lettie picked up one of Ivan's knives. A shaft of sunlight caught the blade sending a flash of light across her face as she held it up.

'We could cut it with this,' she said to Rose, 'it'll

be all the easier to repair afterwards, otherwise we'll have Fauve on our backs.'

Rose's eyes sparkled wickedly as she nodded and suggested she hold the material taut while her sister cut it. The knife was sinfully sharp and sliced through the thin fabric as easily as if it were melted butter. Within seconds the front of the leotard was slashed from neck to navel.

'Now for the crotch,' Lettie said, 'hold it fast for me would you, Rose?'

'Now just a minute—' Danni protested. It frustrated her that they were treating her like a plaything, as though she had no say in the matter.

Rose glanced up at Danni as she squatted down and pulled the damp fabric away from her crotch. She held it taut between her fingers.

'Just trust us, Danni,' she said, sounding uncannily like Ivan, 'soon you'll be screaming with lust.'

'I won't,' Danni said defiantly, hoping she could resist the torment of the vibrator and prove them wrong.

She recoiled as she felt both Lettie and Rose's fingers brushing her sex and then winced as her warm flesh received a cold glance of steel.

'Mind you don't cut her,' Rose warned her sister, 'that wouldn't be much fun.'

The twins laughed and Danni fumed at their amusement at her expense. This was all so embarrassing and unfair. Where the hell was Ivan, why hadn't he come back yet? All at once, a disconcerting thought struck her. Just supposing the whole thing was planned. But no, surely not? Ivan wouldn't dream of doing that to her – would he? Although she was dying to ask the twins to tell her the truth, she didn't dare because deep down she didn't want to know the answer. She preferred to believe that Ivan would return at any moment and be shocked at the way the twins were taking advantage of her.

'There,' Lettie said with satisfaction a moment later, 'one totally free pussy.'

Danni hated that particular description and wanted to say so. She glanced down and noticed how the leotard now hung between her legs. The front flap protected her modesty visually although she could feel the caress of fresh air on her exposed groin. It was unarguably tantalising and she felt all the more embarrassed by her predicament. Her mind was saying one thing while her body was saying something else. Feeling the moisture drying around her vagina as another warm breath of air whipped between her legs she looked anxiously towards the big top entrance, willing Ivan to appear.

'Don't you think this has gone far enough now,' she protested feebly, 'after all, a joke's a joke but—'

From their squatting position in front of her, Lettie and Rose both glanced up at her and then at each other.

'Did you hear that, sis?' Rose said, 'She thinks we're playing a bit of a prank.' Both sisters looked up at Danni again, their expressions completely sincere.

'We both enjoy other women's bodies, Danni,'

Lettie explained, encouraged by nods from Rose, 'and men's. We're not lesbians, we're bisexual and proud of it.' She paused and laughed. 'Apart from anything else, it gives us twice the amount of scope for pleasure. We were hoping you would enjoy our attentions. You will,' she added, more vehemently this time, 'I promise you, you will love what we're going to do to you.'

By this time Danni felt as though she had no option but to give in gracefully. There was no way she could fight them, nor even dissuade them. And in the back of her mind a small voice kept telling her to simply go with the flow. You might enjoy it, the voice said, why deny yourself the promise of pleasure just because the situation is different from what you are used to?

She felt her breath catch and held it as Lettie said to Rose, 'Let's tuck this bit out of the way.'

Warm air caressed her belly as the scrap of fabric hanging down at the front was raised and tucked under what was left of the leotard. She felt incredibly exposed now that she was completely naked from the waist down, with her legs spread and shackled wide apart.

'Pretty little pussy,' Lettie crooned, kneeling on the floor and stroking her hand over Danni's mound. 'Isn't she lovely, Rose?'

The other twin murmured that Danni's sex was indeed lovely and also knelt on the ground to peer between her legs.

Danni felt a flush of shame which started at the tips of her toes and spread throughout her body.

The way the two girls were looking at her most intimate parts and describing what they saw was lewd and yet intolerably exciting. Most of her shame was the result of her own arousal. It didn't seem right to get so turned on by the situation. But aroused she was. She could feel her clitoris swelling and pushing its way between her blossoming outer lips. And her juices were running so freely that they were trickling down the insides of her thighs.

Rose started the vibrator again and stroked it along Danni's sex. A moan escaped Danni's lips. The humming of the instrument sent tingles through her entire body. Her clitoris swelled a little more each time the tip of the vibrator glanced over and around it.

'Nice, huh?' Rose said to her with a smile.

Danni managed to nod. Her whole body felt warm and liquid. If she hadn't been strapped to the board she fancied she might easily have melted into the sawdust. Rose was clever with the vibrator. Somehow, Danni realised, she managed to orchestrate her body to the point of climax and then transfer the pleasure to another part of her anatomy, so that she was left hanging – literally and metaphorically.

The need to orgasm became paramount. Danni heard herself moaning and whimpering, pleading with the girls to let her come.

'Ah, no, not yet,' Lettie teased as she watched her sister draw the tip of the vibrator along the taut length of Danni's inner thigh. 'We want to see how far we can take your pleasure. I promise you, when you do come, it will be explosive.'

Danni didn't doubt it. The vibrator was circling her clitoris again and she felt like exploding now. In her feverish state of mind it seemed to her that her entire body consisted only of her vulva. It dominated every scrap of her senses. She could see it in her mind's eye, all red and swollen and juicy. She could feel the way it throbbed and tingled and moistened. And while her ears were filled with the soft whirring of the vibrator, her nostrils were suffused with the scent of her own arousal.

While Rose stayed kneeling between Danni's outstretched legs and continued to stroke and tease her urgent flesh, Lettie straightened up and stood by Danni's side. Gently, she reached out and parted the front of the leotard so that Danni's breasts were bared. The tanned globes sat high and rounded on her ribcage, the nipples swollen and deeply roseate.

'Lovely breasts,' Lettie breathed admiringly as she simply gazed at them.

Rose glanced up. 'Aren't they?' she concurred, 'Don't they make you feel envious, sis?'

'Mm, absolutely but at least I get to play with them.'

Lettie smoothed her hands up Danni's ribcage and cupped the breasts from underneath, her thumb and forefinger capturing the nipples. She pulled and pinched at them slightly and gave a sigh of satisfaction as they hardened. Smiling straight into Danni's face, which was bright red with a mixture of arousal and mortification, she added, 'You're a very lucky girl to have such a lovely body, Danni. I don't know why you're so shy about revelling in it and showing it off.'

Danni couldn't speak. She tried to but she couldn't. At that point all she could do was signal with her eyes that she was enjoying the twins' caresses. Her lids felt heavy, weighted with lust. It seemed no part of her body went unexplored by the two sisters. While Lettie caressed her breasts, arms and torso, Rose's hands took it in turns to lightly travelled the length of her legs, while she played the vibrator over different parts of her lower body. Softly stroking fingers and the tip of the humming instrument excited the sensitive flesh of Danni's inner thighs, at the backs of her knees, circled her ankles and even stroked between her toes.

A glorious sense of her own womanliness suffused Danni. She felt capable of so much. Her skin and the muscles beneath – stretched taut by necessity of her spread-eagled position – were receptive to every caress. Sensations of voluptuous warmth coursed through every part of her. Her body was an instrument which the twins, through their natural curiosity and sensuality, were able to fine tune and ultimately create harmonious melodies of eroticism.

When she was finally allowed to come, Danni's orgasm was so volatile that she cried out loudly. Her body trembled convulsively until the board – which had been staunch under siege by knives and tomahawks – began to rock. Lettie grasped at it and held it fast without removing her mouth from Danni's breast. Rose, with her fingers buried deep inside Danni, glanced up at her sister.

'Like a volcano erupting,' she said with a hint of amusement. 'I knew she would be like this.'

Returning to reality on the ebbing flow of her orgasm, Danni blushed and smiled weakly.

'I'm sorry,' she said as soon as she had got her breath back, 'I didn't mean to get carried away.'

Rose laughed then and, as she sat back on her heels, her fingers slid out of the moist channel of Danni's vagina. Raising them to her mouth, Rose licked each finger with deliberate relish and a suggestive twinkle in her eye. Turning off the vibrator she stroked the pulsating folds of Danni's vulva tenderly.

'No need to apologise,' she said. 'You obviously loved it.'

'Yes,' Danni said simply.

It shamed her to have to concede defeat after the strength of her denials. Yet at the same time she felt as though another tiny piece of her had been liberated.

Lettie allowed her mouth and hands to slide from Danni's breasts. She left a wet trail down her torso as she sank to the floor. Her lips and tongue pressed to Danni's body for as long as they were able. Then she sat cross-legged and serene beside her sister who copied Lettie's pose.

The warm caress of the late afternoon breeze dried Danni's skin instantly and she felt a small pang of remorse that the encounter, which had seemed so daunting at the start, had now come to an end. To Danni's delight, Lettie's fingers joined those of her sister in a twin caress of her feminine flesh. Lettie stroked her clitoris lightly, smiling knowingly when the tiny bud, so sensitive now, seemed to recoil from her fingers and the muscles in Danni's thighs and groin tensed.

'Can't take any more, huh?' she asked gently.

All three of them jumped when a smoothly accented voice suddenly came out of nowhere and demanded, 'What is this? A case of while the cat is away, I think.'

Ivan! Danni breathed a sigh of relief that he had returned. Then she felt immediately guilty, wondering what he would make of their situation.

'I couldn't stop them,' Danni said as she sensed him walk up behind her.

She felt guilty again then, as though her declaration of helpless innocence betrayed the twins' good intentions. Still, she reasoned, so what if she had enjoyed it? She *had* been helpless. Neither of the twins had given her a choice. What if their actions had turned out to have the opposite effect, leaving her sexuality scarred for life?

The curve of Ivan's lips and the twinkle in his deep blue eyes told Danni that he saw through her charade.

'Danni, Danni,' he murmured, stroking her bare breasts, 'there is nothing to be ashamed of here. Except perhaps—' he paused and glanced down at the twins, who still sat on the sawdust covered

369

floor, their expressions now a little sheepish, 'these two should know better than to take such blatant advantage of someone.'

Displaying characteristic inconsistency, Danni was quick to defend them. 'Oh, I'm sure they didn't mean any harm. And I did – I did—'

'Did what, Danni?' Ivan raised an imperious eyebrow, although the smile in his eyes softened his expression.

'Did enjoy it in the end,' she mumbled, wondering whether to blush or laugh. In the end she did both.

'Come on, you,' Ivan said after a moment. He reached for the strap tethering her right ankle. 'I think it is time I released you.' For a second or two he hesitated and glanced at Rose and Lettie who stood up, grumbling. 'Or perhaps—' he teased. His tone of voice and the insolent expression on his face dared Danni to argue, or plead. When she did neither and simply pretended to ignore him, he laughed again. 'Just joking,' he said, then he added, 'A few of us are going down to the lake for a swim, would you girls like to come along?'

Lettie and Rose agreed eagerly, their faces all smiles. Ivan glanced at Danni as he moved to unfasten the restraints around her wrists.

'Yes, please,' she said, feeling doubly relieved at the prospect of being released and of enjoying a simple pleasure for a change. Going for a dip in a lake seemed like the perfect end to a very odd, but not unpleasant, afternoon.

*

Sunlight glinted off the water of the small, ellipti-
cal lake which was surrounded by a grassy
meadow. Beyond its boundary was a thickly
wooded area of oak, elm, sycamore and silver
birch. The lush emerald grass of the meadow was
strewn with dasies and clumps of clover. And
Danni discovered if she screwed her eyes up
slightly, the meadow looked for all the world like
an unrolled bolt of green and white patterned
fabric.

The surroundings were tranquil and Danni
thought the lake idyllic in the way it shimmered
like a gemstone in the centre of the meadow. The
colour of the glassy water was a brilliant turquoise.
Its iridescence was so inviting that Danni couldn't
wait to wade into the lake's cool depths and swim
until she was completely exhausted. She hadn't
brought a bathing suit or bikini with her. But that
hardly seemed to matter as no one else in their
small group – which consisted of herself, Ivan, the
twins, Randi and Guido – seemed all that bothered
about costumes.

'Skinny-dipping, my second favourite thing in
the whole world,' Lettie claimed dramatically as
she dragged off her T-shirt and jeans. Underneath,
her slim pale body was completely naked.

The twins' white bodies, tinted only by a scat-
tering of freckles, seemed a sharp contrast to those
of everyone else. Although her skin wasn't naturally olive-toned like that of Ivan or Guido, Danni
felt her own golden brown hue was equally attractive. And having a tan always made her feel thin-

ner and more athletic somehow. As she shrugged off the yellow cotton dress she had put on to replace the ruined leotard and scampered quickly down to the water's edge, she felt sublimely free. Perhaps not free enough to parade around with the utmost confidence, like Lettie and Rose, but certainly more relaxed about being naked in mixed company.

Although weakening a little, the rays from the sun were still warm on her back. She felt them toasting her buttocks and shoulders as she stepped gingerly into the water. Recoiling a little from the coolness of the lake, she felt her toes sinking into the mud at the bottom. The water was clear enough for her to see where she was treading. Only a few large pebbles were scattered about on the lake bed and she was able to walk quite confidently into the water until it was waist high. Then she took a deep breath, preparing to submerge the rest of her body in its cool depths.

Fighting the initial shock, which made her want to run back to the water's edge and shiver under a towel, she struck out for the far side of the lake. It was wider than it looked and by the time she was able to touch the bottom again her chest was heaving with the effort of her swim. When she looked up she saw a familiar pair of lean brown legs.

'You look like a particularly beautiful water nymph,' Ivan said. As he squatted down by the edge of the lake, he offered her a helping hand.

Her feet squelched in the mud – a sensation that Danni was surprised to find quite sensuous. All at once, a devilish idea occurred to her. It would serve him right, she thought, and in the next moment she yanked hard on Ivan's arm. Just as she expected, he toppled forward, falling headlong into the lake.

Water droplets sprayed from the ends of his hair as he surfaced, shaking his head like a shaggy dog and gasping for breath.

Danni started laughing. She couldn't help herself and Ivan pretended to look annoyed.

'Cheeky little minx,' he growled with mock ferocity. 'I'll have to make you pay for that.'

Taking her by surprise he grabbed her round the waist and the two of them play-tussled until they fell, gasping and shaking with laughter, onto the muddy bank. Ivan began to tickle Danni and, as she tried to squirm out of his grasp, she became coated with the sticky ooze.

'Mm,' she murmured, squelching her hands into the mud and smearing handfuls over her breasts. After a moment lost in total abandon, she realised Ivan was watching her and not saying anything. 'What?' she said, looking up at him wide-eyed. She noticed he was wearing the sort of wolfish expression that she had seen a few times before – usually as a prelude to lovemaking. 'Are you thinking what I'm thinking?' she asked with only a hint of surprise.

Ivan pretended to look confused. 'How could I know what you are thinking?' he asked. 'The working of your mind is a mystery to me.'

'What about the working of my body?' Danni

countered, mimicking the way he spoke. She couldn't help noticing how hard her nipples had become and felt her body dissolve into the soft mud.

'Ah, that,' he murmured throatily while stroking a questioning hand over her mud-spattered torso. 'Your body is a different matter entirely.'

As his fingers delved between her legs, Danni whimpered with pleasure. Her arousal was instantaneous. Although she sank further into the mud she spread her legs wide apart, her hands coming up to stroke Ivan's chest and shoulders. She smiled at the handprints she left on him and then gasped as she felt his fingers sink inside her.

Her immediate reaction was to try and stop him. 'Don't,' she hissed urgently, 'someone might see.'

'Let them,' Ivan said, fingering her more deeply, 'let them see me caressing you. They will only feel envious.'

She warmed to his compliment and the strength of passion he invoked in her. The others could not be seen from where she lay and Danni soon gave up all pretence at modesty. Churning her sex against his hand she reached down and grasped the hard rod of his penis. For once she didn't fancy putting it in her mouth, not while it was coated with mud. But later she would, she promised herself. Later she would give him as much pleasure as he was giving her.

He took her almost straight away, in a quick hard manner that left them both breathless and temporarily satisfied. Afterwards they rolled around in the mud like playful seals. Danni and Ivan's hair was plastered with mud and long tendrils, thickened with the gooey mass, clung to their faces and necks.

'We must look a sight,' Danni said, wiping a tendril of hair away from the corner of her mouth and streaking her face in the process.

'You look beautiful,' Ivan assured her.

Smiling down at him as she lay on her side, resting her head in her hand, Danni stroked a single muddy fingertip down the length of his torso.

'So do you,' she said.

Resting on the bank of the lake, the waning sun still warm enough to bake the mud onto their naked bodies, Danni and Ivan talked a little about their pasts and about *Cirque Erotique*.

'I can't believe how much less inhibited I feel,' Danni confessed to him, 'coming here has certainly been an eye opener.'

Stroking her breasts absently, Ivan smiled up at her. 'I always like to think of our bodies as erotic treasure chests,' he said sagely, 'with all our desires and needs locked up inside. All it takes is someone with the right key . . .' He allowed his words to taper off and instead brought Danni's mouth down to meet his for a long, lingering kiss.

'You certainly seem to have been my keyholder,' Danni said when they finally broke apart. She looked at him, feeling the poignancy of passion and realising that she wanted him again.

Moving as gracefully as she could, she straddled his body. Her muddy thighs gripped his hips as her hand sought the reassuring hardness of his cock. Her body was undeniably wet and ready for him and, as she positioned herself over his cock and teasingly circled the rim of her vagina with his glans, she found it so easy to slide right down the length of him, engulfing his penis completely.

She ground her hips, watching his changing expression the whole time. There was no doubt he enjoyed being inside her, making love to her, fucking her, whatever . . . And she felt free enough to admit that she enjoyed him. She appreciated his responsiveness and his obvious enthusiasm for her body.

Right now he was reaching for her breasts as they dangled tantalisingly over his chest. A smile of satisfaction crossed his lips and he closed his eyes as he grasped them, his fingers moulding the pliant flesh while she rode him.

With her knees slithering in the soft mud, Danni was forced to grip Ivan really tightly with her thighs. She could feel her excitement mounting by degrees. The hard length of Ivan's cock stroked her inner walls tantalisingly, while she felt the flesh of her labia being stimulated as it rubbed against his pubic bone. Wiping her muddy fingers on a nearby clump of grass, she slid her hand between her legs, stroking her throbbing clitoris until she came in tumultuous waves of sheer pleasure.

With his eyes closed, Ivan was able to concentrate on the delicious movements of Danni's body. His senses delighted to the texture of her vagina, so soft and pulpy, like ripe fruit, yet with an unyielding grip. And the sensation of the soft mud beneath him, the fresh floral scent of the meadow and the delicate warmth of the waning sun combined to embrace him with a voluptuous sensuality.

As his hands cupped and moulded Danni's breasts he felt the soft scratching of her fingernails on his lower belly. A smile touched his lips. She was pleasuring herself. Opening his eyes only a fraction, he watched her covertly, enjoying the obvious proof of her enjoyment. She looked radiant, her cheeks flushed, her gaze sultry and heavy-lidded with lust. He felt her tremble. Sensing the sudden tightening of her body, he knew that she was approaching climax. His hands left her breasts to grip her hips and he slammed upwards into her. He kept up a rhythm of short, fast thrusts until he heard her anguished whimpers and felt the tell-tale spasming of her vaginal muscles.

Still riding him hard, she milked him. The harmonious grip and relaxation of her inner muscles drained him of every last drop of passion. And when they were finally spent he felt the delightful weight and warmth of her naked body as she collapsed on top of him. For a few moments they basked in the aftermath of plea-sure, their bodies still joined. With eyes closed they shared the final abating tremors of their mutual orgasm and the rhythm of each other's heartbeat. The only sounds to break the stillness were the cries of the birds that darted across the blank blue canvas of the sky above them, and the steadying rhythm of their own breathing.

For both of them it was an experience to savour. A perfect moment captured within the landscape of time.

Chapter Nine

BY SATURDAY AFTERNOON, Danni was no longer afraid to swing on the trapeze and had also learned to juggle. She was proud of both achievements but throwing three clubs in the air and catching them ten times in a row struck her as one of the most triumphant moments of her life.

Al was an expert juggler and he showed her how to hold two clubs in her dominant hand, throw one of them and wait until it turned in the air before throwing the single club in her subordinate hand. Time and again she dropped the second club, instead of throwing it, in her eagerness to catch the first. It was frustrating but Al proved very patient. Each time he simply told her to pick up the dropped club and start again.

Taking the clubs from her, he showed her how to throw the clubs high to give herself extra time.

'Every time the club spins, throw the next one,' he said, 'and remember to alternate your hands and concentrate on smooth scoops.'

When she found her skill with three clubs

getting worse instead of improving, he made her go back to using just two clubs and then one, until she regained her confidence again.

'I'm hopeless at this,' she wailed at one point as she scrabbled around in the sawdust picking up not just one dropped club but all three. 'I'll never get the hang of it and it always looks so easy when other people do it.'

'You're not hopeless and you will get it, sweet-pea,' he insisted gently, 'but these things take hours and hours of practice. You can't expect to be brilliant straight away.'

'Oh, but I do,' Danni said grimly as she prepared to throw the first club for the umpteenth time, 'I won't settle for being second best.'

To her annoyance Al laughed. It was a deep rumbling laugh that seemed to echo around the canvas walls of the big top.

'Ain't no worries on that score, honey,' he said, grabbing her around the waist with one hugely muscled arm and squeezing her tight. 'You'll never be second best at anything.'

After that she seemed to do much better. Whether it was Al's compliment, or his confidence in her, she didn't know. What she did know was that if she simply relaxed and concentrated on what she was doing, she could get it right.

Just before lunchtime, Al told her to sit on the ringside and watch him while he showed off a little. He said it in a confident, though not arrogant way that made Danni warm to him even more than she already had.

380

'Guido's a good juggler,' he said as he played casually with half a dozen brightly coloured hoops. Throwing them into the air, he caught them swiftly, one after the other. Then he juggled them for a few more minutes before adding, 'I'd go as far as to say, Guido is proving to be quite a find.'

'Really?' Danni felt compelled to ask, 'Why is that?'

'Aha,' Al said mysteriously, 'you'll have to wait until tonight. A little birdie told me Fauve and Guido have something special planned.'

Danni nodded sagely and didn't bother to press him. After the experience with Meah, she realised that dinner time often included special treats that would never appear on the menus of most ordinary folk.

After her session with Al, Danni returned to her room and changed into a pair of shorts. She teamed them with a skimpy vest top and went outside again to catch the last of the day's rays. The garden lounger was soft and squashy and covered with blue and white ticking. It wasn't long before weariness and the warmth of the sun overcame her and she fell into a light doze.

She awoke to see Fauve and Ivan strolling across the small patch of paddock which had been edged with shrubs and brightly hued bedding plants to form a garden. Ivan's white-blond head was bent to catch what Fauve was saying to him and every so often he smiled and nodded in agreement. When they reached the small wooden bench which stood in the shade of a spiky-limbed monkey puzzle tree, he and Fauve sat down to continue their conversation.

For once, Danni found herself more interested in observing Fauve than Ivan. She hadn't seen all that much of the older woman during the past few days. When she had mentioned it to Ivan he told her Fauve had a lot of business matters to attend to.

'She is a marvellous woman,' he had said admiringly, 'beautiful and intelligent, a truly unbeatable combination.' The comment had incited a small flicker of jealousy in Danni for which she had reproached herself immediately. If it hadn't been for Fauve's generosity she wouldn't be there at all, and would never have met Ivan.

Today Fauve was wearing an ankle-skimming dress of pleated orange fabric. The colour set off her mahogany tan beautifully and her hair had been slicked back with gel. Like a glossy cap it clung to the delicate structure of her skull and made her look younger and more vulnerable, somehow.

Obviously Ivan liked her hair styled in that way, Danni thought to herself, because he kept reaching out to stroke it, or run the back of a crooked finger over her high curving cheekbone. This particular gesture was achingly familiar to Danni and she was forced to close her eyes eventually, deliberately blocking out the vision before envy overcame her completely.

She knew she had no right to feel resentful of

Ivan's relationship with Fauve. They had known each other forever. she reminded herself, Fauve was probably like a sister to him. All the same, she couldn't help feeling a stab of jealousy every time Ivan spoke about the older woman, because he always referred to her in such glowing terms. Obviously, she thought, in Ivan's eyes at any rate, Fauve could do no wrong. She was the brilliant businesswoman, the graceful hostess, the highly skilled artiste. Whereas Danni was – well – just Danni.

Like the sun coming out on a dull day, the realisation struck her that the only way she could keep up Ivan's interest in her was to become more interesting herself. Straight, sexually unadventurous Danni would not do. Ivan had clearly enjoyed the details she had related to him about her encounter with Lettie and Rose. And he had obviously found their later session on the muddy bank of the lake a rewardingly erotic interlude. Afterwards, he had told her that it would go down in his mental catalogue of hedonistic pleasures as one of the most erotic experiences he had ever had. 'I never realised mud could be so sensual,' he confided in her, 'you taught *me* something there.' As a consequence she had glowed with pleasure for the rest of the evening and hadn't minded when he said he couldn't join her in her room that night because he had some important phone calls to make.

'Business,' he had said disparagingly, 'is an irritating curb to enjoyment but also a necessary evil.'

Danni had accepted his explanation without

trying to persuade him otherwise. But the single night of enforced celibacy had left her feeling extremely amorous. She couldn't wait to get him alone later. And, as she lay on the garden lounger soaking up the last of the sun, she noticed how sexy she felt most of the time now.

It wasn't a word she usually used to describe her feelings, yet it seemed the most appropriate right at that moment. She wasn't sure if she could honestly class herself as truly sensual, feeling that there was so much more to pleasure that she didn't know, or hadn't experienced. So *sexy* would have to do. If there was one thing she was sure about, it was that she was far more aware of her body these days.

Before she came to the circus school she had always enjoyed sexual pleasure, whether in the company of someone else or self-induced. But now it seemed her body had taken on a new dimension. It was as though its needs were far more apparent, and urgent, than they had been before. Just lately, she felt as though her body ruled her mind more often than not, rather than the other way around. She was also far more aware of the different permutations for erotic gratification. One-to-one, man-woman, had always seemed the only way to her to achieve sexual fulfilment.

Just lately her rigid notions had taken a bit of a battering. Now she knew it was possible to enjoy licentious pleasures bestowed by a person of the same sex. Her experience with Lettie and Rose had taught her that much. Whether she could actually derive enjoyment from touching another woman was a dilemma she still hadn't managed to resolve. And she wasn't all that sure whether she wanted to find out.

Just at that moment the memory of Meah's chocolate-button nipples sprang into her mind and she licked her lips in an unconscious gesture. Shifting on the garden lounger to make herself more comfortable, Danni realised that her body had started to respond to the image of its own accord. She felt desirous again. Her juices were flowing, her clitoris wakening and starting its gentle pulse.

Stop it! she told herself firmly, you are not a lesbian, Danni, or even bisexual like the twins. Nevertheless, she was forced to admit that, with each passing day, she was beginning to doubt her long-held belief that she was a man's woman through and through.

At dinner that evening she put on the white dress again. Freshly laundered it stood out well against her golden tan. And, though she wasn't sure if it was just wishful thinking, she fancied she looked more svelte in it. Her hips didn't look quite so – well – hippy, she decided as she appraised herself in the mirror, and her stomach looked almost flat.

Feeling daring, she left off her underwear. Just knowing that she was wearing nothing at all under the dress gave her a thrill of excitement. She might let Ivan in on her naughty secret, or then again she might not. Just to sit there at the table, eating and making conversation, with her sex naked under the short dress would be titillation in itself.

Arriving late, she found everyone already gathered around the table. Everyone that was except Guido. Glancing at Meah, Danni couldn't help thinking how lovely the young woman looked in the shiny emerald green dress she was wearing. Although it was far too dressy for a simple meal with friends – which was how she looked upon Ivan, Fauve and the others – Danni thought the dress was an absolutely perfect adornment for a woman who was already beautiful. Plain and simple, with shoestring straps and a hem that ended mid-thigh, it looked like a sparkling jewel with Meah herself as its exquisite setting.

'Where's Guido?' Danni asked Fauve as she took the only empty seat, which was between the older woman and Al.

The chips of black marble that were Fauve's eyes glittered in the light from three long white candles, which stood in the middle of the table and were set in an hexagonal holder of smoked glass.

She smiled warmly at Danni as she said, 'Guido will be here in a little while, *chérie*. He has chosen to be our waiter for tonight.'

Aha, so that's the plan, Danni thought to herself. Obviously the evening was set to involve an element of après-dinner entertainment.

'You look great tonight, sweetpea,' Al cut in, his smile as warm as Fauve's. His eyes were acutely appraising as they flicked over Danni's body.

She felt herself becoming aroused under the

steady gaze that followed his appraisal. Her nipples hardened and she clenched her thighs tightly together to quell the tingling that had started up between them.

'You too,' she managed to gasp.

It was the truth. Normally fabulous-looking anyway, Al was looking particularly delectable in white jeans that clung to his enviably rounded bottom and strong, muscular thighs. With these he wore a lime-green piqué shirt which looked startlingly good in contrast with his tanned skin. Sinewy biceps bulged under the short sleeves and the rest of the fabric fitted like a second skin to his broad torso, showing off every curve of his musculature.

Varying hues of green seemed to be the fashion statement of the evening, Danni noticed as she glanced around the table at the others. Apart from Meah and Al, Ivan was also in green – an olive-green silk shirt, teamed with linen trousers – and Rose was wearing a pair of green and white striped baggy cotton trousers with a drawstring waist. Fauve however, was back in black – a figure-skimming silky dress that ended just an inch or so above the knees – whereas Randi was in his customary blue denim. And Lettie was wearing a shiny silver T-shirt, teamed with a black suede A-line skirt that just skimmed the tops of her narrow thighs.

'How did you fare at juggling, my sweet?' Ivan asked Danni across the table.

Glancing at Al first, she grinned at him. 'OK, I

think,' she replied, 'I kept dropping them at first but Al is such a bully I had to get it right in the end.'

'Good thing too. You keep this lady hard at it, Al,' Ivan said, smiling at them both.

Al laughed a toned-down version of his deep rumble and said, 'Trust me, Ivan, I won't let this little cutie get away with anything. Not even when she turns her big baby blues on me.'

'They're green, actually,' Danni countered, grinning.

As though she were at a tennis match, Danni found her gaze darting back and forth from Ivan to Al, who proceeded to discuss her attributes and her failings as though she wasn't there. She didn't mind. Most of their derogatory comments were mere teasing and they both had plenty of nice things to say about her to counteract the negatives.

It had been agreed that, with the next show only a week away, Al would take over some of Danni's instruction. And, to be honest, Danni thought to herself, she didn't mind at all. She was really beginning to take to the hunky American. Although 'fancy him' might have been a more accurate description. The total opposite of Ivan in every way, he nevertheless had a certain presence that was growing on her in leaps and bounds.

Her reverie was interrupted by the arrival of Guido. At the sight of him in his formal black and white attire, complete with bow-tie, she stifled a smile. He looked like a cross between a typical head waiter and a mafia gangster. So much so that

388

she almost expected to glimpse the outline of a shoulder holster under his jacket.

When he leaned over her to serve her some crisply roasted potatoes cooked with onions and herbs, Danni caught a strong whiff of Giorgio by Armani. This competed heavily with the delicious aroma of the main course which was a very pungent osso bucco. As Guido straightened up and moved away from her to serve Fauve, Danni turned to Al and wafted her hand under her nose while rolling her eyes meaningfully.

Laughing, Al put his arm around her shoulders, drawing her to him. As he put his mouth to her ear he whispered covertly, 'Don't knock the poor guy, he's as nervous as hell.'

As he released her again, Danni straightened up and glanced over her shoulder at Guido, feeling a surge of compassion for the young Italian. Why shouldn't he feel nervous? she asked herself. Just because he was a man didn't mean he should automatically feel more confident about his sexuality than any of the women in the room. Her perception surprised her. For too long, she realised, she had always thought of men as creatures from another planet. Now it struck her that they were only people, with the same hang ups and insecurities as any woman.

'Thank you, Guido,' she said softly, when he returned to her side a few minutes later to pour her a glass of burgundy, 'By the way, you look absolutely gorgeous tonight.'

He flashed her a dark-eyed smile of gratitude.

'Really?' he said in a low voice so that the others couldn't overhear him, 'I feel so self-conscious in this.' He pulled at the jacket and grinned ruefully. 'I tell Fauve she try to turn me into a *pinguino*.'

Danni laughed. 'I take it that means penguin?'

'*Si*,' Guido replied, his pearly teeth flashing brilliantly against the canvas of his olive-toned face, 'but Fauve, she tell me not to be a silly boy.' The admission was followed by a self-deprecating shrug.

The image of Fauve saying this which, Danni guessed, had resulted in a smack on Guido's tight backside, made her grin inwardly.

'She is not a lady you can argue with,' Danni confided in him. 'I should know.'

She remembered how Fauve had insisted on shaving her bikini line and felt a small flicker of arousal. There was something about the older woman's dominant air that excited her, she realised. Tiny, she might be, but Fauve had the confidence and awe-inspiring presence of an amazon. No wonder *Cirque Erotique* was such a success. Only an exceptional person could conceive of the idea and then put it into practice with such flair and enthusiasm. An enthusiasm that, Danni suspected, never waned.

Her sudden admiration for the petite Frenchwoman made Danni turn to her and give her an affectionate smile.

'I just want you to know how much I've enjoyed my stay here so far,' she said.

To her surprise, Fauve looked inordinately

pleased. 'Thank you, *ma chérie*, she responded, bearing an expression of genuine delight. 'It is good to be told I am doing things right.'

Impulsively, Danni reached out and covered Fauve's hand with her own for just for a brief moment. 'Oh, you are,' she said warmly, 'you're a genius.'

The Frenchwoman laughed and clapped her hands with delight, immediately repeating what Danni had just said to everyone else. It came as no surprise to Danni that they all agreed effusively. Then, by unspoken agreement, they all decided it was time to stop talking and start enjoying the delicious meal instead.

For a change, after dinner the small gathering retired to the huge white on white sitting-room to enjoy coffee and Calvados. Danni sat nursing a huge balloon glass. She swirled the amber liquid around the smooth sides of the glass and occasionally took a tentative sip. Unused to drinking brandy, she found it went straight to her head, even on a full stomach.

Replete with good food and bonhomie she felt herself relaxing further into the squashy sofa. Her eyelids felt heavy, her whole body limp with drowsiness. Ivan came and sat next to her, his hand massaging her bare thigh as he talked to her about the forthcoming *grande performance*, as he called it. It was only a week away and he told her that some very prominent people in international business and government circles had already booked to attend.

'What are these people like?' Danni asked. 'Are they perverts or something?' It was a question she had been longing to ask.

She couldn't help wondering if she had overstepped the mark but Ivan's instant laughter filled her with relief.

'Not perverts, my darling Danni,' he said, 'these people are aesthetes.' He turned to look her straight in the eye and took her hands, cradling them between his long, artistic fingers. 'I think you still do not understand the true nature of *Cirque Erotique*,' he continued. 'It is a unique conception. Artistic. Erotic. Think of the skilled, beautiful people you have met already. And there are others just like them. All dedicated to their art and to self-expression.'

'Will I have to make love to all of them?' Danni asked, surprising herself. It was another question that had been bothering the life out of her but she hadn't meant to actually ask it.

Again, to her relief, Ivan shook his head, though his laughter was gentler and his tone compassionate and full of understanding. 'I have told you before, Danni, the performances are similar to ballet and it is, after all, a proper circus. You seem to have the idea that Fauve and I are planning an orgy of some kind. This is not the case, although—'

'What?' Danni interrupted. She gazed back at him wide-eyed.

Behind her ribcage her heart was thumping and she could feel a mixture of anticipation and sexual excitement coursing through her veins. Her chest felt tight, her throat similarly constricted, whereas the rest of her body felt liquid with desire.

He smiled gently and stroked his hands up her arms. 'I was going to say that after the performances, some people feel the need to take things further.'

'In what way?'

Danni felt she already knew the answer but needed to alleviate the mesmerising effect he was having on her. His voice, so low and rhythmic, was hypnotic in itself. And the caress of his hands on her arms, although innocent, was indescribably arousing, stoking the fire of her passion for him.

Just at that moment Lettie bounded over to them with the grace and exuberance of a puppy – a red setter, Danni decided as she watched her long hair fly. She plopped herself down beside Ivan. Although not unwelcome, her arrival succeeded in breaking the spell between Danni and Ivan completely.

Ivan turned to her. 'Danni was just asking me what usually happens after one of our special performances,' he said.

Lettie laughed and tossed her hair over her shoulder. 'Free love,' she declared gaily.

Danni blanched. So it *was* an excuse for an orgy then.

'Only if you want to though,' Lettie added, when she noticed Danni's look of apprehension. Then she giggled and added with an expansive gesture, 'But usually *everyone* wants to.'

After a few minutes Lettie got up and wandered

away again. Then Ivan was summoned to Fauve's study to take another telephone call. Left to her own devices, Danni indulged herself in a spot of people-watching.

On the other sofa, at right angles to her, Guido was seated between Fauve and Rose with Randi sitting on the arm of the sofa on Fauve's left side.

The two women were talking to Guido, their hands massaging his thighs as they spoke. It was obvious to Danni, by their body language, that between them the two women were seducing the young Italian. Randi was watching intently, his eyes never straying from Guido's face, Danni noticed. All at once Danni found herself thinking, he fancies Guido! The surprising perception leaving her feeling oddly aroused.

Never before had she found the idea of male homosexuality a turn on. But, seeing the yearning expression on Randi's face, and understanding that Guido was unwittingly being prepared by the two women for a new experience, gave her an undeniable thrill. It made a change, for once, not to be the object of everyone's attention herself. And it was then she discovered, with startling clarity, that she wasn't the only one who had something to learn about their sexuality.

When Ivan returned to sit beside Danni again, he found her leaning on the arm of the sofa, her chin cupped in her hands as she regarded the four people on the other sofa with a rapt expression.

'Like a lamb to the slaughter,' she murmured without shifting her gaze.

Ivan laughed throatily and she felt his hand slide up her thigh. 'Prude,' he teased. Just at that moment his hand encountered her bare buttock and he added, 'Hang on, I take that back. You, young lady, are not wearing any panties, are you?'

This time she did turn her head. Her cheeks were pink as she smiled coyly at him. 'I wondered how long it would take you to find out.'

By midnight the atmosphere in the expansive sitting-room had changed considerably. Charged with sexual tension, it now provided the setting for the sort of scenario that Danni had been worrying herself about for days. Only she wasn't worried any longer. In fact, she was surprised to discover just how much she was capable of enjoying.

Inflamed by the discovery of her naughty secret – his words – Ivan had proceeded to caress and arouse Danni to such a degree that she hardly offered any protest when he began to make love to her right there on the sofa. Gradually Lettie had drifted across the room to ask politely if she could join in. After only a moment's hesitation, Danni had invited her to join them. She was lying full length on the sofa with her dress pushed up under her armpits and her thighs splayed wide with Ivan kneeling between them.

He caressed her lower body gently, a couple of fingers pushing deeply into her vagina while he stroked her clitoris with his thumb. He had slipped his other hand under her buttocks and now gently

395

massaged them as he concentrated on arousing her.

Danni expected Lettie to start stroking her bared breasts and was eager for her to start doing so, even arching her back provocatively as an open invitation. So her surprise was mingled with a little disappointment when the young redhead opted to kneel behind Ivan and unzip his fly. His cock filled her tiny hands and Lettie began stroking it eagerly to even greater hardness, while all Danni could do was watch and simultaneously take her own pleasure.

Once again she surprised herself by becoming aroused by the sight of Ivan's cock in Lettie's hands. She watched one slim white hand delve into his trousers to cup his balls and felt an answering frisson of desire.

On the other sofa, Fauve and Rose were busy disrobing Guido who, by the expression on his face, was transported into another realm of ecstasy. Meanwhile, Randi was caressing himself, his stubby cock turgid in his broad hands. A moment later he offered his cock to Guido's open mouth and, after only a moment's hesitation, the young Italian man accepted the ample offering between his lips.

'Oh, God!' Danni grunted.

She couldn't help it. The sight of that cock, dark-skinned with a helmet of livid purple, disappearing into Guido's insolent pink mouth was too arousing. The release of her pleasure was beyond her control. Passion surged through her and, as she watched Lettie's hands working furiously on Ivan's cock, and felt the warm spurt of his semen on her belly, she came with an even louder groan and a frantic churning of her hips.

Until that moment Al, who had merely been a voyeur, walked over to the sofa and gently motioned to Ivan to move out of the way. He grasped Danni by the waist and pulled her up into a sitting position on the edge of the sofa. Lettie obligingly unzipped his jeans and he wriggled out of them. Underneath the jeans his tanned body was naked, his belly washboard flat and his cock impressive in its dimensions.

It reminded Danni of a salami – fat, brown and mouth-wateringly delicious. Avidly, she wet her lips, her hands reaching out automatically to enfold him. His cock felt like a solid rod of muscle and she could feel it twitching with excitement, the blood surging through the prominent veins. Glancing up at Al's face, she asked him to stand in front of her. When he did so, she opened her mouth and fed his cock in inch by delectable inch.

Naked now, Lettie moved to sit behind Danni. Her slim legs slid around her hips and Danni could feel the softness of the young woman's pubic hair as it brushed her buttocks. Whimpering with pleasure Danni felt Lettie's hands rubbing her back and shoulders, then her sides and finally the eager, aching globes of her breasts. With her mouth full of Al's cock, one hand gripping his thigh, the other cupping the heavy weight of his scrotum, she felt her desire mount all over again.

'Beautiful, Danni,' Ivan crooned, stroking her hair. 'You make me so proud, so happy.'

His cock, still rigid, stroked her cheek and she felt a drop of semen streak her skin. Her hand left Al's thigh and reached up to caress Ivan instead. It was the first time she had handled two cocks at once and the very lasciviousness of it made her feel suffused with voluptuous abandon.

Al didn't come in her mouth but urged Danni and Lettie at the last moment to caress each other's breasts while his hot fluid jetted all over them. And she was so wrapped up in the moment that it didn't occur to Danni to demur against his suggestion. Her hands cupped Lettie's tiny, uptilted breasts quite naturally and it was only as she felt the exquisite rosebud nipples between her fingertips that she suddenly became aware of what she was doing.

To hell with it! she thought, tossing aside her natural reticence. This was fun – all of it. Nobody was being hurt or shamed by what was taking place. And everyone was over the age of consent. Why not simply abandon her old inhibitions and go with the flow for a change? With her breasts smeared and tacky with semen, Danni put her arms around Lettie and pulled her close. Their naked bodies meshed, bare breasts – one pair golden brown, the other ivory and rosy-tipped – meeting, flesh on flesh. A moment later Danni experienced her first kiss with another woman.

Their lips met, soft and succulent, opening naturally to exchange sweet, feminine breath. Then their tongues, red darting spears of pleasure, stroked and jostled within the wet cavern of their joined mouths. Danni brushed the sensitive tip of her tongue along the juicy inner flesh of Lettie's lips, quivering to the young woman's answering caress. Poignant and achingly delicate, the bliss of their embrace was without parallel.

'Let me go down on you, Danni,' Lettie begged, when they finally pulled apart. 'You've got such a lovely cunt I want to taste it.'

To know that that sweet mouth was capable of producing such crude words only served to heighten Danni's arousal. She felt the jangling of indecision mingle with the pure white fire of indecent desire. Feeling only the merest flicker of apprehension, Danni waited as Lettie stretched herself out on the sofa. Then she knelt obediently, her knees either side of Lettie's head, with her sex positioned over the young woman's wet, pouting lips.

'Lick her too, sweetheart,' Ivan urged. He caressed her bottom and whispered in her ear. The warm breath on her neck was almost as tantalising as the fingers stroking the cleft between her buttocks and the tongue flickering over her throbbing clitoris.

Still, Danni shook her head weakly. 'I can't,' she said in a hoarse whisper, despairing of the prudish rein that still held her back. But even as she spoke she noticed how beguiling the little nest of red curls looked as they nestled between Lettie's pale thighs. Her pubic hair was quite fine and Danni could make out the pouting pinkness of her vulva. The twin lips of her outer labia had parted slightly to reveal the blushing wrinkly folds of her inner flesh. And when, in the next moment, Lettie drew her knees up and let them fall apart wantonly, Danni saw how her vagina streamed with moisture.

'Taste her,' Ivan crooned in her ear, 'try her sweetness for yourself.'

Allowing her arms to take her weight, Danni placed her hands palm down either side of Lettie's hips. The fleshy bloom of the young woman's sex beckoned to her. She lowered her head tentatively, her eyes feasting on the sight of the juicy, blushing flesh. After a moment the need to touch and explore overcame her. Resting all her weight on one palm, she used the fingers of her other hand to stroke the young woman's mound in an experimental way. The hair was soft and springy and the flesh beneath warm to the touch. Her hand slipped between Lettie's legs, the middle finger easing neatly down the slit between her parted labia. Almost of its own volition, it slid into the wet opening of her vagina.

Lettie, moaned and raised her hips slightly, encouraging Danni to explore her more deeply. At the same time her tongue flickered with increasing rapidity over and around Danni's clitoris. Danni felt her breath catch as her senses soared and her lower body became molten with desire. The hard bud of her clitoris seemed to swell even more as Lettie's tongue drummed rhythmically upon it, as though begging the young redhead to give it even more attention.

Fingers were stroking over Danni's sex. She didn't know who they belonged to, though she assumed they were Ivan's. In the next moment she heard him remark to Al about how wet she was. His insolent comment nearly drove Danni to distraction and she found herself sinking another finger into Lettie's hot, wet chasm in response.

More fingers were now holding Danni's sex wide open. Barely coherent with lust, she could feel warm breath exciting the sensitive flesh around her vagina and then a tongue diving into it like a tiny cock. Her protests emerged from her lips as desperate whimpers. Her capacity for pleasure knew no bounds, it seemed.

In the next moment, Fauve came over to kneel beside the sofa. She cupped Danni's dangling breasts in her hands and kneaded them gently but firmly, like dough.

'Pretty, pretty girls,' Fauve said in her light, accented voice, 'you like Fauve to play with you, no?'

I don't care who plays, just don't stop until I come, Danni pleaded inside her head. Her desire exploded in an anguished moan and she felt her juices flooding out of her.

'Delicious,' Al said, 'the purest honey, from a pure honey bee.' And it was then Danni realised that it was his tongue which probed inside her desperate vagina.

'Fuck her, Al,' Fauve commanded gently.

As she turned her head her lips brushed Danni's shoulder, causing Danni to quiver with delight. And the command in itself was a thrill. It sounded so lewd and yet the thought of a stiff cock inside her greedy body excited Danni beyond reason. Eager to encourage him, Danni wiggled her hips.

'Uh, keep still,' Lettie grumbled from between her legs.

Danni almost laughed but she felt too full of arousal and in the next instant her breath was snatched away as she felt Al's cock plunging into her. Unable to support herself on one hand any longer, Danni resumed her all-fours position. To make herself more comfortable she lowered her upper body so that she was resting on her forearms. With her mouth now positioned conveniently over Lettie's sex, she put out her tongue and licked the pink flesh experimentally.

It tasted good. Sweet, like honey, just as Al had described, yet with a musky, slightly salty aftertaste. Lettie's juices were quite different to the flavour of her own, Danni mused as she lapped greedily at the quivering flesh, yet just as delicious. The young woman bucked underneath her as Danni buried her face further between her legs. Her mouth was full of Lettie's dear, sweet flesh now and when she raised her head just for a moment to catch her breath, Danni was aware that her mouth and chin were dripping with the redhead's nectar.

She was grateful that Al thrust only gently, she didn't want to stop enjoying Lettie and was determined to maintain a certain rhythm that she knew would lead to orgasm. Sucking delicately on the young woman's clitoris she ran the tip of her tongue over the sensitive little pearl at its tip. Lettie bucked her hips convulsively and cried out. All the while, Fauve murmured a litany of encouragement and approval.

'So beautiful, so wet,' the Frenchwoman breathed softly, *'les filles sont incroyables.'*

Danni didn't understand all that the Frenchwoman said but her mind, in any case was elsewhere. Between Lettie's legs. Between her own legs where Al still filled her and Ivan's fingers had taken over from Lettie's tongue. The young woman was too suffused with her own pleasure to continue, Danni realised.

A moment later Fauve and Ivan swapped places and Danni felt the delicate trailing of his fingertips over her fiery breasts and nipples and following the length of her spine. The occasional soft scrape of a fingernail on her labia told her that Fauve was now stroking her clitoris. She manipulated it well, as only another woman could, stroking around and around the desperate bud. The extent of Danni's arousal felt intolerably exciting. She heard muted whimpers and knew they were her own.

When she came, a moment later, so did Al. He had no option. Danni's spasming vagina gripped him, her grasping muscles milking him of every drop. And then a moment later Lettie cried out and slammed her sex up against Danni's face, momentarily smothering her. Her clitoris swelled as though it would burst, then receded under its protective hood as her rigid thighs and clenched buttocks gave way to a gentle quiver.

All three collapsed exhausted and Danni's last impression before drowsiness overcame her, was of Guido's beatific expression as Randi drove into him from behind.

Chapter Ten

DRAGON FLAMES OF red and orange flickered around the bulbous head of the metal rod and painted a sunset reflection on the white canvas wall of the circus tent.

'Careful,' Danni warned Ivan, unnerved by the casual way he waved the flaming rod around, 'we don't want to burn the whole place down at this late stage.'

'Don't panic, it's perfectly safe,' Ivan said with a smile that battled with the flaming rod for intensity and warmth. 'Al often juggles with these you know.'

'I don't doubt it,' Danni replied, pursing her lips in a wry smile. 'That man is an American comic book super-hero come to life.'

It was Thursday morning, with only two days left to go before the grand performance. Trying to play down her feelings of nervous anticipation, Danni was determined to concentrate on the business in hand. Which, on this bright and sunny day, was fire-eating. The rod in Ivan's hand was like a gigantic match. It had a long straight stem and bulbous head, which gave a fiery burst at the merest touch of another flame.

'Now, little Danni,' Ivan instructed in a mock patronising way, 'just concentrate and watch me. Take note of how far I put the flame into my mouth. Hear my breath. No, on second thoughts,' he paused and grabbed her hand, placing the palm against the solid wall of his chest, 'feel my breath. Feel how it leaves my lungs.' So saying he leaned his head back and opened his mouth wide.

Fearful of the flame, Danni flinched out of the way as he brought the rod up and held it over his mouth. As he lowered it slowly she heard, and felt, the sharp exhalation of breath which escaped his throat and immediately extinguished the flame.

'There,' he said as he triumphantly withdrew the rod, 'nothing to it. Now you try.'

She tried to demur. No matter how many times Ivan explained the procedure, and despite the simplicity of his instructions, Danni felt certain she would end up, at best, scarring her tonsils for life.

Plenty of saliva and good breathing control were the secrets of fire eating, Ivan had told her. He had demonstrated the necessary breathing technique countless times, his hand pressed to Danni's breastbone to check that she was doing it right. The first couple of times he had done this, Danni had giggled and tried to encourage him to caress her breasts instead of concentrating on the business in hand. But, Ivan could be intractable when he wanted to be, she had discovered. And this was one of those times.

'We will have the opportunity for games later, Danni,' he admonished her gently, treating her to his melting gaze, 'but for now, we work. This is important.'

'Yes, I know,' Danni sighed wistfully. 'OK, let's give it another go.'

She thought she had the breathing right now. The technique necessitated holding a large gulp of air in her lungs, then expelling it sharply from the back of her throat. The puff had to be strong enough to extinguish the flame. If it reached her lips, it would already be too late. The saliva, Ivan also explained, was needed to dampen the flame.

Taking the rod from Ivan's hand, Danni held it nervously, feeling the way her fingers trembled. Her eyes widened as he lit the bulb at the end and it burst into flame. There was no danger of her hair catching fire, as she had previously feared. Danni had scraped it right back off her face and woven it into an untidy plait.

Fauve had offered to redo Danni's hair for her at breakfast but Danni had refused. There was a part of her she still wanted to keep to herself. Fauve might have taken her pleasure from all other parts of her body during the past few days, but her hair, Danni maintained with silent resolution, was entirely her own domain.

Even with her unruly tresses out of the way, Danni still held the flame as far as possible away from her face lest it singe her eyebrows and lashes.

'Don't be frightened of it, Danni.' Ivan counselled her gently. 'You are the mistress of this flame. Remember that. Remember who is in control.'

Right, Danni thought, taking his words very much to heart. I am in charge, so you, Mr Flame, can just go out when I want you to, OK? She felt much better now, having given the instrument in her hand a good talking to.

Breathing deeply for a few moments, she tried to calm the churning panic in her stomach and the rapid beating of her heart. All at once, her lungs felt constricted. Damn it, the air wouldn't go inside them at all!

Ivan moved to stroke the nape of Danni's neck. 'Calm now, sweetheart,' he crooned, 'just be serene and do everything the way I've told you.'

As his words filtered through Danni's ears and into her brain, she felt all her pent-up tension drain gradually from her body. Her shoulders slumped. The knot unwound in her stomach and her lungs suddenly expanded.

Taking a huge gulp of air, she held it and tipped her head back. She wanted to shut her eyes as she brought the flaming tip of the rod down to her face but forced herself to concentrate on it, and on to holding down those deep lungs full of breath. The flame disappeared inside her mouth. She exhaled hard. With one puff it was all over. The flame went out and she withdrew the rod with a beaming smile of achievement.

'Well done, my darling Danni!' Ivan exclaimed.

Taking the rod from her hand, which now trembled with excitement, he threw it to the ground. In the next instant he picked her up off her feet and whirled her around. Then he set her down and composed his thrilled expression into one of total seriousness. 'Now do it again,' he said firmly.

By lunchtime, Danni was as comfortable eating fire as she was eating the plate of sliced chicken and cold roasted peppers which had been put in front of her.

'You're a bit late, you two,' Rose said as she sat down again to finish her own lunch.

'We've been celebrating,' Ivan said without a hint of embarrassment. He ignored the look of amazement Danni flashed at him and Rose's raised eyebrows.

Christ, Danni thought, was nothing sacred! The memory of half an hour ago made her blush. Consumed by success heaped upon success, Danni had encouraged Ivan to take her from behind as she leaned forward over a small stack of hay bales. The encounter had been brief but nothing less than thrilling.

'Did you know you've got straw sticking out of you?' Lettie asked Danni cheerfully as she entered the kitchen through the back door.

As Danni glanced about her person looking for the straw, Lettie walked up to her and removed a long strand which was poking out from under her leotard just above her left hip.

Lettie sat down opposite Danni and began

pleating the golden length of dried grass. 'Heard the news?' she said, glancing at Ivan.

He shook his head. 'What news – an armed raid on the village post office?'

Lettie smiled. 'No, daft thing. I mean the petition.'

Danni, who couldn't help marvelling at the concept of Ivan being described as 'daft' gazed at the young redhead. 'What petition?'

'To stop the circus performances,' Lettie said.

To everyone's surprise, Ivan shot to his feet and slammed his palm down on the kitchen table so that everything on it rattled.

'No!' he exclaimed, his brow creasing with frustration. 'Not again. Where is Fauve?'

'Gone to the bank,' Rose offered. Her skin, normally as pinkly pale as the inside of a radish, blanched even more, Danni noticed.

All at once, it seemed as though a thundercloud had obliterated the strong yellow sun. The interior of the kitchen darkened in direct proportion to Ivan's mood.

'Those imbeciles,' he said venomously, sounding acutely foreign again to Danni's ears, 'they make a mockery of us and of our way of life. What do they know – or care?' He then proceeded to come out with a litany of expletives the like of which Danni had never heard him utter before. Some of them she didn't even understand.

The three young women shared a look of anguish mingled with surprise.

'This is the last straw!' he shouted.

410

'No, *this* is,' Lettie interrupted, picking up the crumpled length of dried grass from the table. Her sudden smile wavered and she fell silent. Looking sheepish, she dropped the straw, realising that Ivan was in no mood for jokes.

Ignoring Lettie's attempt at wit, Ivan strode to the door. He stopped when he reached it and glanced over his shoulder. His expression was black with anger.

'Tell Fauve I am in her study,' he said to no one in particular. 'I want to speak with her the moment she comes back.'

There were a few minutes silence after Ivan had gone, broken only by the ticking of the clock and the faint, occasional chirping of a bird.

'The bastards always try it on,' Lettie said at last.

'Meaning?' Danni asked.

'Meaning the villagers,' Rose supplied for her sister. 'They don't understand us, you see. They're always trying to find ways of stopping our performances and closing us down.'

'But they can't, surely,' Danni protested. 'What goes on here is private. It's none of their business.'

'In places like this,' Lettie cut in dryly, 'everything that goes on is everyone's business. Our mum used to say you can't even shit sideways without someone finding out about it.'

Danni stared at Rose for a moment. Then she felt her lips twitching. 'What an odd expression,' she said.

After another few seconds of introspective silence, all three of them burst into relieved laughter.

411

Fauve arrived to find them collapsed over the table with tears streaming down their faces. When she asked what the joke was all about, Rose told her and then gave her Ivan's message.

The Frenchwoman's expression, which had flickered with amusement, now took on a dark hue similar to that of Ivan's.

'*Bordel de Dieu!*' she exclaimed, flouncing out of the kitchen, clearly on the rampage.

Danni and the twins stared after her in amazement.

'If my memory of French crudities serves me correctly, I think our charming hostess just said "fucking hell",' Lettie muttered.

After lunch, and feeling at a loose end since Ivan's untimely departure from their schedule, Danni wandered into the big top to gaze disconsolately up at the trapeze. She was supposed to have been practising up there again that afternoon. Now, she supposed, that would have to wait until the following day.

She was surprised to feel the soft caress of fingertips on her bare arm and gave a start.

'Meah,' she said when she turned around, 'you made me jump. I was miles away.' Despite the fact that Meah was supposed to be a pupil of the circus school, Danni hadn't noticed her in the big top before.

'I saw you come in here, Danni,' the young woman confessed in her softly accented voice, 'and I follow.'

'Oh?' Danni felt lost for words and merely smiled.

After a moment, Meah resumed stroking Danni's arm. 'I like you, Danni,' she said, looking coy, 'I want that we be good friends.' Her thick, dark eyelashes fluttered as she spoke and Danni thought she could detect a pink flush to the woman's olive-hued cheeks.

'Well, yes,' Danni said, trying to sound brisk but amiable, 'I like you too. Of course I want to be your friend.'

'Then you come with me?' Meah invited as her fingers sought Danni's hand.

Unable to think of a good reason not to, Danni shrugged. 'Sure,' she said, feeling slightly bewildered, 'where are we going?'

Their destination, as it turned out, was Meah's room. Very similar to Danni's in decor, it differed in only two ways. The first was that it had a large brass bed instead of a four poster. And the second was that the room was very neat. Danni couldn't help noticing it's tidiness as she glanced around. She sat down while Meah poured them each a glass of wine and her memory instantly flicked back to the way she had left her own room that morning: the bed unmade, dirty clothes in a heap on one of the chairs and her cosmetics strewn across the surface of the dressing-table.

In comparison, Meah's dressing-table looked as though it had just been polished and bore a rank of bottles and little tubs, arranged according to their height so that they ascended from left to right. Her

413

bed looked as though it had never been slept in and there wasn't a discarded pair of shoes, nor spare item of clothing in sight.

'You're a very tidy person, aren't you?' Danni commented as Meah handed her a goblet of white wine. The glass was tinted green, with little bubbles trapped in its twisted stem.

The young woman shrugged her bronzed shoulders. 'I suppose,' she said. 'Why not to be tidy?'

Why indeed? Danni thought as she watched Meah sit down gingerly on the edge of the bed, as though she didn't dare crease the white satin coverlet. There was nothing wrong with being neat apart from the fact that she believed that life was too short to spend cleaning and tidying things away. She liked to think she subscribed to the Quentin Crisp ethic of housekeeping, which promoted the theory that after the first few inches of dust one failed to notice any further accumulation.

'This wine is nice,' Danni said, for want of something better to say. Then, 'Have you been in this country long?'

'Three years,' Meah replied, 'but I come to the circus school for only five weeks including a visit home. To Mauritius,' she added, as though she thought Danni might assume she meant Croydon or somewhere.

Danni nodded, remembering Fauve's excitement at the young woman's return. 'And what have you enjoyed learning most of all here?' she asked.

She was surprised when a devilish glint touched the dark pools of the woman's eyes and her full ruby mouth twitched at the corners.

'Sex,' she said simply. In an expansive gesture she threw her arms wide open, almost spilling her wine on the pristine bedspread. 'I love it, it is my life now.'

A strange, uncomfortable feeling crept over Danni as she gazed in wonder at the young woman's animated expression. There was something so beguilingly innocent about her, yet at the same time she possessed an animal magnetism. Like a sleek, glossy-haired cat, she exuded a primal heat that screamed out carnal desire from every pore. In was in the way she looked, the way she moved, even the way she sat.

Like now, Danni thought, eyeing the way Meah's proud breasts heaved and thrust provocatively against the simple white cotton top she wore. And how her thighs, barely covered by matching shorts, remained loosely crossed, as though prepared to fall apart at any moment. All it would take, Danni mused, was the merest request, or hint of an erotic caress.

Meah was, she decided, sex incarnate. The living, breathing embodiment of all things licencious. Her hair, which tumbled over her shoulders in thick dusky waves, looked as though it had just been mussed up by a lover. Her easy grace was that of someone who had just tumbled out of bed, still half asleep and consumed by erotic dreams. Sensuality swamped her, from her wriggling brown toes and silky limbs, to her sullen mouth and slumberous eyes.

Good God, I think I fancy her! The realisation brought Danni's covert appraisal to an abrupt halt and she lowered her eyes hastily. She pretended to admire the twisted stem of the green glass and traced it with her fingertips.

It was something she had known all along, she thought, but hadn't wanted to admit, even to herself. From that first evening when she had set eyes on the exotic young woman and coveted the sensation of her milky brown nipples between her lips, the desire for Meah had lain dormant inside Danni's subconcious. Even now, Danni could still recall the musky scent of her arousal and the glossy thatch between her slender thighs, where tendrils of curly hair had become coated with her creamy juices. Her sex had reminded Danni of white chocolate on dark, with a succulent oozing of raspberry filling.

Feeling herself suddenly becoming warm Danni pulled awkwardly at the clingy leotard.

'You are uncomfortable in that thing,' Meah observed. 'You take it off, yes?'

'Well, no I—' Danni began, then stopped. For a moment all she could think about was lying naked beside the dusky young woman. Touching those breasts . . . Between those thighs . . . Did she taste as bittersweet as she looked? she asked herself, feeling her heart begin to pound.

To slake her dry mouth, she took a gulp of wine, then placed her glass on the floor. Standing up she slowly eased the leotard off. Feeling strangely unabashed for once she drew it over her shoulders and peeled it down her body until it spilled around her feet. Then she picked her glass of wine up again and walked boldly towards the bed.

Meah's eyes glittered with excitement. Her red lips parted as Danni walked towards her and, just as Danni reached her, she moved forward and flung her arms around Danni's waist.

Danni gasped with surprise as Meah nuzzled between her breasts. Immediately she felt the wet, exploratory flickering of Meah's tongue.

'Yes,' she murmured, capturing handfuls of the young woman's silky tresses, 'oh yes please.'

Ivan found them entwined together on the bed and was immediately entranced by the sight. Two beautiful women. Naked and unashamed, cloaked only by temporarily satiated bliss. He knew both of them well enough to know that their desire would never be fully assuaged.

Danni was a firebrand, every bit as hot and impulsively reckless as the leaping flames which he had taught her to consume that morning. While Meah tended to simmer. She was the calm before the storm, a tropical heatwave of lust and submissive depravity. Fauve had recognised that much in her right from the start. But then, he reasoned, stepping through the open doorway into Meah's room, no one knew women as well as Fauve.

She had taught him much. And taught him well. He had been young and enthusiastic when he first met her. But without the refinement that he now displayed. Through careful, though wholly pleasurable hours of instruction, during those long sex soaked nights in every corner of the globe, the Frenchwoman had taught him how to please her. How to take his time and appreciate the natural sensuality of the human body.

Then she had encouraged him to practise his newfound art on other women. Those less fortunate than Fauve who hadn't ever known what it was like to be made love to properly. He had a black book as thick as the New York telephone directory and a memory that took him back over many, many bodies and grateful, slumberous smiles.

'If you ever grow tired of the circus, my pet,' Fauve had teased him once, 'you could become a gigolo and be paid for your skill.'

He had laughed off her suggestion. Not because it was a ridiculous notion but because the circus was in his blood. Generations of his family had travelled the world: acrobats, trapeze artists, fire-eaters and lion-tamers. Only he had become a ringmaster and at the one circus which held an unequalled cachet among aesthetic circles – Le Cirque Erotique.

'Ivan?' Danni opened one sleepy eye.

'Yes, sweetheart,' he said, moving to sit on the edge of the bed. He stroked her bare shoulder and glanced at Meah. 'You finally came together then?'

Danni giggled at his pun, knowing it was unintentional and giggled still more at his frown.

'You don't mind, do you,' she asked, wondering if she had misinterpreted his expression. To her relief his face softened into a smile.

'No, silly girl,' he said, 'of course not. I am delighted. Meah has wanted you for so long and you have wanted her, I think.'

She nodded gently. 'Yes, you're right,' she murmured, keeping her voice low so as not to disturb Meah, 'but I only realised I desired her this afternoon.'

He smiled. 'Then it was fortunate I was not around.'

Danni lay back, treating him to an uninhibited view of her naked body. 'How did that business with the petition go – did you manage to sort it out?'

'Not yet,' he said, frowning slightly again, 'but Fauve is – as Al would put it – on the case.'

Just at that moment Meah stirred between them and her heavy-lidded eyes fluttered open. If she was surprised to see Ivan there beside her, she didn't show it.

'Hi,' she said, giving him a sleepy smile. 'You join, yes?'

Ivan hesitated, wondering what Danni would think about it but she smiled and nodded encouragingly.

'Oh yes, do,' she said. 'It would be nice to have a man with us.'

'Ah, so that is all I am to you both, is it?' he joked as he stood up and started to take off his clothes.

'Any cock in a storm,' Danni responded cheekily.

She winked at Meah who gave her a sultry, long-lashed wink back.

As she and Meah moved over to welcome Ivan's long lean body between them, Danni couldn't help marvelling at how far she had come in such a short space of time. At the start of her stay at the circus school she would have been appalled at the idea of sharing Ivan with anyone, even though he had been a brand new lover. Now she felt truly liberated. In body and in mind.

The soft caress of Ivan's hair as he moved to nestle his head between her thighs induced a sigh of pleasure from Danni. Twisting her upper body slightly she began to caress Meah, trailing her fingertips lightly over the brown globes of the young woman's breasts and down over the gently rounded belly to stroke the pulpy flesh between her parted thighs.

Gentle moans filled the air, to be carried away on the late afternoon breeze. The curtains, filmy white, billowed into the room from the open window like interested ghosts – spectral voyeurs who were keen to witness what was taking place on the brass bed.

Danni felt suffused with voluptuous abandon. Her erotic thoughts darted and drifted through her mind as the gentle insistence of Ivan's lips and tongue upon her most intimate flesh carried her to her first orgasm.

He turned to Meah then, whispering instructions to her to move onto her hands and knees so that Danni could wriggle under her and caress her dangling breasts. Pressing his mouth to the open wetness of Meah's sex, Ivan heard her moan and felt the trembling in her body. Danni was suckling her breasts he noticed, her mouth full of one juicy nipple and then the other as her hands rhythmically kneaded both silky brown orbs.

When she had had her fill of Meah's breasts, Danni moved to lie under Ivan instead and took his cock in her mouth. Stroking her lips and tongue down the stem, she paused to lap greedily at his balls before returning to engulf him once again.

They moved in harmony. Their bodies changing position and emphasis until all of them had enjoyed at least one orgasm. Then Danni sat astride Ivan and took his penis deep inside her while Meah straddled his head. As if by silent agreement, the two young women leaned forward to clasp each other's shoulders. They kissed, damp tendrils of dark hair obliterating their faces as their mouths meshed.

Heat surged through Danni. Ivan's cock felt deliciously hard inside her. It stroked her velvety walls and glanced tantalisingly off her G-spot. She tasted Meah's gasps of arousal, felt her body squirming under her hands. At one point she glanced down and noticed how Ivan's tongue speared the young woman. Delving right inside her succulent depths, it finally emerged, glistening with her juices.

The sight drove Danni wild and her fingertips sought the throbbing bud of her own clitoris and massaged it frantically. When she noticed that

Meah was watching her masturbate she felt a further surge of pleasure.

'Come for me, Danni,' Meah whispered, her voice hoarse with passion as she clutched at her own breasts and threw her head back.

Frissons of sublime pleasure coursed through Danni. Meah looked beautiful in the throes of voluptuous abandon. Ivan *was* beautiful. And as for herself, Danni felt as sensual and decadent as a siren luring sailors to disaster as she rode Ivan mercilessly.

Joined together in an erotic trio, they bucked and gasped and fondled and licked. And, a few moments later, all three of them came in a tumultuous expulsion of ecstatic groans.

Chapter Eleven

OF ALL THE feelings Danni had experienced during the past couple of weeks, despair hadn't been one of them. Until now. Sitting on the edge of her bed, her melancholy gaze taking in the bright, airy room and its trappings, she felt acutely homesick. Not for the flat in West London to which she was due to return the day after next but for the place she would be forced to leave – *Cirque Erotique.*

It surprised her that in such a short space of time she could have grown so attached to the circus school and its inhabitants. She had always thought putting down roots involved years of living in the same place and seeing the same old faces: the postman, the Asian couple who ran the late-night grocer's on the corner of her road, even Geoff Wilson, the policeman who religiously walked her particular beat. Now, she thought, she knew better. Belonging wasn't about waving at a familiar face across the street, nor exchanging the same old pleasantries with the old lady nextdoor with nine cats and chronic asthma. It involved getting to know people properly, understanding how they ticked, how they might be feeling at any given time. In all her years as an adult she didn't recall ever feeling as close to anyone as she did to Ivan and the others – even Fauve, who was somewhat remote in comparison.

At that moment Rose popped her head through the doorway that opened out onto the farmyard.

'Hey, misery guts, aren't you coming to get some breakfast?' she asked cheerfully. Her smile faltered when Danni shook her head and deliberately glanced away so that Rose wouldn't be able to see the unshed tears glistening in her eyes. But Rose wasn't to be put off. 'Now, what's all this about?' she persisted, coming into the room and sitting next to Danni. She put a consoling arm around Danni's shoulders and hugged her comfortingly. 'What's the matter, it can't be that bad? Nothing really bad ever happens here.'

Danni turned to look at Rose, her eyes registering the pale pointed face, so like her sister's yet with a more pronounced smattering of freckles across the bridge of her nose. It was this that set the twins apart, making it easier to distinguish one from the other, at least at close quarters.

'I'm dreading going back,' Danni admitted, gulping back a sob. She glanced around and as she did so, the tears were jostled from her eyes and slid slowly down her cheeks in fat, wet drops.

'Oh, crikey,' Rose said, 'you are in a bad way. And I haven't even got a tissue.'

At this, Danni sniffed, then laughed and hiccupped all at the same time. Finally she managed a watery smile. 'I know, I'm just being an idiot,' she said, 'I'll get over it.'

Rose sat back a bit and regarded her thoughtfully. 'Maybe,' she murmured sagely, 'or more likely you won't.' She glanced down at her lap, then up again, fixing Danni with a frank stare. Her pale blue eyes were unblinking. 'I think you're one of us,' she said, surprising Danni. 'Me and Lettie felt just like you do now when it was time to leave. That's why we left home and came here. We haven't looked back. Never been happier, not in our whole lives.'

'And Fauve let you stay here?' Danni asked. 'Just like that.'

Pursing her lips, Rose seemed to consider her question for a moment before answering carefully, 'Not exactly just like that. She gave us both the third degree, I can tell you. Proper put us on the spot she did, wanting to know why we really wanted to stay, as though the relaxed atmosphere and the feeling of being surrounded by really good friends wasn't enough.'

'Was it enough for Fauve?' Danni knew those were exactly the same reasons why she wanted to stay. Somehow, she felt, for a realist like Fauve, they would prove an inadequate explanation.

'Not exactly,' Rose admitted. 'She really kept on digging until we had dredged up all our feelings.'

'And those were?' Danni prompted.

At that, Rose chuckled. 'Well, I'm not going to

tell you, am I? You might come out with the same reasons. The trouble is, if you're only echoing someone else you're not going to sound very convincing.' She paused then added, 'One thing I can tell you, Fauve is a real sucker for sincerity. If she believes you – and believes *in* you – then she'll be your friend for life.' She gave a deep sigh and then stood up, pausing only to plant a gentle kiss on Danni's cheek. 'Why don't you talk to her,' she suggested. 'It can't hurt.'

For a moment Danni felt as if her own private sun had come out again. Then, just as quickly, a cloud of apprehension drifted across it. What if Fauve didn't want her to stay? Danni wasn't even sure if the Frenchwoman liked her all that much. Maybe she was even a little bit jealous of her relationship with Ivan. Danni was a beginner in every sense of the word and not particularly skilled at any of the circus arts which she had learned. Supposing Fauve simply thought she wasn't worth the effort?

'I will talk to her,' Danni said resolutely to Rose. She stood up and walked into the bathroom to blow her nose before coming back into the pretty bedroom. Glancing around, she took the young woman's arm in a friendly gesture. 'Come on,' she muttered, dragging her towards the door, 'the condemned woman must eat a hearty breakfast first.'

Danni tracked Fauve down to her study. It was the first time she had been there and was surprised to discover how different it was from the rest of the rooms in the farmhouse.

Instead of stark, modern simplicity, Fauve's study was a cosy blend of old and new. Antique tables of burnished walnut and mixed wood marquetry stood cheek by jowl with high-backed metal sculpted chairs – like thrones – and steel filing cabinets. The *pièce de résistance* – as Fauve would have described it herself – was her desk. It was a delicate confection of black Chinese lacquer. The modesty panel at the front depicted a typically Chinese scene of a temple and various figures in traditional costume. And the glossy top of the desk bore the incongruous accessory of a word processor.

Seated behind the desk, in a metal and black leather chair, was the enigmatic woman herself. She wore a pair of half-moon glasses perched on the tip of her elegant little nose and she was flicking through the pages of a weighty personal organiser. Covered in black leather, it conveyed the impression that it's owner was a very efficient and popular person.

'I – I did knock,' Danni explained hesitantly, when Fauve glanced up.

The Frenchwoman appraised her silently over the rim of her glasses and motioned to Danni to sit on one of the high-backed chairs opposite her.

'Is there something I can do for you, *ma chère*?' she said, closing the personal organiser and reclining back in her chair. She took off the glasses and placed them on the top of the desk, then sat back again, crossed her legs and clasped her knee with both hands.

'I don't know where to start,' Danni admitted, feeling distinctly uncomfortable.

She found herself staring at Fauve's long red fingernails and wished she hadn't come now. And yet, she told herself firmly, if she didn't take the chance now she would never forgive herself for the missed opportunity.

'Try at the beginning,' Fauve encouraged her with a gentle smile.

Speaking hesitantly at first and then becoming bolder, Danni repeated everything she had told Rose that morning. Just as Rose had said she would, the older woman asked her to describe her real feelings. And Danni did, the words just gushing out before she even had a chance to think about them.

'I just can't bear the thought of going back to my old life,' Danni finished, somewhat lamely she thought, after her outpouring.

'Everything has changed for me since I came here. I'm not the same person any more.'

Fauve was silent for a long time and Danni hardly liked to rush her when she was obviously thinking. With her head turned towards the window she seemed to be gazing at an unseen place, far beyond the boundaries of the front gates and the lane beyond.

While Fauve pondered Danni's dilemma, Danni concentrated on stroking the ears of Delilah, the black labrador. As though grateful for the young woman's undivided attention, Delilah rolled her eyes and settled her chin more comfortably on Danni's lap.

'She likes you,' Fauve said, turning back to Danni and smiling.

Danni nodded wordlessly. Yes, she thought, but is that enough reason to let me stay here?

Presently, Fauve let out a sigh and stood up. She walked to the window and turned, perching her neat jeans-clad bottom on the sill. Then she folded her arms and gazed thoughtfully at Danni. She was wearing the same outfit that she had worn to greet Danni the first day she arrived.

'I do not know what to say to you, *ma chérie*,' Fauve said at last.

Danni groaned inside, desperation gnawing at her. This was it then, this was the big heave-ho.

'But,' the Frenchwoman added, smiling again, 'I 'ave the feeling I should not just say no. I think we need to consider this, you and I. And Ivan,' she said, almost as an afterthought. 'I must ask him what he thinks about all this.'

'He doesn't know,' Danni said quickly. 'I wanted to speak to you first.' She couldn't help noticing Fauve looked surprised.

Then I think it is best if I talk to him first,' the older woman said, 'after all, he is my partner.'

Danni left Fauve's study feeling no more secure about her future than when she had entered. When she met up with Ivan in the big top he couldn't help remarking how worried she looked. To her relief, he seemed to assume that her concerns were about the forthcoming performance.

'I think we will not practise this morning,' he said, taking her arm and steering her towards the exit. 'Al will be here this afternoon to put everyone through their paces but for now we will relax and watch a little film.'

'A film?' Danni's eyes widened in surprise. 'What is it about?'

For the first time since breakfast she felt herself relax as Ivan's warm smile drifted over her. 'The circus, of course,' he said. 'What else?'

If only all cinemas could be as comfortable and as intimate as this, Danni thought as she relaxed further back into the sofa. They were seated in the sitting-room – the only room in the farmhouse that had a TV and video – its hugeness made intimate by the drawn curtains which blocked out the rest of the world.

The video film which they were watching was a complete history of the circus, from its origins in 421 BC, when Socrates was entertained by a troupe of entertainers, and later, in the first century AD, by which time trained animals had started making an appearance. It took them to every country in the globe, depicting various acts and some amazing performers and pieces of equipment.

Danni was particularly taken by a young man named Elvin Bale, who was noted for his skills on the trapeze and had performed with the Ringling Barnum Circus.

'Watch how he does this,' Ivan urged her. He

leaned forward and grasped her knee absently while the television screen flickered with the black and white film. 'Don't blink or you'll miss it,' he added on a cautionary note.

Danni kept her eyes glued to the screen obediently and gasped with amazement as the young man plunged forward from a swinging trapeze and then caught himself by the heels.

'Sensational!' she exclaimed, wide-eyed with delight.

Ivan turned his head and smiled. 'I thought you would enjoy this,' he said. Then he turned his attention back to the film. 'Now watch. This piece of apparatus is called the Whirling Wheel.'

The Whirling Wheel, Danni noted, was a giant wheel of metal and mesh which could spin and revolve at the same time. The contraption was no match for the fearless Elvin Bale, who walked and balanced on it with more grace than the average person on terra firma.

The next scene showed another performer, the unfortunately and inappropriately named Fatini, at the Tower Circus in Blackpool. His act involved something that looked like a street lamp, upon which he balanced on his hands, while the incredibly tall, thin pole swayed dangerously from side to side like a reed in a gale.

Danni was no less impressed by the performers whose acts involved trained circus animals and, by the time the film came to an end, she had temporarily forgotten her despondency. Instead her jade green eyes were glowing when she finally sat back and smiled a thank you at Ivan.

'I feel so inspired,' she said to him while they waited for the video to rewind. 'Right now I could go into the big top and fly like a bird on the trapeze, juggle ten clubs at once and do a hundred backflips.'

'I don't doubt it,' Ivan said, smiling back at her. 'You're a natural, Danni.'

'I am?' She stared at him in amazement.

No one had ever told her that before. Apart from her parents perhaps, who had often commented that she was a natural disaster area. It was then she decided to confess to him her desire to stay, despite knowing that Fauve wanted to speak to him about it first.

'Ah,' he said enigmatically. He looked, Danni thought, quite unsurprised by her admission. 'That explains why Fauve asked me to join her for lunch in private. You have spoken to her about this, I take it?'

'Yes,' Danni said, feeling all her old doubts returning at the mention of Fauve, 'but she didn't look too keen.'

Ivan laughed then and pulled her into his arms. He stroked her hair and shoulders in a comforting, non-sexual way and Danni felt about three years old again.

'Fauve is not the sort of woman to look keen, as you put it,' he told her. 'She prefers to remain inscrutable, like a Chinese Mandarin. But I know she likes you and is very pleased by the way you have settled in here. It is not for everyone.'

'I love it here,' Danni said earnestly, 'the people are so wonderful and friendly. And then there's—' she broke off hastily.

'Yes?' he prompted.

Biting her bottom lip, Danni hesitated. 'I was going to say then there's you, but to be honest I think it's more than that. I feel so free here. I've done things I never dreamed of doing before. And I don't just mean circus things,' she added, blushing.

'I understand, sweetheart,' Ivan said, dropping a kiss on the top of her head. He turned his wrist to glance at his watch. The chrome dial showed it was almost eleven o'clock. 'You must go, Danni,' he said with more urgency and gently easing her away from him. 'Al wants you all to rehearse today and I must try to appease the village idiots. The last thing we need tomorrow night is a petition-waving delegation gatecrashing our performance.'

'Do you think it could come to that?' Danni asked, alarmed. She suddenly had visions of herself involved in some sort of erotic situation and being besieged by photographers from the *Sun* and the *News of the World*. Christ, it didn't bear thinking about, her parents would go spare! She blanched visibly.

'Not if I can help it,' Ivan assured her as he stood up.

His manner was brisk now and Danni decided to make a tactful withdrawal and let him get on with it. She left him with an uncommonly chaste peck on the cheek and wandered off to the big top to find Al and the others.

She awoke on Saturday feeling as though it were Christmas morning and the last day of the summer holidays all rolled into one. She couldn't wait to take part in the grand performance that night and could hardly contain her excitement every time she thought about it. But knowing it would also be the last time she would be together with everyone in the big top made her feel, in the next instant, dreadfully low. It was a seesaw of emotions upon which she couldn't seem to balance. Oh, to be like Elvin Bale, or the great Fatini, they had known how to keep their equilibrium under far more horrendous circumstances.

After breakfast, Fauve invited everyone into the sitting-room to see their costumes. Danni trailed after the chic Frenchwoman wishing she would turn around and say something encouraging. Since the previous morning no mention had been made about Danni's request to stay. Not even by Ivan, who had spent the whole night in her bed.

They had enjoyed a wonderfully sensuous time, made all the more poignant for Danni who hadn't been able to help wondering if it would be their last. She was under no illusions that, on Saturday night, she would be involved in sexual activity with a variety of people, but couldn't be sure if Ivan would be one of them. And being part of a group certainly wouldn't have the same exclusive eroticism as making love in private.

The pendulum swing of Fauve's hips under a tight black skirt stopped at ten to five as she came to a halt in the open doorway to the sitting-room and stood hand on hip.

Glancing over the Frenchwoman's shoulder Danni allowed her mouth to drop open in amazement. For there in front of them were arranged rail upon rail of brightly coloured clothing. Like jewels, the outfits sparkled on the hangers – amazing confections of Lycra and gauze, some hardly more than a wisp of tinted cobweb.

Fauve started up her pendulum motion again and everyone filed into the room. With expectant smiles on their faces, they waited patiently while the older woman walked over to the rails and began handing out items of clothing to their new owners. Occasionally she held a garment in front of herself – a pair of tangerine harem pants; a gauzy shroud of palest pink; a stretchy body-suit of harlequin colours.

'This is for you,' Fauve murmured, handing Danni one of her outfits.

Danni held it up and considered it carefully. It looked as though Fauve had reached up to the sky and snatched a piece of it with which to fashion this garment. Of the palest blue, streaked with white, it was a short floating dress of the purest chiffon. Although it was lovely, doubt crept easily into Danni's mind. There was no disguising the fact that, when she put it on, the garment would be completely transparent.

'Don't worry, sweetheart,' Ivan whispered in her

435

ear, 'you will look so beautiful—'

'I can't wear this, not in front of all those strangers,' Danni interrupted him. Ivan had told her that almost three hundred 'invitations' to the grand finale had been accepted.

'Of course you can,' he said placatingly as he ran a thoughtful hand over her buttocks. 'Remember, you will be there to be admired. For your skill as well as your beauty.'

There was no time to argue with him. At that moment Fauve interrupted them, pressing another garment into her hands. This one looked more like a bikini. Made of black satin, it had long slits at the front of each underwired cup and the pants were crotchless. Silver and white sequins edged the slits and Danni realised straight away that they would merely serve to draw attention to those parts of the body which were exposed.

'This is to be worn with the bikini,' Fauve said, handing Danni a black cape.

It was constructed of panels of ebony chiffon and taffeta and fastened around the neck with a sequined collar. The cape also had a voluminous taffeta hood.

'To hide my blushes presumably,' Danni said, unable to stop the comment from slipping out.

Fauve and Ivan exchanged a glance, then they both looked at her.

Danni felt herself reeling from the intensity of their dual gaze and was grateful when Fauve reached out and put a hand on her shoulder. At least it stopped her from falling over.

436

'We 'ave decided,' Fauve said, 'that if you still want to, you may stay on 'ere.'

It took a few moments for her words to sink in.

'Really?' Danni gasped in amazement, 'Do you really mean it?'

Fauve and Ivan's faces lit up with smiles and the older woman planted delicate, rosebud kisses on each of her cheeks.

'Welcome to *Cirque Erotique*,' she said simply, in a husky voice that sounded choked with emotion. Then she seemed to recover her usual sang froid, turning and clapping her hands together briskly to summon everyone's attention. They all glanced up: Al, Guido, Randi, Meah and the twins, Lettie and Rose. '*Tout le monde*, Danni 'as decided to become the latest member of our *petite troupe estimée*,' Fauve announced in the Franglais that was typical of her and which Danni found so endearing.

A whoop of congratulation went up and, with all the élan of a conjurer, Ivan produced a bottle of champagne. There was a tray of glasses on a black lacquered side table and now he shared the foaming mixture amongst them and handed a glass to each person in the room.

'To Danni,' he said in a simple toast, raising his glass aloft.

'To Danni,' they all chorused.

Glancing around at all of them, Danni felt herself glowing with pleasure. Now, at last, she felt as though she really and truly belonged at *Cirque Erotique*.

A little while later, they all took their costumes back to their rooms. Al's room was next to Danni's and so he walked with her across the courtyard, chivalrously taking command of her costumes. When they reached her room, she invited him in for a cold drink.

'That champagne has made me feel thirsty, would you believe?' she said, laughing.

'Where shall I put these?' Al asked, holding up her costumes – such as they were, she thought, taking them from him and hanging them on the hook on the back of the bathroom door.

She noticed that, for once, he didn't have his long hair tied back in a ponytail. Instead it fell down his back in a smooth chestnut curtain.

'I love your hair,' she said impulsively, stroking it.

'Most women do,' he admitted but without conceit. Grasping her by the wrist, he held the palm of her hand to his mouth and kissed it.

Danni felt herself melt. Next to Ivan, Al was the most attractive man she had ever met.

'Sit down, please,' she said, feeling strangely flustered, 'I should have offered before.'

His eyes twinkled in his nut brown face. 'I'd rather *lie* down, with you, honey,' he said in a voice that was low and filled with promise.

The ache that immediately consumed her body made Danni feel faint. She reeled slightly and wondered whether it was purely by accident that she happened to veer towards the bed as she fell.

She was wearing a pair of shorts and a T-shirt and in moments Al was lying beside her, pushing her T-shirt up, over her head.

Warmth crept over her as stealthily as a cat burglar as Al stroked his broad hand across her bare stomach. Beneath the rose coloured satin bra that she was wearing she felt her breasts swell and her nipples harden. Was this to be her way of life from now on, she asked herself dreamily as he began to pull down her shorts and panties all in one go? What once would have appalled her – the idea of moving from man to man, even man to woman – now seemed as natural to her as breathing.

Sensual exploration combined with erotic gratification was the philosophy of *Cirque Erotique*. Did this mean she now considered sex to be the most important component of her life? Sex and love, she amended mentally. It was inescapable that she loved the others in different ways and felt loved in return. If there was one thing she had learned during the past two weeks, it was that everyone at the circus school respected each other and would never dream of taking advantage.

Everything that had happened to her had been with her consent – whether she had been able to admit it to herself at the time or not. Even when she had been strapped to the board after taking part in Ivan's knife throwing act, she had been the willing victim of the twins. All it would have taken was the simple word 'no' and they would have left her alone. She knew it now and realised she had known it then.

'Dreaming, honey?' Al asked as he moved to kneel between her legs. 'Open wide,' he added, smiling when she did as he asked.

'Thinking,' she corrected him, 'thinking how lucky I am.'

She finished on a gasp as Al spread her outer labia wide apart and ran his tongue down the fleshy slit between them. The silky strands of his hair tantalised the sensitive flesh of her inner thighs and stroked across her belly. Moving easily into the realm of erotic sensation, Danni willingly abandoned all attempts at rational thought for the time being. There would be plenty of time for self-congratulation when she was alone and thoroughly satiated.

Chapter Twelve

EXCITEMENT HUMMED IN the air. The atmosphere, no longer that of a rural retreat, was now one of lavish opulence. Redolent with expensive perfumes, the balmy evening breeze carried with it a strange melée of accented voices, the constant slamming of car doors, the swish of silken coats and dresses and the crunch of footsteps on the gravel path.

Shielded by the curtain, Danni watched the guests arriving, all dressed as if invited to a grand society ball. There were people of all descriptions: tall men in dress suits with willowy blondes on their arms; squat men with bald heads and handlebar moustaches; stout dowagers with throats encircled by diamonds; and arty, eccentric types with ponytails and crushed velvet jackets. Singly or in animated cliques, they streamed into the farmhouse to be greeted by Fauve. Then they would be offered champagne and canapés before being directed to claim their seats in the big top.

The side meadow had been turned into a car

park for the evening and by craning her neck, Danni could make out the gleaming bodywork of Rolls Royces and Mercedes limousines. Such ostentation was interspersed with cars much sportier but none the less expensive, Porsches, Ferraris and Aston Martins being among those that she recognised.

A knock at the door drew her away from the window and she hastened to answer it. She was surprised to see Fauve standing there. Every inch the chic Frenchwoman, she was dressed in a long black sheath of an evening gown which shimmered with sequins and sparkled almost as much as her smile.

'Surprised to see me?' she said, swaying into Danni's room.

Standing back to let her in, Danni nodded dumbly, then said, 'Er, yes, I thought you would be busy with all those guests. I've been watching them arrive.'

Fauve's smile lifted even more. 'It is a wonderful turn-out, *n'est-ce pas*?' She sat in the small chair by the bed and motioned Danni over to her. 'I 'ad to come, to wish you good luck,' she added, sounding slightly breathless, 'you are our protégée after all.'

'Well, thank you,' Danni replied, feeling overawed at being singled out for such attention when she knew the older woman had a much greater duty to her guests.

Gradually, she came to realise that Fauve was appraising her and in the next instant remembered

442

that she was dressed only in her first costume for the evening – the chiffon dress. Short and floaty it danced around the tops of her thighs when she moved and did absolutely nothing whatsoever to disguise the curves and shadows of her naked body beneath. Immediately, she felt like covering up and her hands fluttered nervously in front of her.

'Don't be shy,' Fauve insisted huskily. She reached out to Danni and slid her palms over her stomach, flattening the gauzy fabric against it and pulling it tightly over the firm globes of her breasts. Her pubic hair snagged the chiffon and was clearly visible as a neat, golden brown triangle. Fauve smiled at Danni's blushes. 'You are so beautiful,' she said, 'you must not be ashamed to show off your body.'

'Me, beautiful?' Danni laughed nervously. Although she had been told the same thing by other people during the past couple of weeks, she still couldn't get to grips with the notion.

Fauve's smile changed to an expression of pure desire. 'Yes, you, Danni,' she said. 'And your beauty is not just on the outside but comes from in 'ere.' She smoothed a thumb over Danni's ribs, just beneath her left breast.

Feeling her breath catch, Danni realised that the reason she felt so unsure of Fauve was because deep down she desired the older woman. And it was only now she understood that she had felt the first stirring of erotic longing the day she spoke to her on the phone. Later, when Danni set eyes on

Fauve for the first time, her feelings had been confirmed. At that point she had been largely ignorant of her own latent urges and what she felt inside had gone unrecognised. Danni hadn't known then what it was like to give full rein to her sensuality and that she could enjoy making love to another woman. Thank God, she mused, that she knew better now.

Kneeling down, Danni stroked her palms up Fauve's slender arms in a tender, exploratory gesture. Then, feeling emboldened by the woman's acquiescence, she leaned forward and pressed her lips to the perfectly formed rosebud mouth that glistened with bold red lipstick.

Fauve's mouth opened naturally under hers and she felt the warmth of the Frenchwoman's body as she pressed against it. The sequins prickled through the thin chiffon and she yielded to the sensation of Fauve's hands roaming her back and sliding up under the hem of her short dress to stroke her bare bottom.

'Ah, my sweet Danni,' Fauve murmured when they broke apart, 'this is so wonderful but it will not do. Not now.' She glanced at her elegant gold wristwatch and shook her head regretfully. 'Later,' she promised in a husky voice, 'after the performance. You and I, we will share our first whole night together.'

Shakily, Danni stood up. Trickles of her own juices ran down the insides of her thighs and her body felt hot and heavy, filled with a voluptuous yearning that needed to be assuaged.

'I'm so nervous,' Danni admitted, watching her fingers pleat the hem of her short dress while her mind whirled with anticipation at what was to come – and what would come later.

'You will put on a brilliant performance, I think,' Fauve said, inspiring Danni with confidence.

She stroked a finger delicately up the inside of Danni's thigh and caught some of the fluid on its tip. Holding it to her smudged lips she tasted it and smiled. Oh, yes, her eyes seemed to say, yes, Danni, we will have such fun from now on. Standing up abruptly she smacked Danni lightly on the buttocks and told her to get her things together and scoot over to the big top. Pausing to take the black satin cape from its hook on the back of the door, she draped it around Danni's shoulders.

'Better to wear this,' she advised with a wicked smiled, 'otherwise my guests, they will ravish you a thousand times over before you reach the big top.'

The thought only slightly disturbed Danni, who shivered, but with excitement rather than apprehension.

'Thank you, Fauve, for everything,' Danni said, wrapping the cape around her and reaching for the bikini which matched it.

Fauve made a tutting sound and seemed to shrug off her thanks. 'Just enjoy yourself tonight,' she said, 'and we will talk again after the show. And now I must go. Take care, Danni and *bonne chance*.'

445

As Danni stood in the wings of the big top and surveyed the ring, which was filled with familiar apparatus of all descriptions, she felt as though she would need all the luck she could get just to survive the next few hours. Although Ivan and Al had schooled her well and she knew exactly what she must do and when, she still felt horribly nervous. Never before had she performed in front of an audience and could not have imagined putting on a performance such as this – even for a lover and in total privacy.

Her gaze travelled around the banks of seating which had been erected to form a semicircle around the front half of the ring. The plush red velvet chairs were filling up fast. Divested of their coats, the audience now appeared as a shimmering, jewel coloured sea, their faces as bright and animated as their clothing. Each discovered a pair of opera glasses on their seats and Danni found herself trembling as she imagined the close up view they would have of the performers on display – including herself. No part of her would go unmissed that evening. Three hundred pairs of eyes would be able to share in every visual delight her body had to offer.

'Nervous, Danni?' Ivan spoke softly in her ear.

She glanced around and felt her eyes widening, her body responding automatically to his nearness and the splendid sight of him in his ringmaster's costume. Tight white breeches clung to his lean thighs and followed the curve of his buttocks and the intriguing bulge at his groin. Above these he wore a white silk shirt topped by a red tail coat with black velvet lapels. The breeches were tucked into gleaming black leather riding boots and his white blond hair flowed like a mane from beneath the brim of a black felt top hat. The last and most intriguing addition, one which made Danni's stomach clench with a latent desire yet to be explored, was the black leather whip which he held coiled loosely around his hand.

'You look magnificent,' Danni gasped, her eyes rapidly trying to take in the full beauty of him. She could feel her heart beating fast behind her ribs, her body melting. His stature and the gaze he favoured her with was proud and masterful.

'Thank you, darling girl,' he said softly, appearing totally unfazed by her open admiration. 'And you, of course, look beautiful.'

'I do, don't I?' she said, accepting the compliment for once.

In truth, she did feel beautiful. Rose had helped her with her hair, curling it with tongs and piling the resulting corkscrews on top of her head. The style gave her more height and showed off the sweep of her neck and shoulders which, she had been forced to admit, looked achingly lovely and graceful. And she had grown used to the filmy dress she was wearing, hardly minding now that it drew attention to the body underneath rather than disguised it at all. On her feet she wore pale blue satin ballet shoes to match her dress. And she

447

found herself high stepping as she walked, her heels hardly touching the ground as the balls of her feet took most of her weight.

The combination made her feel beautiful and ethereal, like a rather licentious fairy who flaunted and teased as she floated around. This, she was certain, was the effect Fauve had intended to achieve all along. The Frenchwoman was, Danni recognised now with an emotion close to love, a very clever, very remarkable woman and she felt privileged to be one of her chosen few – a fully fledged member of *Cirque Erotique*.

Music filled the big top, drowning out the hubbub of cosmopolitan chatter. It came from a small orchestra which, Ivan had told her, was one of the finest in Europe. Danni couldn't place the composer of the piece they were playing. She only knew a little bit about classical music yet thought she recognised the influences of Tchaikovsky, Wagner and Dvorak in there somewhere.

'We're on,' Ivan murmured softly in her ear. Then he strode past her and out into the middle of the ring.

He stood there for a moment, tall and commanding, his body turning this way and that, surveying the gathering before him with arms outstretched in welcome. Then he turned and cracked the whip. The black leather thong snaked through the air and fell, biting into the sawdust and throwing up a small cloud.

This was the signal for the opening procession and Danni, along with all the others in their brightly coloured, wantonly revealing costumes, immediately painted smiles on their faces and stepped out to meet the crowd. As she circled the ring Danni keenly felt the sensation of all eyes being upon her. Her breasts and bottom bounced as she skipped lightly on tiptoe. Her hairstyle wobbled on top of her head, one silky tendril falling to caress her cheek and shoulder. Instead of running for cover as she would have done not that long ago, she kept proudly in step. Taking the admiration of the crowd as her due, for once she felt, not as the old Danni, but beautiful and voluptuous in the most perfect, feminine way.

As she came full circle, she broke away with Guido and climbed the ladder to the trapeze. A draught of air snaked across her bare buttocks and whipped between her legs as she climbed. She felt acutely aware of the opera glasses trained on her, knowing how much must be revealed as she mounted each rung of the ladder. Her cheeks felt warm, tinted hot pink with spots of shame. Yet at the same time she was enjoying herself. Being the object of attention was wonderful – shamefully titillating yet overwhelming in its glorious flamboyance.

Below her, for she was no longer afraid to look down, she saw other members of the circus troupe engaged in various acts. Lettie and Rose were on unicycles and Danni could easily imagine the sensation of their naked vulvas pressed against the leather saddles, rubbing lightly as they pedalled. They were wearing dresses similar to her own but in a strong shade of verdant green which suited their colouring beautifully.

From the audience came ripples of applause and gasps of admiration. Danni knew that the evening would gradually warm up in terms of erotic content, while maintaining the overall theme of a traditional circus performance. Beautifully choreographed by Al, the troupe tantalised and teased the audience through carefully executed movements and displays. They caressed each other briefly as they moved together and then apart, slowly warming the atmosphere, charging it with undeniable frissons of concupiscent tension.

Aided by Guido, who cast his hand lingeringly over her breasts and between her legs as she moved, Danni climbed onto the trapeze. She swung to and fro, feeling the air current catch the hem of her dress and lift it. A collective gasp ran around the audience below, diverting Danni momentarily. After a moment she regained her composure. Moving gingerly, she allowed herself to drop down, catching the trapeze with her feet and entwining them around it. Her hold was solid, perfectly safe enough for her to let go with her hands and swing upside down.

Above her, Guido walked the tightrope, his body, lithe and swaying like a reed in tight black Lycra which clung to every curve and delineation of his lean musculature. He crossed easily, skipping the last few feet with the natural grace of one born to his chosen art and bounding lightly to land on the small platform. Then he caught the other trapeze, swung himself down to hang upside down like Danni, then swayed towards her.

Back and forth they swung, caressing each other lightly as they came together. On the third swing, Guido caught Danni's dress which hung down now over her face, and pulled at it, dragging it over her head.

Hanging bat-like and completely naked, Danni watched the ethereal piece of gauze float like thistledown to land on the net below. They hadn't rehearsed this, she thought, shocked for an instant by what had happened. But before she could gather her thoughts, Guido was swinging towards her again, positioned on his trapeze so that he could grasp her around the waist and bury his face between her wide open thighs.

She saw the upside down faces of the audience, opera glasses trained upwards, watching intently as Guido held on to her while they swung. His tongue lapped over her exposed vulva and snaked her outer labia apart. It tantalised her clitoris and glided along her slit, rimming her vagina before following the crease between her buttocks. Her cheeks flared with shame. Short of allowing herself to fall there was nothing she could do except abandon herself to the moment.

A short while later, a tumultuous orgasm weakened her grip and sent her tumbling to the ground. The net caught her trembling body and she scrambled to the edge as gracefully as she could, her face and throat flaming. Only the whispered congratulations of Al and Rose, and eventually Guido when he had descended the ladder, prevented her from feeling as though she had shamed the entire troupe.

'Marvellous,' Al said in a stage whisper as he led her, naked and still trembling, from the ring, 'I couldn't have orchestrated that better myself.'

There was no time to ponder her imagined disgrace. Danni had only a few minutes to put on her second costume of the evening. Fauve helped her to dress, sliding the straps of the bra over her shoulders and fastening it at the back. Then Danni stooped to step into the bikini bottoms.

After appearing stark naked in front of the audience, she didn't think she could feel at more of a disadvantage, yet she was surprised to find that in this outfit she did.

'Let me look at you,' Fauve said, turning Danni around so that the two women faced each other. 'Shoulders back, now,' she admonished gently when Danni tried to hunch her body to shield it. 'Let me see those lovely breasts thrusting.'

Danni stifled a nervous giggle. With her shoulders back and head erect as Fauve instructed she could feel her breasts oozing over the cups, the tips of them swelling obscenely through the slits at the front. To her complete mortification, Fauve rubbed her fingertips over the swelling buds of her nipples, exciting them, making them stand out even more.

'I rouge them,' Fauve suggested, producing a pot of blusher as if from nowhere.

Danni bit her bottom lip as the older woman's

fingers rubbed the tinted powder into her nipples. Then she glanced down. Her nipples seemed huge, all swollen and ripe like juicy berries. She stopped biting her lip to run her tongue over it and then over her upper lip.

'Good enough to eat, eh?' Fauve asked, her dark eyes glinting wickedly. 'Now we attend to your pretty little nether regions.'

Before Danni could offer any protest, Fauve sank to her haunches and considered the view that the split crotch offered. She reached out and touched Danni, making adjustments, easing Danni's outer labia apart and covering them with the satin so that her clitoris and inner labia were exposed. The fabric seemed to grip her labia, holding them in the position Fauve favoured. Then the older woman got to work with the rouge again, reddening Danni's slit so that it matched her nipples and the blush that stained her cheeks.

While she did this, Danni groped blindly for something to hold on to. Her legs were shaking so much and her clitoris, still sensitive from the orgasm that Guido had given her, throbbed and swelled even more each time Fauve's fingertips glanced across it. She stroked on the rouge with exquisite precision, circling Danni's clitoris time and time again until she was whimpering with lust. She felt so desperately aroused that, when Ivan appeared and told them that he was about to call Danni into the ring again, she almost pleaded with him for more time.

His knowing glance swept over her body, lingering

on her quivering vulva and swollen nipples before reaching her face. He fixed her with his mesmerising gaze, his expression at once lustful and commanding.

'Rude girl,' he admonished, smacking her sex lightly so that he was left with a red stain on his fingertips. 'Plenty of time for that later. You must come out and finish the show, our audience awaits.

Danni knew that this time she and Ivan would be performing together. The round, red and white board awaited her, the leather shackles open and ready to receive her wrists and ankles. Part of the grand finale was to be the knife-throwing act for which Ivan was famed. And Danni was to be his assistant. Spread-eagled and tethered, with the most intimate parts of her body diabolically exposed, the blushing flesh contrasting so acutely with the black satin, she was to appear in front of everyone as a sacrifice.

As she walked out into the ring again, her hand tucked reassuringly in Ivan's, she heard a muted ripple of applause. Then, as she positioned herself in front of the board and two young orientals – one male and one female, who Danni had never met before – stepped forward to enclose her wrists and ankles with the restraints, there was a collective gasp of approval.

She tried to concentrate on the oriental couple and blot out the vision of the sea of faces that surrounded her. The couple were dressed from neck to ankle in closely fitting black bodysuits. The bodysuits matched the colour and silkiness of their hair and had zigzag panels of smoky hued gauze across the torso, revealing a nipple here and the under curve of a breast there, as well as their entire pubic area.

They were both around the same age as her, Danni estimated, and she remembered now that they formed part of a small acrobatics troupe from Korea. The girl was a contortionist and had earlier delighted the audience by bending right over backwards. The position had thrown her barely concealed vulva into lewd prominence and she had managed to peer through her legs at the audience, her expression a mixture of feigned surprise and deliberate naughtiness.

Now Danni felt the caress of their fingers as they fastened the restraints and deliberately explored the length of her limbs. It was all part of the act, although Danni had previously rehearsed it with the twins, Lettie and Rose. Ivan strode over and pretended to shoo the couple away. The young woman cowered from the threat of the whip but the young man had to pretend to challenge Ivan. Keeping his eyes fixed on the stony gaze of the ringmaster, he slid his fingers up the inside of Danni's thigh and right into her vagina.

With a small gasp, Danni wriggled her hips as much as the restraints would allow. It wasn't part of the act but the audience loved her 'pretence' at outrage. Pretending to ignore Ivan, the young man turned to smile wolfishly at the audience, taking orders from them to probe Danni more deeply and stroke her clitoris and nipples.

'No,' Danni moaned, moving her head from side to side, trying to deny the way her body responded of its own accord.

'A virgin sacrifice,' Ivan announced. 'What should we do with her?'

The suggestions that came rebounding back from the audience were wholly licentious. They were also wickedly thrilling and Danni felt herself moving onto a higher plane of eroticism. Never before had she been treated like this, her body exposed to hundreds of voyeurs and made more open and moist by a stranger's exploring fingers.

Now the girl joined in, pinching Danni's clitoris lightly, laughing aloud when Danni moaned with desire. Leaving her throbbing clitoris alone for a moment, her hands moved up to Danni's breasts and she began to play with the nipples, pulling and pinching them until they became fully swollen and distended. She smacked Danni's breasts sharply with the palm of her hand, admonishing her for her naughtiness and lack of control.

'Rude girl,' she scolded, echoing Ivan's earlier sentiment as she slapped them again. But in her accent it came out as 'lewd girl', which was still an accurate description, Danni thought, half laughing, half groaning inside her head.

She felt so consumed by desire and by the shameful pleasure she was deriving from the situation she wondered, fleetingly, if she would ever recover. Ever be 'normal' again – whatever that was.

On the front row of the audience, directly in

front of Danni sat an oldish man, steel-haired and distinguished. Beside him sat an incredibly beautiful woman of around the same age, with a bouffant of pale hair that had obviously faded from golden blonde.

They both looked as if they had plenty of 'old money', Danni thought, trying desperately not to meet either pair of eyes. The woman was clothed in a long red taffeta dress, its luscious folds billowing out, exposing only slim ankles and a dainty pair of feet clad in matching satin shoes. Around her throat she wore a simple three string collar of black opals and similar huge, drop opals hung from her earlobes. She looked exquisite, Danni mused, holding in a gasp as the young orientals stroked and tantalised her yearning sex.

Against her will, she found her gaze drawn to that of the man. He wore a traditional black dress suit and looked immaculate but for his bow tie, the meandering ribbon of which hung from his collar. The top button of his pristine white shirt was undone and just occasionally, she noticed, he moved a finger to his throat, as though the collar was still restricting him in some way.

Realising that it was she who was having that effect on him made Danni feel less embarrassed and more voluptuous still. Fixing his pale grey eyes with her own insouciant gaze she pouted slightly and let out a clearly audible whimper. The man flushed, his finger moving to his collar again, battling against it. His eyes could not stay with hers, she noticed, with only the slightest flicker of shame, but kept dropping to that place between her legs where her flesh throbbed and pouted and streamed with the evidence of her arousal.

What Danni didn't realise was that behind her, beyond the limited scope of her vision, various scenes of similar eroticism were being enacted by the other members of the troupe. But for her and the couple on the front row, it was as if she were the only performer and they her exclusive audience.

Turning her head slightly to look at the woman, Danni noticed how she seemed to be totally involved in what was happening. Her bosom was heaving, her breathing short and rapid and two brilliant spots of pink appeared in her cheeks. Her eyes were over bright, sparkling with excitement and the tip of her tongue darted out with increasing frequency to moisten her wide, rosy lips.

Seeing this, recognising the outward signs of the woman's own arousal, Danni felt her passion mount. She wanted more than anything to offer herself to the couple, to enjoy them as they would surely enjoy her. Yet all that would happen between them would be a meeting of minds and a sharing of visual pleasure.

This was her reward, she realised. This was the reason why *Cirque Erotique* was so successful. It was the perfect combination of fantasy and fact. Voyeurs and performers conspiring to meet in an atmosphere of perfect complaisance. The audience gave their money and their appreciation and the members of *Cirque Erotique* gave their bodies and their voluptuous sensibilities in return.

Able now to embrace the true philosophy of the unique band to which she was forever joined, Danni gave herself up to the glorious sensation of giving and receiving. She arched her back, thrusting her hips forward, offering herself to her tormentors and her audience. Then, with a loud cry of joyous abandon, she came . . . and came . . . and came . . .

Afterwards, when the oriental couple stepped back to allow Ivan to continue with his act, Danni hardly noticed the flashing steel blades which whistled towards her to become embedded in the wood. She felt completely at one with the circus troupe and the audience. And as Ivan helped her to step forward and take a bow at the end of the act, her cheeks were flushed with pleasure rather than embarrassment.

They had only a few minutes to compose themselves before Ivan had to go back out into the ring to announce the finale. Fauve surprised them all again by producing a third set of costumes.

'I did not know if they would be ready in time,' she admitted, 'but my seamstresses from the village, they work like demons.'

The costumes were variations on a theme. White silk and satin, trimmed lavishly with matching feathers. Danni's dress, a clinging white sheath, clung to every curve and was cut so low at the back it showed the upper swell of her buttocks and the first inch or so of the crease between them. It dipped low at the front as well and was slit from ankle to waist, around which a matching belt was fastened at the front with a square diamanté clip.

The stark simplicity of the dress set off her tan beautifully. And when she walked, the silk flowed over her body like single cream. With each step a lean, tanned leg appeared and the slit widened to reveal a tantalising glimpse of her pubis.

'Lovely, *ma chérie*,' Fauve enthused, her face wreathed in smiles as she clapped her tiny hands together delightedly, 'and 'ere is the finishing touch.' So saying, she draped a long white feather boa around Danni's throat so that it trailed down her back, the feathers teasing her bare skin.

Danni pulled back the flap of red and white striped curtain that shielded them from the audience.

'So far so good,' she said, 'we haven't been raided by an angry mob of villagers yet.' Then she clapped a hand over her mouth and stared wide-eyed at Fauve. 'Omigod, I shouldn't have said that. It's tempting fate.'

'No need to worry,' Ivan said as he stepped through the curtain to join them, 'Fauve and I have already sorted that out.'

'How?' Danni glanced from one to the other.

Fauve held up a hand and rubbed the tips of her fingers together. 'Money, my darling girl,' she said with a wicked smile.

'It works every time,' Ivan cut in, 'they soon stopped complaining when Fauve and I offered to donate a share of the takings to the fund for a new village hall.'

'Clever,' Danni said approvingly.

'Philanthropy,' Ivan corrected her, 'is a wonderful thing.'

In the main body of the big top, the orchestra started up again. This time Danni recognised the music as Mahler.

'Our closing act,' Ivan said, 'wait one moment, Danni, I have a couple of friends for you.'

Surprise was written all over her face as he disappeared into the throng of performers behind them. She glanced at Fauve who gave her an insouciant shrug in reply. Moments later he returned and Danni felt her stomach contract with alarm. In each hand he held a short black velvet lead. Each lead was attached to a beautiful diamanté collar. And each collar encircled the graceful neck of a sleek black panther.

'We broke our own rules about not involving animals in the circus,' he explained, passing the ends of the leads into Danni's stunned hands. 'Meet Sheba and Cleopatra.'

'I – I—' Danni felt beads of perspiration break out on her forehead.

'Do not worry, *ma chérie*,' Fauve reassured her, 'they are perfectly tame. They come from the local circus and are only for show.'

'They are far less vicious than this little cat here,' Ivan said, squeezing Fauve's shoulder affectionately.

Danni glanced at Sheba and Cleopatra who gave her a blank, yellow-eyed stare in return. Then Cleopatra yawned sleepily and nuzzled Danni's leg.

461

'See,' Ivan added with a broad smile, 'friendly as kittens.'

There was no time to argue with him. It was time to go back out into the ring. With Ivan walking proudly ahead, Danni and the others followed. By the time they had walked a few paces to the centre of the ring, Danni felt quite comfortable with Sheba and Cleopatra and the roar of approval that went up as Danni entered, swathed in her white silk and feathers and leading the sleek black cats, was enough adulation to turn any girl's head.

I was born to this, she told herself proudly, as she stood centre stage, flanked by the panthers and surrounded by all the other performers. Her old life seemed a million miles away now. Consigned to a different era. This was a new beginning and, she knew deep inside, the start of a wonderful, sublimely erotic existence.

Who Dares Sins

Roxanne Morgan

Chapter One

SHANNON GARRETT DROPPED her briefcase into the pannier of the despatch rider's motorcycle. Her folded white linen jacket followed.

The despatch rider stared at her. He moved away from the iron railings at the top of the shop's basement steps, despatch sheet falling to his side.

London's hot summer dust lay in the creases of his leather trousers and biker jacket. He wore heavy boots, and his trousers were padded at thigh and knee. Sweat runnelled down his face. His long fair hair was curly, dusty; and matted with sweat from being under the bike helmet. He was broad across the shoulders. A faint blond stubble covered his cheeks. His eyes were blue. Twenty-five years old, maybe? Twenty-six?

Shannon wordlessly held out the black visored crash helmet that had been resting on his bike. He took it.

'Drive,' she directed. Her voice barely shook.

Shannon swung her leg over the Honda 1000cc motorbike. Her lined linen skirt rucked up to the tops of her thighs, and creased. The leather pillion seat of the bike was hot from standing parked in the summer sun. It moulded itself slightly to her crotch as she sat. She felt the warm leather through her sheer stockings and lace panties.

She leaned forward, her sleeveless shirt-blouse pulling tight over her breasts. To her surprise, her nipples were already hard, painfully erect. I can't believe I'm doing this, she thought.

'Drive,' she repeated, more strongly.

'Look ... this is a wind-up, yeah? Yeah. You've given your mates sitting over there a laugh.' The man met her gaze. 'If you're *serious*, there's no one in the despatch office, we could go round the back—'

'Just drive,' Shannon said.

The young despatch rider shrugged. He grinned, appreciatively, with a crooked grin. Then he put the crash helmet on. Immediately, black visor down, he became anonymous.

He swung himself on to the bike.

Shannon did not look back. She leaned forward and put her arms around his broad, leather-clad torso.

His body leaned to one side as he kicked the bike into life. The powerful engine roared. The casing of the bike vibrated. Shannon put her feet up on the foot-rests. She spread her legs slightly, and forced her body down. The throbbing vibration of the bike, through the leather seat, pressed against her pussy. She eased forward, pressing the front of her panties down on the seat, bringing her clitoris into contact with the leather.

'Drive!' she said. '*Now*.'

The powerful bike roared out of the side street and into London traffic.

The hot wind of summer caressed her stockinged legs like warm oil. Her hair shook free of its silk-covered elasticated band. She tightened her arms around the man's chest as the bike cornered, feeling hard muscle under the creased leather jacket. She felt his breathing quicken. She leaned back slightly and looked down between their bodies. Old leather trousers, worn soft and pliable, stretched across the rider's buttocks.

The bike heeled over, shot between a bus and a taxi, and, to a blare of horns, sped up Tottenham Court Road. Weaving through the central London lunch-time traffic at sixty miles an hour.

She opened her mouth to speak, but the wind snatched the words from her mouth. She realised, No point in talking. He's got a helmet on. Whatever I do, he can't hear me.

Shannon let go with one hand and brought her arm back. She slid her hand down between their bodies, between the hot leather that stretched across his back, and the thin cotton, already marked with sweat and dust, that clung to her small breasts and flat stomach.

She stroked the taut leather trousers where they stretched across his buttocks.

The bike lurched and recovered.

One hand locked around his body, Shannon caressed the tight, spread buttocks of the rider. The bike shot past a red bus. Shannon, behind black sunglasses, gazed up at passengers who – for one shocking millisecond – stared down at her.

She removed her hand from the rider's buttocks and slid it up her own thigh.

The bike slowed, caught by traffic lights. She glimpsed a tube station, a major road junction – and pepple. Hundreds and hundreds of people, in summer suits and dresses, in tourist gear, in T-shirts and tight shorts . . .

Shannon clamped her body against the rider's back. His breathing quickened: she felt his broad chest rise and fall. Her free hand slid secretly up the inside of her stockinged thigh, to her bare cool flesh and suspenders, and then her fingers pushed down inside the front of her lace panties. Warmth met her fingers.

Her pubic hair was soaking. Teasingly, she caressed her little bud, until her inflamed clitoris throbbed.

I can't go through with this . . . can I?

She brought her hand out, and lifted it towards her nostrils.

The lights changed. The bike shot forward.

Shannon whooped, abandoning all caution now. Her legs clamped on to the bike's seat, and again the throbbing of the metal casing aroused her. Behind the anonymous safety of her sunglasses, she laughed at the cars they passed. Streets, trees, lamp-posts, crossing; all gone in a flash, and now they were among high multi-storeyed City buildings.

The despatch rider freed one hand and brought it back behind him. Before Shannon realised, he had grasped her own hand. He pulled her forward. Her sweating body thumped up hard against his muscled back.

He continued to pull her hand forward.

He pressed it down into his crotch.

Shannon closed her hand gently. Worn leather stretched, pushed out by an eight-inch erection. She stroked the length of it. Then, still without entering his clothes, she gripped its girth.

The bike slowed.

Shannon shook her head, frustrated. She hammered with her free hand on his broad back, and then removed her other hand from his throbbing erection. The visored helmet half-turned. Then, the bike began to speed up again. They flashed through canyons between buildings, where towering glass windows glared back in the sun. Seventy m.p.h., seventy-five, eighty . . .

Shannon leaned up against the despatch rider's hot, hard back and slid both her hands around to the front of his body. She stroked his cock through his leather trousers.

His swelling dick hardened, hardened and lengthened. She gripped it tightly and began to move the leather up and down, up and down.

His shoulders stiffened. She felt his arms lock rigid on the handlebars, and the powerful machine swerved coolly between two speeding taxis and shot across three lanes of traffic unscathed. All his muscles tightened; back, shoulders, and powerful thighs gripping the machine.

Shannon moved one hand back. She slid the leather of his pants up and down the shaft of his cock with one hand, and with the other, pressed her fingers into the leather-clad cleft of his buttocks, where his anus should be. His buttocks clamped together, almost trapping her fingers in place. She shifted her hand away from him, pressing her fingers against her spread legs, rubbing her clitoris hard. The bike throbbed in her crotch.

'Ohhh . . .' Shannon slitted her eyes. That they were in London traffic ceased to matter. Fumbling with the fastenings to his trousers, she got one hand down the front. The hot skin of his belly felt slick with sweat. The hard shaft of his cock filled her hand. She ringed it with her thumb and fingers, pulling the foreskin up over his knob. Not able to even see over his shoulder, only able to imagine: is it ivory-coloured, blue-veined, throbbing red, purple . . . ?

Shannon thought, in a bewildered haze, *Never like this, it's never been like this!*

The bike sped suddenly free into sunlight, out of City streets and buildings. With iron-willed determination, the rider wrenched the bike across two lanes and began to parallel the Embankment. Tourists in pastel-coloured shirts stood on pavements. One raised a camcorder to film the Tower of London as Shannon and the bike shot past him.

She could not touch the rider's neck or face. The crash helmet covered him. His head turned slightly. She glimpsed nothing but her own face reflected in the black visor, hair streaming, cheeks flushed. He faced forward again.

Her hand plunged deeper into his pants. At the same time she pushed one finger between her own spread legs, down the front of her lace panties, and slid it in and out of her pussy. Her juices covered her hand, and her hot cleft throbbed.

She slid her other hand down the velvet hardness of his dick. The tangled wet hair at his crotch was springy. She scooped his balls into her hand, pressing against the tautness of his pants. His backbone, where she rode pressed against it, arched.

'Now,' she whispered.

She clamped herself to the despatch rider's back. The sun brought smells of leather and man-sweat, sex-juices, and petro-chemicals from the other traffic. She plunged both hands down the front of his pants, one hand kneading his scrotum, the other gripping the shaft of his cock.

She began to bring him off harder, both her hands on his cock. Her legs clamped tight to the motorbike's sides. She pushed her crotch against the pillion seat.

His chest heaved, and she heard him panting, even over the noise of the cars. His back arched, pressing into her breasts. Her nipples strained at her shirt, and her whole breasts ached. She bent her sweating cheek in to his shoulder, smelling leather, clamping her eyes shut.

'Come on, come *on* . . .' Her hand gripped his cock tight. She moved her hand up and down, his hot skin sliding on the shaft. He swelled again in her hand. The blue sky was above them, and girders. Sun flashed off water. The Thames shone below, as they crested the

470

rise and the bike thundered out on to Tower Bridge. She squeezed and slid, squeezed and slid.

The rider's broad body convulsed in her arms. For a second she was standing, feet on the bike's foot-rests, leaning forward, bottom in the air. Her linen skirt remained rucked up to her hips. She felt hot slipstream on her thighs, above her stockings. Hot slipstream that was cold on the soaking crotch of her lace panties.

The rider's back arched.

Hot semen jetted into her hands, inside his leather trousers. He came, rising up from the metal casing of the speeding bike; came again and again into her hands, pelvis thrusting forward, narrow hips jerking in her straining arms, his taut buttocks momentarily thrust up level with her face.

She pressed her whole face into the back of his crotch. She breathed in the smell of sweat, of leather, of semen like flowers and pollen.

The bike's back wheel skidded.

Shannon jolted into the air, made a wild grab at the rider's waist, and sat down with a thump, legs spread wide.

The bike curved around roadworks, ran a red light, and shot off under London Bridge station.

Frustrated, she pushed her crotch against the throbbing seat of the bike. Just the smell of him on her hands made her breathless with wanting. She writhed her body up against him, grinding her breasts into his spine, ignoring the delicious pain.

The despatch bike swung down into side-streets. Narrow roads between warehouses, chain-link fences. The engine's roar echoed off Victorian brick walls.

With a squeal of rubber, the bike halted under a brick arch.

Shannon heard a tinny voice. She realised it was the despatch rider's radio, echoing under this bridge.

Stunned, hands shaking, she sank back and let go of the rider.

'That's—' She panted. 'Not *fair* – you – I didn't—'

The bike's rider ignored what she was saying.

Before she could move, he had lifted his leg and dismounted from the bike, propping it on its stand. The last echo of the engine died. The hot side-street, deserted, was utterly silent. A gull cried somewhere over the river.

The rider reached up and jerked the strap of his crash helmet. He swung it off his head, pushing broad hands through his wet fair hair. One hand unzipped his leather jacket. It swung open, disclosing a soft sweat-soaked T-shirt. His muscles shone. The man-smell of sweat and semen breathed off him.

'I—'

Before Shannon could say any more, he stepped behind the bike. She had no time to turn. A broad strong hand slapped her back, between her shoulder-blades, and pushed her body down. Shannon sprawled forward on the bike's metal casing. She threw her arms around the front fork.

She felt his knee on the bike's seat beside her. The bike shook, taking the weight of a second person. His panting breath echoed under the bridge.

Shannon found herself sprawled forward, breasts pushed into the hot metal of the bike casing. Her shirt was jerked firmly up. One hand kept her pressed down, his other hand, underneath her, gripped her breasts, kneading them until she bit her lip, and then threw her head back and up. 'Ahhh . . .'

Her feet were still on the rests, pushing her bottom up into the air, higher than her head now.

His hand jerked free, and tugged her skirt up over her buttocks, around her waist.

His fingers hooked under the back of her lace

472

panties and yanked them down.

Summer air swept cool across her naked buttocks and pussy. His hands gripped and caressed her stocking-covered legs, then slid upwards and away.

Behind her, she heard the sound of a zip pulled down.

Unbelievably, she felt herself arch her body down, pushing her buttocks higher.

He straddled her and the bike together.

His muscled thighs pushed against the back of her thighs, his skin hot and running with sweat. Fingers briefly caressed her buttocks. His newly-erect cock slapped against her pussy.

She felt him bring a hand up and guide it in. The thickness of the head of his cock pushed her apart, her soaking juices sliding him in. She pushed her body up and back, against his cock and balls and belly. His shaft slid deep into her vagina. She gripped him, hot and clenching and craving. His strong hands grabbed her hips and pulled her to him as he thrust.

Her whole body arched up.

More than ready, shivering with pleasure delayed, she came in a searing burst of pleasure; came again and again, sweating bare stomach pressed against the leather of the bike seat, arms gripping the hard metal, his firm hands grabbing her waist, his thick sex impaling her, her pussy clenching again and again on his cock, until he came for the second time, and they sprawled together, panting, breathing echoing under the brickwork of Southwark Bridge.

At last, his voice his beside her ear, panting, said, 'I don't even know your name!'

Shannon pushed herself upright. She began to clean and straighten her clothes with shaking fingers, and stuttered something, she herself didn't know what.

His hot semen slid from deep in her pussy and

slicked the seat of the motorbike.

Feeling that, a great relaxation and satisfaction swept through her. She smiled and turned her face towards the sun. 'It's been lovely, thank you. Goodbye.'

' "Goodbye"?' he protested plaintively. 'But won't I see you again, darlin'?'

'No,' Shannon said simply.

His blue eyes were very puzzled. 'I don't get it, doll. Why not?'

'Because I don't want to,' Shannon said. 'That isn't why I did it. Oh – there is something you can give me, though. No, not money. *That.*'

She reached over and tore the first despatch sheet off his pad. His voice echoed down the back-streets towards London Bridge Station. 'But *why . . . ?*'

Shannon smiled reflectively, casting her mind back towards lunch-time.

. . . Shannon Garrett was late for lunch.

The sun beat down into the narrow London streets. Her heeled sandals kicked up dust as she took the short cut through St Giles churchyard and emerged, sweating, below Denmark Street.

She took a moment to check her reflection in a shop window. White blouse and cream skirt, and a white linen jacket; briefcase in hand . . . she peered closer, seeing a woman who did not quite look to be thirty, with curly hair pulled back at the sides – brown hair, but the shop window glass turned it almost auburn.

You could not tell, Shannon decided, that she had been crying. Her eyes were not puffy, or smudged.

Across the road, someone waved.

Shannon picked out Nadia Kay immediately from the throng sitting at the tables outside the Café Valletta. The red-haired woman lifted her hand again, waved languidly, and smiled. Sunglasses hid her eyes. Shannon waved back and crossed the busy road.

'You managed to leave the shop, then?' Shannon sat down beside Nadia, in the meagre shade of a lime tree.

'My father's looking after it for a couple of hours. He's such an old dear.' Nadia removed her sunglasses, briefly displaying eyes with sweepingly long, dark red lashes. A few faint crow's feet hinted that she was a decade older than Shannon. A trickle of sweat ran down her freckled shoulders, across her collarbone, vanished down the neck of her ecru linen dress. 'Shannon, is something the matter?'

'No,' Shannon said unconvincingly.

The scent of human sweat was in the air from the young men and women crowded into the Café Valletta. Not unpleasant. Warm bodies, sleeves rolled up, necklines low. A loud hum of talk. The lunch-time business drinkers: City types, arty types. Shannon took a guilty look round in case any of the other staff from *Femme* magazine should be here. No, no one.

'Corey's getting drinks from the bar,' Nadia remarked, leaning back to look into the crowd inside the café. The sun had already brought a slight flush to her bare, cream-skinned arms. 'I told her to get one for you. What's upset you?'

'It's. . .' Shannon's face crumpled. She sat down next to Nadia in a white plastic chair. 'I've broken up with Tim. I have *finally* done it. I'm glad I've done it!'

Nadia stubbed out a slim cigarette. 'He was never going to leave Julia. I'm glad you realised.'

'Oh, I always knew. It's just that, when I told him, he cried. He cried, Nadia, like always; and he said that he would leave her, it was just the kids, but he would do it, give him time.'

'And you said?'

Shannon took a deep breath. 'I surprised myself. I

said, *I've heard that shit too many times before. Get out.* And – and he *went*. After six years!'

'I shall find you a man,' Nadia announced, when Shannon had stopped crying. 'There's nothing like a new lover to restore your confidence – so long as you don't fall in love with him.'

A new voice said, 'He'll only turn into a wimp, whoever he is.'

A tall girl with short black hair stood over the table, carrying three glasses with care. As she put them down, and smoothed her wet palms down her black summer dress, she smiled at Shannon.

'Only two kinds of men. Wimps and bastards,' Corey Black said.

Shannon dabbed at her eyes. 'I always forget you've been divorced. You seem so young.'

'Married at eighteen, divorced at twenty,' the girl said.

'Tim was a wimp. I always knew that. Except, in bed . . .' Shannon looked at her two friends. 'Wouldn't it be good if we could just have sex with the men we want, without bothering about the rest of it?'

Red-haired Nadia smiled enigmatically. 'Good in theory, but you wouldn't do it, my dear.'

'I would, too,' Shannon growled. 'I know what you think about me. Boring old Shannon, works in an office, with a married boyfriend – what a mouse!'

'My dear, we don't!'

Somewhat mollified by the genuine concern in Nadia's voice, Shannon finished, 'I'd do anything you two would do!'

Corey pointed across the road to the corner of Denmark Street. 'Well, I bet you wouldn't pick *him* up. Not a chat-up. Just a fuck. Go on, I dare you.'

Nadia joined in with the young girl's laughter. 'Yes. We dare you!'

476

Shannon was silent for a minute.

She looked across the road, at the despatch rider.

'If I take the dare,' she said slowly, 'if I bring you proof, then – what do I win?'

Nadia smiled. 'Why . . . you get to dare both of *us*. That seems fair. Don't you think so, Corey?'

'Sure,' Corey said. 'Why not? But I know Shannon! She'll never do it.'

Shannon stood up . . .

Shannon Garrett walked up from the Tottenham Court Road Underground station to the Café Valletta, jacket over her arm, briefcase swinging from one hand. She smiled gently. Sometimes she hummed under her breath.

The lunch-time clientele had left the café-bar two hours ago. It was not yet time for the evening drinkers. Nadia Kay and Corey Black still sat together, lazily, at the table under the lime tree.

'Hey, Shannon!' The younger woman waved.

Nadia silently lifted her glass.

Shannon pulled up one of the white chairs and put her briefcase and jacket carefully on it. Then she threw a piece of paper down on the table, among the empty glasses and Nadia's gold-banded cigarette stubs.

'Proof,' Shannon said.

Corey leaned forward and looked.

A despatch rider's sheet, with signatures as far as 1 p.m. After that, nothing but two scrawled kisses.

The black-haired girl leaned back, a vaguely discontented expression on her face. 'We know you went off with him. We saw. That isn't proof that you *did* anything with him.'

Nadia interrupted. 'Don't be naive, my dear. You only have to look at her.'

'Yes, but—' Corey looked up. Shannon saw her take

477

in the creased skirt and blouse, and what Shannon felt must surely be her burning, flushed face.

Corey suddenly grinned. 'Oh, wow! Shannon, you're going to tell us all about it, aren't you?'

'Maybe.' Shannon called the waiter over and ordered Pimm's and lemonade. She eased herself into another of the white chairs. She reached over and pulled her briefcase on to her lap, and took out two folded pieces of paper. 'But before I do . . . this *was* a dare. Remember what we agreed. I did my part of it – now *I* dare both of you.'

Shannon smiled.

'While I was coming back here on the Tube, I had time to be inventive.'

She held up two folded papers.

'Take one,' she invited. 'Go on. I dare you.'

'Oh, you can't seriously. . .' Corey's voice trailed off. Suddenly bright red, she buried her nose in her own glass of Pimm's and drank deeply. She mumbled, 'It was just a joke. Surely.'

Nadia smiled. When she took off her sunglasses, Shannon saw that the older woman's eyes were bright with amusement, and something more like excitement than her usual pose of ennui. 'Corey, sweets, we *did* agree . . .'

Shannon, her body still tingling, grinned at the girl.

Corey's eyes flashed. 'I can take a dare! No one can say I can't!' She snatched one of the folded pieces of paper out of Shannon's hand.

'Fair's fair,' Nadia agreed. She took the other.

Chapter Two

NADIA KAY PAUSED with her key in the lock of *Ephemera*. One hand was poised to turn the notice beside the shop door from CLOSED to OPEN. She hesitated, staring out from behind her shop window into the Neal's Yard arcade.

Nine-thirty in the morning. A few early tourists.

Irresolute, she turned back into the tiny shop. Brooches, cups, mirrors, rings, carved wooden crocodiles, Victorian bird-cages, beads, bells, hand-made pots, Russian icons – all glittering, brightly-coloured, designed to lure in the wealthy tourist. The shop smelled of amber incense.

She slapped the key down on the mahogany counter top, picked up the phone, and dialled.

A voice answered, 'Features editor, *Femme*, can I help you?'

'It's Nadia,' she said.

'Oh, Nadia, hello. It's okay, there's no one in the office at the moment.' Shannon Garrett's voice still had what Nadia thought to be an uncharacteristic purr in it. 'I was going to call you. I keep thinking – did it happen? It did happen! I can't believe it happened!'

Nadia waited until the younger woman had stopped

bubbling at her.

'I wanted to ask you.' Nadia paused. A not particularly well-dressed man wandered past the shop window, studied two netsuke in the glass cabinet, and continued on. 'Shannon . . . I can't possibly do this!'

'Why not?'

'You make it sound so reasonable! Oh, my dear, a lover is one thing – you know Oscar had his little friends, and he never objected to me having mine. Encouraged it, if anything. But I expected to know their social circle, I expected them to take me out to dinner at least, to entertain me—'

'Did they?'

A pause. 'What?'

'Did they *entertain* you? Nadia, I think that's why I stayed with Tim so long. I'd got tired of being bored from starter through to dessert! That was what was so wonderful about yesterday. I didn't have to ask how he liked his coffee. I didn't have to ask his name. I'm tired of hearing how bad it is at the office, and how his mother preferred his younger brother to him, and how his school life was a misery. I just wanted his body, Nadia, and I had it, and I didn't even have to tell him he was wonderful!'

Nadia chewed her lip.

'Besides,' the voice on the phone protested, 'it was a dare. How long have we known each other, Nadia?'

'Ten years,' she answered automatically.

'And we've both known Corey since she was a young teenager. We've always kept our promises to each other.'

Nadia drummed her fingers on the shop counter.

Shannon's voice on the phone was mischievous. 'Beside, if you back out of a dare, that's probably a double penalty. I quite surprised myself on the train coming back, with what I could think up. By the way,

480

which one did you get? Nadia? Hello?'

'I've just had an idea,' Nadia said. 'Oh, you'll know which one I got when I bring the proof. Lunch on Tuesday, as usual.'

She gently replaced the phone on its cradle.

'Curious, but exciting,' Nadia Kay decided softly, 'hunting young men at my age.'

No one heard her speak. She cruised down the deserted Embankment in her red MG sports car. Unseasonable June rain fell, misting the afternoon and the rustling plane trees. A boat on the river sounded a siren. Her emerald green light raincoat fell back from her sheer-stockinged legs as she shifted down the gears.

The teenage boy was walking down the pavement ahead of her.

He has such clear skin! Nadia thought, amazed. And he's so thin!

No more than fourteen, fifteen. The boy hesitated. He stopped, squatted, and began to re-tie the laces on one of his worn combat boots. Rain drops shone in his red hair. It was caught back from his eyes by a black bandanna. Spots of water darkened the ripped sleeveless black T-shirt stretched across his broad back. His shoulders were wide and freckled. His T-shirt rode up out of the back of his tattered black jeans. Nadia saw pale flesh in the gap.

His eyes flicked up as she slowly cruised the pavement.

His gaze lingered appreciatively on the gleaming red polish of the MG, caressed the classic curving lines of its wing, moved up to the driver – and his gaze became utterly blank.

He gave his boot a last tug, stood up, and loped away down the Embankment.

Nadia swore.

Three separate cars and a taxi blared horns as she swung the MG across the road, crossed the opposite lane, shot up a side-street, and screeched to a halt with two wheels up on the low pavement, outside a grey concrete and glass building.

She stared up the concrete stairs to the entrance, not seeing what she was looking at for fury. Closed glass doors, now streaked with rain. Beyond them, greyboard-lined walls with dog-eared University notices pinned up on them. Young men and women swarmed aimlessly inside the reception area.

Damn him, he didn't even see *me!* He has no right!

The sky darkened above the soot-stained London college. Young men in ragged jeans or combat trousers, and T-shirts with logos, walked inside with rare self-possession. No one looked out through the doors at her. Even the male receptionist ignored her.

'Perhaps I look like someone's mother,' she muttered viciously.

Nadia hit the wheel of her MG with her fist.

Anything over twenty-two doesn't exist, is that it? Bloody hell!

The rain fell harder now. Urban summer rain: it brought with it a strong smell through her half-open car window of road-tar, green plane leaves, and petrol. A boy stepped under the protection of the college entrance. Rain spotted his white t-shirt. He stood with his thumbs tucked under the heavy leather belt of his faded jeans.

She recognised the general area of Temple Underground station. This was one of the side-streets leading up to the Strand. The building had a college name over the door which she vaguely knew.

She took Shannon's scribbled note from the pocket of her light raincoat. It was direct and to the point.

482

I dare you to seduce a young male virgin.

As to that, she thought, now I'm in completely the wrong place! These young men here are eighteen, nineteen, twenty. Anything I'd be attracted to has no doubt long since ceased to be a virgin. Damn that Shannon!

The young men and women swarmed out of the doors. Idly, she noted the boy still waiting under the shelter of the entrance. Too young to be a student, surely?

The rain briefly eased.

The boy moved to the bottom step and looked back at her. Then he looked away. Then back.

He was fair-haired, with hulking shoulders for so young a man, wearing blue jeans with a wide belt, and a white T-shirt, and no jacket. His arms were bare to the rain.

Nadia clapped her battered green silk trilby on to her short red hair, and paused to glance in the rear-view mirror and coax a wisp of a curl out from behind her gold-studded ear. The natural deep red of her hair made her skin appear to glow in the soft afternoon.

The boy came up to her as she locked the car door from the outside.

She looked up from under long lashes.

'Good car,' he said. 'I was just noticing it was a good car. I mean. Sorry. I wasn't staring at you, honest.'

Up close he had long, strongly-muscled legs, and a stomach flat as a washboard. His fair hair flopped over his face, and he stooped, unconsciously, being several inches taller than Nadia. She let her gaze sweep from his Doc Martin boots, up the faded blue denim of his jeans, and linger momentarily at his crotch. A small bulge hinted at a hard-on.

'Are you one of the students here?' she asked.

'Yes – no – if I get my grades, I will be, in October

483

next year. My brother's here already.'

No more than sixteen, then. He made as if to move away, up to the glass doors. He stopped. Nadia watched a dark red flush creep up from the white neck of his T-shirt, up his throat, and darken his face up to his blond hairline.

'Part of this building is older, isn't it?' she said. 'I remember a friend of mine recommended it as having one of the finest small eighteenth-century chapels still extant. Is that so?'

'I know where it is. I could show you. They gave us a tour this morning, for next year's students.' His blush had not faded. 'Please, let me show you. This way's easiest.'

He ducked his head and loped up the side-street, in the rain, turning towards the Strand. Nadia followed, heels tapping on the wet pavement. Every so often the boy looked anxiously back to make sure that she followed. She watched his tight buttocks move under the blue denim.

At the Strand entrance, it was obvious that the building had been impressive once. Nadia entered the wide foyer, noting red-carpeted marble stairs to the upper floors, a high moulded plaster ceiling.

'It's up here, uh, miss, uh.'

'My name is Nadia.' She smiled, letting him precede her up the shabbily carpeted stairs. There were fewer other students here. Two Asian girls passed her, walking down.

There was a tall door ahead. He opened it and entered the chapel. She followed him.

It was dark, even at midday. Dark, and a little cold. She reached up and brushed the wet red hair out of her eyes. Wooden pews stretched out in front of her, down towards the altar, and candy-twist pillars lined the aisle.

His husky, deep young voice behind her said, 'I could wait, if you want. I could show you back out when you've finished.'

Nadia rested one hand on the back of a pew. She unbuttoned her raincoat, letting it swing open over the Chinese-style olive-green silk dress that she wore.

'An interesting late example of a box-pew,' she murmured, turning and stepping past him. She steadied herself with one hand on his bare arm.

The boy's fair skin flushed again. He scowled, half-smiled, standing with his hands dangling at his sides, his eyes fixed on her. There was definitely a bulge in his jeans now, Nadia saw, bulking out the faded fly. She blinked at the sheer size of it.

'Stained-glass windows,' he muttered. Clumsily, he pointed up at the blue and red glass, and brushed his arm against her silk-clad shoulder as he brought it down.

'Oh, yes. How beautiful.' Nadia smiled, apparently oblivious.

'I think,' she said, after the appallingly tedious fifteen minutes she felt obliged to spend studying the chapel and its hideous green- and yellow-painted walls, 'I do think that we should go and have tea somewhere. It's the least I can do, since you've been so helpful – what do you say to Fortnum and Mason?'

The red MG had a parking ticket when they came out. She chuckled and threw it on to the back seat.

He brushed her spine, between her shoulder-blades, helping her into her car. After that she drove rapidly and skilfully through London traffic to Piccadilly in the rain, and, in the windscreen, watched his reflection. His bare arms were spotted with rain, the fair hairs erect. Defined biceps – yes, he lifts weights, she thought. I recognise it from my friends' sons.

Fortnum and Mason, crowded, had its usual perfect

smell of spices and coffee. Nadia took the boy to her favourite table, towards the back, and ordered black coffee and cream gateaux.

'It's very good of you,' the boy said. His accent was good, she noticed, and he seemed well-mannered, if somewhat out of his depth. She grinned to herself.

I very much doubt this is within the terms of Shannon's dare. But what the hell, it doesn't happen every day . . .

Nadia dipped the end of her index finger into her cream cake, and licked at it delicately. 'Pure self-indulgence, don't you think?'

The young man's eyes were fixed on her, pupils wide and dark. She put her cream-covered finger into her mouth and sucked it. Then she held up her finger and ran her tongue up it from root to tip.

'Uh,' he said.

After the end of the tea, she led him out the back way, into the street where the MG was parked.

'You've been so very helpful.' Faint rain misted her skin. 'I would like to give you another reward. If you can think of one.'

He swallowed; she saw his throat move. His brilliant blue eyes fixed on her. With a voice that dropped into huskiness, he said, 'I want to kiss you.'

She put her hands flat against his chest. The cotton of his T-shirt was warm from his body. She felt his pulse under her hands.

'Yes,' she said simply, lifting her mouth.

His lips were soft, and the smell of them suddenly loosened her body. She moved against him, lifting her hands and grabbing his head, and bringing his mouth down. His warm breath feathered her cheek, then his lips fastened hard on hers, and his hot tongue flicked out to touch hers.

The effect was electric. All her senses heightened:

she became conscious of the rain on her face, the silk on her skin, and the huge and warm breathing body of the boy-man pressed against her. Strong arms encircled her, uncertain, as if he thought she might break.

'Oh God, you're beautiful.' His voice cracked.

The bulge in his jeans was enormous. She pressed her body urgently against it.

'I know – a hotel—' Her breathing was rapid. Her head whirled. The hotel was a rendezvous she had often made use of when married to Oscar. She had no memory this time of walking to the small, select street; of making the booking. All she was conscious of was the strong young body next to her, and how he kept stealing glances at her, his eyes darkening with desire.

At last she closed the hotel room door behind her.

'This isn't . . .' She slid her hands up under his T-shirt, startled at the heat of his smooth skin. 'This isn't your first time.'

'That was just *girls*.' He shivered like a horse. She ran a cupped hand soothingly round his beardless cheek.

Nadia slowly unbuttoned the top buttons of her silk dress. Without looking down, she slid one hand down the front of his body, over his belt-buckle, and down the fly of his jeans. She cupped his bulging crotch. His thick cock was hot and hard through the soft material.

His hips thrust forward. Suddenly he grabbed her shoulders, pulling her coat down so that it trapped her arms at her sides, and shoved his face into her breasts.

'You don't – have to hurry—' Nadia staggered back, off-balance. She tried to reach out, but couldn't. The soft counterpaned bed caught her behind the knee.

She sprawled on the bed. One heeled shoe went, knocked flying across the room. The boy fell on top of her. His solid body covered her from her feet to her shoulders, blond hair brushing her lips as he gnawed frantically at her breasts.

'Wait—' One of her breasts was squeezed out of her silk dress. The boy's head darted down. His tongue licked her nipple, hard as a little stone, and then his mouth fastened on her, sucking and biting.

She arched her back, trying to push her bare breast further into his mouth. Both her arms were pinioned. She pulled one leg up, stroking his denim-clad leg with her calf, and then lifted her foot until she could tuck the heel into the cleft of his buttocks. She pulled his body sharply towards her and down, feeling the bulge in his jeans push into her crotch, sliding on her silky knickers.

His startled voice cried, '*Shit!*'

Her body was suddenly free of weight. Nadia's head jerked up.

She lifted herself up on her elbows on the bed.

The boy knelt up between her legs, looking down at himself. His face was scarlet. A wet patch was spreading on the crotch of his jeans even as Nadia looked.

'Oh *no*,' he groaned.

'That,' Nadia said, with a wicked smile, 'is nothing to worry about. It often happens with young men. Fortunately it's easily cured.'

She half sat up, slid her arms out of the sleeves of the raincoat, and lay back again. Slowly and deliberately, she unbuttoned her Chinese silk dress.

'Oh God,' he said, 'I want you!'

Her sheer stockings were held up by a lacy white suspender belt. She wore a lacy white bra, and a tiny pair of white satin knickers. Nadia slid her hands down her body. Over her small, firm breasts, gently curved tummy and slim hips. And then, smoothing the satin behind her, cupping her trim buttocks.

The boy sat down cautiously on the bed. She touched his arm. His skin was white, soft, and the muscle underneath rock-solid. She kneaded it gently. 'I want to watch you undress.'

'You want to watch *me*?' A grin tugged one corner of his mouth.

In one movement he put his arms back over his shoulders and stripped his T-shirt forward and off. Nadia watched the light from the hotel windows fall like water on his solid, bulky shoulders and the defined pectorals of his torso. A thin feather of dark blond hair crept up from the waistband of his blue jeans. She slid her hand from his throat to his navel. His skin was utterly smooth and unmarked.

A tension stiffened his shoulders. More awkward now, he stood. His hands went to his flies again, unbuttoning them slowly, silver button after silver button. Then he took his hands away and slid his jeans and boxer shorts together down his hips, down his thighs, and ended in an undignified tangle, standing on one leg.

'You could have taken your boots off first,' Nadia pointed out demurely. His eyes flashed at her from under dark-blond brows. Then he grinned again. His half-flaccid organ bobbed between his legs as he unlaced his boots.

He's so *big!* Nadia thought. Good grief. How wonderful.

The boots thumped on to the carpet.

He stood, naked. She looked up at him from the bed, the sharply-defined triangular shape of his broad shoulders and narrow hips. Smooth-skinned thighs, heavily muscled, and a rough dark bush of hair at the fork of his body from which his cock sprang, newly erect, with a purple engorged head.

'Politeness has no place in bed,' Nadia said. 'I want

your big, beautiful cock inside me. *Fuck me!'*

She barely got the words out. He tumbled her back on to the sheets, pressing her shoulders down on the pillow, pushing her legs apart with his knees. Then, hesitantly, he lowered himself down. The hot, velvety warmth of his skin pressed against her breasts, her stomach, and between her thighs. She clasped her legs around him, pushing her pubic mound up against his stiff rod.

'I want you!' He bent down and kissed her savagely and inexpertly, his weight almost crushing her.

She slid her arms down his smooth flanks, pressing her palms into his warm skin. Suddenly she clutched at his tight buttocks, pressing him to her. He bit at her collar-bone, gnawing and nipping, and, as she breathlessly gasped, worried at her like a dog, biting down the tender skin over her ribs and across her stomach.

'Woman!' His voice was deep, resonant, breaking at the last on a cracked note.

She rolled over, rising above him. To see him sprawled back on the bed, naked, made her pussy throb. His cock rose taut out of the bush of brown hair at his groin.

She leaned forward and began to lick at the side of the shaft. She heard him moan. Ignoring him, ignoring how hard his reaching hands closed on her breasts, she nibbled at his balls, burying her face in his hot, damp hair. Then she lifted her head, and stroked his cock from root to tip with a slow tongue.

'Oh, Jesus!' he yelled.

She took his thick cock into her mouth and sucked, rubbing her lips up and down the shaft, up and down, until he swelled, and his hips arched under her, and she threw her arms around his buttocks and sucked him until he came.

He lay spent for no more than seconds. 'Oh my God,' she said softly; and got no more words out. His mouth came down on hers. She reached between their bodies, marvelling at his flat muscular stomach. The wisp of stomach-hair tangled in her fingers, and she followed it down to his crotch, caressing his swollen, taut balls. She grasped the shaft of his cock. It swelled again instantly in her hand. She began to tease her pussy with the head of it, brushing the tip against the outer walls of her labia. Her sex swelled, opened, dampened.

'Ahh!' He pushed inside her, pushed deep. She took him, her hips rising, her back arching, feeling him thick inside her, feeling the head of his cock rubbing at the narrowest part of her sex, teasing and exciting, until she wrapped her legs around his waist and rhythmically pulled him deep, deep inside. His young hard body thumped against her spread inner thighs, her crotch, her pussy. Mercilessly she squeezed down on him, until his cock slid in her juices, and his balls banged against her anus. Her sex convulsed. Pleasure lifted her hips, lifted her body, blazed through her; flushing her pale skin pink, loosening every muscle, searing into her.

With a triumphant shout she rolled over, him in her arms, until she came to a rest half on, half off the bed. He curled against her back as his cock shrank and slipped from her. They lay for a long time, together. He touched her body wonderingly, from her slender feet to her soft thighs, from her arms to her breasts, all the time his face alight.

The clock on the hotel mantelpiece chimed four.

'I won't see you again, will I?' the boy said wistfully.

'No. It would spoil it.'

'I just wish I had something I could give you. A gift.' He looked around. 'I don't have anything to give.'

Nadia paused, where she sat on the edge of the bed, half dressed, in white bra, knickers, stockings and trilby hat. She remembered Shannon's scrawled note in her raincoat pocket.

'No gifts. No proof,' she said. She reached across to him, sliding her hands into his half done up denim jeans. His cock was already stiffening.

'I really *do* have to go now,' she breathed. 'I do. I – oh!'

Shannon Garrett sat in the Café Valletta at midday on the Tuesday. It was raining again. The water ran down the windows, streaking the plate glass between the big potted ferns. Resounding chatter from the bar made the Café Valletta sound like a hothouse aviary.

She studied Nadia's piece of paper, on the table. A paper smearily duplicated, with a scrawled signature, and contained in a transparent plastic case.

'A *parking ticket?*' she exclaimed. 'What kind of proof is that?'

'Two parking tickets.' Nadia Kay smiled dreamily. 'You'll believe me when I tell you.'

'Well . . .' Shannon muttered, not convinced.

Corey's voice interrupted. 'That's *my* proof,' she said, throwing a fat envelope down on the table.

Shannon undid the flap. She looked inside. With one finger she paged carefully through the contents. Then she looked up, amazed.

'Corey, there must be five thousand pounds here!'

Corey Black looked smug.

'What happened?' Shannon demanded.

The younger woman took off her leather jacket and slung it over the back of her chair. A waiter took her order for coffee. She sat down.

'OK,' she said at last. 'It was the day after we had lunch last week. I had a shoot with Perry. Last Wednesday . . .'

Chapter Three

'*OK, GIVE THAT* smile! Now turn. Hold it. That face! Those eyes, give me *those eyes*. Head left a little . . . that's it . . . smile! Turn again, other side . . . oh, you're beautiful, yes you are . . .'

The catalogue photographer kept a constant flow of instructions in the air. Corey Black whirled on the spot, smiling, with her back to a white wall, and the umbrella-backed lights in her eyes.

'OK, take five. That's wonderful, sweetheart. Keeps 'em happy at *Homestead*.'

'Uh-huh.' Corey stretched her arms, relieving muscle tension. She grinned, then, and did a perfect glide down past the lights into the little W14 back room. 'Four inches taller and I could have been a cat-walk model. Story of my life.'

'Mail order catalogues pay the rent,' the photographer, Perry, remarked.

Corey shrugged. 'I'm getting enough work as a photographer myself. Modelling is just jam. Portraits, mostly. I hate kid's photo-portraits, but they pay . . . what are you using there?'

Ten minutes' discussion about different makes of camera and speeds of film ate up the coffee break. It wasn't until she had changed into another outfit, and done another sheet of contacts, that she got a chance to speak to Serena.

'Serena. . .' She checked that Perry was deep in consideration of his film stock. 'Want to ask you something.'

'Of course, sweetie.' Serena smiled. She had a sharp exterior that concealed a surprisingly air-headed character, Corey thought. She was elegant, if you had to give her a word, and far, *far* too well-dressed to be a professional photographer's assistant, even as a butterfly-minded hobby.

'What is it?' Serena asked.

'I've got a dare on,' Corey said bluntly. 'With a friend of mine. She dared me to do it for money. I want to do it for so *much* money that it's going to shock her little cotton socks off.'

' "It"?' Serena murmured, her eyes on Perry's back.

'Fuck,' Corey said. 'You know. Sleep with. Leg-over job. Have it off with someone. F-U—'

Serena chuckled. 'No lack of opportunity, sweetie. These days, nice girls do.'

Nice Sloane girls with private school diplomas and long legs, Corey marvelled. Beats me why. But then, I don't move in those circles.

'Is this a career change,' the leggy blonde enquired delicately, 'or a one-off?'

'One-off.'

'Mmm . . . how soon do you want to do this?'

Lunch is on Tuesday, Corey thought. 'How about this weekend?'

'Well, I don't know, sweetie. It's short notice. Tell you what. Leave your answerphone on. I'll see if anyone's giving out invitations.'

Two days later, on the Friday, Corey returned to her flat and played back that day's answerphone messages.

'Corey, darling! I've got a man you simply must meet. He's only going to be in town for a few days. Come to Quaglino's for dinner on Saturday. I may not be able to stay long myself, but I'll introduce you to him. Oh, and don't think I'm being rude, but I can lend you one of my frocks to wear.' Beeep!

Corey Black paused at the top of the white marble steps going down into Quaglino's main dining area.

She wore her favourite lace-up combat boots and torn black leggings. Over the leggings, she had put a long ragged skirt composed of layer upon layer of heavy black lace. This was belted with a wide black leather strap. Its chunky buckle read BITCH. Above that, she wore her favourite black bustier, and her studded, high-cut leather jacket.

She wore no jewellery, except for the heavy skull pendant around her throat. She had spiked her black hair in a soft fall, and smudged Goth black eyeshadow in the sockets of her eyes.

She extended one hand. She wore silver-studded, fingerless leather gloves. She rested her hand on the rail that was composed of golden metal interlocked Qs and looked down across the tables for Serena. The noise level at the densely packed hundred tables dropped.

'Corey!' a voice hissed. 'Oh, sweetie!'

Corey waved and walked down the fourteen marble steps. The chatter of the diners began again. Serena swept to the foot of the steps, between dinner-goers and frantic but organised staff. She glared up. She was wearing an elegant pink suit. 'Just what do you think you're doing?' she snapped.

'*I* like it,' Corey said. 'Well, where is he, then?'

'Coming in here like this, showing me up – I am never speaking to you again, Corey Black!' Serena turned on her high heel and strode elegantly towards a table towards the rear. Corey followed her through the crowds.

I'm not nervous, she thought as she sat down, and then realised that she was being ordered better food and wine than she could appreciate for nerves, by a man she dared not look at. She sneaked a glance. Broad-shouldered in an elegant dark suit, with heavy silver cuff-links: a white-haired American who looked to be in his sixties.

Oh, *what!* she thought.

'Corey and I are just going to the washroom,' Serena trilled. *'Aren't we, sweetie.'*

'He's old! He's American!' Corey protested, in the taupe-plush and mirror-filled Ladies' room. 'I thought you were going to find me an Arab prince or something.'

'You haven't studied *Investor's Chronicle.*' Serena coolly reapplied her lipstick. Her eyes wouldn't meet Corey's in the mirror. 'Sweets, a really rich man wouldn't take the chance of being turned down after a one-off ... His name is William Caryll Jenson. He comes from California. His companies invested early in aerospace information technology. He's rich enough for you. I'd say you could go home with four hundred pounds.'

Corey blinked. 'Do you, ah, that is—'

'Sweetie, I wouldn't get into bed for four hundred pounds. I must go. Ronnie phoned. He wants me to fly out to Bahrain with him tonight – rush invitation.' She patted her crocodile bag. 'Passport. Must run. Give my love to William.'

'Yeah,' Corey muttered gloomily after the blonde left the Ladies', 'I'll tell him "the snotty bitch says goodbye".'

I could just walk out of here. I don't even have to go

496

back to the table. Shannon can stuff her dare.

It's a real shame. He looks kind of nice.

Corey was still irresolute when she left the Ladies'. She realized then that she had left her leather jacket hooked over the back of her chair (worth it if only for Serena's appalled expression) and would therefore have to go back and get it.

She walked back between the crowded tables. The American sat alone at their table, one arm stretched out along the back of another chair. He occupied the space around him, Corey thought, trying to put a word to a feeling. Sheppard and Anderson suit, silk tie, the manicured air of wealth – and yet, that craggy face and silver hair ... For the first time she met his gaze for more than a split second. 'The snotty bitch says goodbye.'

He had a full head of silver hair that spilled unruly curls over his lined brow. More lines creased at the corners of his eyes as he laughed resonantly. He leaned forward and took her hand. 'You're something new, miss, I'll give you that.'

I have to do this, Corey thought. Unconsciously she shifted in her seat. Her mouth felt dry. Mixed in with the apprehension was a curious excitement.

She picked up her fork and prodded warningly at her *fruits de mer*. 'And I'm not going to sit here and listen to you talk about the Californian aerospace industry either. I've got enough friends in engineering already who can bore me rigid.'

He had bright eyes deeply set under hairy brows, and they twinkled when he said, 'What shall we talk about, then?'

He didn't look right in a suit. He was the kind of businessman who would take full weekends off to go rock-climbing and leave behind men half his age, she thought. Or back-packing, or hunting. Something outdoors and physical.

'There is something I always wanted to ask.' Corey took another look around at the raucous, well-dressed diners. 'What's it like to be rich?'

'Come and see,' he said.

He did not drive himself, naturally. Corey followed him into the back of the stretch limo. She felt herself choose, standing there on the London pavement with the hot dusk turning to night. She got into the car.

The excitement buzzing in her head made her hardly conscious of the drive, the entrance to his apartment building, the penthouse lift. She wandered open-mouthed through the sumptuous rooms.

'Here,' he said.

Corey pressed the remote he handed her. The floor-length drapes slid aside. She exclaimed, 'Yes!'

The apartment's bedroom window extended from floor to ceiling, from wall to wall. She approached it cautiously. The lights of London shone twenty-six floors below. She edged closer to the point where carpet and glass met, leaning to look down.

'Bought this little place for my second wife,' William Jenson rumbled. 'Nice view, not that I spent any time looking at it.'

Docklands was dark below. Tower Bridge twinkled. Above Corey, the red and green landing lights of a plane going into Heathrow flashed rhythmically, diminishing into the west.

'Okay.' She turned round. 'What do you want me to do?'

The white-haired man looked faintly amused. With his coat off, and his black tie undone, it was apparent how wide his shoulders were for an old man, how broad his chest. With only the lights from the bedside lamp, his face was shadowed. He said, 'I thought it was your job to know.'

'Uh, yeah,' Corey said. After a moment's thought she unzipped her leather jacket and let it fall heavily to the floor. 'Right.'

He rasped, 'You're not a whore.'

Corey opened her mouth. No words came out. She shrugged.

'No,' she said at last.

'You're not even one of Serena's high-class hustling friends.' His West Coast accent had deepened.

'No.'

Part of her rudeness came, she realised suddenly, from regret. She had sat thigh to thigh with him in his chauffeur-driven limousine on the way to his apartment, and something in the warmth of his flesh, the very male smell of him, had surprised her with its attractiveness. Under other circumstances . . .

'A friend of mine dared me to do it for money. So what?' Corey asked.

'So that makes you a very foolish young woman, and a waster of my time,' the big old man growled. 'Or else . . .' He paused. 'Or else it makes you a very naughty little girl.'

The apartment bedroom was hot. I thought it was supposed to be air-conditioned, Corey thought wildly. A strange warmth began to burn in the pit of her stomach. She looked around at the wide bed, the drinks bar, the tv/voicemail screen in its cabinet, the stomach-turning panoramic window. A soft silence enfolded the room, making it somewhere apart from the rest of the apartment building, apart from the rest of the world.

Corey swung around and faced the craggy, white-haired man. She put her leather-gloved fists on her hips, and her head to one side. 'So I'm a naughty girl. So what happens to naughty little girls?'

'*This.*'

He stepped in close before she could move. She had an instant to smell his expensive aftershave and stare at his spotless white shirt front. Then he reached and grabbed one of her wrists in each of his hands, pushed them behind her back, and transferred his grip on both her wrists to one hand.

He was strong, but old. She could have broken the grip.

He jerked her wrists. She spun until she faced half away from him. His hand lifted her wrists, forcing her forward. Her hair fell into her eyes as she bent, head and shoulders down.

A movement caught her eye. In the uncurtained glass, her reflection was plain against the black night. A skinny, ragged-skirted young woman with booted feet apart on the carpet, bent over forwards, bottom up; and behind her the strong old man, a shadow of white shirt and black tailored trousers.

He lifted her wrists higher. 'Missy, I'll show you what happens to bratty little girls!'

Her upper body was forced down. When he pushed, she was forced to stagger forward. He marched her to one of the plush armchairs, and sat on one arm of it. His strong grip thrust her forward and she sprawled across his lap.

Her balance was gone, her feet off the floor. Head hanging down, hair in her eyes, she squirmed and wriggled, trying first to slide off forward, then backwards, but his grip on her was surprisingly tight.

He ran his free hand over her rump.

She stiffened with the suddenness of it. His palm caressed the thick lace folds of her skirt. Then, with a sudden movement, he flicked her skirt up from her waist, over her shoulders. She squirmed, her bottom up.

Corey felt his fingers under the waistband of her

leggings and panties, tugging them down. The room's suddenly cool air slid over her bare buttocks. His hand removed itself. Pushed against his chest and thighs, she could feel his breathing quicken.

'Bad girl!'

A sharp hand stung her across both buttocks.

Corey yelped in surprise. Reflex action made her struggle. She got one foot to the floor, pushed, and felt his grip on her wrists loosen.

She hesitated for a split second.

The flat-handed blow still stung; she could feel the skin of her bare bottom glow. But the strange warmth in the pit of her stomach had been joined by a growing arousal between her legs. Startled beyond measure, she felt her pussy pulse wet.

Corey let the toe of her boot skid on the carpet. She fell forward again, across the man's thighs. Her unprotected bottom jutted up.

'Trying to get away, hah?' His voice rumbled in his chest. 'I reckon that makes you a real bad little girl.'

The hard hand came down again. This time it struck squarely, and she yowled. He drew his arm back. She wriggled, spreading her legs, arching her bottom up. The next spank caught her thighs and her outer labia.

'Ohhh!' She slid back in surprise. Her sex throbbed.

He dropped his hand between her torso and his body, tugging at the zip of his trousers. She pushed forwards. Her breasts in her tight bodice pressed into his lap, pushing against his hard, hot cock.

Two smart blows stung her left buttock and her right buttock. She squealed, experimentally at first, and then louder when he made no complaint. She felt his cock swell against her cleavage. She braced, getting both feet to the floor and straightening her legs. Her head dipped, and she mouthed the head of his thick, stubby cock.

501

'That—'

'Oh!'

'—is—'

'*Oh!*'

'—bad!'

'Ohhh!'

His calloused hand slapped hard on to her buttocks. A fire exploded. She clamped shut on his hand as she came, taken by surprise. He stood up, spilling her on to the carpet, and delivered one last swat to her stinging backside.

As her breathing quietened, she lay and watched her own sprawled reflection in the black of the glass window.

'May I?' The old man knelt beside her, holding out a glass with a finger of whiskey in it. When she took it, he swung around, stiffly, and sat beside her on the floor, his back against the arm of the armchair. His white hair was streaked with sweat. It fell over his blue eyes in surprisingly boyish licks.

'That was most enjoyable,' he said. 'I hope you had no objection.'

'I could have stopped you,' Corey admitted, 'if I had any objections.'

'My old man used to lay into me with a leather belt when I was a kid,' the man drawled reminiscently. 'Don't suppose he had the slightest idea what he was startin'.'

'My family didn't believe in spanking children.' Corey sipped the whiskey. It went down smoothly. 'I'm twenty-two. The only time I've seen a man spank an adult woman is in old nineteen-fifties cowboy films.'

'I have a video copy of every one,' he said gravely. 'I shall get my chauffeur to drive you to your home, young lady.'

502

Corey rolled over and sat up. The thick plush carpet was soft under her bare bottom. She rolled her leggings down and slipped them off, separated her skimpy panties out from the bundle, and turned her back to pull them on and up.

'You didn't come,' she said, kneeling facing away from him, but watching his reflection in the window.

One of his rough white eyebrows quirked up. 'What are you saying?'

Corey looked over her shoulder and grinned. 'I came but you didn't. I guess that makes me naughty.'

'Missy, I can see that it does.'

'But you'll have to catch me first!'

She intended to run behind the far side of the bed. As she sprang up, he reached forward with startling speed and grabbed her ankle. She sprawled full length on her face on the plush carpet.

Before she could get up, a hand grabbed her belt at the small of her back and lifted her.

'Bad girl!'

His hands pinned her wrists in the small of her back. She felt him grope under her stomach, at her belt-buckle. The leather strap suddenly jerked tight, then loosened, and the belt fell away from her unprotected waist. He caught the buckle and belt-end, doubling it into a thick leather loop.

Once again she felt herself thrust forward over his knee, as he sat down spread-legged on the bed. She pushed forward. Her straining breasts slid on the skin of his thighs, pushed out of the top of her bodice. 'Why am I bad?'

His stubby cock hardened under her body. 'Because you creamed your little panties, missy. *Bad!*'

A hard smack with the leather belt emphasised his words. A rain of blows struck her buttocks, so fast and so sharp that she could not count, only writhe and squeal. She thrust her body up to meet the blows of her own belt. He would not pull her panties down this time. The silky fabric between her legs became soaked with her juices, hot with her desire, until she was twisting and moaning, pushing her mound into his hard-muscled leg. Each blow on her reddened buttocks stung more hotly.

Abruptly he dropped the belt and lifted her, threw her forward on to the bed, rolled her over on to her back, and pulled down her panties. She saw his thick, stubby cock push between her spread thighs, against her hot sex.

'Now!' she screamed. 'Come on, come on, come on, *now*—'

The thick head of his cock pushed into her. She widened her legs and took him, clamping down on him as soon as he was inside her. She gripped his lean buttocks, pulling him down, banging his body into hers, until she felt his hot seed suddenly explode into her, and with that she yelled shrilly and came, her sex convulsing, pushing him back outside with her strength and fire.

'Oh, shit!' she said dizzily. 'That was – that was – that *was*.'

His hot, heavy, bony body sprawled heavily across hers. He lay and panted. Then he lifted a sweat-streaked, lined and wrinkled face, and gave her that smile that was forty years younger than he was.

'I had no idea,' Corey added.

'Missy, I envy you. You have so many years to make use of what you know.'

She stroked his face. 'And you've had so many years.'

'Sure have, missy. And there's a good few left in me yet.'

By the morning, when the chauffeur at last came

and she was woken from her sleep with one arm over the old man's broad shoulder, she stumbled into her clothes, half asleep before her first cup of coffee.

'You did say it was a dare, missy,' his strong voice rumbled.

'Oh – yes. Oh, give me a token five cents or something. That should still count as doing the dare.' She smiled at him muzzily.

Not until she was in the chauffeur-driven limousine did she feel something bulky against her side, and took out from the inside pocket of her leather jacket a thick white envelope.

The lunch-time rain had eased, and the Café Valletta emptied. Music played, over-loud now that the café had few people in it. Strong sun through the windows began to warm the skin of Shannon Garrett's bare arms.

She reached down and prodded the fat envelope. 'What are you going to do with the money?'

'Mmm?' Corey came back from her reverie. 'Oh – I don't know yet. Haven't thought.'

Shannon stood reluctantly. 'I suppose I'd better get back to the office. I'm late. Corey, that was . . . you . . .'

The younger woman shook her head. 'I just keep thinking about it! I tell you, Shannon, I'd do it again if I had the chance.'

'We couldn't possibly do it again,' Shannon protested.

'Scared?' Corey looked up, her eyes an incredibly deep blue in her clear-skinned face.

'No- . . .'

Nadia Kay stubbed out a thin cigarette. 'I don't know when I last felt so *alive*. Shannon, don't leave yet. I have an idea, as I said when I last spoke to you on the phone.'

505

'I'm not going to like this.' Shannon Garrett stood looking down at the two friends whom she had dared. 'Am I?'

Nadia leaned back in her chair. Corey, now apprehensive, sat up and looked at the older woman.

'Well . . .' Nadia tucked a red-gold curl back behind her ear. She removed her sunglassees and gazed across at the two of them.

'First, Corey dared you, Shannon. And then you dared Corey – and dared me as well. I haven't had a turn. I think, to be fair, that I should dare each of you, now. This game isn't over yet.'

Chapter Four

MUSIC LEAKED FROM next door through the living-room wall of Shannon Garrett's terraced house. It was audible even over the television. Shannon sighed. *After all the yelling I did at Tim, I don't think I can complain. Not for a while.* She felt for the remote control, and knocked the early evening news soundtrack up a notch.

She didn't take the world news in.

'Well, Shannon, how was *your* day?' she asked herself. Her voice sounded flat in the empty living-room. 'Last week I broke up with my married lover, then I went for lunch with my friends, went back to the office, made a few phone calls, got on with the job, left early. Oh, and I picked up a total stranger and fucked him. And I loved it!'

Cars went by outside in the narrow east London streets. A bee buzzed in from the open kitchen door and flew in rapid circles before leaving.

I can't believe I said that!

She got up and went to the kitchen. *Too hot to cook.* She poured herself a glass of supermarket red. She looked back into her living room.

Right. Despite anything Nadia says, we've all done a

507

dare. It was very nice. Unfortunately, now it's back to the real world. I'll have to phone and tell her that. That I'm not coming round this evening to discuss it, even. It's ridiculous!

Shannon put the glass down. She walked into the living-room. With the aid of a chair, she reached up and took down the framed Degas prints from the walls. Not much to show for six years.

Without warning, memories flashed in front of her eyes. Lunch-time sex. Her pussy heated. She had to put the last framed print down quickly before she dropped it.

I can't believe I did that in the first place. I certainly can't do it again! But if Nadia can think up a really inventive dare, will either of us feel able to back down? What am I *saying*? Shannon stopped and put her hands to her flushed face.

Back to the real world, I said. Or do I mean – I enjoyed it so much that it scares me?

Nadia's doorbell buzzed. When she looked out of her first-floor window, she saw Shannon standing expectantly on the pavement below. The younger woman was still in her work clothes, with her jacket slung over her arm.

'You got here, then.'

'Uh – yes. I guess.'

Nadia leaned out and looked up and down the street. 'I thought you and Corey were coming together?'

Shannon Garrett shrugged. She looked vaguely embarrassed. 'I thought so too.'

'She won't let us down.' The scent of roses filled Nadia's nostrils, from her window-box. Her side-street was deserted in the evening sun. At the end, where it opened into Baker Street, hundreds of sweating commuters still thronged the pavements.

'Come up.' Nadia triggered the ground-floor door lock. 'I have some iced tea ready.'

She went into the flat's tiny kitchen and emerged with a tray and glasses, which she put on the table in her main room. The white walls were disproportionately high for the room's width, but she loved her Edwardian conversion flat, even if it wasn't really big enough for both herself and all the *Ephemera* stock not currently displayed in the shop.

Voices sounded on the stairs outside the door, one of them Shannon's. When Nadia opened the front door, Corey tumbled in too, panting. Her black hair was slicked up with the heat, and her usually pale cheeks were pink with exertion. Her black cotton summer dress was crumpled.

'I ran all the way from the Tube station!' Corey flung herself down on the sofa nearest the open window. 'Sorry. Got stuck on the phone as I was coming out. Patricia! I'm not even *married* to her limp-click son any more. Men!' She seized a glass of iced lemon tea and gulped it down, the frosting on the glass melting over her fingers.

Shannon looked around, obviously searching for somewhere to hang her jacket that was not already taken up by 1920s antique clothing.

'Put it in the bedroom,' Nadia said, 'then come and sit down.'

'You've got them, haven't you?' the brown-haired woman said as she came back into the room. 'Your dares. I can't believe I'm doing this . . .'

'You don't have to do it if you don't want to.'

'Stop treating us like babies!' The black-haired girl sprawled back on the sofa. She crossed her long legs at the ankles, and folded her arms over her ample bosom. Her eyes were brilliant with excitement. 'And I bet you've made them easy – because you think we won't do them otherwise!'

Nadia put her glass of iced tea down. 'Really, Corey.'

'Oh, I'm sorry. I'm just crabby because of Patricia. I prefer to forget Ben.' Corey smiled winningly. 'You've got a right to your turn to dare us. But I want a proper *competition* – let's see if Shannon and I can do the *same* dare, and see who does it best.'

'She's got a point,' Shannon said, turning back from the window. 'How can we say who wins? We need an objective judge. Not one of us. We could – oh, I don't know. Tell the dares as hypothetical stories to someone.' She paused. 'What about Michael?'

You've thought this out beforehand, Nadia smiled to herself. 'As a gay man, he certainly should be objective. Shannon, my dear, I take it this means that you are doing another dare?'

The brown-haired woman licked her lips. A scent of perfume and faint sweat came off her in the heavy summer's air. She took a deep breath and smiled. 'Like I said. I can do anything you two can do.'

Nadia held out a folded slip of paper. Shannon took it. 'Good grief, Nadia, you have *got* to be joking!'

Nadia smiled. She said softly, 'I dare you.'

Shannon wiped the palm of her hand down her linen skirt.

'Show it to Corey,' Nadia added, 'since you both want the same dare this time.'

The black-haired girl sprang up and leaned to read over Shannon Garrett's shoulder. 'Oh, what! Nadia, I bet *you've* never done that!'

'I'm sure the winner will be equally inventive when it comes to my turn.' Nadia smiled. 'I shall expect you for supper in, shall we say, a week?'

Corey bounced on the sofa. 'It's Wednesday today. Let's make it Friday evening. Thanks for the tea, Nadia, I'm off!'

There was a minute's silence after the girl had gone. The sound of the slammed door and footsteps down the stairs echoed. Nadia heard Corey Black whistling as she walked up the road.

Nadia glanced at Shannon. The brown-haired woman had her head bent over the paper scrawled over with Nadia's unkempt handwriting. She absently rubbed her fingers against her chilled glass, and then stroked the cold moisture against the back of her neck and behind her ears. Her upper lip was beaded with sweat.

'I wonder why Patricia is calling Corey again?' Shannon said absently. 'She didn't like the girl when she *was* her mother-in-law, so why she should call after the divorce . . .'

'Oh, I think they're still waiting for the decree absolute.' Nadia savoured the icy tang of the lemon tea on her tongue. 'Mmm. Friday evening. That doesn't give you a lot of time. I shall invite Michael. You'll be there, Shannon – won't you?'

Shannon Garrett looked up, her expression something between arousal and terror. 'Will I?' she said.

'No,' Shannon said. 'I won't be in today, Arabella. No, there's nothing that needs doing before Monday. Have the subs finished with that piece on nightclubs?'

She talked with her assistant for a few more minutes. Then she folded up the mobile phone and replaced it in her briefcase on the café table. The music of Covent Garden buskers echoed down from the high glass roofs. A pigeon fluttered past her head, one wing skimming her hair. She flinched. Her heart raced.

It's Friday. I don't even have a whole day left! If I don't move fast, I'm going to lose. They'll say I copped out. They'll think I couldn't do it!

Nadia's dare was succinct. *I dare you to fuck two or*

more strangers together.

The crotch of her silk panties grew damp as she visualised it. Shannon shifted in her seat.

How do I find someone – more than one – who's willing? How do I do this!

As she sat up, she gazed around the open-air café. Tourists. Men in jeans and T-shirts, women in pastel cottons. Shannon let her glance stray to the crotches of worn, soft denim jeans.

I might pick one who doesn't speak English!

She giggled, and smothered it in a cough. A man looked up from the next table, caught her eye, and continued his conversation with a colleague while he held her gaze for several seconds.

She felt one of her high-heeled sandals slipping off her foot. She bent down to adjust it. Her silk blouse, unbuttoned at the top, momentarily fell open as she leaned forward. The lace of her bra and the soft warm cleft between her breasts became visible.

Slowly, Shannon sat up again.

The man's gaze moved up to her face.

Two men were sitting at the next table. The one who held her gaze seemed forty-ish, but no older than that. A definite air of authority clung to him. Expertly manicured and shaved, extremely well-dressed. When he turned back to his conversation she let her eyes stray up his back. The suit was well-tailored to his lean body. She caught a scent of expensive aftershave, and under it a hint of male sweat.

The man with him was younger, broad-shouldered, and fair-haired. His suit jacket was thrown over the back of his chair. Sweat marked his shirt under his arms. He appeared harassed. Papers and electronic diaries were strewn across the table between the two men.

As she watched, the older man leaned back and smiled with an expression of utter control.

I know how I do this, Shannon thought. I know exactly how I do this.

Her mouth was dry with anticipation as she stood. Automatically she smoothed down her silk-lined linen skirt. She slung her jacket off one shoulder. And as she passed their table, a hidden flick of her thumb triggered her briefcase catch.

'Oh!' Papers spilled at her feet and across the men's table. 'Oh, I'm so sorry!'

'Please, don't mention it.' The older businessman scooped up papers and handed them to her as she crammed them into her case. He leaned back in his chair. Again, his bright eyes met hers. Laughter lines creased the corners of his eyes. 'Actually, James and I were about done here. Could I perhaps buy you a drink?'

Shannon let the pause hang in the air. The younger man, his cheeks slightly flushed, muttered something apologetic and made as if to rise. Shannon sat down on one of the chairs, blocking his way.

'I'd love to,' she confessed. 'It would be a shame to go back to the office on a day like this. Let's have some wine.'

'Edward—' The younger man seemed anxious.

The dark-haired man waved expansively. He had a long, rangy body which his well-cut suit emphasised. 'We can take a long lunch, I believe.' He still kept his eyes on her face. Shannon moved her shoulders back slightly. Her breasts pressed against the silk of her blouse.

The fair-haired man, James, sat back down. His blond eyebrows gave his face a permanent appearance of startlement. 'Oh. Oh, right. I know a little pub near here. It has a garden at the back,' he suggested. 'It usually isn't as crowded.'

Shannon nodded. 'Then take us there.'

513

She and Edward followed the fair-haired man through the Covent Garden crowds. She was electrically conscious of the older man walking behind her. When the packed tourists' bodies pressed them together, she felt the lean muscle of his thigh press once, lightly, against her buttock. She did not pull away. The chatter and calls made speech impossible. She looked over her shoulder at him and did not smile.

His face was equally impassive.

Some streets away, they entered a pub. Shannon found herself half-blind in the bar, after the sunlight outside. She did not wait to hear what James ordered. She moved towards the open door at the rear.

The high heels of her sandals made her conscious of her walk. They thrust her buttocks and breasts slightly out, for balance. Her skin flushed suddenly warm, knowing she was commanding their attention.

'Through here,' the older man said, his voice educated and controlled. She moved, conscious of his gaze, out into a walled courtyard where traffic noise was almost inaudible, and faint music played in the background.

'I ordered Pimm's, and champagne.' The blond young man was flustered, sweating in his suit jacket. Shannon smiled and sat down on a wooden bench. She patted the seat beside her. After a moment's hesitation, he sat down.

'What's your name?' he blurted.

'Elaine,' she replied without hesitation. It was her second name: Shannon Elaine Garrett.

'If you don't mind,' James said, 'I'll take my jacket off.'

'Why not.' Edward removed his own suit jacket and put it over the back of his chair, which he had drawn up to the end of the table. 'It really is very hot indeed.'

They talked inconsequentially. Towards three

514

o'clock, Shannon realised the pub garden had been deserted for at least an hour.

'I'm afraid if we want any more, we shall have to go in and order it,' the older man, Edward, said. 'They won't come out.'

Shannon glanced up at the windowless brick walls that surrounded them, masked by green creepers in which bees lazily buzzed. The scent of honeysuckle cut through the air, sweet in her nostrils.

The dark-haired man leaned back in his chair with an air of authority, his legs wide apart. The fly of his trousers had a definite bulge. Patches of sweat darkened the underarms of his shirt. He smelt very male now. Despite his increasing laughter, Shannon had watched him enough to know that he had drunk very little alcohol since they arrived. He watched her.

As if oblivious, she sat up on the wooden bench. With a completely erect posture, she slid her linen jacket back off her shoulders and let it fall to the ground. She smoothed her hands over her silk shirt, down her breasts, to her flat stomach.

'Edward, I think I should be getting back,' James stuttered nervously. He was not much older than Shannon. She caught his gaze, looking deep into his pale blue eyes, and held it for a long moment.

'Don't break up the party.' Her voice was husky now. James had a fit body, a squash-player's body. She admired the play of muscles on his forearms as he rolled his shirt sleeves up. Tiny golden hairs caught the sun. Light flashed from the heavy metal band of his watch.

Shannon sat back. The hem of her skirt rucked up, showing the tops of her sheer stockings, and a suspender.

'I always think stockings are cooler than tights in this heat,' she remarked. 'But I am still very hot.'

515

She was completely sober. More glasses of wine had gone into the grass beside the table than down her throat. She wriggled her skirt down over her knees. 'I could always take them off, couldn't I.'

'You could take them off, Elaine,' Edward said. A faint line of sweat shone on his forehead.

Of course I will, Shannon thought with a sense of complete freedom. I'm 'Elaine', I can do whatever I want, and I'll never see these men again.

'But it would be a shame,' the younger man added hastily. 'I've always liked stockings myself – on a woman, that is – I mean—'

'But it's so hot.' Shannon reached up and unbuttoned another blouse button. The cream silk clung to her damp skin. If she moved at all now, her blouse would fall open.

Deliberately, she shifted around on the bench. Slowly she extended one leg on to the grass, her toe pointed. Sheer stockings glimmered in the sun. Slowly she put her fingers either side of her knee and began to slide them upwards. Her skirt began to ruck up.

'Very hot. . .'

Now her fingers glided over the top of her stockings, on to the cool flesh of her upper thigh. Her skirt rode up to expose one suspender.

Her body leaning forward made her blouse fall open. The silk material fell away. The full curve of her breasts, contained by her lace and silk bra, shone in the sunlight. A fine sweat pearled her cleavage. Without lifting her body, she raised her eyes to the men sitting either side of her.

'I – ah – ought to go,' James's voice squeaked beside her. He was holding his briefcase on his thighs, concealing his lap.

Shannon shifted her gaze to the older, dark-haired man, Edward. She unsnapped one suspender, and dropped her gaze from his face to his crotch. His face was impassive. A huge erection strained at the fly of his suit trousers. The dark cloth outlined a thick, long cock. He made no attempt to conceal his arousal.

'James,' she said, 'help me with these.'

'Um—'

'These.' Her fingers slid her skirt up on the outside of her thigh, exposing another white suspender. 'Come and help me undo this. There's a good boy.'

Edward gave a deep chuckle. It might have been that that made a steely determination come into the younger man's eyes.

He put the briefcase down on the table and knelt at her side.

His erection poked out the fly of his trousers. Shannon watched it harden and swell as he saw her looking at him. She slid her tongue-tip over her lips.

The wood of the bench was warm under her pussy. The crotch of her knickers dampened as she shifted, exposing more of the length of her leg. Mesmerised, the young fair-haired man took the suspender in his fingers and unsnapped it.

'There's one at the back.' Shannon straddled the bench and leaned forward until her belly and breasts pressed into the hard wooden surface. She reached behind herself and slid one hand over her skirt-waist, over her buttocks, until she could hitch up the hem of her skirt.

She turned back to lie face-down on the bench. Her breasts pushed up out of the neck of her blouse. They swelled with arousal, her bra now uncomfortably tight.

Her skin shivered as the young man's hard, warm fingers fumbled at the back of her thigh. She heard another suspender unsnap. After a second, she felt his hands begin to roll her stocking down her thigh.

The sun caressed her bare flesh. The scent of

517

honeysuckle was hot and heavy. She held the older man's gaze.

'Edward . . .' She stroked the lacy edge of one bra cup. 'It's so hot, and I'm so uncomfortable.'

'I find myself in some discomfort.' His voice was a rasp. He sat with a straight back, the picture of a proper businessman. He pointed, with an air of authority, at his crotch. 'Perhaps if I were – less uncomfortable. . .'

Shannon reached her hands out and grasped the end of the bench. She pulled herself along it on her belly. The hard wood pushed at her soft, aroused breasts. Her nipples swelled and hardened. Her engorged breasts strained at the now-painful constriction of her bra.

She felt cool air on her other thigh. The young man's hands fumbled at her suspenders there. Her hot skin shivered under his touch.

Now that she was leaning forward on the bench, her crotch was raised, and the bench was not pressing against it. She whimpered with anguish, pushing her buttocks back, but they came into contact with nothing except empty air.

'Do it . . .' She raised her head to look back over her shoulder. The blond man straddled the bench, straddled her where she lay face down. A tiny damp spot marked the crotch of his trousers, where his bulging concealed cock had wept a droplet of liquid. His sportsman's muscles tensed on his forearms.

Wanting, aching, Shannon pushed her toes against the earth. She raised her buttocks slightly from the bench, inviting. The crotch of her knickers was soaking wet.

'Do it!' she repeated.

She did not wait for him to act. Now that she lay with her head at the end of the bench, she could reach

Edward's chair. She put her hands on each side of his chair, and dropped her face into his lap.

'I'm going to suck you dry.' Her mouth was close to his fly. Her moist breath feathered his crotch. He grunted. Both his hands gripped the metal arms of the chair. Involuntarily, his hips jerked up. His crotch pressed into her face.

Shannon strained forward, the bench hard against her stomach and breasts. She mouthed his concealed cock through the fabric of his trousers. He gasped. Slowly she brought one hand forward and unbuttoned his top button. She took hold of the zip and tugged experimentally.

'Oh!' Cool air suddenly brushed her buttocks.

The unseen hands of the young man behind her caught either side of her skirt and rucked it up, wrenching it roughly, until it was around her hips. She felt him grab the back of her panties with his whole fist. There was a second of aching anticipation; then he jerked them down. The sheer fabric tore.

He thrust one hand between her legs, under her stomach. His hand, flat against her belly, felt huge. With one muscular movement he pulled her up from the bench and pressed her forwards.

Shannon's high-heeled sandals got a grip. Now she was resting only her upper torso and breasts on the bench. One hand gripped the dark-haired businessman's zip, the other steadied her against his chair.

The tip of a cock brushed her labia. She jerked, steadied, braced herself. With one single movement she yanked down the zipper on the dark-haired man's trousers. His thick cock sprang free. She plunged her face into the springy dark hair at the base of it. Her tongue dived into the sweaty crevices between his balls and his body. His hips raised. She pushed in, her hot tongue licking behind his balls, teasing the flesh

519

between his legs, tasting salt perspiration. She heard him groan. She mouthed her way back along his hairy upper thighs.

'Tell me what you're going to do,' he groaned. 'Talk dirty.'

'I'm going to suck you off. I'm going to take your big cock in my mouth and I'm going to suck and lick until you come in my mouth. And while I'm doing it, I'm going to tell your friend to fuck me from behind. He's going to fuck me hard. I'm going to suck you dry. Ahh!'

The younger man's hands gripped her waist. His stiff cock prodded her sex. She pressed back. The head of his cock pushed within her lips; withdrew: pushed in, withdrew; with a noise of sucking wetness.

Shannon slid her tongue from root to tip of Edward's cock, inhaling his musky smell. She glimpsed his white knuckles on the arms of his chair. Greedily she lowered her lips over him, taking him into her mouth, sucking first at the tip, then at the quiveringly aroused shaft. His hips began to pump upwards. Sweat stained his white shirt, rucked up out of his suit trousers; she glimpsed his flushed face and sweat-matted hair.

'I'm fucking you!' he groaned. 'James! Fuck Elaine. Fuck her hard. *Now*. Fill her right up!'

From behind her, James's cock slammed into her wet, aching sex. She paused for a split second on toe-tip, adjusting to the rhythm. Then, as he penetrated her from behind, she sucked Edward's cock in the same rhythm that James was fucking her. The thick shaft in her pussy and the thick shaft in her mouth were one thing, one experience; she held and was penetrated simultaneously, thrusting and sucking, thrusting and sucking. The rhythm of the cock swelling in her mouth and the cock fucking in her sex hypnotised her: minutes might have passed, or hours.

James's muscled thighs were hard against the back of

her legs. His hands gripped her body. His hips rammed into her buttocks. His balls banged against her. She felt herself open and flower hotly. The cock inside her mouth hardened, achingly erect, widening her lips.

Her pussy clenched, taking the man behind her deep inside. At the same moment she took the other man's cock deep into her throat. Above her Edward cried out and came, pumping strongly. The excitement of that fired her own orgasm, and as she clamped down on the man whose hips thrust into her buttocks, she heard James cry out as he shot his seed into her waiting sex. Drenched, sweat-soaked, she collapsed down on to the bench with her head in Edward's lap. The hard-muscled body of James slumped down across her back, his breath deep and panting. She experienced a moment of heat: sun, sexual bodies, sweat, semen, and the weight and touch of them both, both men satiated, pressing against her skin.

Her silk-lined skirt was creased, rucked up around her waist. Her blouse was undone. One breast had popped from its constricting bra-cup, the other was still enclosed in silk and lace. One stocking and one sandal had gone. The warm air felt like silk over her bare buttocks. Her panties were a ripped scrap of cloth laying on the grass beside the wooden bench.

Edward's tailored trousers were creased and dark with sweat, and spattered with come. His chest still rose and fell rapidly. She rested her cheek against his thigh. James's weight lay on her body and shoulders. When she glanced back, she saw him with the buttons popped off his shirt, and his suit trousers around his ankles. He wore red wool socks.

In summer! Shannon chuckled. Great body. Shame about the rest. She met his eyes and giggled again, deliciously satisfied. She feasted on the sight of his torso and thighs, and his limp and now-shrinking cock. Her nipples began to harden.

I never did get my breasts sucked, she thought dreamily. Now just let me tell them—

A nearby clock struck.

'Good grief!' Shannon exclaimed. She sat up, spilling the fair-haired man heavily on to the grass. He grunted and winced. She said, 'Is that the time? I have to go!'

Chapter Five

IN THE ENSUING silence, Nadia opened another bottle of wine. Michael Morgan allowed her to fill his glass. He was a young, plump man, elegant as ever in blue jeans and a tailored shirt.

'That was some story, Shannon,' he said admiringly. 'I know straight men who'd find that a real turn-on.'

'Freely adapted from some of the letters we get into the office,' Shannon Garrett said blandly.

Nadia caught her eye and grinned.

'What about mine now?' Corey's voice sounded muffled. The tall girl knelt on the wide window-sill. She peered down into the street. Then she straightened, still kneeling above the drop, and nodded. 'Yeah, I can see it. My bike's OK. It's only a Honda 350, and it's older than God, but it's all mine and I love it.'

Michael raised his glass. 'How about a biker story? That might be even more to my taste.'

'Funny you should say that, Mike.' She sat down and switched her legs into the room. 'I could tell mine like it happened. Like it happened to me, I mean. Shall I?'

'I love a story competition.' He drained his wine

and held the glass out to Nadia. 'Do start.'

The girl put one foot up on the sill. Nadia watched her lean her back against the window's edge. She was wearing an extra-long T-shirt borrowed from Nadia, over bra and knickers. Her leathers were hung up inside the bathroom door, that being the only free hook.

'Right.' Corey smoothed her short tangled black hair back from her face. 'What time is it? Let's say ... about twenty-four hours ago. I was riding the bike back from a shoot in the Midlands. It was almost dark. You know what it's like riding a bike in summer, you get sweaty as hell underneath leather. So I pulled into one of the service stations, I don't know which.'

'No corroborative detail?' Michael queried.

'If I did, and got it wrong, you'd know. Are you telling this story or me? Shut up: it's going to be really good.' She swung her leg down from the sill and came back to the table, plumping down in the seat between Nadia and Michael, looking at them with bright eyes.

'You have to imagine I'm looking for a good fuck. I'm after my prey. And I don't just want one man. One man isn't enough this time.

'So anyway, I pulled the bike into this service station. There was just a bit of orange left in the west, but otherwise the sun had set. The sky overhead was dark. All the service station lights were on. I didn't recognise the place very well.

'Then I realise why I wouldn't recognise it anyway. I've missed my turning, and I haven't come into the bike and car park. I'm round where the lorries and the commercial vehicles park. That's why everything looks different. Once I get my helmet off I see it's a big badly-lit expanse of concrete with the lights of the petrol pumps way off in the distance. I can still hear the cars on the motorway, and I can smell engine oil, and diesel, and the food cooking in the service station café. But it looks like I've parked about a mile away from anywhere or anybody.

'This doesn't look good, I think. I'd been planning to go into the service area and see if I could find a couple of men on their own. Only there isn't anyone all the way out here.

'Just as I'm thinking that I'll have to kick the bike into life again, and go and park in the proper place, there's this roar of an engine, and these incredibly bright halogen headlights hit me in the eyes. I'm dazzled! I put my hand up to shield my face.

'A voice calls out, "Stay where you are, sir!"

'They haven't seen I'm a woman, whoever they are, because I'm in my leathers. Even with the helmet off I've got pretty short hair. Speaking of the leathers, I want to take them off by this time, because I'm getting really sweaty being in them without the slipstream from driving the bike. I don't know what to do, so I just stand still. The headlights go dim, but that doesn't help me, I'm still dazzled.

'The next thing I know, someone grabs me by the shoulders and pushes me round, and shoves me up against some kind of vehicle that I hadn't even seen in the darkness. Someone takes my hands and puts them on the vehicle's roof. What feels like a boot kicks my feet apart, so I have to stand straddled and leaning forward. Then some man's hand pats down my arms and up my legs.

'This voice says, "He's clean. And he's cute!" Then this hand just goes up between my legs and hits my crotch, and all of a sudden he snatches it away like it's on fire.

'I turn round. By this time my eyes have recovered. I can see that what I'm standing next to is a dark jeep, and that the man in front of me is dressed in light and

525

dark brown camouflage jacket and trousers. I can see just well enough in the twilight to tell that he's really blushing.

' "Uh, sorry, ma'am," he says. "I didn't realise."

'I realise he's got an American accent. He's a big man, about six foot two or three, and very broad across the chest. What I can see of his hair is bright blond, but it's shaved so close it just looks like fuzz.

'Another American voice says, "What is it, Gary?" A second soldier comes around the side of the jeep. I realise why I didn't see him at first. He's African American. And this black guy stands about four inches taller than the white guy. He looks at the bike and he looks at me. He's interested. Then he looks again. I can see him look down at my leathers, at my chest, and then at my face again.

'There are lots of military vehicles, now my eyes have got adjusted. Some kind of convoy? These two seem to be the only men with the vehicles. Both enlisted men, not officers. I think the others must be inside eating.

'I look at the second man. I can tell he's fit, as well as big; he's got real muscles. "Parked in the wrong place, huh?" he says.

'This black guy isn't wearing a battledress jacket, just camouflage trousers and a three-quarter sleeve T-shirt in the same US camouflage pattern. Boy, does he fill out his clothes nicely! His hair is closely shaved too, but I think it's kind of a nondescript brown.

' "Perhaps I didn't park in the wrong place." The two of them look at each other, and then at me.

'The first man, Gary, says, "What do you want, ma'am?"

'I look him up and down slowly. I'm starting to get hot now. There's no one around, but I can't tell how long it'll be until any of the others come back. I look him right in the eye and say, "I want a man with a big hard cock in his pants. Big enough to satisfy me. Do you think you've got what it takes?'

'The expression of shock on his face is beautiful. I see the black guy fumbling around for his wallet. I know what he's thinking.

' "I don't want money," I tell them. 'I'm looking for a man who's man enough for me, and I haven't met him yet.'

'They start eyeing each other up. I know any second one of them is going to tell the other to get lost. I don't want a fight, and I don't want one of them to go.

'So I say to Gary, "Why don't you and your friend have a little competition? I'll take you both on. I bet neither of you can make me come.'

'I'm really hot in my bike leathers now. I can feel my T-shirt underneath is wringing wet with sweat. While they're just standing there dumbstruck I reach up and pull the zip on my jacket down. It falls open. The night air on my wet skin is cold. I look down and I can see the cotton material clinging to my breasts, outlining my nipples which are standing right up. I put my arms back and let the jacket slide off, and then I sling it over the bike together with the helmet.

'When I look up again, they're both staring at my breasts. I'm getting really hot in the crotch now. I'm ready to have one of them inside me. I say, "Well?"

'The black guy says, "Look, this is pretty strange, ma'am, and there's something we should tell you." 'His friend Gary says, "You're cute, but we're not really into any kind of fucking except one, ma'am. But if you can take it up the ass, we're your men."

'I put my hands on my hips and stare them up and down. I say, "I can take anything you can give out, but you wimps aren't going to, are you?"

'As I planned, that does it. The big guy, Gary, steps

527

forward and grabs my hands. He twists my wrists into the small of my back, and turns me round, and marches me to the front of the jeep. My biker boots are skidding on the tarmac but I can't get any purchase – I don't really want to, but I'm not going to tell them that! I can tell my struggling is getting them excited. When I push back against Gary he's got a huge hard-on in his pants. It's getting *me* excited too, my pussy is sopping wet.

'Gary is immensely strong. When he pushes me face-down over the bonnet of the jeep, he can hold me there with just one hand. I can't push my body up, and he's holding my wrists behind my back. While I'm face down, I feel another hand – it's the second soldier, the black guy. He's kneeling beside the jeep and putting his hand up between my legs. I clamp my legs together but that's not what he's after. He reaches under my stomach for the fastenings of my leather jeans. I feel him pull down the zip. The leather is suddenly loose around my hips and thighs.

'Someone's hard-on pushes against my leg. I want to cry out, but I can't get my breath. Suddenly my wrists are released. Gary pushes my arms out stretched across the bonnet.

' "Hold on, ma'am," he says. "I'm gonna give it to you right up your pretty little ass."

' "I'm not ready!" I say, and I look over my shoulder while I hang on to the jeep bonnet for dear life. As I look, I see the black soldier. He's got a hand scooped full of something dark and sticky which in a moment I recognise as engine grease. I feel them both moving behind me, and one of them pulls my panties down, and the other slaps a handful of grease up between the cheeks of my buttocks.

'It's cold! But I don't cry out. Both their hands are working into my crack. Soon it's warm. I feel strong fingers circling my arse, teasing the edge of my hole, working the grease into it, making it flexible. I drive my hips against the metalwork of the vehicle. If I could rub my pussy against one of their legs I would come like a dog. I can't bear how hot I'm getting.

'Two greasy hands slide up under my wet shirt and grab my breasts. My nipples are so hard they're tender. Whoever it is massages my breasts until I think I'll go crazy. Then he says, 'She's ready, Johnnie.'

'The hands pull out from under me. I sprawl on the metal bodywork of the vehicle. A man's finger is inserted gently into my anus. It slides in and out, in and out, slowly at first, then faster and faster as I get looser. Soon it's not one finger, it's two. I don't know if they belong to Gary or Johnnie or both men together. I bend further forward.

'Two big hands grab my hips. The hot flesh of a cock-head nudges at my anus. At first it's not able to enter. Then I relax and with a sudden rush it goes in, past my sphincter muscle, and I'm pushed open. The front of my body comes up off the jeep and I brace myself bending forward, gripping with my hands. The man's cock thrusts up my arse and almost lifts me off the ground. Pulsations of heat are running through me. I've been bottom-fucked once before but it's never felt like this. I feel totally helpless.

'He thrusts again, and I'm lifted up on to tiptoes. I can feel his thick shaft rammed up my bottom. I look over my shoulder. As I thought, it's Gary. I can see his belly pressed up against my buttocks, and when he withdraws, I see the glistening shaft of his cock.

'Then I see Johnnie come and stand behind Gary. He's got another handful of that engine grease, and a wicked grin. He undoes Gary's pants and pulls them down around his ankles. Gary doesn't even break the rhythm of his thrust. When Johnnie slams the engine grease between the white guy's legs, his thrust lifts me right off the ground for a second. I'm so wet between my legs I just want something in there, anything. My ass feels so full, I know I'm going to come anyway, any second.

'Johnnie takes hold of the big soldier from behind and bends him over me. Gary's body is hot and heavy. He smells of the open air, and of oil and machinery. I can *feel* the thrust as the black soldier enters Gary. Gary's cock swells inside me until I think I can't take it, but I do. I look over my shoudler and see that I am being fucked up the arse by a big crew-cut blond soldier, who himself is being fucked up the arse by an even bigger black soldier. Their arms glisten with sweat. Their muscles stand out hard and taut. Johnnie reaches right forward past Gary and grabs my breast in his big hand. He squeezes so hard.

'Just that and the sight of them both fucking each other and I lose control. I explode. I come and I come, and I clench so hard that I squeeze Gary's cock right out of my arse. He falls on top of me as Johnnie finishes him with a mighty thrust, and Johnnie comes in Gary's arse, and I roll over and take him so that Gary comes in my hands.

'Then I'm sitting with my back against the side of jeep, on the oily concrete. The concrete is gritty and cold under my bare cheeks. My leathers are round my ankles. The night air is cooling my soaked T-shirt. These two huge guys are leaning either side of me, panting. The blond one's face is running with sweat.

'Then his friend Johnnie says, "Hey, I thought this was a competition."

'He's got this deep, rich voice; it vibrates right down to my toes. I put my hand on his chest. It's huge. He isn't breathing hard, he's hardly broken sweat.

' "Ready when you are, ma'am," he says.

'I look down at his camouflage pants. The fly is open. His black cock is lying out, half-limp, but as I look, it starts to swell up. He looks as big as Gary, if not bigger.

'Gary's balls are wrinkled and not very hairy. He's sitting the other side of me with his big hand around his dick. He's grinning too.

'I put my hands on their shoulders and I push myself up on to my feet. My knees are shaking. The lights of the service station are a long way off. There's no one around that I can see. Cars go whizzing past on the motorway about forty foot the other side of a chain-link fence.

'I lean over the front of the jeep again. The metal hood is cold now. The shock makes my nipples hard. I can feel myself getting wet again. I say, "What are you waiting for?"

'Johnnie walks around the jeep until he's standing on the opposite site, about eighteen inches from my face. "I want you to see what you're getting, ma'am. *All* of it."

'He starts pulling at his cock. He's circumcised. Thankfully, I see that while he's got a good nine inches, it's a bit narrow. For what he's going to do to me, that's ideal. I lie there, bare-arsed, over the hood of the jeep, and the black guy just stands there sliding the satin-black skin up and down his cock and getting harder and harder.

'Something pushes the cheeks of my bottom apart. Hot lips kiss my arse. I flatten my tits down on the bonnet, pushing my bum up, trying to spread my ass as wide open as I can. A hot big tongue darts into my anus. It pulls back, pushes in again; starts to thrust.

' "Hey, man, what you doing there?"

' "Just getting her ready for you, boy," Gary's voice says behind me. I hear him spit, and then he's rubbing

531

the saliva around my anus. I can't help pushing back into his hand. I'm running hot again, I can feel my own juices on my thighs.

' "Stand aside," says Johnnie. I turn my head and watch as he walks around behind me. His cock juts out from his pants, hard and long. He puts his hands on my bum. "Ma'am, I got something here for you."

'I say, "Let me have it!"

'His hands lift my hips and spread my cheeks. The air's cold. The circumcised head of his cock nuzzles at the entrance to my ass.

' "Coming up!" he says, and he shoves it right in. If Gary hadn't loosened me up, I couldn't take it. I feel like I'm being filled right up. I can feel every mch of that cock pushing up inside me. The ring of muscle at my entrance pricks and tingles, and then it doesn't hurt any more. It's getting me really hot.

'There's a heavy pair of hands on my shoulders, pushing me down. Gary's voice says, "Go, boy!"

'While Gary holds me down, the black soldier draws his cock back, then thrusts it up my arse. I feel like I want to lift right off the ground. Push and back, push and back; and my arse swells wide open to take the root of his cock as he jams it up me, shrinks as he draws away, and opens wide as his pile-driving body thuds forward.

'Gary doesn't have his hands on my back any more. I'm panting hard, the breath whistling between my teeth, and I'm trying not to yell or groan, someone might hear us. I look over my shoulder.

'The big blond soldier is down on his knees behind Johnnie. He's got both hands on those taut black cheeks, spreading them, and his face is jammed up in the crack, tonging Johnnie's arsehole like there's no tomorrow. I feel Johnnie groan: it vibrates inside me. My pussy is swelling hot. My arse is so full I can't bear it.

'Gary stands up and drops his camouflage pants again. He takes out his thick cock. It's purple at the head, engorged and erect. Johnnie says, "Oh man, don't do that, man, you're gonna take my mind off my work!"

' "Do it!" I gasp. "Fuck *him* while he's fucking me!"

'Slow and sure, Gary moves in behind the black guy. This time it's the black guy's turn to be pushed forward over me. I can feel his body running with sweat, it soaks into my T-shirt. He's heavy, and hard, and his whole body jolts as Gary sticks it in him.

'That's too much for me. I come again, and again, and then I stick my hand down underneath me on to my clit and come for a third time. I feel his cock shoot it's whole load up me. He fills me right up. Slippery come starts oozing out of me. My body bucks up under Johnnie but I can't shift his weight, so I come again right there under him.

'Gary's body thuds into both of us. The black guy juts his ass up as Gary takes him, and Gary shoots *his* load.

'My knees are shaking so much that I just slide down off the jeep's bonnet and lie there, in a tangle, these two big guys half on top of me, half sprawled over the concrete car park, in a panting heap.

'And when I stopped panting, I said, "Thanks, boys." And I pulled up my leather jeans, and put on my jacket and helmet, and I straddled my bike and I rode away.'

Nadia's flat smelled of vinegar, pasta sauce, and wine. The air was heavy, a storm close at hand. Nadia looked round at her three dinner companions; the two women with their elbows on the tables among the empty plates, in surprisingly similar poses; the man leaning back in his chair.

'Is my story better than hers?' Corey pointed at Shannon.

Michael Morgan's face had a dreamy look.

'That's the best.' He glanced around at the three women. 'I'm sorry: it is.'

'Just because it's got soldiers with big dicks in,' Corey teased.

'What I could tell you about the military, you wouldn't believe. No, knowing you, you might.' He smiled, turning to Nadia. 'Let me guess, that one was from a gay male porn film?'

'I don't know. Was it, Corey?' Nadia asked demurely.

'Something like that . . .'

'That's definitely the best story I've heard in a long time. Sorry, Shannon. Which reminds me,' he said, still slightly absently, 'I told Simon I wouldn't be late home tonight. If you ladies will excuse me . . .'

Not long afterwards, Nadia saw a slightly unsteady Michael to the door. She returned to a room of empty plates and glasses. Shannon had her feet resting on a second chair. Corey balanced one wine glass on top of another. Nadia walked over and took it away from her.

Corey grinned up at her. The young woman's clear blue eyes were bright in her pale face. 'I didn't get on the bike right away, actually. We hung around and got cleaned up and chatted. They were really nice. I won the dare, though, didn't I? I had both my guys.'

'I was interrupted!' Shannon protested. 'I didn't have enough time . . .'

Her face grew soft. Nadia saw her friend's habitual expression of slight primness vanish entirely.

'I know what it's like now,' Shannon continued, 'to just tell a man to fuck me. Or tell him I'm going to fuck him. You know what I thought, with Edward and James? I thought, this could be my best fuck ever.'

534

'Then the clock struck and you turned into a pumpkin.' Corey chuckled.

'I'd hardly got started. But I took the dare. I don't think I *did* lose,' the woman protested hotly. Her faintly freckled face flushed.

Corey grinned at her. 'Michael thinks you did.'

Nadia looked at the remnants of salad on dishes. *I ought to take those out to the kitchen.* She wore her green silk mandarin dress, and bronze sandals: the colours accentuated her copper-red hair. Her creamy skin glistened. *I'll clear up later. After – after I tell them. If I do.*

She crossed to the sash windows and pushed them up even further. 'Michael didn't hear all the stories.'

'What do you mean? Corey told hers, and I told mine.' Shannon's hazel eyes widened. 'What aren't you telling us?'

Nadia savoured the warm air on her face. The breeze did not stir the heavy curtains. Purple-blue clouds gathered over the roof-tops to the south, towards Oxford Street. Heat lightning flashed.

She said lightly, 'I thought I'd make it a real competition.'

Corey punched the air with her fist. 'Yes! You took your own dare!'

'You didn't!' Shannon exclaimed.

Nadia turned. Her eyes narrowed slightly, laugh-lines creasing at the corners. Her full lips smiled. 'I suppose I should have mentioned it to Michael before he judged between you two. I couldn't resist trying out my own dare – but sad to say, it went a bit wrong . . .'

Chapter Six

THURSDAY EVENING. NADIA handed her 1920s fur stole over at the cloakroom desk. As she turned away, she bumped into a tall, fair-haired man in evening dress.

'Um, Nadia, yes. There you are.' The man adjusted his bow-tie.

'Oscar. How very kind of you to invite me.' She let a touch of sarcasm enliven her tone.

He had the grace to look uncomfortable. 'You always used to like these dinners. I thought, well, Diane's away in the States, so . . .'

'So instead of bringing your wife, you'd invite your ex-wife. Innovative.' She smiled and linked her arm in his, having to look up. 'I do enjoy not being married to you any more, Oscar. When you're this insensitive, I can laugh at it.'

He chuckled unwillingly. She looked up at his strong, heavy brows and bewildered face. His thick, rough yellow hair had been chopped into an expensive neat cut.

And in two minutes, evening dress or not, he'll look like he's been dragged through a hedge backwards! Ah, but he's still the most good-looking man I know.

It's just such a *relief* not to want him any more.

'Shall we go in?' Oscar asked.

She squeezed his arm. They went together up the red plush stairs, under the white moulding and gilded scrolls. Nadia mentally priced the Victorian portraits of the Guild founders hanging on the walls. *Hardly investment quality, and I can't think of any other excuse for their existence . . .*

'Miss – Nadia – Kay,' the toast-master at the door boomed. 'Oscar – Trevithic.'

It was far from the first time she had been announced when she arrived at a function, but it still made her smile. Nadia paused on the stairs, looked across the heads of the crowd. The hot air seeping in from London outside made the big, barrel-vaulted hall stuffy. Men were monochromatically splendid in evening dress, women in sparkling sequins. Light glittered from silver cutlery on the spotless tablecloths, where the dinner would be served.

Nadia removed her arm from Oscar's and walked down the two steps into the hall with her head high. She wore moderately high heels, knowing that those and her sheer stockings showed her slim legs to best advantage. Her sheath dress of green satin was beaded from plunging neckline to split hem with tiny pearls and emerald sequins, 30s style. It fitted well enough that she could wear a garter belt and strapless bra without spoiling the line of it. She had styled her red hair into a neat Peter Pan cut, and wore two tiny green stone earrings.

'There's Carol,' she said, a practised moment before Oscar's hesitant discomfort became plain. 'I must go and say hello, I haven't seen her for ages. Be good, darling.'

'Darling, what a wonderful dress!' Carol kissed the air some two inches from Nadia's ear. 'Wherever did you get it?'

Car boot sale, Bodmin, and didn't I have to sleep the night in the MG in a car park to be there early enough? Or was that St Albans?

'It's rather exclusive, I'm afraid,' Nadia said airily.

Working the crowd took her some time. She was unlikely to see any of the contacts she had kept up after she divorced Oscar on any other occasion. Most of them knew of *Ephemera*. Some of them passed her hints and rumours of pieces for sale. By the time she sat down to eat, she was too busy calculating whether she could drive to Sheffield in time to look at a dealer's stock before he opened on Monday to note who she was seated next to.

She glanced around. Oscar sat on far side of the hall, between a blonde woman, and one in orange satin. A voice to her left said, 'Wine?'

'Mmm?'

A rather chunky, middle-aged man with grey hair, seated on her left, indicated the waiter.

'Oh, yes. Thank you.'

Nadia tasted her red wine. Passable.

'I'm Peter,' the middle-aged man continued. 'I'm in manufacturing.'

Nadia took another sip of the wine. The other man, on her right, seemed taken up with his companion to his right, an elegant academic-looking woman in her sixties. 'How interesting,' Nadia said gamely.

Before the end of the soup, she had learned rather more about producing widgets than she had ever wanted to know.

I could leave now, she thought. She leaned back as the bowls were removed. The hall had grown even hotter. Between the body heat of two hundred men and women, and the hot evening sun leaking in through the clerestory windows, she felt herself growing slick with sweat.

I've talked to everybody I want to talk to. I've talked to rather a lot of people I don't want to talk to. This chap Peter is very sweet, but I may hit him with the cruet well before dessert. Perhaps I could just put my hand up and say *Can I go home now, please?*

She beamed down at the glass in her hand. She had been twiddling it by the slender stem. It was empty again. I always drink too much when I'm bored. Oh damn.

And it's Friday tomorrow. I wonder if either of them will have . . . Or if both of them . . .

'You could talk to me,' a voice said, very quietly, to her right. 'I couldn't tell you the difference between a widget and a gadget. Or a Post-Modernist and a Post-Structuralist.'

Glancing past her dinner companion to the right showed Nadia the sixty-year-old academic woman deep in conversation with an African diplomat she vaguely recognised from a previous dinner.

She was conscious of an immediately physical attraction to the man sitting beside her. He was big. Not fat – a physically large body frame slabbed with muscle. And he smelled of something that tantalised her. Cinnamon? Patchouli? Sandalwood.

'Sandalwood.' His voice was deep. His arm next to hers at table had a certain bulk. 'On my hands. I had a shipment of incense to check through.'

She studied him. Like Oscar, a big man. You could never mistake him for a boy. Dark eyes surrounded by laughter-lines looked down at her. His brows were thick and dark. His hair was rough-textured, dark brown with a touch of silver. Good lord, he has big shoulders, Nadia thought. They strained his dinner jacket. She let her gaze move down his body, solid under the evening jacket.

539

His easy movement as he leaned back in his chair shifted the expanse of his shoulders. His body tapered only slightly from a barrel chest to solid hips. His legs when he crossed them were strong and well-muscled under the cloth of his evening trousers. He wore the formal clothing with complete ease.

He's not one of Oscar's circle. Not that class. Lower. Military? she wondered. Police officer? Perhaps. Some kind of non-civilian authority about him – under that politeness, he thinks he knows more about real life than anyone else at this table.

Her attraction was positive and growing. Nadia's fingers itched. She wanted to pull his tie undone. Undo the buttons on the stiff shirt. Rumple the neatly-pressed cloth of his evening jacket.

He'd look good stripped. Slow warmth stirred in her groin at the thought. Damn, I've a good mind to take on the other two at this. I wonder if he has a friend?

'Here.' He refilled her glass. His hands were almost square. His fingers were thick, the nails blunt and strong. With no alteration of tone, he added, 'You have the most beautiful breasts of any woman at this table.'

Nadia looked down before she could stop herself. The green beaded dress clung tightly to her torso. The strapless bra pushed up her cleavage. Two full curves of ivory flesh pushed up from her bodice. She flushed. 'You say that from very little knowledge.'

'I can't think of anything better to investigate. In point of fact,' he said, 'I'm a customs officer. On the river.'

'And you know all about undercover work? I'm sorry: that was obvious.' Nadia put her elbow on the table, and leaned her chin on her hand. She smiled up at him. 'I'm not usually this bad-tempered. I'm hot and bored.'

Well. Not bored. Not now.

Shannon and Corey are off looking for their chances. What about me? What if I were in bed with – *two* men like this one?

Do I dare?

The airless heat brought colour to her cheeks. She shifted in her seat. She let her stockinged leg brush against his solid thigh, through the cloth of his trousers. She wiped slick fingers on her napkin, her hands shaking, almost surprised at the suddenness of her response. *Imagine his bare body, next to mine; and a second man's hands on me . . .*

His gaze swept over the dinner guests. Under the noise of their chatter, he said, 'Formal dinners *are* boring.'

'Such a shame it isn't a Classical occasion.' She waited for an expression of puzzlement. His well-worn features flickered from surprise to quick comprehension.

'Classically Roman,' he completed. 'A Bacchanal. I don't think these people are the type.'

'Not for an orgy,' she agreed whimsically.

That body. A sense of humour. *And* education? Public school, I think. I definitely won't ask for his name. Too good to be true.

She noticed Carol at another table. 'Although one might be surprised. I remember, when I was at boarding school, we all read about the Roman Empress Messalina's competition. There wasn't one girl who didn't fantasise about trying that out.'

'A competition?'

'With a whore,' Nadia said bluntly. 'The best whore in Rome. Messalina invited her to compete for how many men they could get through in one night. Just lined them up and brought them in . . . servants, soldiers from the army, sailors off the streets.'

She looked up at him from under red lashes. She

541

anticipated smelling the spices on his square hands, having his strong fingers on her breasts.

'Perhaps it's the sheer number of her men that impresses me. I have very modest tastes, in reality. The height of my ambition is, oh . . .' She smiled. Her mouth was dry. She sipped red wine. *Here we go: let's just ride at the fence and take it!* Nadia continued, 'Oh . . . to take two men to bed at once, shall we say?'

He did not smile. Oh God, Nadia thought, I've shocked him. Then she noted the stillness of his expression.

The corner of his mouth lifted.

'I admire women. You're all so sensual.' The man spoke with conviction, a calm air of authority. 'All it needs is bringing out.'

'By a man, I suppose?' Nettled, Nadia spoke aloud without meaning to.

'A woman alone has desires that she won't act on.'

'Oh, but I do! The other day – no, never mind.'

In the silence, he looked away from her. A man on the far side of the table, short and young and blond, broke off from dinner conversation to acknowledge him with a nod.

'I would like to kiss the hollows behind yours ears. Your throat. Your breasts.' His voice did not move above or below a conversational tone.

Nadia slid her hand down beside her. When she put her palm on his thigh, she felt a broad leg and strong muscles. The ache in her sex began to grow. She slid her fingers towards his crotch.

He reached down and removed her hand.

'*What?*' She sighed sharply and sat back in her chair. 'Oh God. You're gay. Or you're going to say *Not here, darling* and take me back to some tacky flat.'

His long lashes lowered over his eyes. How can such a masculine-looking man have eyelashes like that? she wondered wildly. They would brush against one's skin so tantalisingly lightly . . .

'Excuse me.' His chair scraped back.

She stared after him as he marched off towards the cloakrooms. He stopped for a moment to speak to the fair-haired man who had acknowledged him. Then he walked on without looking back.

She turned to her main course, and prodded it dispiritedly with a fork.

I hate being turned down. Especially, I hate being turned down rudely. Arrogant son of a bitch!

Some minutes later his chair was moved again. She did not look up.

'Listen to me.' The man's voice was quiet. Something in it caught her attention. She moved her head very slightly to see him standing over her.

'Look down there.' His stubby finger pointed towards the bottom end of the table. Long blue velvet drapes hid the wall. The far end of the table was not occupied. 'Doors to the cloakrooms are at the far end. Go and powder your nose. When you come back, you'll find there's room to walk between the drapes and the wall. Duck down under the end of the table, where it's against the wall. Everyone will think you were bored and left.'

'Under the *table?*' Nadia's red brows lifted.

He stood beside her for a moment before sitting down. Her head was level with his waist. The sharp, elegant line of his dress trousers was broken by an unmistakable bulge at the crotch. This evidence of his calm control broken, by her, made Nadia's mouth dry. She looked up at his face, noting fine sweat just visible above his dark brows.

'You see the effect you have?' He spoke a little helplessly. Before any of the seated diners noticed, he carefully sat down. 'I'm going to drop my napkin. I'll

543

join you under the table. Then – my friend over there will join both of us. There's an hour of speeches to come. We can do anything we like. Except make a sound.'

'I don't think I . . .'

'Go to the cloakroom.'

Nadia stood. The silk lining of her evening dress shifted over her skin. Arousal made the slight sensation a torment. She turned without looking at her companion and walked steadily down between the tables. The knowledge that he might be watching her go, knowing what he had just instructed her to do, made her wet between the legs.

In the Ladies' powder room, the yammering noise of the hall was lost. She stood alone in the heat. If only the hall were air-conditioned. If only I had drunk enough wine that I didn't have to think about this . . .

Abruptly she took the two steps back into the hall. One step sideways from the door and she was behind the drapes. It was a large gap, almost a metre wide, hot and shadowed. She trod carefully along it, not touching the curtains, not making a noise with her heels.

When she got to the end of their table, she ducked down and moved under the tablecloth. The stone floor was cool under her hands. The first trousered and stockinged legs started a few yards away.

Nadia reached back and pulled her high-heeled shoes off. Clutching them in one hand, she moved on hands and knees towards the top of the table. Voices sounded above her head in the sun-drenched dimness. I can always say I lost something, she thought. Possibly my sense of decorum. She stifled a giggle.

Avoiding the tips of shoes, she crawled to where a tiny sequinned evening bag told her her own chair stood.

A white linen napkin dropped near her face. Above her, a voice muttered an apology. What seemed like a huge male body in a dinner jacket suddenly rolled in beside her. She clutched his back, stifling a squeak.

There was just room to kneel, if she bent double. The stone was pleasantly cold under her knees. The man crouched, waiting with his head cocked. The even flow of conversation above them was not interrupted.

'Where—'

His hand was solid over her mouth. She could hardly see him in the dimness. His eyes caught the light. His pupils were wide, and dark, and urgent.

He took his hand from her mouth, and rested it on her shoulder. Nadia obeyed its pressure. She eased away from the table-strut and lay down on her back. Her shoes dropped from her hand. The smell of food and coffee and sweat was overlaid by sandalwood.

His other hand took her other shoulder. Tenderly, he cupped her flesh. He knelt beside her, pressing her down. Nadia's flesh leaped. The stone floor cooled her bare back and shoulders. She crammed her hand into her mouth to stop herself from crying out.

His face was above her for a moment. Then his head dipped. She felt the warmth of his hair pressed against the side of her face. His mouth found her ear, the hollow behind it, and his hot tongue darted into the sensitive flesh.

She shifted sideways, pressing her body up against him. Dust made grey creases on his black trousers. His body was broad, as square as his hands, his hips thick and muscled. The fly of his trousers jutted out. She dropped her fingers to his erection, feeling the heat and hardness fill her hand.

'*Mmm*—' Again, she pushed her fist into her mouth. The toe of an evening shoe grazed her shoulder. She writhed away. Frozen, she waited.

545

Above, conversation continued.

The ache in her pussy was a burning frustration. The need for silence frustrated her doubly. I want to tell him to have me! I want to tell him to pull my panties down and fill me!

His big body crushed against her. She rolled over on to her back. The sheer weight of his torso and hips, his thighs and shoulders, made her thrust her body up against him.

He freed his hands and lifted them to the bodice of her dress. Slowly and with exquisite care he slid the sequinned, beaded material down to her waist. He brushed his palms across her nipples, which were swelling in the strapless bra, and then eased that down. Her breasts, free, felt every whisper of warm air. Her nipples hardened instantly. He lowered his head and began to lick, chasing in spirals with his tongue over first one breast then the other, drawing close to her nipples, and then teasingly moving away.

The dress rucked up under her. It was too tight for Nadia to lift her legs and wrap them around his hips. She slid her hands around his waist, feeling the strong flat muscles of his back through his shirt. Carefully she unbuttoned his shirt. His chest was thickly hairy. She ran her fingers through it, pursued it down to the curled wisps of hair that grew thickly up the centre of his belly. She pulled his shirt out of his trousers. The thick cylindrical bulge in his pants hardened, pushing out the cloth.

With one hand to the side of his head, she drew his ear down to her mouth. She whispered, 'What about the other man – your friend?'

He rolled over on to his back and pulled her on top of him. His hot breath tingled across her cheek. 'You just let me handle this.'

Nadia lay along the warm length of his body, the

underside of the table eighteen inches above her head. She saw his pulse beating at the base of his throat. A rattle of plates brought her heart into her mouth. All conversation died.

Somewhere, towards the head of the hall, someone was striking a glass with a fork.

'My Lord, Ladies, and Gentlemen, pray silence . . .'

Oh my God, the speeches. Nadia let her weight fall on the large man beneath her. Her breasts pressed against his hairy chest, now hot and slick with sweat. He brought his head up and kissed her on the mouth, nibbling delicately at her lower lip, darting at the gap between her lips with the very tip of his tongue, until her hands came around the back of his head, and pressed him to her, and his hot writhing tongue thrust deep into her mouth.

He drew back.

Her breath heaved in her chest. Excruciatingly, she forced herself to silence. Forced herself not to ask *What the hell are you doing?*

Above them, not many tables away, a single voice began speaking.

Oh God, it's Oscar. I forgot he was making one of the speeches. Oh, poor lamb!

Laughter almost stifled her. Under the table, the man's eyes gleamed as he half sat up under her. He dropped his hands to her waist, grasped her evening dress, and eased the bottom hem up. Nadia felt her knicker-clad buttocks and hips exposed to the dusty air. The dress rucked up in a roll around her waist.

His hands slid down, fingers first, under her garter belt, under the edge of her knickers. She could not remain still. She thrust her hips down, grinding them into his crotch. His fingers pushed down into her groin, plunged into the wet hair at her crotch, and touched the entrance to her vagina. She plunged her

547

hips down, trying to drive his fingers inside her; thick, short fingers that felt almost like a cock. She smelled his male sweat: acid, rank, enticing.

Her own sweat ran from her face, her neck; ran down over her breasts, leaving wet dusty trails. She sat back as far as the wooden surface above her allowed. His hand guided her hand to his crotch. She felt his body shudder with suppressed gasps. *That's better.* Millimetre by careful millimetre, she eased down the zip of his fly. The cloth was taut over his straining erection. She thought she heard him groan in his throat.

A thunderous burst of applause ripped the air over her head.

Nadia jumped.

Oh – the end of Oscar's speech. Yes. Of course! Swiftly, she ripped the stranger's fly open, under cover of the noise. His erect penis sprang free. In one movement he grabbed either side of her hips and lifted her, then pulled aside the crotch of her panties, and pulled her down on to his thick, hot cock. His hands grabbed her thighs. He snagged her stockings with his caresses. The suspenders left red imprints on her white skin under the pressure. His hips thrust up, driving him deep inside her. She thrust down. She felt her body filled, pushed apart, by his amazing thickness. Mad with wanting, she plunged her body down.

His arms went around her waist. She was seized and rolled over on to her back in one dizzy second. A man's shoes flew past in her vision: she avoided them only by luck. Above them the hall was utterly silent.

His cock pushed up into her body.

I'm going to make a noise, I know I am. Oh, don't *stop!*

With a strong, unstoppable power he drew his hips

back, and thrust them forward, giving her rising pleasure. His thick cock-head slid out to the lips of her vagina, then plunged in again. Again and again: teasingly, sliding almost out of her, then the thick maleness of him thumping into her hot, aching cleft. The thick hair at his groin smeared her, wet with his sweat and her juices. His balls thudded on her anus.

Her hands reached down and seized his buttocks. Ample handfuls of flesh. As he came forward she pulled him up, up, up into her; driving in; her shoulders bouncing off the stone floor, her body pounded, inch by inch sliding up between the tables.

His cock slid out of her. Cold air hit her hot flesh with an electrifying shock. She let go of him and sat up on her elbows. She caught a look of triumph.

Bereft, aching with unfilled desire, Nadia glanced up and down the underside of the table. Legs. Shoes. Nothing else: no one pretending to drop their napkin. If that was the blond man's seat *there*, he certainly hadn't moved, hadn't made a move to join them—

I've been had. In more ways than one! Rage flashed in Nadia's eyes. She opened her mouth. Above, someone chinked a glass. An elderly, frail voice was making a speech on the far side of the hall. She tried to hush her panting breath. But I still want him, damn it!

His cool hands pushed her thighs apart. No hesitation, no nervousness. His rough hair tickled her sensitive skin and she shivered, simultaneously hot and cold. She ached to grab his cock and shove it up inside her.

His skilled tongue caressed her outer labia. She jerked, as if an electric current convulsed her. His tongue darted into her. He licked, nibbled, and began to swirl his tongue inside her. She flooded with wetness and arousal, one hand fisted and plunged into her mouth. His tongue drew close to her clit. It paused.

549

Then his sucking lips closed around her clitoris.

Only his hand clamped on top of hers held back her scream of pleasure. Her hips bucked. Orgasm peaked and surged through her body, flushing her skin, loosening her muscles, lifting her from the cold stone.

Nadia fell back. His arms steered her carefully to the flagstones. She looked up into his dark eyes, bright in his sweating face. She glared at him. The man lay back on his side, shirt and jacket undone, fly unzipped. His thick, blue-veined cock jutted into the air. She could not resist reaching out and stroking its silken velvet hardness.

He unceremoniously drew down her knickers, pulling her to him. The heat of his hard body warmed her from shoulders to toes. The engorged head of his cock pushed hotly against her bare belly. His hands on her buttocks crushed her to him.

Nadia felt her legs part. The table and cloth and legs forgotten, she wrapped her legs around his hips. He was hard enough that his cock needed no guidance. It slid into her wet and welcoming pussy, pushing the clenching walls apart, teasing her with its solidity.

He rolled over and began to drive into her with solid, rhythmic strokes. She drew her legs up and up. She sensed he would not stop now until he had pleasured her fully again. His thrusts penetrated deep into her core. His large, hard body bruised her breasts and ribs. Her back rubbed against the abrasive dirt on the flagstones. Her mouth wide open, she let her gasps out in almost complete silence. On and on, like a machine, thicker and harder; and she wound her fingers in his hair and clamped her eyes shut, her skin flushing hot, her sex sucking wet with the juices of this second arousal, and he arched up and pounded his come into her waiting body, and the fire between her legs flared into a searing explosion of pleasure so intense it was almost pain.

Nadia sprawled on her back on the floor.

Outside the table, a more prolonged burst of applause sounded.

'What happened to your "friend"?' Nadia demanded in a whisper. 'You didn't talk to that man about this. You lied! You didn't even *mention* this to anyone else! I suggested two men!'

'There aren't two men like me,' he said simply. Sprawled back on buttocks and elbows in the dim light, he looked both rumpled and annoyingly calm.

'You enjoyed it, didn't you?' He smiled in the dimness. 'Sweet woman. It's pretty obvious you just need one man who can bring you out of yourself.'

'I need *what?*'

The applause died away to silence.

Her hands clenched into fists.

Infuriated by his calm control, Nadia glared. She wanted to shout and she wanted to kick him and neither was possible. Do I *really* mind if I'm found here? Wouldn't it be worth it? Just to slap his arrogant face?

'We must do this again sometime.' He leaned over and made as if to hold up the edge of the snowy linen tablecloth.

Nadia grabbed his hand.

He put his mouth against her ear. 'And you told me you were a dare-devil.'

Nadia turned her back on him. It was not easy, she had to push under and past his sweat-soaked body.

Half-naked, her shoes in her hands, she crawled with what she hoped was dignity back towards the blue velvet drapes and the exit to the Ladies' powder room.

'What an arsehole!' Corey flared up.

Shannon was laughing. 'That's sweet! Well, no. You know what I mean. Not sweet, exactly. More . . .'

551

'Irritating,' Nadia completed. She looked demurely under her lashes at her younger friends. 'He did do it so well. It's just that I want to hit him.'

Corey pulled a tendril of black hair forward. It was just long enough for her to suck one end. 'I'd kick him in the bollocks!'

'If he hadn't been so arrogant, I would have enjoyed it immensely.' Nadia stopped, and corrected herself. 'I did enjoy *it*. I would have enjoyed *him*, without wanting to kick him in the – er – bollocks. Regrettably, I didn't acquire his name or telephone number. I thought too much of a good thing was enough. Now,' she said, 'what do we do? Do we accept Michael's verdict? That Corey is the winner?'

There was a moment's silence.

'Oh, what does he know?' Corey leaned her elbows on the supper table. 'We know each other best, after all, don't we? Better than he does. It isn't about 'telling good stories'. It's about *fucking!*'

Shannon smiled affectionately at the girl. The top two buttons of Shannon's silk blouse were open again; the lower one was actually missing. She tugged them together absentmindedly. 'If we're ever going to get a proper winner, let's go back to different dares. Half the fun is tailoring them to each person.'

'I'm not convinced Shannon should have lost, either,' Corey added, with a careless generosity that made Nadia smile. 'Technically I didn't have sex with two guys either, I was there while sex was being had. I wasn't the one in the middle. And I think yours was dead good, Nadia, even if it wasn't a proper dare. I don't think you *can* dare yourself.'

'It's got me through life so far,' Nadia said mildly. 'Shannon?'

The woman pushed her fingers through her curly brown hair. Beyond her, through the window, heat-lightning flickered on the horizon. Ten o'clock and the sunset sky scarcely dark yet. 'The trouble is, it's so difficult to judge, because it's so difficult to know.'

'Yeah. *We* might think Edward and James weren't hunks at all,' Corey confirmed.

She began suddenly to smile.

Nadia sat up, keeping her gaze on Corey, feeling the young woman's contagious excitement. 'But it's been so difficult to get real proof. What do you suggest?'

'I know exactly what we should get. *Photographic proof!*'

Nadia stared.

Corey's young face was alight. 'I've just realised. *I* could develop the films. There wouldn't be any trouble about that, I can do it at home. That's a challenge – not only do you have to take your dare, you have to bring back photographic proof. That'll sort out the winners from the losers!'

Shannon Garrett let out a breath. 'That would be a challenge. How on earth could . . .'

'And I tell you what. As soon as we get a proper winner – they get to choose how we spend William Jenson's five thousand pounds.'

Chapter Seven

NADIA LOOKED CAREFULLY at Corey's flushed face. There was something both frantic and oddly absent-minded about her excitement.

Just as Nadia was forming the thought, Shannon asked, 'Corey, is everything OK? There isn't something bothering you?'

'Not about this,' the girl assured them carelessly. 'Hey, one of you will have to set me a dare, too, so that I get a chance to compete. Well? Shall we do it?'

'I suppose we must.' Nadia laughed helplessly. 'How can we refuse? It does answer the question about the five thousand pounds. But taking *photographs!*'

'You can do it! Make mine a really good dare. Don't go away!' The black-haired girl sprang to her feet and seized her car keys from among a heap of commemorative medallions on a side table. 'Make coffee or something. I'll be back in ten minutes!'

Nadia shook her head. 'Hopeless girl! Where are you going?'

'To get my spare camera!' Corey popped her head back around the flat's front door. 'One of you will need to borrow it. I've already thought of the next dares I'm going to set.'

*

The two women were left alone in a companionable silence.

Nadia moved to the big leather armchair by the stuffed alligator and curled up comfortably. A cooler breeze feathered her skin. A handful of fat rain drops plummeted out of the darkening sky, splashing back from the white-painted window-sill. She let the smell of rain and dust permeate. The only light inside the high room came from the last two dinner candles.

She heard Shannon get up. The other woman went off into the kitchen. Nadia heard her making coffee, finding where everything was with the ease of long familiarity. She had lived here as long as Shannon had known her.

The rattle of the rain increased. Spray bounced in, soaking a row of commemoration pewter pots. Nadia got up out of the armchair and went to lower the window. She left a six inch gap at the bottom, for air.

'I put the percolator on, there's enough for three.' Shannon's hand put a coffee mug into the narrow space on the junk-filled side table that could accommodate it. The younger woman went to stand in front of the window, cradling her mug between her palms. Nadia bent her head and inhaled the coffee smell.

'She's riding that bike in the rain again,' Shannon said.

Nadia smoothed a curl of red hair back behind her ear. 'Do you know, that's just what I was thinking.'

'Do you ever hear from her mother these days?'

'Oh, Maria writes twice a year. The last I heard, she and John were becoming very prosperous in Brazil. She's much happier back at home there than she ever was in London. She always tells me to keep an eye on her "little Corazon".'

'That's Spanish, isn't it?'

'I imagine so. Maria was a Ramirez before she married John Black, or so Oscar used to tell me.' Nadia chuckled. 'Maria makes me feel so old, sometimes! I feel much more as though I were Corey's age.'

The other woman muttered, 'Corey makes me feel as if I were an inexperienced fifteen-year-old. She always did, even when she was twelve!'

Rain drummed ferociously on the dark glass. Nadia sipped her coffee. She smiled up at the woman by the window.

'I think, if we're inventive, we can come up with a dare even Corey will regard as a challenge.'

Corey gave them two carelessly scrawled notes. They gave her a slip of paper, written by Shannon, and signed by them both.

'I have to open the shop *some* days,' was Nadia's firm farewell. 'I do have a living to earn. Let's meet Sunday week.'

Shannon drove home and parked the Rover in the garage block. She walked back around to her house through warm night rain. The moisture clung to her hair, dampened her face.

She stood for a second outside her terraced house.

Corey's folded note was in her jacket pocket. She had deliberately not read it. She paused under the orange glow of the street lights.

Shall I . . . ?

She briskly got out her keys and let herself in.

Her bedroom was warm, even with the windows open. Shannon lay down naked on top of the sheet. Her eyes went to the shadowed shape that was her jacket, hung over the back of her chair. To put the light on, to read whatever was written there: it would be so easy.

Shannon's hand strayed over her thigh and between her legs.

It could be anything. Her fingers moved fast, then slow, then fast again. The dim light from the street lamp glimmered on her breasts and thighs. *Absolutely anything ...*

Do I dare?

Her breathing quickened. A little later, her lips curved in a smile of anticipation, she fell asleep in the hot summer night.

Nadia Kay remained sitting in the big armchair in her living-room. The candles melted down to stubs. Rain spattered the windows. Soft yellow light shone on the walls, crowded with posters and prints, and the boxes of old magazines.

Corey knows me very well. Too well!

She looked down at the scrawled note. Corey's handwriting was extremely flamboyant. Nadia thought, yes, she might well end that one with an exclamation mark! *It deserves it.*

Do I *quite* dare ... ?

Corey pulled the bike up halfway around the North Circular. She stopped on a garage forecourt, under the lights, and took off her gloves and helmet to read Shannon's neat handwriting again.

We dare you to have sex with someone in a supermarket.

Corey's black eyebrows went up. In a *supermarket?*

That's all very well for them to say! Pick up some guy in a supermarket, no problem. I've watched Friday night cruising by the pasta shells. But doing sex in a supermarket – and taking a photograph – the question is, *how?*

557

Three days later she had a grand total of two refusals, four looks of complete incomprehension, and a regretful smile from a gay till assistant.

I need a new approach, she decided.

Corey pushed the shopping trolley ahead of her down the supermarket aisle. There were fewer shoppers around now, on a week-day, with only quarter of an hour to go before closing. The overhead lights had been dimmed in the fresh bread and patisserie counter area. Everywhere else was still bright.

She checked the position of the security guards.

A tall, lean man stood by the revolving door exit. He wore a smart grey uniform. Dark hair. Glasses. Corey thought) Yeah, that one's good.

The second security guard was burly and fair-haired, and probably a year younger than Corey. He caught her eye. An intelligent, sharp face. She ignored him and continued on down the aisle.

It's no good trying to just look suspicious. I have to be suspicious.

She re-ran her fantasy in her head: *I know I've been shoplifting, sir, but if you let me go, I'll be really nice to you* ... A pulse of warmth flickered between her legs. Corey looked at the crowded shelves. She would need to take some small item, to make it convincing. Something not very expensive.

Oh, damn! I don't have pockets.

She came to a dead halt as she turned to go up the neighbouring aisle, and looked down at herself. The June evening was hot. She was wearing black jeans and a scoop-necked T-shirt, and sandals. The trolley so far contained a can of beans and her minuscule shoulder-bag. She had forgotten to bring even a light jacket.

The chatter of shoppers diminished, and she heard

the clatter of the till drawers cease. The last announcement of the store closing sounded over the tannoy. Almost too late to do anything now.

In desperation she wheeled the trolley towards the bakery section where the lights were lowered. The department closed earlier than the others, being out of fresh bread.

Once there, she leaned her arms forward on the rail of her trolley and stared around desperately.

This isn't going to work.

Wait a minute . . .

She remembered once reading an article, probably in *Femme*, about shoplifters who wore baggy knickers, specially designed to hide small articles under their clothing. That'll have to do, Corey thought. I'll improvise. She glanced around. The tannoy binged again. *'This store is now closed. Will nll customers please make their way to the nearest till.'* In a panic, she looked at the shelf nearest to her. She was standing by the cool cupboards. The nearest display was one of hard-shelled meringues. The labels alternately said 'jam-filled' or 'cream-filled'.

Well, they're small, she thought. Quickly she reached out and took a cool, smooth ovoid between her fingers. With her other hand, she pulled the waistband of her jeans open. She realised as she slid the meringue past her belt that she had caught the waistband of her lace knickers, too. The hard-shelled meringue slid down inside her knickers and came to rest just below the curve of her stomach. It was cold against her bare flesh. She looked down. The cloth was loose enough that nothing was visible.

Frantic, Corey looked up and down the aisle. No one. No security guard.

She heard the revolving doors at the front of the store stop moving. Staff called to each other. The doors were locked, grills rattling down. One security guard called a good-night – the older or the younger? No way to tell. Corey nodded in satisfaction. Now to hide until everyone except the last security guard had left.

The cool meringue shell shifted in her jeans as she began to push her trolley. It wasn't enough, she decided. It didn't show. He might just think she was a lost customer, and show her out of the door.

Quickly Corey reached out and picked up two more meringues, and slid them under her waistband, down her knickers. They lodged next to the first. Just visible as a bulge.

Walking carefully, she pushed her trolley quietly a few feet further into the bakery department, where the lights were lowest. She paused by the refrigerated compartments. The filled meringues were cold and surprisingly heavy, pulling the fabric of her jeans and pants down. Perhaps they still weren't enough. Something else, small?

She reached out and picked up one of the cakes. A cream-filled éclair. Not practical, she thought. No—

'Can I help you, miss?' A deep male voice boomed in her ear.

In a complete panic, Corey forgot that she was planning to be discovered. She had her back to the man. Instantly she pulled the neck of her T-shirt forward, popped the cream eclair down her ample cleavage, and let the cloth spring back to conceal it.

'I, er—' she looked over her shoulder, her hands now innocently gripping the handle of the supermarket trolley. With relief, she remembered that she needed to look guilty for her plan to work.

It was the fair-haired guard. Maybe a year or two younger than her. Taller. He folded his arms and looked down at her. He had a sharp face, and long-lashed pale eyes. The top button of his uniform collar was undone, and a curl of gold hair poked out between his shirt buttons. He said softly, 'What have we here, then . . .'

Corey shrugged, and gave a sickly grin. 'I can explain.'

'I've been watching you. Shoplifting is a crime, miss,' he said. There was a glint in his eyes. Corey wondered if she ought to confess all of it, the dare included. I don't want to actually get arrested! she realised.

The young security man padded past her on silent feet. She had no idea how so big a man moved so quietly. The glint was still in his eyes. A grin joined it. He faced her, putting both hands on the far end of her trolley, and leaned forward, so that they were almost face to face.

Corey was dry-mouthed. Without meaning to, she denied it. 'I'm not a shoplifter!'

'Not even a little bit?' His voice sounded cynical now, teasing. Corey thought, this is just the kind of boy who would take up my bargain – but I'm not so sure I want him to.

'Not at all,' she said firmly, brazening it out. 'I just stayed in the shop too long.'

He laughed. His hands clenched on the wire trolley. 'That right, miss? Then if I searched you, I wouldn't find any evidence, would I?'

The cool, heavy meringues rubbed against the soft skin of her belly as she straightened up defiantly. The eclair inside her shirt slipped down a fraction. She was sweating: it was slick against her skin. Her brain raced. If only she had been innocent, she would have demanded to be taken to the store manager's office. As it was . . .

'You won't find anything!' she snapped, lying weakly.

His pale eyes shone as he smiled at her. 'I think I will.'

The shopping trolley shifted under her hands. He moved before she realised it. She had no chance of stopping him. He grasped his end of the shopping trolley and jerked it sharply away from him, towards Corey. Her hands clenched on the rail too late. The hard metal mesh of the trolley smacked into her belly.

There was a soft but audible crunch.

She felt the shells of the meringues in her pants smash. Cold, sticky cream shot across her stomach. Jam-filling drenched her crotch, and slid down her thighs. The trolley moved back an inch. Broken meringue shell crunched in her knickers, plastered across her belly.

'Oh!' Corey gasped. She stood stiff-legged, her face flaming. She looked down.

A dark patch spread on the outside of the crotch of her black jeans. As she watched, a trickle of jam and cream ran out of her jeans leg, down her ankle, and pooled on the floor.

The big young man smiled wolfishly. 'That's evidence of shoplifting, miss – now you can't put them back on the shelves and say it never happened.'

'Oh!' Almost speechless, Corey gritted her teeth and tugged the front of her jeans away from her body. Her fingers slipped on the slimy cloth. The material smacked wetly back against her skin. 'How *dare* you!'

He drew himself up, shoulders straightening. With strong and deliberate movements he put the trolley aside and stepped closer. 'And I don't think that's all, is it? You might as well confess and get it over with.'

She didn't know what to say or do. She blurted, 'I didn't take anything else!'

He was so close to her now that she had to crane her neck to look up at him. His grey uniform jacket concealed a strong, fast body.

In one swift movement he put the palm of his hand flat on her T-shirt, above her cleavage, made a fist of his other hand, and brought it down on top of the first hand with a smart smack.

'No!' she cried out, too late.

The cream-filled éclair smashed inside her shirt. It was cold, being from the cooler cupboard display. Icy-cold cream squirted across her breasts, down the cleft between them, and pushed its way into her bra. His hands kneaded her breasts through the cloth, spreading the sticky cream.

'See,' he said smugly.

He's going to have me arrested, Corey thought in abject humiliation. He's going to take me to the manager's office and the police station *like this*. I'll die!

With that thought came a twinge of arousal. She studied the look in his eye. His face was shadowed now the shop lights were down. Impossible really to read his expression. But, for a security guard, he was taking a long time to sound the alarm . . .

Maybe William Jenson knew what he was saying, Corey reflected. Maybe he did teach me something about what I like done to me. Inside her bra, her cream-smeared nipples were standing up hard as two little pebbles. She began to look at the strong young man with confidence.

'Takes a thief to catch a thief,' she said.

'What?'

'How many other poor little bimbos have you tried this on with?'

The mask of cynicism slipped for a moment. Hurriedly, the young man muttered, 'No, you're wrong, I've always wanted to, but I never—'

Corey's grin became triumphant.

'Well,' she said softly, 'that doesn't surprise me. Because you forgot the one thing you're going to find impossible to explain away.'

He took her arm, preparing to lead her away, turning as he did so. 'What's that?'

She was already moving while he was speaking, and it caught him off-guard. With one hand she reached out to the cold cabinet and grabbed an aerosol can of cream, thumbing off the plastic top. Her other hand seized his leather belt and pulled the back of his uniform trousers, with their knife-edge creases, open. She plunged the nozzle of the can down the seat of his trousers and jammed her thumb on the button.

'You little cow!' His voice shot up an octave.

Both his hands behind him, he grabbed at her wrists, tugging, wrestling, trying desperately to pull her hands away. Corey laughed excitedly. Her fingers were locked into the back of his leather belt. Her hands were slippery now, as the cream pumped into his boxer shorts. She kept her grip.

At last the can fizzled and ran empty.

Corey pried her hands away.

She looked up at the blond security man. His jaw had dropped. He gazed at her, open-mouthed.

'You can't do that!' The waistband of his trousers was smeared with white cream. Nothing else was visible but a huge wet bulge in the seat of his pants. Corey gently reached out, cupped her hands under it, and squashed upwards. He shut his eyes in anguish.

'Explain *that* to your manager,' she exclaimed with satisfaction.

She wiped her sticky hand across his fly. Under her palm, she felt his cock twitch through the slimy material.

She replaced her hand on the stiff bulge of cream in his trousers, pushed it down between his straddled legs, and then put her hands on the outside of his muscular thighs. Firmly, she shut his legs together.

There was an audible squelch.

Still resting her palm against his cock, she reached into the cool cabinet and drew out a heavy cream flan.

'You wouldn't dare,' he husked. When she looked up, the light was back in his eyes. Anticipation. Defiance.

'I'm your nightmare come true, sonny.' She pushed the cream pie right into his face. Under her hand, his cock swelled and lengthened. He lifted his hands to scoop the soft, sticky mess away.

'Come with me – miss.' His index finger hooked over the front of her jeans and tugged sharply. The wet material slid snugly up into the cleft of her buttocks. Denim, sticky with cream, was yanked up between her swelling labia. With no choice, she submitted to the pressure and walked forward. Her knickers clung to her skin inside her jeans, cloth sliding slimily across her stomach. A warmth grew in her pussy, somewhere between power and humiliation.

He drew her down the aisle between the freezers and the bakery department. Corey looked at the meringue cases, the sticky buns, the cream cakes. 'You wouldn't dare. I'll tell.'

'If I can't tell, you certainly can't.' Both his hands dropped to her waist. He spun her around so she faced away from the counter.

She felt his fingers swiftly yank her fly buttons undone. He pulled her jeans down to her knees. Corey opened her mouth to protest. She felt his strong young hands seize her either side of her waist and lift.

Her feet left the floor. She yelped. She had a brief glimpse of his grin as he whirled her around, paused for a second, and then sat her squarely down on the counter – in the middle of a huge chocolate gateau. There was a squelch. Chocolate icing and cream filling shot up between her thighs. Sticky cream filled her vagina. His hands did not loosen their grip, but pushed her down into the chilly mess.

Corey squirmed helplessly. Still holding her, he bent his head and began to nuzzle between her thighs. His tongue found her clit. She squirmed deeper into the cold, smooth, sensual mess. She found herself wriggling to smear. the gateau further over her buttocks and thighs. The lacy material of her frilled knickers grew sopping wet.

At last he stepped back, letting her go. His smeared face was dazzled.

She eased herself gingerly, stickily, down from the counter. Her jeans entangled her knees. She tugged them up as far as they would go, the wet denim clinging to her skin. The tactile sensation of slipperiness aroused her. Her sex was so swollen with lust that she could hardly walk. Faltering, she moved to stand in front of him.

He reached a big hand out, caressing her cream-smeared breast through the wet cloth of her T-shirt. His eyes met hers in wonder. 'My God. I *never* thought I'd get to do this. I want you. Now!'

'There's something you're going to get first.' Corey smiled. 'Or should I say, do first.' She pointed at the cold compartment. 'Fill your pants.'

Even in the shadowed supermarket gloom, she saw his face change. 'No,' he whispered.

Corey stroked the back of her hand up the front of his trousers. He was strainingly erect. She tapped the radio hanging on his belt. 'You wouldn't want me to call the rest of the staff, would you? Maybe I don't care. Maybe I think it'd be worth it, to see your face. Now do what I tell you. I'll say when it's enough.'

He reached out to the boxes with his hands trembling, took a meringue, and put it down the front of his damp uniform trousers. He looked anxiously at

Corey. Smiling, she shook her head.

The blond man hefted three meringues in his big hand, and carefully tucked them down his trousers. Then he shrugged, took down a carton, and emptied that down his pants. Corey saw the heavy, cream-filled ovoids bagging out the crotch of his uniform. She said, 'And again, I think . . .'

He gave her one beseeching look. She was adamant. One by one, he pushed five fragile shells down his trousers, until he paused with the last meringue in his hand.

'Might as well be hung for a sheep as a lamb,' he grinned. Corey felt him tug the front of her T-shirt forward and tuck the meringue down between her breasts. Her skin was hot, flushed: her nipples hard in anticipation. He put his palm on her shirt and slowly and deliberately pushed. There was a minute of aching expectation. The meringue suddenly popped. Her eyes shot open wide. A rush of cold cream squished down her breasts and belly. Cream slid smoothly down over her flushed, aroused skin.

She put his hands on her breasts and pressed them hard against her. While he stood like that, she dropped her hands, flattened her palms, and smacked them both firmly across his belly. She felt the meringues crush under her hands. His eyes shut. He shuddered. His hard cock pushed at her hands through the cream-wet cloth.

'That feels fantastic. I wouldn't have dared . . .' He opened his eyes. His face was flushed. He gazed down at her, worriedly. 'We shouldn't be doing this, should we?'

She slid her hands down his trousers to his crotch, then brought one hand up sharply between his legs. His hard-on was by now rock-solid.

'Games are fun,' she said. And she smiled wickedly.

'Aren't they?'

Shame-faced, he grinned. Corey hooked her ankle behind the young man's leg and yanked. She felt him give way to the movement, falling back on the floor. She measured her length along his body, belly to belly. The smashed meringues inside his pants, between them, smeared her crotch too. She wrenched at the zip of his trousers. She stopped, astride. She stood and pulled her T-shirt off, and bent to pull down her jeans, but by the time he had stripped off his uniform jacket and shirt together, and caught hold of the cuffs of her jeans, pushed her down, and pulled them off in one swift movement. They lay slick flesh to slick flesh, in the running juices of food. She instantly mounted his stiff cock, plunging it deep into her ready sex, crying out with anguish and pleasure together, and came twice before his rapid, frantic strokes climaxed in a first flood of seed.

Some minutes later he prowled off barefoot and stark naked to the wine department. When he came back, he knelt beside her. Corey's flesh jerked as cold liquid fizzed over her breasts and stomach, and ran down between her legs.

'It's champagne,' he whispered. 'I'm washing you in champagne.'

His tongue rasped from the sticky hair around her sex, up over the curve of her belly, dipped into her navel, licked up across her breasts, and finished with a deep, champagne-tasting kiss.

Corey sat up with her back to the freezer compartment. As he knelt up before she, she scooped at random and brought out two handfuls of chocolate cream. She held his eye for a second. Then she pressed both hands over his hard, hot cock.

'Oh, shit!' he groaned.

'Don't worry.' The smell of chocolate and champagne

invaded her senses. Corey ran her fingers through his matted hair and took hold of his cock. She lay down beside him. 'I'll clean you up,' she said, and began to lick, delicately and raspingly.

'That's good . . .' his voice purred deceptively. She felt his body move. Then:

'Oh!' she squealed. Something freezing cold and sticky slammed up between her legs. Her thighs clamped together on his hand, and on an ice-cream gateau from the fridge.

'Fair exchange,' he offered, and bent his head to mouth at the freezing ice-cream now running over her hot labia, sucking her, his tongue chasing into the folds of her flesh.

Not long before the early summer dawn she got up and padded barefoot to the abandoned shopping trolley. She reached into her shoulder-bag.

'You might want to turn your head away,' Corey said.

He asked,'Why?'

Corey held up the tiny camera in her palm. 'You wouldn't want to be recognised, I don't suppose.'

The young security guard reached into the freezer. His hand came out holding a chocolate cheesecake, soft, half-defrosted. 'You hide my face,' he invited.

There was a squelch. The camera's flash fired twice.

Chapter Eight

THE SUMMER'S HOT sun burned through the office windows. Even with the slatted blinds drawn, it was hot and airless. Shannon walked through the open-plan office, between the grey work-station partitions, to her own room. Small, it might be. Shelved from floor to ceiling and spilling back issues of Femme everywhere it also might be. But it's mine, she thought as she closed the door. And God knows I worked hard enough to get it!

She threw her briefcase down on the desk. Her large window slid out the statutory two inches. Petrol-smelling air leaked in from the Strand. Air-conditioning, what's that? she thought, and sat down with a thud. You'd think being owned by an American firm would make some difference . . .

And this isn't what I'm really thinking about.

'Coffee?' Arabella put her head round the office door.

'Oh – no thanks.' She sighed. 'Give me half an hour to shift some of this stuff, and then I'll have some iced tea, if there's any left. Is Jane coming in for her appointment at ten-thirty?'

Her assistant nodded and left.

Shannon knew she had twenty minutes undisturbed at the outside. She picked up the phone and dialled an outside line.

It rang for almost two minutes. Then:

'Mmrh? Whassat?'

'Corey, it's me. Shannon.'

'Um.' There was a pause, in which Shannon could all but see the black-haired girl roll over on her futon and knuckle sleep out of her eyes. Corey's voice sharpened. 'Fuck me, is that the *time*? I'm supposed to be in Hammersmith!'

Shannon sat forward in her chair. She could see nothing through her room's glass walls but heads bent over IBM work-stations. 'Corey . . .'

There was a pause.

'I know what you're going to say.' Corey's voice rode over Shannon's as she finally tried to get out another sentence. She was bright, confident. Shannon thought, She's done her dare. She's actually done it . . .

'Shannon, I'm just going to say one thing. Don't take the dare – *if* you can say you've never fantasised about it. Never. Not even once. OK? Otherwise, believe me, I dare you!'

There was a longer pause.

Shannon heard her own voice crackle down the line. 'Do you know Nadia as well as you know me?'

'I don't know. Do I? Gotta go!' Her phone clicked down in its cradle.

Shannon sat holding the phone until it buzzed its long complaint.

On Saturday morning Shannon stood, undecided, on Waterloo Station concourse.

The sun glittered in through glass windows from a sky tending towards the overcast. Shannon straightened her shoulders. The straps of her bikini top tightened over her collar-bones. She wore a loose shirt and a flowing Indian skirt over the top of her bikini, and a pair of thonged sandals. She carried a light shoulder-bag that held a few beach things and a book, a rolled-up towel and a phone. And a camera.

Her eyes searched the departures board for trains to the coast.

There's always the chance, she mused, that the woman who wrote that article didn't know what she was talking about. Did we publish it? Oh, that's right, it'll be in the August issue.

In which case, it's just as well I'm going before the place gets popular.

Shannon read a book from the time when the train departed until the time some hours later when it drew into the coastal station. She closed the book with no knowledge of what she had been reading. As she put the book away in her bag and queued to leave the train, she thought, No, I can't say I *never* fantasised about it. Damn you, Corey, you brat!

Here, away from London, the air smelled clean. A brilliant sun was hazed whitely over from time to time, and a brisk wind blew. It made the streets comfortably rather than unbearably hot. Shannon paused on her walk from the station and bought herself a broad-brimmed sun hat. She adjusted her sunglasses, looking at the brilliance of the seaside town's streets, thronged with tourists and children eating ice-cream.

It's a bit crowded. Hell, it's a lot crowded.

Oh well, the article did say you had to walk quite a way . . .

She found the sign-posted footpath from the promenade and gratefully left the thronging families behind.

A silence fell amazingly quickly. She climbed up the footpath, away from the town. Traffic noise died. A thin, high song rang out in the blue above her. She dredged the bird's name from childhood memories: a skylark. Its song was drowned out, as she walked further on, by the yelping of gulls.

The rough track climbed more steeply, until it came out on to a grassy plateau. Shannon panted. She stopped and took her shoes off, carrying them in her hand. She dug her toes into the cool grass. A muscle-tension she had been unaware of left her. Whether anything happens or not, she thought, I'm glad I came.

Shannon walked slowly on. Something glittered in front of her. She crested the shallow slope. The sea, sunlit and brilliant, stretched away to the south. The scent of salt was strong. Gulls wheeled and cried. Ahead of her, the path dropped in steep curves down a bank, almost a cliff. It ran into a secluded bay. Cliffs cut the bay off from all sides, except where silver sand ran down to the sea.

Shannon drew a breath. A few tiny figures ran among the foam. Swimmers' heads bobbed like dark pinheads. She could not tell from this distance whether they were all women.

She realised she had been standing still for several minutes.

The sun began to burn her shoulders. She walked on, to where the path dipped over the cliff-edge. She could only watch where she put her feet, then, unable to spare any attention for anything else. The wind whisked her skirts. She grabbed her hat with one hand. The strap of her bag cut into her shoulder.

The breeze died. A warm air brushed her face. Her bare feet stood on the edge of sand. Shannon lifted her head and realised she was down in the secluded cove. The packed sand here was warm and slightly damp under her toes. Groups of people in brightly coloured swimsuits and bikinis ran close to the water-line, laughing, their voices echoing back from the cliffs above.

One of the women in a closer group waved a hand and called, 'Hi! That water's *cold!*'

'Um, I don't think I'll swim yet. Thanks.' Hastily, Shannon moved away. She walked rapidly along the beach, or as rapidly as the sand would permit. 'Idiot!' she muttered to herself. I can turn around right now and go home if I want to.

But I don't want to.

She found a stretch of sand not far from the bottom of the cliffs. The cliffs did not go straight up here. There had obviously been a landslip at some time in the past. The hillocks of earth had long ago become overgrown by long grass and waving wild flowers. Bees buzzed in the heat. Shannon stretched out her towel. She knelt on it and took off her shirt, and then slipped her skirt down over her hips. The thin material of her blue and gold bikini clung to her stomach and hips, and enclosed her breasts tautly. Whether it was the hot sensual afternoon or some other reason, she felt aroused.

She remained kneeling on her towel in the sun. Some yards away, at the shoreline, two young women walked hand in hand in the spreading fans of water. One slipped her arm unselfconsciously around the other's waist. Her hand slid down to cup her companion's bikini-clad buttock.

I guess the article was right, Shannon reflected.

She took her book out of her bag and opened it. She lay down with it in front of her. The soft sand gave slightly under her thighs and hips. When she removed her sunglasses the light was too bright. She put them back, watching the beach from behind their security.

Women of all ages sat in groups on the sand, or

played with frisbees, or swam. She let her eye linger. There were a few very young male children, but no men.

Not far away, a woman on her own was sunbathing on a towel. She looked about twenty-three. Her hair was long, black, and fell in ringlets. Shannon watched the gentle rise and and fall of her ribcage. She thought, a man would watch those breasts swelling out of that bikini-top, with their faint hint of a tan.

The woman stirred. She rolled over on to her front. Shannon caught sight of a strong-featured face, and eyes squinting shut against the sun. Then the young woman was lying face down. Her long legs were freckled with sand that dried from ochre to white on her skin. A man would look at that round bottom, split by an emerald-coloured thong. A man would feel . . . what?

Shannon became aware of warmth between her legs.

She sat up and reached for the sun-block in her bag. The plastic canister felt cool. She squirted the pale liquid into her palm and smoothed it up her arms and shoulders. Her hands slid over the tops of her breasts. She refilled her palm and smoothed the sun-block over her stomach; over her thighs and calves.

'Do your back if you want?'

Shannon's head jerked up. She smiled in confusion. The young woman with the ringlets was standing above her. The white sunlight shone fiercely on her flat stomach, pale thighs, and emerald-green bikini. Shannon looked up. The young woman's mouth was too big for beauty, and her dark eyebrows too thick. Her eyes were half hooded against the sun, but when Shannon made eye-contact, there was a long, level stare coming back at her. Shannon stopped smiling.

'You've got such fair skin, you'll burn,' Shannon said. 'How about if I do you first? Then you can do me.

575

Why don't you bring your towel over here?'

'Sure.' The young woman moved back towards it on long legs. Over her shoulder, she said, 'I'm Laura.'

'Elaine.'

'Hi, Elaine.' The towel flopped into the sand. The woman knelt down on it and plunged forward as if she were diving. She sprawled on her stomach on the sun-warmed material. 'You're right, I'm starting to burn, I'm sore.'

'Don't worry.' Shannon picked up the sun-block. 'I'll fix it.'

The breeze from the sea feathered the fine hairs on her arms. It blew her hair into her face. She squirted a generous quantity of sun-block into her palm. For a moment she hesitated. Then she reached down and rubbed her palm across the middle of the young woman's back, below black flowing hair.

Her hand encountered warm, soft skin that shivered at her touch and then quieted. Laura said nothing. She stroked the liquid across Laura's shoulder-blades, under the thong of her bikini top. Shannon reached down and brushed the woman's hair forwards. Then she stroked her hand across the tops of the woman's shoulders. The cool liquid sank into her fine-downed skin.

Shannon leaned back. This time she rubbed sun-block on both her palms. Then she leaned forward and massaged the young woman's foot. Gradually she worked her way up the calf. She squirted liquid on her hands and found them trembling. Suddenly unnerved, she began on the woman's other foot. She worked the liquid into the firm warm flesh, stroking it up towards the woman's knees.

How can I be sure that . . . ?

I suppose I'm about to find out.

Shannon poured a little liquid into the palm of one

576

hand and carefully tipped it on to the back of Laura's right thigh. The thigh twitched, like a pony when a fly lands on it. As Shannon's hands pressed into the soft, cool flesh, Laura stilled. Shannon pushed her thumbs into the firm warmness, trailed her fingers back down the outside of Laura's leg without breaking contact, she pushed her fingers back up the thigh, up to the cleft where the woman's taut buttock jutted up. She smeared sun-block on to the outside curve of Laura's buttock, which was not covered by the emerald bikini.

Shannon found her hands automatically reach out to pull the knotted thong undone. She stopped. To give just one tug, see the flimsy material fall away . . .

She re-charged her hands with sun-block and began to massage Laura's other thigh, pushing the flesh up, smearing sun-block over the outer curve of that buttock. Her fingers moved up to the indentation where Laura's backbone dipped under the bikini pants. By an effort of will Shannon made her hands move up, up towards the underside of the woman's sharply-jutting shoulder-blades. Shannon's sex throbbed once, warmly. She flattened her palms on the girl's warm back.

'Here, I'll help.' Laura's hand snaked up behind her own back. She grabbed the string of her bikini top and pulled. The knot fell undone. Her hand went back down to pillow her cheek. The emerald green bikini top fell flat on the towel. Shannon saw the firm bare curves where Laura's breasts were squashed under her body.

Trembling, she slid her greasy hands around the young woman's torso. She dipped her fingers down, so far down, not quite daring to touch where the breasts began. With both palms flat, she caressed down to Laura's firm waist.

Shannon felt the crotch of her bikini pants growing

damp. Her breathing quickened. She sat back on her heels. Her nipples began to harden under her bikini top. With a momentary loss of nerve, Shannon thought, *What if she sees!*

I want her to. I really want her to.

'I'll do you now, if you like.' Laura's voice was lazy, deep and dark. She sat up. Creases from the towel were imprinted on the skin of her bare breasts. 'Lie down on your back.'

Shannon did not remove her sunglasses. She eased herself down on her back under the glistening sky. Wind blew a scurry of sand across the towels. Happy voices called from far off: the tide was going out.

Shannon shut her eyes. She felt warmth and moving air. Smells of salt, ozone and sweat permeated her senses. She waited.

A cool, cream-slick hand touched her foot. As Shannon relaxed back, Laura's fingers slid up the outsides of her calves, paused, and sank back down. Up. Down. Rhythmic strokes, smoothing the liquid over her hot skin, almost massaging it in. The firm hands slid up again to her other knee. Shannon lifted her knee slightly. The fingers slid in to the soft hollow behind her knee and out again. The procedure was repeated with Shannon's other knee. Then the hands removed themselves.

It was hardly a second until Shannon felt herself touched again. Flat palms curved around her thighs above her knee. Laura's hands pushed firmly upwards, massaging the muscle, covering Shannon's already-greasy skin in more sun-block. The sensual movement drove her wild. The warmth in her sex was becoming a hot fire of arousal. She moved, bit back a moan.

The hands massaged her other thigh, sliding up into the sensitive skin around her groin, back away, then up again. Shannon tried to keep her hips from lifting. She kept her eyes closed.

Laura's hands left her.

There was a longer pause than normal. Shannon opened her eyes. The young woman had her head bent over the sun-block container. She wore only her emerald bikini bottom. Her breasts were small but full, the nipples a very pale pink. The pressure-marks of the towel had almost vanished now.

Laura straightened. Shannon hurriedly shut her eyes. A moment later, firm hands touched her at the base of her ribs. Sun-block was smeared over her stomach, hot in the sun. The pushing fingers moved upwards, smoothing the skin over Shannon's ribs.

Shannon felt the tips of her fingers slip under the bottom of her bikini top. Laura's hands did not stop. The slick fingers slid up over the curve of her breasts. Her bikini top rode up. Laura's hands moved to cup and hold Shannon's breasts.

The fire in her groin was unbearable. Shannon opened her eyes. The young woman was kneeling above her, blocking the light which shone through her tangled black hair. Her strong hands still cupped Shannon's naked breasts. The pale pink nipples swelled as Shannon watched. Her own nipples hardened.

'I love brown nipples,' Laura said huskily. 'Your breasts are so beautiful.'

Shannon reached up and took the woman's right hand. She held it in her own, and plunged them down under the top of her bikini pants. The tender flesh of her stomach shivered at the sensation.

'You're a virgin with women, aren't you?'

Shannon stuttered. 'Yes. That is, not exactly, but . . .'

'I can always tell.' Laura's heavy brows flirted up. 'I'll tell you a secret. It's better!'

579

Her hand slid down the front of Shannon's bikini pants until the tips of her fingers touched Shannon's curling hair.

With a mischievous grin, the younger woman snatched her hand away.

'What?' Shannon blushed brilliant red.

'Oh, I love a woman who can blush. Two things.' Laura sat up on her heels. 'I want to swim in the sea. I want to be clean. And, it's not as romantic as you think on a beach. Sand gets everywhere!'

'What?' Shannon repeated, hot and bewildered.

'We can go up in the hillocks. There's grass there, it's nice. Meanwhile . . .' She sprang up and ran towards the sea, fleet and fit. Shannon stared, open-mouthed. Then she grinned.

She leaped to her feet and began to run.

Shannon caught up when the younger woman had splashed through the shallows, and slowed her stride in the deeper water. She dived cleanly and shallowly, and seized Laura's legs from behind. A flailing body tumbled over her shoulder and splashed into the water.

'I caught you!' Shannon whooped. She reached out and caught the string on the emerald bikini bottom and tugged. Laura squealed. The scrap of cloth floated away on curving waves. She dived after it.

Shannon romped after her, catching the bikini bottom and holding it over her head. Laura threw her arms around Shannon's stomach and rugby-tackled her over. Both women went back into the salt water with a terrific splash. Shannon heard applause from the beach.

She came up holding Laura in the circle of her arms. The woman's black hair sleeked to head like a seal. Her full, small breasts pushed softly against Shannon's own breasts. Shannon felt two lithe, strong legs lock around her waist. Laura's groin bumped her, ground into her hip as the sea drove them together; and a wave knocked them under and apart. Shannon came up spluttering. Laura was already running up the beach. The woman was naked, bikini bottom in hand.

More sedately, Shannon followed.

She plucked her towel and bag from the sand and followed Laura into the hillocks.

Droplets of water slid down her shoulders, thighs, and calves. The wet cloth of her bikini bottom slid up between her swollen labia. She paused, tugged the garment down and off, and walked on, rubbing herself dry with the towel.

Away from the beach, it was cooler, but still hot. Nothing moved the air. The sound of the waves died. Bees hummed among the yellow flowers in the long grass. The ground under her feet was hot.

Shannon scrambled up one hillock. Another dip opened before her. Marram grass grew thickly along its sea-edge. Low, small-leafed bushes grew on one side. They made a line of shadow along the bottom of the dip. White flesh flashed in the shadow.

Cautiously, she slid down the side of the hillock.

Laura lay in the shade, on her back, one leg bent and drawn up at the knee. The hair between her legs was wiry and dark. Shannon, on hands and knees, reached forward to touch it. Her questing fingers met a springy softness. She pressed in. Laura's eyes were big in the shadows. They did not leave Shannon's face.

Shannon's fingers felt springy damp hair. The tips of her fingers slid into a hot, wet crevice. The woman made a sound, half gasp, half sigh. Her hands grasped Shannon's wrist and pressed her hand down and in.

Shannon lay carefully on the grass. Her hand thrust deep between the young woman's legs. With her other hand she reached out and grabbed Laura's breast.

'I want a woman,' Laura whispered. 'I want a woman who'll fuck me so I can't stand. I want *you*.'

Shannon closed her hand tight over the young woman's breast, squeezing it hard. Her fingers pushed up into Laura's ready sex. Hot flesh throbbed under her. Gently she slid her middle finger in. Hot juices flowed down her hand.

'Am I doing this right?' she whispered. 'I mean, I don't know if . . .'

'That's good. Oh, that's good. Do *that*.'

Shannon began to slide her finger into the younger woman's hot cleft. The breast under her hand swelled. She thrust her stiff finger in deeper, harder. Laura's hips began to lift and move. Her thighs clamped on Shannon's wrist, then loosened. Shannon added another finger, sliding them both into Laura's hot sex. She thrust rhythmically, clenching her other hand. Bulging breast flesh pushed up between her fingers. Without losing the rhythm of her thrusting fingers, Shannon lowered her head and took Laura's nipple in her mouth. So much larger than a man's nipple. It swelled as she sucked and teased it with her tongue.

Laura's hands flattened against the grass. Her back arched. The flesh of her sex convulsed around Shannon's hand. Her body bucked and thrashed as Shannon threw her other arm around her, and her head fell back, mouth open, and she gave a great gasping yell. 'Ahhhh!'

A gull shrieked overhead. Shannon glimpsed white wings against a blue, hazy sky.

The younger woman's sweat-soaked body collapsed against her. Slick skin burned hotly against Shannon as she fell back. They lay breast to breast, belly to belly, thigh pushing against thigh. Shannon's unsatisfied sex ached.

'Is that . . . ?'

'That isn't it. Not by any means.' Again, Laura gave her dark-browed, wicked grin. 'Lie back, little virgin. I'm going to teach you how to fly.'

Grass flattened under her. Shannon stretched back. Her hips writhed. Shadow and sunlight flirted over her sweat-soaked body. The solid figure of the other woman blocked the light again, briefly; then she was dazzled as Laura ducked forward.

The black hair tumbled softly down over Shannon's shoulders as Laura leaned over her. The younger woman, propped up on locked elbows, lowered her head. Her pink tongue flicked out and caught Shannon's left nipple. A bolt of pleasure shot from Shannon's nipple direct to her sex. She lifted her hands to cup Laura's breasts, above her.

The younger woman lowered her body. Her mouth encircled Shannon's nipple. She sucked the breast into her mouth, flicking Shannon's nipple again with her tongue. Pinkness flushed Shannon's skin. She fiercely handled the flesh before her, the woman's shoulders, arms, back, breasts. She pulled Laura's head up and their lips met, tongues thrusting deep into each other's mouths.

With a gasp, Laura broke away. She smelled of salt and perfume, tasted of fire. Shannon flopped back. She felt Laura's hands slide down her ribs, across her stomach, down the insides of her thighs. They pushed her legs apart. Shannon wriggled, drawing her legs up slightly. A hot mouth nibbled at the sensitive flesh inside her thigh and she squealed.

Laura's mouth closed over her sex. The woman's lips sucked at her labia. A strong tongue thrust between them. She moaned, pushing her hips up. The tongue thrust deeper and swirled, sending little bolts of pleasure through Shannon's flesh. She gasped.

The tongue slid forward and up. Shiveringly

delicately, it touched her swelling clitoris. Shannon nearly screamed. Two fingers inserted themselves in her and thrust.

'Oh my God!' Shannon grabbed the woman's shoulders. Her fingers drove deep into the soft flesh. 'Oh God, I'm coming! Oh God, don't stop!'

Fat flesh – two fingers? three? – thumped up into her cleft. Shannon's filled sex convulsed. Waves of pleasure lifted her hips off the ground. She drove her body down on Laura's hand, fiercely milking the last spasm, and fell back drained.

'Oh . . .'

Somewhere outside her dizzy collapse, a woman's voice chuckled. Laura. Shannon opened her eyes to see Laura's face. Her too-wide mouth was grinning. Her lips were wet. She cupped Shannon's cheek with her hand.

'I want you more,' she said.

Shannon's sex twitched. 'Can you – can we – I mean, how long does this go on?'

Laura's eyes twinkled. 'As long as you like, lover. I'm no one-shot wonder. Hey.' She pointed at the spilled contents of Shannon's bag. 'Hey, why don't we take some holiday snaps? I'll give you my address.'

'I'll send you copies.' Shannon laid her cheek on the younger woman's belly. 'You can come up to London. We'll do . . . lunch.'

She nibbled her way down the soft skin of the woman's belly. Laura's springy hair tasted of salt and woman come. She thrust her tongue deep, seeking her swelling bud of flesh; teasing, touching, moving away. The heat between her own legs soared.

Shannon sucked Laura's clit. The woman reached down and thrust short-nailed fingers into her dripping heat. Though she would have sworn it was too soon, a swelling wave of pleasure thundered through

Shannon's heat-soaked body.

The shadows of gulls fell across them all the long July afternoon.

The train rattled and jounced under her. Shannon leaned back against the upholstery, bonelessly relaxed and replete. From time to time she opened her bag and touched Corey's camera. With deep satisfaction, she thought, Let her develop these, that'll teach her to think of me as a mouse!

Her mobile phone bleated.

'Yes?' She kept her voice quiet.

'It's me.' Pause. '*Me*.'

'Oh. *Tim*.' She was grateful now that there were few other travellers in the carriage. Her heart beat faster, her face flamed. 'I told you not to call me!'

His voice was light, sexy, utterly familiar. 'I know. Look, I can't talk right now. Can I see you? I have something important to ask you.'

'I – no. Yes.' She breathed in sharply. 'I suppose so.'

'I'll be at your place at eight.' The connection broke.

By half-past seven her terraced house was spotless. Shannon paced backwards and forwards in the living-room, the day forgotten. The whole downstairs had been knocked into one room by a previous owner. Sunlight shone in through the glass doors that led to the tiny garden. She glanced at the stairs.

I'll put clean sheets on the bed. No, I won't. It'll look as if I was expecting him to . . . oh, he won't even notice! Shall I do it? I might as well. But it might look wrong. I told him we were finished!

At eight-oh-one she was stripping the sheet and duvet cover off. She pulled new bedding covers out of the cupboard and pulled them on. Flick covered her cotton dress. She pulled it roughly over her head, opened the wardrobe, dragged out a skimpy black party dress, and dragged it on.

He's late. Maybe he'll bring flowers. I told him not to come back unless he was prepared to – no, that was the time before. What does he *want*?

At half-past eight, Shannon was propped up on the sofa by the window. She had glass of red wine in one hand, and the remnants of last Sunday's newspapers in the other. When the doorbell rang, she didn't even jump.

She put the wine carefully down. Newspaper broadsheets spilled on to the carpet. She walked to the door and opened it. 'Tim.'

Same old Tim. White shirt, blue jeans; the out-of-office uniform. His old green car parked in the road directly outside. She looked up into his dark eyes. He looked slightly plumper in the face: well-fed, happier somehow.

'Hello.' She saw him register her dress and look puzzled. 'I didn't know you were going out. Never mind, I won't keep you long.'

Shannon stood back silently and let him into the house. She waited to see if he would notice she had taken down the framed prints he had given her.

As far as she could tell, he didn't even look at the walls.

She poured him a glass of red wine. 'Why have you come, Tim? What have you got to say to me that's important?'

He picked the newspapers off the floor and straightened and folded them. In anyone else it would have been a nervous mannerism. When he looked at her, however, he was beaming with an expansive good humour.

'I'm sorry, I probably made it sound more desperate than I meant. It would be an *enormous* favour. I couldn't think of anyone, and then I thought of you – I

586

know you wanted us to stay friends, and this is the kind of thing friends do.'

Shannon stared at him. She turned away briefly, running her fingers along the spines on the bookshelves. When she felt more composed, she said, 'You're not coming back to me, then?'

He still had the smile that melted her.

'We can talk about that when I get back.' He grinned boyishly.

'Get back? Tim, I think you'd better just explain.'

'I'm taking Julia away with me on a month's holiday to Greece,' Tim said, 'to celebrate our reconciliation. The kids are at her Mum's. I wondered if you could drop in on the flat while we're gone, and feed the cats?'

Chapter Nine

THAT EVENING NADIA had decided to keep *Ephemera* open very late, to catch the summer tourist trade. When the bell jangled for what she decided was the very last time, however, she came out into the shop to find Shannon Garrett, words tumbling out of her mouth.

'Nadia, I'm going to kill him!'

'Mmm? Oh, no. This is Tim again, isn't it?' Nadia nodded to herself. She did her best to follow the flood of explanation. 'I thought you'd finished with him.'

'I have! I'm going to kill him,' Shannon finished. 'Then I'm going to cut off his balls and *post* them to Julia. She's welcome to him!'

Shannon stomped past her into the back of the shop. Nadia flipped the shop sign from OPEN to CLOSED, and locked the door. She replaced the green baize covers over the counters, hiding the pieces of 1950s costume jewellery from anyone who might think it worthwhile breaking in. She could hear the other woman's shout clearly from the shop's back room:

'Who does he think he is? 'We'll talk about it when I get back'. No, we won't! I'm sorry for Julia. I'd like to tell her just who she's been married to for the last eight years! But if she doesn't know by now, she must be even more stupid than I was!'

Nadia tugged the curtain across, shutting the front of the shop off from the rear room. She found the woman sitting by the open back door, a glass of Perrier in hand, black party dress rucked up to her knees in the streaming evening sun.

'In a way, I'm glad he did it.' Shannon raised her face. 'There's no danger of me forgetting what he's like now. Not after this! I tell you something, Nadia, I am not going to let him get away with this. Nobody's doing that to me!'

'Why don't you come home with me and have supper? I've got some bits and pieces in the fridge,' Nadia offered.

'I'd like that. Thanks. Oh,' the woman said, as she got to her feet, 'what about – you know? Have you done Corey's dare yet? What was yours?'

Nadia licked her suddenly-dry lips. 'Not yet,' she admitted. 'I've been thinking about it. A great deal.'

Thirty-six hours later, Nadia drew the red MG up on the Wiltshire country house's drive in a swirl of gravel.

I didn't expect to come back here again. It hasn't changed.

After she cut the engine, everything was silent.

She rolled the window down and sat listening. Birds began to sing in the high arch of the sky, above the shimmering full green tops of the chestnuts lining the drive. Hot noon sunlight dappled her face through the leaves.

This is too risky. This is far *too risky. I know these people!*

And, of course, that's Corey's point.

Corey's dare had been simple. *Try the last one again.*

Then she went on to name names.

How many times did I want to do this, when I was living here with Oscar? Hundreds. It would have been . . . unfair. Not discreet. How many times did I think, *If I weren't married*—

A warm breeze blew, bringing the scents of flowers up from the hall gardens. Nadia looked briefly up at the old sun-warmed brick of the main building. The doors were closed. Blinds were down on most of the windows.

Oscar never did like to be here in August. He always preferred London. Me? I could never get used to the green . . .

Suddenly decisive, she opened the MG's door and swung her legs out. Her heeled sandals dug into the gravel. The designer-label green silk shirt-dress slipped, exposing her slightly freckled shoulders. The sun burned her skin as she stood up. She put on her sunglasses, and tucked her car keys into her small, expensive clutch bag. One of the few outfits she had kept after the divorce.

Two brightly-coloured butterflies flickered across the air. She heard bees humming. The hands of the clock on the hall tower pointed to one-twenty.

Ignoring the main door, Nadia walked across to the wrought-iron driveway gates at the side of the hall. She pushed. The hot metal swung back from her hand. She walked in, the crunching of her heels the only noise in that hot silence. She kept moving, past the hall's curtained windows on her left, and the riotous colour of the garden on her right hand, approaching the corner of the building.

She rounded the comer. Immediately opposite her were the stables, single-storey workrooms and garages. A large green Rolls stood on the gravel. Half of it was covered in suds. A male voice was singing, not very tunefully. As she watched, a bucketful of water flew over the roof from the far side, and a man came around the back of the car, carrying a wash-cloth. Richard! she thought. You *are* still here.

He was about thirty; short, stocky and ruddy-faced. When he saw her, his face went momentarily blank. He grinned with equal amounts of surprise and pleasure. She registered the quick flick of his gaze up and down her body before he coughed, looked down, and automatically touched his finger to where his cap-brim would have been.

'Hello, Mrs Trevithic.' He hesitated. 'Sorry, ma'am. Miss, I mean.'

'It's not Trevithic now. It's Kay again. Hello, Richard.'

She straightened her shoulders. The thin silk of her dress strained a little across her breasts, as they swelled slightly with arousal. She looked at the chauffeur. His shoes were brightly polished, and the creases in his black uniform trousers knife-sharp. The only concession he had made to the heat was to take his uniform jacket off and roll up his shirtsleeves. He was wearing a dark blue tie. His sandy hair had been cut very short since the last time she had seen him, and it stuck up in tiny sweaty tufts.

'Mr Oscar isn't here, miss.'

'I know. He's in London.' Nadia walked forward. She rested her hand briefly against the wing of the Rolls. The hot metal burned her fingertips. She moved around and opened the back passenger door on his side of the car and sat down, her legs still outside.

Immediately she was covered in a thin film of sweat. The leather smell of the upholstery permeated the interior of the car. She looked up and out at the chauffeur. 'Aren't you hot, Richard?'

'Yes, ma'am. Miss.'

Nadia leaned back into the car, feeling the expensive

silk slide across her body. She stretched her legs out. 'Do you remember,' she said dreamily, 'all those times you drove me up to London, shopping? It seems so long ago now.'

'I didn't forget that yet, miss.' He scrubbed his big hand across his cropped hair. His eyes squinted against the noon sun. He reached up and tugged at the knot of his tie. His eyes dropped from her face, down to the vee-neck of her silk shirt-dress, down her body, to the long, bare silky length of her legs. 'Nobody's in the house, miss, you've had a wasted journey.'

'Not yet,' Nadia murmured. She made eye contact and held it. His face reddened. It might have been the sun. She rather thought not. She leaned against the back of the seat, stretching one leg, pointing her sandalled toe. Perspiration slicked her skin. If she left the car now she would find the baking noon cool by comparison.

'I used to watch you driving, Richard,' she said. 'Your hands on the wheel. You have strong hands; I like that.'

The blond man glanced at his hands and then put them behind him. He half-turned away and threw the wash-cloth. Nadia heard it splash into a bucket.

'I watched you too.' His voice was rough. He gave her no title. When she looked up, his face was hard.

'That was then,' she said. 'I won't be back here, Richard. This is just a last visit. I'd rather like to celebrate it. Please don't say anything if you feel you'd rather not.'

'My God.' His face above his white shirt collar burned bright red. 'My God, woman. You don't mean it.'

She looked at his strong-featured face. He had the same attractive innocence about his own male appeal.

'I don't say anything I don't mean,' Nadia said simply. 'I'd like to undress you, with my teeth.'

'I used to come home after I'd driven you around all

day, miss.' His voice thickened. 'You'd go into the big house with a dozen shopping bags. I'd go back to the garage and think about how you'd look with your knickers down around your ankles, or your face in my crotch. You got any idea how often I've fucked you?'

Nadia rubbed her palms over her sweat-slick cheeks. She pressed her hands to her sides, pulling the green silk taut across her breasts and stomach. She watched his member stiffen in his pants. It was as big as she had always imagined.

'Tell me what I did.' Her breathing quickened.

He pulled the knot of his tie loose with two quick tugs. He stood with his feet planted slightly apart, coiling the strip of material over one hand. He started to speak, mumbled, shook his head, and then met her gaze with dark hungry eyes.

'You'd be going to get out of the car,' he said roughly, 'and you'd pull your dress up. And you'd be wearing French knickers, silk ones, and I'd see them.'

Nadia drew one of her legs inside the Rolls. She left one outside, her toe touching the gravel. She shifted her buttocks on the leather seat. The green silk shirt-dress rode up her thighs. An edge of ivory silk showed. 'Then what would I do, Richard?'

'Then you'd part your legs,' the chauffeur said, 'so I could see up into your crotch.'

A pumping pulse of arousal went through her sex. Nadia put her clutch bag demurely down on the seat. Then she swivelled on the hot leather, spread her legs, and reached down and pulled her dress up to the very tops of her thighs. He gazed at the crotch of her ivory silk French knickers. Nadia felt herself growing damper. 'And then?'

'And then I'd push you back on the seat.' His strong hands gripped his tie, then threw it down on the gravel. He ducked his head and leaned into the car, pushing his body in. The strong scent of sweat came in with him. His bare forearms were covered in wiry golden hair. He put the palm of his hand on Nadia's left breast.

She eased back on to the seat, the leather upholstery hot under her skin. His hand slid down her dress, over her stomach, down to the pit of her belly. He took each side of her knickers between a thumb and forefinger. Nadia shut her eyes. She felt him pull the material down over her bottom, catching between her and the seat, and then her mound was bare.

'*Jesus Christ!*'

Nadia's eyes flew wide open. Richard's body blocked her view. He swore, backed out of the car, cracking his head on the door-frame, and swore again. He was stuffing his shirt back down the front of his unzipped trousers. Nadia sprawled with her legs apart, her damp sex feeling the summer air, her knickers around her knees.

The same new voice repeated, 'Jee-sus . . .'

'Lee?' Nadia lifted her head. 'Is that you, Lee?'

The newcomer was a young man of about twenty. He had a mass of dark yellow curly hair that fell below his broad shoulders, and the aquiline features of a fifteenth-century angel. His well-muscled chest was brown and bare. His strong legs and thighs were sharply defined under the well-worn soft denim of his jeans, so old they were more faded white than blue. To her joy, Nadia recognised the gardener's assistant Oscar had taken on a few months before their initial separation.

The fly of his soft denim jeans bulked hard and full as Lee gazed into the car. He flushed. 'Sorry, I – sorry, Miss Nadia.'

'Don't go.' Nadia caught Richard's gaze. 'Let's go into the stables. All of us.'

There was a moment's hesitation. Then Richard reached into the car and caught her hands. She came forward as he pulled, and he bent down and scooped his hands under her knees and arms, and set off towards the stable block with fast and powerful strides. She was dimly aware of Lee at the periphery of her vision.

The change from sunlight to stable left her dazzled for seconds.

She felt Richard lower her. Her body tell back against a sweaty bare chest. Hay stroked her legs. She was placed down on some surface that gave. Gazing up, she realised she was in an empty horse-box. Lee was behind her, supporting her upper body. Her legs sprawled wide apart on the hay-strewn floor.

Without preamble, Richard unzipped his fly. His erect cock bobbed out, thick and full. Nadia lifted her hands behind her and encountered the hot, shivering skin of another body. She dropped her hands into Lee's crotch. His prick swelled in his pants.

'Is this—' His voice cracked with anxiety. 'I mean – is this all right? Can we—'

'I always wanted you to fuck me.' Nadia's eyes accustomed to the dusty sunlit gloom. 'I used to watch you both out here. I couldn't do anything. Now I can say it. I want you both inside me.'

Richard knelt ih front of her legs. She eased her hips up and slipped her knickers off. Lee's hands came down from where he knelt behind her head. His dirt-stained fingers fumbled with the buttons of her expensive silk dress. It fell open. He seized her breasts in their ivory satin bra cups. His fingers felt rough and calloused.

Richard's stubbled face pressed between her thighs. She felt his hot breath on her sex. Her flesh loosened and swelled. His tongue flickered into her inner lips.

595

Her back tightened and arched. Lee's mouth came down on hers. His strong tongue thrust between her teeth. Richard's tongue lapped up her sex, over her clitoris, up her belly, trailing saliva up to where Lee's strong wrists showed their corded tendons as he grasped her breasts.

Lee's long kiss ended. Nadia gasped in a breath. 'Every time I saw you in your uniform – every time I saw *you* in the garden – I longed to come up and grab your crotches and drag you in here!'

Lee's mouth dropped to her breasts. His sweating muscled torso leaned over her. He bit and nibbled down her body. Nadia reached up and unbuttoned the top of his jeans. She unzipped his fly. His waiting cock swung down and hung. She drew it down to her mouth and began to lick the shaft. It hardened between her hands. She kept his cock in her mouth, and moved her hands up his body, up his flat belly, to his nipples and the soft hair of his chest, as far as she could reach.

Without warning, Richard's cock pushed between the lips of her sex. She stiffened, then her relaxing flesh drew him into her hot wetness. His first thrust was a delicious fullness. She licked down the base of Lee's cock to his balls, burying her face in his scant soft hair. He smells of sweet grass, she thought, and licked him from balls to anus. His thighs parted, so that he straddled her body below the shoulders. Nadia looked up from between the tight cheeks of his ass, up the length of his muscled back, in time to see Richard put both hands either side of the boy's head, and thrust his tongue down the boy's throat. Richard's cock inside her leaped and swelled. She writhed her hips, moaning.

'Up!' Richard said wetly. He pulled at her with urgency. Not understanding, she was for a moment bewildered. Lee tumbled off. Richard's hands under her arms lifted her upright. Her sandalled feet sought a firm footing in the hay.

The blond man pushed her dress back off her shoulders. Her bra was unhooked from behind. Their hands were everywhere. Nadia felt herself stroked, handled, caressed, fondled, until she did not know who did what. Richard's hips pressed into hers, Richard's thick cock impaled her and held her up.

Something nudged at her anus. She gasped. Her body ran with salt sweat. A thick tongue pushed at the rim of her ass, pushing just inside and then retreating, softening her, making her ring of flesh open and then contract. She felt a handful of saliva smeared over her anus. Then with great and gentle care, Lee put the head of his cock at her entrance and pushed.

Richard's cock thrust up. She grabbed his shoulders to hold herself up, standing almost on tiptoe, even in the heeled sandals. The boy's cock pushed remorselessly in, penetrating her ass. She felt the shaft swell, filling her bottom. For one moment she stood in the hot sweating stable, bare from the waist up, with Richard's cock buried to the hilt in her pussy, and Lee's cock filling her ass.

'Fuck me,' she gasped.

'Now,' Richard grunted. Lee thrust. He thrust. Alternating, they began to pump her, lifting her up on to her toes. Nadia's eyes flew open wide. She lifted one leg and hooked it around Richard's thick muscular thigh for support.

'Oh, yes! Oh God. Do it to me,' she groaned. 'I always wanted this! In the car, on the back seat. In the garden, on my back on the grass. I wanted, I *want*. Do it!'

Richard's hands held her shoulders firmly. Lee gripped her hips. Richard's head was thrown back, his teeth bared, and she felt him swell hot and hard within her. The boy's lips brushed her freckled shoulders, and he began to bite at the skin, nipping and worrying a fold of flesh until it tingled, then licking, then seizing another mouthful. His silk-hard shaft pushed up, prising apart the ring of muscle at her anus. Richard's thrusting began to speed up. She was filled, impaled, bursting with their fullness.

'Oh yes!' She clenched her hands on the chauffeur's biceps. Now Lee's thrusts lifted her up on to her toes every time. Each of the men thrust and withdrew, thrust and withdrew, alternately; and her soft inner flesh grew more swollen, more hot, more full with every stroke. 'Oh yes, oh yes – *oh!*'

The two men thrust together. Two cocks simultaneously filled her. Hot come spurted up into her. Her sex exploded with a searing, intense, prolonged burst of pleasure that blackened her vision, weakened her knees, and left her collapsed back against Lee, head thrown back on his shoulders, arms spread wide, her hot sweat cooling on her bare breasts. Their shrinking cocks began to slip from her.

A voice from the door said, 'Am I interrupting at all?'

Nadia twitched as if stung. She lifted her head, otherwise helpless to move. A dark body leaned on the stable's half-door. With the sun behind him, his face was invisible. She recognised his voice instantly.

The customs officer from the banquet.

Nadia Kay shifted her weight forward. Her sweating skin unpeeled from the gardener'is, behind her. She looked at the man who had been her chauffeur, standing with his uniform trousers around one foot.

'Thank you,' she said coolly, 'I believe that will be all.'

Once outside the stables, furiously buttoning her dress, she swung around to face the customs officer.

598

He was wearing off-duty clothes: soft denim jeans and a white T-shirt, which he filled well enough to catch her attention, and make her annoyed at herself for noticing. She demanded, 'How dare you! What do you mean by coming here! How did you find me?'

'It wasn't difficult to find out what you do. A lot of people at the function obviously knew you. This morning I found an elderly gentleman looking after your shop who said you'd gone into the country.' He shrugged massive shoulders. 'I guessed you might be visiting your old home. I wanted to see you again.'

Nadia finished buttoning her silk dress. She tugged the hem of the damp material firmly down over her thighs. 'Well, now you've seen me!'

Despite her immediate embarrassment, a sense of triumph reasserted herself. Her body hummed contentedly with pleasure: if she had been a cat she would have purred. Her pussy and her ass both throbbed with the afterglow of pleasure, sticky with sweet come.

I have taken my pleasure, she thought, no one can take that away from me.

The big man smiled cherubically down at her. 'I did you some good. The last time we met, the height of your ambition was to have two men in the same *bed*.'

He cocked an eyebrow.

'I've obviously helped you to become more ambitious.'

Nadia blushed. She caught herself stuttering. 'It wasn't like that! It *isn't* like that! This has nothing to do with you.'

'Really?'

'Yes. Really!'

He smiled beautifully. 'Must be a coincidence, then.'

'*What?*' Nadia stood and stared, outraged, as he turned and walked away.

'What makes *you* think *you're* responsible for what I dare do?' she shouted. Her voice echoed off the frontage of the hall. She felt her face colour. The big man did not turn around. He kept on walking. As he got into his blue Vauxhall Astra, she heard him start to whistle.

You did *me* some good—?

Of all the fucking nerve!

When she got back into the MG, she saw Corey's spare camera. Still on the back seat. Still in its case.

'Oh, *bugger!*' Nadia exclaimed.

A crow shot up from the front of the hall and flew away into the distance, squawking.

Chapter Ten

THEY RENDEZVOUSED AT the weekend at Corey's flat.

Comparing their photographic evidence turned out not to be an illuminating experience. Shannon Garrett held up a three-by-five inch print. She turned it around, held it upside-down, and studied the matt surface carefully. 'Is that his dick? I can't tell.'

'The light was bad,' Corey said grumpily. 'Here are yours. She hasn't got much in the tit area, has she?'

'That's *me*,' Shannon said frostily. 'She took one when she was on top. Look, they always look smaller when you're lying down! Don't they?'

'Naturally.' Nadia, Shannon noticed, spoke without smiling. She was sitting in the only chair in the bedroom/darkroom. The older woman prodded the curly strips of paper still glistening with the developing liquid, none of which were hers. 'Richard and Lee had wonderful bodies . . .'

'So you keep telling us,' Shannon muttered. 'There's no need to be so po-faced because you were interrupted.'

'That *man*—'

The doorbell interrupted them.

'You guys stay here.' Corey shifted herself up from the futon and padded to the living-room door. 'I'll deal with it.'

As the black-haired girl disappeared, Nadia looked down at Shannon where she lay on the bed. 'I defy anyone to win anything at all on the basis of photographs like these.'

Corey's screech cut her off. *'You want me to what?'*

Shannon exchanged glances with Nadia. She got up and moved towards the door between the bedroom and the main room, intending to close it.

A frosty voice in the living-room said, 'You heard me. My son has been selected to stand for Parliament. A seat in the Midlands, I believe. You'll remember his interest in politics.'

Shannon mouthed *Patricia* at Nadia, and the r ed-headed woman nodded, and padded over barefoot to join her. Shannon raised her brows. Nadia shook her head, and put her finger to her lips.

'Ben might as well be an MP.' Corey's tone from the other side of the door was scathing. 'He's stupid enough. What's this got to do with me?'

'He plans to stand as an MP. His constituency know he's divorced, and while they frown on it, they can live with it. The last thing I want are those dreadful media people finding out that he used to be married to some half-South American porn model.'

Corey's voice squeaked. 'I've never done porn in my life!'

'You surprise me.' The older woman's voice was icy. 'I have my son's respectability as my concern. Whatever kind of modelling it is you're doing, you are to stop it immediately.'

There was a pause. Shannon, biting her lip, put a hand on the door to the living-room. She felt her movement arrested and glanced down to see Nadia's hand on top of hers.

'You're out of your mind,' Corey mumbled.

Patricia Bright's voice echoed clearly. 'As far as I know, you shouldn't be carrying on a business out of this flat in any case. I understand your lease forbids commercial activity. Possibly your landlord is as yet unaware of what you do?'

Corey snarled, 'So how am I supposed to earn a living?'

'Really, that isn't my concern. I expect you'll find some other young man to take in with your lies, the same way that you took in my Ben. I think we understand each other, dear, don't you? I have to go now: I have to rehearse for my little talk at the Conway Hall. No, don't trouble yourself. I'll see myself out.'

The flat's front door closed with a click.

'We couldn't help hearing.' Shannon stepped into the living-room. 'The old bitch. Oh, Corey!'

She held out her arms as the younger woman burst into a short, furious rage of tears. Shannon hugged her. She was aware of Nadia pouring something into a glass and pushing it into Corey's hands. Corey stepped back, drank, and stopped crying, her face bright red.

'The bitch!' Corey drained the glass. 'OK, I can survive on my photography, but the modelling's only catalogue, it isn't even glamour or porn modelling, and in any case *it's the fucking principle!*'

Shannon manoeuvred the girl into sitting down on the old cane sofa. 'So I dare you to do a porn movie. That would show her.'

'She'd just have me evicted. She's got friends. I'm stuffed . . .' The girl wiped the back of her hand across her eyes and looked up. 'Oh well. Don't worry. I'll think of something.'

'Corey,' Shannon said.

'No, I mean it. Forget it. I'll phone Perry in the morning; tell him I can't make it. I don't want to think about it now.'

'I have an idea,' Nadia said.

Both the other women looked at her.

'Corey, sweets, your storeroom, do you still have the key?'

The black-haired girl glanced at the door at the corner of the far wall of the dormer bedroom. 'I guess so. Why?'

Nadia didn't answer. The girl got up and began to rummage through heaps of cosmetic jars, cheap Goth jewellery and small change on the top of her dresser. Eventually she held up a key.

'I wanted to have it done up as a darkroom,' she said. 'The landlord won't convert it into another bedroom; he might just as well have let me. There's nothing in there, Nadia.'

The red-haired woman uncurled from where she sat on her chair. She stood up lazily, as if the summer heat made her too languid to do anything at all, but Shannon saw there was excitement in her eyes.

'Give me the key.' Nadia took it. She crossed the room and unlocked the door.

Shannon padded after her, peering over her shoulder from the doorway.

The room beyond Corey's bedroom was an unconverted loft. Unlike the bedroom and living-room, the walls were not plastered, but were bare brick. The air was heavy and hot.

Corey reached around her and tugged a string. A bare bulb hanging from the rafters flared into harsh light.

Two tiny dormer windows had been let into the sloping roof. Cobwebs hung from the beams. The room was much longer than Corey's bedroom, and halfway down it was divided by massive wooden cross-beams, one diagonal, one horizontal at waist-height, and one just above floor-level. The rafters had been floored over at some time in the past. Old cardboard boxes were scattered across the floorboards: stacks of magazines tipped over, a non-functioning Hoover resting with its wheels up in the air.

'This will take your mind off your problems,' the red-headed woman announced. 'Corey, sweets, if you don't mind me making a suggestion about how some of your five thousand pounds is spent, I have an idea.'

When Shannon looked at Corey, the younger woman's face was bewildered.

'Well, OK. I guess. Oh, come on, Nadia!' Corey began to smile with anticipation. 'What is it? What's going to happen?'

Nadia prodded distastefully at the nearest cardboard box with her bare foot. 'First, you are going to clear this mess up. Shannon and I will then dust, brush, and scrub this room to within an inch of its life. It's a perfectly adequate room under all the dirt.'

Shannon said, 'Umm . . .'

'While we do that, Corey, you will go out and purchase a reasonable quality camcorder, and whatever you need for home development of the film.' Nadia shrugged her lithe shoulders, beaded with perspiration from the attic's airless heat. Her eyes gleamed. 'We don't yet have a winner of our little competition. It's proving impossible to get photographic evidence outside. Very well. I dare you – Shannon – all of us – to bring our dares back here! *Then* film them. Then we can really judge the winner!'

'What's *this*?' Shannon wiped the back of her hand across her forehead. She had reached the far end of the attic. Dust, wet with her own sweat, smeared her forehead.

Corey clomped across the bare boards. 'Oh, that. It's my old futon frame, the cheap one. I kept it as a spare. Let's put it up.'

A quarter of an hour later, Shannon looked at the bare slatted frame of the futon. She coughed, and sat down on its edge. 'This is far too much like hard work!'

Nadia rested her elbows on the cross-beam in the middle of the room. There was a wet circle on the hem of her summer dress, where she had been kneeling to scrub the floorboards. 'Corey, my dear, what a wonderful contraption. May I suggest a little more in the way of furnishings?'

The younger woman kicked the lowest cross-beam with her foot. 'I'd thought of a couple of ring bolts.'

'Ring bolts?' Shannon said. 'What for? Oh.' She coloured.

'What's wrong with having our very own dungeon?' Corey grinned. The expression faded, suddenly, and she sat down on the lowest beam. Nadia remained leaning on her elbows above her. The young woman said, 'We have to be a bit careful. I don't want any putters knowing where I live. And I don't want my landlord finding out! The trouble is, Patricia's right. If he knew about the darkroom business, he'd go ballistic; as for *this*—!'

Nadia reached down and ruffled her short black hair. 'Don't worry, sweets, we're not stupid.'

'We'll handle the practicalities,' Shannon said. The futon frame was uncomfortable. She stood up. She looked around the cleared, swept, scrubbed dormer room. 'Who's going to be first?'

'Have we all thought of dares?' Nadia asked.

Corey reached into her jeans pocket and pulled out a handful of small change. She selected three coins, giving one each to Nadia and Shannon, and keeping the other for herself. 'Odd one out dares first,' she said.

'Heads,' Nadia announced.

'Tails,' Shannon said.

Corey lifted her hand off her twenty-pence piece. 'Heads. You then, Shannon.'

'I've got one for you, Corey,' Shannon said. Thinking ring-bolts, indeed! 'This *is* a dungeon. It only needs whips and chains! Let's use some of the money and go shopping . . . Then I dare you to put a card up in the phone box down the road, and have whoever comes along and phones in.'

Corey Black stood over Shannon, where the older woman knelt on the floor by the phone. She rested her elbows on Shannon's shoulders. Curly brown hair tickled her bare arms as she steadied the pair of binoculars.

'Got it,' she said crisply. 'OK, answer the phone.'

She felt Shannon's arm move as the woman lifted the receiver to her ear. 'Yes . . . ?' Shannon purred.

The image in the binoculars sharpened. Corey focussed them on the telephone booth twenty yards down the road. It had transparent plastic walls, and she could clearly see the profile of the man inside it, handset in hand.

'Make him talk to you!' she whispered. 'What does he sound like?'

'Shut up!' Shannon put her hand over the mouthpiece. 'Ordinary. He sounds ordinary. *Yes, tell me more . . .*'

The man in the booth stood with his face to its wall, his back to the street. His posture was very upright. His hair was sandy red. He wore a white shirt, a tie, and smart grey trousers. There was a briefcase of some sort at his feet, possibly a jacket; she couldn't make that out.

'He says am I "Mistress Whip"?' Shannon whispered, between panic and hilarity. 'What shall I tell him?'

'Tell him you can arrange a meeting with her, dummy! Ask him what he likes.'

'This one doesn't look too strange, then?' Nadia enquired from the back of the room.

'Normal as hell. Not that that means anything. Wait a sec . . .' Corey focussed on his face. He was fair-skinned, freckled, and slightly baby-faced, so that it was impossible to tell if he were in his early or his late twenties. Fairly tall. Stocky. His reddish-orange hair had a slight curl and was cut short. He shifted his feet, altering his position, and Corey got a clearer look at his features. Well-shaved cheeks, appearing almost scrubbed, with a slight pink tinge. Wide eyes. Very definite jaw and nose, but then, something about his mouth as he talked . . .

She saw the distant figure lift his hand up to the wall of the phone booth. He took down a card – ours! she thought. And now there was no mistake, his face was very pink.

She lowered the binoculars and remembered to whisper. 'What's he like?'

'He says his name's Adrian and he likes "the usual".' Shannon had her hand over the mouthpiece again. 'He says his "safe word" is *blue*. What shall I *tell* him?'

Corey shook her head. 'Look at him. Too tame.'

Nadia came forward out of the shadows. 'Shannon, it's your dare, you decide.'

The telephone handset that Shannon held began to yelp with indistinguishable speech. She leaned over Corey's shoulder, one hand steadying herself. 'I think so, yes.'

'What?' Corey protested. 'He's uptight as hell, look at him!'

'Then he may just be a challenge. The dare is, after all, to *make* a man come.' Shannon smiled. 'I'm going to tell him to go to the junction, turn left, turn left again, go into the yard where the garages are, and stand with his face to the wall until someone comes for him.'

Corey raised the binoculars again. 'Challenge. Yeah. Right . . .'

Adrian Ryan stood facing a brick wall. The noon sun cast his shadow at his feet. Sweat ran down the back of his neck. He felt in his trouser pocket for a handkerchief. Suppose someone comes? he thought, wiping his face. People must get their cars out all the time. What am I going to say if someone asks me what I'm doing?

It had been a momentary impulse. Needing to make a phone call on the way back to the Inland Revenue office, he had pulled his car up beside the phone box purely because it was unoccupied. The picture on the white card tucked behind the call board had attracted his attention.

'Stand right where you are,' a female voice said behind him.

His body jerked with surprise. He straightened his shoulders and resolutely stayed facing the wall.

Something hot and smelly dropped over his head. It felt like sacking. A hessian bag? He couldn't see out of it. He lifted his hands to his face.

Something sharp whipped across his knuckles. He yelped.

'I didn't say you could touch that.' The voice was grim. 'Now turn around. And move when I tell you to!'

A hard object poked him in the small of the back. He stumbled forward a surprised step.

'Move!'

Blindfolded and uncertain of his footing, he began to walk. Now it was too late for such doubts, he was suddenly reluctant to proceed. Previously his adventures had been confined to areas on the continent. Or at any rate, outside London. Away from home.

The hard object poked him in the back again. 'Keep moving!'

Corey pulled the heavy curtains over the dormer windows. She switched on the electric light. The bare bulb swung. The bare frame of the spare futon stood alone in the middle of the floor. The only other furniture now was the heavy cross-beams across the centre of the room, with their thick metal ring-bolts.

The last thing she did was check the video camera was recording.

'She's got him!' Nadia whispered from the bedroom door. 'Is the mobile phone on? We'll be in the car. If there's any trouble, shout.'

Corey grinned at the older woman. 'You still don't think I'll go through with this? It's not me who's in trouble. It's him! Whoever he is.'

The outside door opened. Nadia held her finger to her lips. She silently pulled open the bedroom door and allowed Shannon to come in. A man preceded her. He had a casual jacket on now. Folds of thick sacking had been thrown over his head.

'Stop!' Shannon snapped. The man halted instantly. Shannon broke into a huge grin. She reached past him and handed Corey the short-thonged whip. Corey waved both of the other women away. Both of them backed out of the room in exaggerated silence, tiptoeing. Corey marched over and slammed the door.

His whole body startled.

Corey paced back across the room until she stood in front of the blind-folded man. She bent down and picked a pair of padded manacles off the bed. Then she gripped the man tightly by his left wrist. His muffled head swung wildly, as if attempting to see.

He didn't try to take the bag off. He didn't move his arm.

His wrist was thick and corded with muscle. Corey snapped one manacle shut around it. She reached over and grabbed his other wrist.

'H-hello?' he whispered.

The second manacle snapped shut and locked. Eighteen inches of chain swung between his two wrists.

'Hello, is anyone there?'

She took a firm grip on the metal chain and yanked. He stumbled forward. She prodded him with the whip handle, steering him through the door into the far room.

Corey reached up and snatched the sacking off his head.

The man blinked, staring around wildly. Close up, he might have been five or six years older than her. His red hair was ruffled up by the sacking. His face shone pink and hot. He blinked, and then his eyes fixed on her.

Corey put one hand on her hip. She let the thongs of her whip trail down her thigh. She wore extremely tight leather jeans. She saw his eyes move down to her high-laced combat boots, and then back up to the heavy-buckled belt at her waist. Above it, her breasts were tightly lashed into a leather bustier. It laced up, and it was at least a size too small. Her white flesh squeezed out from between the lacing, and her breasts were pushed up high out of its cups.

Her black hair was slicked straight back. She wore mirrorshades.

'Oh dear.' The man's tenor voice was unsteady. 'I'm

very sorry. I think there's been some kind of a mistake.'

Corey said nothing. She looked him in the eyes. He stood with his manacled hands held slightly away from his body, as if they had nothing to do with him. The colour had left his cheeks.

'Mistake,' he repeated. 'This sort of place . . . I didn't understand, or I wouldn't have come here. It's a mistake.'

'Oh, I don't think so.'

She saw how he almost flinched at the sound of her voice. 'What do you mean? Please, take these things off me.'

Corey kept her gaze on him. She walked a few paces to the left, a few paces to the right, the thongs of the whip stroking her leather-clad thigh. 'So it's a mistake, is it? I'll tell you what. You say to me, "I swear I don't want to be in chains," and I'll take them off you.'

She waited.

His gaze dropped. After a moment, a tide of red rose up out of the neck of his shirt. It flamed his cheeks, and he coloured right up to his hairline.

'No!' he protested finally. 'I *don't* want to be! This sort of thing doesn't do anything for me!'

'And you just phoned out of curiosity. Just to see what it's like. And now you're here,' Corey purred, 'you don't like it. The little boy wants to go home.'

He had very pale blue eyes, she saw, as he lifted his head again. They flashed now. 'Let me go!'

'Don't you think it's a little bit . . . late . . . for that?'

He backed away slowly, staring at her as if hypnotised. The bare brick wall hit him smack between the shoulder-blades. She noticed he didn't try for the door. Safe word, she reminded herself. *Blue.* Hey. He's really into this. This is going to be easy.

This is going to be fun.

She swung the whip against her thigh. The dozen thongs lashed the leather. He winced. She felt a spreading warmth in the pit of her sex. Her eyes began to gleam.

His voice rose. 'You can't keep me here against my will!'

Corey took three paces forward across the bare floorboards. She reached out and caught the chain of the manacles, and jerked it suddenly towards her. She didn't have to pull hard. The stocky man came forward with her movement. He tripped, then, and fell to the floor in front of her. Corey released the chain.

'Don't—' He rolled on to his back. His manacled hands went over his head.

She stood over him and kicked his hands away. 'I didn't give you permission to speak. I didn't give you permission to move. I certainly didn't give you permission to come here with your pathetic little excuses and expect me to believe you. *Get up!*'

He scrambled back on to his feet with his tie askew. The top button of his shirt burst open. Dust marked the knees of his grey slacks. Corey lifted her hand. He quite definitely flinched.

Safe behind the mirrorshades, Corey smiled like a shark. She finished her movement. She tugged his tie straight, and pulled up the shoulder of his check jacket where it was slipping down. She patted his cheek, once, just hard enough to sting.

'Why so worried, little man? I haven't done anything to you – yet.'

'I have to get back to work.'

'I don't think so.'

'You *can't* keep me here!'

'Oh, but I can. Forever, if I like. You don't even know where you are.'

Corey moved a pace closer. The hot, enclosed

dormer room brought a sheen of sweat to her flesh. She stood close to him, her breasts almost touching his chest. His eyes flicked downward. Then he shut them and turned his head away, blushing furiously. Something nudged against Corey's leather-clad stomach.

She let him see her look down and stare at the hard-on in his pants. When she raised her gaze once more, his face was burning. He squeezed his eyes shut.

'You've been lying to me . . .' She let her voice caress him. Then she snapped, 'Down!'

'What?' He opened his eyes. 'I don't know what you mean.'

'Yes you do. You're going to be punished for coming here. You're going to be punished for lying about coming here. And you're going to be punished a *lot* for getting hard without permission. It's all adding up, *boy*.' She let the last word crack. 'What have you got to say for yourself?'

He hung his head sulkily. 'Nothing, I suppose.'

'I don't think you understand where you are,' Corey said. She let the silence stretch. Then, softly, she said, 'You're mine, now.'

He raised his head. His eyes met hers. He moved his hands apart to gesture, and the manacle chain snapped taut, restraining his wrists. He opened his mouth as if to speak. Corey stared him in the eye, knowing he saw only faceless mirrorshades. His colour had subsided now. He paled.

'Please . . .'

Slowly, awkwardly, he sank to his knees on the bare boards in front of her. He bowed his head. His knees were apart, his chained wrists hanging between them. She had to strain to hear his voice. It was barely a whisper.

'Please.' He held up his chained wrists. 'Please! Let me go.'

She said nothing. She waited. At last he forced himself to look up at her. He was sweating again, and his eyes were wild. The lump in the front of his trousers was bigger than before.

Huskily, he said, 'What are you going to do to me?'

'I'm going to give you a lesson. I'm going to teach you to speak the truth.' Corey reached down to grab his chain. Her straining breasts in the leather bustier brushed across his face. She heard him gasp. She twisted her hand in the chain and tugged it up. He staggered to his feet.

She gave him a hard shove. He staggered towards the centre of the room. Corey followed, leisurely. He backed away from her. One of the cross-beams arrested his progress. His heels skidded on the boards, as if he would have backed away through solid wood if he could.

'Now drop your pants,' Corey ordered.

'What?'

'You heard me.'

He drew himself up. Now she was close, it was very apparent he was bigger and heavier than her. She let herself smile.

'You know my name,' she said softly. 'What is it?'

The man, Adrian, locked gazes with her. A stranger, in these few minutes grown very well known: the ruffled, sweaty hair falling into his eyes, the weak mouth, the body that almost imperceptibly trembled. After a minute his shoulders slumped. '"Mistress",' he said.

Her sex throbbed. I've learned, she thought. And one of the things I've learned is, turnabout is fair play.

'I think I'll punish you for not using my name before,' Corey said. 'And for not obeying all my orders, instantly. You *will* obey me. Do you really want to find out what I'll do if you disobey me again?'

This time his voice was clearer, if no louder. 'No, mistress.'

'Then drop your trousers when I tell you!' She smiled. 'I'm not going to do it for you. You're going to do it all on your own.'

She stroked the thongs of the whip up between his thighs. His face paled, and he gasped. The crotch of his trousers strained. In acute discomfort, he said, 'But, mistress, you see what a state I'm in.'

'I didn't tell you to talk!'

She flicked her wrist. The dozen short thongs of the whip lashed, catching him across the front of both his thighs. His cock jumped in his pants.

'I'm sorry!' he gasped. He lifted his chained hands to his trouser belt. He stopped. 'You're not – the mistress isn't even going to look away?'

'Drop your pants.'

He unbuckled his belt. Reluctantly, he unzipped his fly. He shot an imploring glance at her. Corey remained impassive. Slowly, he pushed his trousers down from his waist. They slid down to his ankles. His body was white, his legs long, hard and hairy. Now all he wore below the waist were white boxer shorts, with a huge erection poking out of the front of the material.

'Did I give you permission to do that?' She pointed at his cock.

'No, mistress. I can't help it!'

'Why not?' She grinned at his silence. 'I know why. You know what I'm going to do to you. And you want me to do it. You're hard because you want it. Isn't that right?'

'No,' he protested furiously. His colour was high. He stood with his trousers around his ankles, wrists chained together. 'I don't want anything done to me!'

Corey reversed the whip and slid the hard handle

up the inside of his hairy thigh. She slipped it under the leg of his shorts, and pushed it between his legs, pushing aside his balls. She felt with the hard end of it for his anus. Holding the handle between his legs she grinned, and very slightly lifted.

'No!' He was up on the balls of his feet. His back rubbed against the wooden cross-beam.

She teased the puckered hole with the end of the whip handle. His legs clamped together and his eyes jammed shut. In a strangled voice he whispered, 'Mistress, no!'

'Yes.' She drew the whip handle out. Very lightly, she lashed him across the front of his shorts, and his huge erection. He gasped and bit his lip.

She hooked the handle of the whip over the front of his boxer shorts and pulled them down. The material hung up on his cock. She yanked it free. His erect cock was not large, no more than five inches long, but it was fat and purple and thick. The head oozed a drop of clear liquid.

'Turn around,' she said softly.

He shuffled round, his feet tangled in his clothing, until he was facing away from her. A hot pink colour crept up the back of his neck. He stood there in shirt, tie and jacket, his hands chained, naked from the waist down.

Corey roughly pushed him forwards over the horizontal bar. It was high enough to catch him across the stomach. He bent forward, his buttocks straining. Swiftly Corey ducked under the bar. She rapidly unlocked one manacle, yanked hard, threaded the chain doubled under the lower beam, and locked it around his wrists again. It brought him much further up over the bar. He grunted as he rose on tiptoe.

Swiftly, she cuffed his ankles to the lower beam, threading the chain through ring-bolts. He could move his feet perhaps eight inches apart, no more.

Adrian jerked his hands. The chain had no slack, it was absolutely taut. Now that his hands were chained under the second bar, he was completely unable to straighten up. She saw him realise this. The bar she had bent him over was high enough to be uncomfortable.

'Listen—' He twisted his head round, saw her face, and added, 'um, mistress. I've been punished. You don't have to punish me any more. I suppose I've been humiliated. Now you can just let me go, all right?' His voice lifted on a slightly aggressive note.

Corey smiled. 'You're not very bright, are you?'

She walked behind him, where he would find it difficult to see her, and studied his jutting arse. His hard cock was being crushed between his belly and the wide wooden bar. All the muscles of his legs were under tension as he strained upwards with his toes to keep his body from painfully crushing his cock.

'You're still lying to your mistress,' she said.

'I'm not!'

Corey turned around. She lay down on the bare frame of the futon, on her side, where she could study his upside-down red face. She could see it between his legs. Slowly she undid the buckle of her belt.

She said, 'I'm not going to do anything to you now. Until you beg me to.'

His hot, flustered expression did not benefit from being upside-down. Chains scraped wood as he wrenched his wrists from side to side. One toe slipped. He groaned and scrabbled for a foot-hold, trying to take his body-weight off his cock and balls.

Corey slid her hand down the front of her leather jeans.

'Nothing,' she said, 'until you beg me to do it. And you have to say every word.'

'*Let me go!*'

'No, I don't think so.' Her fingers slid down under the taut leather. The tip of her middle finger found her clitoris. She began slowly to rotate her hand. She could not keep her hips still. She did not try.

'Stop it,' he yelled. 'Oh God, stop it, you're making me hard!'

Corey arched her back. Spasms of pleasure flooded her sex. She withdrew her hand.

'I don't hear you asking,' she said lightly. She re-buckled her belt and began stroking the thongs of the whip between her thighs. Suddenly she rolled over and stood up.

'That's me done.' She jingled the key. 'Sure you don't have anything to say? OK. I'll unlock those cuffs, then.'

'What? No! I mean – that is – oh, hell!'

He slumped forward over the bar.

'Yes?' she enquired.

He said something inaudible.

Corey squatted down beside him. 'I don't think I heard that.'

'I said, I want you to do it.' Colour flamed under his skin. He was sweating. 'Mistress, please. Don't make me say it. Don't humiliate me like this!'

'Tell me that you want it.'

His voice dropped to a rough whisper. 'I – yes. All right, damn you! I want it!'

'Now tell me what you want me to do to you. In detail. Out loud. Otherwise – nothing.'

He hung over the wooden beam, his wrists shackled to the floor. Two buttons had come off his shirt now, and that garment and his jacket were soaked with sweat. His tie had come undone. His bare white bottom jutted up over the bar, and his trousers and pants tangled around his ankles. His taut legs shook with the strain of supporting himself on tiptoe. He hung his flushed, sweating head down.

He forced the words out. 'I want you to whip me.'

'How?'

'Hard,' he whispered.

'Where?'

'On my arse, and on my cock and balls.'

'And why?'

He squeezed his eyes tight shut. 'Because I get hard when you humiliate me, mistress. Damn you, do it to me, *I like it!*'

'Six of the best!' Corey snapped the whip. The short thongs lashed his taut, quivering buttocks. A bright pink stripe burned against his white skin. She drew her hand back. The second blow lashed his other buttock. His body jerked, leaping up from the bar.

'Filth!' she snarled. 'Scum!'

'Yes!' he yelled. 'I am! Please, no more, no more!'

'Too late now.' She drew her arm back to her shoulder and lashed down. The flesh on both his buttocks burned pink. His cock swelled against the wooden bar, and he forced himself up on the toes of his brown shoes. Corey flicked the thongs lightly against his balls.

'I told you, you're mine. Anything I want to do to you, I'll do. And you're going to kiss the whip afterwards and thank me – aren't you?'

'Yes!' His body bucked to the lash. Now he squirmed away from the leather. His buttocks and thighs glowed pink.

As Corey lifted her hand for the last time and lashed him across both buttocks, his legs straightened, his chains drew taut, his body momentarily came free of the bar, and a stream of come sprayed up in an arc from his straining cock. His hips banged the wood as he pumped, hard, in the final spasms.

'Oh God . . .' He sank down until only the chains

and the wooden bar kept him from falling to the floor. White come spattered his shirt and jacket, and dripped from his face.

Corey thrust her fist and the whip under his nose.

When he could speak, he muttered, 'Thank you, mistress.' His lips touched the whip handle.

Corey knelt down and took the manacles off his wrists. He collapsed on to the floorboards.

While he was still there, on his back, chest rapidly rising and falling, she bent down and took the white card out of his inside jacket pocket.

'What?' he raised his head.

Corey shredded the card and tossed it into a corner of the room. She smiled. He still hadn't seen her eyes, or her face, properly. All he could see were reflections in her mirrorshades of his own dishevelled body.

'Won't the mistress see me again?' He rose up on to his knees with difficulty. She realised he was not so much kneeling to her as momentarily unable to get up. His voice changed. 'You're . . . Look, let me come and see you again. I don't care what you want, you can have it. Just – let me come back.'

She looked into his pale blue, desperate eyes. She began to smile. She threw him the hessian sacking. 'Put that on, little boy.'

She reached out and turned the mobile phone off before she said, 'You might be back. You can always dream.'

Chapter Eleven

THE SCREEN FLICKERED to silver-grey as Corey Black's videotape ran out.

Shannon became aware that she was squirming in her seat. She stood up abruptly, and crossed her living-room to pop out the tape.

I never thought I'd be turned on by that sort of thing. But then, when we were listening to it over the mobile phone ...

The sound quality on the video was distorted: you couldn't tell it was Corey's voice. Sitting in the Rover, on the sun-hot leather upholstery, it had been very clear that it was the younger woman's voice. Both she and Nadia had sat silently listening, first with curiosity, then distaste, then amusement; and then with what Shannon recognised in herself as growing arousal.

Nadia had not spoken. She had pressed the button and put the window as far down as it would go. The midday streets were hot. There was no cool breeze.

As a dare, it's going to take some beating. And I bet it cheered Corey up after that visit from Patricia!

Shannon Garrett stood in her terraced house living-room. She tapped the edge of the cassette tape case gently against her lip. An idea flickered across her mind – almost too quick to catch.

She began to smile. A slow smile, but it grew until her lips pulled back wolfishly from her teeth. She nodded her head. *Yes. Oh yes. If we can bring it off . . .*

It took her two goes to key Nadia Kay's number on the dial-recall.

'Nadia? It's Shannon. Yes. Look, I've had an idea, and I know how to make it work, it just came to me in a flash, the whole thing, I just – what? OK. Slowly. I've had an idea. Yes, it's a dare. No, for Corey. I know, but I think she'll like this one. I want to talk it through with you first, though.

'Why will she like it? Because I *think* I've just solved her problems with her ex in-laws.'

'It'd never work!' Corey gaped. 'And how are you going to—'

'Leave the practicalities to me.' Shannon grinned.

'I've already done a dare!'

Nadia Kay said, 'Then it gives you an extra chance to win. What do you say? Don't tell me Shannon's come up with a dare too outré even for you?'

Corey narrowed her blue eyes. 'I'll take that as a compliment. Look – if you prove to me this can be done, I'll do it! But I don't see *how*.'

Ben Bright checked his stride when he saw the white paper caught under the Saab's windscreen wiper.

'Not another damn ticket!' He opened the door and slung his case on to the back seat. Then he reached over the hood and tore the paper out from under the wiper. He bent down slightly to glance at the wheels.

No clamp.

Well, then, things could be worse. And the paper was just that, just a sheet of paper without a plastic cover – fly-sheet advertising, no doubt. Now he came to look, most of the cars parked nearby appeared to have a copy under their wipers.

'Bloody nerve!'

His brain registered the words written on the paper just as he crumpled it up. He stopped. Carefully he unfolded the ball of crumpled paper. A photocopy, yes.

Half a dozen words were followed by a mobile phone number.

Ben slowly sat down in the driver's seat. After a minute he pulled his legs into the car and shut the door. Metal and glass enclosed him in a soundless world. He stared out through the windscreen at the sunlit London road. The pedestrians walking past him might have been on Mars.

I swore I wouldn't do it again. Someone might find out. I can't risk it!

His cream-coloured Armani suit was light enough for the summer day, crisp and creaseless. The knot of his silk tie felt momentarily constricting. He put both hands on the wheel, looking at his Rolex watch.

I could spare two hours. If they could take me now. The amount I can pay, they can damn well take me!

He reached out for the mobile phone.

It took him half an hour of cutting up London traffic, the cooler on full blast, before he found the back street to which he was being directed. The usual run-down area. Almost leafy. A line of houses subdivided into flats and maisonettes; nearly-new cars with off-road parking on concrete frontages.

He parked the car two streets away. The briefcase got locked in the boot. Nothing much of interest in it. He removed from the boot a full sports-bag.

All right. I doubt that I completely discarded the idea that I would do this again. Otherwise why would I keep the bag here?

Bright sunlight dazzled off the pavements. He put on his Raybans. He walked through a darker world, looking for the flat number. There was no name under the bell. He buzzed and gave his first name. The lock clicked open.

The stairs inside were moderately clean. A skylight illuminated the stairwell. His shoes made no noise on the threadbare carpet as he climbed to the top floor. A familiar tightness in his breathing made him stop, and stare upwards.

I can go back. I'm not going to do this again, am I? Oh God, I swore I wouldn't! If Mummy ever finds out . . .

The sports-bag bumped his leg. Prompted, he began to climb again, until he stood on a small landing on the third floor.

Something lay on the mat outside the door. A silk scarf, long and black. There was a piece of paper lying on top. He picked it up, recognising the same handwriting that had printed the handbill. It was succinct.

Put on the blindfold. Knock.

Excitement curdled in his stomach. The same sensation that he had had as a child, when the roller-coaster at the fair winched its way up to the top of the rails and he sat gripping the bar, knowing that now it was too late, there was no way out, he was helpless in the face of the inevitable plunge over the edge.

He put down his bag with shaking hands. He bent and picked up the silk scarf, and wound it around his eyes. He knotted it. Then he reached out and fumbled for the memorised position of the bell. It rang loudly enough to make him jump.

He could not tell the moment when the door opened, if it did. He only knew it must have opened when a hand took his arm and pulled him forward. No word was spoken. He felt himself treading on carpet, then on bare boards; walking quite a way, but he was disorientated now. The hand left his arm.

'Just a moment,' he said. 'Let's discuss your rates and my preferences, before we go any further.'

A husky voice behind him said, 'The ad told you what gets done here. Didn't it?'

Ben Bright swallowed, hard. At last he managed to say, 'Yes. Yes, it did.'

The voice – no, another, different voice – said, 'Then you know all that you need to know. Sit down. Relax. Make yourself comfortable. She'll be ready for you in about five minutes.'

A door closed. He pulled the restraining silk scarf off over his head, in time to see that. Not in time to see who had shut it, they were gone. He nervously finger-combed his hair straight.

The room was hot. Bare brick walls at both ends, rafters and plaster above, and bare planks underneath. Obviously a dormer room, but swept and clean. Curtains shrouded the windows. A high-wattage bulb burned. Horizontal wooden cross-beams divided the room halfway down.

Ben brushed the cream cuffs of his Armani suit. There was a futon base on the floor, the wooden slats bare. A high-backed wooden chair stood beside it. Next to that, on a small table, a large jug of clear liquid and ice stood with a glass. He crossed the room, poured some out, and tasted it. Water. There was a small flask, which proved to contain coffee; and a cup. Apart from that, nothing.

His Rolex ticked the passing time away.

As always, he began to take fright. What if they're a crooked set-up? What if they've just – gone away? He did not quite dare try the door. He sat on the wooden chair and drank the water, and then, as time went by, the cooling coffee. No sounds came from the other room.

And what about the sports-bag, containing his change of clothes? He should have made it clear he wanted to change into his favoured old suit first.

How can they treat a paying customer like this? It's ridiculous! Anger gave him courage to approach the door. He heard noises from the far side of it.

'Put the blindfold on, lovey,' a woman's voice called. It was oddly reassuring how motherly she sounded. Ben pulled the silk scarf out of his pocket and re-fastened it. He heard the door open.

A hand took his arm again. It did not lead him out of the room he was in. Instead, he was sure, it led him further down into the centre of that room. A tug on his sleeve arrested his progress. Something hard banged his shin. He swore, coarsely. Something hard and metallic clamped around his right ankle. There was a harsh, metallic *clang!*

'Oh, now, look!' He reached up with both hands and pulled the silk scarf down. 'That's *quite* enough. This is ridiculous. You haven't even asked me what I want—' His voice died away as it caught up with his brain.

Two women faced him. Both wore identical jeans and summer T-shirts, of blue denim and white cotton. The one on the left was taller and slimmer. Other than that, he could not tell them apart. Both had the hairy heads and fanged muzzles of wolves.

Ben stared at the women wearing the joke-shop werewolf masks.

He went to take a pace forward and wrenched his leg. He looked down.

'Good – God!' There was a chain going through a ring bolt on the lowest wooden beam. It pulled taut between the ring bolt and his ankle. Around his ankle, over his dark blue silk sock, was a fleece-padded metal cuff an inch or so thick. He jerked his leg hard. Even with the padding, the metal dug painfully into his skin. 'Take that off me, you bitches!'

He swung round, breathing heavily. The two women had not moved.

Then he saw that one of them was holding a palm-sized camcorder.

'Put that down,' he said authoritatively. 'Right, I want that turned off *now*, do you understand? I thought you'd learnt better in this kind of business! What about client anonymity?' he bristled.

The taller woman spoke softly. The latex wolf mask blurred her voice. He could just make out her words. 'We find our clients pay well – for anonymity.'

'Oh, that's it, is it? You think you can blackmail me.' His confident tone was a triumph of effort. He shrugged, and leaned back nonchalantly against the waist-high wooden beam. 'Go ahead. Nothing's going to happen. You can't *make* me cooperate.'

At that, the shorter of the wolf women went over to the table. She upended the water jug. Only one drip fell out on to the dusty floorboards. Her louder and harsher voice said, 'You already have cooperated, I'd say. Wouldn't you?'

'I would, yes.'

'What?' Even without seeing either of their faces, he could hear from their tone that they were grinning. Smirking. It began to infuriate him that he couldn't see them. He took a firm pace forward. The chain jerked taut. He almost fell. 'Bloody damn bitches!'

One folded her arms. The other adjusted (with some difficulty, because of the mask) the focussing of the camcorder.

Ben Bright felt a heaviness in his bladder.

Sweat broke out over his forehead. No, no, not like

this! His mind protested; and some distant, traitorous part of his brain whispered slyly. *But this is what you came for. You always swear you'll never do it again, and you always, always do. Why not – enjoy it?*

'No!' He didn't know who he shouted at, himself or the masked women. He shifted uncomfortably from foot to foot. 'I, um, I want you to take this thing off my leg. We can talk about money, whatever you want, just – I want to leave the room.'

'That's sad,' the soft voice whispered through a wolf-mask.

'Tough,' the abrasive one said.

The pressure from his bladder became an undeniable strain. Something in the water, he thought wildly. One part of his mind admired the set-up of the operation. *Golden showers, the hand-bill had read. Toilet training and discipline.*

'Just get the damn camera out of here!' he hissed. 'Look, you've obviously got a very professional operation here, which I'll pay well for, just turn that thing off!'

The taller and thinner of the masked women moved down the room. He noticed she stayed well out of arm's reach.

'Look,' he said, 'let me go. You haven't let me change. For God's sake, this is an Armani suit! This isn't fair. You know I'd pay you well for the real thing, done properly. Look, I know you've put something in the water. Let me get changed quickly.'

He became aware that he was shifting from foot to foot. He forced himself to stand still. The pressure in his bladder was now a pain. The whole bottom half of his body tensed.

'Put your hands behind your back,' her voice said behind him. He hesitated. She said, 'Do you want to be freed or not? Do it!'

629

'I don't see how, what . . .' Reluctantly, he placed his hands in the small of his back. 'What are you doing? What – no!'

Two smart metal clicks sounded. He furiously yanked his wrists apart. Unpadded metal cut into his skin. He swore. He tried to lift his arms over his head, and failed; tried to push them down where he could step over them, and became helplessly entangled in the chain on his ankle. Panting, hair dishevelled, he straightened up. His hands were cuffed tightly behind his back.

The taller woman paced back down the room. She seated herself on the wooden chair. Her wolf mask moved in the direction of the woman with the camcorder. 'I lied,' she said. 'I don't think we should let him go.'

The second woman's voice was softer now. 'I'd let him go.'

'You would?'

'I'd let him go if he told us what he came here to do. In detail. Don't you think?'

'Oh, maybe if he did that.' Both wolf masks turned to face him. Behind the latex, eyes glinted in shadow. Painted white teeth gleamed. 'Maybe.'

He froze, thinking, If I keep very, very still, I may be all right. And if this is what it takes to get me out . . .

He cleared his throat. In a strangled voice, he muttered, 'Water sports. I came for water sports.'

The other woman got up from the chair. She moved back towards the far wall, towards a curtain. Appalled, he thought, She's going to open a window? Before he could speak, she thrust the curtain back.

It was not a window. The curtain concealed a full length mirror.

Ben Bright stared into it. The same bare attic room was reflected, lit by the brilliance of the electric bulb.

The difference was that now he could see the white-suited, tethered figure in the centre of the room. He looked from chained ankle to the arms that he could not bring out from behind his back. He looked up, into his own wide, scared gaze. A man in his late twenties, sharp-suited, smart, with every quality accessory. Chained to a wooden beam like a dog.

'Water sports? You'll have to be more explicit,' the wolf with the camcorder said.

Ben couldn't take his eyes off the man in the mirror. He was standing with such a tense stillness, every muscle locked in place. Now he coloured a bright, ashamed crimson, his fair skin flaring from neck to hairline. 'Let me go!'

'What did you come here for?'

'If I say, will you let me go?' he pleaded.

'Of course.' The seated wolf-woman was businesslike. 'Say we're having our first interview. You're here to tell me what you like. Tell me.'

He bowed his head. 'I . . . like to be pissed on.'

'And?'

'And I like . . . to be trained.' Now he could not look his reflection in the eye. 'To piss in my pants and be spanked.'

The room was quiet except for the camcorder's hum.

'Now will you let me go?' he said. He locked his thigh muscles, his buttocks, anything to ease the pressure of his bladder. One of the women laughed. He looked up.

'You're going to piss in your pants,' the taller woman said. 'But first you're going to ask permission. You don't want to know what happens if you do it without permission.'

'But I have to go!' He could see his own wild face in the mirror. Under the urgent desire to urinate, another arousal pushed at his consciousness. The traitor part of his mind said, They do it so well. You might never get another chance like this.

He tugged at his wrists. Immobile. He stared at the mirror. In a slow, cracked voice, he said, 'Please . . . may I piss?'

'Not enough.'

He swallowed, trying to make his mouth less dry. 'Turn the camera off.'

'No.'

Desperation cracked his voice. 'Please . . . may I piss in my pants?'

His crotch tingled. Without warning, and without volition, he let a small stream of piss dribble from his cock. In the mirror, the chained young man stared down. A small dark patch seeped through the crotch of his trousers.

'Oh dear,' cooed the tall masked woman. 'Oh dear . . .'

'I can't hold it!' he groaned. With that he let go and pissed. A heavy warm stream gushed down his thighs. He saw in the mirror the thick golden stream running out of the leg of his trousers. A vast wet patch soaked the crotch and thighs of his pale suit. He squeezed his eyes shut. Acrid hot piss streamed down his legs for what seemed like minutes.

At last the flow eased.

He shifted carefully from one foot to the other. His eyes were still closed tight. Both his socks squelched in his shoes. The wet cloth of his trousers cooled rapidly. Cold wet cloth slid across his crotch as he moved.

His cock twitched, and stiffened.

Shame heated his face. I can't! he thought. This can't be happening to me!

He opened his eyes. He saw in the mirror what the masked woman must be recording with the camcorder. A young man standing with his hands behind his

632

back, the fly and crotch and legs of his suit soaking wet, and the start of an erection poking out the sopping material.

'Oh, dear God,' he said wretchedly.

The taller wolf-woman said, 'He was being truthful. He does like it.'

'Please,' he said miserably, 'I'll do whatever you want, just give me that film, you can do what you like to me, just, please, don't—'

He stopped begging. His cock was getting harder with every word. He shifted damply from foot to foot, staring around, pretending that he was not here, that this was not happening to him.

It didn't work.

I'm on the roller-coaster now, he thought. Childhood memories became stronger. He had pissed his first long trousers on the roller-coaster at the fair, and his mother had raged coldly at him, and nanny had been ordered to lead him back to the car. Through the crowds. With his wet crotch clearly visible to everybody. It would teach him (she said icily) not to do it again.

Ben opened his eyes. He dismissed the camera with a kind of reckless mental shrug: it's done now. They already have enough for blackmail.

I might as well enjoy the rest.

'I wet my pants,' he whined. He noted the two of them glance at each other again. An air of relaxation came over both. The one with the camcorder circled. 'I wet my pants when you said I shouldn't.'

'Then you're a bad boy,' the tall woman said.

A delicious feeling twisted his stomach. His cock hardened in his wet trousers.

'First,' she ordered, 'you can sit in it.'

'But, please—'

'Little boys must be taught!' She walked around

633

behind him. A few seconds later he felt the right handcuff snap open, and then the left. The cuff on his ankle loosened.

He stood with his arms loose by his sides for a moment. Then, he sank slowly to his knees, and sat down on the urine-wet floorboards. The wood pressed the wet cloth of his trousers up into his crotch. He squirmed.

'I sat in my piss. I sat in my wet pants,' he said. 'Mummy, what do I do now?'

The taller wolf-woman sat on the wooden chair. 'Come and stand here in front of me.'

He walked across the room, stiff-legged. The delicious shame coloured his cheeks. He wanted to wallow in it, rejoice in the freedom.

'Now bend over.'

He felt tears begin to run down his cheeks. Snot leaked out of his nose. He didn't wipe it away. 'No, Mummy, please.'

'You're standing there with your pants soaking wet. Look at that.' She slapped his crotch. His rigid cock throbbed. He bit his lip, almost coming. 'Call that tiny thing a dick? You're a very bad little boy. You have to be punished.'

'Don't hit me, Mummy, please don't.' He snivelled in joyous abandon.

He felt her grab his wrist and pull him down. Her grip shifted to the back of his belt. He fell forward across her lap. There was a short hiatus. He cringed in anticipation.

Her palm caught him hard and squarely across the buttocks. Once, twice, three times.

Helplessly, joyously, sprawled across her, knowing the camcorder must be recording every detail of his humiliation, he came in his pants.

When his last jerking spasms subsided, he fell to the

floor. His come cooled on his limp cock, in his ruined suit trousers. His heaving chest subsided. Airless heat made sweat run down his shaven cheeks, mingling with dust, so that when h,e rubbed his suit sleeve across his face it came away filthy.

He lifted his head just far enough that he could reach over and kiss the toe of the taller woman's shoe.

She reached up and pulled off the latex werewolf mask.

Black, sweaty hair stuck out from her head. White powder dusted it. Her cheeks, with a similar white film of talcum powder from the mask over them, were nonetheless pink with heat. Her eyes shone and danced. Her mouth curved in a wide, wicked, brattish grin.

'Oh my God.' All the breath went out of his lungs. For one moment he fell back on the floorboards, perfectly still. The cream-coloured Armani suit clung wetly to his crotch and legs.

'Omigod . . .' Ben clamped his arms over his head.

He was not aware he had curled up into a tight foetal ball until he felt a hand – her hand – pulling at his shoulder.

He pushed his head further into the darkness of his body and whimpered.

'Ben!'

'I don't believe it.' Tears ran down his cheeks. He uncurled slightly. A wave of heat went from his head to his toes.

With a pathetic attempt at dignity, he got up. He stood in the bare attic room. He tugged helplessly at one creased cuff. His click remained completely limp: his humiliation too deep even for arousal. He couldn't look at his ex-wife.

When she spoke, her voice was oddly soft. 'Hello, Ben.'

He yelled, in anguish, 'How could you do this to me!'

'You're going to tell me you didn't like it?'

'Of *course* I didn't like it! All right – I did. But I didn't know it was you!'

She chuckled. When he raised his head, her smile was rueful.

'You can have a copy of the tape as a souvenir, if you like.'

'What do you want, Corey?' He blushed. 'I admit the settlement after the divorce was shabby. That wasn't entirely up to me, you know. I didn't think you'd stoop to blackmail.'

'I don't want money.' Her voice chilled. Then she relaxed, and he remembered, looking at her clear-skinned face, that she could not be any older than twenty-two, even now; hardly older than that day in the registry office when she was eighteen.

He made to step closer. The slimy material of his suit trousers slid up into his crotch.

'Let me go and change,' he pleaded. 'What do you want, Corey?'

'Nothing.' Her voice became hard. 'I get along fine without you in my life. I would get along even better if your mother kept her nose out of my life. I think you ought to suggest she doesn't call me, or come round here, Ben. I think you ought to suggest that very strongly indeed. OK?'

A few hours afterwards, Nadia closed the shop and went back over to Corey's flat. Shannon met her outside and they went in.

'Edited highlights,' Corey said as she put an unlabelled video cassette down on the table. 'There's about ten minutes of really juicy stuff.'

'Edited?' Shannon queried. She flexed her fingers, cramped from holding the camcorder.

'Oh, well . . .' The younger woman looked curiously shame-faced. 'I blacked his head out, OK?'

Nadia raised one dark red eyebrow.

'Ben won't be giving me any more hassle. I guess I think he's suffered enough.' The young woman's expression hardened. 'This one isn't for Ben. It's for Patricia.'

The three women looked at each other.

Shannon said, 'You're right, this one's better for our purposes. Nadia – over to you.'

'Hello? Is that the Conway Hall? I wonder if you can help me. I understand a Mrs Patricia Bright is giving a talk – to the women's charity groups, yes, that's right. A video presentation. Could you tell me when that is, please? The twenty-fourth. That's this Wednesday, isn't it? At seven-thirty. Thank you very much indeed.'

Nadia Kay crossed Red Lion Square in the evening sunlight and made her way to the entrance of the Conway Hall. She wore a light cotton dress in a Laura Ashley print, and flat sandals, and carried a green clutch bag; her make-up was elegant and discreet.

The woman at the door of the main hall smiled automatically but didn't give her a second look.

Nadia kept the smile off her face. The wooden chairs were filling rapidly. Patricia Bright and two other women were up on the stage. The sounds of a low-key altercation about the portable widescreen colour monitor's position drifted down into the audience.

Nadia, looking blamelessly middle-class, and well as though she might be a patron of a charity group, walked down to the front, and along the back of a row of chairs, and past the video tapedeck on the side of the stage.

She didn't look around. She took the videotape in its

cardboard box off the chair it waited on, and put it into her clutch-bag, and set her own equally anonymous tape down in its place. She took a seat five chairs away down the row. No one spoke to her. No one looked in her direction.

The clock ticked towards seven-thirty.

A woman in a pale pink cardigan came and poked at the innards of the video machine and walked away again. She came back with a brown-haired younger woman. They both peered at the machine. One reached down and popped the tape in. The slot whirred and swallowed it. The younger woman nodded. They both walked away.

Seven-thirty. The hall doors closed. Nadia counted, roughly. Between a hundred and a hundred and twenty middle-class women, most of them slightly better dressed than Patricia Bright.

Nadia sat through the interminable introduction, and Patricia's opening remarks about the worthy poor of Mexico City, without even trying to force herself to listen.

The lights dimmed.

'And now,' Patricia Bright said, 'my little video show.'

'I timed it by the hall clock,' Nadia reported back, hardly able to stand up in the telephone booth. 'Absolute *panic*. She couldn't find the remote to turn it off – or even turn it down. *Nine minutes!*'

Chapter Twelve

THEY MET UP with Nadia Kay in the little upmarket pub at the back of the Conway Hall, rushing in, finding themselves among a crowd of extremely well-dressed women whose conversation (Shannon listened as they pushed towards the bar) revolved in hushed and shocked tones around an 'incident' earlier in the evening.

Shannon rubbed her hand under the bridge of her nose and sniffed, hard. She just managed to keep from laughing.

Nadia signalled from a table at the back of the bar. She was halfway through a slim black cigarette and a brandy. A sheen of sweat covered her forehead. She laughed as Shannon pulled up a plush stool. She reached up to grasp Corey's hand.

'Sweetie, never get me doing anything like that again! I thought I'd wet myself. Oh, but you should have seen their faces!'

'I should have seen Patricia's face,' the young woman commented, fetching a five-pound note out of her leather jacket pocket. 'I wish she did know it was me! Right: who wants what?'

With Corey at the bar, Shannon leaned back in her

wooden chair and concentrated on listening to Patricia Bright's ex-audience. 'How shockingly *unfortunate*,' she murmured, quoting several of the women. 'Nadia, didn't anyone say anything – stop you – see you?'

The red-haired woman shook her head. Her short bob flew. She stroked strands of hair out of the corners of her eyes. 'No. No! It was unbelievable. I suppose people don't notice, that's the truth of it. They don't see anything they don't expect to see.' She threw her head back and laughed. 'It was beautiful. I wish Corey could have seen it.'

The young woman put three glasses neatly on to the table in front of them. 'She's off my back, that's what matters.'

'I don't think you'll hear a whole lot from Ben, either,' Shannon said demurely. 'I do have some good ideas.'

The younger woman grinned, sliding her leather jacket off and hanging it on the back of her chair. The pub's doors were open behind her, letting late evening heat drift in.

'Men!' Nadia said.

A few minutes of peaceful silence ensued. Shannon sipped her wine and soda, and began to feel pleasantly buzzed. The pub noise sounded over her head. Music began to beat from the sound system.

'I've got a dare,' Corey Black said suddenly.

Shannon sat up. She looked at the younger woman, startled.

Corey looked at Nadia.

'I dare *you*,' she said, 'to get your own back on that guy.'

Nadia flushed. 'Which "guy"?'

'Oh, yeah, right. The one you've been whining about ever since you got back from Wiltshire! What do you think, Shannon? Is it a good dare?'

Shannon began to grin.

'We dare you,' she said.

But I don't exactly want to 'get my own back', Nadia thought. I just want to prove a point.

Saturday morning. She drove back early from her father's house in Orpington. She was driving towards rain. Ahead, the sky glowed purple. The sun still shone back brightly from the brick and white plaster walls of houses. Then heavy summer rain-drops began to bounce off the gleaming red bonnet of the MG.

She wound the window up most of the way. Traffic held her up in Brixton. She watched people in light summer clothes crowd into shop doorways. A pair of young black women giggled, holding up plastic carrier bags over their hair, and one of them waved at the sports car and blew Nadia a kiss. She returned it, smiling.

By the time she got to Putney Bridge, buildings gleamed under a clearing sky. Patches of blue showed above the City. She drove towards her flat.

She played her messages when she got in.

Oscar's voice on the answerphone was peevish. '*I do think you might have stayed for my speech last week, Nadia. I know I'm no longer your husband, but it looked bad. I had a hell of a job expinining it to His Excellency. Oh, Diane's back from California, she sends her regards.*' Beeep!

She stretched out a hand to rewind the machine. It beeped again.

'*Sorry, forgot. That customs chap you want to ask about importing antiques from America, his name is Steven Anson. I've got his address here somewhere, hang on—*'

Nadia copied it down on to the phone pad. She smiled as the answer phone beeped and fell silent. Poor Oscar. He probably *does* think I want Steven Anson's address and number for business purposes.

641

Little does he know . . .

Nadia's short red hair shone, slightly dishevelled by driving. The morning light emphasised the faint creases at the corners of her eyes. She stroked a finger along silver-framed photos on the sideboard beside her.

Her finger stopped.

The banner in the picture was for a charity she had raised funds for, not long before she and Oscar were divorced.

Good grief. She blinked at the sudden picture that flashed into her mind.

No. I couldn't. It can't be done!

I wonder. Can it?

It would be ideal . . .

Yes!

She dialled. The deep voice that answered the phone made the pit of her stomach leap.

'Steven,' she said. 'Or is it Steve? Yes. It's me. I'll be at your place in twenty minutes. What? Oh – I'm going to show you who's adventurous.' She listened to the phone quack. 'That's all I'm telling you. No. Now. You can go in on shift, or you can phone in sick and come with me. Choose.'

After a moment, she smiled to herself.

'Good. Twenty minutes. Oh, yes. Wear a track-suit.'

'I phoned the long distance weather forecast,' Nadia said as she slowed the MG to a crawl. 'Fortunately, it's going to be fine all day.'

The hot sun gleamed off the MG's red bonnet as she inched it over the speed bump at the gate in the wire perimeter fence. She sneaked a look at Steve Anson.

The big man sat scrunched down in the car. He wore a scruffy but clean white T-shirt, and blue track-suit bottoms and trainers. His heavily muscled arms glimmered with a faint down that thickened to wiry hairs at his wrists, trapped under his thick watch strap.

'This,' he said. 'Is this where you're bringing me?'

Vast expanses of level green grass stretched out to either side of the single-track tarmac road. With the car going slowly now, there was the hot silence that Nadia had always associated with airfields. Leavesdon Airfield, almost in the middle of Watford, might have been in the middle of Dartmoor for all the human activity visible.

'Look,' she pointed. Over to their right, the bubble-globe of a trainer helicopter gleamed in the noon sun, dipping with great care for a practice-landing. She noted a couple of light planes, Cessnas, waiting to go out. She pulled the sports car off into the car park, on the far side of a thin screen of bushes. Beyond them she could see the single-storey buildings and workshops, and the taller flight tower.

'You're joking.' He looked around and down at her. 'You think we're going to do it in a *plane*?'

'No.' Nadia left it at that. She swung her legs out, got up from the car, and shut its door behind her. She was wearing an olive green track-quit, and very small gold studs in her ears. The wind that always blows across airfields brought the scent of flowers, and aviation fuel, and whipped her red hair forward across her eyes.

'I still know one of the instructors here,' she remarked. Then, leaning one hand on the MG for support, she whooped.

'What's so funny?' the big man demanded.

'Nothing.' She looked up as he came around the car and stood beside her. His thick body smelled slightly of cologne, more of sweat. She rested her hands on his flat stomach, slid them up the T-shirt to his hairy pectorals. 'You look so . . . puzzled.'

'Umm.'

Her hands slid lower, across the sun-warmed cloth of his shirt, down to the waistband of his track-quit. She glanced around, then slid her hand quickly down inside and squeezed his cock. She took her hand out again and inhaled his male scent from her palm. Her flesh swelled and hardened between her legs, and she grew slick.

He put a large hand each side of her head. His rough palms drew her to him, and he touched her lips lightly with his. She inhaled his sweet breath. His lips came down hard. She sucked and bit at his lower lip, tasting him, her body pressed up against him, feeling his hard-on press against her belly through the soft cloth.

'Do you think,' he said raggedly, 'there's anything you'll do that I won't?'

'We'll soon see.' Nadia squeezed his balls lightly through the cloth. 'Better pace yourself, sweets. You have about two hours training to get through first.'

'Training?' he exclaimed loudly. '*Training?*'

'Yeah.' Steve Anson gazed up at.the ninety-foot-tall scaffolding tower. 'Right . . .'

'It's no different from jumping off on to the mat,' Nadia grinned. 'Is it, Frank?'

The bearded instructor chuckled. 'About eighty-six feet different, but it's still the same roll. Remember how you've been taught to fall. The rope and harness simulate the static line jump. That's what you'll be doing later.'

'You go first,' Nadia beamed up at the big man generously. 'I'll watch. I've done this before.'

Once, she added mentally. Now I remember that I don't really *like* heights . . . Whatever possessed me to do this before? There must have been easier ways to raise money than a charity parachute jump.

Steve Anson grunted. She watched him follow the

bearded instructor to the foot of the tower. They both began to climb the steel ladder. It seemed long minutes before they reached the top. There was some delay – you don't realise from down here, she remembered suddenly, that at the top it *shifts* in the wind. Then she saw Steve begin to winch up the rope from the last jump, and saw Frank attach it to his body harness. A rope with enough drag on it to simulate an open parachute.

The sweet, hot air caressed her arms. She spread her track-suit top on the grass and sat down. It will be colder on top of the jump tower. It will be colder in the air.

She deliberately didn't look.

'Hey!' Steve Anson sat down heavily beside her on the grass, some minutes later. 'Just like jumping off on to the gym mat!'

His thick brown hair was windswept, and the sun glinted in its first traces of silver at the temples. His face creased into a big grin. He smelled of exertion now, that male smell that made Nadia want to lean forward and bury her face in his crotch.

'Come on, Miss Kay.' Frank might have been smiling under his beard. 'You don't seem to have forgotten anything. It must be, what, two years? Let's see what you make of the tower.'

Climbing the ladder, she momentarily forgot Steve Anson. She stared down at the mat, below, and thought: Remember how to tuck and roll and fall. I can do this. I have done this. Marcia did it and she's ten years older than I am. Remember to keep my eyes open . . .

'Frank!' She shouted over the wind noise at the top of the tower. 'Can we go up today?'

He squinted at the sky. 'Mmm. About three, I'd say.'

*

The flat-roofed, single-storey building looked as though it had been there since World War II. Nadia entered, avoiding the offices, and made her way down to the canteen. The brick walls were painted white. It had windows in each wall. It was bright, and clean, and it smelled of coffee.

She got sandwiches, and fell into conversation with some of the others there: mostly young men and women, and a couple in their fifties. Steve Anson joined her, seating himself carefully on the wooden straight-backed chair.

'Your mate Frank,' he said, when the conversation drifted away from them – two of the younger women were talking about night-flying in rotary wing aircraft.

'Mmm?'

'He's barking mad, isn't he?'

'No more than anyone who flies.' Nadia smiled. 'There's a certain look in the eye. I've noticed it before. They've all got it. They're extremely careful and responsible people. It's just what they *do*.'

His thigh pressed against hers under the table. 'They're not the only ones with that look,' he rumbled. 'Have you seen yourself in the mirror? Woman, you're mad.'

'Not mad,' Nadia said, 'just mildly annoyed.'

'So you want to test my bottle by seeing if I'll jump out of a plane?'

She muttered tartly, 'Consider yourself lucky I've arranged a parachute.'

Steve threw his head back and guffawed, loudly enough to stop all conversation for a second. She couldn't help grinning. She eased back in her chair, a little bruised and jolted by the training jumps, but relaxed. Her body was at ease with itself, her muscles warmed up; just enough anticipatory nervousness to keep her alert.

'Steve.' She touched his arm.

He had rested his elbows on the formica-topped table. Now he looked at her over the rim of his coffee mug. A dab of milk froth decorated his nose. He grinned. 'What?'

'It isn't vvhether you'll jump Otlt of a plane or not,' Nadia said. 'That's not what I'm interested in. I've had a word with Frank. I think I've talked him into letting me go ahead with this.'

She slid her hand over Steve's warm thigh and into his crotch.

'Tell me,' she said, 'have you ever heard of a tandem jump?'

'You're mad!'

'Completely,' she agreed.

They stood out on the edge of the paved area around the buildings, looking across the airfield runways. Green grass stretched off into the distance. The wind had eased. Somewhere a bird sang.

'A tandem jump is done in a double harness.' She eased her bare arms closer to him, where he leaned on the top bar of the wooden gate. 'Often it's instructor and pupil. It's also a good way for a disabled person to be able to parachute jump. I think I've persuaded Frank we're safe to go tandem.'

Steve Anson gave her a look that was plain bewilderment. 'But . . .'

With confidence and control, Nadia said, 'You jump at ten thousand feet. Static line, square parachute. You have thirty seconds of free-fall. Then there'll be between eight and ten minutes before we have to worry about landing.'

Nadia smiled to herself.

'Track-suits,' she added, 'have no time-consuming belts and zips. You can just pull them down.'

'You *are* mad.'

Around her, now, the air was perfectly still. A hot, windless summer day. Her shadow pooled on the tarmac at her feet. The *whuck-whuck* of a helicopter's rotors sounded from the far side of a hanger. She was silent until it had taken off, the noise thudding away into the distance.

'You don't *have* to do it,' Nadia said.

Nadia slowly pulled on her thin leather gloves.

The aircraft thrummed under her. She sat on the metal-frame set, stomach churning.

'You don't want to skin your hands!' Frank shouted over the engine noise. 'Friction burns can be painful! I'll put you into the harness when we reach ten thousand feet, OK?'

Nadia nodded her head firmly. The air in the body of the plane was chill, through track-suit top and bottom, even with a thick jumper on underneath. The noise was so loud that she could hardly hear herself speak. She sat watching while the bearded instructor put Steve Anson into the double harness: thick nylon straps that encircled his body, came up over his shoulders, around both thighs, and locked centrally at the chest.

'OK?' Frank bawled.

The big man stuck up his thumb.

Using the struts as hand-holds, Frank swung himself forward to the cabin. Nadia saw him leaning over the pilot's shoulder. He tapped the younger man, who half glanced up and slipped one ear-phone off.

Past their heads, through the canopy, she saw a vast sky.

Sharp-edged and perfectly clear, green trees clung to a curved horizon a very long way below. No signs of London. Flying west. And yes, roads down there among the green: one six-lane motorway, a power station on the horizon . . .

A hand grabbed her knee. She jumped.

Steve Anson stroked her cheek. He pointed at the plane's floor, vibrating ten thousand feet above the earth, and his eyebrows went up.

Nadia leaned over and put her mouth to his ear. His flesh was warm under her lips.

'We'll only have five or six minutes to actually do it,' she said. 'Are you up to it?' And she smiled, wickedly.

His lips brushed at her ear. 'You're asking a lot!'

'Perhaps I'd better help you. After all, there won't be any time to spare. You need to be – er – ready to go.' Nadia scrunched up close to him on the wood-covered metal seat. He had put borrowed Doc Marten ankle boots on, and thick leather gloves, and a borrowed thermal track-suit top. Through the cloth, his body had a solid warmth that stirred her groin.

With her eyes on Frank, now leaning on the back of the pilot's seat and looking forward, Nadia spoke into Steve Anson's ear.

'I'd like to have you right here in the plane,' she whispered. 'I'd like to put you down on the floor, and pull your track-suit pants down, and just mount you.'

'Tell me what you'll do.' His breath moistened her cheek. His arm rested down across her back, pressing her into his body.

'I'd stroke your cock, every inch of it. I'd put my hand round, and pull the skin up over your knob, and pull it down; quicker and quicker and quicker. Then I'd straddle you, and push myself down on to you, all hot and wet and swollen with wanting you.'

His breath came raggedly. 'Jesus! Ease up.'

'I'd put my hands under your bum and pull you up inside me. Then I'd gently, gently squeeze.' She stopped, swallowed with a dry mouth. 'I'd put your

649

hands on my breasts. I'd bite your shoulders. I'd feel you thick and hot inside my . . .'

He shifted on the seat, and wiped his hand across his face. 'Oh yeah. I'm ready, all right. Come over here, woman – I've got something for you to sit on!'

'Not right now . . .' Nadia laughed. She looked forward. The plane was still climbing. She sat closer to Steve Anson and the parachute pack fastened to his back, all of them crammed on to a narrow vibrating seat. She squirmed, shifting her pussy on the hard surface.

'We both face forward in the harness,' she said. 'I want to be fucked doggy-style. I'm ready.'

'What if someone sees?'

Nadia gave him a challenging smile. 'What if they do?'

'Okay, people.' The bearded instructor walked back from the front of the plane. 'Time to go.'

Frank's hands buckled the straps of the dual harness around Nadia's body, shoulders and thighs. 'We're at ten thousand feet,' he bawled over the noise. 'Call it a thousand feet a minute, you'll have eight or nine minutes to sight-see. Then think about landing! Remember what you know; you'll be fine. OK?'

'Fine!' Nadia shouted. She forced herself not to react to his touch. With difficulty, crab-like, she moved across the plane, Steve Anson's body pressing into her back. His hard-on jutted into her spine. She shifted her body, bringing her buttocks up so that the soft flesh slid across the front of his track-suit.

Frank attached the static line and slid the panel back. A rush of wind sucked at her body. She gasped. Empty air gaped beyond.

'Ready?' Frank bawled.

Nadia heard Steve shout a reply. She nodded, and, as she had done on the previous occasion, very firmly shut her eyes. She walked forward. Someone slapped her shoulder.

The world tripped out from under her feet.

Her stomach clenched. Both her knees came up to her chest and her arms clamped around them. *Wrong,* a voice in her memory said. A great tug and jerk upwards knocked the breath out of her. Steve Anson's body thumped into her back. She spread her arms, and let her legs relax. Her stomach tumbled, turned. She opened her eyes.

'*Wheeee!*'

The weightlessness resolved itself into falling. Face-down, arms and legs spread wide on the cushioning air. A cold wind rushed at her face. The sky above was a great glass dome, full of light. The circle of the earth was brown, green, grey at the horizon.

'I'm floating!' she yelled, not caring that she couldn't be heard. She looked over her shoulder. The ribbed crimson canopy of the parachute swung above her head, huge at the end of its tethering cords.

Wisps of dark hair whipped at her face. She could not turn her head far enough to see Steve Anson's expression. His body pressed the length of her back. She felt him pull cords, aligning them with landmarks. That little tiny patch of green is an *airfield?* she thought. Oh yes, I remember this . . .

Air rushed past her nostrils, robbing her of breath. The excitement was a swelling rush through her veins. She reached behind herself with a gloved hand and encountered Steve's torso. She pushed her hand between their bodies and cupped her hand over his crotch. His cock was limp.

You just can't rely on some people, Nadia thought dreamily. She began to chafe his flesh through the cloth. The great arc of the sky wheeled about her. That she should be here, now, doing this, fizzed through her body like an aphrodisiac.

She hooked one of her feet up over his ankle, pulling Steve closer down on top of her. With her free hand she reached up under her harness and yanked her track-suit top up. Cold air chilled her stomach and breasts. Her nipples hardened instantly in her lacy bra cups.

Steve's right hand came down and grabbed her breast. They swung wildly in the air. His cock twitched under her hand. She smiled. It swelled until it filled her palm. She pulled her hand away, and stretched out her arms to balance them both in the air.

'Fuck me!' she screamed. Wind whipped her words away.

Blunt fingers probed at her bra. Suddenly both cups were pushed up. Her breasts slipped free. His big hands gripped them. He squeezed, hard. Cold wind and hot flesh covered her. Pleasure stabbed from her nipples to her groin. She felt herself swell, widen, grow instantly wet.

The green was marked now. Hedges demarcated fields, roads snaked across low hills. A line of tiny sparks: reflections from the windscreens of cars, so far below.

I wonder if anyone down there has a pair of binoculars?

Both his hands left her breasts. She gasped, arms still outstretched. The shadow of the canopy whirled across her. His hands slid down her ribs, down to her waist. Fingers hooked under the waistband of her track-quit bottoms and tugged. The elasticated material slid back. With one heave, he pulled her tracksuit bottoms and knickers together down to her calves.

His legs hooked around her knees.

Cold wind froze her front from neck to crotch. Hot flesh heated her back. His hands gripped her by the hips. She strained to spread her legs, almost pushing their bodies apart. The head of his big cock pushed between her thighs. She threw her head back and yelled into the wind, knowing she could not be heard.

His cock thudded against her labia. Both his hands closed over her breasts, and her erect nipples. The head of his cock pushed between her outer lips. Her flesh widened instantly. His hips thrust. The full thickness of his cock slid up into her cleft. Her sex ran wet, hot. Shudders of pleasure chased all over her skin. She reached out with her arms as if she could hold all the sky.

For a full thirty seconds they fell, his cock thrust into her, her flesh clamped down on his erect flesh, joined in mid-air. He wrapped his arms tightly around her bare ribs. Her bra and track-suit top rucked up under her arms. Her track-suit trousers, around her knees prevented her from widening her legs. She bent her knees very slightly.

She felt his chest heave. He thrust. The wideness of him filled her deliciously, thickly. His sweat-slick flesh chafed her thighs and buttocks. He drove himself up into her, hard. Fire focussed between her legs. She tilted her hips. He drove into her doggy-fashion. His hands and arms clamped their bodies together. A cry swelled in her throat.

The world spun. The disc of the earth whirled underneath her falling body. Sun dazzled her eyes. There was nothing but the big cock slamming up between her legs, the balls banging her belly, the hot thickness of him. His pumping picked up speed. Her neck arched.

The houses and school below seemed exactly the size of children's toys. Toy cars drove along the motorway. Toy trees cast summer afternoon shade on thickly-grassed fields.

Oh shit! she thought. This is the height we have to think about landing! Look for landmarks! Prepare – *oh!*

One of his hands grabbed both her breasts in front of her body. His strong fingers dug into her flesh. His other hand, palm flat, pressed her mound up towards him. His hot, naked hips and thighs slammed into her buttocks and the backs of her legs. She hung in the air, their legs intertwined, impaled on his thick cock. Pleasure began to sear up between her legs. Her flesh trembled, spasmed.

Steve Anson came. The feel of his hot come spurting up into her was too much. She flung her head back, body loose in the parachute harness, oblivious of the rushing ground. Her sex convulsed and she thunderously came.

'Quick!' she yelled, as her vision cleared. He could not hear her: she hammered at his body with her fist. The landscape – grass, roads, buildings: the *airfield* – spun and whirled. She felt the cords bite. The canopy's shadow fell across her face. The green grass rushed up.

Bodies together, with total precision, they touched down softly enough to make the tuck-and-roll fall all but unnecessary.

Nadia hit the release catch on the harness.

She lay on her back on the green grass, staring upwards. The blue and sunlit crystal of the sky shone, powerless now that she had firm earth under her again. She began to laugh. She lay half naked, her body hot with satisfaction, with her track-suit rucked up and rolled down, in the corner of the airfield, and she laughed and laughed.

Steve Anson silenced her with a deep kiss.

'Very nice indeed,' she approved. 'My compliments. I shall leave you to deal with the parachute canopy.'

She adjusted her clothes while she watched the big man, bare-arsed, attempt to wind in and control the billowing crimson silk.

Nadia dropped him outside his block of flats.

Steve Anson pushed his fingers through his windswept hair, standing on the pavement by the MG in the evening sun.

'All right,' the big man said. 'All right, I grant you, you got me. That one surprised even me.'

'I thought it might,' Nadia said demurely.

He looked down with dark eyes. 'When do I see you again?'

Nadia shifted the MG into gear.

'When I call you,' she said sweetly. 'If I do . . .'

The three of them met outside the Café Valletta, Monday lunch-time. The leaves of the plane trees were more shabby and dusty in the high summer heat. It took most of the lunch-hour for Nadia to describe her weekend, talking quietly enough not to be overheard by the lunch-time drinkers. Shannon Garrett left her sandwiches untouched. Corey Black drank iced coffee, her heels up on one of the white plastic seats. A stream of black cabs whizzed past the Café Valletta's minute courtyard.

After the congratulations, there was a pause.

'I don't suppose,' Corey said, 'that you have any . . .'

'Photos. Proof. No.' Nadia Kay leaned forward in her chair. She looked at Shannon Garrett. 'As to that – we *still* don't have a winner, do we? But I have an idea.'

Shannon pushed back her brown, curly hair. She said sardonically, 'I generally like your ideas better than I like Corey's.'

Nadia smiled. Her lips had a wicked curve. 'I was thinking, Shannon. You had a good idea yourself, not so long ago. It solved Corey's problem with her flat, and with Ben. And then Corey herself had the idea that I should get my own back on Steven Anson, which was – extremely satisfactory.'

Nadia met Shannon's gaze.

'I have to admit this is partly my idea, and partly Corey's.' She looked at the younger woman, who nodded. Nadia went on, 'Before he leaves for Greece, Shannon – we dare you. Give Tim exactly what he deserves!'

Shannon's eyes lit up.

Her hands clenched into fists.

'Yes,' she said. '*Yes.*'

'Come over to my place tomorrow,' Corey said. She grinned. 'There's a couple of Soho shops I'm going to take Nadia around first. Just for a few bits and pieces . . .'

Chapter Thirteen

THEY GOT BACK to Corey's flat a scant five minutes before Shannon was due.

'I wish you could get all this stuff through catalogues.' Corey held a black PVC bodysuit up against herself. The chains chinked. 'Instead of traipsing halfway across London every time, and having to actually buy it before you know if it suits you. What do you think of this one?'

'Mmm . . . I think it's your size. It doesn't look very durable,' Nadia remarked.

'Well, I'm hardly going to take it back and complain, am I?' The girl tossed the costume back on to the futon. 'You know, I bought this bull-whip once, and by the end of the first weekend afterwards, it *broke*. I tried writing to the credit card company about insurance and they just weren't interested – what's the matter?'

Nadia poised her fingers in front of her curved lips for a moment, and then managed to answer with gravity, 'Nothing. Nothing at all. Are we ready here?'

'I guess so.' The black-haired girl flopped down on the futon. Sunlight shone down from the high windows on to her bare, long legs. She prodded a heap of objects. 'Let's see. Leather mask. PVC bodysuit.

Thigh-boots. Riding crop. Strap-on dildo and harness.'

'Thonged whip,' Nadia said, reaching into the carrier bag beside her chair. She stroked the thin leather thongs between her hands. 'You know, sweets, I just can't understand what men get out of this, myself. Ah well. The enema kit's in the bathroom. Nipple clamps. Cock ring . . . What on earth is *this*?' She held up the last small package she had taken from the shopping bag. It was about eight inches long, and thick enough that she had difficulty closing her hand around it.

Corey reached across and grabbed it. 'That's *lunch*. Chocolate bars, for energy.'

They looked at each other and burst into giggles.

'That has to be all.' Nadia hefted the short-thonged whip. She lifted it and lashed it down on to the futon mattress as the flat's door opened, bringing a breath of summer air. Shannon Garrett walked in.

Nadia beamed at her. 'I think we're more than ready for Tim. It's everything he deserves. Have you worked out how you're going to get him here?'

The curly-haired woman stood in the doorway. She wore a blue cotton print dress and sunglasses. Nadia wished suddenly that she could see her face.

Shannon reached up and took off the sunglasses. Her eyes were red-rimmed.

'I can't go through with it.' Her voice was thick. 'I know you think I'm a mouse, but . . . and I *know* he's a bastard. I just can't help it. I did love him. I'm sorry. I can't do this. And I can't allow you to do it, either.'

A week went past. Then ten days. Shannon's phone stayed silent. Once she caught herself driving past Tim's house on the excuse that he might not have got someone in to feed the two cats. Julia's mother was kneeling on the front lawn, weeding a border. Shannon drove on past, her cheeks hot.

Towards the middle of the month she booked a few days off.

The first morning of her break, she woke and ran herself a deep bath, which she lay in for three-quarters of an hour, reading.

Tim will be back in a fortnight.

She pushed the thought away. She soaped herself, rinsed, and pulled out the plug. A warm breeze drifted in through the bathroom window, raising prickles on her cooling skin. She could smell cut grass from the back garden. She dried herself and sat on the edge of the bath, smoothing body cream into her skin.

I won't see him. I won't phone.

Her cupped palm slid over and around her shoulder, down her arm, stroking across the soft flesh under her bicep. The cream sank into her skin and vanished. She squirted another palmful from the container and smeared it across her breasts. Her hand circled and cupped each slick, heavy breast, smoothing the cream into her skin, and slid down across her stomach to the curve of her belly.

And if he phones me, I won't answer. Or maybe I'll just pick up the phone and tell him that I meant it, I'm not going to be his bit on the side any more.

Her hands slid down her firm thighs, over her knees, down her smooth calves. She stroked cream into her narrow, high-arched feet. Her skin felt warm from the bath, warm from the summer air, clean and refreshed and *handled*.

Maybe I should see him face to face, and tell him. Maybe he'll believe me, this time.

Don't be such a bloody idiot!

If I see him, I'll end up in bed with him; it just seems so natural. And then that's it, I've fucked up.

Come on, Shannon, you told him it was over. Now stick to it!

Shannon belted her long silk robe around her waist and went downstairs. The tiles in the kitchen were cool under her bare feet as she fixed herself cereal, luxuriating in the feeling of being at home, not at work, at eleven o'clock in the morning.

As she went into the living-room, a white envelope caught her eye, on the mat by the front door. She put the cereal down and went to pick it up. The handwriting was familiar.

Nadia? she thought. Oh, fine. What's the matter, you couldn't pick up a telephone and say, Never mind a stupid dare, we're still your friends?

She slit the envelope and took out a sheet of paper.

Sweets, it read.

I've been talking with young Corey, and she and I both think that we need one more dare to decide on the winner of our competition. Therefore, we have both decided to dare you to deal with Tim yourself.

But first – we dare you to go to Gatwick Airport, pick up the first attractive man you see, and fly out with him to wherever he happens to be going!

Corey has transferred some of her 'American' money into your account, for spending. It should cover a standby ticket.

Do you dare?

Don't forget your passport.

Love, Nadia. And, scrawled after, *Do it! Corey. xx.*

Shannon folded the sheet of paper in two and put it into the pocket of her robe. She paced back across the living-room floor, the carpet rough under her bare feet, sat down in the armchair, cradled her bowl of cereal and began to eat.

Nadia. Corey. Don't be so stupid. I don't want dares, I don't want to have sex with another strange man, I just want Tim, and I can't have him!

She wiped a tear that slid down the side of her nose with the hand that held her spoon. Milk spattered her robe.

'Oh, shit!' In a temper, she stood up and slammed down the bowl. 'Oh, all right, then! Oh, what the hell – *I'll do it*.'

Shannon Garrett sat in the viewing gallery of the airport bar.

What caught her attention was the prevalence of bags. Suitcases, rucksacks, matched luggage: all the hurrying crowds of people trailing their baggage behind them on wheeled trolleys or trailers. Armed security of ficers cradled bullpup rifles. She nudged her own overnight shoulder bag with her foot, just to check that it was still there.

'Excuse me, I wonder if you know when the flight for Dusseldorf is leaving?'

Shannon glanced up from her chair. She took in the young, lean, muscled man in blue shirt and casual slacks. He was blond, and he had fair stubble that might pass for a beard in some lights.

'Try looking at the departures board,' she said icily, and turned back to her drink.

She stared down the concourse. Business class, holiday class ... A throng of people passing rapidly through the terminal, pausing only at the chemists and W H Smiths concession stands; or sitting with differing degrees of anticipation and nervousness in the rows of moulded plastic seating. Outside the plate-glass windows, planes roared down the runway at what seemed like two-minute intervals.

You're the third in half an hour, Shannon thought, sparing a glare for the man's departing back. Give me a *break*.

This was a bad idea. I shouldn't have come. I know

Nadia and Corey want me to agree to sort Tim out when he gets back, but I don't want to do that, and I don't want to do this, and what *do* I want to do?

Shannon left her seat, and her untouched drink. She slung her bag over her shoulder and walked down the concourse. Towards the automatic doors that would let her out into the car parks.

Her steps slowed.

I don't know.

She changed direction, moving into one of the seating areas, and put her bag down again. She sat and stared into space.

After some minutes, she became aware that she was staring at the back of a woman wearing a black leather jacket. The woman's hair was black and shiny, and hung in chunky curls. The jacket was a glove-leather version of a biker jacket – Shannon could see the zips up the outside of the forearms, where the woman sat with her arms extended across the backs of the moulded plastic seating. Her shoulders were square. Her lower legs and feet were visible under the seats: she wore sheer black stockings, and ankle boots with a thin, three-inch heel.

Shannon looked away swiftly as the black-haired head began to turn.

I could go back into London. I could go and ask about standby tickets. Maybe I should go on holiday, now I'm here, just a brief break, get away from everything . . .

'Elaine?' a voice said. 'It is Elaine, isn't it? I thought I recognised you.'

Shannon startled and knocked her shoulder bag on to the floor. By the time she picked it up, she could explain her flushed cheeks away as a result of bending over. Small strong hands helped her with the bag.

'Laura,' Shannon said.

The woman's too-wide mouth was sharply defined by crimson lipstick. She had done nothing to the heavy dark line of her brows. The rest of her make-up was either subtle or non-existent, but she had a gloss about her that had not been apparent on the beach.

Shannon held the eye contact. The younger woman met her gaze and did not smile.

Under her biker jacket Laura wore a plain black T-shirt, stretched over her small, full breasts. She was not wearing a bra. Her nipples were two small, hard lumps under the soft cotton.

Shannon let her gaze slide downwards. The woman was wearing a short, tight black leather skirt that barely came down to mid-thigh. The outline of a suspender showed on one thigh, under the leather. Shannon felt her cleft heat, and pulse once.

She squirmed on the plastic moulded seat, staring at the younger woman's ankle boots; anything not to look up and meet those brown-black eyes again.

Then she suddenly, secretly, smiled.

It isn't what they dared me to do. Pretty close, though. I should think it counts . . .

'Actually,' she said, lifting her head, 'it's Shannon. Elaine's my middle name. Shannon Garrett. Have you just flown in?'

The lipsticked mouth opened. Shannon stared at her lips, at her small, square white teeth. She barely registered what the younger woman said.

'Laura Maine. No. I'm flying out to the States at four. I just checked in. I've got a couple of hours to wait.' Still, Laura did not smile, and she held Shannon's gaze. 'Can I buy you a drink?'

Wasn't I supposed to ask you that? Shannon thought wryly. Damn. Oh well. I suppose that means I have to go one better.

'You can buy me a drink,' she said, her belly taut

with anticipation. 'Afterwards.'

The red lips parted. Shannon wanted to reach up and touch their softness with her fingertip. She stayed perfectly still. The other woman slowly nodded.

'Where?' she asked simply.

'I've learned a lot about what I like since I last met you,' Shannon murmured. 'A lot about liking it quick and dirty. A lot about liking it long and slow. A lot about how many different kinds of fucking I like.'

At *fucking*, a slow heat began to rise in the other woman's cheeks. She dropped her eyes briefly. When she looked up, she had begun to smile. 'Buy a ticket. Come to the States with me.'

Shannon stood. She shouldered her bag. She took the younger woman's hand. Laura glanced anxiously around the crowded concourse. She tugged. Shannon tightened her grip.

'What—'

'Next time I'll do what you say,' Shannon whispered, leaning over, her breath feathering the fine hairs of the woman's temple. 'This time you're going to do what I tell you.'

The hand within hers grew warm and still.

Hand in hand, Shannon strode down the concourse. She deliberately walked fast, so that the younger woman had to hurry to keep up. Laura stumbled on her high heels. Shannon grabbed her under the elbow and steered her into the Ladies.

The long tiled and mirrored room was, momentarily, deserted, although some of the cubicles were obviously occupied. Shannon didn't release her grip on Laura's arm. She all but pushed the younger woman into the far-end cubicle. It seemed more spacious than the rest, by virtue of an opaque-glass window.

In a frantic whisper, Laura hissed, 'Just what do you think you're doing?'

Shannon put her hand up. She put four fingers flat on the young woman's mouth, and pushed. The precise red lipstick smeared across her mouth and cheek. Shannon put a hand each side of Laura's head, pulled her forward, and kissed her, thrusting her tongue deep into the woman's mouth, tasting her. The woman whimpered, the stiffness of her body relaxing.

Shannon dropped her hands, pressed them to the woman's body, and slid them up under her arms, under the silk lining of the leather jacket. Zips jangled, she cupped the heavy breasts in her palms.

When their lips parted, Laura said, 'We'll be seen! They'll see more than one person's in here!'

She again pressed her finger to Laura's smeared mouth. Then she put her hands down to the younger woman's waist, and pulled her tight in towards her body. Breasts, bellies, thighs; pressed close together through thin cloth.

Shannon unsnapped the back button of the tight leather skirt. The zip came noisily undone. She felt Laura cringe in her arms. Muffling her face in thick, sweet-smelling curls of black hair, Shannon slid her fingers under the waistband of the woman's skirt and began to ease it down over her round little hips. The pads of her fingers slid over garter belt, suspenders and the cool, naked flesh of the woman's bottom, to the tops of her sheer stockings.

She put her lips on Laura's ear. 'You're not wearing any knickers!'

Shannon's sex grew hotter. She pushed with her thighs, forcing the younger woman back towards the wall. Her calf knocked against the cistern. The black leather skirt slid over Laura's round arse and fell down, hanging up around her knees. For a moment Shannon enjoyed the sight of her: tumbled black curls, smeared lipstick, sweaty skin. The black leather jacket swinging open to disclose short T-shirt, garter belt, black suspenders and stockings, and the curly black tuft of hair at her crotch.

She reached up under the jacket, under Laura's armpits, and hoisted the woman bodily up into the air. Her muscles strained. She stepped forward and sat Laura on the window-ledge. The young woman's body leaped as her nude buttocks came into contact with the cold tiles. She clapped both hands over her mouth. Above them, her wide eyes stared at Shannon somewhere between outrage and arousal, and something that might have been admiration.

Shannon leaned forward. She pushed Laura's thighs apart, easing the woman back against the window. The warm, damp smell of her cleft hit Shannon's nostrils. Breathless, unable to wait, she dipped her head between the woman's cool, suspender-clad thighs. She licked one delicate wet stroke across Laura's clitoris. The body under her hands throbbed.

Her hands bit into Laura's thighs. She felt the woman's small, square hands knot in her hair. She put her mouth down into the woman's sex, burying her face in the hot wet readiness, inhaling the musky woman scent. She let her tongue caress the outer labia; then plunged it hard down into the secret interior. The hands in her hair gripped hard, tugged; she didn't stop. Flickering, first fast, then slow, then relentlessly pushing the woman towards an uncontrollable release, she thrust her tongue deep between Laura's legs. Outside, someone ran a tap into a washbasin. Someone else flushed a cistern, further down the cubicles.

Balanced between the throbbing wetness between her own legs and the delicious likelihood of discovery, Shannon stuck one hand down her own knickers. She rubbed, hard, still thrusting her tongue into the woman's sex. The woman's body jerked. The hands pulled her hair hard. Laura's lithe, muscular thighs suddenly tightened and released. Shannon's own sex exploded. She felt warm wetness slick her whole hand. Laura's hot, sweating body collapsed to lean on top of her, rapid deep breathing stifled.

'You cow!' the young woman whispered. 'I'll pay you back for that! Are you coming to New Orleans with me?'

Despite her flushed, triumphant face, Shannon said coolly, 'I suppose I'd better see about tickets.'

Their seats were not together. At least, Shannon thought, we got on to the same plane.

She sat across the aisle, a few seats back, watching Laura stare out of the window. Her pillar-box red lipstick was again precise. Her leather jacket encased her strong shoulders. She sat with her legs crossed, neat ankle boots just visible from where Shannon was sitting. To anyone else, she seemed a collected, seasoned traveller, perfectly unshaken by take-off or flight. *I* know you're not wearing any knickers, Shannon thought, and felt herself grow hot again between her legs.

She staggered as she stood, stepping into the aisle. The throbbing of the gangway underfoot reminded her they were six miles above the earth's surface. She made her way towards the toilets at the back.

They were mostly unoccupied. She chose one. As she got the door open, a body crashed into her back, pushing her forward into the cubicle. The door slammed shut behind them. Shannon opened her mouth to shout and recognised, in the dim light, Laura's grin. There was not room for two people.

With no preamble, Laura grabbed her and kissed her. Then she put her hands on Shannon's shoulders and turned her around to face the back of the cubicle.

The airframe shook. Shannon glimpsed them both in the mirror. Then a hand took her own left hand, and pulled it down and planted it on the wall at the back of the toilet. Her right hand was similarly pulled down.

Shannon leaned with her weight on her arms, her legs apart, over the empty toilet. She felt Laura's hands stroking her ass. 'What the hell are you doing? They'll throw us off!'

'They won't even notice if you keep quiet.' Laura's eyes gleamed wickedly in the mirror. 'I had to.'

With her head craned, Shannon saw Laura put her handbag down by the sink. The reverberations of flight drummed through her taut, spread legs. Laura opened her handbag. She took out a cream-coloured six-inch vibrator.

'Always such fun to explain to Customs,' she purred. She twisted the end firmly. Shannon heard it buzz even over the flight noise. Her sex grew damp, wet, then soaking in the space of seconds. The tight fabric of her panties rode up into her crotch, irritating her labia.

Laura drew the buzzing vibrator's tip down Shannon's spine, down between her buttocks. It buzzed at the entrance of her anus. Shannon's legs stiffened. She jammed her ass up. The vibrator slid down into the wetness of her sex.

Laura's arm snaked under her body. Her strong hand pulled the front of Shannon's dress down. Shannon felt her breasts squeezed out of her bra cups. They hung free, the skin tingling with sensitivity. The woman's hands stroked her. Fingers circled her nipple. Suddenly they pinched, just hard enough to make Shannon gasp. Her nipples hardened instantly.

The vibrator thrust between her spread legs. She braced herself as it thrust in, prizing her hot flesh apart. The woman's hand, where she held it, thumped into Shannon's crutch with every forward stroke. Her flesh loosened, swelled, streamed with juices. She lifted her hips, her throat stretching as her head arched up and back.

The hand squeezed closed on her breast. The pitiless vibrator was slammed up inside her and kept there, Laura's hand firmly across her fanny. Shannon bit her lip and moaned. Her legs shook. Warm arousal flooded every inch of her skin, then zeroed in on her crutch. She almost screamed with anticipation. Her body peaked. She flooded. Her sex convulsed. The explosion of pleasure knocked her to her knees, sprawled across the open seat of the toilet. Sweat soaked her hair and ran down into her eyes. Every muscle of her body shook with release.

The airplane toilet door clicked closed behind Laura's departing back.

Shannon left it a decent number of minutes before she vacated the cubicle. She tried to tidy herself up. When she walked back down the aisle, her face burned, although no one gave her a second look. The crotch of her knickers was soaking wet.

Laura sat in her seat, gazing out of the window again past her fellow-passengers. She was unchanged but for the tiny smile that remained on her lips for the rest of the flight.

They changed planes at Atlanta. They hardly spoke, neither then nor on the hour-long flight to New Orleans. Travelling into the Big Easy, under an immense blue sky, it was still glorious daylight. Shannon sat thigh to leather-covered thigh with Laura in the taxi. She paid more attention to the feel of that against her sweat-soaked, humid skin than she did to the streets and skyscrapers, and she barely registered the name of the hotel Laura booked them into. She was only aware of the ache in her sex, and her realisation of how much remained untried with this woman's body, this garden of pleasures.

The hotel room was moderately big, with a pair of wide windows that let in the sun. They faced the windowless back wall of a factory, Shannon saw, throwing her overnight bag on to one of the two double beds, and they were on the sixth floor.

A hand slid up between her legs.

Shannon turned around. She reached up and grabbed Laura's shoulders. The black leather was soft and warm under her hands. She pushed the woman back. The edge of the bed caught Laura behind the knees, and she fell backwards with Shannon on top of her.

Pressed warm body to warm body, Shannon found herself running with sweat. She reached up and triggered the air-conditioning, in a desperate attempt to overcome New Orleans' humidity. The material of her summer dress was wet under her arms, across her bust, down her stomach. She lowered her head and put her face into the hot cleft of Laura's breasts. The younger woman struggled to hook her legs around Shannon's hips.

'Oh no,' Shannon said. 'After the plane? I've got a little surprise for you. You may like it. I certainly will . . .'

Without getting off Laura's compact, muscled body, Shannon reached across and tugged the zip of her overnight bag. She fumbled her hand inside, among the change of clothes and bathroom bags.

She brought out her hand, holding the handle of a short-thonged black leather whip.

Laura's eyes brightened. 'No, no,' she whimpered, writhing under Shannon's imprisoning weight. She looked up from under long, long lashes. The lipstick on her wide mouth was mussed again. 'You wouldn't beat me, would you?'

Shannon sat back up, dragging the younger woman across her lap. She lifted the whip, and brought the thongs down on the taut leather stretched across Laura's buttocks. The slap was loud in the room, over the hum of the air-conditioner. Laura yelped.

Shannon raised her arm again. She brought the whip down across the backs of the woman's thighs, in the gap between stocking-tops and skirt. Laura's mound pressed hard down on to her thigh. Her torso shuddered, inhaling a deep, sharp breath. She moaned.

Shannon whipped the thongs down. The flesh of the woman's legs began to glow pink. Her whole body writhed with arousal, under Shannon's imprisoning hand. She wriggled. She pushed her breasts against Shannon's leg. Her tangled black hair flopped down over her face. Shannon brought the whip down with a solid *crack!*

'Please!' the young woman said. 'Fuck me! Fuck me until I can't stand up! Please!'

Shannon reversed the whip in her hand. She thrust the slick, thick leather handle up between Laura's legs. The smooth knob on the end met resistance. Gently, she pushed. The whip handle slid smoothly up into the other woman's sex. Shannon drew it back, thrust it forward, with long, slow strokes. She ground her own sex against the rough cover on the bed, thrusting her wet crutch down with force. As Laura moaned and whimpered, she increased the tempo, thrusting the whip handle with a rapid friction. Laura's head went back and she yelled like a banshee. At the same moment Shannon's sex became too aroused for her to think. She let the young woman fall from her knees on to the floor, and took the handle of the whip, and thrust it up between her own legs. The solid bulk inside her filled her so that she came, and came, and came. She slid down, exhausted, to lie beside Laura.

The younger woman grinned lazily through tangled, sweat-wet hair; reached over, and enfolded Shannon in her warm and welcoming arms.

Chapter Fourteen

SHANNON WOKE TO the fifth day. Not sprawled up against Laura Maine's solid, cat-curled spine, this time, but stretched across warm, empty sheets.

When she could rub the sleep out of her eyes enough to read, the note on the pillow said *Love to do this again sometime.* It added a phone number, then: *P.S. The room is paid up to the end of the week. Enjoy!*

She rolled over and lay on her back for a while. The air-conditioning hummed. Outside, New Orleans gleamed under a blue sky. When she rose, naked, and pushed the window up an inch, she smelled mud, fish, urine, roses, patchouli, fresh bread, seafood cooking, and a dozen other smells she could not name.

I know there's something I was supposed to do.

Oh my God, *Tim!* I forgot the dare about Tim!

She stretched her naked arms up to the sun and stretched; every muscle in her body relaxed, her sex satisfied and content.

In a foreign country, three thousand miles from home.

I *did* forget him, didn't I? He never crossed my mind. So much for the dare.

It was not until several hours later, sitting in a coffee

shop in the French Quarter, that Shannon Garrett suddenly laughed out loud. The waitress gave her a startled look.

'I'll have another hazelnut cappuccino,' Shannon said. She beamed and looked out at the narrow, teeming streets.

Of course. It wasn't a dare. It was a present. A present from Nadia and Corey. And it was just what I needed.

Nadia groped for the phone. She switched the bedside lamp on, knocking a 1950s bedside clock to the floor. She groped for it and looked at the face. She recognised the voice on the phone.

'Shannon Garrett, *do you have any idea what time this is?*'

She listened.

'Really? This, may I remind you, isn't New Orleans! This is London. What on earth is so urgent?'

Nadia Kay listened some more.

When she finally put the phone down on the transatlantic call, she flopped back against her pillows. Her window was just growing light with the summer dawn.

She reached for the phone again and dialled.

'Corey, my sweet. Yes. Yes, I *do* know what time it is. I've just had a call from Shannon. She's in New Orleans. Yes. What did she phone for? Oh,' Nadia said, snuggling down, her eyes on the brightening window. 'She says, thanks. She says, her room is paid for, for the week. She says, would we like to come out and join her?

'She says she's got an idea for some *international* dares . . .'

EROTICA OMNIBUS ONE

DARK SECRET *Marina Anderson*

Answering a job advertisement to assist a world-famous actress, Harriet Radcliffe finds herself plunged into an intense, enclosed world of sexual obsession . . .

SISTERS UNDER THE SKIN *Vanessa Davies*

Louise Andrews has always disapproved of her sexy older sister but when she is persuaded to join Gina as a lap dancer, the pair realise they share more than just a job . . .

EDUCATING ELEANOR *Nina Sheridan*

Helping writer Marcus Grant research his book on women's sexuality, Eleanor Dawes finds her own sensual awareness is ripe for re-education . . .

Buy this book direct from the X Libris website:
www.xratedbooks.co.uk

EROTICA OMNIBUS TWO

MUSICAL AFFAIRS *Stephanie Ash*

A singer-songwriter on her way to the top, Amelia Ashton is determined to sort out her affairs, both musical and otherwise . . .

ETERNAL KISS *Anastasia Dubois*

Searching for an ancient lost book of erotic pictures, archaeologist Venetia Fellowes finds that life can imitate art . . .

SHOPPING AROUND *Mariah Greene*

Unable to decide between her would-be lovers at the large department store where she works, Karen Taylor decides that sampling the goods is half the fun . . .

Buy this book direct from the X Libris website:
www.xratedbooks.co.uk

EROTICA OMNIBUS THREE

PLEASURE BOUND *Susan Swann*

A pair of black kid evening-gloves that breathe new fire into an illicit romance; a daring date to a different kind of peep-show; a music lesson with an inspirational teacher . . .

PLAYING THE GAME *Selina Seymour*

Kate has a hunger that just won't stop, an appetite that demands to be fed – whether at her chauvinistic City firm, or at the château of a new French client . . .

MIDNIGHT STARR *Dorothy Starr*

A beautiful pure silk basque that revives a fading love affair; a hot summer night's fantasy that surprisingly comes true; an elevating encounter with a mysterious man in black . . .

Buy this book direct from the X Libris website:
www.xratedbooks.co.uk

BLACK STOCKINGS

Emma Allan

'Letitia pulled on the basque and fastened the hooks into the eyes, using the tightest possible position. As the feeling of constriction increased she felt her excitement growing. Settling her breasts into the bra cups, she looked at herself in the mirror. She had never worn lingerie like this . . .'

Letitia Drew's new job at Black Stockings Lingerie is the opportunity she has always wanted. But when she finds herself strongly attracted to her charismatic Managing Director, Matthew Silverstone, it soon becomes clear that the feeling is mutual.

When his wife Ursula discovers them together, she demands to join in the steamy action. With the power to sack Letitia unless she co-operates, Ursula plans to take her on a roller-coaster ride of new sexual experiences . . .

Buy this book direct from the X Libris website:
www.xratedbooks.co.uk

Other bestselling X Libris titles available by mail or from www.xratedbooks.co.uk

☐ Erotica Omnibus One		£9.99
☐ Erotica Omnibus Two		£9.99
☐ Erotica Omnibus Three		£9.99
☐ Black Stockings	Emma Allan	£5.99
☐ Legacy of Desire	Marina Anderson	£4.99
☐ Private Parties	Stephanie Ash	£5.99
☐ Perfect Partners	Natalie Blake	£5.99
☐ Teaching the Temptress	Ginnie Bond	£5.99
☐ Lottery Lovers	Vanessa Davies	£4.99
☐ Island of Desire	Zara Devereux	£5.99
☐ Hotel of Love	Dorothy Starr	£5.99

The prices shown above are correct at time of going to press. However, the publishers reserve the right to increase prices on covers from those previously advertised without prior notice.

X
LIBRIS

X LIBRIS BOOKS
Cash Sales Department, P.O. Box 11, Falmouth, Cornwall, TR10 9EN
Tel: +44 (0) 1326 569777, Fax: +44 (0) 1326 569555
Email: books@barni.avel.co.uk

POST AND PACKING:
Payments can be made as follows: cheque, postal order (payable to X Libris Books) or by credit cards. Do not send cash or currency.

U.K. Orders under £10	**£1.50**
U.K. Orders over £10	**FREE OF CHARGE**
E.E.C. & Overseas	25% of order value

Name (Block Letters) _____

Address_____

_____

Post/zip code:_____

☐ Please keep me in touch with future X Libris publications

☐ I enclose my remittance £_____

☐ I wish to pay by Visa/Access/Mastercard/Eurocard

Card Expiry Date

☐☐☐☐☐☐☐☐☐☐☐☐☐☐☐☐☐☐☐ _____